Gaston de Latour

Walter Pater, circa 1889
After a photograph by Elliott & Fry

Gaston de Latour :
The Revised Text

Walter Pater

Based on the Definitive Manuscripts
& Enlarged to Incorporate
All Known Fragments

With Introduction, Explanatory Annotation
& Apparatus Criticus

Edited by
Gerald Monsman

ELT Press   *University of North Carolina at Greensboro*

ELT PRESS

of *English Literature in Transition, 1880–1920*

University of North Carolina Greensboro, NC 27412–5001

E–Mail: Langen@fagan.uncg.edu

NUMBER TEN: 1880–1920 British Authors Series

ISBN   0–944318–09–6

Library of Congress Cataloging in Publication Data 94–062118

Distributed in Europe by Colin Smythe, Ltd.

P.O. Box 6 Gerrards Cross Buckinghamshire England SL9 8XA

Typography & Design

Display & Text Type : ITC Berkeley Old Style
Title–Page / Contents / Dust Jacket
Designed by Robert Langenfeld

CorelDraw 5.0 / WordPerfect 6.1
Negatives–Plates Created Via Electronic Prepress
Printer : Thomson–Shore, Inc. Dexter, Michigan
Production Coordinator Diane Nourse

For Claire

CONTENTS

EDITION TEXT   *Gaston de Latour*

❦ List of Illustrations

❦ ACKNOWLEDGEMENTS

I wish to thank Ms. Catherine Jones and her sisters, residual legatees of Walter Pater's estate, for graciously extending permission for the publication of Walter Pater's *Gaston* manuscripts. Grateful acknowledgements is also made for use of the following manuscripts: Chapters 1–5, 7 by permission of the Henry W. and Albert A. Berg Collection, The New York Public Library, Astor, Lenox and Tilden Foundations; Chapters 8–13 (BNC Archives PP1 B2/1) by permission of the Principal and Fellows of the King's Hall and College of Brasenose, Oxford; fragments at the Houghton (bMS Eng 1150) by permission of the Houghton Library, Harvard University, Cambridge, Massachusetts.

In the preparation of this volume, I gratefully acknowledge the suggestions and editorial assistance of John Sparrow, who graciously loaned his manuscripts, Fredson Bowers, Billie Inman, William Shuter, Sharon Bassett, Peter Medine, Clyde Ryals, Marcel Tetel, Jeffrey Russell, and Don Lawler; of Gita Rajan who as a graduate student provided preliminary research assistance in connection with the annotation of Chapters 2 and 3 on Chartres and Ronsard; of Cindy Craw, Brian S. Lee and others who supplied data via electronic networks; of Lois Olstrad and her colleagues at the University of Arizona Library whose competence and cheerfulness have gone far to offset the budgetarily shortened Library hours, constantly broken electronic machines which replaced card catalogues, and misshelved books; and of Leslie Morris, Curator of Manuscripts at The Houghton Library, who helpfully identified material and mailed photocopies. Especially, I wish to thank Louise Kennelly at *ELT* and my publisher, Robert Langenfeld, for his timely moral support and imaginative efforts with design and production.

In 1992 I received a grant-in-aid from the American Philosophical Society which permitted research at a number of important collections in France and Italy, such as the Bibliotèque Nationale (Paris); the regional university library of Aix-en-Provence/Marseilles; the Biblioteca Nazionale Marciana (Venezia); and The Library, American Academy in Rome; and which permitted consultation with scholars at the Vatican and at the Biblioteca Nazionale in Firenze. Also consulted were a number of specialized collections (books and/or artifacts) at the Louvre (Paris), Musée National de Céramique (Sèvres), and the archives at Chartres, as well as visits to a number of sites central to Pater's descriptions in the novel.

This book would never have seen the light of day without the support of my wife and the patience of my daughters. At least one daughter was left too often stranded at school waiting to be picked up while I blithely pursued a footnote. But this book is for Claire: Gaston's age, this year, when he discovered the Seven Stars.

❦ FREQUENTLY CITED SOURCES
& ABBREVIATED REFERENCES

Parenthetical citation in the Explanatory Annotation to works other than the Edition Text is by author or editor and by volume, book, chapter, page or line number geared to each work's organization. The citation is shortened to only the numerical data if it closely follows a reference in the text to the identifying name. With the exception of *Gaston*, references to Pater's writings are to the *New Library Edition of the Works of Walter Pater*, 10 vols. (London: Macmillan, 1910) and will be cited by abbreviated title and page. Where understood as referencing this novel, *Gaston de Latour: An Unfinished Romance*, ed. Charles L. Shadwell (London: Macmillan, 1896) and "Gaston de Latour," *Macmillan's Magazine* (June–October 1888) are abbreviated as "1896" and "MM."

ABBREVIATED REFERENCES

Aubigné, Agrippa d'. *Histoire Universelle*. 4 vols. Ed. Thierry. Geneva: Droz, 1981–1987.

Baird, Henry. *The Rise of the Huguenots of France*. 2 vols. New York: Scribner's, 1879.

Beyer, Arthur. *Walter Paters Beziehungen*. Halle: Niemeyer, 1931.

Brantôme, Pierre de Bourdeille, Seigneur de. *Oeuvres complète de Pierre de Bourdeille, seigneur de Brantôme*. Ed. Ludovic Lalanne. 11 vols. Paris: Renouard, 1864–82.

Bruno, Giordano. *Dialoghi italiani nuovamente ristampati con note da Giovanni Gentile*. Ed. Giovanni Aquilecchia. 3rd ed. Firenze: Sansoni, 1958.

Clements, Patricia. *Baudelaire and the English Tradition*. Princeton: Princeton University Press, 1985.

Erlanger, Philippe. *Saint Bartholomew's Night*. New York: Pantheon, 1962.

Galignani's New Paris Guide. Paris: Galignani and Co., 1857.

Hangest, Germain d'. *Walter Pater*. 2 vols. Paris: Didier, 1961.

Huguenot Wars, The. Ed. Julien Coudy. Philadelphia: Chilton, 1969.

Inman, Billie Andrew. *Walter Pater's Reading, 1858–1873*. New York: Garland, 1981.

———. *Walter Pater and His Reading, 1874–1877*. New York: Garland, 1990.

La Boétie, Étienne de. *Discourse of Voluntary Servitude*. Ed. Harry Kurz. New York: Columbia, 1942.

Lang, Andrew. *Ballads and Lyrics of Old France*. Portland, Me: Thomas Mosher, 1909.

L'Estole, Pierre de. *Mémoires-Journaux de Pierre de l'Estoile*. 11 vols. Paris: Libraire des bibliophiles, 1875–83.

Levey, Michael. *The Case of Walter Pater*. London: Thames and Hudson, 1978.

Marguerite of Valois, Queen of Navarre. *Memoires de lettres de Marguerite de Valois*. Ed. Françoise Guessard. Paris: Renouard, 1842.

Mérimée, Prosper. *Chronique du Règne de Charles IX*. Paris: Nelson, 1931.

Michelet, Jules. *Histoire de France*. 17 vols. Paris: Librairie de L. Hachette, 1852–67.

Montaigne, Michael de. *Essais*. Ed. Pierre Villey. Paris: Presses Universitaires, 1965.

———. *Essays of Michael de Montaigne*. Trans. Charles Cotton. 3 vols. London: Reeves and Turner, 1877.

Pater, Walter. *Letters of Walter Pater*. Ed. Lawrence Evans. Oxford: Clarendon, 1970.

———. *New Library Edition of the Works of Walter Pater*. 10 vols. London: Macmillan, 1910.

———. *Gaston de Latour: An Unfinished Romance*. Ed. Charles L. Shadwell. London: Macmillan, 1896.

———. *Gaston de Latour*. *Macmillan's Magazine*. June–October 1888.

Pattison, Emilia (Mrs. Mark). *The Renaissance of Art in France*. 2 vols. London: Kegan Paul, 1879.

Ronsard, Pierre de. *Oeuvres complètes de P. de Ronsard*. Ed. Prosper Blanchemain. New ed. 8 vols. Paris: Jannet/Frank, 1857–67.

Whitehead, A. W. *Gaspard de Coligny*. London: Methuen, 1904.

White, Henry. *The Massacre of St. Bartholomew*. New York: Harper, 1868.

Wright, Thomas. *Life of Walter Pater*. 2 vols. London: Everett, 1907.

Wright, Samuel. *An Informative Index to the Writings of Walter H. Pater*. West Cornwall, CT: Locust Hill Press, 1987.

❦ Annotational & Transcriptional Format

ANNOTATIONS

The Edition Text is referenced in the Explanatory Annotation and in the Emendations & Variants by chapter, page, and line number (chapter digits are omitted when inessential) with lemma. In the Explanatory Annotation, a lemma is marked in bold; in the Emendations & Variants, a lemma for an emendation is marked with a scroll bracket and for a variant with a square bracket. Thus a reference to Chapter 8, page 87, line 12 would be cited as: 8.87:12 lemma. Parenthetical citation in the Explanatory Annotation to works other than the Edition Text is by abbreviated references, keyed to Frequently Cited Sources and Abbreviated References. Parenthetical placement in the notes of full publication information is used exclusively for references needing documentation but cited only once.

DIPLOMATIC TRANSCRIPTION

The purpose of the diplomatic transcriptional symbols is to indicate the relation of the printed words to the basic twelve-line holograph page: whether the words are on the line, above or below the line, canceled or not canceled, and with or without a caret. Certain extraneous details such as spatters or inky fingerprints are ordinarily not recorded (as the police would say, Pater left a set of "partials"); but the conditions of paper and ink as well as such curiosities as ten short verticle pencil lines on folio 3 of Chapter 8 will be footnoted selectively; differences in pencil and ink in the text will be indicated consistently with symbols. The spacing between paragraphs has been introduced into the transcription to facilitate readability.

1. ↑▲↓ Interlineations (substitutions, alternatives, augmentations, or cancellations) are indicated with arrows—i.e., pointing to above or below the line of the immediately preceding word. Nested interlineations are represented thus: ↑▲the eye ↑eyes↓↓, the left to right diplomatic placement indicating manuscript interlineations stacked upwards from the line (or, in the most cramped passages, upwards and left to right, tier by tier). In exceptionally inchoate venues, sometimes the interlinear string becomes a de facto base line; I then treat it exactly as if it is one of the primary twelve lines per page. In those rare instances where the interlineation is below the line or, more frequently, where the nesting of interlineations clearly moves downward from a superscript, a reverse notation will be used: ↓▼in fact, the final accession to the throne of France,↑.

2. ~~your basic reject~~ Cancelations will be marked with a strikeout. Double cancelations are not frequent and generally will not be noted: e.g., *doors* (Chapter 9, folio 17) first has a vertical strikeout of the *s*, then a second horizontal line strikes out the whole word.

3. < > Superimpositions of characters (i.e., a lower case overwritten with a capital: "b<B>ible") will be indicated with angle brackets; other unique linear augmentations (squeezed-in letters) also are noted, but the routine filling of slightly too-short-gaps on the line are ignored.

4. ⬧ and ◇ Pater's "index markings" (i.e., markings that serve as a pointer or indicator) are subscript notations in the form of short dashes under possibly uneuphoneous pairs of words or single words in need of reconsideration. They are indicated by the superscript ⬧ preceding the words or syllables under which they are found; the superscript ◇ indicates a canceled index mark; more than a single index symbol indicates the number of words in the following phrase so marked (Pater, one sees, is cautious about overuse of the "it was" construction).

5. / The slash will be used in diplomatically transcribing Pater's notations on his unattached slips to indicate the end of a line, since the lower line is not invariably continuous with the one above. Double slashes are used in rare instances to indicate the end of an original manuscript line recovered from two slips.

6. [ ] Square brackets enclose material supplied by this editor; oftentimes the content is self-explanatory. These are several of the most frequently used symbols:

A) [1 cm] Lacunae and illegible cancelations (even with all the benefits of modern illumination, microscopic analysis, and scanning, some words will not "come clean") will be indicated by square brackets with an indication of interval, rounded off to the closest 0.5 cm. Thus [3 cm] indicates a lacuna of that length; Pater's "the" is typically this length or a little less; and [1 cm illeg canceln] is a measurement of the illegible canceled characters or word(s), not the strikeout line; if the lacuna has an interlineation directly above (indicating Pater has not finally confirmed the wording), its diplomatic ordering will be the same left to right as for stacked alternatives: [3 cm] ⌈Suetonius⌉, with a caret only if Pater used one. Lacunae on Pater's slips will not be marked in the diplomatic transcription because Pater does not observe line-length and gaps do not necessarily signify material omitted.

B) [*sic*] or [?] Although Pater's handwriting often is unusually elegant, in some drafts hastily penned characters may be elided, a mere squiggle alluding to an "-ing," for example. Such elisions (foreshortenings rather than the frank omissions of suspensions and contractions), as well as broken or malformed letters (the undotted "i," the "t" with the wandering cross-bar), will generally be treated as if they were fully formed on the page, as indeed they would have been had he composed on a word-processor! (Pierre L'Esotile's editors say it with a Gallic flair: "*on ne s'est pas cru obligé de respecter certains caprices de plume.*") But in those few instances where a letter has been omitted by mental oversight, not wholly a function of the mechanics of penmanship, or misspelled, or the wrong accent indicated, the inaccuracy will be marked by a [*sic*]. If some uncertainty clouds a word or letter (the cancelation could be an *r* but might be an *a* or just a blob from a spastic pen), the reading (if not specified as *illeg cancln*) will be followed by [?].

C) [¶] Indicates a new paragraph (see Introduction for comment on Pater's paragraphing). When Pater himself employs this symbol, it will be given without square brackets.

D) [**End 14 r**] Square brackets in bold indicate the ends of leaves (r for recto; v for verso) for the BNC holograph; the ends of the Houghton holograph leaves are identified thus: [**End 6 r HOU**].

7. { or {   } Scroll-brackets indicate *pencil* emendations: a single scroll-bracket indicates a pencil *strikeout* of an ink word or punctuation; double scroll-brackets enclose *augmentations* in pencil. This pertains particularly to those emendations in Chapter 8.

8. A{<a>}gain Composites of the above symbols are possible. This indicates a pencil correction by overwriting—the ink capital *A* has been emended in pencil to lower case.

EDITION TEXT

1. [   ] Square brackets enclose material supplied by the editor. When reasonable, missing material has been provided in brackets in the place of Pater's manuscript gaps; such authoritative reasons as the editor has for providing the material will be indicated in the Explanatory Annotation. When lacunae occur and the missing material is unavailable, brackets surround a standard-length space. Brackets will not be used for incomplete manuscript words; and in contrast to the diplomatic transcription, question marks in brackets will not follow words difficult to decipher.

2. No other symbols are introduced into the Edition Text and Pater's holograph symbols, retained in the Diplomatic Transcription, have been converted. Other than initials for names or the typical abbreviations of words, several of Pater's symbols are familiar and several strange. The ampersand (&), the ampersand with a period beneath (which I render &c.) and the ¶ need no explanation. Others, such as an inverted triangle of dots (the symbol for *therefore* overturned) means *because*; T.O. means *turn over* (on slips); and the partial underlining of words, often in pairs, has

been explained as "indexing." The familiar * used to indicate the place at which additional material is to be inserted has a number of unfamiliar surrogates: a circle with a dot at the center; a vaguely H-like figure (++); and the Greek beta (B), among others. Possibly Pater multiplied insertion symbols to avoid confusion as to what material should go where.

 INTRODUCTION

PATER BEGAN WORK on *Gaston de Latour* shortly after or possibly even before finishing *Marius the Epicurean* (1885). Between June and October, 1888, he published the first five chapters of *Gaston* in *Macmillan's Magazine*; then, possibly unable to sustain the monthly pace or, as some have speculated, simply lacking a firm grasp of his plotline, he abandoned serial publication. One other chapter, afterwards revised by Pater for the novel, appeared in August 1889 in the form of an essay on Giordano Bruno in the *Fortnightly Review*. Pater continued to work on the novel intermittently until his death in 1894; and in 1896 the serially published chapters, together with one chapter in manuscript, were reissued by Macmillan in book form as *Gaston de Latour: An Unfinished Romance*, edited by Pater's long-time friend and colleague, Charles L. Shadwell. Were one to speculate as to *Gaston's* intended length and design, one might guess that Pater planned four books or parts, as in *Marius*. Assuming six chapters in a book, Part the First would culminate in the St. Bartholomew's Massacre. The Bruno essay ("novelized" and retitled "The Lower Pantheism") would probably pick up the story a few years later, beginning Part the Second; and Part the Third would commence with the unpublished "*Mi-carême*" (in fact labeled in Pater's hand as "Book iii: Chapter XIII"). The printed portion together with the unpublished material and its lacunae make the extant portion of *Gaston* about one-half the length of *Marius* (although Herbert Horne, who tended to be accurate, noted that Pater had planned a *longer* work than *Marius*).[1]

---

1. Michael Field (pseud. of Kathleen Bradley and Edith Cooper) *Works and Days: From the Journal of Michael Field*, ed. T. and D. C. Sturge Moore (London: Murray, 1933), pp. 118–21.

Shadwell may or may not have had detailed knowledge of motives when he conjectured that Pater became "dissatisfied with the framework which he had begun, and . . . deliberately abandoned it" (1896, p. vii), but his opinion is supported by the *Athenaeum* reviewer (T. Bailey Saunders) who writes of *Gaston*: "Only a part of it had been given to the world; and that part—with which, as Mr. Shadwell suggests, and as the present writer can from his own knowledge affirm, Pater was dissatisfied—had been deliberately abandoned, or rather, perhaps, put aside for future reconsideration."[2] Arthur Symons reported that in 1889 Pater thought he needed two or three years to finish; and Herbert Horne told "Michael Field" that in 1890 Pater had announced to him his intention of sacrificing his vacations in order to complete the novel.[3] As Pater's library borrowings indicate, he seems to have been actively researching the historical background as late as the spring of 1893 when, for the seventh time, he borrowed volumes of Pierre de Brantôme's works from the Taylorian Institution (Inman 2:484). The Shadwell-Saunders "dissatisfied" does not quite suggest simple overcommitment, indicating that the mere press of having to meet serial deadlines did not alone contribute to the termination of its run. The agonizingly slow pace of composition after 1888 indicates a more basic thematic or structural problem—either, as has been suggested, with its ostensibly static gallery of literary portraits or because its complex historical scope was too broad to be distilled fictionally or, even, because themes of sadistic eroticism or moral guilt threatened to surge prominently into its foreground. The sensuous undercurrents of a Sodoma portraying the crucified Christ, for instance, flow sotto voce through Pater as well. The key role played by heteronormativity in nineteenth-century England made issues of sexual response and identity volatile. Ostracism, conflict, and the loss of self-esteem threatened those beyond the pale.

Shadwell spoke of Pater's remaining unpublished chapters (a half dozen, numbered 8–13; Chapter 12 undeniably is highly fragmentary) as "for the most part unfinished: and they have certainly not received that revision which he would have been careful to give them before he allowed them to appear among his published writings" (1896, pp. v–vi). Hence Shadwell withheld the rest because he and Pater's sisters felt that "nothing more remains of his

---

2. Rev. of *Gaston de Latour*, *The Athenaeum*, 17 October 1896: 518.

3. Field, *Ibid.*; Symons, *Figures of Several Centuries* (London: Constable, 1916), p. 331.

writings in a shape sufficiently finished for publication," and that it is "not their wish that any work of his should appear in a form less complete than he would himself have approved" (1896, p. vii). According to Sotheby's sales catalogue of 13–15 October 1942 (p. 86), these "unfinished" writings ("chapters 8–13 on 158 4to sheets") and other of Pater's holograph MSS were presented by Miss Constance Ottley to the Duke of Gloucester's Red Cross and St. John Fund for auction in two lots. The *Gaston* (its 164 leaves apparently undercounted by Sotheby's) reportedly was bought by Scribner's; it subsequently came into the possession of John Sparrow, late Warden of All Souls College, Oxford. Several additional pages, detached during composition or possibly misplaced by Sotheby's at the auction, were acquired by Harvard's Houghton Library when it purchased, in January 1961 from Mr. John Holroyd-Reece of Lincoln's Inn, London, the material originally included in Sotheby's other manuscript lot. The Sparrow holographs, which are now at Brasenose College, represent the most extended of various manuscripts Pater left behind at his untimely death.[4]

There are at least three counterarguments to override Shadwell's hesitation to publish Pater's manuscript chapters. First, the present age has a good deal more tolerance for the "unfinished"; indeed, the more one explores the art of the nineteenth century, the more one comes to appreciate the "fragment" as a major aesthetic category. Artistic success has little to do with completion *per se*, but rather with what the aesthetic object actually accomplishes. Neither art nor life, only the infinite is truly complete. Thus reflecting upon the death of his ninety-year-old grandmother, Gaston realizes that mortality has relinquished "some unfulfilled hope, something greatly desired but not to be, which left resignation, by nature or grace, still imperfect, and made death at four score years and ten seem, after all, like a premature summons in the midst of one's days" (2.24:17–20). Second, all of Pater's writing is always on the way to some further stage of perfection; one never quite arrives at Pater's final "fair copy." Indeed, after the earlier chapters of *Gaston* had been printed in *Macmillan's Magazine*, Pater apparently copied them out again and continued his process of revision; and, of course, his other published works frequently underwent successive revisions, edition after edition. Pater's unpublished chapters are way-stations to a novel that might never have found

---

4. Brasenose College Archives, shelf mark: PP1 B2/1; The Houghton Library, shelf mark: bMS Eng 1150 (4 and 23); The New York Public Library, Berg Collection catalogue listing: Walter Pater, *Gaston de Latour* holograph.

its final form in his minutely attuned sensibility, even had he lived long enough to write its last chapter. Third, Pater's growing reputation demands that this intriguing material be available to readers of his works who wish to understand the later Walter Pater of the 1890s. Pater's study of eroticism in his portrait of Queen Marguerite, for example, is a significant contribution to gender studies in the Victorian period. Since the later Pater is in many ways the most interesting of all the successive Paters—certainly wearier, but also more candid, consummately polished artistically, self-consciously aware of a dawning modernism—this new *Gaston* may come to be seen as his high-water mark intellectually, if not artistically.

Moreover, though Shadwell described the Gaston manuscripts as "unfinished," nowhere do they exhibit Pater's intention to carry out large-scale recastings of material; their intermittent incompletions are limited to the selection of references or words, insertions from above the line or from external slips, and final arrangement of phrases or modifiers. Only in very special instances do passages need substantial reconstruction to make sense, and at those points it is possible to track the chronological contours of Pater's compositional process and derive a reading text that represents the author's intended fair copy. But though several of these unpublished chapters when printed in a reading text appear very polished indeed, their atypically shorter lengths (perhaps 30% shorter than several of the *Macmillan's* chapters) suggest that for the shorter ones further expansions may yet have been intended. A former student of Pater reported to Samuel Wright that Pater once had remarked to him that he never published anything until he had written it out seven times.[5]

"I have known writers of every degree," recalled Edmund Gosse, "but never one to whom the act of composition was such a travail and an agony as it was to Pater. In his earlier years the labour of lifting the sentences was so terrific that anyone with less fortitude would have entirely abandoned the effort." Pater's process of composition began with little squares of paper on which he jotted down quotations, references, or phrases—"*memoria technica*," Gosse calls them—which he

> placed about him, like the pieces of a puzzle; . . . he would [then] begin the labour of actual composition, and so conscious was he of the modifications and additions which would supervene that he always wrote on ruled paper, leaving each alternate line blank. . . . In the first draft the phrase would be a bald one;

---

5. Monsman, *Walter Pater* (Boston: G. K. Hall, 1977), p. 145.

all herself ~~that~~ t day as under Jason's guidance he mounts

the staircase of the Louvre to learn in intimate expo-

sure as much as he cares of perhaps the most beautiful

certainly the most accessible of the ladies of that ~~time~~. such ~~to~~ day.

The martial of this embodiment of tenderness and love

seed of Venus and of Mars :— Brantôme her loyal biographer

~~he attests that with boundless admiration.~~ "her share in

the owning of armies": how   : how   .

That writer who had been neither more nor less than a

mirror of the men and women of his day, their attractive

power and grace, had withdrawn himself from their actual

presence about the time of Gaston's coming to Paris. Had

Fig. 1

P. By no means an empty sheath! She had been just in time to catch sight of the retreating Gaston, whose features are not quite new to her. At supper, amid witty ~~such~~ ~~easier~~ amendments on the lie to be ready for use next day against any compromising rumours of her presence here at so late an hour, she asks his name; and awaits him, all herself, not long after, as, under Jasmin's guidance, he mounts ~~by~~ a private staircase of the Louvre, to learn in intimate exposure as much as he will ~~saw~~ of the most beautiful, ~~and~~ as also the most accessible, of the great ladies of ~~that time~~ that day.

The martial aptitudes in this embodiment of loveliness and love – ~~folly~~ ~~of the~~ ~~fancy~~ ~~Venus~~ seed of ~~Venus~~ Venus and ~~of~~ ~~Belon~~ of Mars – Brantome ~~attests~~ has attested

with boundless admiration: "her share in the moving of armies":
how prosperously at the age of twenty-two her coming had seconded
her courage in a certain warlike mission to Flanders: how ever
in the long later years of banishment or imprisonment at Usson
grim fortress of Louis the Eleventh amid the volcanic mountains
of Auvergne her imperative genius had never desisted the adulterous impossible Queen of Navarre ought to be Queen of France.
What would you have? Even in incomparable pearls as experts
know there is always deduction to be made: il y a toujours
à redire. Well! on those ramparts of old black lightning-
struck lava she had very soon been in command. "In a little
time", says Brantome, "the keeper of the ~~prison found him~~

Fig. 3

~~...prison~~ found himself imprisoner.
~~endevmt prisonnier en...temps,~~ says Brantome
What had he thought of doing? Poor Wretch? Did he think to
~~Pauvre homme! ...voulait... fairé? Voulait tenir~~
hold captive in his cells, the woman whose eyes, whose
~~...captive en sa prison cell qui de ses yeux...~~
many countenances won looks and charms with which the
~~...visage... en ses... et chaines...~~
could at last all the rest of the world like a slave at the oar:
~~le reste du monde comme ung forcat~~

whose observant mind was
That courtly writer, ~~who had been,~~ neither more nor less
held up to
generation,
From a mirror ~~of~~ the men and women of his ~~day,~~ their

attractive power and grace, had withdrawn himself from

their actual presence about the time of Gaston's coming

him
to Paris. Had good or evil chance brought ~~Gaston~~ just
Brantome's
then into, ~~his~~ company or even into the company of his
(name him. less.)
written books Pierre de Bourdeilles, ~~and~~ or de Brantome

Fig. 4

in the blank alternate line he would at leisure insert fresh descriptive or parenthetical clauses, other adjectives, more exquisitely related adverbs, until the space was filled. It might then be supposed that the MS. was complete. Far from it! Cancelling sheet by sheet, Pater then began to copy out the whole—as before, on alternate lines of copy-book pages; this revise was treated in the same way—corrected, enlarged, interleaved, as it were, with minuter shades of feeling and more elaborate apparatus of parenthesis.[6]

This incremental composition ensures an unbroken text at nearly every stage of composition, without the possibility that whole scenes may have been intended for transposition from one chapter to another.

The plates (Figs. 1–4) show how the cancelled leaf 3 was expanded to become leaves 3–5 of Chapter 9 (Pater flips his cancelled page over to use the scrap for his revision; his earlier canceled draft now appears as the verso of leaf 5). One suspects there may have been an intermediate stage of revision in which interlineations occurred of the sort Gosse describes, as they do on leaf 5 when Pater decides to translate Brantôme's passage into English. But like deaths in Greek drama, all the fire of Pater's compositional process has blazed elsewhere; such holographic revisions as are apparent on the manuscript pages signify very little about the mind in creation, its struggles or its deepest intentions. The more inchoate essays at Harvard's Houghton Library are no more revealing; Pater's most intimate voice will probably be in his most polished and public productions. In the *Gaston* manuscripts, one seeks in vain for evidence of prolonged, intense creative wrestling with conceptual and emotional issues; Pater's powerful imagination often seems epitomized by a pedantic preoccupation with narrative housekeeping—insuring that "un-looked for" is corrected to "unlooked-for" (7.69:33).

This "pointillistic" or word-specific compositional style has been surprisingly helpful in deciphering difficult-to-read cancelations; one can often find the identical phrase uncanceled not far away in the text. Pater typically does not give up on a canceled word or phrase until he uses it elsewhere. Towards the end of Chapter 13, Pater's intense determination to use "blond" leads him to try it out again and again—somewhere, anywhere, just get that "blond" in. Obviously some connotative (perhaps in this instance

---

6. Gosse, "Walter Pater" *Critical Kit-Kats* (London, Heinemann, 1896), pp. 262–64; see also E. B. Titchener, "Walter Horatio Pater," *Book Reviews*, October 1894, p. 202.

homoerotic) quality that only "blond" conveyed seemed to him singularly applicable across a specific range of text. As to Pater's comprehensive "outline" or plan of composition, it was either an arrangement of earlier drafts that were cut up (Pater frequently jotted down notes on the backs of drafts cut into "post-it" size squares about 3 1/2" x 2 1/4", though this does not suggest transpositions of blocks of material) or existed only in his methodical mind, much as Mozart is said to have composed without sketches.

If, indeed, the "sisters" (actually this would undoubtedly have been principally Clara, the intellectual sister, who was a classics tutor at Somerville College and later privately taught Greek to Virginia Woolf) did feel the later chapters were too unrevised for publication, it may have been only after Clara had worked on them for an afternoon or two. Clara evidently attempted to transcribe a fair copy of Chapter 13 and her version seems to have benefited from access to her brother's notes or sources, if not his personal oversight. (Possibly also in Chapter 8 Clara may have made pencil emendations, perhaps before Walter's death, in an effort to jump-start a stalled process. Walter then may have overwritten one such emendation on folio 6. On the other hand, these may be exceptionally tentative corrections by Pater himself.)

In one instance in Chapter 13, Clara matches an asterisked slip to an asterisk in the manuscript, precisely as a modern editor would do; and in another place, she reconstructs a heavily canceled passage almost as if she had access to some other draft. But where advice might have been sought from her brother, Clara's version omits difficult-to-read words, phrases, and passages that could have been recovered or reconstructed with small in-put from him; she misinterprets an "index" marking as an underlining and at least once introduces a patently wrong emendation because she was oblivious to the Pauline context of Pater's passage. Were one to assume her draft was for Pater's use, why then did she ignore his preferred 12–line mode for revision (she cramps 21–25 lines on a much smaller sheet). Finally, the striking augmentation (13.129:33–34) describing a Parisian *aubépine* that resembles the hawthorn in the so very English "Child in the House" leaves one wondering: did Pater consciously intend here to create parallel imagery or did Clara after her brother's death draw upon a preeminently Paterian passage to assist in her *own* creative reconstruction? Though she astutely uses Paterian phraseology, these words may not have been specifically intended by Pater to go here. For Clara, no pot is so bent some lid won't fit it—or no plot so broken some "lidden" can't rescue it. I *admire* Clara's desire to make the chapter whole; but if she does go too far (and who dares say for sure), her filling the lacunae in Pater's manuscripts certainly demonstrates one most interesting fact (*contra* Pater's theory, not to mention Flaubert's): there are *many* serviceable *mots justes*.

This, then, was the state of the novel in 1896 when Shadwell published the posthumous edition, reprinted a number of times but never edited anew. Contemporaneous opinion took its cue from Shadwell's brief comments on the novel's stylistic polish, its fragmentary state, and its nebulous plot. Several reviewers followed the line that it was fragmentary because Pater had not thought out Gaston's character and the thread of his personal experience is gradually lost. Most agreed that its "pensive pages" concealed a careful stylistic elaboration that fittingly caped Pater's career. And nearly all accepted Shadwell's edition as definitive. The *Outlook* reviewer baldly declares this volume to be "the last thing of Walter Pater's that will be published"[7]; and T. Bailey Saunders in the *Athenaeum* more circumspectly claims that the seven chapters of *Gaston* are all that were left suitable for publication, but then stumbles even by his own standards when he asserts that those chapters "lacked revision."[8] All voices seem to have agreed that Shadwell's surmounting his reluctance to allow the world to read Pater's unfinished work was a literary event barely surpassed by the composition of the novel itself.

THE PUBLISHED CHAPTERS:
CHOICE OF COPY TEXT & EDITING PRINCIPLES

MOST READERS hitherto have known *Gaston* through the *Macmillan's Magazine* chapters as edited and printed in Shadwell's 1896 volume. Interestingly, a 276–leaf manuscript version of all but one of these published chapters (1–5 and 7) is in The New York Public Library, purchased in December 1958 for the Berg collection from Hamill and Barker (Evanston, Ill.), the antiquarian booksellers having acquired it in England "before 1920" at auction or from another bookseller.[9] Though one generally assumes a holograph precedes first publication, the manuscript of Chapters 1–5 and 7

---

7. Rev. of "Gaston de Latour," *The Outlook*, 27 March 1897: 853.

8. Rev. of *Gaston de Latour*, *The Athenaeum*, 17 October 1896: 519.

9. The holograph and three slips are on ruled, laid writing paper, one edge uneven; the cut edges of some sheets are tinted cobalt (either evenly or in a marbled pattern) and those of other sheets are untinted. The paper measures 9" vertically though a few sheets are very slightly shorter; horizontally, the leaves vary from 7" to 7 7/16". Writing is on the recto only; all corrections are in ink.

that is in the Berg collection turned out to have been copied anew by Pater from the *Macmillan's* printing, just as Pater had done with "Hippolytus Veiled" not long before his death (Evans, p. 153, Letter of April or May 1894). Thus a passage in Chapter 4 of the *Macmillan's* version of "Peach Blossom and Wine" (pp. 396–97), later moved to *Plato and Platonism*, is not in the later Berg holograph. Numerous other emendations of published passages in the Berg holograph suggest that Pater revised *as* he copied the *Macmillan's* text. Probably Pater's intention in copying these chapters anew on alternate lines, twelve textual lines to a page (or occasionally marking multi-line manuscript lacunae with reference dots on the left-hand side of the sheet), was to create space for alterations, should he wish, by interlining so as to create a twenty-four row page. (Pater seems to have reversed George Eliot's practice as instanced by *Daniel Deronda*, for example, where on nearly the same-size sheet she packs two written lines between each ruling.) One also notes that only Chapter 1 of the Berg manuscript is numbered; Pater presumably leaves unnumbered the other chapters in order to allow for the possible insertion of whole pages. Given the existence of the Berg holograph, one realizes that the published chapters of *Gaston* are preliminary (much as James Joyce's serialized chapters in *The Egoist* of *The Portrait of the Artist as a Young Man* were not in final revised form), though they are more finished than the drafts of Chapters 8–13. Because the whole of the novel was actively undergoing a process of composition and revision not long before Pater's death, the narrative's greatest intellectual and artistic unity is achieved by combining the Berg as the base text for Chapters 1–5 and 7 with the BNC/Houghton holographs for Chapters 8–13; Shadwell's printing of Chapter 6, which is the only version known at the present date, will serve as the base text for that segment.

In selecting the Berg as copy text, the question naturally had arisen whether Shadwell made use of the draft now in the Berg collection for his 1896 edition. Apparently he did—but inconsistently. (Did Shadwell perhaps keep this manuscript until his death in 1919, after which it was purchased by Frances Hamill in the trade?) Not only did Shadwell decline to publish the more unevenly finished Chapters 8–13 of Pater's novel-in-progress, but in editing the *Macmillan's* chapters he incorporated a few but disregarded most of Pater's settled emendations found in the Berg manuscript. Just possibly his choice of readings for the 1896 edition may reflect reliance upon some other lost copy text or set of off-prints corrected by the author before his death (for example, Pater lightly revised an offprint of "The Child in the House"—now in the Library of Worcester College—for its private reprinting). The penultimate sentence in Chapter 5 of Shadwell's 1896 edition is found nowhere else and clearly was meant to bridge from the chapter on Montaigne to the following one on the St. Bartholomew's Day massacre. Since Pater discontinued publication in *Macmillan's* with Chapter 5 (all the previous chapters had been marked "To be continued," but not this chapter), one might assume that such a transition sentence may have been canceled in *Macmillan's* proofs when Pater foresaw discontinuing the series and that Shadwell restored it for his edition. But it is also characteristic of a later draft; and if the Berg holograph is the most complete and corrected text, that sentence ought to have been restored to it. Still, this is tenuous evidence for a fair copy later than the Berg and to suppose its existence is ultimately untenable.

Assuming that in 1896 Shadwell combined the Berg holograph with the *Macmillan's* text or its corrected proofs, the most likely explanation for his creating a hybrid text is that by his own standards he wished to guard against corruptions—to be absolutely certain that the words we read are the words not only that Pater wrote but that they were the choices he would have made had he lived long enough to complete his novel. In a letter of 25 January 1896 to Gosse, Clara speaks of Shadwell liking "to make his own emendations from the original MS rather than from the printed article."[10] But Shadwell employs guidelines that destroy any meaningful concept of a critically constructed Edition Text. In the case of divergence, he sometimes prefers the holograph, sometimes the magazine. Among numerous small examples, here is a typical one (chosen in part because I admire the evocative immediacy with which Pater conjures up Ronsard's meal (3.32:26–29), while simultaneously conflating imagery from the poet's "*La Salade*" with Baudelaire's "*Le Crépuscule du soir*"):

Macmillan's Magazine: The snow was falling now in big, slow flakes, a great fire blazing under the chimney, its cipher and enigmatic motto, as they sat down to the leek soup, the hard eggs, and the salad grown and gathered by their host's own hands. (p. 263)

Berg manuscript: The snow was falling now in big slow flakes and ⎰while⎱ a great fire blazed under the chimney with its cipher and enigmatic motto as they

---

10. Monsman, "Editing Pater's *Gaston de Latour*: The Unfinished Work as 'A Fragment of Perfect Expression,'" *Pater in the 1990s*, eds. Laurel Brake and Ian Small (Greensboro: ELT Press, 1991), p. 31.

sat down to the leek-soup the hard eggs and the salad grown and gathered by their host's own hands. (folio 125)

Shadwell's 1896 edition: The snow was falling now in big, slow flakes, a great fire blazing under the chimney with its cipher and enigmatic motto, as they sat down to the leek-soup, the hard eggs, and the salad grown and gathered by their host's own hands. (p. 78)

Shadwell quite appropriately retained the *Macmillan's* punctuation for his edition since in the Berg as well as in the BNC/Houghton manuscripts, Pater frequently withheld his punctuation, especially from the more obvious places such as series, probably intending to finalize the mechanics of his points later after he was certain of the over-arching rhythms he desired to obtain. However, although Shadwell incorporates the Berg's "with," he rejects its "and a great fire blazed." Yet if Shadwell was following no other fair copy, he could be accused of finicky editorial tampering.

Shadwell's conception of Pater as a reviser is one who proposes emendations to himself but, quite frequently, rejects them when it comes time to make his final choice. That may be indeed in some measure Pater's practice, but it is not Shadwell's prerogative to determine those instances by personal preference. Shadwell's procedure, certainly, has the superficial appearance of restrained editorial intervention, but he does not really have a single base text; he blends the manuscript and the magazine wordings together. His editorial preferences are intuitive, graceful; he is reluctant to concede authority to either holograph or magazine versions unless they agree. And even when they agree, he will still sometimes impose his own punctuation or, on his own authority, add a small "that" or "the" or, carried away improving upon the style of Pater, substitute a "however" for Pater's "so" or insert a "nay!" or a modifying "divine" or italicize or transpose material. For example, when Pater described Bruno as presenting "himself in the comely Dominican habit" (7.80:2), Shadwell's sense of precision led him to insert "presented himself *to his audience* in the comely Dominican habit" (italics added).

Is Shadwell's *Gaston* a product of sound editorial practice or of possible malpractice? Shadwell would have believed his method the best posthumous tribute, justifying it as more correct than the hurried product of periodical publication or incomplete revision. But, of course, his text is the creation of a sensibility not Pater's, howsoever Pater may have generated the options among which Shadwell's choices usually are made. By suppressing the apparently less-finished chapters and by disregarding chronology in order to arrive at a single text, he sacrificed what may be considered the rich insights into textual differences, into the physical make-up of the manuscript that reveals process, variables, and emerging intentions—all those "non-essentials" that actually are integral.

Resisting the urge to recreate the light that never was on sea or land—a text rebuilt according to a subjective sense of Pater's intentions—I adopt wording in editing the Berg manuscript that will be either on the line or is an interlineation that fills a linear lacuna or is accompanied by a cancelation or a caret, the practical equivalent to linearity since one assumes such wording has benefited from Pater's more deliberate choice. Canceled material and interlined careted material in the holograph constitute Pater's considered emendations of his text and, unlike in the diplomatic transcriptions of the unpublished chapters, is treated in the Edition Text according to Pater's marked intentions without specific transcriptional notation (a perhaps too-elaborate way of saying holograph revisions have been silently adopted); also, variation in the *placement* of punctuation relative to quotation marks has been silently regularized by the editor, and the form of the chapter headings has been standardized. Significant interlined uncareted material is recorded in the Emendations & Variants. Oddly, in a few instances the uncareted interlineation was the originally published phrasing; but since I am privileging Pater's decided wording in the manuscript, that alternative must go into the variants with all the other provisional (uncareted) interlineations.

Finally, one might be tempted as a working guideline to omit punctuation found in the earlier magazine version but not found in the Berg manuscript, assuming that the Berg manuscript is displaying an apparent evolution toward an overall simplification of punctuation. But large sections of the Berg MS are so lightly punctuated as to be confusing. In some places, series are wholly unpunctuated; that surely is not mere streamlining. Indeed, *any* streamlining of the *Macmillan* punctuation in the Berg MS may be merely an illusion produced by a temporary incompletion sealed by Pater's death. Only Chapter 1 of the Berg appears very nearly definitively punctuated (and perhaps that is why it is the only Berg chapter Pater paginated). As in *Marius* so in *Gaston*, Pater is continuously tinkering with punctuation, seemingly without any consistent theory behind the changes other than his subjective ear for rhythm. Given Pater's accretive compositional style, both the Berg and *Macmillan* texts probably show only an evolving and provisional form of punctuation, particularly when one considers that deadline pressures may have contributed to a more-hasty-than-usual review of the *Macmillan* text; indeed, its punctuation may have been more the product of the compositor than of Pater.

Some streamlining by Pater in the Berg text did involve breaking up clauses joined by a semicolon into two sentences. But although in some places the Berg text is much more lightly punctuated than the *Macmillan*, other chapters of the Berg are more heavily punctuated than the *Macmillan*, though not always consistently throughout. Occasionally when punctuation in these texts diverges, Pater may be substituting a mark in one place for a mark in another place; but more often, where punctuation is present in one text but not in the other, this divergence is the result of incompletion rather than a stylistic choice.

For this edition, all of Pater's existing punctuation in the Berg manuscript has been retained in the form given there (*mutatis mutandis*, Pater is not above the occasional error); additional punctuation will be supplied from the *Macmillan's* version (or for Chapter 7, from the parallel passages in the *Fortnightly*) unless clearly redundant. Moreover, except for Chapter 6 for which there is no other authority than Shadwell's 1896 edition, the presumption is that when Shadwell's mechanics (and occasionally wording) diverge from both the magazine and Berg versions his variants have no authority but his own.

THE UNPUBLISHED CHAPTERS:
COPY TEXTS & PRINCIPLES OF EDITING

TURNING NOW to the BNC/Houghton holographs of Chapters 8–13, the editor is presented with three options and various combinations thereof: facsimile, diplomatic transcription, and reading text. The facsimile would all but put Pater's original working drafts in the hands of scholars; and I am aware from discussions in the 1960s with John Sparrow (after he'd finished "scolding" me about my "speculative" *Pater's Portraits*) that his preference had been for photographic facsimiles to accompany a reading text on facing pages—not unlike the Loeb Library classics with their original Greek or Latin face to face with the translation. Although the expense of facsimile reproduction fell rapidly in the 1970s, the deciphering of Pater's handwriting alternatives (not exclusively in the canceled passages) would remain a major difficulty for readers who had only the manuscript facsimile and its reading text. I therefore included, as part of the Apparatus Criticus to my Edition Text, a diplomatic transcription for those who wish insight into Pater's compositional process or are pursuing a formal analysis. The Edition Text itself I based on the definitive manuscripts (i.e. authoritative and apparently exhaustive, though not entire and finished), enlarged to incorporate or to footnote in its Apparatus Criticus all the fragments or "slips" (Pater's word for them) associated with the BNC and Berg holographs (and those slips at the Houghton that refer directly to the novel's text, excluding notes that may pertain more generally to the historical period).

In the diplomatic transcription, Pater's punctuation or lack of it, lacunae, alternate wordings, cancelations and other stumbles will be retained—this is the garden with real (though altogether engrossing) toads in it. Although the diplomatic arrangement is designed to represent with a high degree of objective accuracy the facts of handwriting on the page, obviously an editorial judgment is made about just where to the right or left of words on the line Pater intended to place extended interlineations without carets. Even among simpler instances, Pater's intention may vie with accidents of spacing: in Chapter 10, folio 21, Pater wrote "by way of 'mystery'" on the line; then because he was avoiding a descender in the line above and the high-flying quotation mark, he centered an uncareted "a" over "way of." Whereas the "a" and the quotation mark could not occupy the same space on Pater's page, diplomatic transcription slightly idealizes the spacing according to Pater's obvious intention: "by way of ⌈a⌋ 'mystery.'" Of course, simply by making these observations, some of the objectivity lost through the enhancement of diplomatic transcription can be recuperated. Moreover, the diachronicity of a diplomatic arrangement can reveal intended logical relationships between passages that the facsimile's synchronicity cannot do (in short, the editor has done the "fundamental brainwork" of *suggesting* what goes with what, though if he is wrong—heaven forfend—the reader can construct alternate scenarios from the data provided.)

Although the diplomatic transcription schematizes to the last detail the structures and is thus of value to the scholar, it can be intrusively awkward, inaccessible to the reader who wishes to pursue the novel as, for example, a milepost in cultural studies. A reading text, on the other hand, makes some compromises with the artifact—it specifies choices upon which the author had not himself finally decided, clears away the debris of canceled passages, supplies missing data, standardizes punctuation and corrects small mistakes. If the diplomatic text is the artifact as unretouched as practicable, the reading text is the novel corrected to the point at which the reader is able to rely upon it as authoritative without an insistent awareness of its problematics. The reading text will edit the manuscript to produce copy almost as if Pater had delivered it as his monthly installment, read proof, revised it for book publication, and handed out complimentary copies (with his calling card so neatly inserted into the flyleaf under four little corner cuts).

The arrangement of headings, the italicizing of foreign words and phrases, and the paragraphing and punctuation in the holograph needed to be formalized. Pater's paragraphing displays an outmoded quirk: he usually does not indicate a new paragraph by indentation, only by whatever fraction of a line concludes the preceding paragraph. When the preceding paragraph ends with a full-length line, his practice is to indent minimally or to indicate a new paragraph with the symbol: ¶. Clearly he expected *Macmillan's* to set the material in the conventional way, but his particular practice suggests a need to do serious composing—his thinking, his "listening" to rhythms—in 6 3/4 inch lines (mere notes on slips being the exception)! Also, Pater had punctuated his manuscript drafts of Chapters 8–13 incompletely (this is also true of the Berg manuscript in many places, as I have noted). Only a few sentences seem to have been fully divided in the later chapters. I have attempted to approximate Pater's published usage (which is not governed by current grammatical rules but by rhythm and emphasis); I have not, however, deleted any appropriate manuscript punctuation Pater may have supplied. As to the placement of commas relative to quotation marks (inside or outside of them), neither the *Macmillan's* version nor, even, the 1896 edition is wholly consistent. Amusingly, in the magazine on a single page, column A may follow the inside rule, column B the outside rule. In the manuscript, Pater tends to an outside placement for commas and an inside placement for such other marks as exclamations and interrogatories. However, Pater's previous novel, *Marius the Epicurean*, and the *Fortnightly Review* use a more current placement of commas and periods inside closing quotation marks, all other punctuation outside except when it is part of the quoted material; and I follow that practice throughout.

Pater's standard abbreviations have been silently expanded: ("wh." to "which" or "cath: ch:" to "catholic church"). Although I have maintained Pater's nineteenth-century orthography, obvious errors have been emended and noted. Pater makes practically no English spelling errors; however, his Renaissance French seems occasionally to have been corrupted in transmission from draft to draft: *vaquasmes* becomes *vasquames*, and the like. But because Pater is notoriously free in quoting from sources (there are strategic purposes behind this), I have not emended deliberate interpolations or deletions or adjustments (though to maintain historical consistency, slight adjustments have been made in the orthography of quotations).

When reasonable I have supplied missing material in brackets in the place of Pater's manuscript gaps; but no authority other than the editor's understanding of Pater's intention should be imputed to it (and that understanding, when requisite, will be given in the Explanatory Notes). In the essay "Style," Pater typified his own approach when he described Flaubert's search for *le mot juste*, "the one word for the one thing, the one thought, amid the multitude of words, terms, that might just do" (*Appreciations*, p. 29). With these words ringing in his ears, an editor might well blanch at the task of selecting among those stacked interlineations (even assuming one has editorial guidelines to apply), not to mention filling empty spaces in the manuscript. Paradoxically, the emptiness is often a powerful clue. If stacks of alternatives suggest Pater was trying possibilities on his ear and sensibility, gaps on the other hand suggest he had a specific word or name at the edge of his thought. Given that a major purpose of editorial work is to make explicit what is implicit, the absent but specific is often easier to identify than it is to decide the variable values of predetermined but competing alternatives of wording.

An example might be the first lacuna in Chapter 11, folio 1, in which Pater speaks of "a new French version of the old Greek of [1.5 cm]." Since Pater is discussing historical accounts of ancient tyrants like Elagabalus, and since possibly the most famous translation in the whole Renaissance was Amyot's Plutarch that is filled with just such portraits of autocratic rulers (Brantôme's editor Lalanne even incorrectly asserts that "Héliogable" [9:542 n.1] was one of them), there can be no doubt as to the name. Moreover, Montaigne, who is foregrounded in Pater's novel, read Plutarch in precisely this translation. And if all this were not conclusive enough, Pater earlier mentioned "the eminent translator of Plutarch, Amyot" (2.23:13). Was Pater deliberately teasing his future editor with such blanks ("if you're good at crossword puzzles, you'll love editing my manuscripts")? Hardly; though since the missing name is so crashingly obvious, one can only imagine Pater hesitated because a mistake (a slip of Pausanias for Plutarch, say) would be so blatant and, hence, embarrassing (as in the instance of "Jacques" de La Mole, when Pater confused the father's name with that of the son). I suggest this hesitation is less a matter of mind / memory than of personality / intellectual *brio*. Thus Pater's manuscript gaps frequently can be filled by inferring the word or name from the continuity, correspondence, or other parallelism the editor discovers between what is missing and what is actually provided. On some occasions I avail myself of what I take to be Clara's principle of filling gaps with "previously-used" material, but only when I am certain I am reconstructing or enhancing an already established authorial intention, not creating an editorial one. (This assumes that if there is only one *mot juste* that ought to go in, even Pater, as those stacked alternatives are always suggesting, does not invariably know which it might be.) Clara's diligence was perhaps too far-reaching; thus when lacunae occur and deep conjecture is only darkness, brackets surround an inarticulate void.

But by far the most important editorial issue to be decided was the matter of interlineations without carets. Interlinear wording with carets and cancelations represents a clear decision on Pater's part, and such wording obviously should be incorporated in any edition; however, without such indicative markings Pater's choice is presumably still pending. When uncareted interlinear alternatives vie with linear wording, the editor's quandary can only be resolved by some indication of preference other than cancelation or careting; that is, the editor privileges one alternative over another either because it has been previously published, or because it is on the line and chronologically prior, or because it is above the line and chronologically subsequent. Since no form of the wording of the BNC/Houghton holographs ever was published by Pater, uncareted interlineations may be taken to have roughly the same or more authority as the linear wording, inasmuch as Pater's last contemplated alternative is most likely a pending revision of an earlier still-pending linear formulation. The interlinear option is thus privileged over the linear wording; under these circumstances, "last is best" is a touchstone of sensible editing. Thus in defining the reading text an editorial parting of paths occurs in the handling of the BNC/Houghton in comparison with the Berg manuscript.

Clearly Pater has signaled his intention to revise by returning even his published text to manuscript fluidity (this is most explicitly the case in Chapter 7). The whole of the novel might be considered at Pater's death to have been undergoing a process of composition and revision, and thus the editorial choice of unmarked alternatives throughout might be governed not by considerations of prior publication or location on the line but by chronological currency—the last written is the first chosen. Yet I sense a greater degree of difference in the Berg manuscript between Pater's provisional interlineations and the previously published wording on the line, albeit revised somewhat, than in the BNC/Houghton manuscript between provisional interlineations and its linear, but never published, wording—the linear text of Chapters 1–5 and 7 clearly seems less provisional than that of Chapters 8–13. Thus uncareted material in the Berg is considered a variation, whereas in the BNC/Houghton it is retained for the reading text itself.

Even with this matter resolved, other ambiguities persist in deriving an authoritative reading text from the BNC/Houghton holograph: confronted with a slipping and sliding pile of nested interlinear alternatives in Chapters

8–13, one is not always able to tell what was chronologically the last written. Pater begins with a twelve-line page; then usually adds his first alternative above the line to begin a twenty-four line page. He then sometimes squeezes in his next alternative *between* the first interlineation and the original line below. So on occasion his chronologically last alternative—sometimes his preferred, sometime a canceled option—may possibly be lower than his initially proposed alternative (thus the diplomatic ordering from the line upwards is *not* consistently chronological).

In a preliminary editing of two chapters that eventually appeared in the *Victorians Institute Journal* as "Walter Pater's Portrait of Marguerite of Valois, Queen of Navarre,"[11] I was mindful of Warden Sparrow's typescript of the material that circulated *sub rosa* for nearly a half century as the only version apart from the original item itself. Sparrow's rendering became part of the way this material was encountered by those few *cognoscenti* who were fortunate enough to see it (I among them so many years ago in his floor-to-ceiling book-lined study where letters from Browning or Rossetti were always slipping from between the pages of their first editions). With a kind of nod (if not Jacques La Mole's flinging of the cap) toward John Sparrow, my editorial stance accorded with his "last is best" guideline, one that I continue to believe is the most defensible for the unpublished chapters. I there applied, however, Sparrow's principle more consistently than did he, who, on a few occasions, lapsed into Shadwell's tendency to make choices inconsistent with any clear-cut rules or, more rarely, to reconstruct passages intuitively. Thus for the *VIJ* text when a choice of wording or a choice of placement of words was encountered, the principle employed had been to select either the uppermost or comparable last alternative Pater contemplated (unless fragmentary, illogical, or producing an ungrammatical, unidiomatic or blatantly uneuphoneous reading), even though Pater's interlineations may not have been locked up definitively with carets and deletions. Pater may not *invariably* have made that choice (indeed, a few seemed to me stylistically inferior to the linear wording); however, sequence can be read as giving one of the strongest indications of the wording Pater was striving for in his next working draft *and* unquestionably supplies the editor with an objective standard that guards

---

11. "Walter Pater's Portrait of Marguerite of Valois, Queen of Navarre: The Hitherto Unpublished Chapters IX and X of *Gaston de Latour*," *Victorians Institute Journal*, 20 [1992], vi, 260–302)

against his editorial preferences being subtly fobbed off on the reader as Pater's own. In Chapter 8, I do not always follow the pencil emendations as did Sparrow routinely in his typescript; for even if made by Pater (the handwriting bears a similarity to that of his juvenile letters; but also to Clara's letters), I am not certain they would have been adopted by him in his fair copy (certainly the penciled *sensual* [Chapter 8, folio 6] seems to have been canceled with forceful consternation).

Of course, when one considers idiom and euphony in word choice, one may be edging half-way toward subjectivity; here the editor's sense of *degree* is crucial. Two examples may illustrate the latitude of editorial discretion permitted. In "Anteros" Pater describes Raoul, about to be executed, as having become "humbler than a little child, . . . may be handled, turned this way and that, as passively as a child already dead" (10.108:35–37). Without caret, he had interlined "dead" above "a child"; but to adopt "a dead child" would create a choppy phrasing coming immediately after "a little child." Perhaps, beyond formal considerations of style, something of the brilliant morbidity of the original phrasing entered into my choice (though that would be an inexcusable editorial lapse).

Again, in *"Mi-carême"* Pater writes: "¶↑?↓ The people of Paris says one ↑Mérimée↓ were at that date ↑a cette epoque day↓ horriblement fanatique: its ↑the↓ pulpits ↑of P.↓ rang just then with fanatical leaguist sermons: . . ." (Chapter 13, folio 9). As reading text, this becomes: "The people of Paris, says Mérimée, were at that day *horriblement fanatique*: its pulpits rang just then with fanatical leaguist sermons: . . ." (13.131:25–26). The suggested paragraphing is adopted because its absence would create an uncharacteristically long block of material. Moreover, because Mérimée is uppermost (happily but irrelevantly also an improved specificity), the name is accepted. Although *"a cette époque horriblement fanatique"* is Mérimée's exact phrase (excluding consideration of those pesky accent marks which always bedeviled Pater), on a left-to-right progression "day" is endmost and so technically is chronologically last. But for purposes of euphony, I retain the original "its pulpits rang" because "the pulpits of Paris" obtrusively rephrases "The people of Paris," a settled reading. Occasionally synonyms written on the line—". . . spread themselves so gracefully, easily, superbly for an hour" (10.102:10–11); ". . . evanescent sympathies attachments affections operative as if through a mere touch in the dark" (10.261:20–21)—might not be coordinates all intended to be retained but alternates among which a final choice had been momentarily postponed. The editor, finally, has to make a judgment, though I was frequently surprised at how little the text was affected interpretively by the selection of any one option rather than another or, even, by my preserving several options; generally, I retained as much as possible without exceeding the upper limits of Pater's practice.

DESIGN & THEME

THE FINAL RESULT of combining the Berg and Brasenose / Houghton holographs has been to produce a wholly new reading text for *Gaston*, startlingly further along in the compositional process and surely closer to Pater's intention of what this text should "ultimately" become. The editor's work stands on the ground of what can be, between the truly needless imperfections of what has been in the 1896 text and the never-to-be-realized excellencies of what might have been had Pater come closer to completing it. William Buckler's explanation as to why he considered *Gaston* a fail-ure—Pater does not portray Gaston's assimilation of environmental surround-ings with as consistent a degree of continuous interiority as he does Marius's[12]—could hardly have been made in the same terms had he had access to this edition; perhaps even with access merely to Shadwell's text Buckler's aesthetic judgment shouldn't have been made. At all events, this new edition makes it clear Pater has taken his definition of what he called a "religious phase possible for the modern mind" (Evans, Letter of 22 July 1883) one important step further.

Pater designed his novel to be the second in a trilogy of which *Marius the Epicurean* had been the first, selecting the complex age of the Valois for its setting. As *Marius* thematized the transition from paganism to Christianity, so *Gaston* is set just following the Reformation, in the troubled see-sawing of the religious wars between Catholicism and Protestantism—"a sort of Marius in France, in the 16th Century" (Evans, Letter of 22 January 1892). Though Pater asserted the definition of a "religious phase" to have been the purpose of *Marius*, manifestly it is only in the Renaissance that "the modern mind" emerged in all its historical complexity. Buckler's assertion that the personali-ties of the eponymous heroes are rendered somewhat differently in terms of authorial focus upon interior processes is comparatively true. But what he should also have noted (since earlier studies had quoted the passage) is that

---

12. William E. Buckler, *Walter Pater: The Critic as Artist of Ideas* (New York: New York University Press, 1987), pp. 275–86.

Pater anticipates (though perhaps Buckler might say, rationalizes) dwelling "at length on what was visible in Paris just then, on the mere historic scene there, forgetful it might seem of the company of Gaston, but only because I do suppose him thoughtfully looking on with us all the while, as essentially a creature of the eye, even more likely than others to be shaped by what he sees" (11.121:15–19): dramatic action is filtered by memory, ideas, and multiple perspectives, dissolved so radically that the fictional protagonist seems almost to be reading about the age in which he lived.

This indirection of representation may be more extreme for Gaston than for Marius but is still only a difference in degree; and, in fact, it positions *Gaston* closer to Pater's other works. Consider this: the transgenerational consciousness of *The Renaissance* that Pater epitomized in Mona Lisa (the "symbol" "summing up in itself, all modes of thought and life") yielded in *Marius* to the more synchronic mentality of its hero. But although Pater is dealing with a single lifespan in the consciousness of Gaston, "strange thoughts and fantastic reveries and exquisite passions" are here again defined as multiple: Gaston is "shaped by what he sees" in sixteenth-century France—and what he sees is what he is. The emphasis is not just upon Gaston's own processes of perception, but upon all those complex relationships (more complex, even, than in Henry James's narratives) between past and present, reality and ideas, public and private, authors and readers—Pater and his nineteenth-century audience, not least. Of course, not all sensations and ideas are equally moral; *Marius the Epicurean* had been intended as Pater's first corrective for hedonistic misreadings of the "Conclusion" to *Studies in the History of the Renaissance*. *Gaston de Latour* would extend that caveat—most particularly to Oscar Wilde.

Accordingly, around 1890, perhaps after a two-year hiatus in composition, Pater's conception of his novel evolved to include a new note of urgency in response to Wilde's critical essays and novel. The first version of *The Picture of Dorian Gray* appeared in July 1890; that August Pater abruptly canceled a trip to Italy in order to "finish" *Gaston* (Evans, Letter of 9 August 1890 & n.3). Wilde's Lord Henry Wotton incessantly misquotes both *The Renaissance* and *Marius*; likewise, Wilde's Gilbert praises Pater and declares that "Art is out of the reach of morals" ("The Critic as Artist," Part 2). Reviewing *Dorian Gray*, Pater remarked that Wilde's novel "fails" to set forth a "true Epicureanism" (i.e., the Paterian theory of life defined six years before in *Marius the Epicurean*) because—if indeed life imitates art—art must be understood to contain the "moral sense, . . . the sense of sin and righteousness," something that Wilde's heroes are bent on losing "as speedily, as completely as they can."[13] Pater saw an important distinction between Wilde's flippant dictum to "Live up to your blue china" and his own strenuous desire "to burn with a hard, gem-like flame." He selected Wilde's witticism as a chapter epigraph for "An Empty House" to inaugurate his 1890 continuation of *Gaston*—at least until he canceled it as a too direct attack upon his admirer.

Wilde had seemed willfully to misread the celebrations in *Marius* and *Gaston* of the awakening power of an influential book. Indeed, Lord Henry even misconstrues Pater's cautionary essay on "Giordano Bruno," which had appeared only a month before the composition of *Dorian* began. Just where Wilde in Chapter 4 echoes Pater's essay, Pater turns his imaginary portrait of Bruno back upon Lord Henry's reflections. In material added to the essay for its "novelized" version, Pater stressed the too enticing dissociation of intellectual positions from moral values—doctrines unintentionally can produce treacherous advice and words may have indirectly fatal consequences (7.81–82). Elsewhere *Gaston*, speculating on Jasmin's "hidden sin," is reassured by his friend's bursting suddenly in with "cheerful noise proper to youth," "gaiety of step" and "sincerity of voice," not unlike the youthful Dorian Gray. But, startlingly, whereas in Wilde's novel the hero of Dorian's golden book originally had been named "Raoul" (a name Wilde canceled in his typescript), in Pater's resumption Raoul is made the pathetic victim of a suicidal idolatry for Jasmin.[14] Could this be Pater's warning about detachment from responsibility in such perilous liaisons? And might Queen Margot also be Pater's editorial on the exaggerated sexuality of Wilde's *Salomé*, just then on the horizon (10.104–105)?

If Gilbert, Dorian, and Salomé are indiscriminate in gazing upon the sensuous and sensual aspects of culture, Gaston will seek his alter ego only in some moral sensibility expressed in and through artistic beauty. All of Pater's fiction depicts the quest for a morally regenerate and incorruptible humanity—in *Marius*, for the "fairest of all, . . . that supreme beauty which must of necessity be unique" (*Marius*, 2:161); in *Gaston*, for "the manifestation, at the moment of his own worthiness, of flawless humanity, in some undreamed-of depth and perfection of the loveliness of bodily form" (3.36:33–34). Shadwell ventures the observation, possibly based on some-

---

13. "A Novel by Mr. Oscar Wilde." Rev. of *The Picture of Dorian Gray*. *The Bookman*, 1 (November 1891), pp. 59–60.

14. Oscar Wilde, *The Picture of Dorian Gray*, ed. Isobel Murray (Oxford: Oxford University Press, 1981), pp. 230–31 n.1.

thing Pater may have told him, that the novel's "interest would have centred round the spiritual development of a refined and cultivated mind, capable of keen enjoyment in the pleasures of the senses and of the intellect, but destined to find its complete satisfaction in that which transcends both" (1896, p. vi). The fundamental pattern in Pater's thought is precisely this typical nineteenth-century paradigm of thesis, antithesis, synthesis—the last stage being somehow implicit but never quite attained permanently. This dialectic, says Pater in his 1893 study of Plato's thought, "does in truth little more than clear the ground . . . or the mental tablet, that one may have a fair chance of knowing, or seeing . . . such possible truth, discovery, or revelation, as may one day occupy the ground, the tablet." Plato causes his readers to suppose, says Pater, "that truth, precisely because it resembles some high kind of relationship of persons to persons, depends a good deal on the receiver; and must be, in that degree, elusive, provisional, contingent" (*Plato*, pp. 188, 187).

But as Pater portrays Jacques's or Raoul's or Tannhäuser's madness and idolatry in his portrait of Marguerite in Chapters 9 and 10, for example, the "dubious double root" (10.104:4) of Eros and Anteros subjugates, torments, and destroys. Only where the hero's sensibilities are more idealizing than in Wilde's tale of a doppelgänger can the imperfect be refined. Like Jasmin's Venetian mirror, "the image might react on the original, refining it one degree further" (8.90:34–35) if the protagonist is properly receptive. The multiplicity of doublings, parallels, and juxtapositions in *Gaston de Latour*, complementary or inverted and ironic (two attached homes for two loving brothers, the fratricidal brothers taking opposite sides in the Religious Wars, Gaston and his clerkly predecessor a century before, King Charles and Gaston, Pater and Gaston, Ronsard and Baudelaire, Circe and Margot, Ulysses and the sailor from Florida, Montaigne and Étienne de la Boétie, Montaigne in his father's cloak, the ghostly doubles Gaston's three friends encounter, Eros and Anteros, Jasmin and his Venetian mirror image, and so on) all allude to the protagonist's own alternatives—either a consuming decadence or a quickening aesthetic response, the "hard, gem-like flame" that passes "from point to point, . . . always at the focus where the greatest number of vital forces unite in their purest energy" ("Conclusion," *Renaissance*, p. 236).

Critics may fly to modish sources, but one aesthetic thesis shaping this novel derives from Pater's very good friend, Emilia (Mrs. Mark) Pattison's *The Renaissance of Art in France* (1879). (Pater's letter of 10 September 1877 to Gosse compliments Pattison's architectural study that appeared in the *Contemporary Review* a year before republication in her book.) She discusses in detail several of the artists and works that reappear in *Gaston*; moreover, Pater not only echoed her syntax and diction, he at times dramatized her critical interpretations. In both Pattison and Pater the focus is upon Huguenot figures, a natural religious and national bias (perhaps even personal, inasmuch as William Sharp reports that the surname *Pater* is Huguenot [15]) but here unusually emphatic. Considering why the French artistic Renaissance faltered, Pattison remarks:

> The obvious answer is—that the wars of religion destroyed, in France, the security and leisure necessary to its perfect development, and that in the chronic disturbance of the bitter struggle between Catholic and Huguenot the best energies of the nation were diverted and absorbed. But when we find that the most distinguished men in France, even in the world of arts and letters, stood not in the ranks of the cause which triumphed, but on the side of that which fell, the obvious answer is insufficient. . . . The temper of the Court, and of those from whom the Court derived its support, was characterised by a supreme moral indifferentism, which rendered it impossible that they should either give an initiative or take a share in this part of the Renaissance movement. . . . [T]he prevailing tone of mind . . . rendered the rejection of the element of renewed moral impulse, then shaping itself amongst the Huguenots, an inevitable consequence. (1:29–30)

As this thesis shaped itself in the creative matrix of Pater's novel ("moral indifferentism" is the sermon Bruno preaches to the Court), it supplied his narrative not with the drama of a sectarian dispute but a deeper ethical theme, that of the poison of decadence over against a moral energy. The art of Catholic Italy, as Chapter 13 of *Gaston* makes clear, shared none of this falling off, this moral "caducity" of France (*Renaissance*, p. 170; 9.95:26). Pattison notes: "A state of moral indifference, whether in an individual or a nation, cannot be fruitful of noble life. It is compatible with startling surprises of momentary enthusiasm, with great emotional facility, which is an affair of temperament rather than of moral conviction, and which can never give the stamina necessary to sequence of action sustained at a high level" (1:30). Poised against Pattison's "stamina" is Gaston's (or Tannhäuser's or Raoul's or Jasmin's or Dante's) metaphoric entrapment in cave, maze, enchanted palace or other snare, an "irresponsible, self-centered" (6.67:1) life-style. Since what

---

15. William Sharp, "Some Personal Reminiscences of Walter Pater," *The Atlantic Monthly*, 74 (December 1894): 803.

one sees is what one Platonistically becomes, the eye must be lifted from its fascination with the Medusan vision. In Chapter 13, Gaston wanders through the Cemetery of the Holy Innocents much like a sinful Dante in Purgatory who, after confession and absolution, will rise to Heaven with his spiritual ideal, Beatrice, as his guiding power. Or, in Emilia Pattison's foursquare words: "Perfect beauty, like perfect love, involves the presence of the moral ideal" (1:20).

Just how the plot of *Gaston* would have capitalized on classical and Christian themes of the epic journey through the dark forest of passion and vice to the "moral ideal" of beauty and love remains unknown. Gaston apparently has a lost child; surely something would come of that. And the parallels to the *Odyssey*, especially the theme of Circe's enchanted captivity and the returned wanderer, suggest that Pater may have had some further Homeric correspondences in mind for his unwritten plot. Pater anticipates Gaston "returning to his home" (1.3:20–21)—a typical pattern in Pater's fiction—and remodeling the parish church in the Italian style. An analogous occasion in "Joachim du Bellay," *The Renaissance* (p. 174), employs a phrase from du Bellay's *Les Regrets* (Sonnet 31, cited by Sainte-Beuve as a "little masterpiece"): "*Heureuz qui, comme Ulysse, a fait un beau voyage, . . . / Et puis est retourné, plein d'usage et raison, / Vivre entre ses parents le reste de son aage!....*"

All one can say is that if Tennyson's *In Memoriam* could be considered by him a *Divine Comedy* in miniature, with its three Christmases and epithalamium, so Pater's plan for "a kind of trilogy, or triplet, of works of a similar character; dealing with the same problems, under altered historical conditions" (Evans, Letter of 28 January 1886), suggests a secularized or classicized version of Dante, whose political allusions in the *Commedia* were the foundation for his allegorical vision. The extent of Pater's concession to religious values in the 1890s is perhaps best gauged by his introduction to Shadwell's translation of the *Purgatorio*:

> An age of faith, if such there ever were, our age certainly is not: an age of love, all its pity and self-pity notwithstanding, who shall say?—in its religious scepticism, however, especially as compared with the last century in its religious scepticism, an age of hope, we may safely call it, of a development of religious hope or hopefulness, similar in tendency to the development of the doctrine of Purgatory in the church of the Middle Age:—*quel secondo regno / Ove l'umano spirito si purga:*—a world of merciful second thoughts on one side, of fresh

opportunities on the other, useful, serviceable, endurable, in contrast alike with that *mar si crudele* of the *Inferno*, and the blinding radiancy of Paradise.[16]

Of course, neither Gaston's sixteenth century nor Pater's nineteenth was like Dante's age of faith. Gaston's model may be one step closer to that of Montaigne's essay "Of Friendship," a perfected mutuality between Étienne de La Boétie and Montaigne that is portrayed in Chapter 5. In the 1890s it was not faith, nor even skepticism or passion, but *hope* for faith and love that occupied Pater's imagination as he struggled with the composition of *Gaston*. Just as Marius found "a quiet hope" (*Marius*, 2:69–70) in the sense of a mystical companion, so too Gaston may unite himself with a very nineteenth-century Beatrice or La Boétie—if not in the flesh, then as a world-conscious-ness or Logos expressed through cultural artifacts, perhaps through his architectural reconstruction of Saint Hubert's church.

Before he died, Gaston's consciousness would have found "a sort of *moral* purity; yet, in the *forms* and *colours* of things" (*Imaginary Portraits*, p. 23); and he would have attained a rapprochement between himself and the diverse expressions of a sixteenth-century aesthetic Huguenot "moral impulse." Gaston's consciousness would have embodied that "hard, gem-like flame" of Renaissance Protestant creativity, received by a kind of artistic Apostolic succession from Marius's classical paganism-turning-Christian (though not yet Catholic); passed onwards from that age of dawning hope to Renaissance Catholic Italian artists, rejuvenated by their discovery of classicism and still in the first flush of a powerful religious enthusiasm; and handed from those old masters to their French Huguenot heirs whose "moral conviction" kept it burning bright, often at the stake in flames or dying in dungeons with resolute glittering eyes, like Bernard Palissy whose awesome artistic tenacity seemed almost to mirror the courage that his religious convictions demanded from him; and from these heroes of creative eminence, handed on to England of the Romantic revolution, in what would have constituted the third, but never-written novel of historical / personal identity.

Is *Gaston de Latour* a success? Maybe only to those who feel intensely about such matters, who are able to believe that a consciousness, a vision of authority, resides within the passionate enthusiasms and austere sacrifices of the cultural heritage. This becomes the vision that frees the guilty eye from

---

16. "Introduction," *The "Purgatory" of Dante Alighiere*, trans. Shadwell, 1892, p. xx; VIII.

the moral corruption of its time and place in order that it may search from the depths of its self-contradiction and, at the last, glimpse that love and innocence outside its power to attain.

I have edited this novel or "historical dream" with intense respect and with a kind of unanticipated obedience to the Horatian maxim of *Ars Poetica*, lines 388–89—as John Sparrow so amiably noted. In its final form, basic choices of method, inclusiveness, and relevance were balanced with practical constraints, with the needs of scholarly readers, and with the uncannily "elusive and allusive" qualities of the Paterian text itself. This will be my fourth book-length publication devoted to Pater. More than a dozen years ago I found myself living, as it were, so closely with Pater that I had begun "to feel like one of those maiden sisters of his." Then this new project evolved into nearly the same sort of curious collaboration that Pater's protagonists, Marius and Gaston, establish with their literary mentors, Marcus Aurelius and Marguerite of Navarre. Gaston, "correcting, annotating the great lady's manuscripts" (10.103:20–21), does exactly what I found myself doing for Walter Pater (at least if one understands "correcting" as applying editorial principles to create the Edition Text). It has been a curious opportunity to move so close to Pater's creative process that I almost *hear* his pen scratch, though his sensibility nonetheless remains something of an enigma. Perhaps the tension or irreducible distance that both Marius and Gaston detected between themselves and their historical mentors also exists, for other reasons, between myself and Pater. But if Pater, even so, can feed such an interest, surely it is time to acknowledge that he is much more than a Sphinx without a secret.

❦ EDITION TEXT

GASTON DE LATOUR

CHAPTER I

A Clerk in Orders

The white walls of the Château of Deux-manoirs composed, before its
dismantling at the Revolution, the one prominent object which
towards the south-west broke the pleasant level of La Beauce, the great cornland of central France. Abode in those days of the family of Latour, it bore
significant record of their brotherly union, century after century as they
rested there. From the sumptuous monuments of their last resting-place,
backward to the very stones of this more lightsome home it was visible they
had cared for so much, even in some peculiarities of its ground-
plan—everywhere was the token of a certain scrupulous estimate of those
incidents of man's pathway through the world which knit the wayfarers
thereon most closely together.

Why this irregular ground-plan?—the traveller would ask; recognising
indeed something of distinction in its actual effect on the eye, and suspecting
perhaps some conscious aim at such effect on the part of the builders, in an
age indulgent of architectural caprices. The traditional answer to that
question, true for once, still showed the race of Latour making much, making
the most, of the sympathetic ties of human life. Work, in large measure, of
Gaston de Latour, it was left unfinished at his death, some time about the year
1594. That it was never completed could hardly be attributed to any lack of
means or of interest; for it is plain that to the period of the Revolution, after
which its scanty remnants passed into humble occupation (a few circular
turrets, a crenelated curtain-wall, giving a random touch of dignity to some
ordinary farm-buildings) the place had been carefully maintained. It might
seem a kind of reverence rather that had allowed the work to remain
untouched for future generations at precisely this point in its growth.

And the expert architectural mind, peeping acutely into recondite motive and half-accomplished purpose in such matters, could detect the circumstance which had determined that so noticeable irregularity of plan. Its kernel was not, as in most similar buildings of that date, a feudal fortress, but an unfortified manor-house—a double *manoir*—two houses oddly associated at a right angle. Far back in the Middle Age, said a not uncertain tradition, here had been the one point of contact between two estates, intricately inter-locked with alien domain, as, in the course of generations, the family of Latour and another had added field to field. In the single lonely manor then existing two brothers had grown up; and the time came when the marriage of the younger to the heiress of those neighbouring lands would part two perfect friends. Regretting over-night so dislocating a change, it was the elder who, as the drowsy hours flowed away in manifold recollection beside the fire, suggested the building here of a second manor-house—the Château d'Amour, as it came to be called—that the two families, in what should be as nearly as possible one abode, might take their fortunes together.

Of somewhat finer construction than the rough walls of the earlier manor, the Château d'Amour stood, amid the change of years, as a visible record of all the accumulated sense of human existence among its occupants. The old walls, the old apartments, of those two associated houses still existed, with some obvious additions, beneath the delicate, fantastic surfaces of the *château* of the sixteenth century. Its singular outline was the very symbol of the religion of the family in the race of Latour, still full of loyalty to the old home, as its numerous out-growths took hold here and there around. A race with characteristics ineradicable in the grain, they went to raise the human level about them by a transfer of blood which was far from involving any social decadence in themselves. A peculiar local variety of character, of manners, in that district of La Beauce, surprised the more observant visitor who might find his way into farm-house or humble presbytery of its scattered townships. And as for those who kept up the central tradition of their house, they were true to the soil, coming back, against whatever obstacles, from court, from cloister, from distant crusade, to the spot where the memory of their kindred was liveliest and most exact—a memory, touched so solemnly with a sense, a conscience, of the intimacies of life, its significant events, its contacts and partings, that to themselves it was like a second sacred history.

It was a great day, amid so many quiet days, for the people of Deux-manoirs—one of the later days of August. The event, which would mark it always in the life of one of them, called into play all that was most expressive in that well-defined family character: it was at once a recognition of what they valued most in past years, and an assertion of confidence, of will, for the future, accordant thereto. Far away in Paris the young King Charles the Ninth, in his fourteenth year, had been just declared of age. In the church of Saint Hubert, the chiefs of the house of Latour, attended by many of its dependents and less important members, were standing ready, around the last hope of their declining years—the grandparents, their aged brethren and sisters, certain aged ecclesiastics of their kindred, wont to be called to the family councils. They had set out on foot, after a votive Mass said early in the old chapel of the manor, to assist at the ceremony of the day. Distinguishable from afar by unusual height in proportion to its breadth within, Saint Hubert's church had an atmosphere, a daylight, to itself. Its stained glass, work of the same hands that had wrought for the cathedral of Chartres, admitted only an almost angry ray of purple or crimson, here or there, across the dark, roomy spaces. The heart, the heart of youth at least, sank, as one entered, stepping warily out of the sunshine over the sepulchral stones which formed the entire pavement of the church, a great blazonry of family history from age to age for indefatigable eyes. An abundance of almost life-sized sculpture clung to the pillars, lurked in the angles, seemed, with those symbolical gestures, and mystic faces ready to speak their parts, to be almost in motion through the gloom. Many years after, Gaston de Latour, an enemy of all Gothic darkness or heaviness, returning to his home full of a later taste, changed all that. A thicket of airy spires rose above the sanctuary; the blind *triforium* broke into one continuous window; the heavy masses of stone were pared down with wonderful dexterity, till not a handsbreadth remained uncovered by delicate traceries, as from the fair white roof touched sparingly with gold, down to the subterranean chapel of Saint Taurin, where the peasants of La Beauce came to pray for rain, not a space was left unsearched by cheerful daylight, refined, but hardly dimmed at all, by painted glass mimicking the clearness of the open sky. In the sombre old church all was in stately order now: the dusky, jewelled reliquaries, the ancient devotional ornaments from the manor—much-prized family possessions, sufficient for the entire array of a great ecclesiastical function—the lights burning, flowers everywhere, gathered amid the last handfuls of the harvest by the peasant-women, who came to present their children for the happy chance of an episcopal blessing.

And the almost exclusively aged people, in all their old personal adornments, which now so rarely saw the light, forming the central group around the young *seigneur* they had conducted hither, seemed of a piece with those mystic figures, with the old armour-clad monumental effigies, the carved and painted imageries of the outer circuit of the choir—a version of the biblical history, for the reading of those who loitered on their way from chapel to chapel. There was Joseph's dream, with the tall sheaves of his elder brethren bowing to his sheaf, like these aged heads around the youthful aspirant of to-day. There was Jacob going on his mysterious way, met by, conversing, wrestling with the Angels of God, rescuing the promise of his race from the "profane" Esau. There was the mother of Samuel, and, in long white linen ephod, the much-desired, early-consecrated child, who had inherited her religious capacity; and David, with something of his extraordinary genius for divine things written on his countenance; onward to the sacred persons of the Annunciation, with the golden lily in the silver cup, only lately set in its place. With dress, expression, nay, the very incidents themselves adapted to the actual habits and associations of the age which had produced them, these figures of the old Jewish history seemed about to take their places, for the imparting of a divine sanction, among the living actors of the day. One and all spoke of ready concurrence with religious motions, a ready apprehension of, and concurrence with, the provisions of a certain divine scheme for the improvement of one's opportunities in the world.

Would that dark-haired, fair-skinned lad concur, in his turn, and be always true to his present purpose—Gaston de Latour, standing thus, almost the only youthful thing there, amid the witness of these imposing, meditative masks and faces? Could his guardians have read below the white propriety of the youth, duly arrayed for dedication, with the lighted candle in his right hand and the surplice folded over his left shoulder, he might sorely have disturbed their placid but somewhat narrow ruminations, with the germs of what was strange to or beyond them. Certain of those shrewd old ecclesiastics had in fact detected that the devout lad, so visibly impressed, was not altogether after their kind: that together with many characteristics obviously inherited, he possessed—had caught perhaps from some ancestor unrepresented here—some other potencies of nature, which might not always combine so accordantly as to-day with the mental requisites of an occasion such as this. One of them, indeed, touched notwithstanding by his manifest piety just then, shortly afterwards recommended him a little prayer "for peace" from the Vespers of the Roman Breviary—for the harmony of his heart with itself: advice which, except for a very short period, he ever afterwards followed, saying it every evening of his life.

Yet it was the lad's own election which had led him to this first step in a career that might take him out of the world and end the race of Latour altogether. Approaching their four-score years, and realising almost suddenly the situation of the young Gaston, left there alone out of what had been a large, much-promising, resonant household, they wished otherwise, but did not try to change his early-pronounced preference for the ecclesiastical calling. When he determined to seek the "clericature," he made a great demand on their old-fashioned religious sentiment. But the fund was a deep one, and their acquiescence in the result entire. He might indeed use his privilege of "orders" only as the stepping-stone to material advancement in a church which seemed wholly to have gone over to the world, and one half the benefices of which were at that time practically in the hands of laymen. In effect however the occasion came to be an offering on their part, not unlike those old biblical ones—a dedication in their old age of the single precious thing left them—the grandchild, whose hair would presently fall under the very shears which a century before had turned an earlier brilliant Gaston de Latour into a monk.

Charles Guillard, Bishop of Chartres, a courtly, vivacious prelate, whose quick eyes seemed to note at a glance the whole assembly, one and all, while his lips moved silently, arrived at last, and the rite began with the singing of the Office for the Ninth Hour. It was like a stream of water crossing unexpectedly a dusty way.—*Mirabilia testimonia tua!* In psalm and antiphon, inexhaustibly fresh, the soul might seem to be taking refuge, at that undevout hour, from the mean business, the sordid languor, of men's lives, in contemplation of the unfaltering vigour of the divine righteousness, which had still those who sought it, not only watchful in the night but alert in the drowsy afternoon. Yes! there was the sheep astray, *ovis quae periit*—the physical world, with its lusty ministers at work, or sleeping for a while amid the stubble, their faces up-turned to the August sun—the world so importunately visible, intruding a little way, with its floating odours, across the old over-written pavement, in that semi-circle of heat at the great open door, upon the mysteries within. Seen from the incense-laden sanctuary where the bishop was assuming one by one the pontifical ornaments, La Beauce, like a many-coloured carpet spread under the great dome, with the white double house-front quivering afar through the heat, though it looked as if you might touch with the hand its distant spaces, was for a moment the unreal thing. Gaston alone, with all his mystic preoccupations, by the privilege of youth, seemed to belong to both, and link the visionary company about him to the external scene.

The rite with which the Roman Church "makes a clerk," aims certainly at no low measure of difference from the coarser world around him in her supposed scholar; and in this case the aspirant (the precise claims of the situation being well considered) had no misgiving. Discreetly, and with full attention, he answers *Adsum!* when his name is called, and advances manfully. Yet he kneels meekly enough, and remains, with head bowed forward, before the seated bishop who recites the appointed prayers, between the anthems and responses of his *Schola*, or attendant singers.—Might he be saved from mental blindness! Might he put on the new man, even as his outward guise was changed! Might he keep the religious habit for ever! "The Lord is my inheritance," Gaston whispers distinctly, as the locks fall, cut from the thickly-grown, black head, in five places, "after the fashion of Christ's crown," the shears in the episcopal hands sounding aloud, amid the silence of the curious spectators. From the same hands, in due order, the fair white surplice ripples down over him. "This is the generation of them that seek Him" the choir sings: "The Lord himself is the portion of my inheritance and my cup." It was the Church's eloquent way of bidding unrestricted expansion to the youthful heart in its timely purpose to seek the best, to abide among the things of the spirit.

The prospect from their road homewards, like a white scarf flung across the land, as the party returned in the late August afternoon was clear and dry and distant. The great barns at the wayside had their doors thrown back, displaying the dark cool space within. The farmsteads seemed almost tenantless, the villagers being still at work over the immense harvest-field. Crazy bells startled them, striking out the hour from some deserted church-yard. Still and tenantless also seemed the manor as they approached, door and window lying open upon the court for the coolness. Rather it was as if at their coming certain spectral occupants started back out of the daylight.—"Why depart dear ghosts?" was what the grandparents would have cried. They had more in common with that immaterial world than with flesh and blood. There was room for the existing household, enough and to spare, in one of the two old houses. That other, the Château d'Amour, remained for Gaston, at first as a delightful, half-known abode of wonders, though with some childish fear, afterwards as a delightful nursery of fancy, of sentiment, as he recalled, in this chamber or that, its old tenants and their doings, from the affectionate brothers, onwards—above all, how in one room long ago Gabrielle de Latour had died of joy.

It was difficult to go back to common occupations. As darkness came on the impressions of the day did but return again more vividly and concentrate themselves upon the inward sense. Observance, loyal concurrence in some high purpose for him, passive waiting on the hand one might miss in the darkness with the gifts therein of which he had the presentiment, and upon the due acceptance of which the true fortune of life would turn:—these were the hereditary traits alert in Gaston, as he lay awake in the absolute, moon-lit, stillness, his outward ear attentive for the wandering footsteps which, through that wide, lightly-accentuated country, often came and went about the house, with weird suggestions of a dim passage to and fro, and of an infinite distance. He would rise, as the footsteps halted perhaps below his window, to answer the questions of the travellers, pilgrims, or labourers who had missed their way from farm to farm, or halting soldier seeking guidance; terrible or terror-stricken companies sometimes, rudely or piteously importunate to be let in—for it was the period of the Religious Wars, flaming up here and there over France, and never quite put out, during forty years.

Once, in the beginning of these troubles (he was then a child leaning from the window as a sound of ricketty small wheels approached) the enquiry came in broken French, *Voulez-vous donner direction?*—from a German, one of the mercenaries of the Duc de Guise, hired for service in the civil strife of France, drawing wearily a crippled companion, so far from home. The memory of it, awakening a thousand fancies, had remained by him as a witness to the power of fortuitous circumstance over the imagination. And one night there had come a noise of horns, and presently King Charles himself was standing in the courtyard, belated, and far enough now from troublesome company, as he hunted the rich-fleshed game of La Beauce through the endless corn. He entered with a relish for the pleasant cleanliness of the place, expressed in a shrill strain of oaths, like flashes of hell-fire to Gaston's suddenly awakened sense. It was the invincible nature of the royal lad to speak and feel on these mad, *alto* notes, and not unbecoming in a good catholic; for Huguenots never swore, and these were subtly theological oaths. Well! the grandparents repressed as best they could their apprehensions as to what other hunters, what other disconcerting incident, might follow; for catholic France very generally believed that the Huguenot leaders had a scheme for possessing themselves of the person of the young king, known to be mentally pliable. Meanwhile they led him with great silver *flambeaux* to their daintiest apartment, that he might wash off the blood with which not his hands only were covered, for he hunted also with the eagerness of a madman—*steeped* in blood. He lay there for a few hours, after supping very familiarly on his own birds, Gaston rising from his bed to look on at a distance, and afterwards on bended knee serving the rose-water dish and spiced wine, as the night passed in reassuring silence; Charles himself, as usual, keenly enjoying this "gipsy" incident, with the supper after that unexpected fashion, among strange people, he hardly knew where. He was very pale, like some cunning Italian work in wax or ivory, of partly satiric character, endued by magic or crafty mechanism with vivacious movement. But as he sat thus, ever for the most part the unhappy plaything of other people's humours, escaped for a moment out of a world of demoniac intriguers, the pensive atmosphere around seemed gradually to change him, touching his wild temper, pleasantly, profitably, so that he took down a lute from the wall and struck out its notes, and fell to talking of verses, leaving a stanza of his own scratched with a diamond on the window-pane—lines simpler-hearted, and more full of nature, than were common at that day.

The life of Gaston de Latour was almost to coincide with the duration of the Religious Wars. The earliest public event of his memory was that famous siege of Orleans from which the young Henri de Guise rode away the head of his restless family, himself tormented now still further by the reality or the pretence of filial duty, seeking vengeance for the treacherous murder of his father. Following a long period of quiet progress—the tranquil and tolerant years of the Renaissance—the religious war took possession of, and pushed to strangely confused issues, a society somewhat distraught by artificial aesthetic culture; it filled with wild passions, wildly dramatic personalities, a scene already singularly attractive by its artistic beauty. A heady fanaticism was worked by every prominent egotist in turn, pondering on his chances in the event of the extinction of the house of Valois with the three sons of Catherine de Medici, born unsound and doomed by astronomical prediction. The old manors, which had exchanged their towers for summer-houses under the softening influence of Renaissance fashions, found themselves once more medievally insecure amid a vagrant warfare of foreign mercenaries and armed peasants. It was a curiously refined people who now took down the armour hanging high on the wall for decoration among newer things so little warlike. A difficult age, certainly, for scrupulous spirits to move in! A perplexed network of partizan or personal interests underlay, and furnished the really directing forces in, a supposed Armageddon of contending religious convictions. Yet religion, the assumed ground of quarrel, seems appreciable all the while only by abstraction from the leaders, the parties, who are most forward in the assertion of its rival claims. What there was of it was in hiding perhaps with the so-called "Political" party, professedly almost indifferent to it, but which had at least something of humanity on its side, and some chance of that placidity of mind in which alone the business of the spirit can be done. The new sect of "Papists" were not the truest catholics: there was little of the virtue of the martyr in militant Calvinism. It is not a catholic historian who notes with profound regret "that inauspicious day," in the year 1562, Gaston's tenth year, "when the work of devastation began, which was to strip from

France that antique garniture of religious art which later ages have not been able to replace." Axe and hammer at the carved work sounded from one end of France to the other.

It was a peculiarity of this age of terror, that every one, including Charles the Ninth himself, dreaded what the accident of war might make, not merely of his enemies, but of temporary allies and pretended friends, in an evenly balanced but very complex strife—of merely personal rivals also, in some matter which had nothing to do with its professed motives. Gaston de Latour passing on his country way one night, with a sudden flash of fierce words two young men burst from the door of a road-side tavern. The brothers are quarrelling about the division, lately effected there, of their dead father's morsel of land. "I shall hate you till death!" cries the younger, bounding away in the darkness; and two atheists part, to take opposite sides in the supposed strife of Catholic and Huguenot.

The deeds of violence which occupy the foreground of French history during the reigns of Catherine's sons might lead one to fancy that little human kindness could have remained in France,—a fanatical civil war of forty years, that no place at all could have been left for the quiet building of character. Contempt for human life, taught us every day by nature, and alas! by man himself—all war intensifies that. But the more permanent forces, alike of human nature and of the natural world, are on the whole in the interest of tranquillity and sanity, and of the sentiments proper to man. Like all good catholic children, Gaston had shuddered at the name of Adretz, of Briquemaut with his great necklace of priests' ears, of that dark and fugitive Montgomeri, the slayer, as some would have it the assassin, of a king, now active, and almost ubiquitous on the Huguenot side. Still, at Deux-manoirs, this warfare, seething up from time to time so wildly in this or that district of France, for the most only became sensible in incidents we might think picturesque, were they told with that intention; delightful enough certainly to the curiosity of a boy, in whose mind nevertheless they deepened a native impressibility to the sorrow and hazard that are constant and necessary in human life, especially for the poor. The troubles of "that poor people of France"—burden of all its righteous rulers from Saint Lewis downwards—these, at all events, would not be lessened by the struggle of Guise and Condé and Bourbon and Valois, of the Valois with each other, of those four brilliant young princes of the name of Henry. The weak would but suffer somewhat more than was usual, in the interest of the strong. If you were not sure whether that gleaming of the sun in the vast distance flashed from swords or sickles, whether that far-off curl of smoke rose from stubble-fire or village-steeple, to protect which the peasants, still lovers of their churches, would arm themselves, women and all, with fork and scythe,—still those peasants used their scythes, in due season, for reaping their leagues of cornland, and slept with faces as tranquil as ever towards the sky, for their noonday rest. In effect, since peace is always in some measure dependent on one's own seeking, disturbing forces do but fray their way along somewhat narrow paths over the great spaces of the quiet realm of nature. La Beauce, vast enough to present every phase of weather at once, its one landmark the twin spires of Chartres, salient as the finger of a dial, guiding by their change of perspective victor or vanquished on his way, offered room enough for the business both of peace and war to those enamoured of either. When Gaston, after brief absence, was unable to find his child's garden-bed, that was only because in a fine June the corn had grown tall so quickly, through which he was presently led to it with all its garish sweets undisturbed: and it was with the ancient growths of mind—customs, beliefs, mental preferences—as with the natural world.

It may be understood that there was a certain rudeness about the old manor, left almost untouched from age to age, with a loyalty which paid little or no heed to changes of fashion. The Château d'Amour indeed, as the work of a later age, refined somewhat upon the rough feudal architecture; and the daintier taste had centred itself in particular upon one apartment, a veritable woman's apartment, with an effect in some degree anticipating the achievement of Gaston's own century, in which the apparatus of daily life became so eloquent of the moods of those to whom it ministered. It was the chamber of Gabrielle de Latour, who had died of joy. Here certainly she had watched, at these windows, during ten whole years, for the return of her beloved husband from a disastrous battle in the East, till against all expectation she beheld him crossing the court at last. Immense privilege! Immense distinction! Again and again Gaston tried to master the paradox, at times in deep concentration of mind seemed almost to touch the point, of that wonderful moment.

Hither, as to an oratory, a religious place, the finer spirits of her kin had always found their way, to leave behind them there the more intimate relics of themselves. To Gaston its influence imparted early a taste for delicate things as being indispensable in all his pleasures to come; and, from the first, with the appetite for some great distinguishing passion, the peculiar genius of his age seeming already awake spontaneously within him. Here, at least, had been one of those "grand passions," such as were needed to give life its true meaning and effect. Conscious of that rudeness in his home, and feeding a strong natural instinct for outward beauty hitherto on what was barely sufficient, he found for himself in this perfumed place the centre of a fanciful world, reaching out to who could tell what refined passages of existence in that great world beyond, of which the echoes seemed to light here amid the stillness. On his first visit one pensive afternoon, fitting the lately attained key in the lock, he seemed to have drawn upon himself, yet hardly to have disturbed, the meditations of its former occupant. A century of unhindered summers had taken the heat from its colours—the couches, the curtains drawn back from the windows, which the rain in the south-west wind just then touched so softly. That great passion of old had been also a dainty love, leaving its impress everywhere in this magic apartment, on the musical instruments, the books lying where they might have fallen from the hands of the listless reader so long since, the fragrance which the lad's movement stirred around him. And there, on one of the windows, were the verses of King Charles, who had slept here as in the most courtly resting-place of the house. On certain nights Gaston himself was not afraid to steal from his own bed to lie in it, though still too healthy a sleeper to be visited by the appropriate dreams he so greatly longed for.

A nature instinctively religious, which would readily discover and give their full value to all such facts of experience as might be conformable thereto! But what would be the relation of this religious sensibility to sensibilities of another kind now awaking in the young Gaston, as he mused in this dreamy place, surrounded by the books, the furniture, almost the very presence, of the past, which had already found tongues to speak of a still living humanity—somewhere, somewhere, in the world!—waiting for him in the distance, or perchance already on its way, to explain, by its own plenary beauty and power, why wine and roses and the languorous afternoons were so delightful. So far indeed the imaginative heat, which might one day enter into dangerous rivalry with simple old-fashioned faith, was blent harmoniously with it. They were hardly distinguishable elements of an amiable character, susceptible generally to the poetic side of things—two neighbourly apprehensions of a single ideal.

The great passions, the fervid sentiments, of which Gaston dreamed as the true realisation of life, have not always softened men's natures: they have been compatible with many cruelties, as in the lost spirits of that very age. They may overflow, on the other hand, in more equable natures and amid happier circumstances, into that universal sympathy which lends a kind of amorous power to the homeliest charities. So it seemed likely to be with Gaston de Latour. Sorrow came along with beauty, a rival of its intricate omnipresence in life. In the sudden tremour of an aged voice, the handling of a forgotten toy, a childish drawing, in the tacit observance of a day, he became aware suddenly of the great stream of human tears falling always through the shadows of the world. For once, the darling of old age more than responded in full to its tenderness. In the isolation of his life there had been little demand for sympathy on the part of those anywhere near his own age. So much the larger was the fund of affection which went forth, with a delicacy not less than their own, to meet the sympathies of the aged people who cherished him. In him, their old, almost forgotten sorrows bled anew. Variety of affection, in a household in which many relations had lived together, had brought variety of sorrow. But they were well-nigh healed now—those once so poignant griefs, the scars remaining only as deeper lines of natural expression. It was visible, to their surprise, that he penetrated the motive of the Mass said so solemnly, in violet, on the Innocents' Day, and understood why they wept at the triumphant antiphons:—"My soul is escaped as a bird out of the snare of the fowler!"—thinking intently of the little tombs which had recorded carefully almost the minutes of children's lives, Elisabeth de Latour, Cornelius de Latour, aged so many years, days, hours. Yes! the cold pavement under one's feet had once been molten lava. Surely the resources of sorrow were large in things. The fact must be duly marked and provided for, with due estimate of his own susceptibility thereto, in his scheme of life. Might he pass through the world, unriven by sorrows such as those! And already it was as if he stept softly over the earth, not to outrage its so abundant latent sensibilities.

The beauty of the world, and its sorrow, solaced a little by religious faith, itself so beautiful a thing: these were the chief impressions with which he made his way outwards, at first only in longer rambles, as physical strength increased, over his native plains, whereon, as we have seen, the cruel warfare of that age had aggravated at a thousand points the every-day appeal of suffering humanity. The vast level, stretching thirty miles from east to west, thirty from north to south:—perhaps the reader may think little of its resources for the seeker after natural beauty, or its capacity to develope the imagination. A world, he may fancy, in which there could be no shadows, at best not too cheerful colours. In truth, it was all *accent*, so to speak. But then, surely, all the finer influences of every language depend mostly on accent; and he has but to think of it as Gaston actually lived in it to find a singularly companionable soul there. Gaston, at least, needed but to go far enough across it for those inward oppositions to cease, which already at times beset him; to feel at one with himself again, under the influence of a scene which had for him something of the character of the sea—its changefulness, its infinity, its pathos in the toiling human life that traversed it. Featureless, if you will, it was always under the guidance of its ample sky. Scowling back sometimes moodily enough, but almost never without a remnant of fine weather, about August it was for the most part cloudless. And then truly, under its blue dome, the great plain would as it were "laugh and sing," in a kind of absoluteness of sympathy with the sun.

CHAPTER II

Our Lady's Church

L ike a ship for ever asail in the distance, thought the child, everywhere the great church of Chartres was visible, with the passing light or shadow upon its grey, weather-beaten surfaces. The people of La Beauce were proud, and would talk often of its rich store of sacred furniture, the wonder-working relics of "Our Lady under the Earth," and her sacred veil or shift—*sacra camisia*—which kings and princes came to visit, returning with a likeness thereof, replete in miraculous virtue, for their own wearing. The busy fancy of Gaston, multiplying this chance hearsay, had set the whole interior in array—a dim, spacious, fragrant place, afloat with golden lights. Lit up over the autumn fields at evening, the distant spires suggested the splendour within, with so strong an imaginative effect that he seemed scarcely to know whether it was through the mental or bodily eye that he beheld. When he came thither at last, like many another well-born youth, to join the episcopal household as a kind of half-clerical page, he found (as happens in the actual testing of our ideals) at once more and less than he had supposed; and could never precisely detach his earlier vision from the supervening reality. What he *saw*, certainly, was greater far in mere physical proportion, and incommensurable at first by anything he knew—the volume of the wrought detail, the mass of the component members, the bigness of the actual stones of the masonry, contrary to the usual Gothic manner, and as if in reminiscence of those old Druidic piles amid which the Virgin of Chartres had been adored, long before the birth of Christ, by a mystic race, possessed of some prophetic sense of the grace in store for her. And through repeated dangers good fortune has saved that unrivalled treasure of stained glass. Now and then the word "awful," so often applied to Gothic aisles, is here for once really applicable. You enter, looking perhaps for a few minutes' cool shelter from the summer noonday; and the placid sunshine of La Beauce seems to have been transformed in a moment into imperious, angry fire.

It was not in summer, however, that Gaston first set foot there: he saw the beautiful city for the first time as if sheathed austerely in repellent armour. In his most genial subsequent impressions of the place there was always a lingering trace of that famous frost through which he made his way, wary of petrifying contact against things without, to the great Western portal, on Candlemas morning. The sad, patient images by the doorways of the crowded church seemed suffering now chiefly from the cold. It was almost like a funeral—the penitential violet, the wandering taper-light, of this half-lenten feast of Purification. His new companions, at the head and in the rear of the long procession, forced every one, even the Lord Bishop himself, to move apace, bustling along, in their odd little copes, out of the bitter air, which made the jolly life Gaston now entered on, around the great fire of their hall in the episcopal palace, seem all the more winsome.

Notre-Dame de Chartres!—It was a world to explore, as if one explored the entire Middle Age: it was also an unending, elaborate, religious function, a life, or a continuous drama, to take one's part in. Dependent on its structural completeness, on its wealth of well-preserved ornament, on its unity in variety, perhaps on some undefinable operation of genius, beyond, but concurrently with, all these, the church of Chartres has still the gift of a unique power of impressing. In comparison, the other famous churches of France, at Amiens, for instance, at Rheims or Beauvais, may seem but formal, and to a large extent reproducible effects of mere architectural rule on a gigantic scale. The somewhat Gothic soul of Gaston relished there something strange, or even bizarre, in the very manner in which the building set itself, so broadly couchant, upon the earth; in the natural richness of tone on the masonry within; in the vast echoing roof of timber, the "forest," as it was called; in the mysterious maze traced upon its pavement; its maze-like crypt, centering in the shrine of the sibylline Notre-Dame, itself a natural or very primitive grotto or cave. A few years were still to pass ere sacrilegious hands despoiled it on a religious pretext:—the catholic church must pay, even with the molten gold of her sanctuaries, the price of her defence in the civil war. At present, it was such a treasure-house of medieval jewellery as we have to make a systematic effort even to imagine. The still extant register of its furniture and sacred apparel leaves the soul of the ecclesiologist athirst.

And it had another remarkable difference from almost all Gothic churches. There were no graves there. Its emptiness in this respect being due to no Huguenot or revolutionary desecration. Once indeed, about this very time, a popular military leader had been interred with honour within the precinct of the high altar itself. But not long afterwards, said the reverend canons, resenting on the part of their immaculate patroness this intrusion, the corpse itself, ill at ease, had protested, lifting up its hands above the surface of the pavement, as if to beg interment elsewhere. Gaston could remember assisting, awakened suddenly one night, at the removal of the remains to a more ordinary place of sepulture.

And yet that lavish display of jewellers' work on the altars, in the chapels, the sacristies, of Our Lady's Church, was but a framing for little else than dead people's bones. To Gaston, a piteous soul with a touch also of that grim humour which, as we know, holds of pity, relic-worship came naturally. At Deux-manoirs too there had been relics, including certain broken children's toys and some rude childish drawings, taken forth now and then with almost religious veneration, with trembling hands and renewal of old grief, to his wondering awe at the greatness of men's sorrows. Yes! the pavement under one's feet had been, might become again for him, molten lava. The look, the manner of those who exposed these things, had been a revelation. The abundant relics of the church of Chartres were for the most part perished remnants of the poor human body itself. Appertaining however to persons long ago and of a far-off, immeasurable kind of sanctity, they stimulated a more indifferent kind of curiosity, though seeming to bring the distant, the impossible, as with tangible evidence of fact, close to one's side. It was in one's hand,—the finger of an Evangelist! The crowned head of Saint Lubin, Bishop of Chartres, long centuries since, but still able to preserve its wheat-stacks from fire; bones of the "Maries," with some of the earth from their grave: these, and the like of these, were what the curious eye discerned in the recesses of those variously contrived reliquaries, great and small, glittering so profusely about the dusky church. Yet its very shadows ministered to a certain appetite in the soul of Gaston for dimness—for a dim place like this—such as he had often prefigured to himself, albeit with some suspicion of what might seem a preference for *darkness*. Physical twilight we most of us love, in its season. To him, that perpetual twilight came in close identity with its moral or intellectual counterpart, as the welcome requisite for that part of the *soul* which loves twilight, and is, in truth, never quite at rest out of it, through some congenital distress or uneasiness, perhaps, in its processes of vision.

As complex, yet not less perfectly united under a single leading motive, its sister volume, was the ritual order of Notre-Dame de Chartres, a year-long dramatic action, in which every one had, and knew, his part—the drama or "mystery" of Redemption, to the necessities of which the great church had shaped itself. All those various "offices" which, in Pontifical, Missal and Breviary, devout imagination had elaborated, from age to age, with such a range of spiritual colour and light and shade, with so much poetic tact in quotation, such a depth of insight into the Christian soul, had joined themselves harmoniously together, one office ending only where another began, in the perpetual worship of this mother of churches, which had also its own picturesque peculiarities of "use," proud of its maternal privilege therein. And the music rose—warmed, expanded, or fell silent altogether—as the order of the year, the colours, the whole expression of things changed, gathering around the full mystic effulgence of the pontiff in his own person, while the sacred theme deepened at the great ecclesiastical seasons. Then the aisles overflowed with a vast multitude, and like a court, combed, starched, rustling around him, Gaston and his fellows "served" Monseigneur—they, zealous, ubiquitous, more prominent than ever, though for the most profoundly irreverent, but notwithstanding this, one and all, with what disdain for the un-tonsured laity!

Well! what was of the past there—the actual stones of the building and that sacred liturgical order—entered readily enough into Gaston's mental kingdom, filling places prepared by the anticipations of his tranquil, dream-struck youth. It was the present, the uncalculated present, that now disturbed the complacent habit of his thoughts. Alien at a thousand points from his pre-conceptions of life, it presented itself, in the living forms of his immediate companions, in the great clerical body of which he was become a part, in the people of Chartres itself (none the less animated because provincial) as a thing to be judged by him, to be rejected or located within. How vivid, how delightful, they were!—the other forty-nine of the fifty lads who had come hither, after the old-fashioned way, to serve in the household of Monseigneur, by way of an "institution" in learning and good manners. And how becom-ingly that clerical pride, that self-respecting quiet, sat upon their high-bred figures, their angelic, unspoiled faces, saddened transiently as they came under the religious spell for a moment. As for Gaston, they welcomed him with a perfect friendliness, kept their best side foremost for an hour, and would not leave his very dreams. In absolute unconsciousness, they had brought from their remote old homes all varieties of hereditary gifts, vices, distinctions, dark fates, mercy, cruelty, madness. Appetite and vanity abounded, but with an abundant superficial grace, befitting a generation which, as by some aesthetic sense in the air, made the most of the pleasant outsides of life. All the various traits of the dying Middle Age were still in evidence among them, in all their crude effectiveness, only, blent, like rusty old armour wreathed in flowers, with the peculiar fopperies of the time, shrewdly divined from a distance, as happens with competent youth. To be in Paris itself, amid the full delightful fragrance of those dainty visible things which Huguenots despised—that, surely, were the sum of good fortune! Half-clerical, they loved nevertheless the touch of steel; had a laughing joy in trifling with its latent soul of destruction. In mimicry of the great world, they had their leaders, so inscrutably self-imposed: instinctively, they felt and underwent the mystery of leadership, with its consequent heats of spirit, its tides and changes of influence.

On the other hand also, to Gaston, dreamily observant, the way they had of reproducing, unsuspectingly, the humours of animal nature was quaint, likeable. Does not the anthropologist tell us of a heraldry, with a large assortment of heraldic beasts, to be found among savage or half-savage peoples, as the "survival" of a period when men were nearer than they are, or seem to be now, to the irrational world? Throughout the sprightly movement of the lads' daily life it was as if their "tribal" pets or monsters were with or within them. Tall Exmes, lithe and cruel like a tiger—it was pleasant to stroke him. The tiger was there, the parrot, the hare, the goat of course, and certainly much apishness. And, one and all, they were like the creatures in their vagrant, short memories, alert perpetually on the topmost crest of the day and hour, transferred so heartlessly, so entirely, from yesterday to to-day. Yet out of them, sure of some response, human heart would break: in and around Camille Pontdormi, for instance, brilliant and ambitious, yet so sensitive about his thread-bare home, concerning which however he had made the whole company, one by one, his confidants—so loyal to the people there, bursting into wild tears over the letter which brought the news of his younger brother's death, visibly fretting over it long afterwards. Still, for the most part, in their perfect health, nothing seemed to reach them but their own boyish ordinances, their own arbitrary "form." Theirs was an absolute indifference, most striking when they lifted their well-trained voices to sing in choir, vacant as the sparrows, while the eloquent, far-reaching, aspiring words floated melodiously from them, and sometimes, with a truly medieval license, singing to the sacred music those songs from the streets (no one cared to detect) which were really in their hearts. A world of vanity and appetite, yet after all of honesty with itself! Like grown people, they were but playing a game, and meant to observe its rules.—Say, rather, a world of honesty and courage. They, at least, were not pre-occupied all day long, and, if they woke in the night, with the fear of death.

It was part of their precocious worldliness to recognise, to feel a little afraid of their new companion's intellectual power. Those obviously meditative souls, which seem "not to sleep o' nights," seldom fail to put others on their guard. Who can tell what they may be judging, planning in silence, so near to one? Looking back long afterwards across the dark period that had intervened, Gaston could trace their ways through the world. Not many of them had survived to his own middle life. Reappearing from point to point, they connected themselves with the great crimes, the great tragedies of the time, as so many bright-coloured threads in that sombre tapestry of human passion. To recall in the obtuse, marred, grieved faces of uninteresting men or women, the disappointments, the sorrows, the tragic mistakes, of the children they were long ago is a good trick for taking our own sympathy by surprise, which Gaston practised when he saw the last or almost the last, of some of them, and felt a great pity, a great indulgence.

Here and now, at all events, carrying their cheerful tumult through those quiet ecclesiastical places—the bishop's garden, the great sacristy, neat and clean in its brown, pensive lights, they seemed of a piece with the bright, simple, inanimate things, the toys, of nature. They made one lively picture with the fruit and wine they loved, the birds they captured, the buckets of clear water drawn for pastime from the great well, and Jean Sémur's painted conjuring book stolen from the old sorceress, his grandmother, out of which he told their fortunes; with the musical instruments of others; with their carefully hidden dice and playing cards, worn or soiled by the fingers of older gamesters who had discarded them. Like their elders, they read eagerly, in racy new translations, old Greek and Latin books, with a delightful shudder at the wanton paganism. It was a new element of confusion in the present-ment of that miniature world. The classical enthusiasm laid hold on Gaston too, but essayed in vain to thrust out of him the medieval character of his experience, or put on quite a new face, insinuating itself rather under cover of the Middle Age, still in occupation all around him. Venus, Mars, Aeneas, haunted, in contemporary shape, like ghosts of folk one had known, the places with which he was familiar. Latin might still seem the fittest language for oratory, sixteen hundred years after Cicero was dead; those old Roman pontiffs, draped grandly, sat in the stalls of the choir; Propertius made love to Cynthia in the raiment of the foppish Amadée; they played Terence, and it was but a play within a play. Above all, in natural, heart-felt kinship with their own violent though refined and cunning time, they loved every incident of soldiering; while the changes of the year, the lights, the shadows, the flickering fires of winter, with which Gaston had first associated his companions, added themselves pleasantly, by way of shifting background, to the spectacular effect.

It was the brilliant surface with which the untried world confronted him. Touch it where you might, you felt the resistant force of the solid matter of human experience: of human experience in its strange mixture of beauty and evil, its sorrow, its ill-assorted fates, its pathetic acquiescence; above all, in its overpowering certainty, over against his own world of echoes and shadows, which perhaps only seemed to be so much as echoes and shadows. A nature with the capacity of worship, he was straightway challenged, as by a rival new religion claiming to supersede the religion he knew, to identify himself conclusively with this so tangible world, its suppositions, its issues, its risks. Here was a world, certainly, which did not halt in meditation, but prompted one to make actual trial of it, with a liberty of heart which might likely enough traverse this or that precept (if it were not rather a mere scruple) of his earlier conscience. These its children, at all events, were, as he felt, in instinctive sympathy with its motions; had shrewd divinations of the things men really valued, and waited on them with unquestioning docility. Two worlds, two antagonistic ideals, were in evidence before him. Could a third condition supervene, to mend their discord, or only vex him perhaps from time to time with efforts towards an impossible adjustment?

At a later date Monseigneur Charles Guillard, then Bishop of Chartres, became something like a Huguenot, and, with the concurrence of ecclesiastical authority, ceased from his high functions. Even now in his relations to a more than suspicious Pope he was but the *protégé* of King Charles. A rumour of the fact, reaching those brisk young ears, had already set Gaston's mind in action, tremblingly, as to those small degrees, scarcely realisable perhaps one by one, though so immeasurable in their joint result, by which one might part from the "living vine." At times he started back, as if he saw his own benighted footsteps pacing lightly towards an awful precipice. At present indeed the assumption that there was sanctity in everything the kindly prelate touched, was part of the well maintained etiquette of the little ecclesiastical court. But, as you meet in the street faces that are like a sacrament, so there are faces, looks, tones of voice, among dignified priests, as among other people, to hear or look upon which is to feel the hypothesis of an unseen world impossible. As he smiled amiably out of the midst of his pontifical array on Gaston's scrupulous devotion, it was as if the old Roman augur smiled not only to his fellow augur but to the entire assistant world. In after years Gaston seemed to understand, and, as a consequence of understanding, to judge his old patron equitably:—the religious sense too had its various species. With a real sense of the divine world, but as something immeasurably distant, Monseigneur Guillard, as the nephew of his predecessor in the see, had been brought by maladroit worldly good luck a little too close to its immediate and visible embodiments. From afar you might recognise a divine agency at its work. But to touch its very instruments, to handle them with these fleshly hands:—well! for Monseigneur, that was by no means to believe because the thing was "incredible or absurd." He had smiled, not, certainly, from irreverence, nor (a prelate for half his life) in conscious incredulity, but only in mute surprise, at the thought of an administration of divine graces—this administration in which he was a high priest—in itself, to his quite honest thinking, so unfitting, so improbable. And was it that Gaston was a less independent ruler of his own mental world than he had fancied, that he derived his impressions of things not directly from them, but mediately from other people's impressions about them that he needed the pledge of their assents to ratify his own? He asked himself at all events, from time to time, could that be after all a real sun at which other people's faces were not irradiated? And sometimes it seemed, with a riotous swelling of the heart, as if his own wondrous appetite in these matters had been deadened by surfeit, and there would be a pleasant sense of liberty, of escape out-of-doors, could he be as little touched as almost all other people by Our Lady's Church, and old associations, and all those relics, and those dark, close, fragrant aisles.

At such times, to recall the winged visitant, gentle, yet withal sensitive to offence, which had settled on his youth with so deep a sense of assurance, he would climb the tower of Jean de Beauce, then fresh in all its array of airy staircase and pierced traceries, and great uncovered timbers, like some gigantic birdnest amid the stones, whence the large, quiet, country spaces became his own again, and the curious eye at least went home. He was become well aware of the power of those familiar influences in restoring equanimity, as he might have used a medicine or a wine. At each ascending storey, as the flight of the birds, the scent of the fields, swept past him, till he stood at last amid the unimpeded light and air of the watch-chamber above the great bells, some coil of perplexity, of unassimilable thought or fact, fell away from him. He saw the distant paths, and seemed to hear the breeze piping suddenly upon them under the cloudless sky, on its unseen, capricious way through those vast reaches of atmosphere. At this height, the low ring of blue hills was visible, with suggestions of that south-west country of peach-blossom and wine which had sometimes decoyed his thoughts towards the sea, and beyond it to "that new world of the Indies," which was held to explain a certain softness in the air from that quarter, even in the most vehement weather. Amid those vagrant shadows and shafts of light must be Deux-manoirs, the deserted rooms, the gardens, the graves. In mid-distance, even then a funeral procession was on its way humbly to one of the deserted churchyards. He seemed almost to hear the words across the stillness.

Those words identified themselves, as with his own earliest prepossessions, so also with what was apt to impress him as the common human prepossession—a certain finally authoritative common sense of the quiet experience of things—the oldest, the most authentic, of all voices, audible always if one stepped aside for a moment and got one's ears into what might after all be their normal condition. It might be heard, it would seem, in proportion as men were in touch with the earth itself, in country life, in manual work upon it, above all by the open grave, as if, reminiscent of some older, deeper, more permanent ground of fact, it whispered then oracularly its secret to those who came into such close contact with it. Persistent after-thought! Would it survive always, amid the indifference of others, amid the verdicts of the world, amid a thousand doubts? It seemed to have reached, and filled to overflowing, the soul of one amiable little child who had a kind of genius for tranquillity, and on his first coming here had led Gaston to what he held to be the pleasantest places, as being impregnable by noise. In his small stock of knowledge, he knew, like all around him, that he was going to die, and took kindly to the thought of a small grave in the little green close, as to a natural sleeping-place, in which he would be at home beforehand. Descending from the tower, Gaston knew he should find the child seated alone, enjoying the perfect quiet of the warm afternoon, for all the world was absent—gone forth to receive or gaze at a company of distinguished pilgrims.

Coming, sometimes with immense prelude and preparation, as when King Charles himself arrived to replace an image disfigured by profane Huguenots, sometimes with the secresy and suddenness of an apparition vanished before the public was aware, the pilgrims to "Our Lady under the Earth" were the standing resource of those (such there were at Chartres as everywhere else) who must needs depend for the interest of their existence on the doings of their neighbours. A motley host, only needing their Chaucer to figure as a looking-glass of life, type against type, they brought with them, on the one hand, the very presence and perfume of Paris, the centre of courtly propriety and fashion, on the other, with faces which seemed to belong to another age, curiosities of existence from remote provinces of France, or Europe, from distant, half-fabulous lands remoter still. Jules Damville, who would have liked best to be a sailor, to command, not in any spiritual ark, but in the French fleet (should half-ruined France ever come to have one) led his companions one evening to inspect a strange maritime personage, stout and square, returned, contrary to all expectation, after ten years' captivity among the savages of Florida. There he knelt among the lights at the shrine, with the frankness of a good child, his hair like a mat, his hands tattooed, his mahogany face seamed with a thousand weather-wrinklings, his outlandish offerings lying displayed around him.

Looking, listening, as they served them in the episcopal guest-chamber, those young clerks made wonderful leaps, from time to time, in manly knowledge. With what eager shrewdness they noted, discussed, reproduced, the manners and attire of their pilgrim guests, sporting what was to their liking therein in the streets of Chartres. The more cynical or supercilious pilgrim would sometimes present himself—a personage oftenest of high ecclesiastical station, like the eminent translator of Plutarch, Amyot, afterwards Bishop of Auxerre, who seemed to care little for shrine or relic, but lingered over certain dim manuscripts in the canonical library, where our scholarly Gaston was of service, helping him promptly to what he desired to see. And one morning early, visible at a distance to all the world, risen betimes to gaze, the Queen-mother and her three sons were kneeling there—yearning, greedy, as ever, for a hundred diverse, perhaps incompatible, things. It was at the beginning of that winter of the great siege of Chartres, and on that same morning the child Guy Debreschescourt died in his sleep. His tiny body with the placid, massive, baby head still one broad smile, the rest of him wrapped round together like a chrysalis, was put to rest finally in a fold of the winding-sheet of a very aged person, deceased about the same hour.

For a hard winter, like that famous winter of 1567, the hardest that had been known for fifty years, makes an end of the weak—the aged, the very young. To the robust how pleasant had the preparation for it seemed—the scent of the first wood-fire upon the keen October air; the earth turning from grey to black under the plough; the great stacks of fuel, brought down lazily from the woods of Le Perche, along the winding Eure; its wholesome perfume, the long, soothing nights, and early twilight. The mind of Gaston, for one, was touched by the sense of some remote and delicate beauty in these things, like an effect of magic as being won from unsuspected sources.

What winter really brought however was the danger and vexation of a great siege. The householders of catholic Chartres had watched the forces of their Huguenot enemies gathering from this side and that; and at last the dreaded circle was complete. They were prisoners like the rest, Gaston and the grandparents, shut up in their little hotel; and Gaston, face to face with it, understood at last what war really means. After all, it took them by surprise. It was early in the day. A crowd of worshippers filled the church of Sainte-Foy, built partly on the ramparts; and at the conclusion of the Mass, the Sacrament was to be carried to a sick person. Touched by unusual devotion at this perilous time, the whole assembly rose to escort the procession on its way, passing out slowly, group after group, as if by mechanical instinct, the more reluctant led on by the general consent. Gaston, the last lingerer, halting to let others proceed quietly before him, turns himself about to gaze upon the deserted church, is half tempted to remain, ere he too steps forth lightly and leisurely, when under a shower of massy stones from the *coulevrines* or great cannon of the besiegers, the entire roof of the place sank into the empty space behind him. But it was otherwise in a neighbouring church, crushed in a similar way with all its good people, not long afterwards.

And in the midst of the siege, with all its tumult about her, the old grandmother died, to the undissembled sorrow of Gaston, bereft, unexpectedly as it seemed, of the gentle creature to whom he had always turned for an affection that had been as no other in its absolute incapacity for offence. A tear upon a cheek, like the bark of a tree, testified to some unfulfilled hope, something greatly desired but not to be, which left resignation, by nature or grace, still imperfect, and made death at four score years and ten seem after all like a premature summons in the midst of one's days. For a few hours the peace which followed it brought back to the face a protesting gleam of youth, far antecedent to anything Gaston could possibly have remembered there, moving him to a pity, a peculiar sense of pleading helplessness, which to the end of his life was apt to revive at the sight (it might be in an animal) of what must perforce remember that it had been young but was old.

That broken link with life seemed to end some other things for him. As one puts away the toys of childhood, so now he seemed to discard what had been the central influence of his earlier youth, what more than anything else had stirred imagination and brought the consciousness of his own life warm and full. Gazing now upon the "holy and beautiful place," as he had gazed on the dead face, for a moment he seemed to anticipate the indifference of age. And when not long after the rude hands of catholics themselves, at their wits' end for the maintenance of the "religious war," spoiled it of the accumulated treasure of centuries, leaving Notre-Dame de Chartres in the bareness with which we see it to-day, he had no keen sense of personal loss.

Chapter III

Modernity

The besieging armies disappeared like the snow, leaving city and suburb in all the hardened soilure of war and winter, which only the torrents of spring would carry away. And the spring came suddenly: it was pleasant, after that long confinement, to walk afar securely, through its early fervours. Gaston, too, went forth, on his way home, not alone. Three chosen companions went with him, pledged to the old manor for months to come; its lonely ancient master welcoming readily the tread of youth about him. "The Triumvirate":—so their comrades had been pleased to call the three; that term (delightful touch of classic colour on one's own trite but withal pedantic age) being then familiar, as the designation of three conspicuous agents on the political scene of the generation just departing. Only, these young Latinists went back for the associations of the word to its Roman original, to the three gallants of the distant time, rather than to those native French heroes— Montmorenci, Saint-André, Guise—too close to them to seem really heroic. Mark Antony, knight of Venus, of Cleopatra: shifty Lepidus: bloody, yellow-haired Augustus, so worldly and so fine: you might find their mimic semblance, more clearly than any suggestion of that triad of French adventurers, in the unfolding manhood of Jasmin, Amadée, and Camille.

They had detached themselves by an irresistible natural effectiveness from the surface of that youthful scholastic world around the episcopal throne of Chartres, carrying its various aptitudes as if to a perfect triple flower; restless Amadée de l'Autrec, who was to be a soldier, dazzled early into dangerous, rebellious paths by the iron ideal of the warriors of "the religion," and even now fitting his blond prettiness to airs of Huguenot austerity; Camille Pontdormi, who meant to be a lawyer in an age in which certain legists had asserted an audacity of genius after a manner very captivating to youth with any appetite for predominance over its fellows—already winsomely starched a little amid his courtly finery of garb, and manner, and phrase; Jasmin de Villebon, who hardly knew what he meant, or wished, to be except perhaps a poet—himself, certainly, a poem for any competent reader. Vain,—yes! a little, and mad, said his companions, of course, with his clinging, exigent, lover's ways. It was he who had led the others on this visit to Gaston de Latour. Threads to be cut short, one by one, before his eyes, the three would cross and re-cross, gaily, pathetically, in the tapestry of Gaston's years, and, divided far asunder afterwards, seemed at this moment, moving there before him in the confidential talk he could not always share, inseparably linked together, like some complicated pictorial arabesque, under the common light of their youth, and of the morning, and of their sympathetic understanding of the visible world.

So they made their way, under the rows of miraculous white thorn-blossom, and through the green billows, at peace just then, though the war still blazed or smouldered along the southern banks of the Loire and far beyond, and it was with a delightful sense of peril, of prowess attested in the facing of it, that they passed from time to time half-ruined or deserted farm-buildings where the remnants of the armies might yet be lingering. It was Jasmin, poetic Jasmin, who, in giving Gaston the book he now carried ever ready to hand, had done him perhaps the best of services, for it had proved the key to a new world of seemingly boundless intellectual resources, and yet with a special closeness to visible or sensuous things: the scent and colour of the field-flowers, the amorous business of the birds, the flush and refledging of the black earth itself in that fervent springtide, which was therefore unique in Gaston's memory. It was his own intellectual springtide; as people look back to a physical spring, which for once in ten or fifteen years, for once in a lifetime, was all that spring could be.

The book was none other than Pierre de Ronsard's "Odes," with *Mignonne! allons voir si la rose*, and "The Skylark" and the lines to April—itself verily like nothing so much as a jonquil, in its golden-green binding and yellow edges and perfume of the place where it had lain—sweet, but with something of the sickliness of all spring flowers since the days of Proserpine. Just eighteen years old, and the work of the poet's own youth, it took possession of Gaston with the ready intimacy of one's equal in age, fresh at every point; and he experienced what it is the function of contemporary poetry to effect anew for sensitive youth in each succeeding generation. The truant and irregular poetry of his own nature, all in solution there, found an external and authorised mouth-piece, ranging itself rightfully, as the latest achievement of human soul in this matter, along with the consecrated poetic voices of the past.

Poetry!—Hitherto it had seemed hopelessly chained to the bookshelf, like something in a dead language, "dead, and shut up in reliquaries of books," or like those relics "one may only see through a little pane of glass," as one of its recent liberators had said. Sure, apparently, of its own "niche in the temple of Fame," the recognised poetry of literature had had the pretension to defy or discredit, as depraved and irredeemably vulgar, the poetic motions in the living genius of to-day. Yet the genius of to-day, extant and forcible, the wakeful soul of present time consciously in possession, would assert its poetic along with all its other rights; and in regard to the curiosity, the intellectual interest, of Gaston, for instance, it had of course the advantage of being close at hand, as with the effectiveness of a personal presence. Studious youth, indeed, put on its mettle, though it may make a docile profession of faith regarding the witchery, the thaumaturgic powers, of Virgil, or may we say of Shakespeare, is yet often actually of listless mood enough over books that certainly stirred the past profoundly. How faint and dim, after all, the sorrows of Dido, of Juliet, the travail of Aeneas, beside quite recent things felt or done—stories which, floating to us on the light current of to-day's conversation, leave the soul in a flutter! At best, poetry of the past could move one with no more directness than the beautiful faces of antiquity which are not here for us to see and unaffectedly love them. Gaston's demand (his youth only conforming to pattern therein) was for a poetry, as veritable, as intimately near, as corporeal, as the new faces of the hour, the flowers of the actual season. The poetry of mere literature, like the dead body, could not bleed, while there was a heart, a poetic heart, in the living world, which beat, bled, spoke with irresistible power. Elderly people, Virgil in hand, might assert professionally that the contemporary age, an age, of course, of little people and things, deteriorate since the days of their own youth, must necessarily be unfit for poetic uses. But then youth, too, had its perpetual part to play, protesting that, after all said, the sun in the air, and in its own veins, was still found to be hot, still begetting, upon both alike, flowers and fruit; nay! visibly new flowers, and fruit richer than ever. Privately, in fact, Gaston had conceived of a poetry more thaumaturgic than could be anything of earlier standing than himself. The age renews itself; and in immediate derivation from it a novel poetry also grows superb and large, to fill a certain mental situation made ready in advance. Yes! the acknowledged, and, so to call it, legitimate, poetry of literature was but a thing he might sip at, like some sophisticated rarity in the way of wine, for example, pleasing the acquired taste. It was another sort of poetry, unexpressed, perhaps inexpressible, certainly hitherto not made known in books, that must drink up and absorb him, like the joyful air,—him, and the earth, with its deeds, its blossoms, and faces.

In such condition of mind, how deeply, delightfully, must the poetry of Ronsard and his fellows have moved him, when he became aware, as from age to age inquisitive youth by good luck does become aware, of the literature of his own day, confirming—more than confirming—anticipation! Here was a poetry which boldly assumed the dress, the words, the habits, the very trick, of contemporary life, and turned them into gold. It took possession of the lily in one's hand, and projecting it into a visionary distance, shed upon the body of the flower the soul of its beauty. Things were become at once more deeply sensuous and more deeply ideal. As at the touch of a wizard, something more came into the rose than its own natural blush. Occupied so closely with the visible, this new poetry had so profound an intuition of what can only be felt, and maintained that mood in speaking of such objects as wine, fruit, the plume in the cap, the ring on the finger. And still that was no dubious or generalised form it gave to flower or bird, but the exact pressure of the jay at the window: you could count the petals, of the exact natural number: no expression could be too faithful to the precise texture of things; words, too, must embroider, be twisted and spun, like silk or golden hair. Here were real people, in their real, delightful attire, and you understood how they moved. The visible was more visible than ever before, just because soul had come to the surface. The juice in the flowers, when Ronsard named them, was like wine or blood, so coloured were things. Though the grey things also, the cool things, all the fresher for the contrast—with a freshness, again, that seemed to touch and cool the soul—found their account there: the clangorous passage of the birds at night foretokening rain, the moan of the wind at the door, the wind's self made visible over the yielding corn.

Thus it was Gaston understood the poetry of Ronsard, generously expanding it to the full measure of its intention. That poetry, too, lost its thaumaturgic power in turn and became mere literature in exchange for life, partly in the natural revolution of poetic taste, partly for its faults. Faults and all however Gaston loyally accepted it; those faults—the lapse of grace into affectation, of learning into pedantry, of exotic fineness into a trick—counting with him as but the proof of faith to its own dominant positions. They were but *characteristics*, as such needing no apology with the initiated, or welcome even, as savouring of the master's peculiarities of perfection. He listened, he looked round freely, but always now with the ear, the eye, of his favourite poet. It had been a lesson, a doctrine, the communication of an art,—the art of placing the pleasantly aesthetic, the welcome, elements of life at an advantage in one's view of it till they seemed to occupy the entire surface; and he was sincerely grateful for an undeniable good service.

And yet the gifted poet seemed but to have spoken what was already in Gaston's own mind, what he had longed to say, had been just going to say: so near it came, that it had the charm of a discovery of one's own. Perhaps that was because the poet told one so much about himself, making so free a display of what though personal was very contagious, of his love-secrets especially, how love and nothing else filled his mind. He was in truth but "love's secretary," noting from hour to hour its minutely changing fortunes. Yes! that was the reason why visible, audible, sensible things glowed so brightly, why there was such luxury in sounds, words, rhythms, of the new light come on the world, of that wonderful freshness. With a masterly appliance of what was near and familiar, or, again, in the way of bold innovation, he found new words for perennially new things, and the novel accent awakened long-slumbering associations. Never before had words, single words, meant so much. What expansion, what liberty of heart, in speech: how associable to music, to singing, the written lines! He sang of the lark, and it was the lark's voluble self. The physical beauty of humanity lent itself to every object, animate or inanimate, to the very hours and lapses and changes of time itself. An almost burdensome fulness of expression haunted the gestures, the very dress, the personal ornaments, of the people on the highway. Even Jacques Bonhomme at his labour, or idling for an hour, borrowed from his love, homely as it was, a touch of dignity or grace, and some secret of utterance, which made one think of Italy or Greece. The voice of the shepherd calling, the chatter of the shepherdess turning her spindle, seemed to answer, or wait for answer—to be fragments of love's ideal and eternal communing.

It was the power of "modernity," as renewed in every successive age for genial youth, protesting, defiant of all sanction in these matters, that the true "classic" must be of the present, the force and patience of present time. He had felt after the thing, and here it was,—the one irresistible poetry there had ever been, with the magic word spoken in due time, transforming his own age and the world about him, presenting its every-day touch, the very trick one knew it by, as an additional grace, asserting the latent poetic rights of the transitory, the fugitive, the contingent. Poetry need no longer mask itself in the habit of a by-gone day: Gaston could but pity the people of by-gone days for not being above-ground to read. Here was a discovery, a new faculty, a privileged apprehension, to be conveyed in turn to one and another, to be propagated for the imaginative regeneration of the world. It was a manner, a habit of thought, which would invade ordinary life, and mould that to its intention. In truth, all the world was already aware, and delighted. The "school" was soon to pay the penalty of that immediate acceptance, that intimate fitness to the mind of its own time, by sudden and profound neglect, as a thing preternaturally tarnished and tame, like magic youth, or magic beauty, turned in a moment by magic's own last word into withered age. But then, to the liveliest spirits of that time it had seemed nothing less than "impeccable," after the manner of the great sacred products of the past, though in a living tongue. Nay! to Gaston for one, the power of the old classic poetry itself was explained by the reflex action of the new, and might seem to justify its pretensions at last.

From the poem fancy wandered to the poet, and curious youth would fain see the writer in person—what a poet was like, with anxious surmises, this way and that, as to the degree in which the precious mental particles might be expected to have wrought up the outward presence to their own high quality. A creature of the eye, Gaston, in this case at least, the intellectual hold on him being what it was, had no fear of disillusion. His poetic readings had borrowed an additional relish from the genial, companionable manner of his life at this time, taking him into the remotest corners of the vast level land, and its outer ring of blue uplands, amid which, as he rode one day with "the three," towards perfectly new prospects, he had chanced on some tangible rumour of the great poet's present abode. The hill they had mounted at leisure, in talk with a village priest, dropped suddenly upon a vague tract of wood and pasture with a dark ridge beyond, towards the south-west. The black notch, which broke its outline against the mellow space of evening light, was the steeple of the priory of Croix-val, of which reverend body Pierre de Ronsard, although a layman, was, by special favour of King Charles, Superior.

Though a formal peace was come, though the primary movers of war had taken hands or kissed each other, and were exchanging suspicious courtesies, yet the unquiet temper of war was still abroad everywhere with an after-crop of miserable incidents. The captainless national and mercenary soldiers were become in large numbers thieves or beggars, and the peasant's hand sank back to the tame labour of the plough reluctantly. Relieved a little by the sentimental humour of the hour, lending, as Ronsard prompted, a poetic and always amorous interest to everything around him, poor Gaston's very human soul was vexed nevertheless at the spectacle of the increased hardness of human life, with certain misgivings from time to time at the contrast of his own luxurious tranquillity. The homeless woman suckling her babe at the roadside, the grey-beard hasting before the storm, the tattered fortune-teller who, when he shook his head at her proposal to "read his hand," assured him (perhaps with some insight into his character) "You do that"—you shake your head negatively—"too much":—these, and the like, might count as fitting human accidents in an impassioned landscape picture. And his new imaginative culture had taught him to value "surprises" in nature itself, the quaint charm of the mistletoe in the wood, of the blossom before the leaf, the cry of passing birds at night: nay! the most familiar details of nature also, its daily routine of light and darkness, beset him now with a kind of troubled and troubling eloquence. The rain, the first streak of dawn, the very sullenness of the sky, had a power only to be described by saying that they seemed to be *moral* facts.

On his way at last to gaze on the abode of the new hero or demi-god of poetry, Gaston perceives increasingly as another excellence of his verse, how truthful it was, how close to the minute fact of the scene around. There are pleasant wines which, expressing the peculiar quality of their native soil, lose their special pleasantness away from home. The physiognomy of the scene had changed: the plain of La Beauce had ruffled itself into low green hills and gently winding valleys, with clear, quick water and fanciful patches of heath and woodland. Here and there a secular oak tree maintained a solitude around it. It was the district of the "little Loir"—the Vendomois; and here in its own country, the new poetry, notwithstanding its classic elegance, might seem a native wild flower, modest enough.

Gaston then came riding with his companions towards evening along the road which had suddenly abandoned its day-long straightness for wanton curves and ascents; and there, as an owl on the wing cried softly, beyond the tops of the spreading poplars was the west front, silver-grey and quiet, inexpressibly quiet, with worn, late-gothic "flamings" from top to bottom, as full of reverie to Gaston's thinking as the enchanted castle in a story-book. The village lay thinly scattered around the wide, grass-grown space. Below was the high espaliered garden-wall, and within it, visible through the open doors, a gaunt figure, hook-nosed, like a wizard, at work with the spade, too busily to turn and look. Or was it that he did not hear at all the question repeated thrice:—Could one see His Reverence the Prior, at least in the Convent Church? "You see him!" was the answer, as a face, all nerve, distressed nerve, turned upon them not unkindly, the vanity of the great man being aware and pleasantly tickled. The unexpected incident had quickened a prematurely aged pulse, and in reward for their good service the young travellers were bidden carry their equipment, not to the village inn, but to the guest-chamber of the half-empty priory. The eminent man of letters, who had been always an enthusiastic gardener, though busy just now, not with choice flowers, but with salutary kitchen-stuff, working indeed with much effort to counteract the gout, was ready enough in his solitude to make the most of chance visitors, especially youthful ones. A bell clanged. He laid aside the spade, and casting an eye at the whirling weather-vanes announced that it would snow. There had been no "sunset." They had travelled away impercep-tibly from genial afternoon into a world of ashen evening.

The enemies of the lay Prior, satirists literary and religious, falsely made a priest of him, a priest who should have sacrificed a goat to pagan Bacchus. And in truth the poet, for a time a soldier, and all his life a zealous courtier, had always been capable, as a poet should be, of long-sustained meditation, adapting himself easily enough to the habits of the "religious," following attentively the choir-services in their church, of which he was a generous benefactor, and to which he presently proceeded for vespers and matins. Gaston and "the three" sat among the Brethren, tempting curious eyes, in the stalls of the half-lighted choir, while in purple cope and jaunty biretta the lay Prior "assisted," his *confidentiaire*, or priestly substitute, officiating at the altar. The long, sad, Lenten office over, an invitation to supper followed, for Ronsard still loved, in his fitful retirements at one or another of his numerous benefices, to give way to the chance recreation of flattering company, and these gay lads' enthusiasm for his person was obvious. And as for himself, the great poet, with his bodily graces and airs of court, had always possessed the gift of pleasing those who encountered him.

The snow was falling now in big, slow flakes, and a great fire blazed under the chimney, with its cipher and enigmatic motto, as they sat down to the leek-soup, the hard eggs, and the salad grown and gathered by their host's own hands. The long stone passages through which they passed from church, with the narrow brown doors of the monks' dormitories one after another along the white-washed wall, made the coquetries of the Prior's own distant apartment all the more reassuring. You remembered that from his ninth year he had been the pet of princesses, the favourite of kings. Upon the cabinets, chests, book-cases, around, were ranged the *souvenirs* received from various royal persons, including three kings of France, the fair Queen of Scots, Elizabeth of England. The conversation therefore fell to, and was kept going by, the precious contents of the place where they were sitting, the books printed and bound as they have never been before—books which meant assiduous study, the theory of poetry, with Ronsard, accompanying its practice—delicate things of art which beauty had handled or might handle, the pictured faces on the walls, in their frames of reeded ebony or jewelled filigree. There was the Minerva, decreed him at a conference of the elegant, pedantic *Jeux Floraux*, which had proclaimed Pierre de Ronsard "Prince of Poets." The massive silver image Ronsard had promptly offered to his patron King Charles; but in vain, for, though so greatly in want of ready money that he melted down church ornaments and exacted "black" contributions from the clergy, one of the things in which Charles had ever been sincere was a reverence for literature.

So there it stood, doing duty for Our Lady, with gothic crown and a fresh sprig of consecrated box, bringing the odd, enigmatic physiognomy, preferred by the art of that day, within the sphere of religious devotion. The King's manuscript, declining, in verse as good as Ronsard's, the honour not meant for him, might be read attached to the pedestal. The ladies of his own verse, Marie, Cassandra, and the rest, idols one after another of a somewhat artificial and for the most part unrequited love, from the Angevine maiden—*La petite pucelle Angevine*—who had vexed his young soul by her inability to yield him more than a faint Platonic affection, down to Helen, to whom he had been content to propose no other, gazed, more impassibly than ever, from the walls.

They might have been sisters, those many successive loves, or one and the same lady over and over again, in slightly varied humour and attire—at the different intervals perhaps of some rather lengthy, mimetic *masque* of love, to which the theatrical dress of that day was appropriate. The mannered Italian or Italianised artists, including the much-prized, native Janet, with his favourite water-green backgrounds, aware of the poet's predilection, had given to one and all alike the same brown eyes and tender eyelids and golden hair and somewhat ambered paleness, varying only the curious artifices of the dress—knots and nets and golden spider-work and clear flat stones. Dangerous guests in that simple, cloistral place, Sibyls of the Renaissance on a mission from Italy to France, to Gaston one and all seemed under the burden of some weighty message concerning a world unknown to him which the stealthy lines of cheek and brow contrived to express, while the lips and eyes only smiled, not quite honestly. It had been a learned love, with undissembled "hatred of the vulgar." Three royal Margarets, much-praised *pearls* of three successive generations (to the curious in these objects purity is far from being the only measure of value) asserted charms a thought more frank, or French, though still gracefully pedantic, with their quaintly kerchiefed books—books of what?—in their pale hands. Among the ladies, on the pictured wall as in life, were the poet's male companions, stirring memories of a more material sort, though their common interest had been poetry—memories of that *Bohemia* which even a "Prince" of court poets had frequented when he was young, of his cruder youthful vanities. In some cases the date of death was inscribed below.

One there was among them, the youngest, of whose genial fame to come this experienced judge of men and books, two years before "Saint Bartholomew's," had been confident,—a crowned boy, King Charles himself. Here, perhaps, was the one entirely disinterested sentiment of the poet's life, wholly independent of a long list of benefits, or benefices; for the younger had turned winsomely, appealingly, to the elder who, forty years of age, feeling chilly at the thought, had no son. And of one only of those companions did the memory bring a passing cloud. It was long ago, on a journey, that he had first spoken, accidentally, with Joachim Du Bellay, whose friendship had been the great intellectual fortune of his life. For a moment one saw the encounter at the way-side inn, in the broad, gay morning, a quarter of a century since; and there was the face;—deceased at thirty-five. Pensive, plaintive, refined by sickness, of exceeding delicacy, it must from the first have been best suited to the greyness of an hour like this.—Tomorrow, where will be the snow?

The leader in that great poetic battle of the Pleiad, their host himself, (he explained the famous device, and named the seven chief stars in the constellation,) was depicted appropriately, in veritable armour, with antique Roman cuirass of minutely inlaid gold and flowered mantle, the crisp, ceremonial laurel-wreath of the Roman conqueror lying on the audacious, over-developed brows, above the great hooked nose of practical enterprise. In spite of his pretension to the Epicurean conquest of a kingly indifference of mind, the portrait of twenty years ago betrayed, not less than the living face with its roving, astonished eyes, the haggard soul of a haggard generation, whose eagerly-sought refinements had been after all little more than a theatrical make-believe—an age of wild people, of insane impulse, of homicidal mania. The sweet-souled singer had no more than others attained real calm in it. Even in youth nervous distress had been the chief facial characteristic. Triumphant, however, in his battle for Greek beauty—for the naturalisation of Greek beauty in the brown cloud-lands of the North—he might have been thinking, contemptuously, of barking little Saint-Gelais, or of Monsieur Marot's pack-thread poems. He, for his part, had always held that poetry must be woven of delicate silk, of fine linen, or at least of good home-spun worsted.

To Gaston, yielding himself to its influence, for a moment the scene around seemed unreal. An exotic, embalming air, escaped from some old Greek or Roman pleasure-place, had turned the poet's workroom into a strange kind of private sanctuary, amid these rude conventual buildings, with the March wind aloud in the chimneys. Notwithstanding, what with the long day's ride, the keen evening, they had done justice to the monastic fare, the "little" wine of the country, the cream, the onions,—fine Camille, and dainty Jasmin! and the poet turned to talk upon gardening, concerning which he could tell them a thing or two—of early salads, and those special apples the king loved to receive from him, mille-fleur pippins, painted with a thousand tiny streaks of red, yellow, and green. A dish of them now came to table, with a bottle, at the right moment, from the darkest corner of the cellar. And then, in nasal voice, well-trained to Latin intonation, giving a quite medieval amplitude to the poet's sonorities of rhythm and vocabulary, the Sub-prior was bidden to sing, after the notation of Goudimel, the "Elegy of the Rose"; while the author girded cheerily at the clerkly man's assumed ignorance of such compositions.

It was but a half-gaiety, in truth, that awoke in the poet even now, with the singing and the good wine, as the notes echoed windily along the passages. On his forty-sixth year the unaffected melancholy of his later life was already gathering. The dead!—he was coming to be on their side. The fact came home to Gaston that this evocator of "the eternally youthful" was visibly old before his time; his work being done, or centered now for the most part on amendments, not invariably happy, of his earlier verse. The little panelled drawers were full of them. The poet pulled out one, and as it stood open for a moment there lay the first book of the *Franciade*, in silken cover, white and gold, ready for the king's hands, but never to be finished.

Gaston, as he turned from a stolen reading of the opening verse, in jerky, feverish, gouty manuscript, to the writer, let out his soul perhaps. The poet's face struck fire too, and seeming to detect on a sudden the legible document of something by no means conventional below the young man's well-controlled manner and expression, he became as if paternally anxious for his intellectual furtherance, and in particular for the addition of "manly power" to a "grace" of mind, obviously there already in due sufficiency. Would he presently carry a letter with recommendation of himself to Monsieur Michel de Montaigne? Linked they were, in the common friendship of the late Etienne de la Boetie yonder! Monsieur Michel could tell him much of the great ones—of the Greek and Latin masters of style. Let his study be in them! With what justice, by the way, had those Latin poets dealt with winter, and wintry charms, in their bland Italy! And just then, at the striking of a ricketty great bell of the Middle Age, in the hands of a cowled brother, came the emblazoned grace-cup, with which the Prior de Ronsard had enriched his "house," and the guests withdrew.

"Yesterday's snow" was nowhere, a surprising sunlight everywhere; through which, after gratefully bidding adieu to the great poet, almost on their knees for a blessing, our adventurers returned home. Gaston, intently pondering as he lingered behind the others, was aware that this new poetry, which seemed to have transformed his whole nature into half-sensuous imagination, was the product not of one or more individual writers, but (though it might be in the way of a response to their challenge) a general direction of men's minds, a delightful "fashion" of the time. He almost anticipated our modern idea, or platitude, of the *Zeit-geist.*—Social instinct was involved in the matter, and loyalty to an intellectual *movement.* As its leader had been himself the first to suggest, the actual authorship belonged not so much to a star as to a constellation, like that hazy Pleiad he had pointed out in the sky, or like the swarm of larks abroad this morning over the corn, led by a common instinct, a large element in which was sympathetic trust in the instinct of others. Here, truly, was a doctrine to propagate, a secret open to every one who would learn, towards a new management of life,—nay! a new religion, or at least a new worship, maintaining and visibly setting forth a single overpowering apprehension.

The worship of physical beauty,—a religion, the proper faculty of which would be the bodily eye! Looked at in this way, some of the well-marked characteristics of the poetry of the Pleiad assumed a hieratic, almost an ecclesiastical air. That rigid correctness; that gracious unction, as of the medieval Latin psalmody; that aspiring fervour; that jealousy of the profane "vulgar"; the sense, flattering to one who was in the secret, that this thing, even in its utmost triumph, could never be really popular:—why were these so welcome to him but from the continuity of early mental habit? He might renew the over-grown tonsure, and wait, devoutly, rapturously, in this goodly sanctuary of earth and sky about him, for the manifestation, at the moment of his own worthiness, of flawless humanity, in some undreamed-of depth and perfection of the loveliness of bodily form.

And therewith came the consciousness, no longer of mere bad-neighbourship between what was old and what was new in his life, but of incompatibility between two rival claimants upon him, of two ideals. Might that new religion, so to term it, be a religion not altogether of goodness, a *profane* religion, in spite of its poetic fervours? There were "flowers of evil," among the rest. It came in part, avowedly, as a kind of consecration of evil, seeming to lend it the beauty of holiness. Rather, good and evil were distinctions inapplicable in proportion as these new interests made themselves felt. For a moment, amid casuistical questions as to one's indefeasible right to liberty of heart, he saw himself, somewhat wearily, very far gone from the choice, the dedication, of his boyhood. If he could but be rid of it altogether! Or, if it would but assert itself, speak, with irresistible decision and effect! Might there be perhaps, somewhere, in some penetrative mind in this age of novelties, some scheme of truth, some science of men and things, which could harmonise for him his earlier and later preferences, "the sacred and the profane loves," or, failing that, establish, to his pacification, the exclusive supremacy of the latter?

CHAPTER IV

Peach–blossom and Wine

Those searchings of mind brought with them from time to time a cruel start from sleep, a sudden shudder at any wide out-look over life and its issues, draughts of mental east-wind across the hot mornings, into which the voices of his companions called him, to lose again in long rambles every thought save that of his own firm, abounding youth. Those rambles were the last, sweet, wastefully spent, remnants of a happy season. The letter for Monsieur Michel de Montaigne was to hand, with preparations for the distant journey which must presently break up their comradeship. Notwithstanding, its actual termination overtook them at the last as if by surprise. On a sudden that careless interval of time was over.

The carelessness of "The Three" at all events had been entire. Secure, on the low, warm, level surface of things, they talked, they rode, they ate and drank, with no misgivings, mental or moral, no too curious questions as to the essential character of their so palpable well-being, or the rival standards thereof, of origins and issues. And yet, with all their gaiety, as its last triumphant note in truth, they were to trifle with death, welcoming, by way of a foil to the easy character of their days, a certain luxurious sense of danger—the night-alarm, the arquebuse peeping from some quiet farm-building across their way, the rumoured presence in their neighbourhood of this or that great military leader—delightful premonitions of the adventurous life soon to be their own in Paris. What surmises they had of any vaguer sort of danger, took effect, in that age of wizardry, as a quaintly *practical* superstition, in the expectation of cadaverous churchyard things, and the like, intruding themselves where they should not be, to be dissipated in turn by counter-devices of the dark craft which had evoked them. Gaston, then, as in after years, though he saw no ghosts, could not bear to trifle with such matters: to his companions it was a delight, as they supped, to note the indication of nameless terrors, if it were only in the starts and cracking of the timbers of the old place. To the turbid spirits of that generation the midnight heaven itself was by no means a restful companion; and many were the hours wasted by those young astrophiles in puzzling out the threats, or the enigmatic promises, of a starry sky.

The fact that armed persons were still abroad, thieves or assassins, lurking under many disguises, might explain what happened on the last evening of their time together, when they sat late at the open windows as night increased, serene but covered summer night, aromatic, velvet-footed. What coolness it had was pleasant after the wine; and they strolled out, fantastically muffled in certain old heraldic dresses of parade, caught up in the hall as they passed through, Gaston alone remaining to attend on his grandfather. In about an hour's time they returned, not a little disconcerted, to tell a story of which Gaston was reminded (seeing them again in thought as if only half real, amid the bloomy night, with blood upon their boyish flowers) as they crossed his path afterwards at three intervals. Listening for the night-hawk, pushing aside the hedge-row to catch the evening breath of the honeysuckle, they had sauntered on, scarcely looking in advance, along the causeway. Soft sounds came out of the distance, but footsteps on the hard road they had not heard, when three others fronted them face to face—Jasmin, Amadée, and Camille—their very selves, visible in the light of the lantern carried by Camille: they might have felt the breath upon their cheeks: real, close, definite, cap for cap, plume for plume, flower for flower, a light like their own flashed up counterwise, but with blood, all three of them, fresh upon the bosom, or in the mouth. It was well to draw the sword, were one's enemy carnal or spiritual; even devils, as wise men know, taking flight at its white glitter through the air. Out flashed the brave youths' swords, still with mimic counter-motion, upon nothing—upon the empty darkness before them.

Curdled at heart for an hour by that strange encounter, they went on their way next morning no different. There was something in the mere belief that peace was come at last. For a moment Huguenots were, or pretended to be, satisfied with a large concession of liberty; to be almost light of soul. The French, who can always pause in the very midst of civil bloodshed to eulogise the reign of universal kindness, were determined to treat a mere armistice as nothing less than Utopia realised. To bear offensive arms was made a crime; and the sense of security at home was attested by vague schemes of glory to be won abroad, under the leadership of "The Admiral," the great Huguenot Coligni, anxious to atone for any share he might have had in the unhappiness of France by helping her to foreign conquests. Philip of Spain had been watching for the moment when Charles and Catherine should call the Duke of Alva into France to continue his devout work there. Instead, the poetic mind of Charles was dazzled for a while by dream of wresting the misused Netherlands from Spanish rule altogether.

Under such genial conditions, then, Gaston set out towards those south-west regions he had always yearned to, as popular imagination just now set thither also, in a vision of French ships going forth from the mouths of the Loire and the Gironde, from Nantes, Bordeaux, and La Rochelle, to the Indies, in rivalry of Spanish adventure. The spasmodic gaiety of the time blent with that of the season of the year, of his own privileged time of life, and allowed the opulent country through which he was to travel all its advantages. Henceforth that low line of blue hills would mean more, not less for him, than of old. After the reign of his native apple-blossom and corn, it was that of peach-blossom and wine. Southwards to Orleans and the Loire; then, with the course of the sunny river, to Blois, to Amboise, to Tours, he traversed a region of unquestioned natural charm, heightened greatly by the mental atmosphere through which it reached him. Black Angers, white Saumur, with its double in the calm broad water below, the melancholy seigneurial woods of Blois, ranged themselves in his memory as so many distinct types of what was dignified or pleasant in human habitations. Frequently, along the great historic stream, as along some vast street, contemporary genius was visible (a little prematurely as time would show) in a novel and seductive architecture, which, by its engrafting of a seductive grace on homely native forms, spoke of a certain restless aspiration to be what one was not but might become—the old Gaulish desire to be mentally enfranchised by the sprightlier genius of Italy. With their terraced gardens, their airy galleries, their triumphal chimney-pieces, their spacious stair-ways, their conscious provision for the elegant enjoyment of all seasons in turn, here surely were the new abodes for the new humanity of this new, poetic, picturesque age. What but flawless bodies, duly appointed to typically developed souls, could move on the daily business of life through these dreamy apartments into which he entered from time to time, finding their mere garniture like a personal presence in them? Was there light here in the earth itself? As he passed below, wild fancy would sometimes credit the outlook from those lofty gables with felicities of combination beyond possibility. What prospects of mountain and sea-shore from those aerial window-seats!

And still, as in some sumptuous tapestry, the architecture, the landscape, were but a setting for the human figures. These palatial abodes challenged continual speculation as to their inhabitants—how they moved, read poetry and romance, or wrote the memoirs which were like romance, passed through all the hourly changes of their all-accomplished, intimate life. The Loire was the river pre-eminently of the monarchy, of the court; and the fleeting human interests, fact or fancy, which gave its utmost value to the liveliness of the natural scene, found a centre in the movements of Catherine and her sons, still roving, after the eccentric habit inherited from Francis the First, from one "house of pleasure" to another, in the pursuit at once of amusement and of that political intrigue which was the serious business of their lives. Like some fantastic company of strolling players amid the hushed excitement of a little town, the royal family with all its own small rivalries, would be housed for a night under the same roof with some of its greater enemies—Henri de Guise, Condé, "The Admiral," all alike taken by surprise—but courteously, ineffectively therefore. And Gaston, come thus by chance so close to them, had not so much the sense of nearness to the springs of great events, as of the likeness of the whole matter to a stage-play with its ingeniously contrived encounters, or the assortments of a game of chance.

And in a while the dominant course of the river itself, the animation of its steady, downward flow, even amid the sand-shoals and whispering islets of the dry season, bore his thoughts beyond it in a sudden irresistible appetite for the sea; and he determined, varying slightly from the prescribed route, to reach his destination by way of the coast. From Nantes he descended imperceptibly along tall hedge-rows of acacia, till on a sudden, with a novel freshness in the air, through a low archway of laden fruit-trees it was visible—sand, sea, and sky, in three quiet spaces, line upon line. The features of the landscape changed again, and the gardens, the rich orchards, gave way to bare, grassy undulations. Only, the open sandy spaces presented their own native flora, for the fine silex seemed to have crept up the tall, wiry stalks of the ixias, like grasses the seeds of which had expanded, by solar magic, into veritable flowers, crimson, green, or yellow patched with black.

It was pleasant to sleep as if in the sea's arms, amid the low murmurs, the salt odour mingled with the wild garden scents of a little inn or farm, forlorn in the wide enclosure of an ancient manor, deserted as the sea encroached—long ago, for the fig-trees in the now riven walls were tough and old. Next morning he must turn his back betimes, with the freshness of the outlook still undimmed, all colours turning to white on the shell-beach, the wrecks, the children at play on it, the boat with its gay streamers dancing in the foam. Bright as the scene of his journey had been, it had from time to time its grisly touches. A forbidden fortress with its steel-clad inmates thrust itself

upon the way: the village church had been ruined too recently to count as
picturesque; and at last, at the meeting-point of five long causeways across a
wide expanse of marshland, where the wholesome sea turned stagnant, La
Rochelle itself scowled through the heavy air, the dark ramparts still rising
higher around its dark townsfolk:—La Rochelle, the "Bastion of the Gospel"
according to John Calvin, the conceded capital of the Huguenots. They were
there the armed chiefs of Protestantism, dreaming of a "dictator" after the
Roman manner, who should set up a religious republic: they were there, and
would not leave it, even to share the festivities of the marriage of King Charles
to his little Austrian Elizabeth about this time. Serried closely together on
land, they had a strange mixed following on the sea. Lair of heretics, or
shelter of martyrs, La Rochelle was ready to protect the outlaw. The corsair,
of course, would be a Protestant, actually armed perhaps by sour old Jeanne
of Navarre—the ship he fell across, of course, Spanish. A real Spanish ship of
war, gay, magnificent, was gliding even then stealthily through the distant
haze; and nearer lay what there was of a French navy. Did the enigmatic
"Admiral," the coming dictator, Coligni, really wish to turn it to foreign
adventure, in rivalry of Spain, as the proper patriotic outcome of this period,
or breathing-space of peace and national unity?

Undoubtedly they were still there, even in this halcyon weather, those
causes of disquiet, like the volcanic forces beneath the massive chestnut
woods, spread so calmly through the breathless air, on the ledges and levels
of the red heights of the Limousin, under which Gaston now passed on his
way southwards. On his right hand a broad, lightly diversified expanse of
vineyard, of towns and towers innumerable, rolled its burden of fat things
down the slope of the Gironde towards the more perfect level beyond. In the
heady afternoon an indescribable softness laid hold on him, from the objects,
the atmosphere, the lazy business, of the scene around. And was that the
quarter whence the dry daylight, the intellectual iron, the chalybeate
influence, was to come?—those coquettish, well-kept, vine-wreathed towers,
smiling over a little irregular old village, itself half-hidden in gadding vine. It
was pointed out at all events by the gardeners (all labourers here were
gardeners) as the end of his long, pleasant journey, abode of Monsieur Michel
de Montaigne, the singular but not unpopular gentleman living there among
his books, of whom Gaston hears much over-night at the inn where he rests,
before delivering the great poet's letter, entering his room at last in a flutter
of curiosity.

In those earlier days of the Renaissance, a whole generation had been
exactly in the position in which Gaston now found himself. An older ideal,

moral and religious, certain theories of man and nature actually in possession, still haunted humanity, at the very moment when it was called, through a full knowledge of the past, to enjoy the present with an unrestricted expansion of its own capacities.—Might one enjoy? Might one eat of all the trees?—There were those who had already eaten and needed, retrospectively, a theoretic justification, a sanction of their actual liberties, in some new reading of human nature itself and its relation to the world around it.—Explain to us the propriety, on the full view of things, of this bold course we have taken, or know we shall take.

Ex post facto, at all events, that justification was furnished by the Essays of Montaigne. The spirit of the Essays doubtless had been felt already in many a mind, as, by a universal law of re-action, the intellect *does* supply the due theoretic equivalent to an inevitable course of conduct. But it was Montaigne certainly who turned that emancipating ethic into current coin. To Pascal, looking back upon the sixteenth century as a whole, Montaigne was to figure as the impersonation of its intellectual licence; while Shakespeare, who represents the free spirit of the Renaissance moulding the drama, hints, by his well-known preoccupation with Montaigne's writings, that just there was the philosophic counterpart to the fulness and impartiality of his own artistic reception of the experiences of life.

Those essays, as happens with epoch-marking books, were themselves a life, the power which makes them what they are having accumulated in them imperceptibly by a thousand repeated modifications, like character in a person. At the moment when Gaston presented himself, to go along with the great "egotist" for a season, that life had just begun. Born here, at the place whose name he took—*Montaigne*, the *acclivity* of Saint Michael—just thirty-six years before, brought up simply, earthily, at nurse in one of the neighbouring villages, to him it was doubled strength to return thither, when, disgusted with the legal business which had filled his days hitherto, seeing that "France had more laws than all the rest of the world," and was—what one saw! he began the true work of his life, a continual journey in thought, "a continual observation of new and unknown things," his bodily self remaining, for the most part, with seeming indolence at home.

Montaigne boasted that throughout those invasive times his house had lain open to all comers, that his frankness had been rewarded by immunity from all outrages of war, of the crime war shelters. And certainly openness—that all was wide open, searched through by light and warmth and air from the soil—was the impression it made on Gaston, as he passed from farmyard to garden, from garden to court, to hall, up the wide winding stair to the uppermost chamber of the great round tower. In this sun-baked place the studious man still lingered over a late breakfast, telling, like all around, of a certain homely epicureanism, a rare mixture of luxury with a preference for the luxuries that after all were home-grown and savoured of his native earth.

Sociable, of sociable intellect, and still inclining instinctively, as became his fresh and agreeable person, from the midway of life towards its youthful side, he was ever on the alert for an interlocutor to take part in the conversation, which (pleasantest, truly! of all modes of human commerce) was also of ulterior service as stimulating that endless *inward* converse of which the Essays were a kind of abstract. For him, as for Plato, for Socrates, whom he cites so often, the essential dialogue was that of the mind with itself. But then such dialogue throve best with, was often impracticable without, outward stimulus—physical motion, a text shot from a book, the queries and objections of a living voice.—"My thoughts sleep, if I sit still." Neither "thoughts," nor "dialogues," exclusively, but thoughts still partly implicate in the dialogues which had evoked them, and therefore not without many seemingly arbitrary transitions, many links of connexion to be supposed by the reader, the Essays owed their actual publication at last to none of the usual literary motives—desire for fame, to instruct, to amuse, to sell—but to the sociable desire for a still wider range of conversation with others. He wrote for companionship, "if but one sincere man would make his acquaintance"; speaking on paper as he "did to the first person he met."—"If there be any person, any knot of good company, *in France or elsewhere*, who can like my humour, and whose humours I can like, let them but whistle, and I will run."

Notes of expressive facts, of words also worthy of note (for he was a lover of style) collected in the first instance for the help of an irregular memory, were becoming, in the quaintly labelled drawers, with labels of wise old maxim or device, the primary rude stuff, or "protoplasm" of his intended work, and already gave token of its scope and variety. "All motion discovers us"; if to others, so also to ourselves. Movement, some kind of rapid movement, a ride, the hasty survey of a shelf of books, best of all a conversation like this morning's with a visitor for the first time,—amid the felicitous chances of that, at some random turn by the way, he would become aware of shaping purpose. The beam of light or heat would strike down, to illuminate, to fuse and organise the coldly accumulated matter of reason, of experience. Surely some providence over thought and speech led one finely through those haphazard journeys!

Yet thus dependent to so great a degree on external converse for the best fruit of his own thought, he was also an efficient evocator of the thought of another—himself an original spirit more than tolerating the originality of others which brought it into play. Here was one who (through natural predilection reinforced by theory) would welcome one's very self, undistressed by, while fully observant of, its difference from his own—one's errors, vanities, perhaps fatuities. Naturally eloquent, expressive, with a mind like a rich collection of the choice things of all times and countries, he was at his best, his happiest amid the magnetic contacts of an easy conversation. When Gaston, many years afterwards, came to read the famous Essays, he found there many a delightful actual conversation re-set, and had the key we lack to their surprises, their capricious turns and lapses. Well! Montaigne had opened the letter, had forthwith passed his genial criticism on the writer, and then, characteristically, forgetting all about it, turned to the bearer as if he had been intimate with him from childhood. And the feeling was mutual. In half an hour's time Gaston seemed to have known his entertainer all his life.

In unimpeded talk with sincere persons of what quality soever—there, rather than in shadowy converse with even the best books—the flower, the fruit, of mind was still in life-giving contact with its root. With books, as indeed with persons, his intercourse was apt to be desultory. Books!—He was by way of asserting his independence of them, was their *very candid* friend: they were far from being an unmixed good. He would observe (the fact was its own scornful comment) that there were more books upon books than upon any other subject. Yet books, more than a thousand of them, a handsome library for that day, nicely representative not only of literature but of the owner's taste therein, lay all around. Turning now to this, now to that, he handled their pages with nothing less than tenderness. It was the first of many inconsistencies which yet had about them a singularly taking air of reason, of equity. Plutarch and Seneca were soon in the foreground: would "still be at his elbow to test and be tested"—masters of the autumnal wisdom that was coming to be his own, from the autumn of old Rome, of life, of the world, the very genius of second thoughts, of exquisite tact and discretion, of judgment upon knowledge.

But the books dropped from his hands in the very midst of enthusiastic quotation; and the guest was mounting a little turret staircase, was on the leaden roof of the old tower, amid the fat, noonday Gascon scenery. He saw, in bird's-eye view, the country he was soon to become closely acquainted with, a country of passion and capacity (like its people) though at that moment emphatically lazy. Towards the end of his life some conscientious pangs seem to have touched Montaigne's singularly humane and sensitive spirit, when he looked back on the long intellectual entertainment he had had in following, as an inactive spectator, "the ruin of his country," through a series of chapters, every one of which had told deeply in his own immediate neighbourhood. With its old and new battle-fields, its business, its fierce changes, and the old perennial sameness of men's ways beneath them all, it had been to him certainly matter of more assiduous reading than even those choice, incommensurable, books of ancient Greek and Roman experience. The variableness, the complexity, the miraculous surprises of man, concurrent with the variety, the complexity, the surprises of nature, making all true knowledge of either wholly relative and provisional: a like insecurity in one's self, if one turned thither for some ray of clear and certain evidence: yet an equally strong assertion all the time of the interest, the power, and charm, alike of man and nature and of the individual mind: such were the terms in which Gaston, reflecting on his long unsuspicious sojourn there, detached for himself, from the habits, the random traits of character, his concessions and hints and sudden emphatic statements, the soul and potency of the man.

How imperceptibly had darkness crept over them, effacing everything but the interior of the great circular chamber, its book-shelves and enigmatic mottoes and the tapestry on the wall—Circe and her sorceries, in many parts, to draw over the windows in winter. Supper over, the young wife entered at last. Ever on the look-out for the sincerities of human nature (sincerity counting for life-giving *form*, whatever the *matter* might be) as he delighted in watching children, Montaigne loved also to watch grown people, when they were most like children, at their games namely, and in the mechanical and customary parts of their existence, as discovering the real soul in them. Abstaining from the dice himself, since for him such "play was not play enough, but too grave and serious a diversion," and remarking that "the play of children is not performed in play, but to be judged as their most serious action," he set Gaston, and the amiable, unpedantic lady to play together, where he might observe them closely, the game turning still, irresistibly, to conversation, the last and sweetest, if somewhat drowsy relics of this long day's recreations.—Was Circe's castle here? If Circe could turn men into swine, could she also release them again? It was frailty, certainly, that Gaston remained here week after week, scarce knowing why, the conversation begun that morning lasting for nine months, over books, meals, in free rambles chiefly on horseback, as if in the waking intervals of a long day-sleep.

CHAPTER V

Suspended Judgment

The diversity, the undulancy, of human nature!—so deep a sense of it accompanied Montaigne always that himself, too, seemed to be ever changing colour sympathetically therewith. Those innumerable differences, mental and physical, of which men had always been aware, on which they had so largely fed their vanity, were ultimate. That the surface of humanity presented an infinite variety, was of course the tritest of facts. Pursue that variety below the surface!—the lines did but part further and further asunder, with an ever-increasing divergency, which made any common measure of truth impossible. Diversity of custom!—what was it but diversity in the moral and mental view, diversity of opinion? and diversity of opinion, what but radical diversity of mental constitution? How various had he found men's thoughts concerning death, for instance, "some (ah me!) even running headlong upon it, with a real affection." Death, life; wealth, poverty; the whole sum of contrasts; nay, duty itself, "the relish of right and wrong"; might seem to depend upon the opinion each one has of them, and "receive no colour of good or evil but according to the application of the individual soul." Did Hamlet learn of him that "there is nothing good or bad but thinking makes it so"?—"What we call evil is not so of itself: it depends only upon us, to give it another taste and complexion.—Things, in respect of themselves, have peradventure their weight, measure, and conditions; but when once we have taken them into us, the soul forms them as she pleases. Death is terrible to Cicero, courted by Cato, indifferent to Socrates.—Fortune, circumstance, offers but the matter: 'tis the soul adds the form.—Every opinion, how fantastic soever to some, is to another of force enough to be espoused at the risk of life."

For opinion was the projection of one's individual *will*, of a native original predilection. Opinions!—they are like the clothes we wear, which warm us not with their own heat, but with ours. Track your way (as he had learned to do) to the remote origin of what looks like folly; at home, on its native soil, it is found to be justifiable, as a proper growth of wisdom. In the vast conflict of taste, preference, conviction, there was no real inconsistency. It was but that the soul looked "upon things with another eye, and represented them to itself with another kind of face; reason being a tincture almost equally infused into all our manners and opinions though there never were in the world two opinions exactly alike." And the practical comment was, not as one might have expected, how desirable to determine of some common standard of truth amid that infinite variety; but to this effect rather, that we are not bound to receive every opinion we are not able to refute, nor to accept another's refutation of our own. Those diversities being themselves ultimate, the priceless pearl of truth would lie, if anywhere, not in large theoretic apprehension of the general, but in minute vision of the particular; in the perception of the concrete phenomenon, at this particular moment, and from this unique point of view—that for you, this for me, *now*, but perhaps not *then*.

Now; and not then!—For if men are so diverse, not less disparate are the many men who keep discordant company within each one of us, "every man carrying in him the entire form of human condition." "That we taste nothing pure": the variancy of the individual in regard to himself: the complexity of soul which there, too, makes "all judgments in the gross" impossible or useless, certainly inequitable, he delighted to note. Men's minds were like the grotesques which some artists of that day loved to joint together, or like one of his own inconstant essays, never true for a page to its proposed subject. "Nothing is so supple as our understanding: it is double and diverse; and the matters are double and diverse too."

Here then, as it seemed to Gaston, was one for whom exception had taken the place of law: the very genius of qualification followed him through all his keen, constant, changeful pondering of men and things. How many curious moral variations he had to show!—"vices that are lawful": vices in us which "help to make up the seam in our piecing, as poisons are useful for the conservation of health": "actions good and excusable that are not lawful in themselves": "the soul discharging her passions upon false objects where the true are wanting": men doing more than they propose, or they hardly know what, at immense hazard, or pushed to do well by vice itself, or working for their enemies: "condemnations more criminal than the crimes they condemn": the excuses that are self-accusations: instances from his own experience of a hasty confidence in other men's virtue which "God had favoured"; and how "even to the worst people it is sweet, their end once gained by a vicious act, to foist into it some show of justice." In the presence of this indefatigable analyst of act and motive all fixed outlines seemed to vanish away. The healthful pleasure of motion, of thoughts in motion!—yes, Gaston felt them moving, the oldest of them, as he listened, under and away from his feet, as if with the ground he stood on. And this was the vein of thought which oftenest led the master back to emphasise contemptuously the littleness of man.—"I think we can never be despised according to our full desert."

By way of counterpoise, there were admirable surprises in man. That cross-play of human tendencies determined from time to time in the force of unique and irresistible character, "moving all together," pushing the world around it to phenomenal good or evil. To such as "make it their business to oversee human actions, it seems impossible they should proceed from one and the same person." Consolidation of qualities pre-supposed, this did but make character, already the most interesting, because the most dynamic, phenomenon of experience, of more interest still. So dispassionate a spectator of a seemingly so average world, a too critical minimiser, it might seem, of all that pretends to be of importance, Montaigne was constantly, gratefully, announcing his contact, in life, in books, with undeniable power and greatness, with forces full of beauty in their vigour, like lightning, the sea, the torrents: overpowering desire augmented, yet victorious, by its very difficulty; the bewildering constancy of martyrs; single-hearted virtue not to be resolved into anything less surprising than itself; the devotion of that so companion-able wife, dying cheerfully by her own act along with the sick husband "who could do no better than kill himself"; the grief, the joy, of which men suddenly die; the unconscious stoicism of the poor; that stern self-control with which Jacques Bonhomme goes as usual to his daily labour with a heart tragic for the dead child at home; nay, even the boldness and strength of "those citizens who sacrifice honour and conscience, as others of old sacrificed their lives, for the good of their country." So carefully equable, his mind nevertheless was stored with, and delighted in, incidents, personalities, of barbarous strength—Esau, in all his phases—the very rudest children of "our great and powerful mother, nature." As Plato had said, "'twas to no purpose for a sober-minded man to knock at the door of poesy," or, if truth were spoken, of any other high matter of doing or making. That was consistent with his sympathetic belief in the capabilities of mere impetuous

youth as such. Even those unexpected traits in ordinary people which seem
to hint at larger laws and deeper forces of character, disconcerting any narrow
judgment upon them, he welcomed as akin to his own indolent but suddenly
kindling nature:—the shrewd wisdom of an un-lettered old woman, the fount
of goodness in a cold heart. "I hear every day fools say things far from
foolish." Those invincible prepossessions of humanity, or of the individual,
which Bacon reckoned "idols of the cave," are no offence to him; are direct
informations, it may be, beyond price, from a kindly spirit of truth in things.

For him there had been two grand surprises, two pre-eminent manifestations of the power and charm of man, not to be explained away—one, within
the compass of general and public observation; the other, a matter of special
intimacy to himself. There had been the greatness of the old Greek and
Roman life, so greatly recorded; there had been the wisdom and kindness of
Etienne de la Boetie, as made known in all their fulness to him alone. That his
ardent devotion to the ancients had been rewarded with minute knowledge
concerning them was part of his good-fortune in belonging to that age, late
in the Revival of Letters. But the classical reading, which with others was
often but an affectation, seducing them from the highest to a lower degree of
reality, from men and women to their mere shadows in old books, had been
for him nothing less than personal contact. "The qualities and fortunes" of the
old Romans, especially, their wonderful straight ways through the world, the
straight passage of their armies upon them, the splendour of their armour, of
their entire external presence and show, their "riches and embellishments,"
above all, "the suddenness of Augustus," in that grander age for which
decision was justifiable because really possible, had ever been "more in his
head than the fortunes of his own country." If "we have no hold even on
things present but by imagination," as he loved to observe,—then, how much
more potent, steadier, larger, the imaginative substance of the world of
Alexander and Socrates, of Virgil and Caesar, than that of an age which
seemed to him, living in the midst of it, respectable mainly by its docility, by
an imitation of the ancients which after all left untouched the real sources of
their greatness. They had been indeed great, redeemed in part by magnificent
courage and tact, in their very sins. "Our force is no more able to reach them
in their vicious than in their virtuous qualities; for both the one and the other
proceed from a vigour of soul which was without comparison greater in them
than in us."

And yet thinking of his friendship with "the incomparable Etienne de la
Boetie, so perfect, inviolable and entire, that the like is hardly to be found in
story," he had to confess that the sources of greatness must still be quick in

the world. That had remained with him as his one fixed standard of value in the estimate of men and things. On this single point, antiquity itself had been surpassed; the discourses it had left upon friendship seeming to him "poor and flat in comparison of the sense he had of it." For once his sleepless habit of analysis had been checked by the inexplicable, the absolute: amid his jealously guarded indifference of soul he had been summoned to yield, and had yielded, to the magnetic power of another. "We were halves throughout, so that methinks by outliving him I defraud him of his part. I was so grown to be always his double in all things that methinks I am no more than half of myself. There is no action or thought of mine wherein I do not miss him, as I know that he would have missed me." Tender yet heroic, impulsive yet so wise, he might really have succeeded in the work which the survivor (so it seemed to himself) was but vainly trying to do. Yet it was worth his while to become famous if that hapless memory might but be embalmed in one's fame. It had been better than love,—that friendship, to the building of which so much "concurrence" had been requisite, that "'twas much if fortune brought the like to pass once in three ages." Actually, we may think, the "sweet society" of those four years, in comparison with which "the rest of his so pleasant life was but smoke," had touched Montaigne's nature with refinements it might otherwise have lacked. He would have wished "to speak concerning it, to those who had experience" of what he said, could such have been found. In despair of this, he loved to discourse of it to all comers,—how it had been brought about, the circumstances of its sudden and wonderful growth. Yet after all were he pressed to say why he had so loved Etienne de la Boetie, he could but answer, "Because it was He! Because it was I!"

And the surprises there are in man, his complexity, his variancy, were symptomatic of the changefulness, the confusion, the surprises, of the earth on which he lives, of the whole material world. The irregular, the unforeseen, the inconsecutive, miracle, accident, he noted lovingly: it had a philosophic import. It was habit rather than knowledge of them that took away the strangeness of the things actually about one. How many unlikely matters there were, testified by persons worthy of faith, "which, if we cannot persuade ourselves to believe, we ought at least to leave in suspense.—Though all that had arrived by report of past time should be true, it would be less than nothing in comparison of what is unknown."

On all sides we are beset by the incalculable—walled up suddenly, as if by malign trickery, in the open field, or pushed forward senselessly by the crowd around us to good fortune. In art, as in poetry, there are the "transports" which lift the artist out of, as they are not of, himself; for orators also, "those

extraordinary motions which sometimes carry them above their design."
Himself, "in the necessity and heat of combat," had sometimes made answers
that went "through and through," beyond hope. The work, by its own force
and fortune, sometimes out-strips the workman. And then, in defiance of the
proprieties, whereas poets sometimes "flag, and languish in a prosaic
manner," prose will shine with the lustre, vigour and boldness, with the
"fury," of poetry.

And as to "affairs"—how spasmodic the relationship, collision or
coincidence, of the mechanic succession of things to men's volition! Mere
rumour, so large a factor in events—who could trace out its ways? Various
events (he was never tired of illustrating the fact) "followed from the same
counsel." Fortune, that is to say chance, the incalculable contribution of mere
matter to man, "would still be mistress of events"; and one might think it no
un-wisdom "to commit everything to fortuity." But no! "fortune too is oft-
times observed to act by the rule of reason: chance itself comes round to hold
of justice"; war, above all, being a matter in which fortune was inexplicable,
though men might seem to have made it the main business and study of their
lives. If "the force of all counsel lies in the occasion": that is because things
perpetually shift. If man—his taste, his very conscience—change with the
habit of time and place, that is because habit is the emphatic determination,
the tyranny of changing external and material circumstance. So it comes
about that every one gives the name of barbarism just to what is not in use
round about him, except perhaps the Greeks and Romans. Perhaps could
those privileged Greeks and Romans actually sit beside us for a while, they
would be found to offend our niceties at a hundred points. We have great
power of taking ourselves in, and "pay ourselves with words." Words, too,
language itself, and therewith the more intimate physiognomy of thought,
"slip every day through our fingers." With his eye on his own labour,
wistfully, he thought on the instability of the French language in particular—a matter, after all, so much less "perennial than brass." In no respect was
nature more stable, more consecutive, than man.

In nature, indeed, as in one's self, there might be no ultimate inconse-
quence: only, "the soul looks upon things with another eye, and represents
them to itself with another kind of face: for everything has many faces and
several aspects. There is nothing single and rare in respect of itself, but only
in respect of our knowledge, which is a wretched foundation whereon to
ground our rules, and that represents to us a very false image of things." Ah,
even in so "dear" a matter as bodily health, immunity from physical pain,
what doubts! what variations of experience, of learned opinion! Already in six

years of married life, of four children so carefully treated, never, for instance, roughly awaked from sleep, "wherein," he would observe, "children are much more profoundly involved than we,"—of four children, two were dead, and one even now miserably sick. Seeing the doctor depart one morning a little hastily, on the payment of his fee, Montaigne is tempted to some nice questions as to the money's worth.—"There are so many maladies and so many circumstances presented to the physician, that human sense must soon be at the end of its lesson: the many complexions in a melancholy person; the many seasons in winter; the many nations in the French; the many ages in age; the many celestial mutations in the conjunction of Venus and Saturn; the many parts in man's body, nay, in a finger. And suppose the cure effected, how can we assure ourselves that it was not because the disease was arrived at its period, or an effect of chance, or the operation of something else that the child had eaten, drunk, or touched that day, or by virtue of his mother's prayers? We suppose we see one side of a thing when we are really looking at another. As for me, I never see all of anything; neither do they who so largely promise to show it to others. Of the hundred faces that everything has I take one, and am for the most part attracted by some new light I find in it."

And that new light was sure to lead him back very soon to his "governing method—ignorance," an ignorance "strong and generous, and that yields nothing in honour and courage to knowledge, an ignorance which to conceive requires no less knowledge than to conceive knowledge itself"—a sapient, instructed, shrewdly ascertained ignorance, suspended judgment, doubt everywhere. Balances, very delicate balances:—he was partial to that image of equilibrium, or preponderance, in things. But was there, after all, so much as preponderance anywhere? To Gaston there was a kind of fascination, an actually aesthetic beauty, in the spectacle of that keen-edged intelligence, dividing evidence so finely, like some exquisite steel instrument, with impeccable sufficiency, always leaving loyally the last word to the central intellectual faculty, in an entire disinterestedness. If on the one hand he was always distrustful of things that he wished, on the other he had many opinions he would endeavour to make his son dislike, if he had one. What if the truest opinions were not always the most commodious to man, "being of so wild a composition"? He would say nothing to one party that he might not on occasion say to the other, "with a little alteration of accent."

Yes, doubt everywhere!—doubt in the far background, as the proper intellectual equivalent to the infinite possibilities of things: doubt shrewdly economising the opportunities of the present hour, in the very spirit of the traveller who walks only for the walk's sake—"every day concludes my expectation, and the journey of my life is carried on after the same fashion"—doubt, finally, as "the best of pillows to sleep on." And in fact Gaston did sleep well after those long days of physical and intellectual movement, in that quiet world, till the spring came round again.

But beyond and above all the various interests upon which the philosopher's mind was for ever afloat, there was one subject always in prominence—himself. His minute peculiarities, mental and physical, what was constitutional with him as well as his transient humours, how things affected him, what they really were to him,—*Michael*, much more than *man*,—all this Gaston came to know, as the world knew it afterwards in the Essays, often amused, sometimes irritated, but never suspicious of postures or insincerity. Montaigne himself admitted his egotism with frank humour:—"in favour of the Huguenots, who condemn our private confession, I confess myself in public." And this outward egotism of manner was but the symptom of a certain deeper doctrinal egotism.—"I have no other end in writing but to discover *myself*." And what was the purport, what the justification, of this undissembled egotism? It was the recognition, over against that world of floating doubt, of the individual mind, as for each one severally at once the unique organ, and the only matter, of knowledge,—the wonderful energy, the reality and authority, of that, in its absolute loneliness, conforming all things to its law, without witnesses as without judge, without appeal, save to itself. Whatever truth there might be must come for each one from within, not from without. To that wonderful microcosm of the individual mind, of which, for each one, all other worlds are but as accidents,—to himself,—to what was apparent immediately to him, what was "properly of his own having and substance," he confidently dismissed the enquirer. His own egotism was but the pattern of the true intellectual life of every one. "The greatest thing in the world is for a man to know that he is his own. If the world find fault that I speak too much of myself, I find fault that they do not so much as think of themselves." How it had been "lodged in its author":—that, surely, was the essential question concerning every opinion that comes to one man from another.

Yet again, even on this ultimate ground of judgment, what undulancy, complexity, what surprises !—"I have no other end in writing but to discover myself, who also shall peradventure be another thing tomorrow." The great work of his life, *The Essays*, he placed "now high, now low, with great doubt and inconstancy." "What are we but sedition? like this poor France, faction against faction within ourselves, every piece playing every moment its own game, with as much difference between us and ourselves as between ourselves and others. Whoever will look narrowly into his own bosom will hardly find himself twice in the same condition. I give to myself sometimes one face and sometimes another, according to the side I turn to. I have nothing to say of myself, entirely, and without qualification. One grows familiar with all strange things by time; but the more I frequent myself and the better I know myself, the less do I understand myself. If others would consider themselves as I do they would find themselves full of caprice. Rid myself of it I cannot without making myself away. They who are not aware of it have the better bargain. And yet I know not whether they have or no."

One's own experience!—that, at least, *was* one's own. Low and earthy, it might be: still the earth was, emphatically, good, good-natured; and he loved, emphatically, to recommend the wisdom, amid all doubts, of keeping close to it. Gaston soon knew well a certain thread-bare garment worn by Montaigne in all their rides together, sitting quaintly on his otherwise gallant appointments—an old mantle that had belonged to his father. Retained, as he tells us, in spite of its inconvenience, "because it seemed to envelope me in him," it was the symbol of a hundred natural, perhaps somewhat material, pieties. Parentage, kinship, relationship through earth,—the touch of that was always and everywhere like a caress to him. His fine taste notwithstanding, he loved, in those long rambles, to partake of homely fare, sometimes paying largely for it. Everywhere it was as if the earth in him turned kindly to earth. "Under the sun," the sturdy thistles, the blossoming burrs also, were worth knowing.—"Let us grow together with you!" they seem to say. Himself was one of those whom he thought "Heaven favoured," in making them die, so naturally, *by degrees.* "I shall be blind before I am sensible of the decay of my sight, with such kindly artifice do the Fatal Sisters entwist our lives. I melt, and steal away from myself. How variously is it no longer I!" Never would he carry a furry robe at midsummer, because he might need it in the winter.—"In fine, we must live among the living, and let the river flow under the bridge without our care, above all things avoiding fear, that great disturber of reason. The thing in the world I am most afraid of is fear."

Health, the survival of youth, "admonished him to a better wisdom than years and sickness." Was there, in short, anything better, fairer, than the beautiful light of health? To be in health was itself the sign, perhaps the essence, of wisdom—a wisdom, rich in counsel regarding all one's contacts with the earthy side of existence. And how he could laugh!—at that King of Thrace, for instance, who had a religion and a god all to himself, which his subjects might not presume to worship; at that King of Mexico who swore at his coronation not only to keep the laws, but also to make the sun run his annual course; at those followers of Alexander, who all carried their heads on one side, as Alexander did.

The natural second-best, the intermediate and unheroic virtue (even the Church, as we know, by no means *requiring* "heroic" virtue) was perhaps actually the best, better than any heroism, in an age whose very virtues were apt to become insane; an age "guilty and extravagant" in its very justice; for which, as regards all that belongs to the spirit, the one thing needful was moderation. And it was characteristic of Montaigne, a note of the real serviceableness there was in his thoughts, that he preferred to base virtue on low, safe grounds. "The lowest walk is the safest: 'tis the seat of constancy." The wind about the tower, coming who knows whence and whither?—could one enjoy its music, unless one knew the foundations safe twenty feet below-ground? Always he loved to hear such words as "soften and modify the temerity of our propositions." To say less than the truth about it, to dissemble the absoluteness of its claim, was agreeable to his confidence in the natural and incidental charm, the gaiety, of goodness—"that fair and beaten path nature has traced for us," over against any difficult, militant, or chimerical virtue.—"Never had any morose and ill-looking physician done anything to purpose." In that age, it was a great thing to be just blameless. Virtue had its bounds, "which once transgressed, the next step was into the territories of vice." "All decent and honest means of securing ourselves from harm, are not only permitted but commendable." Any man who despises his own life, may "always be master of that of another." He would not condemn "a magistrate who *sleeps*, provided the people under his charge sleep as well as he." Though a blundering world, in collusion with a prejudiced philosophy, has "a great suspicion of facility," there was yet a certain easy way of taking things which made life the richer for others as well as for one's self, and was at least an excellent make-shift for disinterested service to them. With all his admiration for antique greatness of character, he would never commend "so savage a virtue, and that costs so dear," as that, for instance, of the Greek mother, the Roman father, who assisted to put their own erring sons to death. More truly commendable was the custom of the Lacedaemonians, who when they went to battle sacrificed always to the Muses, that "these might, by their sweetness and gaiety, soften martial fury." How had divine philosophy herself been discredited by the sour mask, the sordid patches, with which, her enemies surely! had sent her abroad into the world. "I love a gay and civil philosophy. There is nothing more *cheerful* than wisdom: I had like to have said more wanton."

Was that why his conversation was sometimes coarse? "All the contraries are to be found in me, in one corner or another"; if delicacy, so also coarseness. Delicacy there was, certainly, a wonderful fineness of sensation. "To the end," he tells us, "that sleep should not so stupidly escape from me, I have caused myself to be disturbed in my sleep, so that I might the better and more sensibly taste and relish it.—Of scents, the simple and natural seem to me the most pleasing, and I have often observed that they cause an alteration in me, and work upon my spirits according to their several virtues.—In excessive heats I always travel by night, from sunset to sunrise.—I am betimes sensible of the little breezes that begin to sing and whistle in the shrouds, the forerunners of the storm.—When I walk alone in a beautiful orchard, if my thoughts are for awhile taken up with foreign occurrences, I some part of the time call them back again to my walk, to the orchard, to the sweetness of the solitude, and to myself.—There is nothing in us either purely corporeal, or purely spiritual. 'Tis an inhuman wisdom that would have us despise and hate the culture of the body. 'Tis not a soul, 'tis not a body, we are training up, but a man; and we ought not to divide him. Of all the infirmities we have, the most savage is to despise our being."

There was a fineness of sensation in these unpremeditated thoughts which seemed to Gaston to connect itself with the exquisite words Montaigne had found to paint his two great affections, for his father and for Etienne de la Boetie—a fineness of sensation perhaps quite novel in that age, but still of *physical* sensation. And in pursuit of fine physical sensation he came, on his broad, easy, indifferent passage through the world, across the coarsest growths which also thrive "under the sun," and was not revolted. They were akin to that ruder earth within himself, of which a kind of undissembled greed gave token; his love of "meats little roasted, very high, and even, as to several, quite gone," while, in drinking, he loved clear glass, that the eye might *taste* too, according to its capacity. They were akin also to a certain slothfulness. "Sleeping," he says, "has taken up a great part of my life." And there was almost nothing he would not say; no story, no fact, from his curious, half-medical reading he would not find some pretext to tell. Man's kinship to the animal, the material, and all the proofs of it—he would never blush at. In truth, he led the way to the immodesty of French literature, and had his defence, a sort of defence, ready.—"I know very well that few will quarrel with the licence of my writings, who have not more to quarrel with in the licence of their own thoughts."

Yet when Gaston, twenty years afterwards, heard of the seemingly pious end of Monsieur de Montaigne, he recalled a hundred always quiet, but not always insignificant, acts of devotion, noticeable in those old days, on passing a village church, or at home in the little chapel—superstitions, concessions to other people. Strictly appropriate recognitions, rather, they might seem, of a certain great possibility, which might lie among the conditions of so complex a world. Here was a point which could hardly escape so reflective a soul as Gaston's. At a later period of his life, at the harvest of his own second thoughts, as he pondered on the influence over him of this two-sided thinker, the opinion that things as we find them would bear a certain old-fashioned construction, seemed to have been the motive, however secret in its working, of Montaigne's sustained intellectual activity. A lowly philosophy of ignorance would not be likely to disallow or discredit whatever intimations there might be in the experience of the wise or of the simple, in favour of a religion, which from its long history had come to seem like a growth of nature. Somewhere among men's seemingly random and so inexplicable apprehensions, might lie the grains of a wisdom more precious than gold or even its priceless pearl. That "free and roving thing," the human soul,—what might it not have found out for itself, in a world so wide? To deny, at all events, would be only to *limit* the mind, by negation.

It was not however this side of Montaigne's double philosophy which recommended itself just now to Gaston. The master's wistful tolerance, so extraordinary a quality in that age, attracted him, in his present humour, not in regard to those problematic heavenly lights that might find their way to one from infinite skies, but rather in connexion with the pleasant quite finite objects of the indubitable world of sense so close around him. Backing the world's challenge to make trial of it, here was that general license which his own warm and curious appetite demanded at the moment of the moral theorist. For so pronounced a lover of sincerity as Monsieur de Montaigne, there was certainly a strange ambiguousness in the result of his lengthy enquiries, on the greatest as well as on the lightest matters, and it was inevitable that a listener should accept the dubious lesson in his own sense. Was this shrewd casuist only bringing him by a round-about way to principles he would not have cared to avow? To the great religious thinker of the next century, to Pascal, Montaigne was to figure as emphatically on the wrong side, and not merely because "he that is not *with* us, is *against* us." It was something to have been, in the matter of religious tolerance, as on many other matters of justice and gentleness, the solitary conscience of one's age. But could he really care for truth who never even *seemed* to find it? Did he fear, perhaps, the practical responsibility of getting to the very bottom of certain questions? That the actual discourse of so keen a thinker appeared often inconsistent or inconsecutive might be a hint perhaps that there was some deeper ground of thought in reserve, as if he were really moving, securely, over ground you did not see.—What might that ground be? As to Gaston himself,—had this kindly entertainer only been drawing the screws of a very complex piece of machinery which had worked well enough hitherto for all practical purposes? Was this all that had been going on, while he lingered there, week after week, in a kind of devout attendance on theories, and, for his part, feeling no reverberation of actual events around him, still less of great events in preparation? These were the questions Gaston had in mind, as he thanked his host one morning with real regret, and at length took his last look around that meditative place, the manuscripts, the books, the emblems, the house of Circe in the tapestry on the wall.

CHAPTER VI

Shadows of Events

We all feel, I suppose, the pathos of that mythic situation in Homer, where the Greeks at the last throb of battle around the body of Patroclus find the horror of supernatural darkness added to their other foes; feel it through some touch of truth to our own experience how the malignancy of the forces against us may be doubled by their uncertainty and the resultant confusion of one's own mind—blindfold night there too, at the moment when daylight and self-possession are indispensable.

In that old dream-land of the *Iliad* such darkness is the work of a propitiable deity, and withdrawn at its pleasure; in life, it often persists obstinately. It was so with the agents on the terrible Eve of St. Bartholomew, 1572, when a man's foes were those of his own household. An ambiguity of motive and influence, a confusion of spirit amounting, as we approach the centre of action, to physical madness, encompasses those who are formally responsible for things; and the mist around that great crime, or great "accident," in which the gala weather of Gaston's coming to Paris broke up, leaving a sullenness behind it to remain for a generation, has never been penetrated. The doubt with which Charles the Ninth would seem to have left the world, doubt as to his own complicity therein, as well as to the precise nature, the course and scope, of the event itself, is still unresolved. So it was with Gaston also. The incident in his life which opened for him the profoundest sources of regret and pity, shaped as it was in a measure by those greater historic movements, owed its tragic significance there to an unfriendly shadow precluding knowledge how certain facts had really gone, a shadow which veiled from others a particular act of his and the true character of its motives.

For, the scene of events being now contracted very closely to Paris, the predestined actors therein were gradually drawn thither as into some narrow battle-field or slaughter-house or fell trap of destiny, and Gaston, all unconsciously, along with them—he and his private fortunes involved in those larger ones. Result of chance, or fate, or cunning prevision, there are in the acts great and little—the acts and the words alike—of the king and his associates, at this moment, coincidences which give them at least superficially the colour of an elaborate conspiracy. Certainly, as men looked back afterwards, all the seemingly random doings of those restless months ending in the *Noces Vermeilles* marriage of Henry of Navarre with Margaret of France, lent themselves agreeably to the theory of a great plot to crush out at one blow, in the interest of the reigning Valois, not the Huguenots only but the rival houses of Guise and Bourbon. The word, the act, from hour to hour through what presented itself at the time as a long-continued season of frivolity, suggested in retrospect alike to friend and foe the close connexion of a mathematical problem. And yet that damning coincidence of date, day and hour apparently so exactly timed, in the famous letter to the Governor of Lyons, by which Charles, the trap being now ready, seems to shut all the doors upon escaping victims, is admitted even by Huguenot historians to have been fortuitous. Gaston, recalling to mind the actual mien of Charles as he passed to and fro across the chimeric scene, timid, and therefore constitution-ally trustful towards older persons, filially kissing the hand of the grim Coligni—*Mon père! Mon père!*—all his *câlineries* in that age of courtesy and assassinations—would wonder always in time to come, as the more equitable sort of historians have done, what amount of guilty foresight the young king had carried in his bosom. And this ambiguity regarding the nearest agent in so great a crime, adding itself to the general mystery of life, touched Gaston duly with a sense of the dim melancholy of man's position in the world. It might seem the function of some cruel or merely whimsical power, thus, by the flinging of mere dust through the air, to double our actual misfortunes. However carefully the critical intelligence in him might trim the balance, his imagination at all events would never be clear of the more plausible construction of events. In spite of efforts not to misjudge, in proportion to the clearness with which he recalled the visible footsteps of the "accursed" Valois, he saw them, irresistibly, in connexion with the end actually reached, moving to the sounds of wedding music, through a world of dainty gestures, amid sonnets and flowers, and perhaps the most refined art the world has seen, to their surfeit of blood.

And if those "accursed" Valois might plead to be judged refinedly, so would Gaston, had the opportunity come, have pleaded not to be misunderstood. Of the actual event he was not a spectator, and his sudden absence from Paris at that moment seemed to some of those he left there only a cruelly characteristic incident in the great treachery. Just before that delirious night set in, the news that his old grandfather lay mortally sick at Deux-manoirs had snatched him away to watch by the dying bed, amid the peaceful ministries of the religion which was even then filling the houses of Paris with blood. But the yellow-haired woman, light of soul, whose husband he had become by dubious and irregular Huguenot rites, the religious sanction of which he hardly recognised—flying after his last tender kiss, with the babe in her womb, from the ruins of her home, and the slaughter of her kinsmen, supposed herself treacherously deserted. For him, on the other hand, "the pity of it," the pity of the thing supplied all that had been wanting in its first consecration, and made the lost mistress really a wife. His recoil from that damaging theory of his conduct brought home to a sensitive conscience the fact that there had indeed been a measure of self-indulgent weakness in his acts, and made him the creature for the rest of his days of something like remorse.

The gaiety, the strange devils' gaiety of France, at least in all places whither its royalty came, ended appropriately in a marriage—a marriage of "The Reform" in the person of Prince Henry of Navarre, to Catholicism in the person of Margaret of Valois, Margaret of the "Memoirs," Charles's sister, in tacit defiance of, or indifference to, the Pope. With the great Huguenot leaders, with the princes of the house of Guise, and the Court, like one united family, all in gaudy evidence in its streets, Paris, ever with an eye for the chance of amusement, always preoccupied with the visible side of things, always Catholic—was bidden to be tolerant for a moment, to carry no firearms under penalties, "to renew no past quarrels," and draw no sword in any new one. It was the perfect stroke of Catherine's policy, the secret of her predominance over her sons, thus, with a flight of purchaseable fair women ever at command, to maintain perpetual holiday, perpetual idleness, with consequent perpetual, most often idle, thoughts about marriage, amid which the actual conduct of affairs would be left to herself. Yet for Paris thus Catholic, there was certainly, even if the Pope were induced to consent, and the Huguenot bridegroom to "conform," something illicit and inauspicious about this marriage within the prohibited degrees of kinship. In fact, the cunningly sought papal dispensation never came; Charles, with apparent unconcern, fulfilled his threat, and did without it; must needs however trick the old Cardinal de Bourbon into performing his office, not indeed "in the face of the Church," but in the open air outside the doors of the cathedral of Notre-Dame, the Catholics quietly retiring into the interior, when that starveling ceremony was over, to hear the nuptial mass. Still, the open air, the August sunshine, had lent the occasion an irresistible physical gaiety in this hymeneal Assumption weather. Paris, suppressing its scruples, its conscientious and unconscientious hatreds, at least for a season, had adorned herself as that fascinating city always has been able to adorn herself, if with something of artifice, certainly with great completeness, almost to illusion. Whatever gloom the Middle Age with its sins and sorrows might have left there, was under gallant disguise to-day. In the train of the young married people, *jeunes premiers* in an engagement which was to turn out almost as transitory as a stage-play, a long month of masquerade meandered night and day through the public places. His carnality and hers, so startling in their later developments, showed now in fact but as the engaging force of youth, since youth, however unpromising its antecedents, can never have sinned irretrievably. Yet to curious retrospective minds not long afterwards, these graceful follies would seem tragic or allegoric, with an undercurrent of infernal irony throughout. Charles and his two brothers, keeping the gates of a mimic paradise in the court of the Louvre, while the fountains ran wine—were they already thinking of a time when they would keep those gates, with iron purpose, while the gutters ran blood?

If Huguenots were disgusted with the frivolities of the hour, passing on the other side of the street in sad attire, plotting, as some have thought, as their enemies will persuade the Pope, a yet more terrible massacre of their own, only anticipated by the superior force and shrewdness of the Catholics, on the very eve of its accomplishment—they did but serve just now to relieve the predominant white and red, and thereby double the brilliancy, of a gay picture. Yet a less than Machiavellian cunning might perhaps have detected, amid all this sudden fraternity—as in some unseasonably fine weather signs of coming distress—a risky element of exaggeration in those precipitately patched-up amities, a certain hollow ring in those improbable religious conversions, those unlikely reconciliations in what was after all an age of treachery as a fine art. With Gaston, however, the merely receptive and poetic sense of life was abundantly occupied with the spectacular value of the puissant figures in motion around him. If he went beyond the brilliancy of the present moment in his wonted pitiful, equitable after-thoughts, he was still concerned only with the more general aspects of the human lot, and did not reflect that every public movement, however generous in its tendency, is really flushed to active force by identification with some narrower personal or purely selfish one. Coligni, "the Admiral," centre of Huguenot opposition, just, kind, grim, to the height of inspired genius, the grandest character his faith had yet produced—undeterred by those ominous voices (of aged women and the like) which are apt to beset all great actions, yielded readily to the womanish endearments of Charles, his filial words and fond touching of the hands, the face, aged at fifty-five—just this portion of his conduct let us hope being exclusive of his precise share in the "conspiracy." And the opportune death in Paris of the Huguenot Queen of Navarre only stirred question for a moment: autopsy revealed no traces of unfair play, though at a time credulous as to impossible poisoned perfumes and such things, romantic in its very suspicions.

Delirium was in the air already charged with thunder, and laid hold on Gaston too. It was as if through some unsettlement in the atmospheric medium the objects around no longer acted upon the senses with the normal result. Looking back afterwards, this singularly self-possessed person had to confess that under its influence he had lost for a while the exacter view of certain outlines, certain real differences and oppositions of things in that hotly coloured world of Paris (like a shaken tapestry about him) awaiting the Eve of Saint Bartholomew. Was the "undulant" philosophy of Monsieur de Montaigne, in collusion with this dislocating time, at work upon him, that, following with only too entire a mobility the *experience* of the hour, he found himself more than he could have thought possible the toy of external accident? Lodged in Abelard's quarter, he all but repeats Abelard's typical *experience*. His new Heloise, with capacities doubtless, as he reflected afterwards regretfully, for a refined and serious happiness, although actually so far only a man's plaything, sat daintily amid her posies and painted potteries in the window of a house itself as forbidding and stern as her kinsmen, busy Huguenot printers, well-to-do at a time not only fertile in new books and new editions, but profuse of tracts, sheets, satiric handbills for posting all over France. Gaston's curiosity, a kind of fascination he finds in their dark ways, takes him among them on occasion, to feel all the more keenly the contrast of that picture-like prettiness in this framing of their grim company, their grim abode. Her frivolity is redeemed by a sensitive affection for these people who protect her, by a self-accusing respect for their religion, for the somewhat surly goodness, the hard and unattractive pieties into which she cannot really enter; and she yearns after her like, for those harmless forbidden graces towards which she has a natural aptitude, loses her heart to Gaston as he goes to and fro, wastes her days in reminiscence of that bright passage, notes the very fineness of his linen. To him, in turn, she seems, as all longing creatures ever have done, to have some claim upon him—a right to consideration—to an effort on his part: he finds a sister to encourage: she touches him, clings where she touches. The gloomy, honest, uncompromising Huguenot brothers interfere just in time to save her from the consequence of what to another than Gaston might have counted as only a passing fondness to be soon forgotten; and the marriage almost forced upon him seemed under its actual conditions no binding sacrament. A marriage really indissoluble in itself, and for the heart of Colombe sacramental, as he came afterwards to understand—for his own conscience at the moment, the transaction seemed to have but the transitoriness, as also the guilt of a vagrant love. A connexion so light of motive, so inexpressive of what seemed the leading forces of his character, he might, but for the sorrow which stained its actual issue, have regarded finally as a mere mistake, or an unmeaning accident in his career.

Coligni lay suffering in the fiery August from the shot of the ambiguous assassin which had missed his heart, amid the real or feigned regrets of the Guises, of the royal family, of his true friends, wondering as they watched whether the bullet had been a poisoned one. The other Huguenot leaders had had their warnings to go home, as the princes of the house of Navarre, Condé and Henry of Bearn, would fain have done—the gallant world about them being come just now to have certain suspicious resemblances to a prison or a *trap*. Under order of the king the various quarters of Paris had been distributed for some unrevealed purpose of offence or defence. To the officers in immediate charge it was intimated that "those of the new religion" designed "to rise against the king's authority, to the trouble of his subjects and the city of Paris. For the prevention of which conspiracy the king enjoined the Provost to possess himself of the keys of the various city gates, and seize all boats plying on the river, to the end that none might enter or depart." And just before the lists close around the doomed, Gaston has bounded away on his road homeward to the bed of the dying grandfather, after embracing his wife, anxious, if she might, to share his journey, with some forecast of coming evil among those dark people.

The white badges of Catholicism had been distributed, not to every Catholic (a large number of Catholics perished), to some Huguenots such as La Rochefoucauld, *brave guerrier et joyeux compagnon*, dear to Charles, hesitating still with some last word of conscience in his ear at the very gate of the Louvre, when a random pistol-shot, in the still undisturbed August night, rousing sudden fear for himself, precipitates the event, and as if in delirium he is driven forth on the scent of human blood. He had always hunted like a madman. It was thus "the matins of Paris" began, in which not religious zealots only assisted, but the thieves, the wanton, the un-employed, the reckless children, *les enfants massacreurs* like those seen dragging an insulted dead body to the Seine, greed or malice or the desire for swift settlement of some long-pending law-suit finding here an opportunity. A religious pretext had brought into sudden evidence all the latent ferocities of a corrupt though dainty civilisation; and while the stairways of the Louvre, the streets, the vile trap-doors of Paris, run blood, far away at Deux-manoirs Gaston watches as the light creeps over the silent cornfields, the last sense of it in those aged eyes now ebbing softly away. The village priest, almost as aged, assists patiently with his immemorial consolations at this long, leisurely, scarce perceptible ending to a long, leisurely life, on the quiet double-holiday morning.

The wild news of public disaster, penetrating along the country roads now bristling afresh with signs of universal war, seemed of little consequence in comparison with that closer grief at home, which made just then the more effective demand on his sympathy, till the thought came of the position of Colombe—his wife left behind there in Paris. Immediate rumour, like subsequent history, gave variously the number—the number of thousands—who perished. The great Huguenot leader was dead, one party at least, the royal party, safe for the moment and in high spirits. As Charles himself put it, the ancient private quarrel between the houses of Guise and Châtillon was ended by the decease of the chief of the latter, Coligni de Châtillon—a death so saintly after its new fashion that the long-delayed vengeance of Henri de Guise on the presumed instigator of the murder of his father seemed a martyrdom. And around that central barbarity the slaughter had spread over Paris in widening circles. With conflicting thoughts, in wild terror and grief, Gaston seeks the footsteps of Colombe, of her people, from their rifled and deserted house to the abodes of their various acquaintance, like the traces of wrecked men under deep water. Yet even amid his private distress, queries on points of more general interest in the *event* would not be excluded. With whom precisely, in whose interest had the first guilty motion been?—Gaston on the morrow asked in vain as the historian asks still. And more and more as he picked his way among the direful records of the late massacre, not the cruelty only but the obscurity, the accidental character, yet, alas! also the treachery, of the public event seemed to identify themselves tragically with his own personal action. Those queries, those surmises were blent with the enigmatic sense of his own helplessness amid the obscure forces around him, which would fain compromise the indifferent, and had made him so far an accomplice in their unfriendly action that he felt certainly not quite guiltless, thinking of his own irresponsible, self-centered, passage along the ways, through the weeks that had ended in the public crime and his own private sorrow. Pity for those unknown or half-known neighbours whose faces he must often have looked on—*ces pauvres morts!*—took an almost remorseful character from his grief for the delicate creature whose vain longings had been perhaps but a rudimentary aptitude for the really high things himself had represented to her fancy, the refined happiness to which he might have helped her. The being whose one claim had lain in her incorrigible lightness, came to seem representative of the suffering of the whole world in its plenitude of piteous detail, in those unvalued caresses, that desire towards himself, that patient half-expressed claim not to be wholly despised, poignant now for ever. For he failed to find her: and her brothers being presumably dead, all he could discover of a certainty from the last survivor of her more distant kinsmen was the fact of her flight into the country, already in labour it was thought, and in the belief that she had been treacherously deserted, like many another at that great crisis. In the one place in the neighbourhood of Paris with which his knowledge connected her he seeks further tidings, but hears only of her passing through it, as of a passage into vague infinite space; a little onward, dimly of her death, with the most damaging view of his own conduct presented with all the condemnatory resources of Huguenot tongues, but neither of the place nor the circumstances of that event, nor whether, as seemed hardly probable, the child survived. It was not till many years afterwards that he stood by her grave, still with no softening of the cruel picture driven then as with fire into his soul; her affection, her confidence in him still contending with the suspicions, the ill-concealed antipathy to him of her hostile brothers, the distress of her flight, half in dread to find the husband she was pursuing with the wildness of some lost child, who seeking its parents begins to suspect treacherous abandonment. That most mortifying view of his actions had doubtless been further enforced on her by others, the worst possible reading, to her own final discomfiture, of a not unfaithful heart.

Chapter VII

The Lower Pantheism

"Jetzo, da ich ausgewachsen,
Viel gelesen, viel gereist,
Schwillt mein Herz, und ganz von Herzen,
Glaub' ich an den Heilgen Geist." —HEINE.

Those who were curious in tracing the symmetries of chance or destiny felt now quite secure in the observation that of nine French kings of the name, every third Charles had been a madman. Over the exotic, nervous creature who had inherited so many delicacies of organisation, the coarse rage or *rabies* of the wolf, part doubtless of an inheritance older still, had asserted itself on that terrible night of Saint Bartholomew, at the mere sight, the scent of blood in the crime he had at least allowed others to commit; and it was not an unfriendly witness who recorded that, the fever once upon him, for an hour he had been less a man than a beast of prey. But, exemplifying that exquisite fineness of cruelty which is proper to ideal tragedy, with the work of his madness all around him, he awoke next day sane, to remain so—aged at twenty-one—seeking for the few months still left him to forget himself in his old out-of-door amusements, rending a consumptive bosom with the perpetual horn-blowing which could never rouse again the gay morning of life.

"I have heard," says Brantôme, of Elisabeth, Charles's queen, "that on the Eve of Saint Bartholomew, she, having no knowledge of the matter, went to rest at her accustomed hour, and sleeping till the morning was told, as she arose, of the brave mystery then playing. 'Alas!' she cried; 'The king! my husband! does he know it?' 'Ay, Madam!' they answered; 'the king himself has ordained it.' 'God!' she cried; 'How is this? and what counsellors be they who have given him this advice? O God, be pitiful! For unless Thou art pitiful I fear this offence will never be pardoned unto him'; and asking for her 'Hours,' suddenly betook herself to prayer, weeping."

Like the shrinking, childish Elisabeth, the Pope almost wept at that dubious service to his Church from one who was, after all, a Huguenot in belief; and Huguenots themselves pitied his end.—"*Ah, ces pauvres morts! que j'ai eu un meschant conseil. Ah, ma nourrice, m'amie, ma nourrice, que de sang, et que de meurtres!*"

It was a peculiarity of the naturally devout Gaston that, though yielding himself to the poetic guidance of the Catholic Church in her wonderful, year-long, dramatic version of the story of redemption, he had ever found its greatest day least evocative of proportionate sympathy. The sudden gaieties of Easter morning, the congratulations to the Divine Mother, the sharpness of the recoil from one extreme of feeling to the other, for him at least never cleared away the Lenten preoccupation with Christ's death and passion. The empty tomb, with the white clothes lying, was still a tomb: there was no human warmth in the "spiritual body": the white flowers, after all, were like those of a funeral, with a mortal coldness, amid the loud Alleluias, which refused to melt at the startling summons, any more than the earth will do in the March morning because we call it Spring. It was altogether different however with that other festival which celebrates the Descent of the Spirit, "the tongues," the nameless impulses gone all abroad, to soften slowly, to penetrate all things, as with the winning subtlety of nature, or of human genius. The gracious Pentecostal fire seemed to be in alliance with the sweet, warm, relaxing winds of that later, securer season, bringing their spicy burden from unseen sources. Into the close world, like a walled garden, about him, influences from remotest time and space found their way, travelling unerringly on their long journeys as if straight to him, with the assurance that things were not wholly left to themselves; yet so unobtrusively that a little later the transforming spiritual agency would be discernible at most in the grateful cry of an innocent child, in some good deed of a bad man, or unlooked-for gentleness of a rough one, in the occasional turning to music of a rude voice. Through the course of years during which Gaston was to remain in Paris, very close to other people's sins, interested, all but entangled, in a world of corruption in flower (pleasantly enough to the eye), those influences never failed him. At times it was as if a legion of spirits besieged his door:—"*Open unto me! Open unto me! My sister, my love, my dove, my undefiled!*" And one result, certainly, of this constant prepossession was that it kept him on the alert concerning theories of the divine assistance to man and the world,—theories of inspiration.

On the Feast of Pentecost, on the afternoon of the thirtieth of May, news of the death of Charles the Ninth had gone abroad promptly with large rumours as to the manner of it. Those streams of blood they were full of blent themselves fantastically in Gaston's memory of the event with the gaudy colours of the season, the crazy red trees in blossom upon the heated sky—like a fiery sunset, it might seem, as he looked back over the ashen intervening years. To Charles's successor (he and the Queen-mother being now delightfully secure from fears, however unreasonable, of Charles's jerking dagger) the day became a sweet one, to be noted unmistakably by various pious and other observances, which fixed still further the thought of that Sunday on Gaston's mind, with continual surmise as to the tendencies of so complex and perplexing a scene.

Charles's last words had asserted his satisfaction in leaving no male child to wear his crown. But the brother, whose obvious kingly qualities, the chief facts really known of him so far, Charles was thought to have envied,—those gallant feats of his youth, *de ses jeunes guerres*, his stature, his high-bred beauty and eloquence, his almost pontifical refinement and grace,—had already promptly deserted the half-barbarous kingdom which had been but the mask of banishment. He delayed much, however, on his way to his new kingdom, passing round through the cities of Venice and Lombardy, seductive schools of the art of life as conceived by Italian epicures, of which he became only too ready a student. On Whitsun-Monday afternoon, while Charles "went in lead," amid very little private or public concern, to join his kinsfolk at Saint-Denys, Paris was already looking out for its new king, following, through doubtful rumour, his circuitous journey to the throne, by Venice, Padua, Ferrara, Mantua, Turin, over Mont Cenis, by Lyons, to French soil, still building confidently on the prestige of his early manhood. Seeing him at last, all were conscious in a moment of the inversion of their hopes. Had the old witchcrafts of Poland, the old devilries of his race, laid visible hold on the hopeful young man that he must now take purely satiric estimate of so great opportunity, with a programme which looked like formal irony on the kingly position, a premeditated mockery of those who yielded him, on demand, a servile reverence never before paid to any French monarch? Well! The amusement or business of Parisians, at all events, would still be that of spectators assisting at the last act of the Valois tragedy, in the course of which fantastic traits and incidents would naturally be multiplied. Fantastic humour seemed at its height in the institution of a new order of knighthood, the enigmatic splendours of which were to be a monument of Henry's superstitious care, or, as some said, of his impious contempt, of the day which had made him master of his destiny,—that great Church festival, towards the emphatic marking of which he was ever afterwards ready to welcome any novel or striking device for the spending of an hour.

It was on such an occasion, then,—on a Whitsunday afternoon, amid the red hues of the season, that Gaston listened to one, who, as if with some intentional new version of the sacred event then commemorated, had a great deal to say concerning the Spirit; above all, of the freedom, the indifference, of its operations, and who would give a strangely altered colour, for a long time to come, to the thoughts, to the very words, associated with the celebration of Pentecost. The speaker, though understood to be a brother of the Order of Saint Dominic, had not been present at the mass—the daily University red mass, *De Spiritu Sancto*, but said to-day according to the proper course of the season in the chapel of the Sorbonne, with much pomp, by the Italian Bishop of Paris. It was the reign of the Italians just then, with a doubly refined, somewhat morbid, somewhat ash-coloured, Italy in France, more Italian still. What our Elisabethan poets imagined about Italian culture,—forcing all they knew of Italy to an ideal of dainty sin such as had never actually existed there,—that the court of Henry, so far as in it lay, realised in fact. Men of Italian birth, "to the great suspicion of simple people," swarmed in Paris, already "flightier, less constant, than the *girouettes* on its steeples"; and it was love for Italian fashions that had brought king and courtiers here this afternoon, with great *éclat*, as they said, frizzed and starched, in the beautiful, minutely considered dress of the moment, pressing the learned University itself into the background. For the promised speaker, about whom tongues had been busy, not merely in the Latin quarter, had come from Italy. In an age in which all things about which Parisians much cared must be Italian, there might be a hearing even for Italian philosophy. Courtiers at least would understand the Italian language, all the curious rhetoric arts of which in their perfection this speaker was rumoured to possess. And of all the kingly qualities of Henry's youth, the single one which had held by him was that gift of eloquence, which he valued also in others,—an inherited gift perhaps, for amid all contemporary and subsequent historic gossip about his mother, the two things certain are, that the hands credited with so much mysterious ill-doing were fine ones, and that she was an admirable speaker.

Bruno himself tells us, long after he had withdrawn himself from it, that the monastic life promotes the freedom of the intellect by its silence and self-concentration. The prospect of such freedom sufficiently explains why a young man who, however well-found in worldly and personal advantages, was above all conscious of great intellectual possessions, and of fastidious spirit also, with a remarkable distaste for the vulgar, should have espoused "poverty, chastity, and obedience," in a Dominican cloister. What liberty of mind may really come to in such places, what daring new departures it may suggest even to the strictly monastic temper, is exemplified by the dubious and dangerous mysticism of men like John of Parma and Joachim of Flora, reputed author of a new "Everlasting Gospel," strange dreamers, in a world of rhetoric, of that later dispensation of the Spirit, in which all law will have passed away; or again by a recognised tendency, in the great rival Order of Saint Francis, in the so-called "spiritual" Franciscans, to understand the dogmatic statements of faith *with a difference.*

The three convents in which successively Bruno had lived, at Naples, at Città di Campagna, and finally the Minerva at Rome, developed freely, we may suppose, all the mystic qualities of a genius, in which, from the first, a heady southern imagination took the lead. But it was from beyond monastic bounds he would look for the sustenance, the fuel, of an ardour born or bred within them. Amid such artificial religious stillness the air itself becomes generous in under-tones. The vain young monk (vain of course!) would feed his vanity by puzzling the good, sleepy heads of the average sons of Dominic with his neology, putting new wine into old bottles, teaching them their own business—the new, higher, truer sense of the most familiar terms, of the chapters they habitually read, the hymns they sang, above all, as it happened, every word that referred to the Spirit, the reign of the Spirit, and its excellent freedom. He would soon pass beyond the utmost possible limits of his brethren's sympathy, beyond the largest and freest interpretation such words would bear, to words and thoughts on an altogether different plane, of which the full scope was only to be felt in certain old pagan writers—pagan, though approached, perhaps, at first, as having a kind of natural, preparatory kinship with Scripture itself. The Dominicans would seem to have had well-stocked, liberally-selected, libraries; and this curious youth, in that age of restored letters, read eagerly, easily, and very soon came to the kernel of a difficult old author, Plato or Plotinus,—to the real purpose of thinkers older still, surviving by glimpses only in the books of others, but who had been nearer the original sense of things—Empedocles, for instance, Pythagoras, Parmenides, above all, that most ancient assertor of God's identity with the world. The affinities, the unity, of the visible and the invisible, of earth and heaven, of all things whatever, with one another, through the consciousness, the person, of God the Spirit, who was at every moment of infinite time, in every atom of matter, at every point of infinite space; Aye! *was* everything in turn:—that doctrine, *l'antica filosofia Italiana*, was in all its vigour, like some hardy growth out of the very heart of nature, interpreting itself to congenial minds with all the fulness of primitive utterance. A large thought! yet suggesting, perhaps, from the first, in still, small, immediately practical, voice, a freer way of taking, a possible modification of, certain moral precepts. A primitive morality,—call it! congruous with those larger primitive ideas, with that larger survey, with the earlier and more liberal air.

Returning to this ancient "pantheism," after the long reign of a seemingly opposite faith, Bruno unfalteringly asserts "the vision of all things in God" to be the aim of all metaphysical speculation, as of all enquiry into nature. The Spirit of God, in countless variety of forms, neither above, nor in any way without, but intimately within, all things, is really present, with equal integrity and fulness, in the sunbeam ninety millions of miles long, and the wandering drop of water as it evaporates therein. The divine consciousness has the same relation to the production of things, as the human intelligence to the production of true thoughts concerning them. Nay! those thoughts are themselves actually God *in* man: a loan to man of His assisting Spirit, who, in truth, is the Creator of things in and by His contemplation of them. For Him, as for man in proportion as man thinks truly, thought and being are identical, and things existent only in so far as they are known. Delighting in itself, in the sense of its own energy, this sleepless, capacious, fiery intelligence evokes all the orders of nature, all the revolutions of history, cycle upon cycle, in ever new types. And God the Spirit, the soul of the world, being therefore really identical with the soul of Bruno also, as the universe shapes itself to Bruno's reason, to his imagination, ever more and more articulately, he too becomes a sharer of the divine joy in that process of the formation of true ideas, which is really parallel to the process of creation, to the evolution of things. In a certain sense, which some in every age of the world have understood, he, too, is the creator; himself actually a participator in the creative function. And by such a philosophy, Bruno assures us, it was his experience that the soul was greatly expanded: *con questa filosofia l'anima mi s'aggrandisce; mi se magnifica l'intelletto!*

For, with characteristic largeness of mind, Bruno accepted this theory in the whole range of its consequences. Its more immediate corollary was the famous axiom of "indifference," of "the coincidence of contraries." To the eye of God, to the philosophic vision through which God sees in man, nothing is really alien from Him. The differences of things, those distinctions, above all, which schoolmen and priests, old or new, Roman or Reformed, had invented for themselves, would be lost in the length and breadth of the philosophic survey: nothing, in itself, being really either great or small; and matter certainly, in all its various forms, not evil but divine. Dare one choose or reject this or that? If God the Spirit had made, nay! was, all things indifferently, then, matter and spirit, the spirit and the flesh, heaven and earth, freedom and necessity, the first and the last, good and evil, would be superficial rather than substantial differences. Only, were joy and sorrow also, together with another distinction always of emphatic reality to Gaston for one, to be added to the list of phenomena really "coincident" or "indifferent," as some intellectual kinsmen of Bruno have claimed they should?

The Dominican Brother was at no distant day to break far enough away from the election, the seeming "vocation," of his youth, yet would remain always, and under all circumstances, unmistakeably a monk in some predominant qualities of temper. At first it was only by way of thought that he asserted his liberty—delightful, late-found, privilege!—traversing, in strictly mental journeys, that spacious circuit, as it broke away before him at every moment upon ever-new horizons. Kindling thought and imagination at once, the prospect draws from him cries of joy, of a kind of religious joy, as in some new "Canticle of the Creatures," some new hymnal or antiphonary. "Nature," becomes for him a sacred term.—"Conform thyself to Nature!" With what sincerity, what enthusiasm, what religious fervour, he enounces that precept, to others, to himself! Recovering, as he fancies, a certain primeval sense of Deity broad-cast on things,—a sense in which Pythagoras and other "inspired" theorists of early Greece had abounded, in his hands philosophy becomes a poem, a sacred poem, as it had been with them. That Bruno himself, in "the enthusiasm of the idea," drew from his axiom of "the indifference of contraries" the practical consequence which is in very deed latent there, that he was ready to sacrifice to the antinomianism, which is certainly a part of its logic, the austerities, the purity, of his own youth for instance, there is no proof. The service, the sacrifice, he is ready to bring to the great light that has dawned for him, occupying his entire conscience with the sense of his responsibilities to it, is the sacrifice of days and nights spent in eager study, of plenary, disinterested utterance of the thoughts that arise in him, at any hazard, at the price, say! of martyrdom. The work of the divine Spirit, as he conceives it, exalts, inebriates him, till the scientific apprehension seems to take the place of prayer, oblation, communion. It would be a mistake, he holds, to attribute to the human soul capacities merely passive or receptive. She, too, possesses initiatory powers as truly as the divine soul of the world, to which she responds with the free gift of a light and heat that seem her own.

Yet a nature so opulently endowed can hardly have been lacking in purely physical or sensuous ardours. His pantheistic belief that the Spirit of God is in all things, was not inconsistent with, might encourage, a keen and restless eye for the dramatic details of life and character however minute, for humanity in all its visible attractiveness, since there, too, in very truth, divinity lurks. From those first fair days of early Greek speculation, love had occupied a large space in the conception of philosophy; and in after days Bruno was fond of developing, like Plato, like the Christian Platonists, combining something of the peculiar temper of each, the analogy between the flights of intellectual enthusiasm and those of physical love, with animation which shows clearly enough the reality of his experience in the latter. The *Eroici Furori*, his book of books, dedicated to Philip Sidney, who would be no stranger to such thoughts, presents a singular blending of verse and prose, after the manner of Dante's *Vita Nuova*. The supervening philosophic comment re-considers those earlier, physically erotic, impulses which had prompted the sonnet in voluble Italian, entirely to the advantage of their abstract, incorporeal, theoretic equivalents.

Yet if it is after all but a prose comment, it betrays no original lack of the sensuous or poetic fire. That there is no single name of preference, no Beatrice or Laura, by no means proves the young man's earlier desires to have been merely Platonic; and if the colours of love inevitably lose a little of their force and propriety by such deflection from their earlier purpose, their later intellectual purpose as certainly finds its opportunity thereby, in the matter of borrowed fire and wings. A kind of old scholastic pedantry creeping back over the ardent youth who had thrown it off so defiantly (as if love himself went in now for a University degree) Bruno developes, under the mask of amorous verse, all the various stages of abstraction, by which, as the last step of a long ladder, the mind attains actual "union." For, as with the purely religious mystics, "union," the mystic union of souls with one another and their Lord, nothing less than union between the contemplator and the contemplated—the reality, or the sense, or at least the name of such union—was always at hand. Whence that instinctive tendency towards union, if not from the Creator of things himself, who has doubtless prompted it in the physical universe, as in man? How familiar the thought that the whole creation, not less than the soul of man, longs for God "as the hart for the water-brooks"! To unite one's self to the infinite by largeness and lucidity of intellect, to enter, by that admirable faculty, into eternal life—this was the true vocation of "the spouse," of the rightly amorous soul. *À filosofia è necessario amore*. There would be degrees of progress therein, as of course also of relapse: joys and sorrows, therefore. And, in interpreting these, the philosopher, whose intellectual ardours have superseded religion and physical love, is still a lover and a monk. All the influences of the convent, the sweet, heady incense, the pleading sounds, the sophisticated light and air, the grotesque humours of old gothic carvers, the thick stratum of pagan sentiment beneath all this—*Santa Maria sopra Minervam!*—are indelible in him. Tears, sympathies, tender inspirations, attraction, repulsion, zeal, dryness, recollection, desire:—he finds place for them all: knows them all well in their unaffected simplicity, while he seeks the secret and secondary, or, as he fancies, the primary, form and purport of each.

A light on actual life, or a mere barren scholastic subtlety, never before had the pantheistic doctrine been developed with such completeness, never before connected with so large a sense of nature, so large a promise of the knowledge of it as it really is. The eyes that had not been wanting towards visible humanity turned now with equal liveliness on the natural world in that region of his birth, where all the colour and force of nature are at least two-fold. Nature is not only a thought or meditation in the divine mind; it is also a perpetual energy of that mind, which, ever identical with itself, puts forth and absorbs in turn all the successive forms of life, of thought, of language even. What seemed like striking transformations of matter were in truth only a chapter, a clause, in the great volume of the transformations of the divine Spirit. The mystic recognition that all is indeed divine had been simultaneous with a realisation of the largeness of the field of concrete knowledge, the infinite extent of all there was actually to know. Winged, fortified, by that central philosophic faith, the student proceeds to the detailed reading of nature, led on from point to point by manifold lights, which will surely strike on him, by the way, from the intelligence in it, speaking directly, sympatheti- cally, to a like intelligence in him. The earth's wonderful animation, as divined by one who anticipates by a whole generation the Baconian "philosophy of experience":—in that, those bold, flighty, pantheistic speculations become tangible matter of fact. Here was the needful book for man to read, the full revelation, the story in detail of that one universal mind, struggling, emerging, through shadow, substance, manifest spirit, in various orders of being,—the veritable history of God. And nature, together with the true pedigree and evolution of man also, his gradual issue from it, was still all to learn. The delightful tangle of things!—it would be the delightful task of man's thoughts to disentangle that. Already Bruno had measured the space which Bacon would fill, with room perhaps for Darwin also. That Deity is everywhere, like all such abstract propositions, is a two-edged force, depending for its practical effect on the mind which admits it, on the peculiar perspective of that mind. To Dutch Spinosa, in the next century, faint, consumptive, with a hold on external things naturally faint, the theorem that God was in all things whatever, annihilating their differences, suggested a somewhat chilly withdrawal from the contact of all things alike. But in Bruno, eager and impassioned, an Italian of the Italians, it awoke a constant, inextinguishable appetite for every form of experience,—a fear, as of the one sin possible, of limiting, for one's self or another, the great stream flowing for thirsty souls, that wide pasture set ready for the hungry heart.

Considered from the point of view of a minute observer of nature, the Infinite might figure as "the infinitely little"; no blade of grass being like another, as there was no limit to the complexities of an atom of earth, cell within cell. And the earth itself, hitherto seemingly the privileged centre of a very limited universe, was, after all, but an atom in an infinite world of starry space, then lately divined by candid intelligence, but which the telescope would one day present to bodily eyes. For if Bruno must needs look forward to the future, to Bacon, for adequate knowledge of the earth, the infinitely little, he might look backwards also, gratefully, to another daring mind, which had already put that earth into its modest place, and opened the full view of the heavens. If God is eternal, then, the universe is infinite and worlds innumerable. Yes! one might well have divined what reason now demonstrated, indicating those endless spaces which a real sidereal science would gradually occupy.

That the stars are suns: that the earth is in motion: that the earth is of like stuff with the stars:—now the familiar knowledge of children:—dawning on Bruno as the calm assurance of reason on appeal from the prejudice of the eye, brought to him an inexpressibly exhilarating sense of enlargement in the intellectual, nay! in the physical atmosphere. And consciousness of unfailing unity and order did not desert him in that broader survey, which made the utmost one could ever know of the earth seem but a very little chapter in the endless history of God the Spirit, rejoicing so greatly in the admirable spectacle that He never ceases to evolve from matter new conditions. The immoveable earth as we term it, beneath our feet! Why, one almost felt the movement, the respiration of God in it. And yet how greatly even the physical eye, the sensible imagination (so to call it) was flattered by the theorem. What joy in that motion, in the prospect, the music! The music of the spheres,—he could listen to it in a perfection such as had never been conceded to Plato, to Pythagoras even.

> *Veni Creator Spiritus,*
> *Mentes tuorum visita,*
> *Imple superna gratia,*
> *Quae tu creasti pectora.*

Yes! The grand old Christian hymns, perhaps the grandest of them all, seemed to blend themselves in the chorus, to be deepened immeasurably under this new intention. It is not always, or often, that men's abstract ideas penetrate the temperament, touch the animal spirits, affect conduct. It was what they did with Bruno. The ghastly spectacle of the endless material universe— infinite dust, in truth, starry as it may look to our terrestrial eyes—that prospect from which the mind of Pascal recoiled so painfully, induced in Bruno only the delightful consciousness of an ever-widening kinship and sympathy, since every one of those infinite worlds must have its sympathetic inhabitants. Scruples of conscience, if he felt such, might well be pushed aside for the "excellency" of such knowledge as this. To shut the eyes, whether of the body or the mind, would be a kind of sullen ingratitude: to believe, directly or indirectly, in any absolutely dead matter anywhere would be the one sin, as being implicitly a denial of the indwelling spirit.—A free spirit, certainly, as of old! Through all his pantheistic flights, from horizon to horizon, it was still the thought of liberty that presented itself, to the infinite relish of this "prodigal son" of Dominic. The Divine Spirit had made all things indifferently, with a largeness, a beneficence, impiously belied by any theory of restrictions, distinctions, of absolute limitation. Touch! see! listen! eat freely of all the trees of the garden of Paradise, with the voice of the Lord God literally everywhere:—here was the final counsel of perfection. The world was even larger than youthful appetite, youthful capacity. Let theologian and every other theorist beware how he narrowed either. "The plurality of worlds!"—How petty in comparison seemed those sins, the purging of which was men's chief motive in coming to places like this convent, whence Bruno, with vows broken, or obsolete for him, presently departed. A sonnet, expressive of the joy with which he returned to so much more than the liberty of ordinary men, does not suggest that he was driven from it. Though he must have seemed to those who had loved surely so loveable a creature to be departing, like the "prodigal" of the Gospel, into the farthest possible of far countries, there is no proof of harsh treatment on their part, or even of an effort to detain him.

It happens, most naturally of course, that those who undergo the shock of spiritual or intellectual change sometimes fail to recognise their debt to the deserted cause:—how much of the heroism, or other high quality, of their rejection is really the product of what they reject. Bruno, the escaped monk, is still a monk; and his philosophy, impious as it might seem to some, a very new religion indeed, yet a *religion*. He came forth well-fitted by conventual influences to play upon men as he had been played upon. A challenge, a war-cry, an alarum, everywhere he seemed to be but the instrument of some subtly materialised spiritual force, like that of the old Greek prophets, the "enthusiasm" he was inclined to set so high, or like impulsive Pentecostal fire. His hunger to know, fed dreamily enough at first within the convent walls as he wandered over space and time an indefatigable reader of books, would be fed physically now by ear and eye, by large matter-of-fact experience, as he journeys from university to university; less as a teacher than as a courtier, a citizen of the world, a knight-errant of intellectual light. The philosophic need to try all things had given reasonable justification to the stirring desire for travel common to youth, in which, if in nothing else, that whole age of the later Renaissance was invincibly young. The theoretic recognition of that mobile spirit of the world, ever renewing its youth, became the motive of a life as mobile, as ardent, as itself, of a continual journey, the venture and stimulus of which would be the occasion of ever new discoveries, of renewed conviction.

The unity, the spiritual unity, of the world:—that must involve the alliance, the congruity, of all things with one another, of the teacher's personality with the doctrine he had to deliver, of the spirit of that doctrine with the fashion of his utterance, great reinforcements of sympathy. In his own case, certainly, when Bruno confronted his audience at Paris, himself, his theme, his language, were alike the fuel of one clear spiritual flame, which soon had hold of the audience also; alien, strangely alien, as that audience might seem from the speaker. It was *intimate* discourse, in magnetic touch with every one present, with his special point of impressibility; the sort of speech which, consolidated into literary form as a book, would be a dialogue according to the true Attic genius, full of those diversions, passing irritations, unlooked-for appeals, in which a solicitous missionary finds his largest range of opportunity, and takes even dull wits unaware. In Bruno, that abstract theory of the perpetual motion of the world was become a visible person talking with you.

And as the run-away Dominican was still in temper a monk, so he presented himself in the comely Dominican habit. The reproachful eyes were to-day for the most part kindly observant, registering every detail of that singular company, all the physiognomic effects which come by the way on people, and, through them, on things, the "shadows of ideas" in men's faces, his own pleasantly expressive with them, in turn. *De Umbris Idearum*: it was the very title of his discourse. There was "heroic gaiety" there: only, as usual with gaiety, it made the passage of an occasional peevish cloud seem all the chillier. Lit up, in the agitation of speaking, by many a harsh or scornful beam, yet always sinking, in moments of repose, to an expression of high-bred melancholy, the face was one that looked, after all, made for suffer-ing,—already half pleading, half defiant, as of a creature you could hurt, but to the last never shake a hair's breadth from its estimate of yourself.

Like nature, like nature in that opulent country of his birth, which the "Nolan," as he delighted to call himself, loved so well that, born wanderer as he was, he must perforce return thither sooner or later at the risk of life, he gave *plenis manibus*, but without selection, and was hardly more fastidious in speech than the "asinine" vulgar he so deeply contemned. His rank, unweeded eloquence, abounding in play of words, rabbinic allegories, verses defiant of prosody, in the kind of erudition he professed to despise, with here and there a shameless image—the product not of formal method, but of Neapolitan improvisation—was akin to the heady wine, the sweet, coarse odours, of that fiery, volcanic soil, fertile in such irregularities as manifest power. Helping himself indifferently to all religions for rhetoric illustration, his preference was still for that of the soil, the old pagan religion, and for the primitive Italian gods, whose names and legends haunt his speech, as they do the carved and pictorial work of that age of the Renaissance. To excite, to surprise, to move men's minds, like the volcanic earth as if in travail, and, according to the Socratic fancy, bring them to the birth, was after all the proper function of the teacher, however unusual it might be in so "ancient" a university. "Fantastic!"—from first to last that was the descriptive epithet; and the very word, carrying us to Shakespeare, reminds one how characteris-tic of the age such habit was, and that it was pre-eminently due to Italy. A man of books, he had yet so vivid a hold on people and things, that the traits and tricks of the audience seemed to strike from his memory all the graphic resources of his old readings. He seemed to promise some greater matter than was then actually exposed by him; to be himself enjoying the fulness of a great out-look, the vaguer suggestion of which was sufficient to sustain the curiosity of the listeners. And still, in hearing him speak you seemed to see that subtle spiritual fire to which he testified kindling from word to word. What Gaston then heard was, in truth, the first fervid expression of all those contending views out of which his written works would afterwards be compacted, of course with much loss of heat in the process. Satiric or hybrid growths, things due to ὕβρις, insult, insolence, to what the old Satyrs of fable embodied,—the volcanic South is kindly prolific of these, and Bruno abounded in mockery: it was by way of protest. So much of a Platonist, for Plato's genial humour he had nevertheless substituted the harsh laughter of Aristophanes. Paris, teeming, beneath a very courtly exterior, with mordant words, in unabashed criticism of all real or suspected evil, provoked his utmost powers of scorn for the "Triumphant Beast," the "Installation of the Ass," shining even there amid the university folk—those intellectual bankrupts of the Latin Quarter, who had so long passed between them so gravely a worthless "parchment and paper" currency. In truth, Aristotle, the supplanter of Plato, was still in possession, pretending, as Bruno conceived, to determine heaven and earth by precedent, hiding the proper nature of things from the eyes of men. "Habit"—that last word of his practical philosophy—indolent habit! what would this mean in the intellectual life, but just that sort of dead judgments which, because the mind, the eye, were no longer at work in them, are most opposed to the essential freedom and quickness of the spirit?

The *Shadows* of Ideas, *De Umbris Idearum*: such, in set terms, had been the subject of Bruno's discourse, appropriately to the still only half emancipated intellect of his audience:—on approximations to truth: the divine imaginations, as seen, darkly, more bearably, by weaker faculties, in words, in visible facts, in their shadows merely. According to the doctrine of "Indifference," indeed, there would be no real distinction between substance and shadow. In regard to man's feeble wit, however, varying degrees of knowledge might constitute such a distinction. "Ideas, and *Shadows* of Ideas": the phrase recurred often; and, as such phrases will, fixed itself in Gaston's fancy, though not precisely according to the mind of the speaker; accommodated rather to the thoughts which just then pre-occupied his own. As already in his life there had been the *Shadows of Events*,—the indirect yet fatal influence there of deeds in which he had no part, so now, for a time, he seemed to fall under the spell, the power, of the *Shadows of Ideas*, of Bruno's Ideas; in other words, of those indirect suggestions, which, though no necessary part of his doctrines, yet inevitably followed upon them. What, for instance, might be the proper practical limitations of that telling theory of the "coincidence," the "indifference," of "opposites"?

To that true son of the Renaissance, in the light of those large, antique, pagan ideas, the difference between Rome and the Reform would figure, of course, as but an insignificant variation upon some deeper and more radical antagonism between two tendencies of men's minds. But what of an antagonism deeper still? Between Christ and the world? say:—Christ and the flesh? or that so very ancient antagonism between good and evil? Was there any real place left for imperfection, moral or otherwise, in a world wherein the minutest atom, the lightest thought, could not escape from God's presence? Who should note the crime, the sin, the mistake, in the all-embracing operation of that eternal spirit, which must be incapable of misshapen births? In proportion as man raised himself to the ampler survey of the divine work around him, just in that proportion would the very notion of evil disappear. There were no weeds, no "tares," in the endless field. The truly illuminated mind, discerning spiritually, might do with impunity what it would. Even under the shadow of monastic walls, that had sometimes been the precept, which larger theories of "inspiration" had bequeathed to practice. —"Of all the trees of the garden thou mayest freely eat!—If you take up any deadly thing, it shall not hurt you!—And I think that I, too, have the spirit of God!"

Bruno, a citizen of the world, Bruno at Paris, was careful to warn off the vulgar from applying the decisions of philosophy beyond its proper speculative limits. But a kind of secrecy, an ambiguous atmosphere, encompassed, from the first, alike the speaker and the doctrine; and in that world of fluctuating and ambiguous characters, the alerter mind certainly, pondering on this novel "reign of the spirit"—what it might actually be—would hardly fail to find in Bruno's doctrines a method of turning poison into food, to live and thrive thereon—an art, to Paris, in the intellectual and moral condition of that day, hardly less opportune than had it related to physical poisons. If Bruno himself was cautious not to suggest the ethic or practical equivalent to his theoretic positions, there was that in his very manner of speech, in that rank, unweeded eloquence of his, which seemed naturally to discourage any effort at selection, any sense of fine difference, of *nuances*, or proportion, in things. The loose sympathies of his genius were allied to nature, nursing, with equable maternity of soul, good, bad, and indifferent, rather than to art, distinguishing, rejecting, refining. Commission and omission! sins of the former surely would have the natural preference. And how would Paolo and Francesca have read this lesson? How would Henry, and Margaret of the *Memoirs*, and other susceptible persons then present, read it, especially if the opposition between practical good and evil ran counter to, or did not wholly coincide with, another distinction, the "opposed points" of which, to Gaston for one, could never by any possibility become "indifferent"—the distinction, namely, between the precious and the base, aesthetically; between what was right and wrong in the matter of art?

CHAPTER VIII

An Empty House

Beauty and ugliness: no! one could never persuade one's self that these were "coincident" or "indifferent" in this Paris of the Renaissance—this garden of all the trees of which according to Bruno's doctrine, Bruno's new religion, one might freely eat. Art, certainly fine art, with which just then Paris was so industriously occupied, had and must have its preferences, its distinctions, was indeed at its height of dainty conscience now, as was borne in upon Gaston one day, when, to renew old acquaintance, he made his way through the quiet monastic neighbourhood of Saint-Germain-des-Prés to the abode of Jasmin de Villebon, as poetic, as "aesthetic" as ever, and at present a very ornamental court official advancing rapidly in the royal favour.

In that choice place, a little *hôtel* or town-house, of which his father's death had left this youthful mirror of French fashion the master, one had a favourable opportunity for estimating what we now call aesthetic culture was come to under the last of the Valois. It was a Gothic house of the later fifteenth century, when, in anticipation of the exotic elegance of that Medicean taste which would ere long supplant it altogether, the national architecture was already losing its medieval precision, and therewith its strength. To the trained eyes of that day, eyes, we may suspect, in collusion with certain inward tendencies towards relaxation of the *moral* fibre, it was delightful to see the severe structural lines give way till they vanished, or figured as but graceful pencillings on a quiet surface jealous of all emphatic relief. The column lost its capital and roved softly into the arch, rippling now for ornament rather than support, above the pleasant windows which betrayed, through their fine-grained glass, the fastidious comfort that reigned within. Above, towards a roof still acutely pitched against the rain, the patterned slates, wont to protect a loosely plastered wall, did duty now as ornament. Year by year the snow, the clinging icicles were reducing the little heads of baked clay below the sill, enlarged from old Roman coin or cameo, into veritable likeness of the antique. Beneath them the ashlar was planed into something like a marble surface, to remind one of the real marble of Italy, and attracting the hand to test its pearly smoothness, while lower still about the doorway, inserted like gems in a homely setting, was real artists' work on plinths of porphyry or jasper. Borrowing from Bramante, from Raffaelle, the "arabesque" pilasters which divided the continuous window of the ground-floor no longer prison-like and medieval, the Northern builder had associated them to the actual neighbourhood, and the thistles and field-flowers, interlaced in emphatic love-knots, were sympathetic with a natural flush of purple here or there in the precious stone. It was *à la mode* indeed,—the taste of the year,—this highly conscious Italianised manner; and yet (triumph of the élite, of "those who know," in every age, even when dealing with the modes, the fashions, they have not invented for themselves!) everywhere the individuality, the will of the owner showed through.

The owner after all was absent. An unexpected summons to courtly duty (as polite servants and a silken-corded letter explain), a royal invitation that was like a command, had caused him to break his engagement, as nothing else on earth could have done. Would Gaston make himself at home for awhile, eat, and drink of the choice wine set ready, amuse himself with the books, the pictures, say! the toys? It looked comfortable enough with the fragrant wood fires on this sunless though summer day; and if the owner was absent, all around seemed eloquent concerning him, leading Gaston on his side, as he lingered there, agreeably entertained hour after hour, to all sorts of casuistic considerations concerning the man and his abode, applicable generally, in truth, to the mood of that age as reflected in the mirror of all-accomplished Paris.

An age great in portrait-painting, it found after all its aptest self-expression, its own veritable *likeness*, in a dwelling like this. In such places, that sensuous and highly coloured life described by Brantôme, still in rapid movement on his animated pages, might seem to have passed over from action to art, to have composed itself for the eye as a thing to be *seen*, a sort of "still life," with an exclusive view to spectacular effect. It was a world in which all there was had been emphasised in forms of sensation and told as ornament, as visible luxury or refinement besetting one everywhere: plain, white light was no more. For they took pains, those people, and made their work, as they understood it, *complete*. If the one thing the philosophic Bruno could not away with was indolence, the life expressed here was certainly not an indolent life, however trifling to one or another its business might seem. In this age of scholars and of artists, some of the most perfect fruits of art had been here assorted with a perfect scholarship—a scholarship that could think for the whole and each several part with equal solicitude. The very flowers, the dishes set ready for a small company, had been made accomplices in this intention. The exhibition of every-day life as a fine art now happily solving the last minutest difficulties of the material it had to deal with, was complete. As Gaston passed from stair to stair, these walls seemed to shut him off more and more, as by some mutual repulsion, from the crude world outside. Here at least it might seem that all select things whatsoever, all that would really pass with the select few as in any sense productions of fine art, were strictly congruous with one another, begetting by mere juxtaposition something like the unity of a common atmosphere.

And as you may sometimes explain an enigma in the world of events by seeing or coming to know an actual person, to appreciate a personal influence, so here, breathing this atmosphere and amid the peculiar complexion of shadow and light in Jasmin's house, Gaston for the first time was able to define for himself something, a humour, a quality, a character, that was all about one in the Parisian life—something physiognomical, closely connected, therefore, as effect or cause with what must be moral in its operation.

In fact, the portraits, what purported to be the life-likeness of those who would be at home here, reigned in this room, and that as from a throne. At first, indeed, they might have seemed but extraordinary conditions of the atmosphere about them; or, less fancifully, only members of an ornamental scheme, in their places on the panelled walls, so congruous were they in their ebony and green and gold with the wholly inanimate objects around. It was to second thoughts that they explained this atmosphere, by referring one to the original secret of its composition in certain strong personal predilections. Amid all their exotic Italian tendencies, these people had had a measure of old Gallic or Gothic energy within them, forcing their peculiar tastes, their peculiar standard of distinction, as law upon others. To harmonise the living face with its lifeless *entourage*, to make atmosphere, is, we know, the triumph of pictorial art. Here, such sifted atmosphere as Leonardo or Titian could weave for his portraits, had overflowed the frame and become a common medium, for visitors to this privileged place to move in as freely as they would. How these pictured people saw or liked to see things, had determined a new visual faculty, if it were not rather an endemic infection of the eye;

which helped to explain certain visible peculiarities of the living world beyond these enchanted walls, and might be for Gaston a guide to some further refinements of selection therein. Here, certainly, the impulse had worked consistently with itself. Jealous, exclusive, of whatever was not significant of its own humour, there had been, as this place clearly witnessed on nearer survey, all sorts of shrewd rejections, in what seemed at first sight to be a very catholic aesthetic taste, and within the circuit of its influence, the concord of things disparate, the resultant harmony of effect was entire.

Such elaborately balanced harmonies have, however, as we know, a certain hazard in their conditions, and are apt to be easily disturbed. After all, it was not quite true that all really beautiful things went well together. A book he picked up for its binding, one of many lying ready to hand, struck the jarring note. Not [*Le Songe*] of Polyphile with [brilliant French engravings,] not *L'Heptaméron des nouvelles* [of Marguerite of Navarre,] not [,] but a little volume printed at Lyons purporting to be the ["*sentences*"] of the virtuous emperor [Marcus Aurelius.] In all the disguises of the Euphuism of the day, it had come with all sorts of conscious and unconscious transmutation by the way, through the Spanish from a Latin forgery, and was but a faded product of an age of translations, adaptations, mistranslations. But from its faint pages did emerge for the first time to Gaston's consciousness, the image of the antique, strenuous emperor in his life-long contention towards the old Greek "sapience," disinterested, brave, cold. Well! the atmosphere of that lofty conscience seemed absolutely unassimilable by the alembicated air Gaston was here breathing. To conceive of that at all, to keep the outline of it before him, all that was actually around him must be shut out even from the mental eye. And then certain products of pagan sculpture, nude fragments, arm or hand or torso or braided head, whose well-worn beauty he had scarcely noticed till this moment, amid the lively demand on his attention of the more directly sympathetic work of contemporary art, reinforced that dissonant note. Emphasised now by the suggestions of [the *Thoughts*], they presented an almost satiric contrast to everything else around them. Under that softly gilded light, set with much consideration as Giorgione might have set the jewel of his human flesh, and amid the rich apparel of the place, that delicately mellow old marble would not really blend. The shadowy ebony and green about it might have been the defiling earth from which it was but lately arisen after long burial. Creature of the fresh air, the fresh sun of Italy, of Greece, it shuddered amidst these tricky indoor splendours of the age of the Valois, and refused to be really, effectively associated with them, even by the graceful intervention of such recent imitators of the antique manner as Michel

Colombe or Germain Pilon. In contrast with Jean Goujon's daintily clothed voluptuousness of form, the pagan marble might have been primitive humanity itself—naked yet unashamed, fresh from its Creator's hand and unmistakably before the Fall. It seemed to protest that certain forms, certain refinements in the clothing of a later world were more suggestive of carnal thoughts than the unadorned uncovered flesh. And at least it started questions, some very irritant questions: Did this novel mode of receiving, of reflecting the visible aspects of life commit one to an intellectual scheme, a *theory* about it, the remoter *practical* alliances of which one could not precisely ascertain at present, but would inevitably be led to in due course? Was this odd grace no more than the superficial expression of an intellectual aristocracy "differenced" from the rest of the world by mere fashion and taste, or did it involve other differences from the vulgar, less innocent? Was it indeed their shame these people were seeking to hide under a fascinating exterior, which might conceivably become the vesture, the ritual of a new and a very profane religion? Or, did one's own perhaps crude sense of incompatibility between things, certainly attractive apart, merely indicate that there was some higher level of culture in these matters one had not yet reached? For there might be a mental point of view already attained by some, from the height of which the opposition between the thoughts of Henri and Marguerite de Valois and the thoughts of Antoninus, between the sophisticated colour and form of contemporary art and the antique white sculpture, its white soul, must disappear. There was certainly something over-charged, something questioning and questionable, in the expression of these portraits which became almost caricature in the purely imaginary faces: an air which the very furniture of the period seemed mockingly to reflect. But again, was it only that art had reached its highest power of expression, and must soon become "mannered," with an expressiveness really beyond anything there was to express? Meantime the artistic mode of the day, professedly derivative from the genial traditions of Italy, had put on the wan Transalpine complexion of Dürer's *Melancholia*, the out-look of a mind exercised absorbingly, but by no means quite pleasurably, by with a bewildering variety of thoughts.

It might perhaps be that, after all, things as distinct from persons, such things as those one had so abundantly around one here, were come to be so much that the human being seemed suppressed and practically nowhere amid the works of his hands, amid the objects he had projected from himself. Could there be in this almost exclusive preoccupation with things, to which indeed a sincere care for art may at any time commit us, something of that disproportion of mind which is always akin to mental disease? The physiognomist remarks certainly that the most characteristic pictured faces of that day have an odd touch of lunacy about them. It was a habit of the time, symptomatic of much else in it, partly through its minute love of art, partly in cynic disillusion, to expend strong feelings on small objects. In that world of Parisian fashion, fashion as you know having its very being in the felicitous management of slight or unsubstantial things, there might well be no place left at all for considerations beyond them—how, in a word, shadow matched substance. Shadow and substance!—had not Bruno declared that shadow and substance, the outside and what was within, great and little, were to the eye of reason "seeing all things" indifferently "in God," themselves "indifferent" or "coincident"? Had one here in Jasmin's dainty house, in visible presentment, only a slightly ironic form of that doctrine? It was the triumph of art certainly, "in the end of days"—this transfiguration of the indirect, of the secondary and accidental matters of existence, deftly extracting pleasure, a refining pleasure, out of the useful, the barely necessary—though with this consequence, at least in this instance, that the sheath became too visibly more than the sword, or, say, the house than the master, than Jasmin himself, in fact, touching if you found him out of spirits for a moment, enviable, delightful company for half an hour, but surely of no consequence to any one at all, and whom you scarcely missed while his evening suit in cloth of silver and pearls, marvellously *godronné*, a "symphony in white," lay ready there to be looked at like the other high-priced objects around. Was the house then empty after all? Was it not the essential man? His "effects" we say, with unconscious irony, of a man's goods—the French themselves of the bag or box he has with him, and power thus passing away from man into his works, it was as if he were already dead.

Dead!—suggestive therefore of melancholy thoughts, depressing to a creature of the senses—such thoughts as broke in upon Gaston from time to time through his own years of eager preoccupation with the sensuous aspects of life, the prosecution of the aesthetic interests discovered to him for the first time to-day. His search for the lost child, if it had ever indeed existed, proving hopeless, gradually ceased altogether at last, under the fascination of the scenes across which it had impelled him; while his uncertainty as to the mother's death left him, though no priest, yet in a kind of priestly celibacy after all, responsible, it might seem, only to himself, his own needs or tastes, in the disposal of his time. Surely the near, the visible, the immediate, was prevailing with him over what was distant and unseen, over remote hypothesis or conjecture. That it had so prevailed was an opportunity, in that matter of aesthetic culture, to make full use of which would be in accordance with the opportunist doctrines of Bruno and Montaigne still fresh in his ear. Yet it was from a great distance, comparatively, that these voices came which had been about him here all day. Were they notes of birds flitting about the lonely towers of the neighbouring abbey, above the great trees of the Pré-aux-Clercs, or the calling rather of children at play, hungry children at play with something of an effort, solicitous, at moments agonised, as if turned suddenly upon some one passing out of ear-shot, parent or friend? It was as complaining voices, certainly, with a touch also of the significance of that cry Augustine heard one day in the neighbourhood of another great city, that they settled into Gaston's memory. They would be identified by some trick of association with similar sounds haunting ear or fancy through the years that followed, till they came to seem like an acoustic peculiarity of Paris itself—this haunted medieval Paris with those strange, later, dubious (no! certainly holy) Innocents of Saint Bartholomew's Eve still "green in earth" there. Querulous always, invasive and reproachful, they would divert all other sounds into their peculiar note, and were apt to reinforce the distress of every distressful moment. They grew as time went on to be the voices of grown boys sweeping by, resonant, sonorous, the voices of young men at last, masterful, deliberate, expressive, increasing firmly in due order to what the age of the lost or dead child would have grown to be. Piercing now the velvet walls about him, otherwise exclusive of everything but what belonged to the merest foreground of existence, they rendered this long unoccupied day in Jasmin's house a complete epitome of Gaston's subsequent years in Paris.

An opportunity, I said, for the furtherance of the aesthetic life:—and it was telling already, as Gaston became aware, surprised by a certain fineness new to himself in his own reflexion from a Venetian mirror, of lustrous depth and hardness, presumably faithful. Like Wilhelm Meister's approving mentor, the looking-glass assured him that his eyes [were more deep set, his forehead broader, his nose more delicate and his mouth much more pleasant]. If according to the Platonic doctrine people become like what they see, surely the omnipresence of fine art around one must re-touch, at least in the case of the sensitive, what is still mobile in a human countenance. The period, as artistic periods at all events do, had found its expression in a recognised facial type, and Gaston too was conforming to it. Did portraiture not merely reflect life but in part also determine it? The image might react on the original, refining it one degree further. Given that life was a matter of sensations, surely he too was making something of its "brief interval" between the cradle and the grave. Here was the perfected art of the day, and it was a miracle of dainty scruples, of discernment at least between physical beauty and all that was not that: a practical condition quite at the opposite end of the scale from those rank, unweeded natural growths tolerated by Monsieur de Montaigne, promoted by the doctrines of Bruno. And he might "live up to" it. At least for a while it might take the place of conscience, and by way of proxy represent its larger, vaguer pretensions through the dimness of the world.

—To keep one animated and physically clean, quick and white, as it had certainly kept frail Jasmin de Villebon, who now, spite of all courtly softness burst suddenly into his dwelling with all the cheerful noise proper to youth, with a gaiety of step, a sincerity of voice putting to flight Gaston's late surmises as to hidden sin. His companions promptly retreated from the door, stood for a few moments in the moonlight, and shouted good-night with a laugh as pleasant as his own at the sight of his twinkling light above, and in the confusion of their departure Gaston too slipped forth; he would stay neither to test impressions nor taste the dainty supper; in effect, he had renewed old acquaintance. Yes! the house, the style, was the man.

CHAPTER IX

A Poison–daisy

"The earth with her bars was about me."

That laugh in the moon-lit street was partly at sight of a well-known object,—*assez recognoissable pour estre doré, et de velours jaune garny d'argent,*—the carriage of Queen Margaret of Navarre, who had stepped forth lightly at the street-corner and, gliding along the shadowed side of the way, presently ascended Jasmin's stairs, by appointment, to solicit in person the favours of that reluctant youth. "At the Court of France 'tis the women solicit the men":—So, savage old Jeanne d'Albret had warned her son, Margaret's husband, when he first came to Paris, from which he was now far enough away in his rude little mountainous dominion. "Queen Margot," Marguerite—pearl, or daisy—so called as if for the very purpose of suggesting satiric fancy, but with a face, at all events, as irreproachably white as the moon-light, unlike the women of her time, is used to go unmasked on the very boldest errands. She, certainly, is by no means an empty sheath! Call her rather, amid the many classic revivals of the hour, memories of "the magnificent, ancient, empresses, of time past, as Suetonius and others describe them," delightfully to her loyal biographer Brantôme:—Call her a new and perhaps lovelier Faustine, at home and popular among men of the sword. Like Faustine, she had had "a share in the moving of armies"; might have been called like her, in dubious sense, "*Mother* of the Army."—

By no means an empty sheath! She had been just in time to catch sight of the retreating Gaston, whose features are not quite new to her. At supper, amid witty amendments on the lie to be ready for use next day against any compromising rumours of her presence here at so late an hour, she asks his name; and awaits him, all herself, not long after, as, under Jasmin's guidance, he mounts a private staircase of the Louvre, to learn in intimate exposure as much as he will of the most beautiful, as also the most accessible, of the great ladies of that day.

The martial aptitudes in this embodiment of loveliness and love—of the seed of Venus and of Mars—Brantôme has attested with boundless admiration: "her share in the moving of armies": how prosperously, at the age of twenty-two, her cunning had seconded her courage in a certain warlike mission to Flanders: how even in the long later years of banishment or imprisonment at Usson, grim fortress of Louis the Eleventh amid the volcanic mountains of Auvergne, her imperative genius had never deserted the adulterous, impossible Queen of Navarre, not to be Queen of France.—What would you have? Even in incomparable pearls, as experts know, there is always deduction to be made: *il y a toujours à redire*. Well! on those ramparts of cold, black, lightning-struck lava, she had very soon been in command. "In a little time," says Brantôme, "the keeper of the prison found himself her prisoner. What had he thought of doing, Poor Wretch? Did he think to hold captive in his cells, the woman whose eyes, whose comely countenance, were locks and chains with which she could set fast all the rest of the world like a slave at the oar?"

That courtly writer, whose observant mind was neither more nor less than a mirror held up to the men and women of his generation, their attractive power and grace, had withdrawn himself from their actual presence about the time of Gaston's coming to Paris. Had good or evil chance brought him just then into Brantôme's company, or even into the company of his written books, Pierre de Bourdeilles or de Brantôme, incapable as he seems by nature and training of any kind whatever of "second" thoughts, must certainly have reinforced those earlier theoretic or abstract influences upon him of Bruno and Montaigne. For it is precisely according to their intention, their abstract conception of things, that the chronicler represents the living world of persons and their deeds around him, *paints* it, we may truly say, so lively, so gaudy are the hues of his vocabulary, his palette. The mere habit and carriage of Brantôme himself upon the stage of Parisian life would have concurred alike with the "new gospel" of the philosophic monk, as with the Gascon worldling's summarised experience of the world, in a challenge to make free trial, a free realisation, of the doctrine of "indifference," of moral indifference. The business of war Brantôme had learned under that "great captain, Monsieur François de Guise," though in his day King Charles the Ninth, that sincere lover of letters, who had had a true literary gift of his own, had valued in him not so much the soldier as the unflagging story-teller. "Gentleman in Ordinary of the King's Chamber," "born a mere gentleman," as he observes of another, "he had the heart of an emperor in his bowels." "To every place where illustrious rivals contested the prize of glory," he had made his way. Mars and Love, he says, "make war alike: the one and the other has his sword, his clarion, his camp." He frequents both, yielding himself always easily, genially, and with no misgiving, to the world on its march, careless what the issues may be, so only for his part he feels it to be in motion. Unembarrassed by abstract questions, a lover of every sort of hazard, he passes lightly over what might shock others in the undeniable mere brilliancy of men's doings, the brilliancy of their sins, of their generosity. *Ces beaux faicts!*—those gallant deeds, he has seen, or read of in history:—there is nothing in all that, he would protest, "but what I could achieve as gallantly, at a push!" Chagrinned in some way by Charles's successor, he shut up, or parted with his court braveries, and in the retirement of a country-house turned, finally, at about the age of thirty-five, from the actual world to feed in memory on its carefully hived sweetness, with a pen in hand he could use as adroitly, as gaudily, as the sword. He is visibly anxious for "name and fame" in transmitting to his executors the manuscript work of his remaining years. When he is gone, they will print his books, fruit, as he boasts, of his own shining natural abilities, *faictz et composez de son esprit et de son invention.* "The said books will be found in velvet covers of various shades respectively, together with a large volume of 'Ladies' covered, that, in green velvet, all curiously *gardéz* and fairly corrected. Fine things are to be found there: grave histories, in effect, stories, high speech, witty sayings, such as no one will omit to read, methinks, that has once peeped within." Those books, the [*Grands capitaines étrangers*], the [*Grands capitaines françois*], the [*Livre des dames*], were not published till [1665], [fully seventy] years after Gaston's end, and it was just as he came thither that the writer had quitted Paris. Failing Brantôme, however, and his gallery of eloquent portraits, there still was the original, the living thing itself, precisely as he had left it:—left it, however, (observe!) under a genial sunshine, sunset as it proved, which truly was now turned to colours very different from those of any kind of normal day, or night.

Those wild fervours of love and battle, of sin, such as, for Brantôme and his like, count as but the ordinary degree of blood-heat, have their reactions. As upon Charles himself on the morrow of the great crime, a sort of *atome* of nervous prostration had settled visibly on Paris, with certain sullen effects of colour, if not immediately agreeable, at least profoundly interesting to the duly trained aesthetic sense. Art, art achieved, and reaching just now its last refinements, the finest intelligence of its own motives and capacity, must needs minister to the mood of the day with somewhat low-pitched "symphonies" in black and grey, with "harmonies" in iron and steel, or at the gayest, in steel and silver—rusty steel, tarnished silver. Iron armlets, necklaces, necklets, iron chains, how daintily decorative we may conceive, became the fashion among, well! among *Les belles ferronières*, in the years which saw or felt all around the first beginnings of "The League," and cherished ever in the precious metals the cloudy lustres of the baser. It was as if they felt some sensible affinity for colours of the earth, earthy, of the sudden earth under rain or in decay—which made silver look like iron. The night-mare work of Bernard de Palissy is, in fact, fairly representative of the age. Like that masquerade figure of his, shading half-blindedly its own little candle, one groped one's way mentally, morally about all-accomplished Paris, as if in the rambling purlieus of some vast theatre, among the traps, the lofts and ladders and peep-holes, upon the artificially illumined stage, where the actors not seldom reached the height of real lust, real madness, and in real fury drew swords on one another. Partly moulding, in part merely obsequious to the preferences of its day, the taste of the reign of Henry the Third was but the appropriate last word of an art from the first largely derivative, that so carefully "forced" Renaissance art dear to the French court, which borrowing from Italy its patience, its subtlety and refinement, had not cared or not been able to derive also its buoyant, red, natural life-blood. In Raffaelle, in Titian, even in the dreamy Umbrians, the thoughtful Lombards, how full the pulsation, how stalwart the growth. The artists of the new *Italy in France* had contrived to infect it with the visible malaise which went properly with their own moral, perhaps physical, "caducity":—exotic contemporary writers had introduced the word. The old, intransigeant, native art itself, in Jean Cousin for instance, had lost its "Gallic" gaiety. Well! even the most powerful art, the hand of Veronese himself, must needs after all be contented not with broad day, but at best with a sort of algebraic system of symbols thereof. So, Gaston, as he looked back upon these years, seemed to have been dealing in them not with facts at all, perhaps, but only with "effects" of art, at the clearest under that sort of merely pictorial daylight in which the artist can but make terms with darkness.

For there was much in his own mental condition at this time, in his own changed sense of life, which made him sympathetic with those peculiarities of the surrounding atmosphere. The sombre air of Paris, as if of that ashen hue which is proper to penitence, befitted certain remorseful shadings of his own thought, a certain sense of broken ideal there, a haunting desire to *repair*, an offended moral delicacy which, however exaggerated, was inalienably a part of himself, as, the search for the child ceasing, he settled down into a mere spectator, thrust, it might seem, from action upon contemplation in a world where, while action seemed so dubious, so compromising to the scrupulous conscience, there was still so much to see, to understand, perforce to admire. As he assumed his place to watch, to take his share, perhaps, to take at least an intellectual part as sympathetic as might be in the dramatic action before him, the voices of Giordano Bruno and of Monsieur de Montaigne were indeed almost physically in his ears, both alike recommending, though from opposite points in the speculative circle, their doctrine of "indifference": yes! of moral indifference. It presented itself, in fact, as neither more nor less than the nicely weighted theoretic equivalent to the actual situation.

Readers will call to mind that place in the *Odyssey* where Ulysses approaches the palace of Circe, as in that memorable tapestried scene on the wall of Monsieur de Montaigne's study, its pleasant-seeming solitude in the midst of the magic island, the clear voice singing which makes one forget everything beside, as she suddenly appears at the doorway and calls to *him*:

$$\text{ἡ δ' αἶψ' ἐξελθοῦσα θύρας ὤιξε φαεινὰς}$$
$$\text{καὶ κάλει·}$$

Just such singing welcomed Gaston now, seemed to draw him magnetically up the spiral Gothic stair-case of the old palace of the Louvre to the modish and modern, half-Italian apartments of Queen Margaret. From the various levels, as he ascended, "the city of pleasure" (consciously Paris was already that) became more and more completely visible in what was artistically perhaps the most fortunate moment of its history. The red-tiled, fantastically crested houses wound along deep and narrow lanes close about the vast monastic precincts, the vast "hôtels" and palaces all alike climbing for light as high as they could in the thickly over-built space between *La Cité*, old Roman Lutetia, with its gothic towers of *Notre-Dame* on the island in the divided Seine, and the bosky circle of clerical or seigneurial gardens beyond the fiercely marked line of rampart bristling with iron. The sun-light seemed to rest by preference on the broad, white, cheerful masses of the half-classic Renaissance masonry, which had pushed their way amid the sombre medieval brickwork, threatening to supersede the Middle Age with its sad memories altogether, though with still uncompleted towers, abrupt galleries, and stairways into the air.

Immediately below, filling the atmosphere with the acrid perfume of coarse wild flowers, the old disused tile field stretched away to the delicately pillared central *pavillon* of the Tuileries. Nothing was finished. You heard the crisp sounds of the chisel even then at work. The fresh, daintily carved cornices ran into the hanging masses of unwrought masonry, as daringly as the weeds might do into masses of hanging ruin. The very staircase up which Gaston and his companion seemed drawn now by a shrill dominant singing above them, was itself but a remnant of the Middle Age, emphatic upon the voluptuously smoothed surface of the Medicean facade completed by the eminent Pierre de l'Escot on two sides only of the old feudal court-yard. The Louvre of the Valois, where the "Matins of Paris" had begun, to the inmost recesses of which their bloody service had penetrated, the few favoured Huguenot courtiers rushing for shelter to Margaret's chamber, under her coverlet, "because they were used," said popular satire:—the visitor to Paris may conceive the place as intermediate between the forbidding circular donjons of Louis the Eleventh and the later, official splendours of Richelieu and the Napoleons, the foundations of those ancient feudal towers still remaining traced out now, instructively, in white on the nineteenth-century asphalt pavement.

At the sound of male footsteps the royal lady was astir and flinging wide the doors upon them suddenly, like Homer's sorceress, thrilled her curious visitors, who trod their way softly into what might seem the dimness, the discreet order, the perfume of some religious rite just concluding, as the virginal treble music died away. It was nothing less than an oratory, this very characteristic apartment of Queen Margaret, with its relics and rich reliquaries, its recesses for devotion, was partly also a student's chamber as seriously arranged for its purpose as any monastic *scriptorium*: the tapestries (profanely storied, it must be said) excluding daylight might seem appropriate as a security also against the intrusion upon this charmed area of any quite simple thoughts from the world without. In fact, its cunning occupant had well considered her business, understood the best way of presenting her personal gifts, and might, with other than clerkly motives, be shy even at this remote height of undraped windows. Clerkly this sovereign beauty of her day certainly was; writing, writing constantly with a sort of really classic instinct for the genius of her native tongue, and that clerkliness did but add the more to the impression of cunning and wizardry about her, again like that of Homer's Circe—δεινὴ θεός. On those classic pages which have survived her, taking all the world into her confidence about all her people and herself, doubtless with much adroit suppression of truth amid their seeming candour, though by way of what some may think a quite "ruinous" apology, all, so far as language is concerned, is clear, straight-forward and—prosaic!

Friendly Brantôme had seen many strangers come to France, to the French court, expressly to gaze on that unique beauty of which the fame was gone through all Europe. He finds it pleasant to remember her (how many years afterwards!) at Blois on one particular occasion, with "her palm," how at a certain procession he and others had no profit of their devotions—our Palm-Sunday devotions—*car nous y vaquasmes peu pour contempler ceste princesse, et nous y ravir plus qu'au service divin.* "Bacchus," he observes in another place, always ready for quaint prattle about the old pagan gods,—Bacchus gives men fine blood, Ceres fair flesh: but (here is the point) could have given neither one nor the other so long as men and women lived, not on bread and wine, but on chestnuts or acorns. Certainly Queen Margaret's beauty, *qui est telle que le beau parler de Maistre Jehan Chartier, le suttilité de Maistre Jehan de Meun, et la main de Foucquet ne sauroyoient dire, escrire ne paindre*, being nevertheless a carnal product of the carnal things of Ceres and Bacchus—carnal, as the massive white throat testifies—came of fine living, of fine feeding, to speak candidly, of very dainty meal and wine, through many generations of those who had lived "softly," as a matter of course, "in kings' houses." The paleness Ronsard and his friends had cherished in their girlish mistresses had been a paleness not less used than that of white wild-flowers to open-air French sun-light: that of Margaret on the other hand, with her Italian derivation, a quality which, at least out of Italy, will never seem altogether a thing of nature. With all the blue-veined, well-compact lustre of flawless physical health, it was the pallor, nevertheless, of a thing kept studiously, like white lilac or roses in winter, from the common air or, you might fancy, in the dark; and there was almost oriental blue richness, blackness, in the king-fisher wings or waves of hair which over-shadowed *ce beau visage blanc* so abundantly, yet with lines so jealously observed along the proud, firm, smooth flesh, making you think, by its transparent shadows, of cool places around—yes! around dangerously deep water-pools, amid a great heat. Like such water, the black eyes surprised you by their clear dark blue, when in full sunlight for a moment as the trees opened above.

That this beauty, excellent as Gaston found it, had the air of an instrument for men's perdition about it, had been the remark of an unfriendly, perhaps disappointed, male visitor. But it was a devoted friend of Margaret's own sex who, dying and desiring to die piously, must needs thrust her from the bedside: *Retirez-vous, Madame, je vous prie, car il me faut prier et songer à mon Dieu, et vous ne me faites que ramentevoir le monde, quand je vous regarde.*

Of many minor arts at their perfection in that artistic age, perhaps the most characteristic is the enamel of Limoges, with its exquisitely pencilled miniatures, delicately veined, brightly jewelled, and detached in sharp outline on the lustrous or dark-blue surface, like a solitary reflection in a mirror. Why had the dainty powers of hand involved in it come to just this or stopped just here, one asks before the now priceless achievements of this seemingly irrecoverably lost art—hard or, as it is at its best, harsh surely in spite of the manifold refinements of handling which delight the connoisseurs in such things—connoisseurs such as Margaret herself, the panels of whose apartment, where the quite fresh or natural colours were to be found only in some out-of-the-way material—green ivory, green garnets, white peacocks' feathers—had been filled with sumptuous plaques from the hand of Léonard the Limousin himself. And (the thought occurred to Gaston) she had herself, perhaps, a superficial resemblance to this stuff, as he sat and watched her and Jasmin at play with chessmen wrought of it—a miracle of artistic dexterity in their way. She might have been the cunning *Bella Donna* whose physiognomy haunts so much of the art-work of that age, the visible form or presentment of an unseen force moulding and remoulding, after its own pattern, all one saw around one in that choice little world of Paris where she had played so large a part—δεινὴ θεὸς!—the genius of cruel or unkindly, as opposed to kindly, love.

CHAPTER X

Anteros

"The earth with her bars was about me."

The physiology of love, from the days of Plato to our own—the days of Stendhal and Michelet—has had its students analysing, more or less ingeniously, the phenomena of its diseased or healthy action, not always with entire theoretic disinterestedness, yet driving, amid the complexities, the thousand-fold casuistries of what is after all the most practical of subjects, at the very practical distinction of a blessing or a curse in it—Eros or Anteros. The essence of such distinction, however, has perhaps been touched most truly by William Blake in his fantastically wise little poem of "The Clod and the Pebble," where he contrasts the Love which must needs please another with that which can only please itself, the Loves which respectively must serve or be served, be possessed or in possession, the Love that would fain do costly sacrifice with the Love that would so willingly extort it. Unselfish love, as we know, has its flights, its extraordinary passages, and the selfish, even more, its caprices of self-pleasing, of demand on the voluntary yet so ruinous servility of others: their bodily or mental decrease—their suicide let us say!—as just one grain of incense, consumed, wholly consumed, on the red coal. Such impious claim to sovereignty centres, of course, in the consciousness of some inalienable, incommunicable personal distinction, most properly of that physical beauty which flushes the veins, and therewith his imagination, his reason, his force of will, with physical appetite, scarcely anything man covets being in ultimate analysis desirable by him except through links of association however remote, of identification however supposititious, with the desire of the bodily eye.

Fastus inest pulchris, sequiturque superbia formam.

How many enigmas on the stage of human life are really covered by the recondite relationships of what we may call erotic humility to erotic pride.

In the age of the Valois, among people of an extraordinary force of will, ready to assert to the utmost the whole of what they felt and were, an age of courtiers and ceremonial, of continual self-presentation therefore, which, with senses refined by a lovely though decadent art, felt the full significance of personality in its sensible manifestations,—in such an age, we might perhaps trace the steps by which the desire of physical, of carnal beauty, becomes a sort of religion, a profane and cruel religion, as cruel religions there are or have been. Was such sentiment, wasteful, despotic, and strangely exclusive where it is present at all, a natural and normal condition of certain types of human mind at all times, or the wholly artificial creation of a somewhat visionary art and poetry, invading a phase of actual life from which ordinary motives had departed: or had it come, already in full development, from Italy (as infection comes, wrapped up with costly furniture and the like) to set a fashion, and remodel everything else after its own new pattern? Had it escaped from the grave of antiquity, reopened there with all that antiquity had known, the over-powering literature, the sins, the exotic sin which imperial Rome in its days of decadence had learned from those old-world subjects, who were become in turn the masters of its thought, sins like those of Tyre and Sidon, which neither the blood of primitive martyrs nor the consecrations of the Middle Age had yet detached from its very stones? So the student of moral ideas, of historic fact, may ask, shocked or merely curious. There at all events it was: *Amor, L'Amour*, in every form of selfish pity and terror, of sorrow and joy, "enthroned in the land of oblivion," of forgetfulness of all beside itself, the carnal, consuming, and essentially wolfish love, though so humanely learned in the remotest delicacies of human form, the shading of the eyelid, the curvature of the lip, colours, lines as immaculate seemingly as those of opening flowers,—the love or lust that will not be contented with anything less than the consumption, the destruction of its object, as if it had been a literal eating and drinking of it, which meant only to pluck all that, to take another like a flower from its stalk or a grape from the wall, suck out the juice and fling away the rent skin, chiefly by way of gaining pleasant assurance to itself of its own sovereignty.

Its sovereignty enthroned for the moment in the person, the reprobate beauty, of Margaret, that golden daisy of France, golden or yellow, or at least not white (but then, even liturgically, yellow or gold, however dusky, does duty for white): *moy*, as she writes, *qui suis fille de roy, et soeur de roys*, herself indeed queen, Queen Margot of little Navarre, but who thought it not worth while to secure by average decency of life the throne of France: preferred rather to be queen, empress, deity, if it might be, of men's hearts, and found in plenty her willing, devoted, thirsty subjects. Yes! there were the virginal, the really white flowers of both sexes whose floral perfection, like some triumph of the gardener's art, of the old Adam bringing his curious skill so far, might be thought to justify the heated shade, the morbid, *terne*, "secondary" colours, all that was artificial or medicated in the air of the world around them, upon which, like veritably spiritual things in their transformed earthiness, they stole, opened, spread themselves so gracefully, easily, superbly, for an hour, yet with so delightful a sense of mystery, as if they drew their nurture from nethermost darkness. They swarmed here, those luscious heavy-petalled blossoms, these momentarily beautiful faces, lips, eyes, with your own eyes on which you might forget, or desire to forget, all beside, and over which, for the like of Margaret, some cruel assertion of empire might have the sweetness of an embrace. From forgotten old houses in remote corners of France, like choice furniture or untouched portraits, they had come on demand; and with the lapse of a month or a year, in this singular atmosphere, the exotic personality, the hand, the eye, the lip, the inflammable fancy within of which these were eloquent, had even surpassed the utmost imaginings of the exotic fine art which had discovered to others as to themselves their high aesthetic value. You seemed to expect, to have known something of them before they came; after a few minutes' intercourse, to have known them always. They filled a place made ready for them by the books, the pictures, the very fashions of the day—nay! more than filled it, they superseded all this daringly. And might this be, perhaps, the fulfilment of Gaston's early boyish dreams of [some great distinguishing passion] awaiting him here—somewhere among these faces, pathetic, appealing, in spite of their pride, passing so constantly about him by day, and at night fixed steadily upon the dark wall of the brain?

Unkindly or cruel love, the worship of the body, the religion of physical beauty, with its congenital and appropriate fanaticism, a servitude based on the most potent form of that relationship of the weak to the strong, noted by Aristotle as the elementary ground of slavery in human nature itself—most potent because, in effect, the servitude of the insane to the sane—the "impassioned love of passion," love for love's sake as a doctrine and a discipline, a science and a fine art all in one, its evocative power over what finely educated senses must straightway declare delightful, desirable, in the sphere of imageries, colour, music, words refining the very lips that uttered them, the anatomy of the thing of his own free experience, the strange delight of such servitude for the master and, stranger still, for the servant in it, was for a time, for months that grew to years, almost exclusively to occupy the mind of Gaston, at home in this singular place like Circe's enchanted island, or like the maze on that old cathedral floor at Chartres, such mazes as savage fingers no less than the finest ones have been led to trace, likest of all to that labyrinth of land and water, of streams and pathways, in the background of [Leonardo's *La Gioconda*], revolving perpetually into themselves. An air of casuistry about it, stimulating pleasantly the reflective action of the brain as its romance coaxed the fancy, that odd savour of a remote and curious scholarship of love in which Queen Margaret seemed a graduate, a doctor, had from the [beginning] a fascination for the studious youth, himself before all things a scholar, a fastidious scholar. His own conscious clerkly distinction was, in truth, to the taste of Margaret, as the final expression of the taste of that day, the hour, the moment, the present moment for which alone, professedly, those who were of it thought and wrought. For both of them, as both alike absorbed students, fellow-students, there was certainly a wonderful charm when, as with the poet of the *Vita Nuova*, with Petrarch, with sinful Abelard of old here in Paris, such grave thoughts as seem naturally alien from carnal love enter its service, put on its livery, become its accomplices. The trim, discreet, almost priestly scholar correcting, annotating the great lady's manuscripts, nominally a very proper secretary, was conscious of, while he suggested to her, the question (of a kind seductive for the thoughtful) in what exact proportions a cool, grave, self-possessed intelligence might coexist with the physical throb of youth, could conspire with it, as he came and went on his learned business, entertaining and himself entertained, in what by his good fortune was a kind of mutual indifference. For, as with physical delicacies, if you wished to sip, as you might wine, to enjoy in veritable connoisseurship the singularly attempered character of the so gifted Margaret, a calm though kindly indifference was, in fact, the proper condition for doing so—an indifference which would have formed, in truth, one of the three constituent chapters in that book on the physiology of love which she might have penned with triumphant suitability to the humour of her generation.

The unkindness of its two other chapters—of that cruel eagerness to consume the reluctant lover, and then of that cruel weariness of a lover found too facile, which allowed, nay encouraged him to consume, to destroy himself by sacrifice, delightful surely in its degree to him also—these chapters in Margaret's supposed Physiology of Love Gaston read, we might say, carefully to the end, as one might really read a book, occupied, that is to say, often feverishly enough in brain-work with philosophic or casuistic questions

concerning, for instance, the entanglement of beauty with evil,—to what
extent one might succeed in disentangling them or, failing that, how far one
may warm and water the dubious double root, watch for its flower, or retain
the hope, or the memory, or the mere tokens of it in one's keeping? Amid a
hundred palpable though quickly evanescent affections, operative as if
through a mere touch in the dark, a form seen but for a few moments, or a
name only, with the fancied voice and eyes and hands that might pertain to
it, he found himself at times almost as suppliant as the people about him to
what claimed for service on bended knee and with consciously self-forgetful
heart. Enthralled constantly by the spectacle before him, more and more
exclusively detached by it from the claims of anything beside, yet chilled to
the heart by a wretched sense of brevity, of decay and hasting in it, he lived
ever in dread of some great and over-whelming temptation. Was it he, in fact,
who suffered the exclusion, the detachment, thus paying a penalty? Was there
something, some one he had disloyally neglected, who had now put him
aside, deserted him in just distress or anger and pain, fluttering away from
him as from a soiled place, and now he must bear the consequences? *In
omnibus his peccaverunt adhuc*: said the Psalmist: *Et defecerunt in vanitate dies
eorum*: Therefore their days did He consume in vanity, and their years in
festinatione,—in distresful hasting no-whither. And was it really thus after all?
Was it so with himself?

If Queen Margaret's chamber was like some place of strange worship,
herself at once its idol and priestess, its chief relic was as ghastly as church
relics usually are, a dead man's face, with the stamp of his violent end,
mummied and brown, lying there exposed among the best prized objects of
the lady's personal property, mounted in a kind of shrine or pyx of good
goldsmith's work, and set with gems picked from milady's own jewel-case.
Precisely such fantastic love, love as a servitude, an idolatry, a voluntary
humility, had come naturally to the liking of one Jacques La Mole, gay-
flowering sprig from an old stock rooted deep in the province of [Provence],
as he first sauntered hopefully into Paris, on a path which crossed at last at
the fatal point of conjunction, on the fatal day and hour, the so inexorable
path of Margaret, then also at her freshest, and henceforth the monarch of his
soul; and thereupon the entire sheaf of his gifts and gaieties had kindled into
fire, a pyramid of sweet aromatic flame moving to its end before her as she
went onward. Plotting recklessly with the madman's hare-brained wit he had,
in that world of very cunning plots, in fact almost as frankly as he unsheathed
always for her sake his first youthful sword, he played for her a wild game for
[well-nigh two] years, in which not even he, not even love's fanatics, could

maintain he had won the prize at stake. Shortly in course of time, you see him pass into a sordid prison, into dim torture-chambers in the keeping of those who will rack the young limbs this way and that, to squeeze out, if they can, truth about the doings of more stealthy enemies than he, of the powers that are; and when he emerges again to suffer in public, and as if voluntarily, by way of a slight offering, to fling his life to her, sitting there to watch, she has no effective or natural sympathy for the young man, with form already ruined, his shattered arm making shift to fling cap in air gallantly, does watch however, puts out no hand to save him, only makes a point of carrying the severed head, thus offered and duly accepted by her, away with her, to set it among her choicest winnings. *Ci-gît* [Jacques La Mole,] and [may God] have mercy on his soul or on what may still be left unconsumed of it.

There, then, ever in the presence of Margaret, actually upon an altar with unbleached funeral wax lights amid the curtained space of her little oratory, like the smirched moth upon the candle, was the ugly brown face, made thus ugly for her sake. The graceful Jasmin sees it there, recoils instinctively, hates the very place where it is kept, seems to detect the scent of it here, there, underneath pleasanter perfumes, wishes to be gone as usual, having in truth no great care for Margaret, one of her reluctant lovers or claimees, in which matter he will pay the cost almost as heavily as that former, too prompt lover, whilom owner of the embalmed lips and eyes, so winning and eloquent once, so repulsive now.

Yet Jasmin, too, so light of step, picking his way through an unclean world as if along a silken list, with a daintiness which makes almost every one he meets instinctively yield him the best side, he too has done, does his part in crushing living sentient things there in his brief passage, though he has no liking for ghastly relics in the pleasant chambers of his memory or his house.—

About this time, for the diversion of Paris, a choice company of Italian players, brought thither by King Henry, presented there in masquerade, by way of a "mystery" or "morality," their own version of a legend people since have come to know well, the legend of Tannhäuser. The romantic knight, as we remember, on his dreamy medieval journey, stumbles amid the eery old cliffs and woods of Germany into the hiding-place of Venus herself, not dead but still alive, though if she peeped forth she would see a Gothic church steeple. Well! once for all Tannhäuser is hers, gives her his heart, himself, a thing not recoverable, makes his efforts to break the spell, goes to Rome seeking absolution from the Pope, returns again, however, to the cave (his heart there all the time) and to hell, as we feel, forever, though a pretty afterthought hints at final restoration.

Those Italian players took their subject a little on one side, so to speak, put the *Venustas*, the quality of Venus, not on a goddess but on a god, and made the adoring fanatical lover a woman, the old Eve, mother of us all, as through many forms she takes her way through the world, ever one and the same from age to age, with desire towards [her lord] ruling over her, betrayed again and again into the realm of some irrepressible male idol, supposed in this particular case to be [   ], seeking now and then, if it may be, the ministry of some wholesomer kind of religion, but always returning again at last underground to her madness and idolatry, usually, as was truly said, to nurse her deity in sickness. Well! The Franco-Italian version followed her, then, the self-immolating, longing feminine soul, from age to age always the same (the constant repetition of its sad fortunes was the force of the thing), with such fantastic knowledge as stage-players in that loosely pedantic age could come by, of the ways, the looks, the raiment of men and women in old Assyria transformed mistily on the stage to ancient Egypt, Judaea, Corinth, Rome, to humanity, like this very theatrical company did, presenting a single piece in all the towns and provinces in turn, onward to medieval Nuremberg and modern Venice, and coming down to the last generation, discreetly stopped at their own, not from lack of contemporary instance, as the reader is aware, but as leaving the theme confidently to the fancy, the experience, of a fashionable Parisian audience late in the sixteenth century.

Only, be it remembered, such female souls are not necessarily lodged in women's bosoms. In a certain episode of Jasmin's fantastic experience, the idolatrous or servile attitude unveiled itself in the person of a lad who had realised towards him, as it were, the very genius of slavery as a natural affection of the human mind. See them together, just able to move away from one another in play for a few minutes, at the door of the farm-house in the old French country, foster-brothers, Jasmin *fleurdelisé* and Raoul, as delicately made as he though less softly clad: the wild flower, if it be really wild, is not essentially less delicate than the growth of gardens. Raoul, come through generations of cottagers on the wholesome woodside where nice wild-flowers naturally abound, seems indeed cut, so to speak, on the same pattern and of the same stuff as his play-fellow from the manor-house, yet somehow, by some natural tendency in the inward, unseen, elementary settlement of things, one will be a master, indeed, and the other a "servant of servants" to his brother. What strange disturbance is this within him, like the battling of a wounded bird in his bosom, when Jasmin leaves the place for the first time, this overwhelming discovery, in a moment, that the other who seems already far off along the road homewards, is necessary to his being, the sickness with which he turns back to his own place in the world, so sufficient an hour ago, the suddenly formed but unalterable determination—to find his one solace, to nurse at any price the hope to see Jasmin again with unchanged ways towards himself. He is told that the other will forget him, that it must and ought to be so, in his unimaginable home far up there at the fine castle lined with silk and gold, yet he wonders what that other may be doing now and now, there or there. Yes! forgetful doubtless of him. A few days ago he would not have understood that thus it could be with him, this dislocation of a part of himself, like a thing cut in two yet alive still, as Plato fancied, seeking, seeking blindly, to be one again with its fellow, its self.

The Castle, however, after all is not so far off, is distantly visible up there on the rising ground, while he is down in the cottage, and he does see his lord again from time to time and actually with a sort of kindness on both sides, the luxury of pride on this side working with perfect reciprocity and ease around the luxury of humility on that other, nature itself having formed some to rule and some to serve. For so decided is the opposition of the mutual instincts which determine such relationship found to be, that we may surely suppose them the result of some original, primitive, purely physical or animal divergency in the cerebral molecule or germ, parted asunder, set over against each other more and more in each generation, the fatally fixed opposites in a necessary contention and subsequent collusion of soul like two distinct yet, as the older doctrinaires fancied, natural species now. Yes! the seigneurial species of soul and the servile species, a mass of instincts, susceptibilities, consequent issues, gathered gradually from of old through generations of forefathers whose abode had been in meagre cottages, in their lords' stables, in dark cells, torture chambers, surviving with all fitness in the modest person of this young servitor or serf in fifteen-hundred-and[-seventy-something], side by side with the perfectly blown flower of the old primitive or eternal germ of mastery, of the natural superior in Jasmin. His servant loves him the more, would fain serve him in some very costly manner, as he returns finer, daintier, each time from school, from court, from incredible foreign places, a perfect mystery of superiority, like some young pontiff in his silk and lace and *godron* in the view of that loyal, simple, confident creature, feeling that strange ache within when the other of course departs again, not less through habit but more than at the first anticipating now, each time, the tale of emptied days, as it will be told over again, as freshly as ever, from point to point, for him thus deserted by his comrade, his master. He thinks of all the pleasures, the glories that the other goes to, his own indeed and right for him, but is not envious. And now, coming again, he makes his servitor, though he cannot handle the pen, a sort of poet at last, as he consciously associates that gallant presence with the flashes, the changeful beauty and pride, of all other outward things, the lily and the rose on Our Lady's altar, the moving ocean of fresh green leaves, the immaculate snow. Drilled by his own loyal painstaking into a fit attendant enough, like some choice kind of dog, he is permitted at last, to his unspeakable delight, to follow his lord to Paris, throws himself without question into the young man's life there, his friendships, hatreds, intrigues, and as fate leads at length, his heart aflame with the mere hope to please such a master to the uttermost and in costliest fashion, follows up some fancied passing quarrel of his, hunts down with a suddenly developed cunning, and takes his lord's vengeance on the person of a young seigneur of higher rank than Jasmin's own. In the inattention, with the indifference of spirit which follows a great deed, he lightly permits himself to be taken red-handed, guilty of a crime, the murder of a [nobleman] by a servant, for which he will be "broken on the wheel," certainly to the passing regret of Jasmin, though shocked at such a crime as that. They crowd in where he is to "suffer" on the hot fine morning, an indifferent world going to market or returning on their way home from a wedding, on their way to funerals, taking their cakes to the baker, or their cattle to the butchery, regretful only not to be able to stay and see it out, people wholly unused to question the justness of "public acts of justice": a pavement of heads, children who thought he must indeed "be wicked to have suffered so" or that he couldn't feel the blows, or hid their faces and wept, religious persons who would have prolonged his lifetime, kept him alive between those blows or added to their number, to secure a truly penitent passage for him from the world, this world of racking eyes about him in the Place de Grève. Amid this heat of the gaudy, thirsty June morning, how enviable those more aristocratic sight-seers who sit at nicely shaded windows, and those who have found standing place in that long shadow across the square of the belfry of the old Hôtel de Ville, where all has been made ready for the sufferer. He, at least, emerging from the shadowy prison gate, seemed even thus to find the heat, the sun-light, the wide air, a momentary pleasantness; and shivers partly with cold as they strip away his scanty clothing. Under the constraint of the last few days, he is become humbler than a little child, is pressed onward, may be handled, turned this way and that, as passively as a child already dead. A priest of course stands as near him as may be, but he doesn't listen, looks only for the master, in his [bewilderment] might mistake another for him. When they bind him at last to the great fixed upright wheel, like Saint Andrew on his cross, not blindfold, facing the multitude, having only his loose white shirt upon him at the bosom (it will be nothing in the way of the iron bar), the women, perhaps for the first time in his brief life, in a luxury of grief feel that he belongs or ought to belong to them, to their proper world, *Amor Lacrimosus*, bound there to the wheel, like a rose on the trellis. The executioners forgot the rag for blindfolding the lad's eyes; a score of handkerchiefs are handed over the heads of the crowd. People speculate with [suppressed] breath on the effect of the first blow of the iron bar in hands of iron across the legs, are hushed, as if for distant music or an eloquent voice, as they await the sound of the next and the next, this way and that, with pause between, over the extended arms, the stomach, for the last stroke upon the open bosom, which does not always kill immediately, the body with every limb broken hanging there to die, after all, in the course of nature, till the public [labourers] come who will reduce it to ashes. As people pass away around it, they hardly know whether it breathes still, a few only get near enough to ascertain the truth of the relieving rumour which passes through the crowd that the boyish criminal is dead.

Yet Jasmin shuddered at, could not bear the neighbourhood of the relic Margaret had snatched triumphantly from a scene such as that, key-note as it was for the entire scenery of the whole world here about him, to [Gaston] and his thoughts at this time, a great Place de Grève. Again and again revolutionists tried to purge it, that Parisian one, but by fresh crimes of their own.

"Intention," the mental act by which you peer into and exhaust the infinitude of qualities lying within the compass of a single object or phenomenon, is ever necessarily (as logicians tell you) in inverse proportion to "extension," to any larger or more liberal survey of the area which the name of such object or phenomenon generally denotes. The interests, the one interest, revolving perpetually round and round again into itself, which occupied the thoughts of Gaston at this time, had a marked exclusiveness. Observe, touch, taste of all things, indifferently!—So his philosophic guides had steadily recommended—guides he might seem indeed to have encountered quite casually on his way, whose theories, nevertheless, presented to him as he then actually was, seemed to come to him with nothing less than axiomatic force.

Yet it was to this their advocacy of the larger and more liberal acceptance of life had in fact committed him—to this exclusive preoccupation with what was certainly but a limited department of the great garden; and as he looked back afterwards, it was noticeable that just here for him life had contracted to its narrowest. As he contemplated ever more and more intently a single exotic sentiment with its interpretation in art, in literature, in life, other interests, manifold, once his, fell away around it, leaving it there alone, thrusting it forward upon him as if in an otherwise empty world, but yes! with the bell of doom hanging there under the sunless sky. *In vanitate, in festinatione deficiunt dies—anni.*

Presenting itself at first as only the proper antidote to the too narrow and scrupulous conscience of a religious childhood, a restrained youth, the theory of "indifference" had but subjected him to a sort of conscience more exclusive still, to this impassioned love of passion—call it what you will. *Amans amavi...*: so in ever-revolving circle, through every tense of the verb "to love," does Augustine describe the like of it in himself. Here certainly, for a while, was for him the single and all-exclusive touch-stone of reality, of value in things. Not the conscious art only, the literature, the music of the age, but the very furniture about one was full of it and of nothing else—the wine one drank, the cup that held it, the platter one took it from, and above all those graceful fashions, with perhaps the loveliest masculine dress the world has seen, how faithfully, how daintily it followed, displayed, yet made a mystery of, the person, the natural form within, relieved the finely bred, much cared for hand and head. And then the shoes. Common people's seemed to belong to what soiled them, these designed rather to mark with scornful emphasis dainty opposition to the earth they trod on.

And glancing across his mirror (how that age doated on its mirrors!), Gaston saw himself also closely enough conformed to the aesthetic demand of the day, that he too had taken the impress and colour of his age, the hue (like the insect on the tree) of what mentally he fed on. With the jealousy, the exclusiveness of the herbalist, for instance, who must complete his series at any cost, or of the grammarian or any other specialist, it was as if he [had been] gathering, under lock and key in the hot-house of an over-excited fancy, a collection of very rare flowers of human life. Nay! this tiny red drop at the bottom of the cup, so to figure it, into which the whole world seemed expressed, who should say it was not worth all beside? And its hue infected not merely all objects of sense, but the sense itself. The eye, the fancy, the very fibre and fabric of his brain being saturated by it, "the earth with her bars" was "about" him in his very sleep; and at this time, after fifteen years' using, that little Prayer for Peace, as useless at last, or insincere, or perhaps profane, for a while departed from his lips.

CHAPTER XI

[The Tyrant]

Was Margaret after all indeed the mirror of her time, or that other, her brother, on the throne? In an age so spontaneous and sincere, in its devotion to antiquity wearing its well-dusted antique lore like some fresh flower of to-day, the features of "The Tyrant," as Suetonius and Lampridius had conceived him, must of course have come in evidence, to be welcomed or otherwise along with other types. Would it have been with a shudder or with a sense of encouragement at the discovery of a spirit so akin to his own, with a blush or only a satiric laugh perhaps, the whirligig of things coming round again to the same point so funnily, that in the Latin pages of Lampridius, Dion, Herodianus, or in a new French version of the old Greek of [Plutarch], King Henry might recognise his likeness under a portrait in which vicious inclinations and a kind of reprobate beauty are blent in proportions of which we can hardly get at the secret? Many resemblances to himself in the shameful young Roman emperor, who had polluted afresh by taking the impiously divine name of Elagabalus, he could not fail to notice. Fondling of a woman he afterwards banishes to a remote Syrian town, but who, as the sister of an empress, had tasted something of the splendours of the imperial court like the French queen-mother, like Catherine, now all cunning, now all audacity, always without scruple for the child she has early dedicated to the service of an impure religion in the magnificent temple of the Sun-god at [Emesa], at fifteen he issues from the mystic shelter of his boyhood, himself like a fascinating idol in her hands. He delights the eyes of the debauched soldiery, as they see him gracefully performing the functions of his office, delights their very souls when, victims thus of a clever *coup d'etat*, they accept him as at least the illegitimate son of their late indulgent murdered emperor, as their emperor to be, with passing flashes of the courage, of the military gifts they can really understand.

He is still, notwithstanding, true to his priestly education, himself at heart a priest of the hot, mad Assyrian sun-god whose worship is a prostitution, whose name Elagabalus, adding to it the whole gaudy load of official names and titles, he has taken for his own, by whose favour, surely, he is now on his imperial progress, till with the assent, the acclamation of a senate and a populace doating in their turn on the lax, florid, sentimental features, still extant on his coins, on the strange voluptuous Syrian nature, the wild dances and barbaric hymns, his supposed possession of magic gifts, the largess, doubtless, of carefully hoarded wealth, he stands on the Palatine hill, the jewelled mitre glittering on his head, to lay there the foundations of the temple of his own tutelary deity, for whom he is jealous, and who shall cast the native gods of Rome into obscurity. But, like the young French monarch returning from Cracow to Paris, he had loitered, fatally for himself, on that so delightful journey. The roses had seemed to come down on him from above, and from the earth at the touch of his feet, of his chariot-wheels. All he comes in contact with blossoms or is transformed into gold. Only, somewhere among them, like Henry of France, he has left behind him his understanding, and appears at times a madman. His people soon tire of a frantic superstition, such as this he appears really attached to, of the lad's cruelties, of a sensual cruelty apparently for its own sake, of the grave folly which establishes a senate of women under the presidency of his mother, an earlier Catherine de Medici, for the decision of questions of attire and etiquette, his marriage to a Vestal virgin, his polygamy, his coarse favouritism, the dreamy profanity with which he solemnises the nuptials of his impure god to Pallas of Troy, to Urania, to all the goddesses of Italy, the secret human sacrifices, the open murders. He could hardly have sinned so much in the time, objects the shrewder student of what historic writers liked so well, doubtless, to tell of him. For, alas! for the degeneracy of a later age, of a Northern latitude, in this matter of life as a fine art (one of the minor merely decorative or amusing arts), Elagabalus had managed to pack his entire story into the incredibly brief term of three years, and died at eighteen along with the still doating mother, cut to pieces suddenly by the swords of his former admirers, the victim of art, of his poetry, his own poetic soul, you might almost say of his religion!

King Henry's masquerade, his gloomy theatrical reproduction of the part of the insane young Roman emperor, had a run after all of not less than [fifteen] years. He dies by the hand of an assassin, a fanatical monk, at the age of [thirty-seven], in Gaston's [thirty-seven]th year, with taste surfeited, one might fancy, of such toys as he really cared for. Meantime the storm gathering around, joining cloud to cloud, does but enhance, at least for sensitive spectators, the theatrical effect of the thing, a tiny, flowery, madly lighted island, whence the music and satiric laughter are heard across the black waves which must presently engulf it. Gay as those revellers seem, they have at heart the melancholy proper to the insane. Pluck one of them by the sleeve, and you'll hear also the weeping of the madman, for a moment aware of his madness and what must come of it. But since we are, all, or the more sensitive of us, educated, formed, transformed, brought to be what we are in a large measure by what we *see*, perforce or by chance or choice, sympathetically or otherwise, to follow for a few pages that singularly blent scenery, may further the interpretation of Gaston's character as he stands there for a while to watch the actors; so closely that for a time he seemed actually to be of their company, fascinated by the sense of a certain beauty there, he could not wholly have explained even to himself, of the saving animation and gaiety, it might be, with which a worthless thing was done, the pathetic grace with which the infatuated, the doomed, pass to their destruction, as he was always on the alert also for redeeming traits in vitiated human nature. The estimate of an age, of its characteristics, as seen in its effects upon a sensitive mind:—that, after all, is the utmost we can come by in converse with even the strictest of historians.

Votre État baye de tous côtés, comme une vieille masure. Où sont vos noblesses? Où sont vos soldats? Votre trône est à qui veut le prendre. Vous touchez la ruine.—It was the warning of Louis of Nassau, a shrewd politician not unfriendly to the throne of the Valois, in the year next after that fatal one of Saint Bartholomew. Ten years had since passed by, and now the faithful chronicler of his time, Pierre de l'Estoile, noting events from day to day, seemingly with no prejudices, records precisely how *Le Roi* is [behaving] *comme* [*s'il n'y eust plus eu de guerre, ni de Ligue en France;*] *faisait tous les jours festins nouveaux, comme si son Estat eut été le plus paisible du monde.* As if blinded, however, by heaven or by himself, he did thus with an all but empty purse, on the verge of public bankruptcy. *"On n'entendait parler que des choses effroyables."* It was as if they felt, knew—these people, Catherine and her flying cortege—their hour, the end of their world all but upon them, and were bent desperately now on gathering up what they really cared for most—they and their like, the fragments that remained under the threatening ferment, to the curious eye revealing [their] character. The historian observes about this time that *la huitième guerre civile avait commencé,*—the eighth: and, in fact, we know that for a whole generation war, civil war, had been like a part of the established condition of things, its shocking incidents mixed up with the perennial picturesque of nature, and the pretty artifices of that gracefully self-indulgent age. Smoldering like a fire, creeping like a serpent among the corn, raising its metal coil here or there in declared battle, war, or the spirit of it, its immediate causes were everywhere, in men's families, in men's very selves, in Gaston for instance, a war between that profoundly rooted sensuousness within, which held him there gazing sympathetically year after year on what the religious mysticism, which formed the other half of his nature, bid him fly from for immediate refuge in the wounds of [Jesus Christ]. The reader sees him, it is to be hoped, pleased or at least interested, yet regretful, sorrowfully puzzled for himself and others, curious, indulgent, not however very self-indulgent, and certainly not with a made-up mind. And on the larger scene of battle also, various long-smoldering oppositions had formed at last very definitely into two camps, hostile even to death. The eighth civil war, the war of the three Henries, *des trois Henri*, had commenced, says the historian. But in truth among the many parties into which France was split, Henry the Third and what friends he had scarcely counted for one at all. The League being set now so decisively against "The Cause," you might think that legitimate royalty as a third party might ally itself to either, to each in turn, with the futile subtlety of old Catherine's hopeless policy. No! The other two will squeeze number three out "of the way" between them. It was beside any question of the insignificant claims of Henri de Valois, and all but over his crushed person, that Henri de Guise and Henri de Navarre were to fight out their battle.

—"The Cause" led by Henri de Navarre, "The League" under Henri de Guise, loosely representative, respectively, of the Huguenots, of the Catholics:—It would be impossible for the King to take the leadership of either, though invited, perhaps half ironically, to do so by one and the other. The Huguenots are less than a tenth part of the French people, but shrewd and rich far beyond that proportion: the Reformation, *armed* Protestantism. Their Catholic neighbours are really afraid of these men, who *will* pray openly after their own fashion in defiance of law, but who pray standing upright in their armour. The crime or accident of the Eve of Saint Bartholomew has left their general condition unchanged, adding only a profound sense of wrong. "They were cats," as the Queen-mother, Catherine, knew—"those Huguenots!—*que vos Huguenots qui se trouvent toujours sur leurs pieds.*" All over France they are drawing more and more compactly together, hope to conquer

France for the Reformation, failing that are ready to dismember her by the conquest of a part.

You may read in a certain old Suabian chronicler whose grimy blacksmith's hands handled a pen forcibly, how a famous Italian smith constructed a singular flower of iron. It was like the stealthy formation of the League over against those Huguenots, *une armée* of terrible armed men—*d'hommes sortant de la terre.* They loved, those genial old Swiss and South German masters, to curb, smooth, and curl their harsh rude metal into trellis work of honey-suckle, spiked lilies, bossy roses: and now, here was a cunning Italian more than emulating their art, being determined for once to do the like while retaining under the undulous leaves all iron's native poignancy and defiance. How he contrived, polished, veiled his machinery, you were tempted to try with the finger amid the graceful foliage, touched the hidden spring perchance, and found your wrist imprisoned in a moment in a circle of bristling points, while the central stamen slid through the hand, like a great poignard from its sheath, or the fang of a steely serpent. Flashing suddenly like that upon the Huguenots, upon King Henry, the League, "The Holy Union for [Defense of the Catholic, Apostolic, and Roman Faith]" (the supremacy, in fact the final accession to the throne of France, of the house of Lorraine, somewhat hypocritically of catholicism, only so far as was compatible with that) had been cunningly shaped to its end in secresy for years, and was at last, after a shock of incredible conflicting rumour, now actually in evidence, first of all in Picardy, patient, humble and devout, its broad waves of corn and grass and stately grey churches in large sympathy with the sky, Picardy, where catholicism still seems a thing of the soil, the earth itself, so to speak, still naturally green with it. It was not for the Pope certainly: he disavows it, with many another false or ambiguous volunteer in his service; nor for the king, though satirically challenged to assume its headship—of the *Sainte Union*—if a true son of the church he be; nor for the clergy, whose fanaticism it is ready to betray; nor for Christ, nor, as it pretends, for the poor whom He loved, "the impoverished French people"; "the poor of France!"—nor for France, which it is as ready to sell to Spain as the Huguenot to dismember, nor even for any section of it, nor in the proper sense for any political interest at all, but simply bent on taking advantage of all men's religious or other enthusiasm by the way, the unscrupulous conspiracy of a family, a family with a nest of murderous enmities within its own bosom, something of the unnatural tragic horror of some old Greek play. With that unerring relentlessness, for once, which fiction supposes in the "secret society," as such, it spreads from Picardy to Normandy to Champagne, from North to South, into the streets of Paris, closes gradually and therefore all the more firmly, locks itself together, round the court, the throne, the person of the king, from whose light head it would pluck the crown, has its Judith, or [Jael], or [Jehu], in the person of the Duchesse de Montpensier, the *soeur furieuse* of Henri de Guise, ostentatiously resident in Paris. She carries at her girdle, strange heirloom, the scissors which made a tonsured monk of the *fainéant*, and shall do the like for Henry the Third.

The court, as we saw, with its sweet-lipped leader, its Queen Margot, was gracefully pedantic, classical, ready to sell anything, to sell itself for a song really old, and its enemies catch a trick so taking for the moment, in learned but not necessarily far-fetched parallels, minatory, significant, between the present and the past in ancient Rome, or say! in ancient Tyre even, or in [Babylon]. They had their theories also, in an age ambitious of metaphysic views, abstract theories, yet practical in this, that they give to vague or passing enmities or discontent that intellectual coherence, that unity of idea, by which they may appeal to the imagination. A certain old theory for instance *du gouvernement des sires du fleur de Lys*, that recommends itself to the house of Lorraine. Legitimately, France must of necessity be governed by a member of the royal family, but not necessarily by its hereditary head: and that convenient theory is reinforced by an appeal still more disquieting to recondite historic fact. Older than the House of Capet, the House of Lorraine, Henri de Guise and his natural issue are the legitimate heirs not merely of the personal rights of Charlemagne, but of the apostolic benediction upon him, the patronage of the Roman see to which, Observe! we are faithful. And the opportunity is come at last for a restoration of the crown to its legitimate owners. Nay! they represent, in a past older than Charlemagne even: Pharamond, Clodion le Chevelu. *Retourne, Chilpéric! Clovis, revéille-toi!* says the Anonymous Sonnet, chalked on the walls, the house-doors, of Paris, on the doors of the Louvre.

Le tuer ou le tondre, to slay the usurping tyrant who fails even of the conventional title to reign, or make him a monk, a capucin, with those shears of the new Judith, La duchesse de Montpensier; *lui faire suivre sa vocation*: there are genuine precedents for either course in our old French history. Pope Sixtus the Fifth, who does not think much of what the Leaguers and their like boast to be doing for *him*, asked at length *s'il serait bon d'attenter à la vie du Roi*, answers of course honestly with a decided negative. Old Jewish history, old Roman history, however, seemed to give a different answer to Huguenot and to certain new-fangled "republicans" of that early date as to the righteous treatment of Tyrants, and the end of Henry the Third might already be foreseen.

For to the classic fantasies of a court paganised under the mask of catholic zeal, to the antique, poetic or pedantic pretensions of the rival Guises, the Huguenots reading their Bible in French, oppose in their turn, like our English puritans, ardent defenders of the *Évangele*, of the New Testament, though they profess to be, certain grim reminiscences of the Old, and were terribly in earnest about them. Tyrannicide, that is to say assassination, is *duty*, surely, nay! heroic piety, in certain cases about which "armed Protestantism" may develope a Protestant casuistry. Men's thoughts were then hard at work all around on the nature and basis of royal and all other authority, on the very basis of society itself. Those fervid Hebrew reminiscences of the past meet half-way a wholly different range of thoughts which anticipate the future. *Les rois tiennant leur couronne du peuple, et peuvent le "forfaire" pour félonie envers le peuple, comme un vassal "forfait" son fief envers son seigneur.* Those forcible, metallic words are heard in a new connexion. Full-fledged republican theories of "social contract," Elective Monarchy, *la "sacro-sainte autorité de l'assemblée nationale,"*—present themselves in folios or pamphlets or audacious talk, and lend a sufficiently threatening import to the assembling of the States-general with immense popular enthusiasm at Blois, whither, already his people's prisoner, King Henry goes to preside, playing the desperate hand of Louis the Sixteenth—to preside over the debates which may end in "improving away" himself. The League itself, "for mutual protection *sans nulle acception de personnes*," had already mastered some of the revolutionary slang of 'ninety-three.

And our brother of Alençon, Anjou and the rest, *Monsieur*, our sullen younger brother!—how far may we count on the loyalty, the family sentiment of one of our own blood, our own naughty blood who, should we fail of legitimate offspring, is our natural heir, yet who sees us but a few years older than himself and wedded to maiden health fresh from the fields of [Jarnac and Moncontour]. So acutely, in fact, does he understand the advantages, the temptations of his position, that he is terribly afraid lest we be beforehand with *his* very existence and, to add to our perplexities, is for ever escaping from an affectionate home, as from a prison, to our avowed enemies in England or the Netherlands, or within the bounds of France, or at our very doors. Our mother, truly, does not fail in the blind love of a cat for her offspring, of herself, but is failing in whatever dubious political craft may once have been hers, her old tricks which no longer deceive, is anxious still, however, to manage for us, to occupy us with delightful aesthetic fatuities, that all the serious things of life may be left to her, and has blundered badly more than once of late. Our version, then, of Elagabalus in the North is not an unmixed success. Of the personal gifts appropriate to that part we are undoubtedly possessed, but circumstance, the accidents we cannot compel, go for more than half in the production of such magnetic effects as that wonderful progress from Syria to Rome, or the brilliancy of our own youth. We are Christians, after all, of a sort, not pagans, very craven ones indeed, hampered at every move, at least by the susceptibilities of others, and in a Northern latitude every thing moves slowly, while rapidity of the action in passion was, as may be perceived, an essential in the success of the piece which that blood-stained, flowery young Roman emperor played out to its end in three years. The mistake of prolonging such a piece beyond the natural life of its floral decorations is nothing less than ruinous. *Dès lors*, says the historian, *le roi était comme seul*. To whom shall we turn?

Well! With Louise at one's side, *princesse si belle et bien formée*, still, of course, to the hope of offspring of our own. A cry, a wail, poignant as that of biblical Leah, or Rachel, goes up from every church in France, that *Le Roi pourroit tost avoir belle et abandante lignée*, and gives a kind of shrill, startling, sharply expressed outward accent to Gaston's silent preoccupation with the fate of his own lost child, to his increasing desire, as the years increase, that he might feel less alone, while those haunting voices of the children, grown now to youth, come to him too reproachfully to be borne, out of some dim background of the world immediately about him, with its manifold outrages on human kindness. King and Consort proceed once more to the sanctuary of his youth, to the church of Chartres, to the feet of Our Lady Under the Earth, as to the hem of her veritable garment there, take away with them the copy of it to be worn by themselves in faith.

But in vain! Ostentatiously, in late Lent after a too prolonged carnival, *Leurs Majestés* visit in turn every church in Paris, to hear Mass with a special "intention" that male offspring may be given them as they so greatly desire—the male line which may succeed to the crown of France. Henry dedicates a new or fresh piece of The True Cross replacing an older relic stolen lately from La Sainte-Chapelle, the chapel of Our "Palace," fallen doubtless into miserable Italian keeping, to the great consternation of Parisians, always devout at least up to that level. Hypocrite! think his people as they see him pass in somewhat abject devotion, along the foul streets, muttering prayers as best he can amid a pressing crowd of sordid "penitents." Still, there really are complexities of human temper at times a little beyond the *people*. True! Meantime, observes the chronicler, not withstanding all its miseries, they manage to be gay in Paris, to dance and laugh, he says; amorously of course, to put the last refinements upon the low octave of colour then prevailing, *couleurs de sacristie* almost, art's latest triumph surely, in bringing by a subtle economy out of so little, effects so rich. A banquet in one colour, or a combat by torch-light of *quatorze blancs contra quatorze jaunes*, in the courtyard of the Louvre. If those comedians we have ordered from *Venise* would but come to teach us what little remains to be learned of the full meaning of life!—Brown satin, grey silk enriched with black velvet, set up with rich dark fancy stones and heavy unbleached lace! What a flutter of expectation along the double row of courtiers when [Henry] enters the presence chamber in that new toilet, contrasting, the white aristocratic pâté of his face, while the silent unheeding monarch, "the tyrant," cons—a Latin grammar! *qui sembloit*, says [L'Estoile], *presager la déclinaison de son Etat*, is actually learning anew to decline, keeps all the world waiting for that. And had not that other delightful young decadent Byzantine emperor, kept the grey-beard ministers waiting, while he fed his favourite pigeons, studied their dietetic whims, their markings, their dainty tumbles over the jasper floor, an achievement of nature, a spectacle for infinite power, infinite leisure, worth surely all protocols, movement of armies and the like; all the world beside. For contrast, *pour rehausser* the effect of all that, across those dim *couleurs de sacristie*, as if revealed by sudden lantern flash amid shadows, the uniforms, crude, truculent, barbaric, of the Swiss guards who serve us, a regiment of mercenary guards already in attendance, again like a presage of 'ninety-three, against revolutionary outrage on our sacred person. Nay! our aesthetic doings shall have a purpose beyond any merely momentary satisfaction. Pentecost, that day we have always piously observed as so conspicuously our day of good-fortunes, shall be further honoured by a new order of knighthood, a band of young men tall and "proper," dear to our heart, and devoted to us, who may defend us—*ces épées dorées*—in the undisguised hand-to-hand battle in one's very chamber, to which we seem to be coming, among these rambling stairs and narrow passages of our hôtel, or prison, de Saint Paul. The insignia and apparel of the Order, its copes, with [altar and desks] you might still see not long since in the *Musée des Souverains de France*, along with the [silver baptismal font] of St. Louis and [Charlemagne's prayer-book] and [the armour in which Henry II died].

Fear, wild sudden fear, the chief performer stricken by it:—that is of course a distinctly appropriate effect in such a scene of tragi-comedy, the sort of effect to which orchestra and spectators gradually attune themselves. As if angry heaven itself in the form of a beggar forced its way in to threaten, through the serried guards, amid all the morbid luxuries of this bankrupt court, comes the bold remonstrance of a single just man here or there, representing the wretched condition of "the poor," that is to say of the people of France. *Pour dix qui vivent grassement ici il y en a dix mille qui ont disette.* In still less considerate form, the same reproach penetrates to the royal cabinet as anonymous printed matter, pasquinades in French or Latin, that irrepress-ible *liberté Françoise de parler* now chatting through a press whose agency is already everywhere. Outside, the learned and curious were already collecting the handbills, tracts, sheets for posting all over Paris, very popular in intention though often quaintly learned in the form or even in the very language in which they were written:—*Le Réveille-matin*, journal of the Huguenots who could cut as sharply with the pen as with the sword, says L'Estoile, who has soiled many of his pages with such lying or truthful satire of the day—silly acrostics which repack the letters of the royal name, *La Vie de la Royne-Mère qu'on appelle vulgairement La Vie de Sainte Catherine.* She herself read and laughed at, could have done it better, added something to it. *Rithmes parlant des roines Frédégondes, Brunehilde, Jézébel.*—*Des bruits de Paris c'est-à-dire menteries*, yet they pass from hand to hand, things erewhile people would not have dared to whisper, printed now. And about this time, *exhumée pour ainsi dire du tombeau de son auteur,* Le Discours de la Servitude Volontaire, that terrible declaration de La Boétie against royalty, is published for the first time.—A circle of hissing tongues all about, round the court and its gaieties, with fangs of set steel below.

The reader remembers perhaps the sad case of the traveller who must needs die or sleep for an hour as he traverses a desolate forest. The place abounds in ants, terrible red ants. But he gathers the brush wood carefully together in a great circle on a clear space, and lights a great fire all round him to keep the insects away. Then he lies down to sleep in the midst, but wakes with the hissing of a circle of venomous serpents all round his blazing ring, only waiting till the fire burns itself out.

Strange! It is this conscious or unconscious imitator of faineant old Roman or Byzantine emperor-deities, who becomes "majesty" for the first time in France, half in personal vanity, half in fear, shrouds himself to be adored, changes the old easy accessibility of a French monarch into a curious system of etiquette through which it is difficult for ordinary people to penetrate. The people of Paris, the poor, have their suspicions, and with more or less shrewdness put their own disloyal construction on the studied mystery of their master's life, disseminate their rumours. He makes a shadow where he goes artfully. Great is gossip; and the mysterious, even if it be not the mystery of hidden crime, secures its full further advantage to gossip. Meantime the rival Henry, Henri de Guise, now veritable *Roi de Paris*, comes hither on his selfish business, leader of that solemn league and covenant, yet with florid abundant face and hair, like the sun; and, as if he made the flowers they threw about him to grow there, playing his part with a delightful ease and a kind of jovial natural royalty over common people. Parisians always sympathetic, ever at home straightway with a cheerful countenance, like him none the less for that manly or brutal scar across the check. That it repeats oddly the accident of his father's youth, who had been *Le Balafré* before him, doubles the prestige of the thing. It is like a sign impressed by heaven—or hell. They credit him, as people will sometimes credit creatures only a very little stronger than themselves, with almost diabolical personal force.—Is it powder of gold, or of steel, that he takes in his meat?—*Bon Prince!* Meantime the flowers are rained gently upon him. He is well-nigh stifled with the close pressure of affection. The simple rubbed their chapelets *contre lui pour les sanctifier.*

I have dwelt thus at length on what was visible in Paris just then, on the mere historic scene there, forgetful it might seem of the company of Gaston, but only because I do suppose him thoughtfully looking on with us, all the while, as essentially a creature of the eye, even more likely than others to be shaped by the things he sees. With a look, a manner, a manner of speaking also, which infallibly win royal kindness, he penetrates that awful reserve, does but feel at rest, a certain repose of temper, amid the dainty selections and adjustments which prevail amid these last pale lustres of the court of the Valois, awed sometimes by its deeper shadows, its darkness, wistful, curious, but himself certainly uncontaminate as if invisibly shielded, and always with great pity, a great indulgence. *J'ay une merveilleuse lâcheté,* says his tutor, Michel de Montaigne (might have said for him), *vers la miséricorde et mansuétude.*

There are certain half-domestic animals which draw very near to men's lives, their firesides, only to be the objects of their hatred; the last of the Valois set Gaston thinking of them. The tyrant—*le tyran aux abois*; it was like one of these animals, and he pitied it as one must pity the very rat which sheds tears at last, they say who know it best. And then, according to his habit, he looked back and saw in thought his contemporary, the hopeful lad, eloquent and brave, "*spirituel,*" in this man whose name was to be infamous: and that he could do so without effort was a proof, surely, of surviving moral capacity, as if some discerning artist, from the malignant caricatures which remain as the veritable likeness of so personable a monarch, were to put together for himself such a portrait of Henry the Third, as happens to have been preserved, in a certain old picture gallery not far from Venice: winsome lad there! *puer ingenui vultus ingenuique pudoris*. You had but to look closely, kindly, even now, and there were redeeming touches amid the ruin to which he was actually come.

To the disciple of Montaigne, his doctrine of the "ondoyancy" of the world, it came naturally of course to note the unexpected taking place in us, after all reassuringly, to the discredit of many an obvious forecast about men's souls, those surprises which Montaigne had taught him to prize in man as in nature, the mixture of motives, the afterthoughts, the repentances, saving inconsistencies, returns upon one's self, of the conscience of right; dews of paradise, call them in fact, penetrating even to hell, which leave seemingly damned souls at the worst but dubious ones after all. The devil, the [*savant chimiste*], says [Baudelaire], is [the alchemist of boredom], and as such an *ennuyant* because a really inexpressive character; and for one's own sake as a mere spectator who claims at least to be interested, we are anxious to find those saving inconsistencies in evil, which reassure us as with a hopeful indication of latent redeeming forces still at work here or there below the surface, very deep it may be, to regenerate after all in ways beyond our limited power of calculation. It brought him, then, a flattering sense of his philosophic capacity, that he could note without prejudice the self-denying assiduities of royalty about a childish death-bed at this time. It was pitiful enough, indeed, to think of what became of some other children, stricken, forced to suffer in their earliest days, so large a part of the penalty of the political offences or mere unsuccess of their fathers, the young children of Coligni, or Gabriel Montgomery. Little Madame Elizabeth, the daughter of [Charles IX], she at least, for one, felt what sweetness there was in Henry's kindness. The courtly array about her bed of suffering had for once its justification in pleasing distracting a sick child. The little princess—with perhaps mistaken scruples they tried to make her understand she was dying, but didn't succeed. Though she admitted in truth her inability to say her long prayer, said her short one, and then died, *pleurée et regrettée, à cause de son gentil esprit et de sa bonté et douceur*. The white queen, mother of the tiny princess, soon after departed finally alone to her old German home. That was like another child's funeral, with universal regret for a train of such white deaths, so to call them, of women and children, amid red ones. Ah! how people wept in that Paris which meant to have sold itself for the minor graces of life. And here was the other queen, praying, full of contending terrors, that the king her husband may repudiate her, and the like. Ah! Pity of Heaven, of [Notre-Dame de Cléry], of [Notre-Dame de] Chartres, *Me donnez masle lignée!*

There was one artist in France to whom, though he knew how to be a courtier, a sort of primitive greatness, something of the proper and the natural dignity of art and life, had still remained in the midst of that world of self-satisfied decadence in both. Let him give us, ere we part from it, a glimpse of those persistent moral forces in things, such as he afforded from time to time, with an effect of ironic contrast to the age of Henry the Third, and without which no picture of that age can be complete. Jean Cousin, a sort of Michelangelo in France, has an imagination like his occupied not by the low-pulsed middle-period, so to call it, of his own day, but with its energetic origins and issues of human life, the Creation of Adam and Eve, Eva Pandora, the Last Judgment: the naked realities, so to speak, of human destiny, displayed in a world which had come to find dress the most important thing in life, and draped sculpture more significant than the nude. Here indeed, under a certain Italian influence, all the little things of existence were become marvellously refined, but with a refinement, however, which was in truth but the garment's hem, the outermost aura of the great art of Italy itself, and it was to this that the soul of Cousin had reverted, or rather perhaps to the old Gothic vigour of his native France itself. For he had in fact a predilection not explained by the mere conditions of demand and supply at that moment, for work in that conspicuously medieval and French manufacture of painting on glass, though he refined immeasurably at every point in the process upon all earlier achievements in it. While he knows more than all the old secrets of its [embroidered draperies] and ruby and gold, he can also draw with the truth and largeness of a master, though still with an eye to the particular destination of his drawing. He can also think profoundly, and has, again like Michelangelo, and in sympathy with the finer spirit of that age generally, his dreams of old Roman greatness, like that from the realisation of which his hand has just now rested. To-day, then, King and court, with whom, unfitted though they are for more than a superficial understanding of his aims, the aged master nevertheless has his credit, proceed in gay summer weather fitted for the excursion to the old chapel of the castle in the forest of Vincennes, to gaze on his latest achievement there in the colours they love. The new window gleams out amid the shadows of the old gothic chapel, a marvel of many-coloured gold, clear as crystal, like in the Apocalyptic vision itself, and they listen readily while the aged painter deferentially, with ironic deference is it? explains the subject ("I can always leave off talking when I hear a master play!") concerning which, though like veritable connoisseurs they profess an almost exclusive care for form and handling in art, they are straightway curious.—What the splendid figure with crown and sceptre is doing:—A fine subject in fact, perhaps the greatest art can deal with, though certainly not yet worn-out by artists: the Sibyl, summing up all [modes of thought and life]: Augustus [kneeling at her feet]: the Mother and the Child, all the pathos of human flesh which the eternal Son has now wrapt about himself. Aye! a Gospel subject, the speaker asserts to the ignorant questions with which, with rapturous comments on the [Madonna], they begin presently to distract Cousin's further speech, who seems, indeed, [like a ghostly cricket]. For their master, being visibly put out [by God's favor to] Augustus, was supposed to have merited [a male heir himself. Henry's unavailing quest for progeny] is one horn of the royal dilemma, and the light [of that visionary company, the heavenly court,] glares actually on the other, the opposite form of it, with the effect of an unkindly, ironic contrast, like a blow in the face, as from the lightning-flash, the thunder-clap which suddenly darkens the place on the June evening, at which modern royalty, in a wicked rage, pulls out a rattling rosary and begins to patter to itself, with the mien of a veritable coward: a model of such as the artist perhaps took note for professional use.

CHAPTER XII

A Wedding

(for motto, an epitaph)

To crown the lad's good fortune, a husband of the Queen's lineage has been found for Jasmin's pretty but penniless sister; and glad for once to find himself *in loco parentis*, he was astir almost with the first light of the flighty March morning, to prepare himself for the duty of giving away the bride. With thoughts almost insanely preoccupied by the marriage relation, and making pleasure as the serious business of life, Henry, and those who led or were led by him, always made the most of weddings and contrived to spend a long time upon them. The significance of this day now actually come at last, bringing that final, sacred distinction to him and his, flushes Jasmin's face suddenly as he wakes from his perfectly dreamless sleep of youth, collects his thoughts in a moment, springs from the bed, and looks forth, anxious first of all concerning the weather. While he slept, the world visible from his window had arrayed itself in virgin white. The grey spires of Saint-Germain-des-Prés had lodged the crisp snow-flakes on their way along the north-east wind blowing steadily since nightfall, and stood there more monastically chaste than ever, panelled and picked out afresh on that side, he could have fancied, with snow-white Italian marble.

The silver, and white linen, the purple and white flowers, of the wedding table, are scarcely less virginal, set there ready for the royal and other guests in the long low chamber of the Palais des Thermes, the *Hôtel* which the Abbot of Cluny had inserted so daintily amid the smoke-black hollows of the haunted old Roman bath of the Emperor Julian. Should the reader visit the place, he is recommended to acquaint himself with its fantastic change of fortunes. The Abbot left [   ] who, by royal favour, will keep house there for awhile rent-free. Bride and bridegroom, the aged cardinal [Pierre de Gondi] who officiates [   ] waited long for Jasmin in the [Flamboyant] Gothic chapel, made shift at last to perform the due ceremonies in his absence, with an uncomfortable sense of incompleteness in the rite, though royalty, as such paternal over all its subjects, good-naturedly takes upon itself the duty of giving away the bride, a genuine country lass, and here like a caged bird too much fluttered to be quite aware what is doing with her. As they pass from the restraint of the sacred place, a babble of wonderment ensues. But for his duty towards the bride, pale now as the snowdrops, half-fainting at the breakfast table with fatigue and fear, the king himself would have gone to seek him in his lodgings. Refusing meanwhile to take his place, he sends instead two pages, two wedding posies of silken flowers detached from his very person. Let loose from "the presence" into the reviving air, they fly over the crisp snow, the buckram of their court dress yielding this way and that to natural boyish movement within it, with a gracefully comic air of ruffled feathers, making those who watch them from the window laugh even now, as they run more speedily than would have been credited, though on tip-toe and glancing suspiciously at their satin shoes.

Jasmin, as we know, had not forgotten his duty, was not likely to forget of that kind, had been full of it over-night and, up betimes, could hardly occupy the interval by the most leisurely of toilets, pausing now and then to examine the pictures from his old nursery on the wall, himself at six years old as [   ]. Handling his mirror very carefully not to break it ominously at such a moment, he compares the infant face with his own, and just then a red dash across it of foggy sun-light makes him think, with a little laugh, of that evening not so long ago when he "had met himself."

Even the toilet of a Parisian in the reign of Henry the Third does not last for ever. The beautiful male dress of the day is complete, the head stiff in the collar starched heavily with rice. There was no more to be done, and just then the lad feels aware of an empty stomach and summons his valet, who serves him with a little delicate bread and wine, himself tasting the latter first *pour faire l'essai*, as is done always in these treacherous days with persons of importance. At last, then, he descends the stairs, himself looks forth from the door along into the street for the chair which is to carry him to the wedding, not due to come, however, for half an hour yet, as he notes by the much-prized watch at his [   ]; which stopped, half-crushed in his hand, a few minutes later, marking at least for others the critical point of his little destiny. The snow on the ground is still freezing. Impatient at the delay, he will try his foot upon the untouched, crisp particles in the delicious, frosty, virgin air. Like an opal, a mass of opals, his white satin holds its own, is not shamed even face to face with the virgin snow, flashes, rather, against the level morning sunlight upon the hard white road-way.

With a kind of ultimate indifference on both sides, how pleasant could Margaret, Queen Margot, be to those whom the fortune of the hour brought her. Only, if her heart moved at eye or hand, if that malediction of her love, entered into the [   ], it was equally fatal to slave or rebel, to La Mole as he lifted [his shattered arm], to Jasmin now, in his twenty-ninth year, as he sets forth, in profound peace with himself and all things, self-centered, free from any embarrassing lien on any person besides, devoted, if to any one, to the King, who has used him so kindly. . . .

CHAPTER XIII

Mi–carême

"He shall drink of the brook in the way."

The foreground of life, its sins, its beauty and sorrow, the spectacular contrasts of the incidents, the actors from which one could not take one's eyes:—the reader, it is hoped, can still see Gaston through the admiration and distress, the perplexity also, excited in him as he gazes thereon, so absorbed, preoccupied in truth with its immediate effects that he finds but scant occasion for noting what at some other time might have been discernible by him in a more or less remote background, where, it must be said, the religion of his youth is now little more than a vanishing point. Its old formalities recurring to his mind, now and again, he admitted to himself, with mixed feelings, that in all probability he must have long since ceased to be in what he had been taught to identify as "a state of grace," while that little Prayer for Peace from the Roman Vespers had departed from his lips.

The misgivings which, in a nature such as his, survive of course positive belief, were apt also to accumulate upon him in the darkness, following naturally whereon mere physical daylight in its turn would dissipate them altogether for a while; and it was on a spring morning that, having left his bed earlier than was now his habit, Gaston paced the streets of Paris, to air a haunted fancy, so to speak, himself after a few moments' exercise, all alive to the early freshness and very glad, might one say *grateful?* as he crosses from side to side to walk continuously in the sun, Yes! *grateful*, to be thus alive.

There were no signs, however, of early or late rising in the spot to which, after a while, this cheerful circuit brought him, though in one sense the most populous in Paris, the old Cemetery of the Innocents, with its *milliers sur milliers de cadavres*, over which the yellow light was winning its way kindly, the lowliest graves then casting long shadows.—They haunted him everywhere still, those Innocents, the young children slain or lost: who in irony, surely, had lent their name to this most aged place, with its defiant, unashamed presentment, of mortality by day, of the misdeeds of the living by night, the thieves, the courtesans who haunted this place of ill fame, sheltered by its horrors, or relishing the better the dregs of sin amid the coarse or crude associations of death, the grave-diggers' careless ways, the odours, the corrupt colours—*sur cette terre pestiférée du grande cimetière des Innocents, la nuit, erraient des filles, logeaient prés des charniers, et faisaient l'amour sur les tombes.* La belle Huissière, at least, had found a permanent lodging at last; Gaston read her epitaph on the weathered stone.—

> *Ce fut le plus grand jour d'esté*
> *Que trepassa la belle Huissière—*
> *Or donques, Messieurs, qui avez,*
> *Vivans, caressé cette Dame,*
> *Dites au Ciel ce que sçavez,*
> *Pour le salut de sa pauvre âme.*

Let the reader think of what he may have seen of ancient historic grave-yards, of [Vysehrad at] Prague, the Alyscamps at Arles, St. Pancras, if he likes, as Gaston walks there amid [the tombs], with the increasing heat of the sunshine upon his pathway, upon himself, but thrust all that back, deep into the grotesque gloom of the middle age. Ah! they needed long changing there, those old soiled bodies in the dark, through these endless, unnoted mornings, and the [heavenly] ones long in making; though the earth for her part seemed anxious to give up its ragged dead already, or at least to be but a careless keeper of the bones, having made its natural use of the body's juices. As if mistaking the jubilant sunshine of this first summer day for the resurrection morning, the occupant of a nameless old stone coffin had tumbled forth. Hanging luxuriantly in the irregularities of the wasted mouldered grey walls, an immense *aubépine* of immemorial age flowered above it, filling its hollows with nests of fiery crimson; had flowered, as if with a second youth of late years, miraculously, it had seemed to the crowds who had come to visit it, being *arrosée, rajeunie, fortifiée*, drinking strength to blossom anew from the blood of the heretic it had come by, after the carnage of Saint Bartholomew. The industrious L'Estoile has chronicled the fact, and surmise:

[*Le lendemain de Saint-Barthelemy, environ midy, on vid un aubespin fleury au cimetière Saint-Innocent. Si-tost que le bruit en fut espandu par la ville, le peuple de Paris y accourust de toutes partz: on commença aussy à crier miracle et parce qu'il y avoit tout plein de catoliques qui interprétoyent le reverdissement de l'aubespin pour le reverdissement de l'estat de France, un meschant huguenot caché, composa la épigramme suyvantz:*

Hinc, quàm faecundus sit cruor iste, nota!

Qui, reliquis herbis rabido morientibus aestu,

Germinat, et caelo semina digna movet.]

Left to itself, the churchyard earth abounded with veritable field-flowers of the more acrid coarser kinds, with a sort of savage abundance of pollen flung around about them. As if for a parable, it sent up sparkling water too from the very midst of its defilements. And was it also by way of parable that Jean Goujon in his turn had designed this graceful fountain to utilise it for the thirsty, or to quench the *bénitiers*, little holy water fonts at the graves?—with just those particular imageries of youth and vigour, the nymphs you may still see amid their native reeds and water-lilies at [the Louvre]. In the low-rippling lines of the low white marble reliefs, they seem to be in motion with the water amid which they are yet so firmly, carnally, embodied. Perhaps Jean Goujon only meant to cheer the gloom of the place with these graceful creatures, though he had but emphasised it by passing contrast—what Adam of Brescia says:

[*Chè l'immagine lor vie più m'asciuga*
Che il male ond'io nel volto mi discarno.]

Reading the epitaphs, as he steps casually, even then for the most part formal or trivial, but with here and there a veritable cry of distress of the dead for the dead, he too comes presently as if by accident to "the brook in the way":

[*Ed ecco più andar mi tolse un rio,*
Che in ver sinistra con sue picciol'onde
Piegava l'erba che in sua ripa uscìo.]

—finds it, feels those drops of water welcome in this Inferno, or Purgatorio, say, of Paris, in the sounds, the lights, which enfold him, take possession of him as he enters a certain church door at the road-side, one of those later Gothic flowery churches which then enriched Paris, and in which the last dainty arts, fittest it might seem for [courtly festivites], spent themselves on divine service. The well-informed visitor to Paris will remember, perhaps, St[-Gervais], St[-Étienne], St. Médard, and take a hint from them, their dainty morsels of stained glass, the *jubé*, of the genius of that refined place, in which Gaston, for a moment, becomes once more the creature of the influences of his consecrated boyhood. Its builder was very happy, or very acute, for while it adapted as if under mere awkward necessity to the lines of the adjoining streets, its very enforced irregularities were full of expression. No soul of man, or thing, or place, nothing is ever like another, it seemed to say, be as formal as you will. An acute artist might have conceived just such a curious system of proportions as he was here committed to, for their own sake, or welcomed the site which enforced them on him. The more careful gaze seemed to find some special fineness of self-recollection in the lines of *jubé* and arch, as if the wayward free fancies of the builder had been effectually called upon to recollect themselves here,—where they were and what they were doing. And it had this effect, it gave what, for the mere formal style of the place, would otherwise have been but one sanctuary among many others not unlike it, a cachet of its own, and as regards the soul of Gaston, here to-day, the *peculiarity* which won him. Crowded for foot-hold, on the odd irregular space among the streets around, it went, as if one-sidedly, as best it might, but with markedly united determination, all the higher into the air above them. The light fell placidly on the remote, high stone spaces: and the windows, they were like the natural brightness of a fine day. It was like religion, like the catholic church, subduing, tempering itself with indulgence, the infinite patience of an infinite superiority, to the wayward or petulant soul.

The people of Paris, says Mérimée, were at that day *horriblement fanatique*: its pulpits rang just then with fanatical leaguist sermons: but the movement, however, which makes fanatics of the coarse, lighting on finer souls produces there its finish of religion, its finer flowers: and that age had its revival of ritualism also, as we should call it: its curés who were miracles of personal devotion; its churches where worship was more select, careful than elsewhere; its revival of [liturgy] with a more correct consideration than had prevailed of late for sacred seasons, points of ritual, above all with a great development of such church music as lifted the age of [Palestrina]. The ritualistic Gaston, then, is reminded by the rose-purple, the "flowers of pensive hope," a certain reserved gaiety breaking through the Lenten severity, that it is the season of *mi-carême*, [Laetare] Sunday, with its thoughts of manna in the wilderness, of the miraculous feeding of the fainting multitudes, and yields himself, as he could do more readily than most men, to its suggestions—this lover of pensive places, of the sanctuary especially, where humanity lays aside its vulgarity for a while—at least looks its best for a while—and if one addresses you, it is proper to reply, hush!—lingers, reaches irresistibly to look, to listen. *Respiremus*—let us take breath a little, recover our strength, pleads the collect. The door closes on the world behind him, but it is like coming into the open air, like leaving a mad-house: not he alone had thought of the people who gave it its colour, its character, as a sort of *aveuglés* or madmen, desperate, of himself as infected perhaps with their misfortune. Well! the ritual of to-day was full not of miraculous feeding only, but of the cure of the sick and the insane, of demons cast out. The Epistle, still on that peculiar line of thought, explained how Abraham had two sons—*unum de ancilla, et unum de libera,* and how he that was born after the flesh persecuted [him that was born after the Spirit.] And as he thus lingered, seated himself, at least to gaze as an outsider might, for half an hour, on what the accident of his morning's walk had thus presented as if generously for his refreshment, his thought takes its way back stade upon stade, the [grand passions], the [world so importunately visible], the [great ecclesiastical seasons], to descend and rest at last in the midst of his consecrated boyhood, when thoughts such as these had come so naturally to him. Decorated or soiled, as he is with, well! the vanities, that can hardly belong to a beautiful and venerable place like this, he seems to see that other world with the place he has but deserted for a time still kept for him there; as one predestined from eternity in spite of all to sit there among the elect. The Gospel for the Mass proper for the day tells of the lad and the provision he had made or induced others to make for his carnal refreshment: lifted now to so wondrous use, a service so unparalleled. A carefully sensuous boy, surely, with his loaves and fishes, yet with a hunger for eternal things which had brought him so far. What had become of him? and of this strange privilege of his early life? Had it remained as the hour of the redemption of his body and soul, or only as an almost incredible incident of a dreamy boyhood, as he looked upon which, and the sentiment it recalled, he could but exclaim: "My wickednesses are gone over my head!"

But the Mass proper to the day completed, a less graciously [cheerful] office begins. In a little while, the place transforms itself, under the hands of diligent sacristans, into a house of emphatic earthly mourning, crudely black and white, and from the depths of the great brazen *serpents* groan the first notes of the funeral psalm, the funeral service of a not undistinguished military officer, as the great white satin scutcheons, spread amply on the velvet pall, indicate. A little band of the soldiers of his regiment are on duty in their uniforms, form the guard of honour around the heavy coffin, and at its foot, braced stiffly also in fresh boyish uniform, stands the son of the deceased, a lad of sixteen years perhaps, of modest yet manful bearing, such as those haunting nestlings to Gaston's fancy were now well-nigh grown to be, almost, as we know, to his bodily ear. Yes! verily it might seem; with palpable accent to his bodily ear to-day.—Why, by what ill-timed disfavour, had he roved hither this morning to be moved uselessly by another's distress; for as they lift the coffin at last awkwardly, the Mass for the Dead being now over, with a cruel hollow grating over the stones, the lad (that young Frenchman!) who had kept his footing there so manfully throughout, lost all on a sudden his forced composure, doubled himself and, his face on his sleeve, literally lifted up his voice and wept aloud.

The cry of another's grief, after all of a very youthful grief, which ere the day was to be over might in all likelihood be superseded by other thoughts comfortable enough, did but leave Gaston all the readier to follow his route further from home, as he had designed to do in fulfilment of a certain old promise to visit a friend, far beyond the gloomy boundaries of Paris, to Fontainebleau, then a favourite place of retirement of the court. He meant to leave Paris altogether soon, its close streets, its colours of decay, its sin, its nightmares, and even this temporary escape from it into the "peaceful sanctuary of his youth" was irresistibly reassuring, as the wheels passed lightly over the roads southeastwards. Even the suburban streets, as he drove away at that fresh early hour, seemed already to anticipate the country, be full of pleasant country thoughts; a scent of watering was in the air: more and more as the prospect widens, the peace, the gaiety of the country reigns sole in his thoughts. The very work-people, the toiling travellers on foot, the very beggars, in a series of [homely] vignettes, seemed graceful, blond, well-clad, light-footed. The acacias along the road lifted their bouquets of tender verdure as high as they could into the late April sun, below them the *étroits sentiers*, between the vines, would take one deeper into the country-side—vines, the winding village streets of [Vitry,] of [Choisy] all but hived in them. The finger of the fresh morning breeze was restless everywhere through the dazzling symphony in white and green. Still recording the notes in it more directly congruous with his own leading sentiments, he notes a young man resting that the boy he accompanies may rest in the rare shade: they seem as *gaie* and *babillard* as the young birds, yet, as he thinks, resemble himself. As he comes towards the end of his journey, he notes the thing again for a moment as he passes, in the garden now of a *riant* miniature Italian villa beyond the gilt trellis ironwork, with its [wreaths of flames or flowers]: there they stand, blond, matutinal, making an idyll of the carefully kept garden beds and grass, the pathways of fine sand. And over this *gentil*, friendly *campagne*, the forest at last with its grey rocks, its immemorial oaks and beeches of Pharamond and St. Louis, spread, *moutonnés*, over gentle hill and vale under universal shadowless sunlight, till the golden green stood triumphant upon the large noonday blue.

Towards evening would he care to visit, asks his hospitable friend, a rare place of which he holds the key: *le cabinet des peintures du roi*—of laughing Francis I. The works of [Raphael], and [Titian], and [Michelangelo], above all of the great Milanese master Léonard de Vinci hang just as he had left them, by the orders of Francis the First. It was a favourable hour for seeing them, this slanting afternoon light.

The expansion of the animal spirits in Gaston, as he passed to-day, through the light and air of his route to Fontainebleau, this white place, was like a physical parallel to the mental relief, to a certain larger and richer genial sense of things, of which this creature of the eye now became aware in himself, yielding straightway to the influence of what he saw on the walls around him. He surrendered his taste to the genial spell of Italian art, the power of Leonardo and [Michelangelo], and their peculiar reading of life. The Renaissance of Italy transferred to France, in a hundred minor ["effects"] coloring life, had, in fact, as all that is really growing will do, conformed itself to the soil [of France], allying itself to, and was become the minister of what reigned already in men's hearts or fancies there, the barren, the unkindly love, which centered in Margaret's [erotic pride], in the [boyish Raoul] broken on the wheel in the Palace de Grève. How potent had been the spell over Gaston's [fancy]. Looking to-day from the derivative to the source, or to the rock whence it was hewn, he found amid a development of form and colour and poetic suggestion, so much richer than this Northern one, a larger heart also, the genius not of an unkindly—as we call barren earth unkindly—but of a kindly love, a manifestation of nature and man, as if under the genial light of God's immediate presence. The reader may estimate for himself the significance of this discovery for one to whom art, and the sensible preferences of art, had become the substitute for conscience, dislocated or dissipated by the negative philosophy of ["indifference"]; what a force it had in the future [experiences of Gaston], colouring so to speak of his spirit: it gave a coherency to the growing suggestions of Gaston's own mind and purpose. His visit to this place actually set him on a long series of explorations among the art-treasures of Paris itself, what there might be like it there to see, to hold converse with through the eye,—a cheering resource during the remainder of the time he stayed there—and was like the later stage of a long education. Kindness, the kindness of [Cupid] to [Psyche], forgetting

itself in the love of visible beauty, the eyes, the lips kindled to the reproduction of its like, renewing the world, handing on, as a ground of love and
kindness for ever, the beauty which had kindled it, the likeness of, or an
improvement upon, itself, kindling a like love in turn, linking paternally,
filially, age to age, the young to the old, marriage, maternity, childhood and
youth,—the kindness by which [Christ] cherishes the failing heart in [his
Apostle Peter]— consecrated by indefeasible union with the [Godhead], who
looks favourably also on the virginity, the restraint which in fact secures the
purity, the ardency therefore, of the creative flame: this was what Gaston
found in those untouched revelations of the mind of [Leonardo] and
[Michelangelo], those mature Italian masters, promoting still further that
increasing preoccupation with the greater unchangeable interests of life with
which he entered upon the coming new and later phase of his own maturer
manhood. Here art, according to its proper ministry, had been at once the
interpretation and an idealisation of life.

❦ EXPLANATORY ANNOTATION
TO THE EDITION TEXT

CHAPTER I : ANNOTATION

A Clerk in Orders

1:17   **La Beauce**   Stretching southwest of Paris nearly to Orleans, La Beauce is an unrelievedly flat but fertile wheat-growing region, including such towns as Chartres, Châteaudun, Étampes, and Pithiviers.

1:18   **family of Latour**   Apart from being a well-known sixteenth-century name in one form or another (de la Tour), Montaigne's son-in-law was François de Latour.

1:25   **irregular ground-plan**   Pater's friend, Mrs. Mark Pattison, described the château of Azay le Rideau that the Paters had visited in 1877: "It is built on two sides of a square, one side of which is prolonged somewhat and then abruptly truncated at an outward angle. This unsymmetrical ground-plan is a trace still retained of earlier days" (1:59). Regularity in plan distinguished Renaissance from medieval châteaux. Though the L-shaped Azay itself is clearly far too grand to serve as the original for Pater's imaginary structure, the germination of Deux-manoirs may well lie in Pattison's description abstracted as pattern from Azay's very different historical prominence and visual impact. Likewise, the brotherly friendship may have been inspired by Montaigne's essay, "Of Friendship," concerned with "true and perfect friendships" that rise to more than biological fraternity.

1:32   **1594**   In this year the Religious Wars wind down as Henry IV is crowned in Chartres and Paris surrenders to him.

1:32–36   **never completed . . . carefully maintained.**   This is a touch perhaps borrowed from Montaigne's essay, "Of Vanity," in which, speaking of his father's plan for "building at Montaigne where he was born," the essayist writes: "wherever I have taken in hand to strengthen some old foundations or walls, and to repair some ruinous buildings, in earnest I have done it more out of respect to his design, than my own satisfaction; and am angry at myself, that I have not proceeded further to finish the beginnings he left in his house, and so much the more, because I am very likely to be the last possessor of my race, and to give the last hand to it" (3.9:951 B,C).

3:2–3   **King Charles the Ninth**   Charles IX, King of France, ascended to the throne at the age of ten and, during his short life (1550–1574), reigned over a country sadly divided by a series of religious wars between Catholics and Huguenots; a pawn of his mother, Charles and Catherine broke the fragile but unfolding peace with the massacre of Huguenots on Saint Bartholomew's Eve.

3:3–4 church of Saint Hubert An imaginary church; according to legend, St. Hubert, Bishop of Liège (died 727), while hunting on Good Friday saw an image of the crucified Christ between the antlers of a stag. Pater may have intended some correspondence to Gaston's career in Hubert's subsequent turn from worldly life to religious service.

3:26 Saint Taurin This seems to be an imaginary saint.

4:2 Joseph's dream Genesis 37:5–8. Two of Joseph's dreams foretold a time when parents and brothers should bow in obeisance before him, which occurred when the brothers, who had sold him into Egyptian slavery, came to Egypt to buy grain; Joseph, now a high court official, recognized and forgave them.

4:4–6 Jacob . . . Esau Genesis 32:1–32. Having stolen Esau's birthright, Jacob on his flight had a vision in which God assured him of the covenant blessings; years later, Jacob wrestled with an angel and in consequence his name was changed to Israel and he was blessed.

4:6 Samuel I Samuel 2:18. As a child, Samuel lived at the tabernacle, assisting Eli in his ministrations, and became after Moses the earliest of the great Hebrew prophets and the last of the judges; he annointed both Saul and David. An ephod is an upper holy garment—plain linen worn by the ordinary Jewish priests and twisted linen embroidered with gold, blue, purple and crimson for the high priest. Pater's reference to "a dedication" (1.08:08) of Gaston is partly an echo of Samuel as boy-priest.

4:8 David Founder of a dynastic monarchy in Israel; Christ belonged to the "House of David." This and the other windows recall scenes from windows at Chartres and elsewhere, except that St. Hubert's subjects are atypically all from "old Jewish history," unlike those of Chartres that include the Nativity, Passion and Resurrection. However, all are prefigurations of Christ and the the new covenant: David, the first king of the Jews; Joseph, betrayed but forgiving; Jacob, "rescuing the promise of his race"; and Samuel, a heroic symbol of faith.

4:10 Annunciation The announcement of the Incarnation related in Luke 1:28–35 (celebrated the 25th of March); favorite subject of medieval and Renaissance artists.

4:32 little prayer "for peace" One of a number of such petitions in the *Liturgy of the Hours* (or *Breviary*); referred to again at the end of Chapter 10 and in Chapter 13 (13.128:28). One famous prayer for peace ("Lord, make me an instrument of your peace . . .") is traditionally ascribed to St. Francis of Assisi (1182–1226); another by St. Francis de Sales (1567–1622) would be slightly too late for this story. Pater's Marius has a similar personal prayer (*Marius*, 2:217).

5:2–3 the ecclesiastical calling Marius was likewise a boy–priest; the "earlier, brilliant Gaston" may be a complementary double whose history may have had a role to play in the plot, but Gaston's darker double in this calling is Elagabalus (11.1–3).

5:7–8 one half the benefices   "There were one hundred and seventeen bishoprics, fifteen archbishoprics, and countless abbeys and priories, in the gift of the Crown, and one and all were looked upon as the legitimate spoil for favourites and ladies of the court. 'All that is needed to have a benefice in France,' remarked the Venetian Contarini, 'is to be the first to ask'" (Whitehead, p. 286). Like Gaston, Pierre de Ronsard, the subject of Chapter 3, became a cleric in minor orders though never ordained a priest, having received his tonsure from a bishop related to the family (thus made eligible for benefices, if not for marriage).

5:14   Charles Guillard, Bishop of Chartres   (1514–1573); bishop during the reigns of Henry II and Charles IX (1553–1573); Pater notes Guillard's Calvinist doubts of transubstantiation and, indeed, makes him a kind of Browningesque Bishop Blougram. This explains the ironic echo of Luke 1:2 in the deleted epigraph from the following chapter (see variants, 313.14:11).

5:17   Office for the Ninth Hour   The office for the ninth hour after sunrise is called None from the Latin *nonus*, ninth (3 p.m.), often in practice recited earlier, inasmuch as it is also the derivation of "noon."

5:18   *Mirabilia testimonia tua!*   Psalm 119:129. "Thy testimonies are wonderful: therefore doth my soul keep them."

5:23   sheep astray, *ovis quae periit*   Isaiah 53:6: "All we like sheep have gone astray; we have turnd every one to his own way; and the Lord hath laid on him the iniquity of us all"; also Psalm 119:176: "I have gone astray like a lost sheep; seek thy servant; for I do not forget thy commandments."

5:36   a clerk   from Greek *kleros*, clergy or, in allusion to Deuteronomy 18:2, "inheritance": "Therefore shall they have no inheritance among their brethren: the Lord is their inheritance, as he hath said unto them."

6:1   *Adsum!*   "Here am I!" This seems an echo, translated in this fashion, of I Samuel 3:3–8.

6:6–7   "The Lord is my inheritance"   Deuteronmy 18:2; see note above for **clerk** (5:36).

6:8   five places . . . Christ's crown   after the five wounds in hands, feet, side; the crown of thorns was placed by the Roman soldiers on Christ's head to mock him (Matthew 27:29).

6:11–12   "This is the generation . . . my cup."   Psalms 24:6 and 16:5.

7:9   Religious Wars   Between 1562 (Condé's race to Orleans) and 1598 (the Edict of Nantes granting religious toleration), the crown was little more than a pawn in the hands of those nobles who sided with the Reformation (Huguenots) and those who sided with Catholicism, though certainly in the upper strata of the nobility, if not among the lesser gentry and commoners, the ultimate issue was less religious toleration than a naked power struggle for the throne prompted by the derelictions and political weakness of the Queen-mother Catherine's three sons.

7:13   *Voulez-vous donner direction?* Would you point out the route?

7:14   **mercenaries of the Duc de Guise** Possibly Pater meant the Protestant prince Condé, though if he did it would be unlikely that assistance could be expected from the Latours. Although Charles IX's forces were bolstered by Swiss auxiliaries—and Henry III employed Swiss mercenaries in Paris (whose lives Guise ostentatiously saved on the Day of the Barricades)—such German mercenaries as were typically used, called "reiters" (from the country of Martin Luther), were at the disposal of the Huguenots, not the Royalists or Catholics. L'Estoile writes of "the advance of the German mercenaries which are said to be brought into France by the Prince of Condé and other noblemen" (1:32–33, November 1574).

7:32–33   **a madman—*steeped* in blood** Charles "was addicted to the chase 'even to frenzy,' passing whole days and nights in the woods. . . . Under date 22d March, 1571, Smith writes to Burghley from Blois: 'Inordinate hunting, so early in the morning and so late at night, without sparing frost, snow, or rain, and in so despotic a manner as makes her (Catherine) and those that love him to be often in great fear.' . . . Sometimes he and his madcap associates would tear along the roads, decapitating any unlucky donkey he might encounter, or transfixing stray pigs with his hunting spear. Then, as if maddened by the sight of blood, he would dabble in their entrails like a butcher" (White, pp. 322–323). The following is a typical account of Charles given by an observer, the Venetian Sigismondo Cavalli, not long before the King died: "he tries to tire himself out, remaining on horseback twelve and fourteen hours in succession; he goes about in this way, hunting and running after the same animal, the stag, through the forests for as much as two or three days at a time, stopping only to eat and not resting a moment at night" (Coudy, p. 234). Charles' fondness for hunting is cited by nearly every commentator on his reign; for Pater, clearly a foreshadowing of St. Bartholomew's where Charles is driven forth to his "surfeit of blood." John Addington Symonds cites the princes of Anjou, among others, in his discussion of "Haematomania, Bloodmadness" in *Renaissance in Italy* (New York, 1888) 1:109, 589–591. Various episodes of bloodshed in *Marius*—the "manly amusement" of the area or the "ceremony of the dart" (Chapters 14 and 18)—may be a counterpart in the earlier novel.

8:11   **Henri de Guise** Françoise de Lorraine, duc de Guise was assassinated in 1563 at Orleans by a Huguenot spy whose unreliable confessions implicated Cologny; the duke's son Henri (1550–1588) inherited his father's titles, including ultimately his sobriquet *le Balafré*. See 11.114:15; 121:7.

8:20–21   **three sons of Catherine de Medici** Catherine was the Italian wife of Henry II and mother of the succeeding three kings of France (Francis II, Charles IX—both clearly of uncertain bodily and mental health—and Henry III, morally debilitated);

Catherine was a woman of courage, perhaps of necessity unprincipled in her attempts to shield the crown against factional hostilities; but to fill out the implications of her daughter Marguerite's picture of life at the Louvre, one could say she corrupted her sons with overindulgence and a sense of prerogative.

8:23   **softening influence**   Emilia Pattison devotes two paragraphs to this change: "Strongholds rapidly made way for *leiux de plaissance* . . ." (1:22–25). The Latour's "Château d'Amour" (2:14, 18; 6:28; 10:18) which "refined somewhat upon the rough feudal architecture" seems to draw creatively upon Pattison's perception.

8:33   **"Political" party**   As a party, the *politiques* were royalist partisans, nationalistic Catholics neither supportive of the Huguenots nor adherents of the Holy League which they considered a tool of Spain. Pierre de l'Estoile, Pater's main historical source for the reign of Henry III, was the classic *politique*.

8:37   **not a catholic historian**   Reference not traced; possibly Michelet.

9:23   **Adretz**   François de Beaumont, baron des Adrets (c. 1512–1587) was one of the Huguenot's most fierce leaders whose policy, as he revealed to the Huguenot historian D'Aubigné (2.3:7–9), was to pay back cruelty in its own coin. According to D'Aubigné, Adrets considered it an act of courtesy when he returned in wagons to their own forces 300 horsemen, each with a foot and a hand cut off (though brutal, this made sense militarily since Adrets did not have the burden of imprisoning them, nor would they effectively take up arms against him again; it also demoralized those who had to fight against him in the future). See also Brantôme (4:32–36).

9:23   **Briquemaut**   Briquemaut, François de Beauvais, seigneur de (c. 1502–1572), a Huguenot leader executed, in a patently retroactive attempt to justify the St. Bartholomew's Massacre, for allegedly plotting against the lives of the royal family (D'Aubigné, 3.5–6.1). Pater, however, confuses Briquemaut with his comrade-in-arms, Armand de Clermont, sgr. de Piles (or Pilles) who, at Saint-Jean-d'Angély, had made a necklace of priests' ears. Piles had accompanied Jeanne d'Albret to Paris and was among those in Henry of Navarre's retinue who bravely died in the Louvre early in the morning of St. Bartholomew's.

9:24   **Montgomeri**   Gabriel de Lorges, Count of Montgomery (c. 1530–1574) accidentally killed Henry II with whom he was tilting. In 1562 he joined Condé's army, and in 1574 he was captured at the surrender of Domfront. In vengeance for the death of her husband, Catherine de' Medici ordered him beheaded in the Place de Grève (1574).

9:35   **four brilliant young princes**   Henry de Bourbon, King of Navarre; King Henry of Valois; Prince Henry of Condé; and Duke Henry of Guise.

10:24   **died of joy**   Montaigne in "Of Sorrow" alludes to "the Roman lady, who died for joy to see her son safe returned from the defeat of Cannae" (1.2:14 A). In Hardy's *Two on a Tower* (1882), Vivette dies of joy, in the last scene.

10:34 **great distinguishing passion** This should be connected with the "Conclusion" to *The Renaissance* in which "high" or "great passions may give us this quickened sense of life, ecstasy and sorrow of love. . . . Only be sure it is passion—that it does yield you this fruit of a quickened, multiplied consciousness. Of such wisdom, the poetic passion, the desire of beauty, the love of art for its own sake, has most" (p. 238–239). If *Marius* was meant to be a corrective to the "thoughts suggested" (p. 233), as Pater states in the footnote explaining his reason for restoring the "Conclusion," possibly *Gaston* fulfills the same function.

12:1   **human tears falling** This is the theme of *"Sunt Lacrimae Rerum"* (Chapter 25 of *Marius*) from Virgil's *Aeneid*: "they weep here / For how the world goes, and our life that passes / Touches their hearts" (1:462).

12:12 **Innocents' Day** The Feast of the Holy Innocents is celebrated on 28 December to commemorate Herod's massacre of the children of Bethlehem (Matthew 2:16).

12:13–14 **"My soul . . . fowler!"** Psalm 124:7, with perhaps an adjustment in number from Psalm 91:3 and Proverbs 6:5.

12:23 **beauty . . . sorrow** The same combination of qualities occurs in the final four paragraphs of "The Child in the House" (*Miscellaneous Studies*, pp. 189–196), an almost Wordsworthian combination of beauty and fear, as in *The Prelude*.

12:35 **companionable soul** This is not unlike Wilhelm Meister's "communion with the Invisible Friend" in Book 6 of Goethe's *Wilhelm Meister's Apprenticeship*, though it correlates particularly with the "winged visitant" (02.21:22) and "some one . . . fluttering away from him" (10.104:16–18) in the later chapters of this novel, as well as with the "divine companion" of *Marius* (2:70–71) and with various images of the soul as a bird, both in *Marius* (1:22) and in "The Prince of Court Painters" (*Imaginary Portraits*, pp. 14–15) or "The Child in the House" (*Miscellaneous Studies*, pp. 184, 196).

CHAPTER II : ANNOTATION

Our Lady's Church

14:11   **Our Lady's Church**   The time period for this episode is between c. 1564 (assuming "about the age of twelve years" in "The Child in the House" [*Miscellaneous Studies*, p. 195] and Pater's own age of thirteen when he went to Canterbury also apply here) and the winter of 1567–1568. Notre Dame de Chartres, the fifth church on that site at Chartres, was dedicated October, 1260, to the Assumption of Our Lady, mother of Jesus (Luke 1:32–35), whose body, preserved from corruption, was taken up into heaven to be reunited with her soul.

14:18   **"Our Lady under the Earth"**   By 1024 a crypt, still the largest in France, had been completed by the bishop Fulbert, often called the Socrates of the Chartres Academy. This crypt contained a much-venerated Romanesque wooden statue (publicly burnt at the French Revolution) that, according to church records, had superseded a virginal fertility figure worshiped by the Druids, discovered with an altar on this spot. The druidic *Virgo paritura* (from c. 100 B.C.), revitalized in the worship of the "sibylline Notre-Dame" (15:30), initiates a mother/whore motif: Our Lady looks forward to the image of the Tiburtine Sibyl at the end of Chapter 11, but she has her corrupt expression also in Marguerite of Valois (Chapters 9 and 10).

14:19   *sacra camisia*   Charles the Bold, grandson of Charlemagne, presented the cathedral with its most famous relic acquired from his grandfather, the Sancta Camisia or holy chemise (now in the cathedral treasury)—a cloth believed to have been worn by Mary when she gave birth to Christ. In Chapter 11, the repeated pilgrimages to the shrine of the "*Virgo paritura*" by King Henry III and his queen, seeking an heir to the throne, are explained by this relic. L'Estoile (1:113, 23 January 1579) describes how Henry III was ridiculed for ordering Virgin-blessed T-shirts from Chartres for himself and his queen to assist their procreation.

14:22   **fragrant place**   Letter of July 1915 from Robert William Raper to Edmund Gosse (Gosse Papers, Perkins Library, Duke University): "At one of the Master of Balliol's week-end dinner-parties I sat between John Addington Symonds and Swinburne, whom he had never met; and Symonds asked me to introduce him, which I did. They talked across me, and at once plunged into an animated conversation concerning the prevailing perfumes of flowers in various pleasure resorts in Italy. Their enthusiasm for these fascinating fragrances reminded me a little of Pater, who, when asked by me if he would care to come to see our Trinity Chapel, said, 'No, but I should like to smell it if I might' (remembering the aroma of the cedar wood)."

15:6–8   **that famous frost . . . Candlemas morning**   Pater too had entered his cathedral school, at Canterbury in 1853, on Candlemas morning; and "that famous frost" is certainly a memory of his own, for *The Annual Register of 1853* (London, 1853) records the weather during his first month of school as exceedingly severe and snowy. Candlemas refers to the candles blessed at the feast celebrated 2 February in commemoration of the presentation of Christ in the temple and of the purification (from childbirth, according to the Mosaic Law) of Mary (Luke 2:22–39). The chapter's action is bracketed between this "famous frost" and "that famous winter of 1567" (23:25).

15:23   **Amiens . . . Rheims or Beauvais**   Like Ruskin, Pater preferred the early innovative Gothic, of which Chartres is a prime example, over these later more formal models. He has two rather forgettable essays (both 1894) on Amiens and Vézelay.

15:29   **mysterious maze**   Chartres' labyrinth, dating from 1200, is set into the floor of the nave in black stone. At one time, a brass plate fixed at its center depicted Theseus with Ariadne's thread and the Minotaur, allegorical figures perhaps meant to portray the path man must travel to salvation. The cathedrals of Sens, Arras, Amiens, Reims and Auxerre formerly had comparable labyrinths.

16:3–4   **corpse . . . protested**   Beyer (pp. 82–83) cites the account of this legend in Guillaume Doyen's *Histoire de la ville de Chartres, du pays chartrain et de la Beauce*, 2 vols. (Chartres: de Deshayes, 1786) 2:73.

16:23   **Saint Lubin**   The chapel of St. Lubin is under the high altar; Lubin was born in the reign of King Clovis, became Bishop of Chartres 544 and died 587. This relic and all others, save for a part of the Sancta Camisia, were destroyed during the French Revolution.

16:25   **the "Maries"**   Though some confusion attends their identities, the holy women at the sepulchre of Christ (Matt. 28:1–11; Mark 16:1–8; Luke 24:1–11; John 20:1–9) were a familiar subject of medieval art (e.g., Duccio's *Three Marys at the Tomb* on a panel from the back of his *Maestà* at the Siena Cathedral). Lucien Merlet's *Catalogue des reliques et joyaux de Notre Dame de Chartres* (Chartres, 1885) describes a "reliquaire des Maries" with earth from their tombs (Wright, p. 256).

17:1–2   **Pontifical, Missal, and Breviary**   The Pontifical contains the forms for sacraments and rites performed chiefly or wholly by a bishop; the Missal contains the words and chants for the celebration of the Mass throughout the year; the Breviary contains the daily offices or prayers for the canonical hours, the appointed times of devotion (matins with lauds, prime, terce, sext, none, vespers, and compline).

17:6   **mother of churches**   The principal or oldest church in a country or district, particularly the cathedral of a diocese; here, perhaps, not without an awareness also of its dedication to the mother of Jesus, its glass, portals and porches the palace of the Queen of Heaven.

18:5   **touch of steel** The military-religious conjunction appears in "Lacedaemon" (1892) in *Plato* and "Emerald Uthwart" (1892) in *Miscellaneous Studies*, this latter story dealing with another period of cathedral schooling and vocation (400 years later) and, therefore, a not insignificant pattern for the unfinished *Gaston*.

18:17   **Exmes** Pater leave a lacuna here in the Berg holograph, but the name can be supplied from *Macmillan's Magazine*. Its sui generis character, naming a partner in what is undeniably an erotic activity, suggests the uncommon possibility of an anagram (though probably not "sex me") or some other private connotation. Michael Levey in *The Case of Walter Pater* (London: Thames and Hudson, 1978) p. 63, associates Exmes-the-tiger with a bull-like classmate from Pater's schooldays. In "Prosper Mérimée" (1890) Pater echoes contemporary anthropological theories of animal totems; he postulates "a humanity as alien as the animals. . . . Were they so alien, after all? Where there not survivals of the old wild creatures in the gentlest, the politest of us?" (*Miscellaneous Studies*, p. 28). Chartres and Gaston's friends display a "strange mixture of beauty and evil" (20:5–6), a discord explored later in this work and one that had been prefigured in Pisa and Marius's friend Flavian in Pater's earlier novel.

18:23   **Camille Pontdormi** One of Gaston's "Triumvirate" of friends, as described at the beginning of the next chapter (3.25:37–26:2). In his poverty, Camille resembles Flavian in *Marius* (1:50); the reference somewhat later to the boys' singing sacred music with words from the streets also recalls Flavian's poetic refrain (1:99).

19:20   **Jean Sémur** There seems to be little connection between the name of Gaston's fellow clerk and Semur, now Semur-en-Auxois, near Dijon, mentioned in Pater's "Vezelay" as having a cathedral (*Miscellaneous Studies*, p. 137).

19:30   **Venus, Mars, Aeneas** Venus is the Roman goddess of beauty and sensual love; Mars the Roman god of war. Celebrated by Lucretius as a goddess of fertility, Venus is thus related to Virgil's fantasy that she was mother of Rome. In the *Iliad* and *Aeneid*, Aeneas is a Trojan prince, son of Venus and Anchises, and ancestor, according to Virgil, of Julius Caesar and Augustus. Aeneas' career of wandering and battling echoes that of Homer's hero—Aeneas' quest of the divinely appointed but unknown goal clearly also underlies Gaston's vicissitudes. Aeneas loses his wife in the confusion of warfare, as does Gaston; his dalliance with Dido is perhaps a more overt relationship than Gaston's with the Queen of Navarre; and his descent into Avernus foreshadows Gaston's "dark period" (19:5).

19:33   **Cicero** Marcus Tullius Cicero (106–43 B.C.) Roman statesman, orator, and author. Pater praises his "musical" prose and "sumptuous good taste" in "Style" (*Appreciations*, pp. 11, 36).

19:33–34 **Roman pontiffs** bishops; members of the council of priests forming the most important part of the Roman Catholic religious body. Their official language, of course, is "Choice Latin, picked phrase, Tully's every word," which Browning's dying bishop craved ("The Bishop Orders His Tomb").

19:34–35 **Propertius made love to Cynthia** Sextus Propertius (c. 50–between 15 and 2 B.C.), Roman elegiac poet who called Hostia, his mistress, Cynthia.

19:35 **Amadée** Amadée de l'Autrec, another of Gaston's "Triumvirate" of friends (see 3.25:35–37).

19:35 **Terence** Publius Terentius Afer (born between 185 and 195, died c. 159 B.C.), Roman writer of comedies noted for their moral opinions, characterization, and exquisite style.

20:28 **"living vine"** The Catholic Church as the representative of Christ restates John 15:1–6 in which Christ depicts himself as "the true vine," a passage theologically related to Christ as a "quickening spirit" (I Corinthians 15:45).

21:24 **tower of Jean de Beauce** Jean Texier (also known as de Beauce) was architect for the stone northwest tower, begun about 1506 and completed by 1513, as a replacement for the old lead-covered wooden one that had been struck by lightning and burnt. In the ornate flamboyant Gothic style, it stands beside the earlier twelfth-century southwest octagonal stone spire.

21:38 **"new world of the Indies"** Peter Martyr Anglerius' *Decades of the New World*, describing the natives of Hispaniola, had been partially translated into French as early as 1532. Such other contemporary accounts as Jean Ribaut's *Terra Florida* and Renaud de Laudonnière's *Hakluyt*, together with numerous actual French voyages, created at this time an intense interest in the Americas. Ronsard, subject of the next chapter, in "*Complainte contre fortune*" (1559) denounced new world colonization as a despoilation of nature (*Meslanges*, Book 2).

22:37 **Jules Damville** Apparently an imaginary figure, though a well-known aristocratic name at this time (appears in Brantôme).

23:3 **savages of Florida** Although not absolutely impossible, a decade's captivity at this date would imply that this Frenchman had arrived in "Florida," as the whole southeast coast of North America was called, sometime before Captain John Ribaut had made the first (1562) of his several voyages, supported by Admiral Coligny, to found a New France in North America; earlier French voyages to colonize South America would fit better Pater's dates for this chapter.

23:13 **translator of Plutarch, Amyot** The famous French translation of Jacques Amyot, a French bishop and classical scholar, of *Les vies* (1559) in two folio volumes was for all practical purposes the first in French (an abridgement had appeared the year before); see L'Estoile's "portrait" (4:368–369). Montaigne, who read the *Parallel*

Lives in Amyot's translation, owes much of the style and method of his *Essais* to Plutarch (c. 46–post 120); and it is to Montaigne that Plutarch's reputation in the Renaissance owes its first stimulus.

23:20   **great siege** Marching on Paris from the southeast in the depth of winter, the Huguenots detoured, for the sake of provisioning, through the rich lands of La Beauce and arrived at Chartres on 23 February 1568; though the city wall was breached, the town stubbornly resisted Condé's army. A month later, over the objections of Coligny, an insincere peace reflective only of mutual fatigue was signed at Longjumeau.

23:21   **Guy Debreschescourt** Beyer (pp. 85–86 n.1) asserts that the historicity of the death and strange funeral of this child cannot be established.

24:1–2   **church of Sainte-Foy** Beyer (pp. 85–86 n.1) likewise maintains that the shelling and collapse of the roof of Sainte-Foy is not historically established; however, it is an analogue to Marius' narrow escape from the rock landslide (*Marius*, 1:166). Huguenot artillery in this campaign was limited to five siege-pieces and four light culverines or long cannons.

24:33   **spoiled**   or "despoiled" (15:32). Brantôme mentions Huguenot disfiguring of several churches other than Chartres. Although the city of Chartres was besieged in 1568 by the Prince of Condé and again in 1591 by Henry IV, at which time several cannon balls hit the church with one breaching the West Rose window, the cathedral otherwise survived the sixteenth-century religious wars almost unscathed. Far greater ravaging occurred in the eighteenth century, first with modernizing and subsequently with the despoliation of "the accumulated treasure" (24:33–34) at the French Revolution. Also during the Revolution the "vast echoing roof of timber, the 'forest'" (15:28) above the stone vaults, was stripped of its lead; later it burned and was replaced with copper-covered cast-iron. Pater's connection of the despoiled church with the grandmother's "dead face" (24:31)—a connection of body with edifice that occurs also in "The Child in the House" (*Miscellaneous Studies*, p. 196)—determines Gaston's future quest for the recovery of the human and religious ideal in a more indestructible form.

Chapter III : Annotation

Modernity

25:11   **Modernity**   Pater portrays the poets of the Pléiade, led by Pierre de Ronsard (1524–1585), as modernists of the Renaissance. This group, its name taken from seven Hellenist poets named after the constellation of seven stars, transformed medieval French literature through the inspiration of classical literature. Sainte Beuve portrays Du Bellay, one of Ronsard's "Pléiade," as "intensely modern" because the writer aims to portray "his most intimate moods" (Inman 1:313). But Pater also connects through analogy the sixteenth and nineteenth centuries: Ronsard is to Gaston as Baudelaire is to Pater (a self-reflexive analogue noted in Monsman's *Walter Pater's Art of Autobiography*, pp.137–38; afterwards developed in Patricia Clements's *Baudelaire and the English Tradition*, pp. 88–98). In Pater's "Romanticism" (1876), three significant references to Baudelaire establish his knowledge of both *L'art romantique* and *Les fleurs*, though doubtless as early as 1868, in his review of the poetry of William Morris, Pater displayed familiarity with Baudelaire. As a source for Pater's characterization of Ronsard, Baudelaire's study of Constantin Guys, particularly "*La modernité*" in *Le peintre de la vie moderne*, is used in *Gaston* "both to steal and to acknowledge and to keep both actions carefully veiled from all but the select few among his readers" (Clements 89).

25:20–21   **"The Triumvirate"**   At King's school, Canterbury, Pater met Henry Dombrain and John Rainier McQueen. The three companions, all of Huguenot descent, were called the "triumvirate" by their school principal and comrades (Levey, 52; T. Wright 1:87). In 1561 a Catholic triumvirate had been formed by Duke François de Guise, Constable Anne de Montmorency, and Marshal de Saint André, dedicated to the extirpation of the Huguenots. Guise was assassinated at Orleans, Saint André killed at Dreux and Montmorency captured. There were two Roman triumvirates, the first, in 60 B.C., was informal, consisting of Julius Caesar, Pompey, and Crassus; the second, in 43 B.C., was legalized: it included Mark Antony (83?–30 B.C.), orator and general whose exploits with Cleopatra were recorded by Plutarch, "shifty" Lepidus (d.13 B.C.), and Octavian (63–14 B.C.), i.e., Julius Caesar who became the first emperor, Caesar Augustus.

25:31   **Jasmin, Amadée, and Camille**   These three are imaginary figures. Jasmin de Villebon—his "clinging" (26:5) suggests the fragrant night-blooming jasmine vine. Baudelaire's "strange flowers," says Théophile Gautier, are cultivated in preference "'to lilies and roses, jasmine and forget-me-nots and violets, the innocent flora of small volumes bound in straw-yellow or pearl-gray covers'" (quoted in Inman 2:306). Jasmin's connection with Oscar Wilde or Wilde's Dorian (Chapters 8, 10) suggests a newly minted beauty-evil doubling for this flower. Amadée de l'Autrec—either an echo of Jules Amadée "Barby" d'Aurevilly, the aesthete and commentator on Baudeliare, or of Amadys Jamyn, Ronsard's poet-secretary at Croixval, according to Blanchmain (p. 19). Camille Pontdormi—Émile Zola's *La Conquète de Plassons*, a story of murder with a character called Camille, read by Pater (Inman 2:461) in 1884; also, Alexander Dumas' heroine, Camille, in *La Dame aux Camelias* (1848) may have popularized the name. But all three names are also familiar sixteenth-century surnames: Villebon is the name of a chateau in the region; Brantôme's works mention a Pontdormi and a de Lautrec.

26:7   **threads to be cut short**   A foreshadowing of future plot action, in allusion to the three Fates, that for Jasmin clearly was meant to occur in Chapter 12; also, forces weaving and unweaving as threads is an image from the "Conclusion" to the *Renaissance*, the scientific version of the old classical myth.

26:24–25 **refledging of the black earth**   as the young birds acquire their feathers, so in spring the earth covers itself once again with verdure.

26:29   **Ronsard's "Odes"**   The *Odes* and *Amours* (1550 and 1552; published collectively in 1560) included the famous short ode beginning "*Mignonne, allons voir si la Rose*" ("A Cassandre," *Les odes* 1:17, Blanchemain, 2:117); its theme of the "carpe diem," of spring as a metaphor for death and regeneration, opened the way to Pater's allusion to Proserpine in the following line. "The Skylark" is *"L'alouette"* (*"Hé Dieu! que je porte d'envie"*) in *Gayetez et epigrammes* (Blanchemain, 6:348). In *The Renaissance*, Pater quoted, as an example of Ronsard's poetry, the stanzas beginning: "*Avril, la grace, et le ris / De Cypris . . .* ," then noted "that is not by Ronsard, but by Remy Belleau" (p.159) of Ronsard's circle. Gaston's discovery of Ronsard's odes parallels the episode of the "golden book" of Apuleius that Flavian and Marius enjoy in *Marius the Epicurean*.

27:4   **reliquaries of books**   Pater rephrases du Bellay's *La Deffense* which he had quoted in "Joachim du Bellay," *The Renaissance* (p. 163): "Greek and Latin, dead languages shut up in books as in reliquaries—*péris et mises en reliquaires de livres*." A few pages previously, Pater quoted du Bellay: "'Those who speak thus . . . make me think of the relics which one may only see through a little pane of glass, and must not touch with one's hands. That is what these people do with all branches of culture, which they keep shut up in Greek and Latin books, not permitting one to see them otherwise, or transport them out of dead words into those which are alive, and wing their way daily through the mouths of men'" (p. 161). Pater repeats this image again: (*Renaissance*, 163). In a parallel maneuver, Baudelaire's "Epistle to Sainte-Beuve" (1844) expresses a desire to move away from the rigidity of the classics and extols "triumphant and mischievous" inventions in rhyme, claiming that eager young men "awaited with hungry ears pricked, and drank like a pack of hounds" the ideas from his new *Fleurs du mal.*

27:15   **witchery . . . Virgil**   Baudelaire's dedication of *Les fleurs* to Théophile Gautier was: "*Au poète impeccable au parfait magicien ès lettres Françaises*"—"the perfect magician of French literature." Blanchemain notes that Ronsard had memorized Virgil and could quote him on any occasion, "*les beaux passages de Virgile . . . entirèment par coeur*" (Blanchemain, 8:10); Pater owned Blanchemain's 1867 edition of Ronsard's *Oeuvres complètes* (Inman 1:300). Later in this paragraph, Virgil becomes a protagonist in the battle between the ancients and the moderns; Pater's "Romanticism" (retitled "Postscript" in *Appreciations*) is his most extensive commentary on this contention beween ancients and moderns and, perhaps covertly, a defense of the French decadents.

27:18   **Dido . . . Juliet . . . Aeneas**   Virgil transforms the myth of Dido, Queen of Carthage, so that she falls in love with Aeneas, shipwrecked on the Carthaginean coast, and kills herself when he forsakes her. Juliet is the heroine of Shakespeare's first romantic tragedy who stabs herself after Romeo, thinking her dead, had died from self-administered poison.

28:10   **turned them into gold**   In *Project d'Epilogue* (1887), Baudelaire says "You gave me your mud and I've turned it into gold" (Clements, p. 92).

28:10–11   **the lily in one's hand**   Both *Punch* (in 1880) and Gilbert and Sullivan's "Patience" (in 1881) had ridiculed Oscar Wilde's "lily in the hand." Wilde's friend, Douglas Sladen, recalled that as an Oxford undergraduate Wilde once "banished all the decorations from his rooms, except a single blue vase of the true aesthetic type which contained a 'Patience' lily" (Ellmann, *Wilde*, pp. 87–88).

28:19   **count the petals . . . golden hair**   Baudelairean allusion yields to Pre-Raphaelite reference, to those painters enthralled with the texture of the visible world, piling form upon form in their pictures, so that butterflies, grass, and plants can be identified by genus and species.

29:11   **love's secretary**   *Sonnets pour Hélène*, "*Je fuy les pas frayez du meschant populaire*," 1:26.

30:10   **"impeccable"**   Baudelaire was described as "impeccable" by Swinburne in his *Blake* (Swinburne, *Works* 16:65); and Baudelaire himself had dedicated his revolutionary *Fleurs* to an "impeccable" Gautier.

30:18   **creature of the eye**   A similar phrase, "lust of the eye" (from I John 2:16) appears in "The Child in the House," *Miscellaneous Studies*, p. 181.

30:28   **priory of Croix-val**   Blanchemain (8:29) notes that Ronsard exchanged a benefice in 1566 for a prebendary at Tours and also was granted by Charles IX the priorship of Croixval in Vendômois, situated on a tributary of the Loire.

30:30   formal peace The edict of pacification of St. Germain-en-Laye (8 August 1570) concluded the third civil war; a limited religious toleration was guaranteed, property and offices were restored, the judiciary reorganized to promote equity for Huguenots, and four cities designated as Huguenot havens.

31:13   *moral* Possibly an allusion to Wordsworth, for whom "nature" was "The guide, the guardian of my heart, and soul / Of all my moral being" ("Tintern Abbey," lines 110–111). Also in Pater's "The Prince Of Court Painters" in *Imaginary Portraits* Watteau achieved "a sort of moral purity, yet, in the *forms* and *colours* of things" (p. 23).

31:21–22 secular oak . . . Loir Oaks that have lived through ages or centuries along the Loir, a branch of Loire, that flows through the region of Vendômois where Ronsard's priory was located, about 20 miles north of Tours and 65 miles southwest of Chartres.

31:32–33 visible through the open doors, a gaunt figure A characteristic technique of Pre-Raphaelite art accentuates intimacy by framing its subject, such as the gaunt figure of Ronsard, as if the viewer were glimpsing the scene through a window or door ajar. A slip accompanying the Brasenose holograph defines Pater's own technique of "imaginary portraiture" in his novel: "Imaginary: because—[ ] and portraits, because they present, not an action, a story: but a character, personality, revealed especially, in outward detail." Pater's technique of portraiture presents historical characters in imaginary dialogue—like Landor's *Imaginary Conversations* that includes a dialogue between Scaliger and Montaigne.

31:36–37 a face, all nerve, distressed nerve In 1541, due to a severe fever, Ronsard became partly deaf and left the court of Francis I; between 1566–68 he suffered, among other symptoms, an intermittent fever and went into retirement at Croixval. Pater's image constructs another connection with the nineteenth-century decadents: Baudelaire's Poe, for example, was "*l'écrivain des nerfs.*"

32:3–6 enthusiastic gardener . . . youthful ones Beyer (p. 84) has shown that Pater draws upon Claude Binet's *Discours de la vie de Pierre Ronsard* (1586) as background to this chapter: "*Il prenoit aussi singulier plaisir à jardiner, ... Il incitoit fort ceux qui l'alloient voir et principalement les jeunes hommes*" (pp. 45, 49). Clements argues that Pater's phrase, "choice flowers," alludes specifically to Baudelaire's *Les Fleurs*; equally significant was Pater's realization that Ronsard had used this image to describe the fantastic style of the Pleiad: "that special flower, *ce fleur particulier*, which Ronsard himself tells us every garden has" (*Renaissance*, p. 167). So says Ronsard in "Preface sur La Franciade" (Blanchemain, 3:34).

32:10–11 enemies . . . Bacchus Ronsard, ridiculed and satirized by Huguenot poets, not only responded with satirical verses but even promoted a rumor that, dressed as Bacchus and crowned with a laurel and ivy wreath, he led a goat through the streets to ritual sacrifice (Blanchemain, 8:33).

32:19   *confidentiaire*   close assistant

32:27   **chimney with its cipher**   Mottoes engraved over the windows and doors of Ronsard's ancestral home, the château de la Poissonnière, included sayings such as *Veritas filia temporis* (Truth is the daughter of time) and over the fireplace of the central hall with its family coat-of-arms: *Non falunt futura merentem* (The worthy will not lack future rewards) (Blanchemain, 8:1, 3).

32:28   **leek-soup . . . salad**   In *Les fleurs* Baudelaire's *"Le Crépuscule de soir"* depicts a tired scholar preparing to retire to a simple meal, the precious yet fleeting experience of "evening spent / at a fireside—fragrant soup, a friend" (lines 35–36). Ronsard's *"La Salade,"* in *Sixiesme livre des Poëmes* (1569), describes the poet and his amanuensis, Amadys Jamyn, going to collect herbs and greens from the fields for their evening meal.

33:3–9   **Minerva . . . reverence for literature**   Binet: *"Chacun sçait le pris proposé à Thoulouze aux Jeux Floraux. . . . et par decret public, pour honorer la Muse immortelle de Ronsard, . . . lui envoyerent une Minerve d'argent massif de grand pris et valeur: laquelle Ronsard ayant reçeuë, presenta au Roy, qui l'eut fort agreable, l'estimant d'avantage qu'elle ne valoit, pour avoir servy de marque à la valeur infinie d'un tel personnage"* (pp. 22–23). Ronsard offered this silver statue won in the Floral Games at Toulouse to Henry II, not Charles (Blanchemian, p. 21).

33:15–18   **Marie, Cassandra . . . Helen**   Ronsard's first *Amours* memorialized his unrequited love for Cassandra de Salviati. His second and third *Amours* (1555–56) extolled Marie, the country girl from Anjou; Marie de Clèves, wife of Henri de Condé and mistress of Henry III, is another of Ronsard's figures of desire. Among Ronsard's finest poetry, the *Sonnets pour Hélène* (1578), are the verses addressed to Hélène de Surgères, a maid of honor in the court of Catherine de Medicis.

33:16–17   *La petite pucelle Angevine*   "Chanson," *Amours* 2:1, "The little maid of Anjou" (line 1), who was Marie de Bourgueil.

33:25   **Janet**   Jean Clouet and his son François, *both* called Janet (the son using his father's nickname), were court portrait painters and draughtsmen. Jean (c. 1485–1541), painter and *valet de chambre* to Francis I, represented an older Flemish tradition influenced by the Italian high Renaissance style, often drawing portraits of members of court in black or red chalk; his famous oil of Francis I hangs in the Louvre. François (c. 1510–1572), influenced by northern-European naturalism, often glazes backgrounds in his oils in cool blues and greens; he portrayed his "gallant ladies" with jewelled chains and other stylish ornaments. A three-quarter face of Charles IX by François hangs in the Louvre; the king wears a gold embroidered black velvet coat, his right hand carrying his gloves resting on a red velvet sofa. Another of his portraits of the king is now in Vienna's Kunsthistorisches Museum.

33:30–35 Sibyls . . . royal Margarets These figures reflect Pater's theme of the pagan gods (or goddesses) in exile, like Bacchus, with a hidden or forbidden knowledge; this connects with Baudelaire's theme of beauty entangled with evil. Pater's interpretation of Leonardo's Medusa in *The Renaissance* or Marius's Medusa presents the clash harshly; Leonardo's *Mona Lisa*, an embodiment of the Hegelian idea of history as accumulation, embraces these antinomies—and others as well. The three Margarets are: Marguerite of Navarre (1492–1549), author of the *Heptameron* and grandmother of Henry IV; Marguerite (1523–1574), daughter of Francis I; and Marguerite of Valois (1553–1615), author of the *Mémoirs* (*vide* note 10.92:19). Latin *margarita* means pearl.

33:35 "hatred of the vulgar" Unidentified, but certainly suggestive of aestheticism's defiance of bourgeois values.

34:14 Joachim du Bellay (1512–1560). Fellow member with Ronsard in the *Pleiade* and its reintroduction of classical literature and techniques into French poetry, Du Bellay is portrayed in Pater's *Renaissance* in terms of his contribution to emergent poetic theory and practice and to the landscape of La Beauce. From 1553 to 1557 du Bellay was in the service of Cardinal du Bellay in Rome. The emotional isolation expressed in *Les Regrets* turned to physical suffering upon his return to France when in 1557, exhausted and aged by affliction, he visited Ronsard. This friendship is yet another instance of pairings, such as that between the Latour brothers or Montaigne and Étienne de la Boetie. Like Ronsard with a "distressed nerve," du Bellay is "refined by sickness." Pater's theme of genius in the ill or misshapen body (as with de la Boetie) may be attributable to Baudelaire.

34:19 Tomorrow, where will be the snow? See D. G. Rossetti's translation of Villon's ballad on the brevity of beauty and love, "The Ballad of Dead Ladies," refrain: "But where are the snows of yester-year?"

34:22 depicted appropriately The frontispiece in Ronsard's *Amours* edited by Muret (1572) profiles Ronsard with a laurel crown and in brocade robe (Blanchemain, 8:69); the appropriateness of this depiction may lie in its explicit contrast to and veiled connection with the satiric image of Ronsard as Bacchus with goat.

34:28 haggard soul of a haggard generation Possibly an echo of the precursors of Decadent writers of the eighteen-nineties; from Baudelaire's flowers of evil and Joris Karl Huysmans *à Rebours*, from Swinburne's elegy for Baudelaire and George Moore's flowers of passion to such younger Paterides as Arthur Symons, Lionel Johnson, and Oscar Wilde, the *maladie du fin de siècle* and *ennui* became evidence of a "loosening of the moral fibre" or exhausted idealism.

34:35–36 Saint-Gelais . . . Marot Saint-Gelais was a popular poetaster who denounced the innovative features of the Pleiad, as did the writer Clément Marot; the metrical Psalms of Marot and Bèze became the marching songs of Huguenot soldiers. Beyer (p. 85) cites Binet on the connection between Ronsard and his rival Saint-Gelais.

35:8–10   **talk upon gardening . . . king loved to receive**   Binet: "*Il scavoit de beaux secrets pour le jardinage, fust pour semer, planter, ou pour enter et greffer en toutes sortes, et souvent en presentoit des fruictz au Roy Charles, qui prenoit à gré tout ce qui venoit de luy*" (Beyer, p. 84).

35:15   **Goudimel**   Claude Goudimel (c. 1520–1572) was a French composer who "set Ronsard's songs to music" (*Renaissance*, p. 169), though primarily known for his settings of Clément Marot's translation of the Psalms. He became a Huguenot and was killed in Lyons in the spreading of St. Bartholomew's Massacre of 1572.

35:15   **"Elegy of the Rose"**   The *Amours* (1552) contained supplementary musical settings (three by Goudimel) for nine of its *chansons*—chiefly sonnets; however, the subprior sings the elegy to "Marie" (either the peasant girl or the princess) from the much later *Amours* 2:2, "*Comme on voit sur la branche au mois de mai la rose.*" Sainte-Beuve's *Tableau historique* (1869), a copy of which Pater owned (Inman 1:336), did much to restore Ronsard's reputation and expressed high regard for this elegiac sonnet. Pater's friend, Andrew Lang, whose translations of the Pleiad Pater praised (*Renaissance*, p. 175), entitles this "His Lady's Tomb" (*Ballads and Lyrics of Old France*, p. 23) and misdates it as 1550.

35:22   **"the eternally youthful"**   unidentified

35:26   *Franciade*   A French national epic, in imitation of the *Aeneid*, commissioned by Charles IX but abandoned after his death as a fragment in four books, published in 1572.

35:35–36   **Monsieur Michel de Montaigne**   See 42:33–34; and for Montaigne's estimate of Ronsard, see 43:13. In "Apology for Raimond de Sebonde" (2.13.514 A), Montaigne quotes Ronsard's "*Remonstrance au peuple de France*" (lines 64–78) written five years before the time of this imaginary incident.

36:13   *Zeit-geist*   German word meaning "time-spirit," initially used and defined by Pater in "Romanticism" (reprinted as "Postscript" in *Appreciations*); Pater invokes the concept also several times in *Plato and Platonism* to describe a common intellectual environment.

36:39   **"flowers of evil"**   A translation of Baudelaire's title, *Les fleurs du mal*; compare this reference with Pater's discussion of "the entanglement of beauty with evil" (10.104:2). As Pater's most explicit reference to nineteenth-century French decadence, this temporal cross-cutting to Baudelaire suggests an effort to deal with a current issue though historical hindsight. Whereas in 1876 Pater had dared to defend and praise Baudelaire in "Romanticism," the following year in "The School of Giorgione" he instead borrowed from Baudelaire without naming him (Hill, *Renaissance*, pp. 388–89). It must have become evident to Pater that Baudelaire's flowers of evil were regarded with continuing, perhaps even growing, hostility by "most Englishmen" (so W. J. Courthope had implied in the *Quarterly Review*). Thus when Pater republished "Romanticism" in 1889 as the Postscript to *Appreciations*, he presumably feared Baudelaire's "unhealthy" reputation and suppressed all mention of his name, actually substituting Hugo's in its place. Only a major *apologia* could absolve Pater of the charge of decadence; accordingly, as *Marius* had been an attempt to deal "more fully" with the aesthetic philosophy, so *Gaston* would continue the discussion of the relation of art to moral values.

37:10–11 "**the sacred and the profane loves**" Whatever else this familiar antithesis may allude to, Pater was familiar with Titian's "Sacred and Profane Love," twin Venuses symbolizing nature's generative forces and divine, eternal love.

CHAPTER IV : ANNOTATION

Peach–blossom and Wine

38:16 **east-wind** cold and dry air currents originating in the polar regions flow more or less from east to west, resulting from the axial west to east rotation of the earth; conversely, warm and moist equatorial winds are westerly.

39:21 **three others fronted them face to face** The doppelgänger motif in Pater has been addressed generally in the Introduction (Design & Theme section); more specifically, this incident might be related to T. Gautier's story, "*Le chevalier double*" (1840) in *Romans et contes* (Inman 2:325) and to D. G. Rossetti's picture, *How They Met Themselves*.

39:33 **concession of liberty** In August of 1570 the Treaty of Saint-Germain-en-Laye concluded the savage third War of Religion, giving the French Protestants a measure of political freedom and religious toleration. As its corollary, Charles IX's Edict of Pacification, sanctioning the peace, disbanded the warring factions. The fortified Huguenot city of La Rochelle (42:3–14), under Jeanne of Navarre (6.64:8; 9.92:8) and Coligny, became a nearly independent republic, its walls protecting the Protestant leaders should the Peace prove insubstantial.

39:38–39 **Huguenot Coligni** Gaspard de Coligny, Seigneur of Châtillon, Admiral of France (1519–1572), assassinated in the St. Bartholomew's Massacre. Initially leading the French successfully against the Spaniards, he afterwards became leader of the Huguenots, opposing the Guises whose leadership of the Catholic party veiled their desire to wrest the throne from the Valois. As Admiral, he supported colonizing expeditions to the New World that challenged the monopolies of the kings of Portugal and Spain; his settlement in Florida had been slaughtered in 1565 by the Spanish. Coligny wished to divert France from its civil wars toward support of the Dutch in expelling Spain from the Lowlands, a policy that Catherine feared would embroil France in a disastrous war with the darling of the Pope, Philip II.

40:2–3 **Duke of Alva** Ferdinand Alvarez de Toledo, Third Duke of Alva (1507–1582), a Spanish general—ambitious, sadistic, egocentric, cautious and treacherous. In 1567 his army marched into the Netherlands, defeating William of Orange; he despotically persecuted to the death any who were even suspected of religious or political dissent from Spanish hegemony. After the Netherlands threw off the Spanish yoke, its great Renaissance flowering occurred, described in Pater's "Sebastian van Storck." Pater's phrase "devout work" is an ironic jib at Alva's pretense of religious purpose—here, theoretically, supporting Catholicism on behalf of the French monarchy; in actuality, making Catherine and Charles puppets of Philip.

40:6–7   **south-west regions**   Nantes is on the estuary of the Loire, Bordeaux on the estuary of the Garonne and La Rochelle, between them, is on the ocean. Gaston follows the Loire valley and its river, which had been an important means of commerce until the railway superseded it only a quarter century before Pater's time. Even today the route offers picturesque views: river sandbanks, poplar trees, vegetable fields, and chateaux silhouetted on the banks. Ronsard, du Bellay and the other seven poets named after the constellation of the Pleiades were established in the Loire Valley, singing the praises of its women and flora.

40:18   **Black Angers, white Saumur**   Angers, former capital of Anjou, lies southwest of Paris on the banks of the Maine river; it and its near neighbor Saumur, on the Loire, were centers of Protestantism. From the thirteenth century, Saumur had been linked with Angers under the rule of princes of Anjou. The blue-black slate from nearby quarries that covered the houses of Angers caused it to be called the black city. Whereas in the west (Black Anjou) construction utilized various forms of schist, in the east the predominating material was limestone (White Anjou).

40:30–31   **flawless bodies**   This is a material and social variant on the novel's motif of the quest for a moral and regenerate humanity, anticipatory of the Pauline body "raised in incorruption" (2 Corinthians 15).

41:7   **Francis the First**   (1494–1547) Embroiled in territorial wars with Italy for most of his reign, Francis also was a patron of painters and writers, including Leonardo da Vinci; his numerous palatial building projects placed an enormous strain on the royal purse but produced the greatest Renaissance chateaux. However, Pater's references to the court of Francis as a "fantastic company of strolling players" and French politics as "a stage-play" suggest a court ultimately less a center of culture than of perfected decadence. Jaques's melancholic speech, "All the world's a stage, / And all the men and women merely players" (*As You Like It*, 2.7.139–140), may be considered the locus classicus of this motif which appears so often in this novel. Pater is conveying a vision of society that is profoundly antithetical to the Victorian sense of life's necessary moral earnestness. His use of this image may convey the courtly "moral indifferentism" that Emelia Pattison alleged limited the high-water mark of arts and letters in sixteenth-century France.

41:8   **"house of pleasure"**   Pater translates a French locution that Pattison and others had used to describe "the *house* air, which now crept over fortified *château*. Strongholds rapidly made way for *lieux de plaisance*" (1:23). Of course, the other connotation of "brothel" is also intended.

41:29   **ixias**   corn lilies (iridaceae), producing on thin wiry stems in late spring to early summer spikes of dainty star-like flowers, white, yellow, scarlet or blue. Pater did not realize the ixia had been introduced into Europe from its native South Africa in 1792.

42:5–6 **La Rochelle . . . John Calvin** La Rochelle, a fortified Protestant port north of Bordeaux, resisted many assults during the Reformation period, finally in 1628 forced by famine to surrender. In this connection a Berg slip, canceled with a single top-to-bottom line, asserts: "—vrais Hug^{ts}, qui savaient / mieux le metier de / se diffendre que de' / assaillir.": "—true Huguenots, better at defending themselves than at suddenly attacking." Baird (2:583) describes La Rochelle anticipating attack in 1573: "With Puritan simplicity and faith, the reformed inhabitants of La Rochelle had named the strong work at the northwestern angle of the circuit the "Bastion de l'Évangile," or the "Bastion of the Gospel"; . . . upon the ability of the Rochellois to defend the Bastion of l'Évangile must depend the salvation of the city." Calvin (1509–1564) was a French Protestant reformer based in Geneva and influential on the side of Condé and Coligny. In *Marius*, Pater mentions "the faulty theology of John Calvin" (2:101), thinking of its inflexible definition of salvation.

42:9 **marriage of King Charles** Elizabeth of Austria, daughter of the Emperor Maximilian of Germany, was married to Charles on 26 November 1571 at Mézières, with processions, speeches, banquets and masques that lasted for months. The Huguenots were absent, feeling their safety precarious.

42:10 **Austrian Elizabeth** See 122:31

42:13–14 **Jeanne of Navarre** See 6.64:8; 9.92:8

42:23 **the Limousin** A predominantly rural province in the Massif Central, originally part of the kingdom of Aquitaine, the capital of which is Limoges.

42:29 **chalybeate** Impregnated with iron, as mineral waters; or resembling iron in taste or action.

42:33–34 **Monsieur Michel de Montaigne** Montaigne (1533–1592) the essayist is portrayed in Chapter 5, "Suspended Judgment," as skeptical and relativistic in matters of reason and knowledge, a lover of diversity, spontaneity, and flux. Just as Pater's Marius had been imaginatively present when Aurelius' *Meditations* were first enunciated, so here Gaston encounters future works, even before the first books of the famous *Essais* appeared in 1580.

43:4 **eat of all the trees** Genesis 3:2–3: "And the woman said unto the serpent, We may eat of the fruit of the trees of the garden: But of the fruit of the tree which is in the midst of the garden, God hath said, Ye shall not eat of it, neither shall ye touch it, lest ye die." The account begins at Genesis 2:16; see 7.78:27–28.

43:14–16 **Pascal** Blaise Pascal (1623–1662), French mathematician and religious philosopher, noted for *Lettres provinciales* (1657) and *Pensées sur la religion* (1669). Pater restates Pascal's closing evaluation of Montaigne (from *Entretien avec Saci sur*

Épictète et Montaigne, 1660), one that he also earlier had quoted in *Marius* 1:150 and later repeated in his posthumous essay, "Pascal," *Contemporary Review*, February 1895. See 7.78:15.

43:29–30 **"France had more laws than all the rest of the world"** "Of Experience" (3.13.1066 B): "*Car nous avons en France plus de loix que tout le reste du monde ensemble. . . .*"

43:31–32 **"a continual . . . things"** "Of Vanity" (3.9.973 B): "*L'ame y a une continuelle exercitation à remarquer les choses incogneuës et nouvelles. . . .*"

43:34–35 **house had lain open** "Apology for Raimond de Sebonde" (2.12.438 A): "My house has long been open to men of knowledge and is very well known to them. . . ."

44:11 **dialogue was that of the mind with itself** Matthew Arnold, "Author's Preface," *Poems* (1853): "the dialogue of the mind with itself has commenced."

44:14 **"My thoughts . . . still."** "Of Three Commerces" (3.3.828 C): "*Mes pensées dorment, si je les assis.*"

44:21–22 **"if but . . . person he met"** "Of Profit and Honesty" (3.1.790 B): "*Je parle au papier comme je parle au premier que je rencontre.*"

44:22–25 **"If there be . . . I will run!"** "Upon Some Verses of Virgil" (3.5.843–844 B): "*S'il y a quelque personne, quelque bonne compaignie aux champs, en la ville, en France ou ailleurs, resseante ou voyagere, à qui mes humeurs soient bonnes, de qui les humeurs me soient bonnes, il n'est que de siffler en paume, je leur iray fournir des essays en cher et en os.*"

45:13 **genial criticism on the writer** "Of the Education of Children" (1.26.171 A; 1.25 Cotton): "Since Ronsard and Du Bellay have brought renown to our French poetry, every little apprentice I know is doing more or less as they do, using noble words and copying their cadences." And "Of Presumption" (2.17.661 A): "As for poets writing in French, I think that they have raised poetry as high as it ever will be and that in those qualities in which Ronsard and Du Bellay excel I find them close to the perfection of the Ancients."

45:23 **books upon books** "Of Experience" (3.13.1069 B): "*et plus de livres sur livres que sur autre subject. . . .*"

45:30 **"still be at his elbow to test and be tested"** "Upon Some Verses of Virgil" (3.5.875 B): "*Plutarque . . . s'ingere à vostre besongne et vous tend une main liberale et inespuisable de richesses et d'embellissemens.*"

46:3 **"the ruin of his country"** "Of Physiognomy" (3.12.1046 C): "*je l'ay plus de moitié passée en la ruine de mon pays.*"

46:20   **Circe**   The sorceress in Homer's *Odyssey*, Book 10, who turned Ulysses's companions into Swine, mentioned only in passing in the *Essays.*

46:27–28   **"play . . . diversion"**   "Of Democritus and Heraclitus" (1.50.303 C): *"Je le hay et fuy, de ce qu'il n'est pas assez jeu, et qu'il nous esbat trop serieusement, ayant honte d'y fournir l'attention qui suffiroit à quelque bonne chose."*

46:28–30   **"the play . . . action"**   "Of Custom" (1.23.110 C; 1.22 Cotton): *"les jeux des enfans ne sont pas jeux, et les faut juger en eux comme leurs plus serieuses actions. . . ."*

CHAPTER V : ANNOTATION

Suspended Judgment

47:11   **Suspended Judgment**   "Of Cripples" (3.11.1030 B): "*je suis d'advis que nous soustenons nostre judgement aussi bien à rejetter qu'à recevoir*" (Pierre Villey edition): "I am of opinion that we ought to suspend our judgment, whether as to rejection or as to reception" (Cotton translation). Pater owned an 1877 edition of Charles Cotton's translation (first edition, 1685–1686) of *Les Essais*, edited by William Carew Hazlitt (Inman I:335). Cotton's rather free translations, coupled with Pater's condensings and splicings together of phrases, has produced a weaving together of quotations or echoes from the *Essays*; the smaller embedded fragments often float free of Montaigne's more substantial passages and, though undoubtedly verbal borrowings from Cotton if not from Montaigne, have sometimes eluded identification. When Cotton's essay numbering diverges from that of the Villey edition, I shall so note; but Pater's text ordinarily follows Cotton so closely that to provide his translation would be redundant. Though Montaigne's essays are chockablock with morbid little anecdotes, Pater emphasizes his theoretical attitudes and conceptual passages, particularly stressing, as does Jules Michelet's *Histoire de France* (10.271), Montaigne's skepticism.

47:25–27   **"some (ah me!) . . . affection" . . . "relish"**   Essay title "That the relish of good and evil depends in a great measure upon the opinion we have of them" (1.14.54 B; 1.40 Cotton): "*J'ay veu quelqu'un de mes intimes amis courre la mort à force, d'une vraye affection. . . .*"

47:28–29   **"receive no colour . . . soul."**   "Of Vanity" (3.9.955 B): "*La garde ou l'emploite sont de soy choses indifferentes, et ne prennent couleur de bien ou de mal que selon l'application de nostre volonté.*"

47:30–31   **"there is . . . makes it so"?**   *Hamlet* II.ii.256

47:31–38   **"What we call evil . . . risk of life."**   "The Relish of Good and Evil" (1.14.50 A; 1.40 Cotton): "*Or que ce que nous appellons mal ne le soit pas de soy, ou au moins, tel qu'il soit, qu'il depende de nous de luy donner autre saveur, et autre visage, car tout revient à un. . . .*"; "Of Democritus and Heraclitus" (1.50.302 C): "*Les choses à part elles ont peut estre leurs poids et mesures et conditions; mais au dedans, en nous, elle les leur taille comme elle l'entend. La mort est effroyable à Ciceron, desirable à Caton, indifferente à Socrates*"; "That the relish of good and evil depends in a great measure upon the opinion we have of them" (1.14.53 C; 1.40 Cotton): "*Toute opinion est assez forte pour se faire espouser au pris de la vie.*"

48:7–10 "**upon things . . . exactly alike**" "That we Laugh and Cry for the Same Thing" (1.38.235 A; 1.37 Cotton): "*mais nostre ame regarde la chose d'un autre oeil, et se la represente par un autre visage: car chaque chose a plusieurs biais et plusieurs lustres*"; "Of Custom" (1.23.112 C; 1.22 Cotton): "*La raison humaine est une teinture infuse environ de pareil pois à toutes nos opinions et moeurs, de quelque forme qu'elles soient: infinie en matiere, infinie en diversité*"; "Resemblance of Children" (2.37.786 A): "*Et ne fut jamais au monde deux opinions pareilles.*"

48:21–22 "**every man . . . condition**" "Of Repentance" (3.2.805 B): "*chaque homme porte la forme entiere de l'humaine condition.*"

48:22–23 "**That we taste nothing pure**" Essay title "That we Taste Nothing Pure" (2.20.673 A): "*Nous ne goustons rein de pur.*"

48:24 "**all judgments in the gross**" "The Art of Conference" (3.8.943 B): "*Tous jugemens en gros sont lâches et imparfaicts.*"

48:26 **grotesques which some artists . . . joint together** Giuseppe Arcimboldo (1527–1593) painted faces of fruit and vegetables, fish, fire, books and twigs—pictures now in the Kunsthistorisches Museum, Vienna.

48:28–29 "**Nothing . . . diverse, too.**" "Of Cripples" (3.11.1034 B): "*Il n'est rien si souple et erratique que nostre entendement: . . . Et il est double et divers, et les matieres doubles et diverses.*"

48:33 "**vices that are lawful**" "Of Profit and Honesty" (3.1.796 B): "*Il y a des vices legitimes, comme plusieurs actions, ou bonnes ou excusables, illegitimes.*"

48:33–35 **vices . . . conservation of health**" "Of Profit and Honesty" (3.1.791 B): "*les vices y trouvent leur rang et s'employent à la cousture de nostre liaison, comme les venins à la conservation de nostre santé.*"

48:35–36 "**actions good . . . themselves**" See above 48:33: "Of Profit and Honesty" (3.1.796 B).

48:36–37 "**the soul . . . wanting**" Essay title (1.4.22 A): "*Comme l'ame descharge ses passions sur des objects faux, quand les vrais luy defaillent.*"

48:39–49:1 "**condemnations . . . condemn**" "Of Experience" (3:13.1071 C): "*Combien ay-je veu de condemnations, plus crimineuses que le crime?*"

49:3–4 "**even to the worst . . . justice**" "Of Profit and Honesty" (3.1.798 B): "*Et à ceux mesme qui ne valent rien, il est si doux, ayant tiré l'usage d'une action vicieuse, y pouvoir hormais coudre en toute seurté quelque traict de bonté et de justice. . . .*"

49:10–11 "**I think . . . full desert.**" "Of Democritus and Heraclitus" (1.50.303 A): "*et il me semble que nous ne pouvons jamais estre assez mesprisez selon nostre merite.*"

49:15–17 **"make it their business . . . person"** "Of the Inconstancy of our Actions" (2.1.331 A): *"Ceux qui s'exercent à contreroller les actions humaines . . . il semble impossible qu'elles soient parties de mesme boutique."*

49:31–33 **"those citizens . . . country."** "Of Profit and Honesty" (3.1.791 B): *"aux citoyens plus vigoureux et moins craintifs qui sacrifient leur honneur et leur conscience, comme ces autres antiens sacrifierent leur vie pour le salut de leur pays. . . ."*

49:35 **Esau** Named so because he was "all over like a hairy garment" (Genesis 25:21–26).

49:35–36 **"our great and powerful mother, nature"** "Of Cannibals" (1.31.206 A; 1.30 Cotton) *"nostre grand et puissante mere nature."*

49:36–37 **As Plato . . . door of poesy,"** "Of Drunkenness" (2.2.347 A): *"Et comme Platon dict que pour neant hurte à la porte de la poësie un homme rassis. . . ."*

50:5 **"I hear . . . foolish."** "Of the Art of Conference" (3.8.937 C): *"J'oy journellement dire à des sots des mots non sots."*

50:7 **"idols of the cave"** Francis Bacon enumerated five kinds of "idols," bad habits of mind that cause error; "idols of the cave" are prejudices unique to a specific person.

50:14 **Étienne de la Boétie** (1530–1563) best remembered as a friend of Montaigne, he was a distinguished jurist, diplomat, poet, and, owing to an early essay on soverignty, the founder of modern French political philosophy. Because of its radical views on universal natural rights, his *Discourse of Voluntary Servitude* circulated only in manuscript until it was published anonymously and incompletely in the Huguenot *Reveille-Matin* (1574). Montaigne makes it clear in "Of Physiognomy" that "a very beautiful soul" (3.12.810), such as the homely La Boétie's, to some extent colors the perception of physical attributes.

50:20 **"The qualities and fortunes"** See 50:25–26: "Of Vanity" (3.9.996 B).

50:23 **"riches and embellishments"** "Upon Some Verses of Virgil" (3.5.875 B): *"Plutarque . . . s'ingere à vostre besongne et vous tend une main liberale et inespuisable de richesses et d'embellissemens."*

50:25–26 **"more in his head . . . country"** "Of Vanity" (3.9.996 B): *"J'ay eu plus en teste les conditions et fortunes de Lucullus, Metellus et Scipion, que je n'ay d'aucuns hommes des nostres."*

50:26–27 **"we have no hold . . . but by imagination"** "Of Vanity" (3.9.996 B): *"les choses presentes mesmes, nous ne les tenons que par la fantasie"* (imagination is given as a variant).

50:33–36 **"Our force is . . . than in us."** "Of Ancient Customs" (1.49.299 A): *"nos forces ne sont non plus capables de les joindre en ces parties là vitieuses, qu'aux vertueuses:*

car les unes et les autres partent d'une vigueur d'esprit qui estoit sans comparaison plus grande en eux qu'en nous."

50:37–39   **"the incomparable . . . in story"**   "Of Friendship" (1.28.184 A; 1.27 Cotton): *"Estienne de la Boitie . . . en cette partie des dons de nature, je n'en connois point qui luy soit comparable. . . . si entiere et si parfaite que certainement il ne s'en lit guiere de pareilles, et, entre nos hommes, il ne s'en voit aucune trace en usage. Il faut tant de rencontres à la bastir, que c'est beaucoup si la fortune y arrive une fois en trois siecles."*

51:3–4   **"poor and flat . . . it"**   "Of Friendship" (1.28.192 A; 1.27 Cotton): *"Car les discours mesmes que l'antiquité nous a laissé sur ce subject, me semblent lâches au pris du sentiment qui j'en ay."*

51:7–11   **"We were halves . . . missed me."**   "Of Friendship" (1.28.193 A; 1.27 Cotton): *"Nous estions à moitié de tout; il me semble qui je luy desrobe sa part, ... J'estois desjà si fait et accoustumé à estre deuxiesme par tout, qu'il me semble n'estre plus qu'à demy."*

51:16–17   **"concurrence" . . . "'twas much . .. three ages."**   See 50:37–39: "Of Friendship" (1.28.184 A; 1.27 Cotton). Also Cotton uses "concurrence" in each of the following: "into a concurrence of desires" (1.28.186 A; 1.27 Cotton); "with equal concurrence" (1.28.189 C; 1.27 Cotton); "the reason is the concurrence of our wills" (1.28.190; 1.27 Cotton); "and that absolute concurrence of affections being no other than one soul in two bodies" (1.28.190; 1.27 Cotton).

51:17–19   **"sweet society" . . . "was but smoke"**   "Of Friendship" (1.28.193 A; 1.27 Cotton): *"si je la compare, dis-je, toute aux quatre années qu'il m'a esté donné de jouyr de la douce compagnie et société de ce personnage, ce n'est que fumée, ce n'est qu'une nuit obscure et ennuyeuse."*

51:20–21   **"to speak . . . experience"**   "Of Friendship" (1.28.192 A; 1.27 Cotton): *"je souhaiterois aussi parler à des gens qui eussent essayé ce que je dis. Mais, sçachant combien c'est chose eslongnée du commun usage qu'une telle amitié, et combien elle est rare, je ne m'attens pas d'en trouver aucun bon juge."*

51:25   **"Because it was He . . . I!"**   "Of Friendship" (1.28.188 C; 1.27 Cotton): *"Par ce que c'estoit luy; par ce que c'estoit moy."*

51:32–35   **"which, if . . . unknown"**   "Folly to Measure Truth and Error by our own Capacity" (1.27.180 A; 1.27 Cotton) *"desquelles si nous ne pouvons estre persuadez, au moins les faut-il laisser en suspens"*; "Of Coaches" (3.6.908 B): *"Quand tout ce qui est venu par rapport du passé jusques à nous seroit vray et seroit sçeu par quelqu'un, ce seroit moins que rien au pris de ce qui est ignoré."*

51:38–52:1   **"transports . . . their design."**   "Various events from the same counsel" (1.24.127 A; 1.23 Cotton): *"Les saillies poëtiques, qui emportent leur autheur . . . non* *plus que les orateurs ne disent avoir en la leur ces mouvemens et agitations extra-ordinaires, qui les poussent au delà de leur dessein."*

52:2–3 **"in the necessity . . . through"** "Of the Art of Conference" (3.8.936 B): *"J'ay autrefois employé à la necessité et presse du combat des revirades qui ont faict faucée outre mon dessein et mon esperance. . . ."*

52:5–7 **"flag, and languish . . . fury"** "Of Vanity" (3.9.995 B,C): *"Mille poëtes trainent et languissent à la prosaïque; mais la meilleure prose ancienne (et je la seme ceans indifferemment pour vers) reluit par tout de la vigueur et hardiesse poetique, et represente l'air de sa fureur."* In this connection one recalls that Pater's ambition at Oxford was to be a *"prosateur"* (Monsman, *Walter Pater* [Boston: G.K. Hall, 1977], p. 142).

52:11–12 **"followed from the same counsel."** Essay title (1.24.124 A; 1.23 Cotton): "Various events from the same counsel."

52:12–13 **Fortune . . . mistress of events"** "Various events from the same counsel" (1.24.127 A; 1.23 Cotton): *"la fortune maintient tousjours la possession des evenemens."*

52:14–16 **"fortune . . . justice"** Essay title (1.34:220; 1.33 Cotton): "That fortune is oftentimes observed to act by the rules of reason."

52:18 **"the force . . . the occasion"** "Of Repentance" (3.2.814 C): *"La force de tout conseil gist au temps; les occasions et les matieres roulent et changent sans cesse."*

52:27–28 **physiognomy . . . our fingers."** "Of the Art of Conference" (3.8.930 B): *"qu'elle fut eschapée et fondue entre leurs doigts. . . ."*

52:30 **"perennial than brass"** Horace, *Odes* 3.30.1: *Exegi monumentum aere perennius*

52:33–37 **"the soul looks . . . things."** "That we laugh and cry for the same thing" (1.38.235 A; 1.37 Cotton): *"mais nostre ame regarde la chose d'un autre oeil, et se la represente par un autre visage: car chaque chose a plusieurs biais et plusieurs lustres"*; "Of Coaches" (3.6.908 B): *"Il n'y a rien de seul et de rare eu esgard à nature, ouy bien eu esgard à nostre cognoissance, qui est un miserable fondement de nos regles et qui nous represente volontiers une tres-fauce image des choses."*

53:2–3 **"wherein . . . involved than we"** "Of the Education of Children" (1.26.174 A; 1.25 Cotton): *"que cela trouble la cervelle tendre des enfans de les esveiller le matin en sursaut, et de les arracher du sommeil (auquel ils sont plongez beaucoup plus que nous ne sommes). . . ."*

53:6–18 **"There are so many maladies . . . light I find in it."** "Of the Resemblance of Children to their Fathers" (2.37.782 A): *"Il luy est proposé tant de maladies et tant de circonstances, qu'avant qu'il soit venu à la certitude de ce point où doit joindre la perfection de son experience, le sens humain y perd son latin; . . . tant de complexions, au melancolique; tant de saisons, en hyver; tant de nations, au François; tant d'aages, en la vieillesse; tant de mutations celestes, en la conjonction de Venus et de Saturne; tant de* *parties du corps, au doigt. . . . E puis, quand la guerison fut faicte, comment se peut il asseurer que ce ne fut que le mal fut arrivé à sa periode, ou un effect du hazard, ou l'operation de quelque autre chose qu'il eust ou mangé, ou beu, ou touché ce jour là, ou le mérite des prieres de sa mere grand?";* "Of Democritus and Heraclitus" (1.50.302 C): *"Car je ne voy le tout de rien: Ne font pas, ceux qui promettent de nous le faire veoir. De cent membres et visages qu'a chaque chose, j'en prens un tantost à lecher seulement. . . . Et aime plus souvent à les saisir par quelque lustre inusité."*

53:19–22 **governing method . . . knowledge itself** "Of Cripples" (3.11.1030 B, C): *"Voire dea, il y a quelque ignorance forte et genereuse qui ne doit rien en honneur et en courage à la science, ignorance pour laquelle concevoir il n'y a pas moins de science que pour concevoir la science."*

53:33–34 **"being of so wild a composition"** "Of Cripples" (3.11.1033 B): *"Quoy, si les plus vrayes no sont pas tousjours les plus commodes à l'homme, tant il est de sauvage composition!"*

53:35 **"with a little alteration of accent"** "Of Profit and Honesty" (3.1.794 B): *"Je ne dis rien à l'un que je ne puisse dire à l'autre, à son heure, l'accent seulement un peu changé. . . ."*

53:39–54:2 **"every day concludes . . . fashion"** "Of Vanity" (3.9.978 B): *"Mon dessein est divisible par tout: il n'est pas fondé en grandes esperances; chaque journée en faict le bout. Et le voyage de ma vie se conduict de mesme."*

54:12–14 **"in favour of the Huguenots . . . public."** "Upon some Verses of Virgil" (3.5.846 B): *"En faveur des Huguenots, qui accusent nostre confession privée et auriculaire, je me confesse en publicq, religieusement et purement."*

54:15–16 **"I have . . . discover myself."** "Of the Education of Children" (1.26.148 A; 1.25 Cotton): *"Je ne vise icy qu'à découvrir moy mesmes, qui seray par adventure autre demain, si nouveau apprentissage me change."*

54:25–26 **"properly of his own having and substance"** "Of Managing the Will" (3.10.1009 B): *"l'ame . . . . peut voir et sentir toutes choses, mais elle ne se doibt paistre que de soy, et doibt estre instruicte de ce qui la touche proprement, et qui proprement est de son avoir et de sa substance."*

54:27–30 **"The greatest thing . . . themselves."** "Of Solitude" (1.39.242 A; 1.38 Cotton): *"La plus grande chose du monde, c'est de sçavoir estre à soy"*; "Of Repentance" (3.2.805 C): *"Si le monde se plaint de quoy je parle trop de moy, je me plains de quoy il ne pense seulement pas à soy."*

54:34–35 **"I have . . . to-morrow."** See 54:15–16 "Of Education of Children" (1.26.148 A; 1.25 Cotton).

54:36–37 "now high, now low . . . inconstancy" "Of the Art of Conference" (3.8.939 B): "je . . . loge les Essais tantost bas, tantost haut, fort inconstamment et doubteusement."

54:37–55:9 "What are we . . . have or no" "Upon Some Verses of Virgil" (3.5.866 B): "qu'est-il de nous aussi qui sedition et discrepance?"; "Of the Inconstancy of our Actions" (2.1.337 A): "Nous sommes tous de lopins, et d'une contexture si informe et diverse, que chaque piece, chaque momant, faict son jeu. Et se trouve autant de difference de nous à nous mesmes, que de nous à autruy"; "Of the Inconstancy of our Actions" (2.1.335 B): "et qui y regarde primement, ne se trouve guere deux fois en mesme estat. Je donne à mon ame tantost un visage, tantost un autre, selon le costé où je la couche. . . . Je n'ay rien à dire de moy, entierement, simplement, et solidement, sans confusion et sans meslange, ny en un mot."

55:25–27 "I shall be blind . . . no longer I!" "Of Experience" (3.13.1105 C): "qu'il me faudra estre aveugle formé avant que je sente la decadence et vieillesse de ma veuë. Tant les Parques destordent artificiellement nostre vie."

55:28–31 "In fine . . . fear." "Of the Art of Conference" (3.8.929 C): "Somme, il faut vivre entre les vivants, et laisser courre la riviere sous le pont sans nostre soing, ou, à tout le moins, sans nostre alteration"; "Of Fear" (1.18.76 C): "C'est ce dequoy j'ay le plus de peur que la peur."

55:32–33 "admonished . . . sickness." Pater paraphrases, including surrounding material: "Of Repentance" (3.2.816 C): "La santé m'advertit, comme plus alaigrement, aussi plus utilement que la maladie."

55:33–34 the beautiful light of health "Of Experience" (3.13.1093 B): "d'un esclair la belle lumiere de la santé."

55:36–37 King of Thrace "Of the Inequality Amongst Us" (1.42.261 C).

55:38 King of Mexico "Of the Art of Conference" (3.8.935 B).

56:1 Alexander "The Inconvenience of Greatness" (3.7.919 B).

56:10 "The lowest . . . constancy." "Of Presumption" (2.17.645 B): "La plus basse marche est la plus ferme. C'est le siege de la constance."

56:13–14 "soften . . . our propositions." "Of Cripples" (3.11.1030 B): "J'ayme ces mots, qui amollissent et moderent la temerité de nos propositions. . . ."

56:16–17 "that fair . . . traced for us," "Of Moderation" (1.30.198 C; 1.29 Cotton): "du beau et plain chemin que nature nous a tracé."

56:18–19 "Never had any . . . to purpose." "Of Diversion" (3.4.830 B): "jamais medecin laid et rechigné n'y fit oeuvre."

56:21–22 "All decent . . . commendable." "Of Constancy" (1.12.45 A): "Au rebours, tous moyens honnestes de se garentir des maux sont non seulement permis, mais loüables."

56:23 "always be master of that of another" "Various Events from the Same Counsel" (1.24.128 A; 1.23 Cotton): "*quiconque aura sa vie à mespris, se rendra tousjours maistre de celle d'autruy.*"

56:23–24 "a magistrate . . . as he." "Of Managing the Will" (3.10.1021 B): "*Je n'accuse pas un magistrat qui dorme, pourveu que ceux qui sont soubs sa main dorment quand et luy. . . .*"

56:29–30 "so savage a virtue . . . dear" "Of Moderation" (1.30.198 C; numbered 1.29 Cotton): "*Et n'ayme ny à conseiller ny à suivre une vertue si sauvage et si chere.*"

56:32–34 Lacedaemonians . . . martial fury." "Of Profit and Honesty" (3.1.802 B): "*Avoit il pas emprunté de ses ennemis l'usage de sacrifier aux Muses, allant à la guerre, pour destremper par leur douceur et gayeté cette furie et aspreté martiale?*" This Lacedaemonian custom is cited earlier in "Of Glory" (2.16.628 B).

56:36–38 "I love . . . wanton." "Upon Some Verses of Virgil" (3.5.844 B): "*J'ayme une sagasse gaye et civile, et fuis l'aspreté des meurs et l'austerité. . . .*"; "Of the Education of Children" (1.26.160 A; numbered 1.25 Cotton): "*Il n'est rien plus gay, plus gaillard, plus enjoué, et à peu que je ne dise follastre.*"

57:4–6 "that sleep should . . . relish it" "Of Experience" (3.13.1112 B) "*A celle fin que le dormir mesme ne m'eschapat ainsi stupidement, j'ay autresfois trouvé bon qu'on me le troublat pour que je l'entrevisse.*"

57:6–8 "Of scents . . . virtues." "Of Smells" (1.55.315 C): "*Les senteurs plus simples et naturelles me semblent plus aggreables. Quelque odeur que ce soit, c'est merveille combien elle s'attache à moy, et combien j'ay la peau propre à s'en abreuver.*"

57:8–9 "In excessive heats . . . sunrise." "Of Vanity" (3.9.974 B): "*et aux extremes chaleurs, les passe de nuict, du Soleil couchant jusques au levant.*"

57:9–11 "I am betimes . . . storm." "Of Managing the Will" (3.10.1017 B): "*Je sens à temps les petis vents qui me viennent taster et bruire au dedans, avant-coureus de la tempeste. . . .*"

57:11–14 "When I walk . . .myself." "Of Experience" (3.13.1107 B): "*voyre et quand je me promeine solitairement en un beau vergier, si mes pensées se sont entretenues des occurences estrangieres quelque partie du temps, quelque autre partie je les rameine à la promenade, au vergier, à la douceur de cette solitude et à moy.*"

57:14–15 "There is nothing . . . purely spiritual." "Upon Some Verses of Virgil" (3.5.892 B): "*Pouvons nous pas dire qu'il n'y a rien en nous, pendant cette prison terrestre, purement ny corporel ny spirituel. . . .*"

57:15–16 "'Tis an inhuman wisdom . . . body." "Of Experience" (3.13.1106 B): "*Moy, qui ne manie que terre à terre, hay cette inhumaine sapience qui nous veut rendre desdaigneux et ennemis de la culture du corps.*"

57:17–18   **"Of all the infirmities . . . being."**   "Of Experience" (3.13.1110 B): "*et de nos maladies la plus sauvage c'est mespriser nostre estre.*"

57:27–28   **"meats . . . gone"**   "Of Experience" (3.13.1101 B): "*En toutes celles qui le peuvent souffrir, je les ayme peu cuites et les ayme fort mortifiées, et jusques à l'alteration de la senteur en plusieurs.*"

57:28–29   **clear glass . . . capacity**   "Of Experience" (3.13.1084 C): "*Tout métail m'y desplait au pris d'une matiere claire et transparente. Que mes yeux y tastent aussi, selon leur capacité.*"

57:30   **"Sleeping . . . my life."**   "Of Experience" (3.13.1096 B): "*Le dormir a occupé une grande partie de ma vie. . . .*"

58:15   **priceless pearl**   Matthew 13:45–46; see 9.92:26.

58:34   **"he that is . . . *against* us."**   Matthew 12:30 "He that is not with me is against me."

CHAPTER VI : ANNOTATION

Shadows of Events

60:11   Shadows of Events   The events alluded to are, specifically, the murders of St. Bartholomew's Eve (24 August 1572). Chapter 7 suggests the relation of this title to Bruno's philosophy: "As already in his life there had been the *Shadows of Events*,—the indirect yet fatal influence there of deeds in which he had no part, so now, for a time, he seemed to fall under the spell, the power, of the *Shadows of Ideas*, of Bruno's Ideas" (7.81:31–34). In *Marius*, Pater had contrasted the immediacy of the world with the young boy's secluded, shadowy existence; so also for Gaston, Pater described "human experience, in its strange mixture of beauty and evil, its sorrow, its ill-assorted fates, its pathetic acquiescence; above all, in its over-powering certainty, over against his own world of echoes and shadows, which perhaps only seemed to be so much as echoes or shadows" (2.20:5–8). These "two antagonistic ideals" (2.20:18) of tangible reality and contemplative withdrawal seek a harmony.

60:14   situation in Homer   Patroclus, the close friend of Achilles, was killed by Hector; the "supernatural darkness" is described in Book 17:591–647.

60:23   Eve of Saint Bartholomew   Sixteenth-century historians questioned whether the massacre had been premeditated or was a sudden seizing of opportunity, and they assessed the complicity of those responsible variously (nineteenth-century historians, such as John Lingard and John Allen, continued to be no less partisan in their exonerations or condemnations; the *Westminster Review*, January 1827, examines this controversy). Brantôme, the consummate courtier, claims that Catherine was *manipulated* into acquiescing in the massacre for self-defense after the Huguenots were angered by the attempt on Coligny. Pater, more plausibly, implies she incited the Guises to revenge themselves on Coligny, expecting that Coligny's followers would in turn kill the Guises, thereby decreasing the pressure upon the monarchy from both sides. Though the attempt on Coligny may not have originated with Catherine, when it miscarried she either panicked or cold-bloodedly took advantage of the opportunity to eliminate the Huguenot leadership, detonating a wider massacre. Pater believed Charles's complicity remained "unresolved" even in the nineteenth century; but accounts from the first seem relatively clear-cut about his domination by Catherine and his brother Anjou, the future Henry III. Catherine cynically convinced her impressionable son that unless he struck first, their lives were immediately at risk from Huguenot reprisal. Charles moved from an initial anger at the attempt upon Coligny's life (he smashed his tennis-racket he was so upset) to a belated but bloodthirsty participation in the massacre two days later (enthusiastically potting Huguenots with an arquebuse from his Louvre window). Probably the real risks Catherine intended to lessen were long-term: renewed civil strife (since the Huguenots now saw they could no longer rely on the king for protection) or a war with Spain if Coligny recovered and marched into Flanders with Charles in support of his charismatic "father." The latter eventuality she avoided; the former, of course, her blunder primed and ignited.

61:10   *Noces Vermeilles* **marriage**   "marriage of blood" or "blood-red wedding," a reference to the massacre that followed the marriage. The father of the future Duke of Sully "had predicted darkly that 'if these nuptials took place in Paris, the wedding favours would be very red'" (quoted in Whitehead, p. 256).

61:10   **Henry of Navarre with Margaret of France**   The third civil war had concluded advantageously to the Huguenots with the peace of St. Germain-en-Laye in 1570, causing dissatisfaction among the militant Catholics. In 1572 the marriage of Henry of Navarre, the emergent head of the Huguenots, with King Charles XI's sister Margaret (or Marguerite, "Queen Margot"; see 9.92:19) was designed to foster religious reconciliation. Unlike Coligny, Henry was no paragon of Huguenot leadership; the Venetian ambassador to Paris once observed him eating cherries and throwing the pits at the Huguenot preacher in the pulpit. Numerous Protestants attended the ceremonies on August 17 (betrothal) and 18 (wedding), described at firsthand by the Huguenot historian Agrippa d'Aubigné (3.6.3; passage translated in Coudy, pp. 180–181).

61:17   **famous letter**   Immediately after the assassination attempt on Coligny, Charles had written his governors, including François de Mandelot, the governor of Lyon, asking that it be made known he intended to punish the perpetrator and insisting that everyone without exception must observe the edicts of pacification. Probably as a protective measure, Charles also shut all but two, tightly guarded, gates of Paris. Mandelot and others again were written on the 24th of August, Charles claiming the massacre was the work of Guise; verbal instructions at this time may have included orders to eliminate Huguenots. Neither written dispatch, however, seems to be Pater's "famous letter" since neither depicts what Pater terms "guilty foresight."

61:23   *Mon père*   When in September 1571 Coligny was summoned back to court, Charles "called him his father and after three embraces, the last cheek to cheek, said graciously as he wrung the old man's hand, 'Now we are going to keep you here; you won't be able to escape us if you wish'" (d'Aubigné 3.6.1; "old" here was early fifties). D'Aubigné reports that when Charles visited Coligny after the assassination attempt, he used the same term of respect, several times.

61:23   *câlineries*   cajoleries, fondlings

62:37   **degrees of kinship**   Henry's grandmother was a sister of Francis I, Marguerite's grandfather, making bride and groom second cousins (the common great-grandparents were Charles, Comte d'Angoulême and Louise of Savoy); although a papal dispensation was required, both because the parties were within the degrees of consanguinity prohibited by the Church and because of their different religions, the Pope's refusal was entirely because Navarre was considered a professed heretic. Marguerite dutifully married Henry (despite his heavy body odor) though she was (or at least had been until Charles intervened) pursuing an affair with the Duke of Guise; at the ceremony, she is reported to have remained silent and had her head nodded from behind by the hand of her brother Charles. Though Catherine suspected Henry and "Margot" failed to consummate their union, the two certainly were not chaste when it came to liaisons with others—nor unduly concerned with consanguinity: by her own admission, "Margot" had an early sexual history as mistress for her brother Henry and, after Guise, she performed the same role for brother François. See Erlanger, pp. 61–62.

63:1 **old Cardinal de Bourbon** "old" Charles of Bourbon (1523–90) was allied with Henri de Guise and the League; before Guise's assassination in 1588 he had hoped to succeed Henry III as Charles X.

63:6 **hymeneal Assumption** The principal feast of the Virgin Mary, the Feast of the Assumption is observed on August 15, celebrating the ascent of her body ("transla-tion" in theological terms) into heaven after death. Here the Feast is connected with the marriage (thus, hymeneal).

63:12 *jeunes premiers* "juvenile leads" or "leading couple"—a theatrical phrase, tying in with Pater's on-going metaphor of Paris as theater.

63:20 **Louvre** The entertainments connected with Margot's wedding included balls, banquets, and on the 20th an allegorical masque in the great hall of the Petit-Bourbon adjoining the Louvre—Paradise, defended by Charles and his brothers as three knights, and Tartarus to which the unsuccessful invaders of Paradise (Huguenots, significantly) were condemned (Erlanger, pp. 131–132). On Sunday morning the 24th, the festivities segued into a slaughter when many of the Huguenot retainers of Henry were trapped in the palace, disarmed and slaughtered (Charles watching from a window, shouting that none should escape); a few did flee to Margot (one actually jumped in bed with her, he shouting, she screaming hysterically) and were saved by her intervention.

64:4 **ominous voices** L'Estoile, 12:376 (7 July 1572): "A peasant woman of Châtillon, a subject of the late Admiral, came to him as he was preparing to mount his horse to come to Paris for the wedding of the king of Navarre, threw herself at his feet, putting her arms around his knees with great affection and crying out: 'Ah, my good master, why go to your destruction? I will never see you again if you go to Paris, for you will die there and everyone who goes with you. At least,' she said weeping, 'if you have no pity for yourself, have pity on madame and your children, and on so many good people who will perish on your account.'" Also: "'How often have I predicted it to him! How often have I warned him!" exclaimed Theodore Beza, in the first paroxysm of grief at the assassination of his noble friend" (Baird, 2:554).

64:7   **aged at fifty-five**   Coligny was born February 16, 1519; therefore, he would have been at his death in August of 1572 only fifty-three years of age.

64:9   **Huguenot Queen of Navarre**   Jeanne d'Albret (1528–1572), mother of the bridegroom, who died of natural causes (according to her autopsy) before the wedding. Coming from Italy, where poisoning was a fine art, Catherine de Medici had an unproven notoriety as a poisoner; scented gloves from Catherine's glover, René, had been given to Jeanne (Erlanger, pp. 95–96): "Monsieur René, Italian, . . . lived only by murders, robberies, and poisonings, having poisoned among others the queen of Navarre shortly before Saint Bartholomew," writes L'Estoile (12:380). Marguerite describes in her *Mémoires* Jeanne's death-bed scene and the Court hypocrisy that she witnessed.

64:24–25 **repeats Abelard's typical** *experience.*   Pater retells the "legend" of Abelard and Heloïse in "Two Early French Stories" in *The Renaissance*: "You conceive the temptations of the scholar, who, in such dreamy tranquillity, amid the bright and busy spectacle of the 'Island,' lived in a world of something like shadows; and that for one who knew so well how to assign its exact value to every abstract thought, those restraints which lie on the consciences of other men had been relaxed" (p. 4). Abelard lived in the Latin Quarter, the location of the University of Paris.

64:29   **Huguenot printers**   Protestantism was the first mass movement to take advantage of the revolutionary new medium of printing to influence opinion. Robert Estienne, royal printer for Francis I, with his son Henri was a well-known firm, as was that of Antoine Vincent of Lyons; but many informal syndicates of printers in Paris, Lyon, Geneva and elsewhere carried the burden of polemical debate.

65:9   **Colombe**   Prosper Mérimée's dissimilar, action-oriented novel, *Chronique de temps de Charles IX* (1829), had a romance between a Huguenot male and a Catholic female at the moment of the Saint Bartholomew's Massacre, a reversal of religious affiliations; since Pater uses a quotation from this novel in Chapter 13 (13.131:25) and discussed the novel at some length in his lecture on Mérimée (1890), this is likely the seed of the idea for the love-affair of Colombe and Gaston. Mérimée does not suggest that the Pope cynically encouraged or sanctioned the massacre nor that a frantic monarchy resorted to an impulsive atrocity, but rather that St. Bartholomew's was the result of an unanticipated explosion of popular violence.

65:18   **bullet had been a poisoned one**   When the court went to visit the wounded Coligny, Catherine darkly (a propos of the assassination of the elder Guise) observed that poisoned bullets if successfully extracted could not cause death; a medical attendant replied that Coligny already had been given an antidote as a precaution against poison as a complication.

65:19–20   princes . . . Condé . . . Henry of Bearn   The two princes of Navarre—Henri, Prince de Condé (1552–1588) and Henri de Bourbon, Prince of Béarn (Henry of Navarre)—were first cousins. Condé's marriage to Marie de Clèves, to a lesser extent than Navarre's, had been meant to link Catholic and Huguenot. Immediately after the assassination attempt on Coligny, the cousins had asked Charles's permission to leave the court because they felt they could not remain safely, but the king begged them to stay.

65:25–28   "to rise against . . . enter or depart."   From the Register of the Paris city hall (23 August 1572): "His Majesty more fully and particularly explained to the provost of merchants how on that same evening certain rebellious personages of the new Religion had conspired together against him and his state, even threatening him; in consequence of which he told the provost of merchants to provide and give orders for his safety, that of the queen mother, his brothers, and his realm, and for the peace, repose, and tranquility of the city and of his subjects. And, to forestall further plots and prevent them from carrying out their evil intentions, he enjoined and commanded the provost of merchants to seize the keys to all the city gates, so that no one could enter or leave through them, and to have all the boats on the side of the city drawn up and fastened with chains, and to forbid and prevent anyone from taking them, and to arm all the captains, lieutenants, ensigns, and bourgeois of the wards, and to have the city patrolled by men capable of bearing arms, and to have them ready in the cantons and at the crossroads of the city to receive and execute His Majesty's commands" (*Registres des déliberations du bureau de l'Hôtel-de-Ville de Paris 1449–1614* [Paris: Bonnardot, 1883]; translated in Coudy, p. 190).

65:29   lists   Paris is here an area for a tournament or place of combat, another quasi-theatrical image.

65:33   white badges of Catholicism   A number of contemporary accounts describe arm bands and white crosses on hats as the protective emblem for Catholics; but because in the confusion "everyone was allowed to kill whomever he pleased, whether or not that person belonged to the Religion, provided he had something to be taken or was an enemy . . . it came about that many papists themselves were slain." This anonymous Protestant witness also describes "*les enfants massacreurs*," children who participated in the killing (relevant passages quoted in Coudy, pp. 204–205). Coligny's body was dragged about the streets for three days "*par les petits enfans*" (quoted in Baird, p. 459 n2).

65:35–37   La Rochefoucauld . . . random pistol shot   "brave warrior and merry companion" Jean de Mergey recounts in his *Mémoires* La Rochefoucauld's exit from the Louvre. Later when the king's assassins knocked on his door, he thought it one of Charles's practical jokes; Michelet says his throat was cut before he had stopped laughing. The Duke of Anjou, the future King Henry III, describes how he, Charles and the Queen mother "heard a pistol shot, but could not tell just where it was or whether anyone had been hit. This sound, however, wounded all three of us, entering our minds in such a way that it affected our senses and our judgment, and filled us with terror and fear of the great disorders that would take place" (quoted in Coudy, pp. 192–194, 196–197).

66:1   **madman**   Brantôme (5:255–256) describes the King as having become "more passionate than anyone else. . . . He incessantly shouted, 'Kill, kill!'" Charles's curious sociopathology was probably rooted in a powerful paranoia and a coward's viciousness, which erupted as events spun towards chaotic violence.

66:3   **les enfants massacreurs**   See 65:33.

66:7–8   **vile trap-doors**   L'Estoile (12:380) describes a "rascal" named Thomas who killed a good Catholic named "Rouillard, councillor of the court of Parliament and a canon of Notre-Dame. . . . After holding him three days, he cut his throat and threw him into the water through a trap door he had in his house."

66:12   **double-holiday morning**   Shadwell's note: "Sunday, August 24, Feast of S. Bartholomew" (p. 159). Contemporary accounts suggest that Sunday would have been a work day for many but for the coinciding feast, allowing Parisians the leisure to kill their neighbors.

66:18–19   **the number of thousands**   The following are the various calculations: "The most exaggerated estimate is that of Péréfix, Louis XIV's tutor and later Archbishop of Paris, who speaks of a hundred thousand dead. Bosseut, writing at about the same time, gives the lowest figure—six thousand. Sixty thousand, stated Sully: forty thousand, asserted de Thou, and ten thousand of these in Paris: the Jesuit Bonamy reckoned four thousand in Paris and twenty-five thousand in the provinces, thus going beyond the figure of fifteen thousand that the Protestant Crespin gives in his *Martyrologue*—which the abbé Novi de Caveirac later contradicted with great care and no impartiality. Papyre Masson, the king's historiographer, Conon, Geizkofler and the reports in the English archives all arrive at results that are very close to one another—two to three thousand Huguenots killed in Paris, about ten thousand throughout the provinces. Petrucci and Zuniga speak of three thousand in Paris. According to Brantôme, Charles IX 'took very great pleasure in seeing pass under his windows more than four thousand bodies of people killed or drowned, floating down upon the river'" (Erlanger, pp. 191–192).

66:24–25   **presumed instigator . . . martyrdom**   Francis, Duke of Guise, was treacherously (so the etiquette of warfare in those days defined the act) assassinated in 1562 by Poltrot de Meré, a Huguenot spy, who accused Coligny of abetting his deed; Coligny denied his involvement. Francis's son, Henry, insured that Coligny was among the first to die in the 1572 massacre.

67:4   *ces pauvres morts!*   these pitiful dead! See 7.69:7 where this phrase occurs attributed to L'Estoile's account of the dying Charles IX; since it does not appear here in L'Estoile, Pater may have found his quotation elsewhere, perhaps from some historian completely other than L'Estoile, combining it with L'Estoile's words.

CHAPTER VII : ANNOTATION

The Lower Pantheism

68:11   **The Lower Pantheism**   This chapter was originally published in 1889 as an essay in the *Fortnightly Review* entitled "Giordano Bruno. Paris: 1586." This was the decade in which essential collateral documentation (*Documenti intorno a Bruno*, ed. Domenico Berti, 1880) on the life of Bruno emerged (in 1889 Berti also reissued in revised and expanded form his influential biography of Bruno) and in which Bruno's Latin works (*Opera latine conscripta*, ed. Francesco Fiorentino *et al*, 1879–1891) and vernacular works (*Le opera italiane di Giordano Bruno*, ed. Paul de Lagarde 1888) appeared in complete and scholarly editions. Also, at this time the first English translation of the *Eroici furori* (75:14) was published.

For the novel, the *Fortnightly* chapter was retitled "The Lower Pantheism," in a somewhat heavy-handed ironic allusion to Tennyson's poem, "The Higher Pantheism." Nature may indeed be a manifestation of God; but the higher truth, warns Tennyson, is that there are dimensions of that revelation which mortals cannot perceive or understand. Bruno (1548–1600) sojourned in Paris a number of times during 1581–1586, expounding the Pantheistic notion that God is one with the forces and laws of the universe. In 1586, Bruno returned to Paris where he held a public debate at the Sorbonne in which he disparaged Aristotelian philosophy and defended his new pantheism, the event after which Pater loosely patterned *Gaston's* fictional episode. *Camoeracensis Acrotismus* (Paris, 1586), Bruno's subsequently entitled invitation to this debate, sets forth his central ideas that, we learn from the diary of Guillaume Cotin, the librarian of the Abbey of St. Victor, were expounded on 28–29 May 1586, "*les mercredy et judy de la sepmaine de Pentecoste*" (*Documenti della vita di Giordano Bruno*, ed. Vincenzo Spampanato [Firenze: Leo Olschki, 1933], pp. 44–45). The 1574 burial of Charles on Pentecost blends with the Pentecost of Bruno's discourse, no longer for the novel specifically during 1586, inasmuch as this date has been removed from the heading. The imagined title of Bruno's Pentecostal address is taken from *De Umbris Idearum*, a 1582 work (see below), in form quite unlike the address described here. As Pater did with Aurelius' *Meditations* in *Marius* or with Montaigne's *Essais* in Chapter 5 of *Gaston*, he weaves a cento of Bruno's later published contents into a hypothetical discussion or address: ideas in a book presented in their emergent form "become a visible person talking with you" (*Plato*, p. 198).

68:14–17 *"Jetzo . . . Geist."* From Heinrich Heine's *Travel Pictures (Reisebilder)*, "The Harz Journey" (*"Die Harzreise"*), 1824. The speaker's faith has evolved from an early preference for God the Father's material creation to an appreciation of God the Son's self-sacrificing love to, finally, an emphasis upon the spiritual power of the third person of the Trinity: "Now, grown up, I've read and traveled / Through the world from cliff to coast, / And my heart puts all its faith now / Firmly in the Holy Ghost" (inset in the essay, the poem is entitled "Mountain Idyl"; Pater's stanza is from Section ii).

68:23–24 **coarse rage or** *rabies* In *Marius the Epicurean*, "Manly Amusement" (1:238), Pater describes rabies as an indication of Diana in her character as the "cruel, moonstruck huntress" (possibly in allusion to Martial's *De Spec.* 18). The allusion in *Gaston* thus links St. Bartholomew's with rituals of slaughter and sacrifice in the earlier novel.

68:26–28 **not an unfriendly witness . . . beast of prey** Probably Braôtome's description of the king shouting "Kill, kill" (6.66.1). According to an account attributed to the king's brother, the Duke of Anjou (*Discours d'un personnage d'honneur et de qualité*), Charles, under pressure from Catherine and his counselors, exhibited "a sudden change and remarkable and strange metamorphosis" (Coudy, p. 188); a nineteenth-century historian developed the trope of the huntsman king: "Charles, who had just been telling his mother that 'the weather seemed to rejoice at the slaughter of the Huguenots,' felt all his savage instincts kindle at the sight. He had hunted wild beasts, now he would hunt men: and calling for an arquebuse, he fired at the fugitives, who were fortunately out of range" (White, p. 426).

68:33 **perpetual horn-blowing** When in 1573 Charles fell ill at Vitry-le-Français as the court traveled to Lorraine, his physicians diagnosed the cause as excessive exertion in hunting and in trumpet blowing.

68:35–69:4 **"I have heard . . . weeping"** Brantôme (9:598; *Discours* 8.1: "Isabelle d'Autriche"): *"J'ay ouy raconter qu'au massacre de Sainct-Barthellemy, elle, n'en scaichant rien, non pas senty le moindre vent du monde, s'en alla coucher à sa mode accoustumée; et ne s'estant éveillée qu'au matin, on luy dist à son réveil le beau mystère qui se jouoit. Hélas, dist-elle soudain, le roy, mon mary, le sçait-il?—Ouy, madame, repondit-on, c'est luy-mesme qui le fait faire.—O mon Dieu! s'escria-elle, qu'est cecy? et quelz conseillers sont ceux-là qui luy ont donné tel advis? Mon Dieu! je te supplie et te requiers de luy vouloir pardonner; car, si tu n'en as pitié, j'ay grand'peur que ceste offance soit mal pardonnable.' Et soudain demanda ses heures et se mit en oraisons et prier Dieu la larme à l'oeil."* Pater's translation here—"this offence will never be pardoned unto him"—seems to follow an older edition: *"cette offense ne luy soit pas pardonnée,"* *Oeuvres* 5:297 (Paris, 1823).

69:7–9 **"Ah! ces pauvres . . . morts!"** Predominately from l'Estoile's *Mémoirs de quelques princes hommageables* in the appendix to his *Mémoires-Journaux*. The phrase

"Ah! these pitiful dead," which Pater also quoted separately at the end of Chapter 6, is not in L'Estoile: "the king began to say to her, heaving a great sigh and crying so hard that the sobs interrupted his words: 'Oh! my nurse, my friend, my nurse, so much blood, so many murders! Oh! what wicked advice have I had!'" (12:389). L'Estoile's passage concludes with Charles describing his mental torment. His Huguenot nurse's comforting response may suggest just how much she was aware Charles was a pawn of Catherine's political apparatus.

69:18   **"spiritual body"**   "So also is the resurrection of the dead. . . . It is sown a natural body; it is raised a spiritual body. There is a natural body, and there is a spiritual body" (I Corinthians 15:42–44). See 13.129:27.

69:25   **Pentecostal fire**   The seventh Sunday after Easter (Whitsunday) the descent of the Holy Spirit on the Apostles is celebrated. "And when the day of Pentecost was fully come . . . there appeared unto them cloven tongues like as of fire, and it sat upon each of them" (Acts 1:3).

69:32   **grateful cry of an innocent child**   See 8.90.7–8.

69:36   **world of corruption in flower**   See 3.36.39 and 13.130.1–8

69:38–39   *"Open unto me . . . my undefiled"*   Song of Solomon 5:2.

70:3–5   **On the Feast of Pentecost . . . blood**   Compare L'Estoile's similar wording (entry of this date, 1:3): "Sunday, 30 May, the Feast of Pentecost 1574, at three o'clock in the afternoon, Charles IX, King of France, worn out by a long and violent illness and loss of blood, . . . died." Baird observes: "That the king, whose guilty acquiescence in the murderous scheme of Catherine, Anjou, and Guise, had deluged his realm in blood, should himself have perished of a malady that caused blood to exude from every pore in his body, was certainly sufficiently singular to arrest the attention of the world" (2:638).

70:9   **Charles's successor**   Henry the Third, King of France (1551–1589), brother of Charles IX and of Marguerite of Navarre, spent most of his brief reign (he was assassinated) fighting off the ambitious Guises, who openly aspired to his throne. In Chapter 11, Pater compares him to the "insane young Roman emperor," Elagabalus, who treated "life as a fine art (one of the minor merely decorative or amusing arts)" (11.112.30–31) and who also was assassinated, a victim of his religion of self-worship.

70:15   **Charles's last words**   What Charles apparently meant by asserting "his satisfaction in leaving no male child to wear his crown" was that under Salic Law only males could inherit the kingdom and that both France and its king would be miserable if the ruler were not an adult. See D'Aubigné, 2:129; Baird, 2:637.

70:18   *de ses jeunes guerres*   the wars of his youth; see 11.117:28–29.

70:20   **the half-barbarous kingdom**   Poland; Henry forsook the crown of Poland, leaving Cracow one step ahead of the pursuing Poles, to assume the crown of France.

70:25   **"went in lead"**   coffins for distinguished corpses were lined with lead; therefore, the phrase means "to be buried." Thus in the "Address to the Nightingale" of Richard Barnfield (1574–1627): "All thy friends are lapp'd in lead." The foregoing was falsely attributed to Shakespeare (*Passionate Pilgrim*, 21.24); the following is from *I Henry 6*: "Speak softly, or the loss of those great towns / Will make him burst his lead and rise from death" (1.1.64).

71:13   **Order of Saint Dominic**   The Dominicans are an order of medicant preaching friars founded in 1215 by St. Dominic, Domingo de Guzmán (1170–1221). Bruno took his vows in the Dominican Order in 1566, living at the Dominican convent in Naples where Thomas Aquinas had been buried; he became a priest in 1572. All his surviving works were written between 1582 and 1592. By the time Bruno was burned at the stake in Rome in 1600, his outspokenness (mixed in equal parts of sarcasm and impetuosity) had earned him, as one commentator observes with only minimal hyperbole, the unusual distinction of having sufficiently angered the Calvinists, the Lutherans, *and* the Catholics so that at one time or another each would gladly have done the deed.

71:14   **red mass, *De Spiritu Sancto***   This *Messe Rouge*, so called because the celebrant and the university professors and doctors were all vested or gowned in red, was celebrated in honor of the Holy Spirit as the source of wisdom; it was not a "daily" but an annual mass celebrated at University convocations and, at Sainte-Chapelle, to inaugurate the judicial year.

71:16   **Italian Bishop of Paris**   Earlier, the bishops of Paris had been saints and intellectuals associated with the university; however, during the sixteenth century the bishops were of a more political character. Pierre de Gondi, Cardinal-Bishop (1569–97) of Paris during the Wars of Religion, figures in many accounts of the period, such as Pierre de l'Estoile's *Mémoires-Journaux*, more as a political than a pastoral cleric. The son of an Italian banker, whose wife was a favorite of Catherine de Medici, Gondi entered his church "not through the door but through the window"—appointed by Charles IX rather than, as required by the Edict of Orleans, elected to his diocesan charge.

71:22   **"flightier . . . than the *girouettes*"**   Anti-Italian prejudice was widespread owing to wealthy Italian financiers and courtiers who attached themselves to the widowed queen mother, Catherine. The classic expressions of this xenophobia are recorded in L'Estoile (6 July 1575; 23 September 1578): 1:69–82; 266–68. Consult also Émile Picot, *Les Italiens en France au XVIe siècle* (Bordeaux: Féret, 1918).

72:7   **John of Parma and Joachim of Flora**   John of Parma (c.1208–1289) was an Italian monk in minor orders who became a professor of theology at Paris and a church diplomat under Pope Innocent IV, but later was imprisoned for thirty years in a convent for heterodox beliefs. Joachim (c. 1145–1202), called Flora or Floris from the monastery of San Giovanni in Fiore of which he was both the founder and abbot, was an Italian mystic of noble birth; author of the *Concordia novi et veteris Testamenti* (first printed, Venice, 1519) and the *Expositio in Apocalypsin* (Venice, 1527), among other works. The power of his ascetic mysticism led Dante to include him among the souls in bliss in the "Paradiso."

72:13–14 **Naples, at Città di Campagna, and . . . Minerva at Rome** Bruno's first convent at Naples (1563) was the Monastery of San Domenico; he was admitted to the priesthood (c. 1570) at Città di Campagna near Salerno; see 76:8 for Minerva.

72:21 **new wine into old bottles** Matthew 9:17, Mark 2:22, Luke 5:37, 38

72:33–36 **Plotinus . . . Empedocles . . . Pythagoras . . . Parmenides** Plotinus (204–269), Roman (Egyptian-born) philosopher, whose Neoplatonism regarded nature as the shadow of reality; God is the source and goal of everything. Empedocles, (495–435 B.C.), Greek philosopher and statesman, the leader of the democracy in his city of Agrigentum, Sicily; in hylozoistic fashion he believed that all things have the power of thought and that earth, air, fire, and water never change absolutely, only relatively. Pythagoras (flourished circa 500 B.C.), Greek philosopher and mathematician, is most extensively treated in Pater's "Plato and the Doctrine of Number" in *Plato* (1893); the ancient Pythagorean belief in a divine reason ordering by rational mathematical laws the universe of human minds and physical phenomena underlies Bruno's metaphysics. Parmenides, fifth century B.C. Greek philosopher, believed that there could be only a single, eternal, unchangeable substance; and because change is inconceivable, the world of sense is an illusion. These thinkers were all concerned with nature and mind: substance, number, change or stasis.

73:2 *l'antica filosofia Italiana* the ancient Italian philosophy

73:10 **"the vision of all things in God"** Such a brief, typical idea may be found in several contexts; however, notable allusions to God in things occurs in Bruno's *Spaccio della bestia trionfante* (1584): "God as a whole (though not totally but in some more in some less excellently) is in all things" (*Dialoghi*, p. 777); and again in the Fifth Dialogue of *De la causa, principio e uno* (1584): "Thus by a very definite analogy one sees how the one infinite substance can be whole in all things, albeit in some finitely, in other infinitely—in this with less, in that with greater, measure" (*Dialoghi*, p. 337).

73:32–33 *con questa . . . l'intelletto!* "With this philosophy my mind was enlarged and the intellect increased" (*Il candelaio* [or *The Candle Bearer*], ed. Vincenzo Spampanato [Bari: Laterza, 1923], p. 7). This dramatic satire of religious and social affectation has, perhaps unfairly, been overwhelmed by the far greater bulk of Bruno's didactic work.

73:36 **of "indifference," of "the coincidence of contraries"** Pater's presentation of Bruno's failure to distinguish good and evil values is similar to ideas Pater also finds in Swedenborg's *Arcana Coelestia*, Balzac's novel *Séraphîta*, and a number of "brainsick mystics" (Inman 2:65, 312–313). Specifically in Bruno this Neoplatonic notion is found *passim* in the Fifth Dialogue of *De la causa, principio e uno* (*Cause, Principle, and Unity*) (1584) and *De l'infinito universo e mondi* (*On the Infinite*) (1584)—works undoubtedly indebted to Nicholas of Cusa's concept of infinity, though Bruno locates in material reality the unity-of-opposites that Cusanus ascribed to God. Here is one of the most likely phrases in *De la causa*: "*vegnono ad essere uno e indifferente gli contrari*" (p. 336): "the contraries coincide as one and indifferent."

74:9–10   **intellectual kinsmen of Bruno**   Stoics; the emperor Aurelius was "indifferent" (Chapter 14) to the slaughter in the arena: "He was revolving, perhaps, that old Stoic paradox of the *imperceptibility of pain:* which might serve as an excuse, should those savage popular humors ever again turn against men and women." In contrast, Marius is aware of "a fierce opposition of real good and real evil around him" (1:240–241).

74:19   **"Canticle of the Creatures"**   Saint Francis of Assisi's "Canticle of the Sun" (1225) is also known as the "Praises of the Creatures"; in assonated prose of his native Umbrian dialect with occasional rhymes, Francis expresses his joyous love of nature—sunlight, moon and stars, air, rain, fire, mother earth and even death. "Canticle" derives from the Latin *canticulum,* a little song.

74:20   **"Conform thyself to Nature!"**   See, for example, *La cena de le ceneri* (or *The Banquet of Ashes*), ed. Giovanni Aquilecchia (Torino: Giulio Einaudi Editore, 1973), p. 72, in which Bruno says the painter in his art must shape himself to nature: "*et conformarsi con l'arte a la natura*"; also in one of Bruno's Latin poems: "*Naturaque sit rationi / Lex; non naturae, ratio*": "nature must be law for human reason, and not reason for nature" (*De Immenso et Innumerabilibus,* in *Jordani Bruni Nolani Opera Latine Conscripta* 3 vols. in 8 parts, [Naples and Florence: F. Fiorentino *et al,* 1879–1891], Vol. 1, Part 2, p. 275); similar phraseology occurs *passim* in *De l'Infinito.*

74:25   **philosophy becomes a poem**   This is an apt description of the *Eroici furori* (1585). Pater was, perhaps, in advance of modern scholarship in calling attention to Bruno's literary expression of his philosophy, the songs and sonnets interpolated in his prose treatises; drawing heavily from Lucretius, Bruno also painted a "poetical" picture of the cosmos, albeit in Latin prose rather than in hexameters.

74:28   **antinomianism**   The doctrine taught by John Agricola in sixteenth-century Germany that faith frees Christians from the obligations of the moral law, only faith being necessary to salvation. As to the lack of "proof" that Bruno's own sexual "purity" was sacrificed to his antinomianism, Pater should have given more weight to the unfolding testimony in the prefatory letter to Sir Philip Sidney in the *Eroici furori,* in which Bruno admitted he "never had a desire to become a eunuch" or believed in being sexually "tied"; indeed, he later confessed that in sexual conquests he aspired to rival King Solomon (Angelo Mercati, *Il Sommario del processo di Giordano Bruno,* [Città del Vaticano: Biblioteca Apostolica Vaticana, 1942], p. 102).

75:10   **the Christian Platonists** Medieval/Renaissance writers who, following Plato, believed that the material world is the image of the eternal Ideas. The relation between Christian mysticism and developments of Plato's doctrines was rooted in the writings of Plotinus and Dionysius the Areopagite; in the Renaissance, this Neoplatonism was developed by Ficino's translations and commentaries on Plato and Plotinus, by Pico della Mirandola's *Commento*, and typically expressed by Edmund Spenser's *Foure Hymnes* (1596) which expound the relationship between earthly and heavenly love. Unlike his predecessors, such as Marsilio Ficino, Bruno was not a consistent Platonizer, but the indebtedness of his influential *Eroici furori* (1585) to Platonic love treatises and of his *De umbris* (1582) to Neoplatonic metaphysics is unmistakable.

75:14   ***Eroici Furori*** *De gli eroici furori* (1585), a collection of love poems heavily influenced by Ficino's commentary on Plato's *Symposium*, published in England and dedicated to Sir Philip Sidney. The first English translation by L. Williams, *The Heroic Enthusiasts*, was published just as Pater was working on *Gaston* and the Bruno portrait, 1887–89.

75:16   **Dante's *Vita Nuova*** Composed at the beginning of the fourteenth century, it celebrates in verse and commentary the supernatural quality of Beatrice's life; belatedly printed only a few years before Bruno's *Eroici* which parallels it. Like Dante, Bruno in the *Eroici* is poet, protagonist, and commentator.

75:21–22 **no Beatrice or Laura** See 10.103:18.

75:30   **a long ladder** Between earthly love and beauty and their heavenly counterparts there are progressive stages (seven, according to the worthiest authorities) by which the physical lover mounts to the mystical vision of Love and Beauty. Pater drollfully characterizes the poetry of Dante, Petrarch, and Bruno as leaning the neo-Platonic ladder up against the edifice of Christianity.

75:37–38 **"as the hart for the water-brooks"** "As the hart panteth after the water brooks, so panteth my soul after thee, O God" (Psalm 42:1, King James Version).

76:1–2 *A filosofia è necessario amore* Love is necessary for philosophy

76:8   *Santa Maria sopra Minervam!* The church and Bruno's adjoining monastery at Rome facing the Piazza Minerva, erected primarily in the thirteenth century on the site of Domitian's ruined temple to Minerva and other sacred edifices. The name epitomizes the "thick stratum of pagan sentiment beneath" the Christian. Francis I's "cabinet" (see 13.134:6) contained a cast of Michelangelo's "Christ" from this church.

77:1–4 **Bacon . . . Darwin . . . Spinosa** The empirical-scientific spirit of Pater's earliest published studies owes much to biological, chemical, physical, and geological science; however, only Francis Bacon (1561–1626) and, less frequently, Charles Darwin (1809–1882) are among modern scientists directly quoted or named (with a single mention of Isaac Newton). The "delightful tangle of things!" (76:38) is not merely a generalized reference to the scientific empiricism heralded by Bacon's *Novum Organum* (1620), but an echo of the "tangled bank" passage at the end of Darwin's *Origin of Species* (1859). Baruch Spinoza (1623–1671) and seventeenth-century rationalism owes much to Bruno's understanding of a unifying, superior intelligence in the world of experience, to his "pantheism." Pater's most extended treatment of Spinoza's philosophy is in his imaginary portrait of "Sebastian van Storck" (1886), not long before he undertook his study of Bruno.

77:39   **The music of the spheres**   A Pythagorean-Ptolemaic notion that eight of the ten spheres carrying planets surrounding the earth produce sounds according to their differing rates of motion—or at least that the siren (says Plato) or angel (says Shakespeare, Milton) who sits upon each planet's sphere harmonizes her song with all the others.

78:4–7   **"Veni . . . pectora."**   "Come Creator Spirit," first stanza of the familiar hymn of the Roman Breviary, variously ascribed to St. Ambrose, Charlemagne, and Pope Gregory, sung on Pentecost Sunday, among other occasions: "Come Creator Spirit and visit the souls that are Yours; fill with heavenly grace the hearts that You created."

78:15   **Pascal**   See 4.43:14; "'The silence of those infinite spaces,' says Pascal, contemplating a starlight night, 'the silence of those infinite spaces terrifies me" (*Renaissance*, p. 42), a passage Pater found in the *Pensées* 3:206 (*Oeuvres de Blaise Pascal*, ed Léon Brunschvicg [Paris, 1921], 13:127).

78:25   **"prodigal son"**   Parable (Luke 15:11–32) of the son who spent all his patrimony and became a wanderer until the father's welcome to the returning sinner; *prodigal* is rooted in the Latin for "driven forth" (78:36–79:1).

78:27–28   **eat freely of all the trees of the garden of Paradise**   Genesis 2:16–17: "And the Lord God commanded the man, saying, 'You may freely eat of every tree of the garden; but of the tree of the knowledge of good and evil you shall not eat, for in the day that you eat of it you shall die." See 4.43:4.

78:31–32   **"The plurality of worlds!"**   Though the *Causa* speaks of "*innumerabili mondi*" (p. 229), the phrase belongs to *De l'infinito: "alla pluralità e moltitudine di mondi*" (*Dialoghi*, p. 358) or again, twice on the same page, "*la pluralità di mondi*" (p. 512).

80:6   *De Umbris Idearum   On the Shadows of Ideas* (1582) published in Paris and dedicated to Henry III, a Neoplatonic book of celestial imagery; both terrestrial objects and their zodiacal archetypes reflect or shadow the Ideas in the divine mind. Pater does not seem to have drawn upon more than its title for his interpretation of Bruno.

80:15   **the "Nolan"**   Bruno was born in 1548 at Nola, a small Neapolitan town near Vesuvius and called himself "the Nolan."

80:17   *plenis manibus*   with full hands; i.e., liberally, generously

80:18–19 **rank, unweeded eloquence** Hamlet I.ii.135–37: "'Tis an unweeded garden, / That grows to seed, things rank and gross in nature / Possess it merely."

80:31–32 **"Fantastic!" . . . Shakespeare** In both "'Love's Labours Lost'" and his "Shakespeare's English Kings" Pater uses this adjective: "Some of the figures are grotesque merely, and all the male ones at least, a little fantastic"; ". . . like any other of those fantastic, ineffectual, easily discredited, personal graces, as capricious in its operation on men's wills as merely physical beauty" (*Appreciations*, pp. 169, 204).

81:5 **insult, insolence** These are synonyms for Pater's Greek term: hubris.

81:8 **Aristophanes** Athenian comic dramatist (c.448–c.385 B.C.) at the time of the Peloponnesian War; Robert Browning's "Aristophanes' Apology" (1875) perhaps called attention to the psychology of the dramatist's satire. Among his most famous satires are "The Clouds," "The Birds," "The Frogs."

81:11 **"Triumphant Beast," the "Installation of the Ass"** This incorporates the earlier reference to "the 'asinine' vulgar" and refers to *L'asino cillenico del Nolano* published as an addendum to the *Cabala del cavallo pegaseo* (1585) in which authority, particularly that of the universities and the church, is satirized as disguising ignorance. One of the speakers, an Ass, is the same as the Triumphant Beast of the *Spaccio della bestia trionfante* or *The Expulsion of the Triumphant Beast* (1584); this "natural ass" also is indebted at least partially to the ass of Apuleius's *Metamorphosis*, previously the topic of "The Golden Book" (Chapter 5) of *Marius the Epicurean*.

82:13 **no weeds, no "tares"** The Parable of the Tares, Matthew 13:24–30.

82:36–37 **Paolo and Francesca** Dante, *Inferno* 5:73–142. Francesca, the daughter of the Lord of Ravenna, was married to Gianciotto, son of the Lord of Rimini. She fell in love with Gianciotto's brother, Paolo, as they read erotic passages in the "Romance of Launcelot of the Lake" (a French prose-work of the thirteenth century); for their adultery, both were killed by the enraged Gianciotto (the details of which are given by Boccaccio, translated by Leigh Hunt in his *Stories from the Italian Poets*, Appendix 2). Pater's comment about how Paolo and Francesca would have "read" Bruno's lesson raises the issue of the poisonous book, a question that had dogged Pater personally at least since the publication of *The Renaissance*. In *Plato*, Pater remarks that effective writing is never lifeless, that was "not the way in which, as Dante records, a certain book discoursed of love to Paolo and Francesca, till they found themselves—well! in the *Inferno*; so potent it was" (p. 120).

82:37–38 **Margaret of the *Memoirs*** See 9.92:4.

82:39–83:1 **ran counter to . . . distinction** The morally good and evil, the aesthetically precious and base, do not coincide but form independent axes of co-ordinates, insinuating that moral and aesthetic values might turn out to be mutually self-cancelling (Pater's unrevised wording was: "traversed diametrically another distinction"). Perhaps Wilde's "Preface" to *Dorian Gray* may not just be a response to journalistic attacks on the serialized novel as "poisonous" but specifically a reply to Pater: "There is no such thing as a moral or an immoral book. . . . The morality of art consists in the perfect use of an imperfect medium. . . . No artist has ethical sympathies."

CHAPTER VIII : ANNOTATION

An Empty House

84:11   **An Empty House**   The emptiness of Jasmin's house recalls the similar emptiness of Marcus Aurelius' chambers in *Marius* 2:36; but its decor may well allude to Oscar Wilde's residence at 16 Tite Street, Chelsea, famous as the House Beautiful or, for an Oscar closer to Jasmin's age, to Wilde's undergraduate's rooms in Magdalen, furnished with Pre-Raphaelite lilies and large blue china vases. Pater originally had intended Wilde's flippant aphorism, "Live up to your blue china," to serve as an epigraph for this chapter; but he subsequently canceled it. The earliest of Wilde's sayings to attain renown, this witticism was attacked as "a form of heathenism" in a St. Mary's sermon and received still wider currency with a drawing in *Punch* (October 1880). *Gaston*, continued anew, was designed to answer Wilde's misguided discipleship, notifying readers that burning with a hard, gem-like flame does not equate with a China-vase-and-tea-cup-perfected existence.

84:16–17   **Bruno's doctrine . . . might freely eat**   See 7.78:27–28; 82:17–19; also 4.43:4.

84:22   **Jasmin de Villebon**   For possible meaning of this name, see 3.25:18.

84:25   **that choice place, a little *hôtel***   In "Joachim du Bellay" in *The Renaissance* Pater had written that "the poems of Ronsard, with their ingenuity, their delicately figured surfaces, their slightness, their fanciful combinations of rhyme, are the correlative of the traceries of the house of Jacques Coeur at Bourges, or the *Maison de Justice* at Rouen" (p. 156). One may also compare this *hôtel* with the first of the "curious" houses in *Marius*, Chapter 20. This architecture of Italy in France also looks forward to the art of Jean Cousin (11.123:7); Pater's style seems strongly Ruskinean, as if this were a passage from *The Stones of Venice* (1851–1853).

84:27   **aesthetic culture**   As early as Pater's undergraduate essay, "Diaphaneitè" (c. 1864), he exhibited an indebtedness to German aesthetic sources such as Fichte's lectures on *The Nature of the Scholar* (1794, 1805), Schiller's letters on *The Aesthetic Education of Man* (1795), and G. H. Lewes' *The Life of Goethe* (1855). In 1865 Matthew Arnold in *Essays in Criticism* had discussed the "function of criticism," to which Pater's discussion of "aesthetic criticism" in his Preface to *The Renaissance* (1873) alluded. By 1877 an anonymous essay entitled "Aestheticism" describing "a form of culture, an intellectual atmosphere," had appeared in *The Oxford and Cambridge Undergraduate's Journal* (Inman 2:372–375). Wilde's influential aestheticism in the last decade of the century was owing to the publication of *The Picture of Dorian Gray*, a redaction of Pater's aestheticism in *The Renaissance*. If Wilde's novel had a moral, it was not thereby in Pater's opinion a moral book, since its author clearly had an inclination for the atmosphere of exotic depravity in which his characters moved.

84:33   **relaxation of the *moral* fibre**   The connection of the moral fibre with architectural characteristics is typical of Ruskin's *Stones of Venice*. That esteem for "stiffening of the moral fibre" at such quintessentially Victorian schools as Dr. Thomas Arnold's was rather morbidly offset at the end of the Victorian period by an interest in the loosened fibers of Wilde's sphincter to which medical authority testified at his trials.

85:4   **ashlar**   Hewn or squared stone used for facing; here we have plain or plane ashlar dressed smooth (rather than quarry-faced, herring-bone, or any number of other forms).

85:8   **plinths**   Courses of stones or single blocks serving as bases for statues or decorative friezes.

85:8   **from Bramante, from Raffaelle**   Both Umbrians from Urbino, their work embodies the stately, intellectual order and balance typical of the High Renaissance. Donato Bramante (1444–1514), an architect, is noted for his classic unities of space and for the sculptural effects of his interior and exterior masses; he began the construction of St. Peter's Cathedral. Raffaello Santi (Raphael) (1483–1520), primarily a painter, was the manager in charge of St. Peter's after Bramante's death; his other works include various forms of architectural decoration and paintings, such as "The School of Athens" that creates figures in a centralized, symmetrical architectural setting.

85:9   **pilasters**   A columnar projection with a capital and base, structurally a pier but handled architecturally as a column, advancing from the wall a quarter to a third of its width.

85:15   **"those who know"**   literally, *cognoscenti*

86:7   **life as a fine art**   In *Marius* Lucius Verus treats life as a fine art, in the folding of a toga and taking of snuff; in Chapter 11, Henry like Elagabalus treats "life as a fine art" (112:30–31). The added mention of "all select things whatsoever" (86:11) seems an echo of Tennyson's "Palace of Art."

86:33   *entourage*   here, the "setting" or "frame"

86:34   **Leonardo or Titian**   See Pater's chapter on Leonardo (1452–1519) in *The Renaissance* (pp. 98–129) and 10.103:8; Titian is again cited at 95:22. Both artists were part of Francis I's "cabinet": 13.134:6.

87:12   [*Le Songe*] of **Polyphile**   An influential Platonic allegory or dream vision of the
Quattrocento by the Dominican friar Francesco Colonna (1433–1527), published
anonymously at Venice by Aldus Manutius as *Hypnerotomachia Poliphili* (1499).
Manutius, the greatest of Italian Renaissance printers, produced a book worthy of his
reputation, famous for its typography and eerie woodcuts. The French translation by
Jean Martin (who *"possédait la culture italienne la plus raffinée"*)—*Le songe de Polyphile*
(1546)—was published by Jacques Kerver and illustrated with engravings adapted
from the Italian cuts either by Martin's friend Jean Goujon or, according to Pattison
(2:30, 79–83), by Jean Cousin. Apart from the topic of courtly love, its lengthy
architectural fantasies—the idealized temples, ruins and gardens—contributed to
Franco-Italian art theory. Martin's translation, with its "aesthetic" engravings, might
well epitomize "*l'architecture nouvelle*" of Jasmine's hôtel and "*l'époque nouvelle*" of his
life style. The title and phrase that fill Pater's lacunae are from Pattison: "The Italian
fifteenth-century 'Hypnerotomachia Poliphile' becomes 'Le Songe de Poliphile' of
sixteenth-century Paris; on every page are signs of the influence of another mind and
of another age. And again, in these brilliant French engravings it is plain, I think, that
Cousin is the draughtsman who in them resumes and gives expression to the
tendencies of his day, as he indeed was eminently fit to do" (2:79–80).

87:13   [*L'Heptaméron* . . . **Navarre,**]   Marguerite of Angoulême, sister of Francis I and
Queen of Navarre (1492–1549), composed in imitation of Boccaccio's *Decameron* a
collection of amorous and ribald tales drawn from court scandals, entitled *The
Heptameron* (meaning "seven days"), written by her according to Brantôme (8:126)
in her idle hours when traveling; the framing device for these tales is a flood that
confines at an inn the travelers who tell these stories.

87:14–15   ["*sentences*"] of . . . [**Marcus Aurelius**]   Marcus Aurelius Antoninus
(121–180), Roman Emperor and important character in Pater's *Marius the Epicurean*.
Shortly after his arrival in Rome, Marius listens to a discourse by Aurelius, the ideas
and images of which Pater derived directly from the *Thoughts* or *Meditations*, but
selected by Pater to enhance the emperor's distinctive awareness of the shortness of
life, the closeness of death, and the vanity of existence. In *Gaston*, terms or phrases
such as "strenuous" and "lofty conscience" here characterize Aurelius somewhat
differently. Pater owned the edition he here describes: *Le Livre de Marc-Aurèle, Le
Empereur et Eloquent Orateur*, trans. R. B. de la Griesse (Lyon: par Jean de Tournes,
1544). Dedicated to Marguerite of the *Heptameron*, its "purported" contents are "*la
vie, nobles & vertuex exercices profondes & haultes sentences de l'eloquent Marc Aurele
Empereur.*" The epithet "virtuous" is probably taken from this "vertuex"; the
description of its "transmutation" through Spanish from Latin derives from extended
title: "*tradoict de vulgaire Castillan en Francois . . . fidelement reneu et verifié jus les
exemplaires Latins, & Castillan, dont la esté extraict ledoct liune*" (Inman, 1:335).

87:15   **Euphuism**   A prose romance by the Elizabethan writer John Lyly, entitled *Euphues*, gave its name to an artificially elegant style employing excessive antitheses, alliterations and mythological similes and allusions.

87:31   **Giorgione**   Giorgione da Castelfranco (c. 1478–1511), a Venetian painter discussed in Pater's "The School of Giorgione" (1877) and included in the third edition of *The Renaissance* (1888); according to Pater, Giorgione excelled in harmonizing matter and form in ideal instants of life.

87:38–39   **Michel Colombe or Germain Pilon**   Like architecture, French sculpture shifted gradually from its Gothic traditions to an Italian Renaissance style, as illustrated in Colombe's relief, "St. George and the Dragon" (1508–1509) in the Louvre. His work has been called "distinguishably French" but with "deeper affinities" to Italian work. Germain Pilon (c. 1535–90), the greatest sculptor of the later sixteenth century, also merged his native Gothicism with elements from ancient sculpture and from Michelangelo, seen especially in his tomb for Henry II and Catherine de' Medici (1563–70) in the church of St. Denis, Paris. In "Aucassin and Nicolette," Pater conceives "a continuity between . . . the sculpture of Chartres . . . and the work of the later Renaissance, the work of Jean Cousin and Germain Pilon, and thus heals that rupture between the middle age and the Renaissance which has so often been exaggerated" (*Renaissance*, p. 3).

87:39   **Jean Goujon**   See 13.130:13–14.

88:27   **"mannered"**   Derogatorily, an adherence to peculiarities of style; here also a disparaging reference to the artistic advent of imbalance and restlessness in the Mannerist style, a revolt against the Italian High Renaissance after the death of Raphael.

88:29–30   **Transalpine complexion of Dürer's *Melancholia***   Situated across ("trans") or on the other (north or west) side of the alps ("alpine")—opposite to cisalpine, "this side"; the *Melancholia* (1510) of Albrecht Dürer (1472–1528) is filled with unresolved anxieties and perplexities, reflecting the spirit of nascent Mannerism in Italy. In his essay on "Winckelmann" in *The Renaissance*, Pater refers to Winckelmann's "ardent attraction towards the south. In German imaginations even now traces are often to be found of that love of the sun, that weariness of the North (*cette fatigue du nord*), which carried the northern peoples away into the countries of the South" (*Renaissance*, p. 179).

89:19–20   **cloth of silver and pearls, marvellously *godronné***   Ornamented in loops of interwoven strands: "*Les mignons étaient poudrés, frisés, godronnés comme leur maître*" (Jules-Étienne-Joseph Quicherat, *Histoire du costume en France . . . jusqu'à . . . XVIIIᵉ siècle* [Paris: Hachette, 1875] p. 421). Cotton translates Montaigne's use of this word (in "The Affection of Fathers" [2.8.400 C]) as "tricked." Pater may have in mind Oscar Wilde's *Picture of Dorian Gray* in which Dorian "appeared at a costume ball as

Anne de Joyeuse, Admiral of France, in a dress covered with five hundred and sixty pearls" (Chapter 11). When Joyeuse married the sister of Henry III, according to L'Estoile, Pater's usual authority, king and bride (others say bridegroom) "were so covered with pearls and precious stones that it was impossible to count them," and at each of the seventeen parties "the lords and ladies appeared in a different costume, most of them of gold and silver cloth enriched with embroidery and precious stones of infinite number and great price" (Entry of 7 September 1581; 2:22). Earlier (10 December 1577) at another wedding, "the King made the thirtieth in a masquerade of thirty gentlemen and thirty ladies of the court, all dressed in cloth of silver and white silk embroidered with pearls of great number and price" (1:224–225).

89:20   a **"symphony in white"**   See T. Gautier's "Symphony in White Major" and J. A. M. Whistler's series of paintings by that name, *Symphony in White III* having been sent for exhibit at the Royal Academy. Aware of how his own name and writings cropped up in Oscar Wilde's "The Critic as Artist" (1890), Pater may be alluding here to Gilbert's comment on "the Impressionist painters of Paris and London. . . . Some of their arrangements and harmonies serve to remind one of the unapproachable beauty of Gautier's immortal *Symphonie en Blanc Majeur*, that flawless masterpiece of color and music which may have suggested the type as well as the titles of many of their best pictures. . . . Their white keynote, with its variations in lilac, was an era in color" (Part 2).

90:3   **Pré-aux-Clercs**   A famous students' common-area in the Faubourg St. Germain, to the north of the Abbey of St-Germain-des-Prés: "the university claiming jurisdiction over this ground, the students used to repair thither for their diversion, and it consequently soon became a constant scene of debauchery, duelling, and confusion, to the great scandal of the reverend fathers and peaceful *bourgeois* of St. Germain" (*Galignani's . . . Guide*, p. 367).

90:7–8   **that cry Augustine heard**   Saint Augustine (Aurelius Augustinus) of Hippo (354–430) described in the *Confessions*, his spiritual autobiography, hearing in Milan a child's voice chanting "*tolle lege*": "Take up and read" (8.12); and the Bible passage on which his eyes first fell effected his conversion. Augustine's doctrine of salvation provided the theological foundation for Luther and Calvin's Protestantism, tieing him to the Huguenots; his abnormal sense of sin ties him to Gaston.

90:13   **"green in earth"**   *Romeo and Juliet* IV.iii.42: "bloody Tybalt, yet but green in earth."

90:26–28   **Wilhelm Meister . . . eyes . . .**   Johann Wolfgang von Goethe, *Wilhelm Meister's Apprenticeship* (8.1); after this description, Werner looks at himself in the mirror. Unlike Dorian's picture which reveals evil, Jasmin's mirror refines the beholder.

90:36   "brief interval"   A phrase associated in the Conclusion to *The Renaissance* with Rousseau's *Confessions*, the brevity of life's "interval" (p. 238) is the keynote of Pater's aesthetic philosophy.

91:1   **rank, unweeded natural growths**   Echo of *Hamlet* I.ii.135–37; see 7.80:18–19.

91:2   **he might "live up to" it**   See note for 84:11; though the phrase is canceled in pencil, to correspond with the ink cancellation of the epigraph, this echo of Wilde's aphorism nevertheless is retained here not only because of the equivocal authority of the pencil cancellations but also because living up to one's aesthetic image is a striking reversal of *Dorian Gray* and is integral to the focus of Pater's novel.

Chapter IX : Annotation

A Poison–daisy

92:11   A Poison-daisy   The daisy was the device of Queen Marguerite; thus Lord Henry Wotton in Oscar Wilde's *Picture of Dorian Gray* has "on a tiny satin-wood table . . . a copy of 'Les Cent Nouvelles,' bound for Margaret of Valois by Clovis Eve, and powdered with the gilt daisies that Queen had selected for her device" (Chapter 4). Generally the daisy is not poisonous—unless as here it has become an anticipation of Baudelaire's *fleurs du mal* or the sort of perceived morality that caused the *Daily Chronicle* in an unsigned review to term Wilde's novel "a poisonous book." In the final published chapter (7) of *Gaston*, "The Lower Pantheism," Pater described Paris as "a world of corruption in flower" (69:36) and had described Bruno's philosophy as an attempt to turn "poison into food" (82:26).

92:14   "The earth . . . about me."   Jonah 2:6: "I went down to the bottoms of the mountains; the earth with her bars was about me for ever: yet hast thou brought up my life from corruption, O Lord my God." As a prayer or psalm of thanksgiving after deliverance from the land of the dead, Jonah's allusion to death and resurrection harks back to the motif of entrapment in cave, maze, enchanted palace or other snare and also looks ahead to Lenten imagery in Chapter 13. Pater considered but cancelled an alternative epigraph from Shakespeare's *King John* I.i.213: "Sweet, sweet, sweet poison, for the age's tooth!"—certainly supportive of his chapter title but equally a covert reference to what in Wilde's novel Dorian recognized as Lord Henry's "fascinating, poisonous, delightful theories" (Chapter 6) and, even, the episode of Sibyl Vane's suicide by poison.

92:18–19   assez . . . d'argent   "quite recognizable because it was gilded, and lined with yellow velvet trimmed with silver . . ." *Mémoires de Marguerite de Valois* (Marguerite of Navarre); actually on this occasion in 1574 she visited a nunnery in Lyons with a company of friends and ladies-in-waiting, although malicious gossip did create quite a stir.

92:19   Queen Marguerite of Navarre   or of Valois or of France (1553–1615); daughter of Henry II of France, her political marriage of 1572 to Henry of Navarre, afterwards Henry IV of France, was dissolved by mutual consent; she became, in her apartments at the Louvre, a center of learning and fashion. She was the author of poetry and of the *Mémoirs*, a vivid account in epistolary form of court events from 1565 to 1582; it was composed about 1595 during her confinement in the Auvergne (1586 onwards), reportedly as a corrective to Brantôme's worshipful but inaccurate portrait of her.

92:23   **Jeanne d'Albret**   See 6.64:9. Queen of Navarre; daughter of Henry d'Albert, titular king of Navarre, wife of Antoine de Bourbon, and mother of Henry IV of France; she was a zealous supporter of the Huguenot (Protestant and Calvinist) cause. Her description of Court customs was contained in her letter to Henry of 8 March 1572 from Blois where she had come to arrange his marriage with Margot.

92:26   **pearl, or daisy**   *Marguerite*, pearl (from Latin *margarita*); but also, especially in France, any one of several flowers of the aster family, especially the common garden and field daisy. L'Estoile records (2:305, December 1585) the pun on pearl: "*La Margueritte de haut prix*" (Matthew 13:45–46: "the kingdom of heaven is like . . . one pearl of great price"). Pater's satiric punning (perhaps indebted to the bawdry of Shakespeare's *Much Ado about Nothing*) intensifies below in the imagery of the sword in the "sheath": a sheath or scabbard in Latin is *vagina*.

92:30–32   **"the magnificent, ancient, empresses . . . Brantôme**   Brantôme, Pierre de Bourdeille (1540–1614); served as a page at the court of Margaret of Navarre, later as a soldier and diplomat, withdrawing from court life after the death of Charles IX to write his memoirs—vivid, first-hand accounts of people and events, not always factually reliable. This quotation and many of the others descriptive of Marguerite here and in the next chapter come from his *Book of the Ladies* (*Des Dames, Première Partie* also called *Dames illustres*), "Discourse 5: Marguerite, Queen of France and Navarre" (8:76): "*Bref, ceste reyne est en tout royalle et libéralle, honnorable et magnifique; et, ne desplaise aux impératrices du temps passé, leur magnificences descriptes par Suétone, Pline et autres. . . .*"

92:33   **Faustine**   Faustina, Annia Galeria, the Younger (d. 175 AD); Roman empress, wife of Marcus Aurelius. Pater creates a brief pen-portrait of her in Chapter 13 of *Marius the Epicurean*, a "marvellous but malign beauty" he calls her at the end of that novel.

93:5–6   **the seed of Venus and of Mars**   Giovanni Battista Rosso's *Mars and Venus* (c. 1529), presented to Marguerite's grandfather, Francis the First, was an allegory of the peace of Cambrai, with Francis as Mars and Eleanor of Portugal as Venus. The National Gallery, London, also had acquired a *Venus and Mars* (1481) by Botticelli. Brantôme alludes to Venus' amours with Mars: 9:376–377.

93:7–8   **age of twenty-two**   Actually Marguerite undertook the journey to Flanders in 1577, her twenty-fourth year, as described in her *Mémoires*.

93:10   **Louis the Eleventh**   King of France (1423–1483). Henry III, before his assassination, had imprisoned Marguerite in the Château d'Usson in Auvergne; afterwards, she continued living there—immorally, by most reports.

93:14   *il y a toujours à redire.*   "there is always something with which to find fault"

93:15–20   "**In a little time . . . the oar?**"   Brantôme (8:71): "*Car celluy qui la tenoit prisonnière en devint prisonnier dans peu de temps, encor' qu'il fust fort brave et vaillant. Pauvre homme! que pensoit-il faire? Vouloir tenir prisonnière, subjette et captive en sa prison, celle qui, de ses yeux et de son beau visage, peut assubjectir en ses liens et chaisnes tout le reste du monde comme ung forçat!*"

93:38   **François de Guise**   Son of the founder of the ducal house of Guise (1519–1563); after his assassination, his son Henry succeeded him in duchy and titles. See Brantôme (4:187–281).

94:1–13   "**Gentleman in ordinary . . . at a push!**"   Montaigne's duty at court also was "Gentleman in ordinary to the bedchamber" (Mark Pattison, *Essays*, ed. Henry Nettleship [Oxford: Clarendon, 1889], p.344) and this may have been equally in Pater's mind; certainly Pater is confusing (or conflating) Brantôme with Pierre de l'Estoile's graphic account (1:322–323; 19 August 1579) of the slaying of Bussy d'Amboise who, also as a favorite of Alençon, perhaps seemed a Brantôme-like figure: "He loved to read historical accounts, among others the Lives of Plutarch; and whenever he would read of a noble or brave exploit by one of those old Roman captains: 'There is nothing in all that (he would say) that I couldn't do just as gallantly if it were necessary [at a push].' He also used to say that though he was born a mere gentleman, he had in his bowels the heart of an emperor."

94:11   *Ces beaux faicts!*   Pater's three words after the dash effectively translate Brantôme's phrase.

94:18   "**name and fame**"   See Tennyson's "Vivian," *Idyls of the King*: Merlin's charm caused its victim to "lay as dead / And lost to life and use and name and fame," lines 73–74.

94:21   *faictz . . . invention*   "made and composed by his intellect and his ingenuity" (for the sake of the quotation, Brantôme's *mon* became *son*). Pater then loosely translates into English the rest of this quotation from the *Testament et codicilles de Brantôme* (10:126–127): "*mes livres, qui j'ay faictz et composez de mon esprit et invention, et avecques grande peine et travaux escrits de ma main, . . . lesquelz on trouvera en cinq volumes couvertz de velours tan, noir, verd, bleu, et un en grand volume, qui est celui des Dames, couvert de velours vert, et un autre couvert de vélin, et doré par dessus, qui est celuy des Rodomontades, qu'on trouvera tous dans une de mes malles de clisse, curieusement gardez, qui sont tous très-bien corrigez avecques une grande peine et un long temps. . . .*"

94:26–28   [*Grands capitaines . . .* **fully seventy**]   Brantôme's *Oeuvres* were borrowed by Pater from the Taylorian and Brasenose College libraries on numerous occasions between 1886 and 1893 (Inman 2:497); three titles comprise his most famous writings: *Great Foreign Leaders*, *Great French Leaders*, and *Book of the Ladies* (which includes both *Dames illustres*, in which Margaret is portrayed, and *Dames galantes*, titles that were invented by Brantôme's later editors for the more simply titled *Premier* and *Second livre des dames*). Although in his "*Testament*" Brantôme specifically cites only *Dames* and *Rodomontades* (10:127), this latter volume is so negligible Pater probably did not have it in mind. Gaston, we are told in Chapter 1, died "about the year 1594" (1.1:32); we also learn there that 1562 was "Gaston's tenth year" (1.8:38–39), so the dates for his short life are *circa* 1552–1594 (he dies, somewhat older than Pater's typical aesthetic hero, about his forty-second year of age).

94:36   *atome*   "little bit" or "hint"

95:2–3   **"symphonies" in black and grey, with "harmonies"**   Not only had Whistler painted the *Symphony in White* pictures (see 8.89:20), but in 1872 the *Arrangement in Gray and Black* (known as *The Painter's Mother*) was accepted for exhibition by the Royal Academy; another of his famous works was entitled *Harmonies*. Whistler's work typified an artistic artifice that had prevailed over more conventional values and, even, Ruskinian indignation.

95:6   **Les belles ferronières**   "the gallant ladies with jewelled chains on their heads"—thin chains, of course, of precious metals. Francis the First acquired a portrait by Leonardo's pupil or by the master himself, formerly inaccurately designated *La Belle Ferronière*, now in the Louvre; mentioned in "Leonardo da Vinci," *The Renaissance* (p. 112).

95:7   **"The League"**   Henry, Duke of Guise, founded the League in 1576 both to defend Catholicism against the Huguenots and to overthrow King Henry III (the successor of Charles IX) and place himself upon the French throne. See further 11.115:15.

95:8–10   **It was . . . like iron.**   Théophile Gautier's phrase "*couleurs metalliques*" describes Baudelaire's "strange flowers, unlike those of which nosegays are usually formed; they have the metallic colouring . . . of . . . those exotic blooms . . . grown on the black loam of rotten civilizations" (quoted in Inman 2:306). This ambiguous imagery is in contrast to Pater's representation of decadence in the "Preface" to *The Renaissance*; there he speaks of "that subtle and delicate sweetness which belongs to a refined and comely decadence," illustrated by "an aftermath, a wonderful later growth" of the Renaissance "put forth in France" (pp. xii–xiii).

95:11   **Bernard de Palissy**   (c. 1510–1590), a Huguenot potter and scientific writer on crystals and salts (*Admirable Discourses*, 1580) whose "rustic" earthenware dishes and ewers were decorated with plants and animals (he used actual casts of snakes, fish, frogs and lizards), as well as monsters and allegorical or mythological figures; though at one time patronized by Catherine de' Medici, he died in the Bastille, a martyr to his religious beliefs. Pattison devotes the final chapter of her study to Palissy, referring to his "*Plait aux mascarons*" (2:283) and similar figures.

95:22   **Raffaelle, Titian** Raphael or Raffaello Santi (1483–1520) and Titian or Tiziano Vecellio (1477–1576) are contrasted with the Italianate decadence of Paris—its "caducity" or falling off of vigor and freshness. Thus, for example, Jasmin's townhouse is presented (almost with Ruskinian dogma) as architecturally "losing its medieval precision, and therewith its strength," and "in collusion with certain inward tendencies towards relaxation of the *moral* fibre," the "severe structural lines" giving way "till they vanished" into mere "ornament" (8.84:31–37).

95:24   *Italy in France* In "The Lower Pantheism" Pater describes "the reign of the Italians just then, a doubly refined, somewhat morbid, somewhat ash-coloured, Italy in France, more Italian still" (7.71:16–18). The lack of underlining there suggests that "Italy in France" is not meant to be a book title. Ever since Giorgio Vasari described Francis's Fontainebleau as *quasi una nuova Roma* (a kind of new Rome), historians have applied to his court such expressions as *une Italie française*. In "Leonardo da Vinci" in *The Renaissance*, Pater's penultimate paragraph begins and ends: "France was about to become an Italy more Italian than Italy itself. . . where, in a peculiarly blent atmosphere, Italian art dies away as a French exotic" (p. 128). Also in *Gaston's* Chapter 11, "The Tyrant," Pater calls Jean Cousin "a sort of Michelangelo in France" (11.123:8).

95:27   **Jean Cousin** Cousin, the Elder (c. 1490–1560/1), chiefly painted on glass, though oils, sculpture, and woodcuts are also attributed to him; he worked in the provinces and, Pater implies, was not influenced by the court painters of Francis I at Fontainebleau where Italian art and artists were fostered. See also 11.123:7.

95:29   **Veronese** Paolo Veronese (1528–1588); his intricate patterns of mathematical proportions resisted the imbalance of Mannerist art and looked back to the classic symmetries of the High Renaissance.

96:2   **the child** See 6.67:22.

96:14   *Odyssey* Book 10:312–13: "*hê d' aips' exelthousa thyras ôixe phaeinas / kai kalei*," "Suddenly coming forth, she flung the glittering doors wide and welcomed me in." The parallels in Pater's novel to the *Odyssey*, especially the theme of Circe's enchanted captivity and the returned wanderer, suggest that Pater may have had some further mythic correspondences in mind for his unwritten plot. At Francis I's Fontainebleau, which Gaston visits in Chapter 13, the largest and most ornate gallery, now no longer extant, depicted the whole history of Ulysses; to its courtly promenaders, the Circe episode was not without its traditional allegorical meaning of the snares of carnal pleasure ultimately escaped.

96:32   **Lutetia** Here where Julius Caesar convoked an assembly of Gallic tribes was the town on the island in the Seine that became Paris (Gallic *Parisii*, Roman *Lutetia Parisiorum*); *Ile de la Cité* is the river island's present name.

97:10   **Pierre de l'Escot**   or Pierre Lescot (1510–1578), a French architect, whose study of Roman ruins made him the founder of French architectual classicism; he was employed by Francis I on a wing of the Louvre called *de l'Horloge*.

97:11   **"Matins of Paris"**   Matins, together with Lauds, is the canonical hour for morning prayers, an ironic allusion. The massacre of Huguenots began at two o'clock on the morning of the Feast of Saint Bartholomew, August 24, 1572, and spread outward from Paris in the days that followed. Marguerite's account of the Huguenot courtiers sheltering in her chamber (*Mémoires*, Letter 5) is given in Michelet also (9.24.312–313).

97:16–17   **Richelieu, Napoleons**   Richelieu, de, Duc (1585–1642), French cardinal and statesman; Napoleon Bonaparte (1769–1821), Emperor of France, his son Napoleon II (1811–1832), and Napoleon III (1808–1873).

97:27   *scriptorium*   the writing room of a medieval monastery where records and manuscripts were written and illuminated.

97:37   **Homer's Circe**   Book 10:136: "*deinê theos*," "the dread goddess"

98:1–2   **all . . . is clear, straightforward and—prosaic!**   Discussing the portrait work of Léonard Limosin, Pater's very good friend, Emilia Pattison, writes: "The very choice of colour betrays more science and less sympathy. . . . There are no suggestions of romance in line or colour to soften the fretful lines of the face . . .or dignify the narrow ferocity . . . or enlarge the sombre intensity. . . . *All is clear, and certain, and prosaic.* Nothing is forgiven, nothing felt; the secret of each life has been penetrated with skilled indifference" (2:226–227, italics added). Though he adapted Mrs. Pattison's description of Léonard's enamels to Marguerite's prose, Pater clearly was using this book for more than historical data.

98:8–9   *car nous . . . divin.*   Brantôme (8:38): "because we spent little time there [i.e., at devotions] in order to admire this princess, who delighted us more than divine worship."

98:13   **chestnuts**   In the golden age, people ate what the earth produced naturally; but for refined courtiers, acorns and chestnuts were fodder for roaming pigs.

98:13–15   *qui est . . . ne paindre*   "which is such that the beautiful utterance of master Jehan Chartier, the subtlety of master Jehan de Meun, and the hand of Foucquet would not be able to express, to write nor to paint"; Jean Chartier (c. 1385–1462), a monastic chronicler of Saint-Denis whose history of Charles VII appears in *Les Grands Chroniques de Saint-Denis* (1477); Jean de Meung (fl. 1280), co-author of the allegorical dream romance, *Roman de la Rose*, a naturalistic, even cynical, depiction of the relationship between the sexes; Jean Fouquet (c. 1420–1481), a founder of the French artistic school who had spent several years in Italy, combined the northern tradition of Gothic sculpture and illumination with both a Flemish eye for natural detail and an Italian feel for order, balance and harmonious unity.

98:28–33 *ce beau visage blanc* "this beautiful white face" Brantôme says Marguerite's "*cheveux naturels*" were "*fort noirs*" (8:35); as an image for her eyes, "deep water-pools" offer a royal analogue for the beguiling water that destroyed Hyacinthus.

98:34–35 **instrument for men's perdition** Pater may be attibuting to Don Juan of Austria a hostility that Brantôme certainly does not impute, but the Don's remark is doubtless Pater's source: "though the beauty of this queen is more divine than human, she is created more to ruin and damn men than to save them" (8:26).

98:38–39 *Retirez-vous . . . vous regarde.* "Withdraw, Madam, I beseech you, because it is necessary for me to pray and to think upon my God, and when I look at you, you make me see nothing but the world all over again"—i.e., made her remember the baser things of this world rather than turning her mind to religious concerns. L'Estoile 1:239 (12 April 1578), relates that this was addressed to Margot two days before *la princesse de la Rochesurion* died.

99:12–13 **Léonard the Limousin** (c.1505–1580), a painter-enameller, was given by François I the overall direction of the workshop in Limoges which produced goblets, candelabra, reliquaries, and other objects; he is especially associated with four paintings that adorned the tomb of Diane de Poitiers. Pattison (2:225) reports that one of Léonard's oval plaques portrayed Margot and another portrayed Margot's mother.

99:16 *Bella Donna* "beautiful lady," another phrase describing the *femme fatale*; also, of course, the name of a poisonous plant, the deadly nightshade, its berries having been a cosmetic.

CHAPTER X : ANNOTATION

Anteros

100:11 **Anteros** The title continues the contradictory effect of the "poison-daisy"; the child of Venus and Mars, created to stimulate his brother Eros, Anteros ("love in return" or "anti-Eros") represents either love's complementary fulfillment or, as the beginning of Pater's fourth paragraph remarks, an "unkindly or cruel love." Alluded to in Pausanias's *Description of Greece* (*Attica*, Chapter 30) as the avenger of slighted love, this minor god is associated with the suicidal love of two young men for each other.

100:13 "**The earth . . . about me**" Jonah 2:6; see 9.92:14. Pater previously had quoted this verse in *Marius* 2:104, defining it as a Dantesque descent into and escape from Hell.

100:16–17 **Plato . . . Stendhal and Michelet** *De l'amour* (1822) by Stendhal [Marie-Henri Beyle] (1783–1842) and *L'amour* (1858) by Jules Michelet (1798–1874) were Pater's immediate references; Plato's *Symposium* is the ancient counterpart (*Plato*, p. 137). In fact, however, Pater's inspiration is Ronsard's verse with its pervasive antithesis of cruelty and beauty. The "unkindly or cruel love" (102:31), already introduced in the last line of the preceding chapter, had appeared in Andrew Lang's translation of Ronsard's "Chanson" to the beautiful Marie "of evil will," who is "cruel and unkind" (*"Fleur Angevine de quinze ans,"* *Amours*, 2:1; Lang, p. 18).

100:23–24 "**The Clod and the Pebble**" One of William Blake's (1757–1827) "Songs of Experience" (1794) contrasting submissive with selfish love.

100:39 *Fastus . . . formam.* Ovid, *Fasti* (1.419): "Disdain is present in beautiful people, pride in their appearance follows" or "But the lovely are disdainful, and pride on beauty waits."

101:20–21 **Tyre and Sidon** The two most ancient Phoenician towns on the Mediterranean coast of what is today Lebanon, alluded to frequently by biblical and classical writers alike as wealthy, noted for purple dyes; but, according to Christ, in need of repentance and of sitting in sackcloth and ashes, precisely the same as the Ninevites to whom Jonah preached (from which the chapter epigraph derives).

101:24 *Amor, L'Amour* "Love" in Latin and French—cognates linguistically and psychologically.

101:25 "**enthroned in the land of oblivion**"   Abelard presented in Chapter 6 "enthroned . . . in such dreamy tranquillity . . . . dividing the elements of human passion, its care for physical beauty, its worship of the body" (*Renaissance*, pp. 4–5) is a gentler parallel to Gaston. The "forgetfulness" of this love also doubles the milder relationship described in Chapter 13, "forgetting itself in the love of physical visible beauty" (13.134:39–140:1).

101:38 *moy, as she . . . roys* Brantôme (8:64): "I . . . who am the daughter of a king and a sister of kings"; Pater paraphrases in English Marguerite's last honorific: "*et femme de roy.*"

102:6 *terne*   "dull," "lusterless," or "spiritless"; Pater's linear word was "sad," "triste" was the first interlineation, and *terne* was merely the uppermost interlineation; as so often elsewhere, there is little to prefer in the uppermost or last squeezed-in alternative rather than in a previous alternative.

102:7 **medicated** This unusual word also occurs in "Poems by William Morris," *Westminster Review* 34 (1868): 302, in a passage descriptive of Provençal love and its idolatry (La Mole [104:30] was from Provence). In both contexts the word has a witchy connotation, meaning to tincture or impregnate with any substance that vivifies or enchants, as the incense on the coal (100:32).

102:26 [**some great distinguishing passion**]   Pater inserted a note in parenthesis above the lacuna in his manuscript: "(repeat)." The four parenthetical words supplied have been repeated from Chapter 1 (10:34). Such passions, Pater notes there, "have not always softened men's natures: they have been compatible with many cruelties" (1.11:32).

102:33 **Aristotle** This idea also appears in "Lacedaemon," *Plato and Platonism* (pp. 216–217). Although unequal role relations are cited in the *Nicomachean Ethics* (8.8:1158b), Pater's primary reference is the *Politics* (1.5:1254a,b): "from the hour of their birth, some are marked out for subjection, others for rule. . . ; for in all things ... a distinction between the ruling and the subject element comes to light. . . ; some men are by nature free, and others slaves, and . . . for these latter slavery is both expedient and right."

102:35 "**impassioned love of passion**"   Phrase attributed by Pater in "Dante Gabriel Rossetti" to Mérimée (*Appreciations*, p. 212) and again cited in his lecture on Mérimée.

103:4 **maze . . . Chartres** See 2.15:29. The maze connects with Pater's imprisonment and wandering motif; his sentence, its form an analogue of the meaning and almost Joycean in its preposterous revolving into itself, merely says in synopsis: "Unkindly or cruel love . . . was for a time . . . to occupy the mind of Gaston."

103:7 [**Leonardo's** *La Gioconda*] Pater's reference to a "labyrinth of land and water, of streams and pathways" is surrounded by verbal echoes from Pater's famous passage on the Mona Lisa: "the remotest delicacies of human form, the shading of the eyelid, the curvature of the lip, . . . the love or lust" (101:28–29) of Margot and her lovers. Here "the exotic personality, the hand, the eye, the lip" are "the fulfilment of Gaston's early boyish dreams" (102:17–27) of poetic passion and the desire for beauty—and not unlike so many "portraits" of Wilde's Dorian Gray.

103:17–18 *Vita Nuova* . . . **Petrarch** . . . **Abelard** Three instances of profoundly intellectualized love: that of Dante Alighieri (1265–1321), author of the *Vita Nuova* (a spiritual autobiography completed c. 1307), for Beatrice; of Francesco Petrarch (1304–1374) for Laura; and of Peter Abelard (1079–1142) for Héloïse (this last, analyzed in Pater's "Two Early French Stories" in *The Renaissance*, had been presented there as less physical, less "sinful" than here).

103:37 **Margaret's supposed Physiology of Love** An investigation into the functions and hygiene of sex (at whatever level of the figurative or psychological) is a topic worthy of Havelock Ellis; perhaps a volume of Paul Bourget, with whose work Pater was generally acquainted, may have suggested Pater's imaginary title: *Physiologie de l'Amour Moderne* (Paris: A. Lemerre, 1891), which had appeared serially in *Vie Parisienne* beginning September 1888 (d'Hangest, 2:364 n.15).

104:3 **the dubious double root** The entanglement of beauty with evil had been foreshadowed in the moral-aesthetic axes of "The Lower Pantheism" (7.82:39–83:4), an issue urgently posed by Baudelaire for nineteenth-century aesthetes generally and by Wilde's aestheticism for Pater in particular.

104:16 **fluttering** the "winged visitant" of 2.21:22.

104:17–20 *In omnibus . . . festinatione*, **in distresful** Psalm 78:32–33 (Psalm 77 in Vulgate). *In omnibus . . .*: "For all this they sinned still. . . ." Pater follows the standard Renaissance English translations (Geneva, King James), except that he provides a more accurate rendering of the words translated by the Vulgate as *cum festinatione*; the Israelites' forty-years' wandering in the wilderness, with which this verse is customarily connected, is here an implicit analogue to Gaston's moral wandering. Pater's spelling of "distresful" was obsolete even in the 1890s, but is retained for its biblical undertones.

104:29 **Jacques La Mole** Pater may have first encountered the story of the embalmed head of Jacques La Mole (or Joseph de Boniface, seigneur de La Mole, or La Molle) in Stendhal's *The Red and the Black* (1831), "Queen Marguerite" (2.10); or in Alexandre Dumas' *Queen Margot* (1845). Nor could Pater have missed the reference in Wilde's *Dorian Gray* to Madame de Ferrol who was asked by Dorian, apropos of her several husbands, if "like Marguerite de Navarre, she had their hearts embalmed and hung at her girdle" (Chapter 15). This both recalls Adretz's "necklace of priests' ears"

(1.9:24) and anticipates the scissors hung at the girdle of Madame de Montpensier (11.116:4). Pater also must have heard Wilde discussing another predatory princess and her trophy on a silver shield well before *Salomé*'s1892–93 censoring (in London) and publication (in Paris). Pater did his background reading on La Mole in Pierre de l'Estoile's *Mémoire pour servier à l'histoire de France depuis 1515 jusqu'en 1574* (included as an appendix to the *Mémoires-Journaux*, 12:387–88); he may have consulted d'Aubigné (4.6:6) and other contemporary accounts, though the detail of the embalmed head is amply footnoted in Lalanne's edition of Brantôme (9:122–123). Pater's puzzling use of "Jacques" is possibly explained by a too-hasty check of the given name in Lalanne's "*Table alphabétique*," in which Jacques, the unfortunate lover's father, is also listed. Pater probably assumes Marguerite took La Mole for a lover (her *Mémoires* are far too discreet to reveal anything of this sort) not long after her own disappointing marriage, less than two years before his execution; modern scholarship dates the beginning of the affair to January 1574 (Phillipe Erlanger, *La Reine Margot* [Paris, 1972], 115). One wonders if Pater would have allowed the uneuphoneous "province of Provence" to stand in his final draft.

105:4   **more stealthy enemies than he**   A group known as the "Malcontents" attempted to overthrow the government, but many of those implicated (including Alençon and Navarre) were too powerful to be punished without upheaval; La Mole (partly because he was Margaret's lover) and the Count de Coconnas (with Mole, one of Alençon's favorites and a notoriously bloodthirsty murderer on Saint Bartholomew's Eve) were pawns of suitably inferior rank.

105:11   **Ci-gît . . . God]**   "Here lies . . ." L'Estoile supplies an epigram-epitaph that puns on the Latin form of La Mole's name: "*Mollis vita fuit, mollior interitus*" (Mole/Soft was my life, annihilation made softer); but this is too ambitious for Pater's lacunae. In "A Study of Dionysus," Pater had used an English version for the victim torn to pieces: "Here lieth the body of Dionysus, the son of Semele" (*Greek Studies*, 20). Customarily, after "Here lies . . ." the name of the decedent follows with some form of *ne a* with town and date, and then *decede* with date; here, the data of town and dates seem an historical overload.

105:32   **Tannhäuser**   A German *minnesinger*, he is associated with Abelard in "Two Early French Studies" in *The Renaissance* as the victim of a rebellious love that became "a strange idolatry, a strange rival religion" (p. 24) to Christianity. Wilde's Dorian listened to the opera of "Tannhäuser" and saw "in the prelude to that great work of art a presentation of the tragedy of his own soul" (Chapter 11). Like Tannhäuser, Mole and Raoul are infected with a tendency toward servitude—with greater or lesser nobility or foolishness, they are victims of an ever-revolving web of passion. Circe/Margot's web also imprisons Gaston, but Pater's circumspection suggests a sin so subtle it is less infatuation, sadism, lust, avarice or Baudelaire's gangs of demons boozing in the brain than a decadent beauty from which he cannot lift his eyes. Still, Tannhäuser in the cave of Venus and Jonah (of the epigraph) who has fled the presence of the Lord "to the bottoms of the mountains," are certainly analogues for Gaston's moral entrapment and exile.

106:4   *Venustas*   "beauty," "charm," or "attractiveness." Probably no such play was actually given, though Pierre de l'Estoile notes (1:179), for example, that in February, 1577, a troupe of Italian players called *I Gelosi* performed before King and court at Blois and later at Paris. As an indirect echo of Sibyl Vane's infatuation with Dorian Gray (painted as Paris and Adonis), this epitomizes Lord Henry's observation that "women . . . remain slaves looking for their masters" (Chapter 8).

106:5   **Eve, mother of us all**   Genesis 3:20: "And Adam called his wife's name Eve; because she was the mother of all living."

106:7   **[her lord]**   Genesis 3:16: "and thy desire shall be to thy husband, and he shall rule over thee." Pater's lacuna suggested he was seeking another noun, possibly in ironic counterpoint to the biblical "husband." I have been unsuccessful in identifying the particular legend of the "male idol" to which Pater refers.

106:30   *fleurdelisé*   "marked with an iris-flower," i.e., the heraldic lily.

106:37   **"servant of servants"**   Genesis 9:25: "Cursed be Canaan; a servant of servants shall he be unto his brethren."

107:11   **as Plato fancied**   One speaker in the *Symposium* described man as a whole divided by Zeus into two half-beings, male and female, who are impelled by love to reunite once again into the perfect whole. Socrates adds that love is not the happiness of possession but the insatiable yearning to possess; whereas Plato suggests a spiritual or ideal desire, Pater bases it in a decadent carnality.

107:29   **fifteen-hundred-and[-seventy-something]**   The time-setting for this chapter is during the reign of Henry III, 1574–1589. La Mole was beheaded in 1574, though by the time Gaston sees the relic, it seems to have been in Margot's chamber for some time. Although in the *Fortnightly* Pater dated Bruno's discourse as 1586, historically it could have been delivered as early as 1581 (Pater deleted the date when he revised this earlier chapter). If he overlooked the date of Marguerite's removal from her cramped chambers in the Louvre to larger quarters, Pater did know that in 1586 Marguerite was exiled to Usson. All this narrows the time-frame for the chapter as a whole to the early 1580s. But since the year pertaining to the manuscript hiatus is antecedent to Raoul's execution which itself predates the chapter's present, it would likely be in the 1570s. See below 108:16 for a date from L'Estoile.

107:35   *godron*   A large round coil, such as a starched ruff or jabot. In Chapter 8, Jasmin's evening suit is described as being "cloth of silver and pearls, marvellously *godronné*" (8.89:20), i.e., ornamented like pleats in a coil.

108:16   **murder . . . by a servant**   In his entry for September 1574 (1:23), L'Estoile refers to a young servitor named Pierre le Rouge who was broken on the wheel in the

Place de Grève for the brutal murder of his noble master; several similar executions for servant-master crimes are noted in May and July 1582, L'Estoile wondering what sort of "calamity controls valets this year" (2:72). The historical name may have coalesced with an imaginary one from Oscar Wilde's *Dorian Gray*, inasmuch as Dorian's golden book was to have been called (canceled in manuscript) "*Le Secret de Raoul* par Catulle Sarrazin."

108:28 **Place de Grève** According to Stendahl and others, La Mole had been beheaded also at the Place de Grève ("bank of the river"; afterwards called Place de l'Hôtel-de-Ville), a site of public executions from 1310 to 1832; at the French Revolution, this was one of the earliest locations of the guillotine. There is a splendid engraving in the Bibliothèque Nationale, Paris, of the execution (hang-and-burn form) in the Place de Grève of the Protestant martyr Antoine Du Bourg (1559), showing a facade with six large windows, five or six heads at each window, hard-working executioner and assistant, soldiers, and an impressive throng of heads, with a cityscape at the far end of the crowd. The ladies at the windows and two others beside the cross in the square are in exactly the dresses in which the facile court painter, François Clouet, depicts his noble subjects—Marguerite, Catherine, Jeanne d'Albret (whose features resemble each other no less than that of their nearly identical habiliments).

108:34 **shivers partly with cold** Pater interlined a question mark above "cold," presumably because he twice mentioned the "heat" of the day; assuming fear is not the cause, Raoul might shiver here with exhaustion or with mortal coldness, but hardly from lack of heat.

109:1 **Saint Andrew on his cross** According to tradition, St. Andrew suffered martyrdom in Patrae about A.D. 70 on a cross shaped like an X (crux decussata). The French criminal is spread-eagled on a carriage wheel and his legs and arms systematically broken. La Mole's epigram-epitaph might well characterize Raoul, inasmuch as "*mollior interitus*" means "destruction has made pliable, milder."

109:5 **Amor Lacrimosus** Tearful Love; a contrivance of Renaissance and Pre-Raphaelite amatory verse and art. In Pater's early writing there is no mention of the suffering of the superior few; later Pater's views changed to emphasize this element (Inman 2:343–46). Raoul's emotional hero-worship results in his execution by a society that has no sympathy for this love. Similarly, the young men in "Emerald Uthwart" (1892) are stripped of rank in a ritual of degradation that makes them victims of their inspiration.

109:11–12 **the last stroke upon the open bosom** The executioner gave the tortured criminal a finishing blow on the breast to end his misery, the *coup de grâce*.

109:14 **public [labourers]** Executioner's assistants are *valets du bourreau*. Carlyle describing the guillotine alludes to "the Headsman and all his valets" (*The French Revolution*, 5.3:1); and Arnold Bennett's *Old Wives' Tale* (1908) translates these *valets* as "workmen in blue blouses" (3.3).

109:21 thoughts at this time Gaston's Paris "thoughts" of death were alluded to in 8.89:26–29; and Margot's "relic" as their haunting analogue, for Gaston's mind as well as Jasmin's, is suggested by a BNC slip, Chapter 10.263:n.4.

110:5–6 *In . . . anni* See 104:18–21; in this abbreviated version, the verb *deficio* is now in the present tense.

110:10–11 *Amans amavi* "Loving, I have loved . . ." or "I the lover have loved." Possibly Pater is thinking of the opening paragraphs of the *Confessions* (Book 3), in which Augustine, plunging into Carthage's caldron of unholy loves, says, *Quaerebam quid amarem, amans amare . . .:* "I was looking for something to love, for I was in love with loving." Some form of the word for "love" (exclusive of the words for "lust" and "desire") occurs fourteen times in twenty lines, including such constructions as *amare et amari* ("to love and to be loved") and *amare amabam* ("in love with love"). One is reminded of Dante's similar repetition of the word: *Amor, che a nullo amato amar perdonna . . . . (Inferno* 5.103): "Love, that exempts no one beloved from loving . . . ." Pater refers to this episode both in *Gaston* ("The Lower Pantheism") and *Plato* (p. 120).

110:36 **Prayer for Peace** See 1.4:32. At this point, Gaston's state of mind anticipates and is paralleled by that of Prosper Mérimée in Pater's critical portrait. Mérimée's exclusively intellectual focus stripped life of its unseen possibilities; more enhancing is an appreciation of "half-lights," a skeptical probabilism that accepts uncertainty but clings, in greater or lesser degree, to hope: "Fundamental belief gone, in almost all of us, at least some relics of it remain—queries, echoes, reactions, after-thoughts; and they help to make an atmosphere, a mental atmosphere, hazy perhaps, yet with many secrets of soothing light and shade, associating more definite objects to each other by a perspective pleasant to the inward eye against a hopefully receding background of remoter and ever remoter possibilities" (*Miscellaneous Studies*, p. 15). Gaston's prayer may be just such an "echo," valuable as emotional chiaroscuro in a world of otherwise unrelievedly naked acts and passions.

CHAPTER XI : ANNOTATION

The Tyrant

111:11 **[The Tyrant]** Pater's titles often verbally take their cue from the opening and, to a lesser degree, closing paragraphs of their chapters. For example, Chapter 9, "A Poison-daisy," opens with an allusion to the meaning of Margot's name as a daisy and closes with the image of the poisonous belladonna; or Chapter 10, "Anteros," cites the god at the outset and then alludes in the penultimate paragraph to Augustine's caldron of unholy loves. The first paragraph of Chapter 11 puts "The Tyrant" in title form, in quotation marks; Pater repeats this appellation in his fourth from the last paragraph in the chapter. Furthermore, nearly every important document of political history to which Pater alludes in this chapter, ancient or modern, features the word "tyranny" or "tyrant" in English, French, or Latin.

111:14–15 **her brother** Henry III, 1551–1589 (reigned 1574–1589). L'Estoile everywhere discusses the king's duplicity, extravagances, and minions. At ruinous expense, Henry III promoted the careers of his minions, assisting these personable young sycophants to the openings they desired. Margot's cruel love and Henry's tyranny are, of course, thematic siblings.

111:17 **Suetonius and Lampridius** *The Lives of the Twelve Caesars* by Suetonius (69–c. 140) is not a source for the life of Elagabalus though the historian notes unstintingly various royal cruelties, abuses of power, and "unnatural" lusts; Aelius Lampridius was a Latin writer of the latter part of the fourth century, contributing the life of Elagabalus, among others, to the *Scriptores Historiae Augustae* (the *Augustine History*). Pater draws many of his impressions either from Lampridius's account or at second hand from a source such as Edward Gibbon's *Decline and Fall of the Roman Empire* (1:6).

111:23 **Dion, Herodianus** Other principal sources for the reign of Elagabalus: Dio or Dion Cassius (c. 150–235), a soldier and politician, wrote *The Roman History* from the landing of Aeneas in Italy to his own day (Elagabalus figures in Books 79–80); Herodianus or Herodian of Antioch, who flourished in the early third century and was an imperial civil servant, produced a *History of the Roman Empire* (Elagabalus is treated in 5.5–8).

111:24 **[Plutarch]** See 2.23:13 where Pater had cited "the eminent translator of Plutarch, Amyot."

111:28 **Elagabalus**   (or Heliogabalus), a Roman boy-emperor, born in Emesa 204 A.D. and assassinated in Rome 222. Ordained in youth as a high priest of the Syro-Phoenician sun god Elagabol (also known as Baal), he assumed the deity's name. His reign of three years, nine months was infamous for its debauchery, including human sacrifices made to him. L'Estoile (1:337, September 1579) quotes a satiric verse on Henry III: "*Cest Heliogabal, empereur des Rommains, / Ne se contenta pas de la mère Nature / Qui donne le tetin à toute créature, / Mais exposa son corps aux barbiers inhumains, / Affin d'estre changeé, par l'oeuvre de leurs mains, / Au sexe feminin.*" Pater's euphemism, "coarse favouritism" (112:25), refers in part to the policy of appointing officials whose sole qualification was the enormous size of their male members.

111:35 **[Emesa]**   Syrian city (today called Homs) where the temple of the sun god was located.

112:11 **Palatine hill**   Site of the imperial palace at Rome, so called from the day of the festival of Pales, a pastoral deity, when Romulus laid the foundation of the city at the foot of the hill.

112:26 **Cracow to Paris**   Though Pater's manuscript (11.3:03) waffles between Warsaw and Cracow (which suggests Pater composed without ready references other than his slips), L'Estoile records that notice of Catherine's regency pending the return "*du Roy Henri III*'" was sent "*à Cracovie en Polongne*" (1:13); Michelet (10.5:47) also identifies the city as Cracow.

112:26 **Pallas of Troy; Urania**   In Troy a talismanic statue called the Palladium, said to have fallen from heaven and representing the goddess Pallas Athena, was believed to guarantee the safety of the city. Herodian is Pater's source: "Even though this statue had not been moved from the time when it was first brought from Troy, except when the temple of Vesta was destroyed by fire, Elagabalus moved it now and brought it into the palace to be married to his god. But proclaiming that his god was not pleased by a goddess of war wearing full armor, he sent for the statue of Urania which the Carthaginians and Libyans especially venerate. . . . The Libyans call this goddess Urania, but the Phoenicians worship her as Astroarche [Astarte], identifying her with the moon" ("Macrinus, Elagabalus," *History of the Roman Empire*, 5.6). Oscar Wilde mentioned this incident in Elagabalus' reign as included in the poisonous novel that influenced Dorian Gray (Chapter 11); at this place in his text, Wilde's catalogue of ancient figures impersonated by "Raoul" recalls Pater's interpretation of the sinister Mona Lisa (*Renaissance*, p. 125), including his "as . . . as" construction.

112:30–36 **life as a fine art . . . masquerade**   This is an idea Wilde had found in Pater's *Renaissance*, but in King Henry Pater is satirizing Lord Henry's notions of how "now and then a complex personality took the place and assumed the office of art, was indeed, in its way, a real work of art, Life having its elaborate masterpieces, just as poetry has, or sculpture, or painting" (Chapter 4). Pater had used the metaphor of

Paris as a stage before in Chapters 6 and 9; the fondness of Henry III for fantastic costumes is a leitmotif of L'Estoile's assessment of his extravagance.

112:38 **fanatical monk** a Jacobin monk, Jacques Clément, intensely devoted to the League. L'Estoile (3:304, August 1589) notes that unexpectedly stabbed at eight in the morning, the king was literally caught with his pants down: "*n'avoit encores ses chausses attachées.*"

113:22–24 *Votre etat . . .ruine* Louis of Nassau (1538–1574), younger brother of William I, the Silent, prince of Orange. His friendship with Gaspard de Coligny acquainted him also with Charles IX. Pater probably found the quotation, which he "rearranged," in Michelet: "Now, he said to Charles IX, you touch ruin; your State is engulfed on all sides, cracked as an old tumbledown cottage where one patches the foundation all the time but cannot prevent it from falling apart. . . . Where are your nobles? Where are your soldiers? Your throne is yours to lose" (10.1:49).

113:28–30 *Le Roi . . . monde* L'Estoile (3:122, February 1588): "*Fait aussi masquarades et ballets, tout ainsi qu'en la plus profounde paix du monde, et comme s'il n'y eust plus eu de guerre, ni de Ligue en France*"; "He also provided masquerades and balls, just as if the times were those of greatest peace in the world, and as if there were no war and no League in France." This does not appear in L'Estoile for 1582 as Pater implies, though a good bit of 24 September to 16 October 1581 was spent in festivals; *festins et masquarades* are mentioned elsewhere also (2:182–183, March 1585; 3:123, March 1588). Pater transposes and misquotes, for style's sake—or perhaps because he took his notes in English and was recomposing back into French without the benefit of the text. Reconstructed according to Pater's configuration, the passage would read: "The king is behaving as if there were no war and no League in France; every day he has made new banquets, as if his State had been the most pleasant in the world."

113:32–33 *"On . . . effroyables."* "One hears dreadful things spoken."

113:34 **flying cortege** Catherine's "flying cortege" or "flying squadron" were her ladies-in-waiting who informally apprised her of court intrigues and political affairs.

113:38 *la . . . commencé* "the eighth civil war had begun"; this does *not* seem to be in L'Estoile near the appropriate date. Between 1562 and 1587, eight civil wars blended into a single struggle punctuated with uneasy truces. The "War of the Three Henries" was the eighth war.

114:15 *des trois Henri* Henry III, King of France, and Henri de Lorraine, duc de Guise, fought Henri de Navarre, future King Henry IV. The "War of the Three Henries" errupted after the collapse of the Treaty of Nemours (1585); but the Huguenots' victory at Coutras was shortly reversed by the Duke of Guise. Henry, merely the husk of his younger (reluctantly) military self, was murderously jealous of Guise's larger share of glory (L'Estoile, 3:75, 79; November and December 1587).

114:29–30   **less than a tenth . . . proportion**   Mérimée, *Chronique,* writes: "The population of France was nearly twenty million souls. It was calculated that at the time of the second civil war the Protestants were not more than a million and a half; but they were proportionally stronger in wealth, soldiers, and generals" (*Préface*). Or: "One presumes that there were never in France more than fifteen or sixteen hundred thousand Reformed. . . . France had fully fifteen million inhabitants. Thus the Protestants formed no more than the tenth part" (quoted from M. Lacretelle, *Histoire de France* [2:169–70] by Baird [2:159 n.3]).

114:36   *que . . . pieds*   "those Huguenots always land on their feet." Baird attributes Catherine's remark to the year 1574; he cites an earlier edition of L'Estoile's memoirs by Michaud et Poujoulat and gives *"se retrouvent tousjours"* (2:630) instead of Pater's variant.

115:1–2   **Suabian chronicler . . . famous Italian smith**   Such a Swabian (Pater's spelling is a permissible variant) chronicler has not been identified; neither has the Benvenuto Cellini-type Italian craftsman. But the pen in the hand doubles the poniard that pierces the palm, linking admirer and victim in the same image—a familiar variation on the circumstances of Mole or Raoul.

115:4–5   *une . . . terre*   an army of men leaving earth

115:15–16   **Holy Union**   In 1584 when Henry of Navarre became heir apparent, Henry, Duke of Guise, lead the Holy League, *La Sainte Union,* with the aim of seizing the country by a *coup d'état,* "under this clever masquerade and holy pretext of religion . . . they call themselves true defenders and assertors of the Roman, Catholic, and Apostolic faith, against those who make profession of the new opinion or Pretended Religion of Reform [i.e., Protestantism]" (L'Estoile, 2:184, March 1585). The covert purpose was to wrest control of the country from Henry III for the House of Lorraine, the truth of which even Pope Sixtus acknowledged.

116:2   **de Montpensier**   Catherine Marie de Lorraine, Duchesse de Montpensier (1552–1596), daughter of Françoise de Guise, sister (*"soeur furieuse,"* according to one of Pater's slips) of Henri de Guise, married to Louis II de Bourbon. L'Estoile (3:119, January 1588) notes that when ordered by the King to leave the city, she "had the impudence and shamelessness to say that she carried at her belt the scissors that, within three days, would give the third crown to Brother Henry of Valois" ("Brother" in the religious sense; also, the pope wears a triple crown but Henry's would be the crowns of Poland and France and his tonsure). This echoed a remark of the wife of Marshal Retz who had said that "the whole trouble could be settled with a pair of scissors," alluding to the possibility that the king ought to end his days immured by the Guises in a cloister, much as Childeric had been forced by Pepin to receive a tonsure and enter a religious order. As "the new Judith" (or "the 'Judith of the party,'" as another Pater slip notes), the Duchess is like the eponymous heroine in the apocryphal Book of Judith who cut off the head of Nebuchadnezzar's general

Holofernes. Judith's story is often compared to that of Jael (Judges 4:21); also the assassin Clément as the Duchess' instrument had been confirmed in his mission by comparison to Judith and Jehu (2 Kings 10:11). Judith, Jael, and Jehu are all divine instruments of political justice upon powers of darkness in high places.

116:5   *fainéant*   Henry III; the word means "indolent." Although Louis IV had also been so titled (L'Estoile, 4:398), Henry III was spoken of with contempt as a Sardanapalus (Assyrian king), "*un prince fainéant, enyvré de luxe*" (L'Estoile, 2:350, July 1586).

116:11   [Babylon]   Among several more-political allusions to this Babylonian anti-Christ, the most explicit parallel is the one L'Estoile gives as a Latin epitaph for a murderer: "Paris now is what Babylon was" (5:169, May 1592).

116:14–15   *du . . . Lys*   "government by the lords of the heraldic lily" Reference here is to the Salic and other fundamental laws that at this time were undergoing political scrutiny; the House of Lorraine claimed descent from Charlemagne, whereas the Valois were merely descended from Hugh Capet, a usurper just six centuries previously!

116:25   *Retourne . . . revéille-toi*   Quoted in L'Estoile (1:104, December 1575): "Return, Chilperic; wake-up Clovis!" (Sonnet IX). Both are ancient French kings prior to Charlemagne.

116:28–30   *Le tuer . . . vocation*   "To kill him or to tonsure him" "to make him pursue his vocation"

116:33–34   *s'il . . . Roi*   "if it would be a good move to assassinate the king"

116:34–35   **Old Jewish history, old Roman history**   Saul (I Samuel 15:28) and Julius Caesar, among others; although Étienne de la Boétie's *Discourse of Voluntary Servitude* (1574) cites these in particular, Pater is probably thinking specifically of Theodore Beza's *Right of Magistrates* (1574) which is particularly rich in such examples. Michelet (10.9:83–98) devotes a chapter to Catholic theories of tyrannicide as background to the assassination of William of Orange (and, later, Henry III).

117:4   *Évangile*   Gospel, and all that it implies of the Reformation doctrine of salvation by faith. See 4.42:5–6.

117:12–13   *Les rois . . . seigneur*   "Kings hold their crown from the people, and can forfeit it for crimes against the people, as a vassal forfeits his fief to his lord." This appears *prima facia* to be Pater's precis of the pseudonymous *Protest Against the Tyrant* (*Vindiciae contra tyrannos*, 1579; *tyrannos* is Greek, meaning "lord," but the sixteenth-century reader could translate it as "despot") possibly by Philippe du Plessis-Mornay, "First Question": "if the vassal does not honor the fealty he swore, his fief is forfeited and he is legally deprived of all prerogatives. So also with the king: if neglecting God, he goes over to His enemies and is guilty of felony towards God, his kingdom is forfeited of right and is often actually lost." But because Pater's quote is French and because Pater's king is answerable for felony not to God but to the people, I'm inclined to believe that Mornay's apparent source, Theodore Beza's *Right of Magistrates* (*Du droit des magistrats*, 1574), may have been uppermost in Pater's mind, even though it is a less succinct formulation: "a king or even an emperor . . . forfeits his fief if . . . he commits felony against his vassals . . . Furthermore, even supposing that the lord could not forfeit his fief for crime against the vassal, the fief of the vassal is clearly forfeited for crime against his lord. But the emperor himself . . . owes homage to the empire of which he is the chief and sovereign vassal, and this applies as much or even more to the posture of kings with respect to their kingdoms. Therefore, there can be no doubt that their fiefs are forfeited if they commit crimes so extreme as to become infamous and obdurate tyrants" (Chapter 6).

In the wake of the St. Bartholomew's massacre, French theorists—the Protestant ones taking their clue, most likely, from John Calvin's magisterial *Institutes of the Christian Religion* (1536)—circumscribed the powers of kingship and claimed popular rights in such works as Boétie's *Discourse* (written about 1549 but printed—by Huguenots, much to Montaigne's disgust—only in 1574) and again not only in Beza's *Magistrates* but also in his friend François Hotman's *Franco-Gallia* (1573): "the writer showed by irrefragable proofs that the regal dignity was not hereditary like a private possession, but was a gift of the people, which they could as lawfully transfer from one to another, as originally confer" (Baird, 2:615). Elsewhere, in Jean Bodin's works a defense of the people's rights was balanced with an absolute monarchy and, not long after in England, John Milton's propagandistic polemics defended the abridgment of tyranny (shortening it by a head). One recent account of political theorizing post-1572 is Robert Kingdon, *Myths about the St. Bartholomew's Day Massacres 1772–1576* (Cambridge: Harvard, 1988), which includes a discussion of the *Discours politiques*, printed in Goulart's *Mémoires*, as the least known but most extreme statement on tyrannicide (pp. 173–182). All this ultimately led to such "republican theories of 'social contract'" as, for example, Rousseau's *Du contrat social* (1762) and the French Revolution. The "new connexion" with Beza's thesis (the old had been the St. Bartholomew's Massacre) is the "assembling of the States-general."

117:15 **republican theories** Ideology of those who support a government having a chief of state who is not a monarch, here a reference to the French Revolution (1789). In a night, the nobility of the Revolution had voted away their privileges. In consequence of the murder of the Duke of Guise and his brother the cardinal, the doctors of the Sorbonne absolved the people from obedience to Henry III: "one could remove the power of government from the hands of incapable princes if one suspected their ability to administer" (L'Estoile, 1:77–78, December 1587).

117:18 **Blois** The first of this set of meetings of clergy, nobility and commoners called by the King on November 1576; the States-general advanced constitutional demands and refused the king's request for grants of money.

117:22 *sans . . . personnes* without favor to anyone in particular

117:23 **revolutionary slang of 'ninety-three** In 1793 Louis XVI and Marie Antoinnette were executed, and the Terror of Robespierre and his followers turned Revolution into mere vengeance and madness.

117:24 **Alençon** François de Valois, Duke d'Alençon, youngest son of Catherine, brother of Henry III and heir apparent, often called simply "Monsieur"; died 1584.

117:28–29 **[Jarnac and Moncontour]** Given that "fields" is here in Pater's sense typically a military term, these battles of 1569 are the only likely references. As the Duke of Anjou, Henry fought successfully against the Huguenots, an important factor for the Poles in his election as their king (though in person he was quite a disappointment to them). True, in 1573 Henry was appointed to conduct the siege of La Rochelle; however, the royal army suffered unexpectedly large losses and Henry's election to the crown of Poland came just in time to save embarrassment.

117:34 **Our mother** Henry Baird, in *The Huguenots and Henry of Navarre* (New York: Scribner's, 1886), observes of Catherine's letter informing the King in Poland of his brother's death: "This production . . . reveals the existence of a certain kind of grief, and of a cool calculation that seems never to have forsaken her. The grief is natural enough, but thoroughly selfish in its origin and manifestation, and quite under the control of the writer's will" (pp. 18–19). Of Catherine's performance as regent and power behind the throne, L'Estoile grudgingly observes on the occasion of her death: "She was seventy-one years old, and carried her age well for a woman as homely and fat as she was. She ate well and maintained herself well, but did not satisfactorily understand the affairs of state, although in the thirty years since her husband died she has had as great an importance in them as any Queen in the world" (3:231, January 1589).

118:11–12 *Dès ... seul* "from then the king was alone"

118:13 *princesse ... formée* "such a gorgeous and shapely princess" L'Estoile: "the Queen-Mother found this marriage good, and anticipated that from such a gorgeous and shapely princess the king would be able to have handsome and abundant children; which is the thing (according to common rumor) the said Queen-Mother desires most (or least, according to others) in the world" (1:51, 14 February 1575).

118:15 **Leah, or Rachel** "And when the Lord saw that Leah was hated, he opened her womb: but Rachel was barren" (Genesis 29:31).

118:15–16 *Le Roi ... lignée* "The King would be able to have handsome and abundant children" See above (L'Estoile, 1:51, 14 February 1575).

118:23 **Chartres** L'Estoile records three important pilgrimages of king and queen together to Chartres for purposes of fertility: 26 January 1582 (2:56); 25 June 1582 (2:71); 12 April 1583 (2:121). Other visits are recorded singly or are referenced only sporadically. The most significant are 23 January 1579 (1:306–307), September 1580 (1:369), December 1586 (2:361). Pater's description is based in a generalized way on the two January pilgrimages of 1579 and 1582.

118:27 *Leurs Majestés* **visit in turn every church**   A common reference to "their Majesties" in L'Estoile. There does not seem to be a late Lent pilgrimage, but earlier in November 1575 "the king visited all the churches of Paris to pray and give alms with great piety"; and with the Queen, he went in a coach "to the convents in the vicinity to add to his collection of little lap dogs." Similar visits to Paris churches occurred in August 1576, July 1578, and December 1582 (L'Estoile, 1:93; 1:151; 1:263; 2:95).

118:30 **The True Cross**   See L'Estoile (1:125–126, 15 April 1576); the theft had been recorded in May 1575 (1:58). The chapel was built by St. Louis in the mid-thirteenth century to shelter the Crown of Thorns and other relics, for which the king (more saintly than witting) had paid staggering amounts.

118:35 **muttering**   L'Estoile: "the king goes on foot to the churches of Paris . . . accompanied by only two or three persons, and holds in his hand large-beaded rosaries, reciting and muttering prayers as he goes through the streets. They say this was done on the advice of his mother, to make the people of Paris see how devout a Catholic he was, . . . to encourage them to dig deeper into the purse [i.e., to give him money]. But the people of Paris (although they are easily imposed on in matters of religion) were not deceived, and composed the following verse in the form of a lampoon or jib which was posted up on the streets: The king, in order to get money, has played the beggar, the pauper, and the hypocrite" (1:151–152, August 1576). At the chapter's end, in describing Henry's terrorized "patter" as the storm comes up outside Cousin's window, Pater echoes L'Estoile's description of Henry's religious "muttering."

119:1 *couleurs de sacristie*   colors of the sacristy (where the vestments are kept); hence, colors of the liturgical seasons.

119:3 *quatorze jaunes*   L'Estoile: "in the great and beautiful walks . . . of the Louvre gardens, the King held a tourney of fourteen Whites against fourteen Yellows" (2:33, 16 October 1581).

119:4 **comediens**   *I Gelosi*, Italian players (see 105:29–30). Henry's desire to learn from them "the full meaning of life" is ironic inasmuch as, perhaps not least in L'Estoile's estimation, they seem to have initiated in Paris a topless craze of jiggling breasts: "their comedies taught nothing but fornication and adultery, and served as a school of depravity for the youth of both sexes in Paris. And truly their influence was so great, principally among the gallant ladies and young girls, that like soldiers . . . they exposed their breasts and pecs which constantly oscillated, made by these gallant ladies to go rhythmically like a clock or, better yet, like a blacksmith's bellows which pumps up the fire to serve at their forge" (1:192–93, June 1577). Despite court orders forbidding performances, they continued performing "with the express permission of the king" (following July entry).

119:11 *qui . . . Etat* L'Estoile: "he also took up the study of grammar, to learn to decline. . . . This word seemed to presage the decline of his power" (1:93, November 1575).

119:18 *pour rehausser* in order to accentuate

119:20 **Swiss guards** The popular uprising in May 1588 had occurred when Catherine ordered several companies of soldiers, including Swiss mercenaries, into Paris to thwart the League.

119:25 **a new order of knighthood** the Order of the Holy Ghost, commemorating the third person of the Trinity that on Pentecost descended upon the apostles

119:27 *ces épees dorées* these golden swords

119:29 **hôtel . . . de Saint Paul** A collection of buildings purchased by Charles V in the fourteenth century as royal residences; only its fifteenth century extension, the Hôtel de Sens, was afterwards inhabited by the king. In 1605 Queen Margot returned from exile to take up residence here. With peaked turrets, winding stairways and dungeon, it is one of the best-preserved noble mansions still extant in Paris.

119:31 *Musée . . . France* In the nineteenth century, the Louvre was organized into "museums"; that of the "Souverains" composed five rooms on the *premier étage*, including the former sleeping chamber of Henry IV.

119:30–33 **altar . . . died** Pater's lacunae are filled with contents appropriate to this narrative singled out for mention in the well-known *Galignani's Guide* (pp.172–74).

120:2 *Pour ... disette* "For ten who live here off the fat of the land, there are ten thousand who live in poverty." Note the punning on the "dis-diz" sounds, suggesting that Pater savored the sounds of his French quotations.

120:5 *liberté ...parler* French liberty of speech; L'Estoile's epigraph for the divisional title-page of his *Registre-Journal*: "It is as little in the power of any earthly ability to withhold the French liberty of speech, as to bury the sun in the earth, or to enclose it within a hole" (1:ix).

120:9 *Réveille-matin* The *Réveille-matin des François* (1574), a Huguenot propaganda publication, printing parts of Boétie's *Discours* and many other opinions of the period. In L'Estoile's no less biased political opinion, it was "worthless" as fact (1:31, October 1574).

120:12–13 *La ... Catherine* L'Estoile: "At this time the *Life of the Queen Mother*, which has been popularly renamed the *Life of Saint Catherine*, was printed and circulated.... and the Queen herself has read it laughing to split her sides and saying that if they had consulted her first she would have given them details they didn't know or had overlooked and they could have made a bigger book" (1:27–28, September 1574). Possibly authored by Henri Estienne, this and the *Reveille-matin* were the two most popular pamphlets (both translated into several languages) in reaction to the events of St. Bartholomew's Eve.

120:14–16   **Rithmes . . . menteries**   Rhymes telling of queens Frédégondes, Brunehilde, Jézébel.—Parisian rumors, that is to say lies

120:17–18   *exhumée . . . Le Discours*   exhumed, as it were, from the tomb of its author, *The Discourse*; see above 117:12–13; 5.50:14.

120:32   **old easy accessibility**   L'Estoile: "His Majesty . . . acted more severely and made himself more inaccessible than his kingly predecessors, which the nobility, unaccustomed to such a style, found very unusual; . . . he would not permit them to talk while eating nor to approach him" (1:22, September 1574).

120:39   *Roi de Paris*   L'Estoile writes that after Henry had Guise assassinated, "a scrap of rug was thrown on his poor dead body, and it was left there for some time exposed to the mockery of the courtiers, who called him *the fine King of Paris* (a name his Majesty had given him)" (3:199, December 1588).

121:7   *Le Balafré*   Henry was so nicknamed, "Scarface," because of a scar "from his left ear across his cheek" (L'Estoile, 1:91, October 1575; D'Aubigné, 2.3:20).

121:11   *Bon Prince*   L'Estoile: "Good prince, now that you are here we are saved" (3:137, May 1588); this epithet is also in Michelet (10.13:147).

121:13   *contre . . . sanctifier*   against him in order to hallow them

121:24–26   *J'ay . . . mansuétude*   Montaigne, *Essais*: "That men by various ways arrive at the same end" (1.1.8 B): "for I have a marvellous propensity to mercy and mildness."

121:27–30   **half-domestic animals . . . the rat**   In a Houghton holograph fragment dubbed "Reflections by Lake Geneva," Pater muses how attitudes change "when animals, once feared, have become half domestic, so that we are no longer repelled by them and give them at least poetical justice. The rat shedding tears, as they say, when hunted down at last, has to my mind the same sort of pathos as the hunted witch whose *act d'accusation* is precisely that she cannot shed human tears at all" (Eng bMS 1150).

121:29–30   *le tyran aux abois . . . he pitied*   the tyrant at bay; the ferocity of rats, too, when brought to bay is well known. But Pater discriminates between the sin and the sinner, condemns the one and pities, perhaps because he understands him too well, the other.

121:38–39   **picture . . . *pudoris***   brilliant lad, his face modest and noble; Pattison describes a portrait of Henry III at Hampton Court as an "energetic boy . . . at the age of ten or twelve years . . . beneath the round fulness of the young face which here look out shining with native brilliance from the sober background of quiet brown ... this unostentatious treatment . . . calculated to give value to the rich colour of the flesh tints, to the limpid radiance of the eyes, and to the striking air of life and health which animates the head" (2:131, 335).

122:10–11   **The devil** . . . *ennuyant*   Nowhere else is the devil linked so famously to boredom as in Baudelaire's prologue to *Les fleurs du mal,* "*Au lecteur*" (also in *Une Mort héroïque* he nicknames boredom "*ce tyran du monde*"). In "To the Reader," Baudelaire says the devil causes man's sins, and:

> *Dans la ménagerie infâme de nos vices,*
> *Il en est un plus laid, plus méchant, plus immonde!*
> . . . .
> *C'est l'Ennui!—l'oeil chargé d'un pleur involontaire,*
> *Il rêve d'échafauds en fumant son houka.*
> *Tu le connais, lecteur, ce monstre délicat,*
> *—Hypocrite lecteur,—mon semblable,—mon frère!*

Pater's remark upon "those saving inconsistencies in evil" has much in common with Baudelairean ambiguities that resist definite interpretation.

122:22   **Coligni** . . . **Montgomery**   When Gaspard de Coligny was assassinated, his soon-to-be-distinguished son, François de Châtillon, was fifteen; Coligny's children were "degraded" from their rank as nobles, and pronounced "'ignoble, villains, *roturiers*, infamous, unworthy, and incapable of making a will, or of holding offices, dignities or possessions in France.'" Catherine de' Medici's vengeance had Gabriel Montgomery beheaded for treason in the Place de Grève (q.v. 10.108:28); his children "the judges had declared to be degraded to the rank of 'roturiers'" (Baird, 2:496; 634 n.2). Above "the young children" Pater had interlined "the degraded pauper," doubtless using "degraded" to mean loss of rank, possibly thinking either of François or of Montgomery's young son, who eventually did succeed to his father's rank.

122:23   **daughter of [Charles IX]**   L'Estoile notes in his first entry in the *Mémoires*, recording the death of Charles IX: "He left one daughter, about nineteen months old, named Isabella [Marie-Élizabeth] of France, by his wife Madame Isabella [Elizabeth] of Austria" (1:3, May 1574). The governess of the "little princess" was Brantôme's aunt; Brantôme describes one visit of Henry III to her sick-bed at which "*la petite madame Izabelle de France*" behaved less like Pater's sentimentalized dying child than a spoiled brat (8:145–146). Yet ultimately both Brantôme and L'Estoile paint a sentimental picture: "In short, she had the most courage and greatest spirit that ever was seen in such a young little thing as that" (8:147), says Brantôme.

122:28–29   **died . . . *douceur***   L'Estoile: "died, was mourned and regretted on account of her gentle spirit and her goodness and sweetness" (1:239, 2 April 1578).

122:29–30   **The white queen**   Elizabeth of France: *"la reine Blanche"* is a name given to widowed queens (Brantôme, 8:54). L'Estoile (1:95) records her departure, December 1575.

122:35–36   **husband may repudiate her**   L'Estoile: "the Queen, his wife, lay sick with anxiety (it was said) because she could not have children and because she had heard that for this reason the King would repudiate her" (1:219, 7 October 1577).

122:37   *Me … lignée*   "Give me male lineage!" L'Estoile: "the day after Easter, the King with the Queen his wife left from Paris and went on foot to Chartres, and from Chartres to Cleri, to make their prayers and offerings to the *Belle Dame* solemnly venerated in the churches of these places, so that by their intercession it would please God to give them the male lineage [*donner la masle lignée*] that they so much have desired" (2:121, 12 April 1583). Reporting an earlier pilgrimage to Chartres, L'Estoile (2:56) on 26 January 1582 relates a similar idea: "to give them the heir who would succeed to the crown of France" (see also 2:127, 25 June 1582).

123:5   **Jean Cousin**   See 9.95:27; together with other nineteenth-century scholars, Pattison did not realize there were two Cousins, father and son. Though contemporary scholars date the father's death around the year Charles IX came to the throne, Pater follows Pattison who believed him "living in 1589, having attained a great age" (2:57). The life of Cousin the Younger does indeed reach to about 1594. Pattison's study of Cousin, that already in 1871 had appeared prior to her *Renaissance of Art*, seems to have been Pater's principal interpretative source: "The art for which the Court cared was not the severely restrained work of Cousin, but the product of facile fingers equally ready to paint official pictures of state ceremonies, to decorate triumphal arches, the frame of a mirror, or the panels of a coach. . . . Cousin's work . . . . shows something of that true severity vivified by infinite tenderness, as in Michel Angelo, which can only reside in a great nature, and which inspires fear perhaps in the weak or servile . . . . Whether he paints on glass, or draws on wood, or carves in marble, he is the same Cousin, touching everything with fire and dignity, and for the most part with simplicity. In his later days he was to a certain extent infected by the temper of the Italian decadence, and his manner, in consequence, is sometimes strained and pompous, but it is never vulgar" (2:4–5). Cousin's connection with *la Réforme* seems confirmed by his address in Paris on the Rue des Marais, called "*la Petite Genève.*" Borrowing Pattison's linkage of Cousin with Michelangelo and Pattison's evaluative terms, Pater dramatizes her perception of the misfit of Cousin's genius in a facile Court and, in Henry III's reaction, the fear it inspired in the weak.

123:8–9   **Creation . . . Judgment**   "The Creation of Adam and Eve," not a known work of either Cousin, Elder or Younger; "Eva Prima Pandora" (before 1538, Louvre; cited in Pattison 2:35–39), and "The Last Judgment" (Louvre; cited in Pattison 2:48–51; now ascribed to Cousin, the Younger). Pater's pun on primary/nude in "the naked realities" (11.22:12) may have been prompted both by his awareness that the "Eva" is the first notable French painting of a nude and by the multiplicity of nude forms among the damned in "Judgment." Pater particularly would have responded to Pattison's description of Eve, paralleling in its understated way his purple passage on Leonardo's Mona Lisa—the eyelids of both these knowledgeable women are a little weary. Cousin's use of light in the "Eva" has been cited by others as suggesting familiarity with Leonardo, its Mannerist qualities indebted to Titian and Giorgione.

123:21; 124:4   [embroidered draperies] . . . [Madonna]   Pattison discusses an "obscure process" to create "magical shot effects" with ruby glass and "interwoven golden patterns" that also involved a technical break-through by which Cousin painted thin lines with "enamel colours," thus "executing the embroidered ornaments of . . . draperies on one and the same piece of glass" (2:62–65). It is evident that the popular contrast of "technical skill in colour or design" with "definite subject or situation" that Pater outlines in his "School of Giorgione" in *The Renaissance* (pp. 131, 137) also constitutes the basic misinterpretation of the Court in this paragraph. Thus I have chosen Pattison's "embroidered . . . draperies" as the element of "technical ... design" supplementing the colors; whereas below, the curiosity of the courtiers about the subject suggests filling the lacuna with a contrast to "form," either with "matter," "subject," or, more explicitly, with "Madonna." By dwelling upon this one-sided element of subject in his artistic achievement, the courtiers distract Cousin from his explanation.

123:29–30   old chapel . . . new window   St. Louis added a Holy Chapel to the manor-house within the walls of this "mediaeval Versailles" (Charles IX died, as L'Estoile notes on May 1574, "au Chastel de Vincennes-lès-Paris"). A new Sainte-Chapelle (modeled after the one by the same name in Paris) had replaced the original; it was begun in the fourteenth century (1379) and only completed with a Flamboyant Gothic façade during the reign of Henry II (1552). The subjects of its windows by Cousin the Younger, known as "The Last Judgment" (completed 1558, now much damaged), were taken from the Apocalypse or Book of Revelation (Pattison, 2:31–32). The left window at the end of the nave includes a recognizable likeness of Diane de Poitiers, mistress of the infatuated Henry II, completely naked among the heavenly crowd except for a blue ribbon in her golden hair. Little is known of Cousin's career during the reign of Henry III, and Pater has imaginatively transposed the much earlier "Tiburtine Sibyl" (1530; Pattison dates it c. 1545) from a chapel on the right side of the choir ambulatory in the Cathedral of Sens, perhaps taking his cue from the fact that Cousin later repeated this scene for a nearby chapel in a chateau at Fleurigny.

123:34–35   "I can . . . master play!"   Robert Browning, "A Toccata of Galuppi's," line 27. At 124:5 I use Browning's similie for Galuppi, "like a ghostly cricket," to epitomize the irrelevance of Cousin's explanations for the inattentive courtiers.

123:39   the Sibyl   Pattison describes the subject of the "Tiburtine Sibyl" at Sens: "the appearance of the infant Christ and his mother in glory, to the Emperor Augustus, whose attention is directed to the vision by the Cumaean or Tiburtine Sibyl. . . . The Sibyl of Sens, standing in the centre before us, uplifts her arms with an air of inspired authority above the kneeling figure at her feet. The attitude of the Emperor, the movement of his outstretched hands, are full of bewildered and awestruck amazement.... Over all, thrones the central motive, the glorious apparition, radiant with heavenly light, and hushed in a quiet not of earth; yet within the reach of the hopes and fears which trouble the children of men, for the soft pressure of the Infant against His mother's cheek has a loving delicacy of touch" (2:24–26). In *Marius* Pater wrote, considering Christian maternal affection: "what a sanction, what a provocative to natural duty, lay in that image discovered to Augustus by the Tiburtine Sibyl, amid the aurora of a new age, the image of the Divine Mother and the Child, just then rising upon the world like the dawn!" (2:113–114).

123:39–124:1   [modes . . . feet]   The phrases are from Pater's description of the Mona Lisa ("Leonardo da Vinci" in *The Renaissance*), a figure comparable to the Sibyl: "The fancy of a perpetual life . . . summing up in itself, all modes of thought and life" (p. 125); and from Pattison's description of the kneeling Augustus.

124:5–9   their master . . . court,]   Henry III presumably is annoyed by God's inferior treatment of him in contrast to Augustus, inasmuch as the blessed male child is offered, spiritually, to the Roman but not, physically, to him. Reconstruction of the missing material is a bit iffy, but Pater's intention here does not seem unclear.

CHAPTER XII : ANNOTATION

A Wedding

125:19 *in loco parentis* in the place of a parent

125:29 **grey spires of** *Saint Germain des Prés* Originally this eleventh-century Romanesque church had three square towers, but the twin transept towers were truncated during restoration in the nineteenth century, leaving only the tower with double-arched mullioned windows above the façade, one of the oldest in France; during restoration, its stone spire was replaced with a lighter wooden one.

125:36–37 **Palais des Thermes . . . Hôtel . . . Abbot of Cluny** The old residence of the Abbots of Cluny was finished by Jacques of Amboise between 1485 and 1500 over the ruins of palace baths (*thermes*), now known to predate by 150 years the reign (361–363) of Julian (born 331), who was said to have been proclaimed Emperor here by his troops. The Palais des Thermes once was thought to be the seat of Roman rule in Gaul and afterwards the residence of the early Frankish monarchs. The present assumption is that the structures were public Roman baths destroyed by the barbarians. Mary Tudor, while residing in the Hôtel de Cluny, married the duke of Suffolk in its Flamboyant Gothic chapel, one floor above the ground. In the seventeenth century, the residence housed papal nuncios, including the French cardinal and statesman Jules Mazarin. After the Revolution, it belonged to an odd assortment of owners, finally becoming a museum in 1844.

126:2–3 **[Pierre de Gondi]** See 7.71:16

126:3–4 **[Flamboyant] Gothic chapel** "The ceiling is supported in the middle by a round pillar, from which the ribs extend along the vault, and terminate on brackets against the walls. The vault is loaded with tracery. The chapel receives light from two single pointed windows flanking a recess, in which are three double windows with tracery" (*Galignani*, p. 410).

126:27 **"had met himself"** Jasmin's encounter with his doppelgänger occurs in 4.39:7–29; Gaston was not with Jasmin, Amadée, and Camille when they encountered their ominously prophetic doubles.

126:32–33 *pour faire l'essai* in order to test; i.e., for poison

127:8–9 **La Mole as he lifted [his shattered arm]** See 10.105:9: "his shattered arm making shift to fling cap in air gallantly"

CHAPTER XIII : ANNOTATION

Mi–carême

128:9   **Chapter XIII**   Above the chapter heading in holograh is "Book iii" (see Introduction, p. xvii). Clara's transcription omits this division heading because when she began to copy out the chapter she knew there never would be a Book III.

128:11   **Mi-carême**   *Le dimanche de la mi-carême* is the fourth or mid-Lent Sunday, called "Laetare" or "Rejoice" Sunday from the first word of the Introit, Isaiah 66:10; also called "Mothering Sunday" either from the indulgence granted by Mother Church on this day or from the ancient custom of visiting the mother church at mid-Lent; called also "Simnel Sunday," simnel being a fine wheat flour used in a rich fruit cake sometimes coated with almond paste and baked for mid-Lent (and for Easter and Christmas). The cakes were eaten at mid-Lent to commemorate the feast given by Joseph to his brethren, the first lesson of this Sunday, and also the feeding of the five thousand (John 6; and in Matthew 14, Mark 6, 8, and Luke 9), the Gospel of the day. Lent (from ME *lente*, springtime) falls between Ash Wednesday and Easter, hence the emphasis in this chapter on new beginnings, natural and spiritual. The special signs of joy are flowers on the altar, the organ at Mass and Vespers, and rose-coloured vestments instead of purple.

128:14   **"He shall drink . . . way."**   Psalm 110:7 (King James Version); a reading in the liturgy for this Sunday.

128:27   **"a state of grace"**   Though St. Thomas Aquinas, Luther and Calvin stress rather differing facets, in essence grace is a state of sacred purity or freedom from sinfulness enjoyed by the soul that fulfills God's will; Catholics assert that if lost through sin, contrition and absolution are necessary for its restoration.

128:27–28   **little Prayer for Peace**   See 1.4:32 and 10.110:36.

128:36   *grateful*   Compare *Marius*: "He had often dreamt he was condemned to die; . . . and waking, with the sun all around him, in complete liberty of life, had been full of gratitude for his place there, alive still, in the land of the living" (2:223–224).

128:39   **Cemetery of the Innocents**   Founded a millennium earlier along a Roman road, the Cemetery of the Holy Innocents, with its twelfth-century Church, had been during the ancien régime a popular place for strolling. Just before the Revolution, owing to a newly acquired sense of urban hygiene, its two million skeletons (those that were not powdered and made into bread during the siege-famine of 1590) were moved to old Gallo-Roman quarries south of Paris, christened "the Catacombs," and the old burial ground became an herb and vegetable market.

128:39–129:1   *milliers . . . cadavres*   thousands upon thousands of corpses

129:9–11   *sur cette. . .tombes*   "on this pestilential earth of the great Cemetery of the Innocents, whores wander at night, sheltering near the ossuaries and copulating on the tombs." There were frequent reports on the nocturnal activities and health conditions in the cemetery, its mephitic gases nearly asphyxiating people.

129:11   **La belle Huissière**   A huissière was, nominally, a female porter (its masculine form so translated by William Cotton for his edition of Montaigne) or groom who assisted gentlemen dismounting their steeds; more specifically, for horsemen in need of a mount, "belle" herself was a sharp little filly who would go the distance. A consummate paroxysm transported this beautiful hostler to bliss eternal in the month and year of L'Estoile's entry (1:65–66, June 1575).

129:14–19   *Ce fut . . . âme*   "It was in the broad light of summer day / When the charming maid expired— / Give gold, Gentlemen, you who have, / Living, caressed this Lady, / Tell Heaven what you know, / For the salvation of her wanton soul." Clara (following Walter's practice of omitting ellipses) splices the initial lines of this epitaph to its concluding fifth quatrain (L'Estoile [1:66] records "*à Dieu*" rather than Clara/Walter's "*au Ciel*"); Clara's citation is in the original French, presumably following Pater's practice, as in the "Du Bellay" essay in *The Renaissance*.

129:22   **Vysehrad**   or (in Bohemian) Vysehradsky hrbitov, the most famous of the Prague cemeteries and final resting place of the creators of Czech culture, has an ancient past; the Old Jewish Cemetery (*Stary zidovsky hrbitov*), dating from the first half of the fifteenth century, is an alternative possibility inasmuch as its gravestones have been jumbled in a manner suggestive of the changes in the burial grounds to which Pater compares it.

129:22   **the Alyscamps**   Before the desecration of its sarcophagi, mausoleums, and nineteen churches and chapels during the Renaissance and afterwards, this necropolis on the Aurelian Way at the gates of Arles had been in use since Roman times, greatly expanding after the Christian saints Genesius and Trophimus were buried there. The removal of these and other bodies have left this cemetery as deserted as those of Holy Innocents and St. Pancras.

129:22   **St. Pancras**   The churchyard of St. Pancras Old Church (St. Pancras-in-the-Fields, built about 1350 though by no means the first church on this spot), was for many years after the Reformation the chief burial-place for Roman Catholic families. In the 1860's the construction of a railway destroyed much of the cemetery and, as with Holy Innocents, many bodies were moved elsewhere and the remnants of this burial ground became the St. Pancras Gardens.

129:27 [heavenly] ones Clara's emendation missed her brother's gentle ironizing of the Apostle Paul's theme of the "changed" in I Corinthians 15:36–55.

129:33 *aubépine* hawthorn, white-thorn, or may; the verbal echo of the hawthorn in "The Child in the House" is perhaps Clara's augmentation or possibly Walter's deliberate parallel.

129:36 *arrosée . . . fortifiée* watered, rejuvenated, strengthened

130:1–8 [Le lendemain . . . This flowering that Gaston sees is conflated in Pater's imagination with the earlier effoliation L'Estoile chronicles: "The day after Saint Bartholomew, about midday, they saw a hawthorn bloom in the cemetery of the Holy Innocents. As soon as the rumor became known in the city, the people of Paris rushed there from every quarter . . .: they began then to proclaim a miracle. . . . and because there had been many catholics who interpreted the blooming again of the hawthorn to be the blooming anew of the state of France, . . . a wily hidden Huguenot . . . composed the following: '. . . So, note how eloquent this blood is! / That, unseasonal vegetation, dying in the burning summer, / Grows mightily and sinks roots worthy of heaven'" (12:378–79). This hawthorn that had been bare of leaf and flower for four years, miraculously blooming out of season, was so widely recorded that it became part of the permanent lore of the Massacre. It was described in contemporary pamphlets, published letters, memoirs; later, even Michelet gave a condensed account (9.26.324–325).

130:13–14 Jean Goujon A Huguenot and one of the most distinguished sculptors of his century, Goujon collaborated with Lescot on the restoration of St. Germain l'Auxerrois and on the Louvre. He died before 1568 in exile on account of being a Protestant, if indeed Bolognese documents do refer to him; according to a tradition cited by Pattison (1:212), he was a victim of the St. Bartholomew massacre.

130:14 fountain A collaboration of the architect Pierre Lescot and the sculptor Jean Goujon, who previously had worked together on rebuilding the Louvre, the imposing Fountain of the Innocents (its reliefs carved 1547–1549) stood, until moved and remodeled, in the Cemetery's corner at Rue St-Denis and Rue aux Fers. The original low reliefs of graceful nymphs with their water jars, reflecting a shift away from Gothic traditions toward Renaissance classicism, are now in the Louvre. Its history, from construction to display in the Louvre, is given in Pattison (1:194–199). Again, Pater seems to forge his interpretation from her suggestions: "the weird sisters of the Fons Nymphium seem never to have lost their power. . . . For their beauty has a strange ascetic calm and the sensuous curves of line which might fascinate the common gazer are checked in the full swell of voluptuous expression; across the delicate sentiment which plays about the slight suggestions of movement and of gesture, falls the faint shadow of the past, tingeing with vague melancholy the subtle and singular charm which for ever obeys these spirits of the floods" (2:195–196).

130:15 *bénitiers* holy-water basins or founts

130:21–22   **Adam of Brescia**   *La Divina Comedia*, "Inferno" (30:68–69). At the instigation of the counts of Romena, Adam counterfeited the coin of Florence and in 1281 was burnt for his crime. Once before, in "Demeter and Persephone" (*Greek Studies*, p. 123), Pater cited Dante's figure. For Oscar Wilde's Gilbert in "The Critic as Artist" (Part 2), "Adamo" epitomizes the mood of the "Inferno": "Through the dim purple air fly those who have stained the world with the beauty of their sin, and in the pit of loathsome disease, dropsy-stricken and swollen of body into the semblance of a monstrous lute, lies Adamo di Brescia, the coiner of false coin. He bids us listen to his misery; we stop, and with dry and gaping lips he tells us how he dreams day and night of the brooks of clear water that in cool dewy channels gush down the green Cassentine hills." Pater's "drops of water" (13.130:35) relate to Dante's lines:

> I had while living much of what I wished,
>
> And now, alas! a drop of water crave.
>
> The rivulets, that from the verdant hills
>
> Of Cassentin descend down into Arno,
>
> Making their channel-courses cool and soft,
>
> Ever before me stand, and not in vain;
>
> For far more doth their image dry me up
>
> Than the disease which strips my face of flesh. (30:62–69)

130:31–33   [*Ed ecco . . . uscio.*]   *La Divina Commedia*, "Paradisio":

> And lo! my further course a stream cut off,
>
> Which tow'red the left hand with its little waves
>
> Bent down the grass that on its margin grew.

Dante continues:

> All waters that on earth most limpid are
>
> Would seem to have within themselves some mixture
>
> Compared with that which nothing doth conceal
>
> Though dark its movement, very dark, in tune
>
> With the shade perpetual, that never
>
> Ray of the sun lets in, nor of the moon.
>
> With feet I stayed, and with mine eyes I passed
>
> Beyond the rivulet, to look upon
>
> The great variety of the fresh may-branches. (28:25–36)

Across the brook in the terrestrial paradise is a lady who leads Dante, now on the way to salvation, towards Beatrice to whom he confesses and repents, providing yet one further analogue for Gaston's moral wandering.

130:37 **a certain church**   If not, certainly not unlike, the Church of the Holy Innocents, accommodating in an ad hoc manner through the centuries numerous functions.

130:39 **courtly festivities**   L'Estoile makes a similar comparison, in reverse order, September 1581: "In fact, the cloth of gold and silver, from the masques and chariots to the luxury even in the livery of the servants, the velvet and embroidery of gold and silver, was no more spared than if they had been given in God's honor" (2:23).

131:2 **St. Médard**   A beautiful fifteenth-century church not completed until the seventeenth century. Many windows have old stained glass; in one chapel St. Anne, Mary, and Christ are portrayed. Though stylistically mixed, St-Gervais and St-Étienne-du-Mont, cited to complete the accompanying lacunae, might be remembered by a "well-informed" visitor; both are noted for Flamboyant vaulting and have excellent specimens of period glass influenced by Italian art (the former with glass thought to be by Cousin [Pattison 2:44–45]). St-Étienne, the best known of the three, also has a Valois association: the foundation stone for its new facade, enlarged during the sixteenth century, was laid by Queen Margot. Possibly the still-more-famous St-Germain-l'Auxerrois (the royal parish church of the Valois, its bells signaling the Massacre of St. Bartholomew) or the obscure St-Merry, both with fifteenth-century Flamboyant features and period glass, also may have been in Pater's nearly-well-enough-informed memory.

131:12 *jubé*   A carved wooden or stone screen; Lescot and Goujon collaborated on such a screen at St. Germain l'Auxerrois (some reliefs from which were seen by Pater at the Louvre); St-Étienne has a choir enclosed by an elaborate stone *jubé*, circa 1600, the only remaining roodscreen in Paris.

131:25 *horriblement fanatique*   Mérimée: "The people of Paris were at this time terribly fanatical" ("*Préface*," *Chronique*).

131:33 **[Palestrina]**   Italian composer and reformer of ecclesiastical music (1526?–1594); putting noble and majestic sentiment in the place of the profane words and melodies common in masses, he became the legendary savior of church music.

132:3 *Respiremus*   "Let us take a breath"; in the liturgy for the day, Ezekiel 37:9.

132:6 *aveuglés*   blind persons

132:10–12 **Abraham . . . Spirit**   Galatians 4:22–29; quotation of verse 22 is from the Latin Vulgate: "the one by a bondmaid, the other by a freewoman."

132:15 **stade upon stade**   a Greek measure of length; hence, level upon level. Compare this with the dying Marius: "he would try to fix his mind, . . . like a child thinking over the toys it loves, one after another, . . . on all the persons he had loved in life—on his love for them, dead or living, grateful for his love or not, rather than on theirs for him—letting their images pass away again, or rest with him, as they would" (2:222–23).

132:15–16   [**grand passions . . . ecclesiastical seasons**]   For Gaston contemplation may center on places, aesthetic instants, sounds or silences, as well as persons—or even something as inward as his present state of gratitude for life. But apart from such miscellaneous events or motifs as the new window of Cousin (11.123:32–34), the little Prayer for Peace (1.4:32; 10.110:36; 13.128:28), and the winged visitant (2.21:22; 10.104:17)—the latter two both noted for their absence—Gaston's adult experiences up to this point include no specific moments of *bien-être* or "ideal instants" (*Renaissance*, p. 150); rather, moments such as the voices of children "reinforce the distress of every distressful moment" (8.90:15–16). The three lacunae below are most effectively completed by allusions to more general pleasures such as came to Gaston first in "boyhood." I limited possible options to the initial chapters but selected from them such typical phrases that also would apply to his adult experiences.

132:26   **What had become of him?**   When Pater entitled his first piece of prose fiction "Imaginary Portraits / 1. The Child in the House," he remarked to his editor of this autobiographical composition: "I call the M.S. a portrait, and mean readers, as they might do on seeing a portrait, to begin speculating—what came of him?" (Evans, Letter of 17 April 1878).

132:30   **"My . . . over my head!"**   Psalm 38:4; in the liturgy for the day.

132:34   **brazen** *serpents*   Obsolete bass wind-instruments with mouthpieces and fingerholes, consisting of long conical trumpets bent several times in serpentine form.

133:10   **lifted up his voice and wept**   Phraseology borrowed from Job 2:12.

133:16   **Fontainebleau**   Thirty-six miles southeast of Paris and situated in the midst of a picturesque forest, the château was built for Francis I (incorporating some features of earlier structures, such as in the Chapel of the Trinity a Doric arch from the time of St. Louis) and decorated with the aid of Italian and French artists (the Fontainebleau school). In Pater's day the quiet town surrounding the palace was a fashionable summer resort.

133:18–20   **peaceful sanctuary . . . southeastwards**   La Beauce: "this goodly sanctuary of earth and sky about him" (3.36:31–32). The direction of Gaston's route has been emended; Pater originally wrote "south*west*wards," the direction of Chartres and La Beauce, which would explain why Pater understood this to be for Gaston an escape into the "sanctuary of his youth."

133:25   [**homely**]   Adjective supplied from Pater's discussion in "The School of Giorgione" of French landscape scenery, its roadways and river-banks as interpreted by Alphonse Legros (*Renaissance*, p. 135).

133:27   *étroits sentiers*   narrow footpaths

133:29   [Vitry,] of [Choisy]   Compare these villages with the one in 4.42:31–31. The old Paris-Fontainebleau route (today N305–D25–N7) ran along the southwest (left) bank of the Seine by such villages as Vitry, Choisy-le-Roi, Athis-Mons, and the town of Corbeil. Any old towns along the route would serve Pater's purpose; these two are six and nine miles from Paris, respectively.

133:33–34   *gaie* and *babillard*   merry (*fem.*); talkative

133:36   *riant*   cheerful

133:37   [wreaths of flames or flowers]   Phrase supplied from "An English Poet" in which Pater's describes a French boy and a French-German honeysuckle-trellis of "metal hand-work with its dainty traces of half-vanished gilding" (*Fortnightly Review* 129 [April 1931], 440).

133:39   *gentil . . . campagne*   graceful . . . country fields

133:39–134:2   forest . . . Pharamond and St. Louis   Pharamond, traditionally called the first king of France, c. 420 AD; Louis IX (Saint), 1214–1270 (reigned 1226–70). The road from Paris approaching the town and royal residence of Fontainebleau passes for several miles through a very ancient forest. Many varieties of trees, some very old, grow among rocks, ravines, and meadows; formerly it abounded in stags, deer, and other wildlife. Louis IX loved to hunt at Fontainebleau, calling it his "*chers déserts*"; it was, however, under an "oak" in the *bois* of Vincennes that St. Louis sat and administered justice.

134:2   *moutonnés*   fleecy

134:6   *le cabinet . . . roi*   "the collection of royal art"; paintings and bronze casts of ancient statues brought from Italy. Which paintings Francis's collection contained is only partially known; but Italian artists that it included in addition to Leonardo (and his "Mona Lisa," among other of his works) were Michelangelo, Titian, Raphael, Giulio Romano, Andrea del Sarto, Fra Bartolommeo, and the work of the goldsmith-sculptor Cellini, to note several. Francis's collection contained the portrait of a mistress of a Sforza duke, *La Belle Ferronière*, that served as Pater's touchstone for Italianate Parisian dress (9.95:6). The king displayed these works in a wing added by him to the keep. Its upper floor was a long gallery and the ground floor, where the king displayed his paintings, contained baths and steamrooms. Those not damaged beyond repair by the humidity eventually formed the nucleus of the collection in the Louvre.

134:8   Léonard de Vinci   Pater abbreviated "L. de V.," an Italy-in-France spelling, used to enhance the sense that Gaston is a Frenchman.

134:17   [Michelangelo]   Here and at the end of the paragraph (135:10), I have linked Michelangelo and Leonardo; not only do their critical portraits stand side by side in

The Renaissance, but in his phrase "those mature Italian masters" Pater echoes his epithet "maturity" and his description of Michelangelo's status as one of the "old masters" in the final paragraphs of his essay in *The Renaissance* (pp. 95, 97).

134:22–24 **Margaret's . . . fancy]** The terms "erotic pride," "boyish," and "over-excited fancy," as applied to Marguerite, Raoul, and Gaston respectively, all derive from "Anteros."

134:32 **["indifference"]** Although another term for "negative" philosophies occurs in "An Empty House" where Pater cites the "opportunist doctrines of Bruno and Montaigne" (8.89:39), the noun form "opportunism" seems awkward. Because it is not native to this text, I have resisted using the more famous Paterian term "flux" from Pater's "Conclusion" to *The Renaissance.*

135:4 **linking paternally, filially** Compare the dying Marius' sense of "the link of general brotherhood," "certain considerations by which he seemed to link himself to the generations to come in the world he was leaving" (*Marius,* 2:217, 221).

135:6 **[Christ . . . Apostle Peter]** No instances in *Gaston* fit this description, but in *Marius* there is a perfect match: "The legend told of an encounter upon this very spot, of two wayfarers on the Appian Way, as also upon some very dimly discerned mental journey, altogether different from himself and his late companion—an encounter between Love, literally fainting by the road, and Love 'travelling in the greatness of his strength' [Isaiah 63:1], Love itself, suddenly appearing to sustain that other" (*Marius,* 2:171). Peter describes his "*Quo vadis?*" encounter in the "Acts of Peter and Paul," an account in the Apocrypha.

❦ APPARATUS CRITICUS
TO THE EDITION TEXT

DIPLOMATIC TRANSCRIPTION:
BRASENOSE/ HOUGHTON HOLOGRAPHS

EMENDATIONS & VARIANTS

An Empty House.

"~~Live up to your the china~~". ~~Archbishop's Saying.~~

Beauty and ugliness: no! one could never persuade one's self
these
That ~~they~~ were "coincident" or "indifferent" in this Paris of the Renais-

sance—this garden of all the trees of which according to Bruno's
Bruno's
doctrine, his new religion, one might freely eat. Art certainly

fine art with which just then Paris was so industriously occupied

had and must have its preferences its distinctions, was at its height
indeed

of dainty conscience now as was borne in upon Gaston one day when

to renew old acquaintance he made his way through the quiet mo-

nastic neighbourhood of Saint Germain des Pres to the abode of Jasmin

at present
de Villebon as poetic as "aesthetic" as ever and now a very ornamental

court official advancing rapidly in the royal favour.

Fig. 5

An Empty House. [1]

"~~Live up to your blue china~~".

~~Apochryphal~~ [sic] ~~Saying.~~

[1 cm] Beauty and ugliness: no! one could never persuade one's self that {~~they~~[2] ↑these↓ were "coincident" or "indifferent" in this Paris of the Renaissance—this garden of all the trees of which according to Bruno's doctrine{,} {~~his~~ ↑Bruno's↓ new religion{,} one might freely eat. Art certainly fine art with which just then Paris was so industriously occupied had and must have its preferences its distinctions{,} was ↑▲indeed↓ at its height of dainty conscience ⁺now as was borne in upon Gaston one day when to renew old acquaintance he made his way through the quiet monastic neighbourhood of Saint Germain des Pres to the abode of Jasmin de Villebon as poetic as "aesthetic" as ever and ⁺now ↑at present↓ a very ornamental court official advancing rapidly in the royal favour. [End 1 r]

↑2↓ [¶] In ⁰~~this~~ ↑that↓ choice place, a little "~~hôtel~~ ↑▲or town-house,↓ of which {~~the death of~~ his father<'s> ↑▲death↓ had left ⁰this youthful ↑▲mirror ↑~~looking-glass~~↓ ↓[3] ⁰~~mirror~~ of French fashion the master, one had a favourable

---

1. This chapter of 26 leaves, written on recto only, is not numbered by Pater as chapter eight; consecutive pagination in upper right corner begins with folio 2. Faint pencil headings on fol. 1 in an unknown hand are: *Chap VIII* (above chapter title); *Gaston* (in upper righthand corner); underneath this *Packet 15*; and *(8)* (superimposed on the packet number). Paper: fols. [1], 8 (8 7/8" x 7 7/16"), "cobalt" edge; fols. 2–7 (9" x 7") "COLLARD" watermark, no tinted edge; fols. 9–23 (9" x 7") "cobalt" edge; fols. 24–26 (9" x 7 1/8") "cobalt" edge.

2. A single scroll-bracket indicates a pencil *strikeout* of a word or mark in ink; carets and commas enclosed in double scroll-brackets are *augmentations* in pencil. If the handwriting is Clara's, this and other pencil emendations lack clear-cut authority; however, see notes 13 and 21. In creating the Edition Text, a number of such emendations will be adopted for established editorial reasons.

3. This is the first of many instances where the upwards ordering of interlineations is presumably unchronological. Apparently Pater initially struck out the linear *mirror* and interlined *looking-glass*; he then struck out his interlineation and returned to *mirror*, squeezing the word in between the two strikeouts. Although the above

opportunity ↑▲for↓ ~~of~~ estimating what {↑▲that which↓} ↑▲we ↑▲now↓ call↓ "aesthetic ◇culture was come to under the last of the Valois. It was a Gothic house of the later fifteenth century when ~~anticipating~~ ↑▲in anticipation of↓ the exotic elegance of ~~the~~ ↑▲that↓ Medicean taste which ◇~~was~~ ↑▲would↓ ere long ~~to~~[4] supplant it altogether{,} the national architecture ◇was already losing its medieval precision and therewith its strength. To the ↑ ◇~~cultivated↓~~ trained eyes of that day{,} eyes we may suspect in ◇collusion with certain ↑▲inward↓ tendencies towards **a**[5] relaxation of the *mor*◇*al* fibre it was delightful to see the severe structur◇al lines give way till they vanished or figured [**End 2 r**] ↑3↓[6] ~~but~~ as ↑▲but ↑~~as but only as↓~~↓ ~~more~~ graceful pencillings on a quiet surface jealous of all emphatic relief. The column lost its capital and roved softly into the arch rippling now for ornament rather than support ~~around~~ ↑▲above↓ the pleasant windows which ~~betrayed the~~ ↑that↓ ~~still more fastidious taste~~ ↑wh↓ ~~that ↑wh↓ ↑ing thro' their fine~~ ↑grained↓ ~~glass tha↓~~ trayed through their fine-grained glass the fastidious comfort that ↑▲reigned within.↓ Above{,} towards ~~the~~ ↑▲a ↑a↓↓ roof still acute◇ly[7] pitch◇ed against the rain the pattern◇ed slates wont to protect a loose◇ly plaster◇ed wall ~~now~~ did duty ↑▲now ↑now↓↓ as ornament. Year by year the snow the ↑▲clinging↓ icicles ↑▲were ↑redue◇ed↓↓ ~~clung~~ reducing the little heads of bak◇ed clay ~~below~~ ↑▲below ↑under↓↓ the sill{,} enlarg◇ed from old Roman coin or cameo into veritable likeness of the antique. ~~Below~~ ↑▲Beneath↓ them the ashlar ↑▲was↓ ~~is~~ planed into something like ↑to↓ a marble surface to remind one of the real [**End 3 r**] ↑4↓ marble of Italy and ~~seems to~~ ↑seem◇ed↓ attract<ing> the hand to test its pearly smoothness, while lower still about the doorway inserted like gems in a homely setting was real artists' work ↑▲on↓ ~~in~~ plinths ↑plates[?]↓ of porphyry or jasper. Borrowing from Bramante from Raffaelle the "arabesque" pilasters which divided the continuous window of the ground-floor no longer ↑medie↓ prison-like ↑▲and medieval{,}↓ the Northern builder had associated them to the actual ↑▲neighbourhood{,}↓ ~~neighbourhood~~ and the thistles ↑▲and field-

---

diplomatic ordering makes fewest assumptions, in more complex venues where the scholar may be assisted by a chronological reconstruction, the following ordering may be given: "youthful ↑▲~~looking-glass~~ ↓mirror↑↓ ◇~~mirror~~ of . . . ."

4. Cancelation has a superimposed character resembling an *l*.

5. Deleted *a* is also circled.

6. Ten seemingly random vertical pencil lines, one to two cms. in length, occur on primary lines five, seven, and eight.

7. On folios 3 and 4, Pater uses a single index stroke under *ly*'s and double strokes under *ed*'s.

flowers↓ interlaced in ↑in↓ emphatic love-knots were sympathetic with a natural flush of purple here or there in the precious stone. It was à la mode ↑the taste of the year ↑à la mode↓ ↓ this indeed, ↑▲—the taste of the year,—↓ this highly conscious Italianised manner; ↑▲and↓ yet <(>triumph of the élite, of "those who kno ↑know",↓ in every age ↑▲even when ↑even in↓ ↓ dealing with ↑▲the modes{,↓ the fashions{, [End 4 r] ↑5↓ they have not invented for themselves!<)> everywhere the preference ↑▲individuality↓ the will ↑individuality↓ of the own°ers[8] ↑▲owner↓ showed through.[9]

[¶] The own°er ↑master↓ after all was absent. A°sudden ↑▲An unexpected↓ °summons to courtly duty (as polite servants and a silken-corded letter explain) a royal invitation which ↑that↓ was like a command had caused him to break his engagement as nothing else on earth could have done. Would Gaston make himself at home for awhile, ↑▲eat, and↓ drink of the choice wine set ready, amuse himself with the books ↑▲the↓ pictures say! the toys? It looked comfortable enough with the fragrant ↑▲wood↓ fires on this day sunless ↑▲though summer ↑tho'summer↓ ↓ winter day and if the owner was absent all around ↑▲seemed↓ seemed eloquent concerning him leading Gaston on his side, [End 5 r] ↑6↓ as he lingered there ↑fully↓ agreeably entertained hour after hour to {♦all sorts[10] {↑♦ every kind of↓} of casuistic consideration{s concerning the man and ↑and↓ the house ↑his ↑the↓ abode↓ applicable truly ↑▲generally, in truth,↓ to the mood of that whole ↑▲generation↓ age as seen ↑▲age as reflected↓ in the mirror of ♦all-accomplished Paris.

[1 cm] An age great in °portrait-painting, it found after all its[11] aptest self-expression{,} its ↑▲own↓ veritable portrait ↑°likeness↓ in a dwelling °like

---

8. First s is canceled separately and then the whole word is canceled.

9. The initial period is smeared, so a second period is added.

10. all sorts deleted in pencil; ♦every kind of interlined in pencil. Under the e of every, in addition to a pencil mark, there is a small ink dot, as if Pater with a pen had pondered the suggested correction.

11. In the margin adjacent to this word, the author has left a partial fingerprint in ink.

↑°such[12] as↓ this. In °such places that ↑▲sensuous and {s̶e̶n̶s̶u̶a̶l̶}[13] ↓ highly
coloured ↑▲life↓ described by Brantôme,[14] s̶t̶i̶l̶l̶ ̶i̶n̶ °s̶u̶c̶h̶ ̶v̶e̶h̶e̶m̶e̶n̶t̶ ̶a̶c̶t̶i̶o̶n̶, still
in °s̶u̶c̶h̶ rapid movement on his l̶i̶v̶i̶n̶g̶ ↑▲animated ↑life-° l̶i̶k̶e̶↓ ↓ pages, h̶a̶d̶
↑▲might seem to have↓ passed over from action to art to have composed itself
for ↑▲the eye, e̶y̶e̶s̶ ↑t̶o̶ ̶b̶e̶ ̶t̶h̶e̶ ̶e̶y̶e̶↓ ↓ b̶e̶i̶n̶g̶ ̶s̶e̶e̶n̶, as a ↑▲thing to be *seen*, a↓
sort of "still life", with an exclusive view to spectacular effect. °°It was[15] a
world in which all there °was had been emphasised [**End 6 r**] ↑7↓ in forms
of sensation and told as ornament as ↑▲visible↓ luxury or refinement
besetting one everywhere t̶h̶e̶ ̶v̶e̶r̶y̶ ̶a̶t̶°m̶o̶s̶p̶h̶e̶r̶e̶ ↓[0.5 illeg cancln] ↑ s̶e̶e̶m̶e̶d̶
t̶o̶ ̶h̶a̶v̶e̶ °t̶a̶k̶e̶n̶ ↑a̶c̶q̶u̶i̶r̶e̶d̶ ↑f̶o̶u̶n̶d̶↓ ↓ c̶o̶l̶o̶u̶r̶. ↑:p̶l̶a̶i̶n̶,̶ ̶w̶h̶i̶t̶e̶ ̶l̶i̶g̶h̶t̶ ̶d̶a̶y̶l̶i̶g̶h̶t̶ ↓w̶a̶s̶
n̶o̶ ̶l̶o̶n̶g̶e̶r̶ ↓m̶o̶r̶e̶↑. ↑t̶h̶e̶r̶e̶ ̶w̶a̶s̶ ̶n̶o̶ ↓a̶n̶↑ w̶h̶i̶t̶e̶ ̶l̶i̶g̶h̶t̶↓ ↓ ↓:plain, white light was
no more.↑ For they °took pains those people and made their work ↑task↓ as
they c̶o̶n̶c̶e̶i̶v̶e̶d̶ ↑▲understood↓ it *complete*↓?↑[16]. If the one thing the
philosophic Bruno could not away with was indolence the life expressed here
was certainly not an indolent life,{<,>} however trifling to one or another its
business might seem. In this age of scholars and o̶f̶[17] ↑?↓ ↑▲of↓ artists some
of the most perfect fruits of art had been ↑▲here↓ assorted with ↑by↓ a perfect
scholarship{—}a scholarship that could think ↑c̶a̶r̶e̶ ̶b̶e̶t̶h̶i̶n̶k̶ ̶i̶t̶s̶e̶l̶f̶ ̶o̶f̶↓ for the
whole and each ↑the↓ [1 cm illeg cancln] several part with equal solicitude.
A̶n̶d̶ ̶i̶t̶ ̶m̶i̶g̶h̶t̶ ↑▲?* H̶e̶r̶e̶,[18] a̶t̶ ̶l̶e̶a̶s̶t̶,̶ ̶i̶t̶ ̶m̶i̶g̶h̶t̶↓ s̶e̶e̶m̶ ̶t̶h̶a̶t̶ ̶a̶l̶l̶ ↑▲s̶e̶l̶e̶c̶t̶↓ b̶e̶a̶u̶t̶i̶f̶u̶l̶
t̶h̶i̶n̶g̶s̶ ↑▲w̶h̶a̶t̶s̶o̶e̶v̶e̶r̶↓ w̶h̶a̶t̶e̶v̶e̶r̶,̶ ̶a̶l̶l̶ ̶t̶h̶a̶t̶ ̶w̶d̶ ̶r̶e̶a̶l̶l̶y̶ ̶p̶a̶s̶s̶ [**End 7 r**] ↑8↓[19] The
very flowers, the dishes set ready for a small company had been made
accomplices in this intention. The exhibition of every day life as a fine art now

---

12. Index strokes are double under the four occurances of *such* in primary lines seven
and eight.

13.   In pencil, *sensual* is interlined and underlined; Pater's straight and wavy
strikeouts are superimposed in ink. One likely interpretation is that Clara interlined
sensual as an alternate to *highly coloured* and that Pater struck it out, inserting his own
alternative *sensuous and* to complement *highly coloured.*

14.   small ink comma enlarged by pencil

15.   double index stroke under *was*

16.   Pater is questioning his underline.

17.   The *of* is also circled.

18.   This comma and the three carets are separately canceled also.

19.   The size and watermarks of the paper of folio 8 match folio 1 exactly; Pater's
handwriting is neater, more compact; his ink a bit lighter here. This suggests a
redrafting of the text that had continued from folio 7; the canceled material at the end
of folio 7 reappears at folio 8, primary line 6.

happily solving the ↑{minutest↓ last minutest difficulties of the material it had to deal with{,} was complete. As Gaston passed from stair to stair these ↑▲walls ⁰seemed to shut him off↓ more and more as by some mutual repulsion{,} from the ↑▲crude↓ world outside. Here ↑▲at least↓ it might seem that all select things whatsoever all that would ↑▲really↓ pass with the select few as in any sense productions of fine art were strictly congruous with one another begetting ↑▲by mere juxtaposition↓ something like the unity of a common atmosphere.

[0.5 cm] And[20] as you can ↑may↓ sometimes explain an enigma ↑▲in the world of events↓ by seeing or coming to know an actual person{,} to appreciate a personal influence{,} so here breathing this atmosphere and amid the peculiar complexion of shadow and light in Jasmin's {↑▲house↓} Gaston for the first time was able to define for himself something{,} a humour{,} a qualit quality{,} a character{,} that was all about one in ↑the↓ Parisian life—something physiognomical closely connected therefore as effect or cause with what must be moral in its operation its operation. **[End 8 r]** ↑9↓ ↑▲well organised↓ group of like-minded ⁰persons ↑▲animated by a ↑some[?]↓ common↓ ⁰purpose ↑emotion,↓↓ a school

[¶] [1 cm illeg canceln] In fact, the portraits, ↑▲what purported to be the ↓veritable↑ veritable likeness ↑▲life-likeness↓ of those who would be at home here▲↓ the presumable likeness of such persons, were here reigned in this room & that as from a throne. At first indeed they might have seemed but ↑▲extrordinary[sic]↓ conditions of the atmosphere ↑▲about them; ↑of the place ↓around them.↑↓↓ itself. or, less fancifully, only ↑▲parts of ↑members of↓ ↑a scheme of↓ an ornamental scheme↓ in their places on the panelled walls so congruous were they in their ebony and green & gold with the ↑▲objects ↑wholly inanimate↓↓ things about them. ↑▲wholly inanimate objects around.↓ It was on ↑for to ↑to the↓↓ second thoughts that they explained that ↑▲this↓ atmosphere by referring one to its ▲ source in a↑?↓ ↑the original secret of its composition in certain↓ strong ⁰personal ⁰predilection<s> ↑choice↓. There had been ↑▲those↓ people at least in the generation preceding who amid all their exotic Italian tendencies, ↑▲even↓ then **[End 9 r]** ↑10↓ in fashion, ↑Amid all their exotic Italian th tendencies these people↓ had had a certain primitive ↑▲measure of↓ old Gallic or Gothic

---

20. From this point to the end of the folio, primary lines are double density.

°~~force about~~ ↑in↓ ↑energy within↓ them{,} {~~and~~ {~~had~~ ²¹{~~forced~~ ↑forcing↓ their peculiar taste<s> ↑tastes↓, their peculiar ↑~~peculiar~~↓²² standard of distinction, as law~~, natural law, on~~ ↑{upon}<▲upon>²³↓ others. To harmonise the living face with its ~~inanimate~~ ↑lifeless↓ *entourage*↑?↓, to make atmosphere, is, ↑▲~~of course~~ ↑we know,↓↓ the triumph of °~~portrait~~ ↑pictorial↓ art. Here ~~the~~ ↑such↓ °sifted atmosphere ↑▲as↓ ~~wh.~~ Leonardo ↑~~Lionardo~~↓ or Titian ↑~~Moretto~~↓, °~~weaves~~ ↑▲could weave↓ for his °portraits, had overflowed ↑~~spread beyond~~↓ the frame & become ~~the common~~ ↑a↓ ↑a common↓ medium, for visitors to this privileged place to ~~breathe~~ ↑move in↓ as freely as they would. How these ↑▲g pictured↓ people saw or liked to see things had determined ↑~~defined~~↓ a new ↑▲visual↓ faculty, {~~it~~ if it were not rather ↑~~perhaps~~↓ an ~~epidemic infection~~} ↑endemic↑?↓ affection[*sic*]↓ of the eye; ↑▲~~was an explanation of~~ ↑which helped to explain certain↓↓ ~~it explained the visible~~ [End 10 r] ↑11↓ ↑▲visible↓ peculiarities of the living world ↑▲beyond these ↑[2 cm illeg cancel] ↑[1.5 cm illeg cancel]↓↓ enchanted walls and might be for Gaston a ~~practical~~ guide to some further ↑▲~~might be a practical guide to G.~~↓↓ ~~outside, was a guide to further~~ refinements of selection therein. °~~And at least~~ ↑Here, certainly ↑~~certainly~~↓↓ the ~~generative~~ impulse ↑▲~~here~~↓ had ~~understood,~~ °~~and has~~ ↑▲~~worked~~ ↑▲~~had been~~↓↓ consistently with, itself. Jealous, exclusive, of whatever ↑~~all that~~↓ was not ~~consistent~~ ↑significant↓ of its own humour, there had been, as this place ↑▲clearly↓ witnessed on ~~closer~~ ↑nearer↓ survey, ↑▲all sorts of shrewd↓ ~~fine~~[?] rejections, in what ↑▲seemed at first ~~sy~~ sight to be a very catholic aesthetic↓ ~~looked like a free, or to say the least a very catholic~~ ↑~~aesthetic~~ ↑artistic ~~liking~~↓↓ taste, and within the circuit of its influence ↑~~operation~~[?]↓, the concord of things disparate, the resultant harmony of effect was entire.

[¶] Such elaborately balanced harmonies ↑▲have↓ ~~have~~ however as we know a certain hazard in ↑~~hazard about~~↓ ~~their~~ ↑▲their conditions ↑~~in their conditions~~↓↓ ~~as we know~~ and are ↑▲apt to be↓ easily disturbed. After all °°it

---

21. Both pencil and ink strikeout; the pencil strikeout is continuous through all three words.

22. The puzzling fact of identical words, linear and canceled interlinear, is explained by Pater having left a lacuna on the line, interlining *peculiar* above the blank space, deciding he wanted the word, inserting it on the line and then canceling it above the line. In the preceding revision, the linear word had been singular; when the *s* of *tastes* was brought down to the line, the interlinear alternative was canceled.

23. Ink superimposed upon the identical word in pencil, as if Pater is confirming Clara's suggestion. Did Pater receive pleasure in writing *upon* upon *upon*?

was not quite true ↑It was not quite true after all↓ that all really beautiful
things [**End 11 r**] ↑12↓ went well together. A book he picked up for its
binding, one of many lying ready to hand, struck the jarring note. Not [4 cm]
of Polyphile with [4 cm] not [2.5 cm] Heptameron [3 cm] not [4 cm] but a
little book ↑volume↓ printed at Lyons purporting to be the [2 cm] of the
virtuous emperor [8 cm] ↑{▲Disguised in↓ In all the [3 cm] ↑{▲}disguises↓
of ↑{▲}the↓ Euphuism [2 cm] ↑▲of the day↓ it had come with all sorts of
conscious and unconscious transmutation by the way{,} through the Spanish
from a Latin forgery ↑{▲}and↓ was but {the ↑a↓ fade [*sic*] product of an age
of translations{,} adaptations{,} mistranslations{.} Yet ↑{But {Only,↓ from its
[2 cm] ↑{▲}faint↓ pages did emerge for the first time to Gaston's
consciousness{,} the ↑an↓ image of the antique strenuous emperor in his life-
long contention towards the old Greek "sapience" disinterested, [**End 12 r**]
↑13↓ brave, cold. Well! the atmosphere of that lofty conscience seemed
absolutely {impenetrable ↑{▲}unassimilable↓ by this ↑{the↓ alembicated air
Gaston was now ↑{here↓ breathing. To conceive of that at all, to keep the
outline of it before him, all that was actually around him must be shut out
even from the mental eye. And ↑{▲}then↓ certain {works ↑products↓ of pagan
sculpture{,} nude fragments arm ↑{▲}or hand↓ or torso or braided head{,}
whose well-worn beauty he had scarcely noticed till this moment amid the
lively demand on his attention of the more directly sympathetic ↑{products↓
work of contemporary art reinforced that dissonant note. Emphasised now by
the suggestions of [4 cm] ↑(name of bk.)↓ they presented an almost satiric
contrast to everything else around them. Under {the ↑{▲}that↓ softly gilded
light, set with much consideration as Giorgione might have set the jewel [**End
13 r**] ↑14↓ of his human flesh ↑{▲}and↓ amid the rich apparel of the place the
↑that↓ delicately mellow old marble {did ↑would↓ not really blend. The
shadowy ebony and green about it might have been the defiling earth from
which it was but lately arisen after long burial. Creature of the fresh air
↑{▲}the fresh sun↓ of Greece{,} of Italy{,} ↑{of Greece↓ it shuddered amidst
the ↑{these↓ tricky indoor splendours of the age of the Valois {refusing ↑and
refused↓ to be ↑{▲}really↓ effectively associated with them even by the
graceful intervention of such recent imitators of the antique manner as Michel
Colomb [*sic*] or Germain Pilon. In contrast with Jean Goujon's {half
↑▲daintily↓ clothed voluptuousness of ◆form the pagan marble might have
been primitive humanity itself{—}naked yet unashamed fresh from {the
↑{▲}its↓ Creator's hand ↑{▲}and↓ unmistakably before T{<t>}he Fall{,} and
↑{It↓ seemed to protest that certain ◆forms{,} certain [**End 14 r**] ↑15↓
refinements in the clothing of a later world were more suggestive of carnal

thoughts than the unadorned uncovered flesh. {At ↑And at↓ least it started
questions{,} ↑{▲}some↓ very irritant questions: Did this novel mode of
receiving{,} of reflecting the visible aspects of life commit one to an
intellectual scheme{,} a *theory* about it ↑{▲}of↓ the remoter *practical* alliances
{of̶ which {o̶n̶e̶ could not precisely ↑{▲}be ascertained↓ {a̶s̶c̶e̶r̶t̶a̶i̶n̶ at present
but would ↑{m̶u̶s̶t̶↓ inevitably be led to in due course? Was this odd grace no
more than the superficial expression of an ↑{▲}intellectual↓ aristocracy
"differenced" from the rest of the world by mere fashion and taste or did it
involve other differences from the vulgar{,} less innocent? Was it ↑{▲}indeed
↑{r̶e̶a̶l̶l̶y̶↓ ↓ their shame these people were seeking to hide under a fascinating
exterior, which might conceivably become the vesture{,} the ritual of a new
[**End 15 r**] ↑16↓ and ↑{▲}a↓ very profane religion? Or, did one's own perhaps
crude sense of incompatibility between things certainly attractive apart merely
indicate that there was ↑{▲}some↓ {a̶ higher level of culture in these matters
one had not yet reached? {T̶h̶e̶r̶e̶ ↑{▲}For there↓ might be a mental point of
view already attained by some, from the height of which the opposition
between the thoughts of Henri and Marguerite de Valois and ↑{▲}the
thoughts↓ {t̶h̶o̶s̶e̶ of ↑{▲}Antoninus{,}↓ between the sophisticated colour and
form of contemporary art and the antique white sculpture its white soul
↑would disappear ↑{m̶u̶s̶t̶↓ ↓ {d̶i̶s̶a̶p̶p̶e̶a̶r̶e̶d̶. There was certainly something
over-charged ↑{▲}something↓ questioning and questionable in the expression
of these portraits which became almost caricature in the purely imaginary
o̶n̶e̶s̶ ↑▲faces:↓ an air which the very furniture of the period seemed
↑{▲}mockingly↓ to ↑{✶}{c̶a̶t̶c̶h̶↓ {reflect.[24] [**End 16 r**] ↑17↓ m̶o̶c̶k̶i̶n̶g̶l̶y̶.
↑{▲}But {a̶g̶a̶i̶n̶↓ A{<g>}ain, was it only that art had reached its highest power
of expression and must soon become "mannered" with an expressiveness
↑{▲}really↓ beyond anything there was to express? Meantime the artistic
mode of the day professedly derivative from the genial traditions of Italy had
put on the {s̶i̶c̶k̶l̶y̶ ̶N̶o̶r̶t̶h̶e̶r̶n̶ ↑wan Transalpine↓ complexion of Dürer's
Melancolia [*sic*] the out-look of a mind exercised absorbingly but by no means
quite pleasurably by ↑with↓ a bewildering variety of thoughts.

[¶] It might perhaps be that after all things as distinct from persons{,} such
things as ↑{▲}those↓ one had so abundantly around one here, were come to
be so much that the human being seemed suppressed and practically nowhere
{a̶m̶o̶n̶g̶ ↑{▲}amid↓ the works of his hands{,} ↑{▲}amid↓ the objects he had
[**End 17 r**] ↑18↓ projected from himself. {M̶i̶g̶h̶t̶ Could there be in this almost

---

24. Six spaced periods in pencil underneath *reflect* indicate *stet.*

exclusive preoccupation with things to which ↑{▲}indeed↓ a sincere care for art may at any time commit {~~one~~ ↑us↓ something of {~~the~~ ↑{▲}{a ↑that↓↓ disproportion of mind {~~that~~ ↑which↓ is always akin to mental disease. The physiognomist remarks certainly that the most characteristic pictured faces of that day have an odd touch of lunacy about them. It was a habit of the time symptomatic of much else in it partly through {~~that~~ ↑its↓ minute love of art partly in cynic disillusion to expend strong feelings on small objects. In that world of Parisian fashion{,} fashion ↑{~~as you know~~↓ after all having its very being in the felicitous management of slight and ↑or↓ unsubstantial things there might well be no place left at all for considerations beyond them—how, in a word, shadow matched substance. [**End 18 r**] ↑19↓ Shadow and substance!—had not Bruno declared that shadow and substance{,} the outside and what was within{,} great ↑{~~little~~↓ and little ↑{~~great~~↓ were to the eye of reason "seeing all things" indifferently "in God" themselves "indifferent" or "coincident?" Had one here in Jasmin's dainty house in visible presentment only a slightly ironic form of that doctrine? It was a ↑{~~the~~↓ triumph of art certainly, "in the end of days"—this transfiguration of the indirect{,} ↑{▲}of the↓ secondary ↑{▲}and↓ accidental matters of existence deftly extracting pleasure, a refining pleasure, out of the useful, the ~~barely~~ ↑▲barely↓ necessary—though with this consequence, at least in some instances{,} ↑{~~in this instance~~↓ that the sheath became too visibly more than the sword or say the house than the owner{,} ↑{~~master~~↓ than Jasmin himself in fact{,} touching if you found him out of spirits [**End 19 r**] ↑20↓ for a moment, enviable delightful company for half an hour but surely of no consequence to any one ↑{▲}at all{,}↓ and whom you scarcely missed while his evening suit in cloth of silver ↑{▲}and [2 cm illeg canceln] pearls marvellously *goudronné*[25] a "symphony in white"↓ lay ready there to be looked at like the other high-priced objects around. Was his ↑the↓ house then ~~emp~~ empty after all? Was it not the very ↑{~~essential~~↓ man? His "effects" we say, with unconscious irony, of a man's goods—the French themselves of the bag or box he has with him{,} and power thus passing away from man into his works it was as if he were already dead.

[1 cm] Dead!—suggestive therefore of melancholy thoughts depressing to a creature of the senses{—}such thoughts as broke in upon Gaston from time to time through his own years of eager preoccupation with the sensuous aspect↑s↓ of life,{<,>} the prosecution of the aesthetic [**End 20 r**] ↑21↓

---

25. Underline and accent mark both in pencil.

interests discovered to him for the first time to<->day. His search for the lost child if it had ever ↑{▲}indeed↓ existed proving hopeless{,} gradually ceased altogether at last {amid ↑under↓ the fascination of the scenes across which it had impelled him{;} while his uncertainty as to the mother's death left him though no priest yet in a kind of priestly celibacy after all{,} responsible it might seem only to himself{,} his own needs or tastes in the disposal of his time. Surely the near the visible the immediate was prevailing with him over what was distant and ↑{or↓ unseen over remote hypothesis or conjecture. That it had so prevailed was an opportunity in {the ↑that↓ matter of aesthetic culture{,} to make full use of which would be in accordance with the opportunist doctrines of Bruno and Montaigne still fresh in his ear. Yet it was from a great distance **[End 21 r]** ↑22↓ comparatively that {certain ↑these {those↓ voices came which had been {with ↑about↓ him here all day. Were they notes of birds flitting {round ↑{▲}about↓ the lonely towers of the neighbouring abbey above the great trees of the Pré-aux-Clercs[26] or the calling rather of children at play{,} hungry children at play with something of an effort{,} solicitous{,} at moments agonised as if turned suddenly upon some one passing out of ear-shot{,} parent or friend? It was as complaining voices certainly with a touch also of the significance of that cry Augustine heard one day in the neighbourhood of another great city{,} that they settled into Gaston's memory{,} ↑{They would↓ to be identified by some trick of association with similar sounds haunting ear or fancy through the years that followed{,} till they came to seem like an acoustic peculiarity of Paris itself—this haunted medieval Paris with those **[End 22 r]** ↑23↓ strange later dubious (no! certainly holy) Innocents of Saint Bartholomew's ↑Eve↓ still "green in earth" there. Querulous always, invasive and reproachful, they would **[1.5 cm]** ↑{▲}divert↓ all other sounds {to ↑into↓ their peculiar note and were apt to reinforce the distress of every distressful moment. They grew as time went on to seem ↑{be the↓ voices of grown boys sweeping by{,} resonant{,} sonorous{,} ↑{*}{the↓ voices at last of young men ↑{at last↓ masterful{,} deliberate{,} expressive{,} {firmly increasing ↑{▲}firmly↓ in due order to what the age of the lost or dead child would have grown to be. Piercing now the velvet walls about him otherwise exclusive of everything but what belonged to the merest foreground of existence they made ↑{rendered↓ this long ↑{▲}unoccupied↓ day in Jasmin's house like ↑{a complete↓ an epitome of Gaston's subsequent years in Paris.

---

26. Accent and hypens in pencil.

[¶] An opportunity I said for the {improvement ↑furtherance↓ of the aesthetic life:—↑▲and it was telling [**End 23 r**] ↑23<4>↓ [27] ↑▲already as Gaston could not but note ↑became aware↓↓ surprised by a certain fineness new to him ↑▲himself↓ in his own reflexion from a Venetian mirror of lustrous depth and hardness presumably therefore faithful. such as that foppish age prized ↑loved↓⁚ Like Wilhelm Meister's approving mentor the looking-glass assured him that his eyes &c. [1.5 cm] If according to the Platonic doctrine people ↑once↓ become like what they see surely the omnipresence of fine art around one must re-touch at least for ↑▲in the case of ↑with↓↓ the sensitive what is still mobile in a human countenance. The period as artistic periods at all events do had found its expression in a recognisable ↑recognised facial↓ type and he ↑Gaston↓ too was conforming to it. Portraiture did ↑▲Did portraiture↓ not merely reflect life ↑▲but↓ in part also it formed ↑determined↓ it. The image might react on the original ↑▲refining it↓ & refine it one ↑▲degree↓ grade[?] further ↑still↓. Given that [**End 24 r Hou**] ↑24<5>↓ life was a thing ↑matter↓ of sensations↑?↓ ↑▲surely he ↑▲too↓ was making↓ he ↑▲too↓ must be making something ↑the best↓ of its "brief" interval" [28] between the cradle & the grave. Here was the perfected art of the day and it was a miracle of dainty scruples of discernment ↑▲at least↓ between physical beauty and all that was not that: a practical condition of things quite at the opposite end of the scale from those rank unwd[?] unweeded natural growths by tolerated by ↑▲Mʳ de↓ Montaigne promoted by the doctrines of Bruno. He ↑▲{And he↓ {might "live up to" it.[29] It ↑▲At least for a while it↓ might take the place ↑▲of conscience↓ {at least for a while of conscience and represent ↑maintaining ↑representing↓↓ by way of proxy ↑▲represent its larger, vaguer↓ its vaguer and more pretensions through the dimness of the world.

[¶] —To keep one animated and physically clean, ↑white↓ quick and [**End 25 r Hou**] ↑25<6>↓ white ↑quick↓ as it had certainly kept frail Jasmin de [1 cm] ↑▲Villebon↓, who, now, spite of all courtly refinement ↑softness↓ burst

---

27. Folio pages 24–26 are separated from the BNC manuscript and are found at the Houghton. Because these sheets were originally numbered 23–25 (their current pagination is produced by an overwriting of the 3, 4, and 5 with a 4, 5, and 6) and because they are in a more hasty hand and uncorrected by Clara, these Houghton sheets may belong to an earlier draft, the final pages of which Pater annexed to his current draft and renumbered.

28. Pater is trying out a one or two word quotation.

29. The preceding seven words are deleted in pencil, presumably to agree with the deletion of the epigraph.

suddenly into his dwelling with all the cheerful noise ↑~~bruit~~↓ proper to youth, with a gaiety of step, a sincerity ↑~~frankness~~↓ of voice ↑~~utterance~~↓ putting to ~~rout~~ ↑▲flight ↑~~flight all surmises~~↓↓ Gaston's ↑▲late↓ surmises as to hidden sin. His companions promptly retreated from the door stood for a few moments in the moonlight ~~to~~ and shouted good-night with a laugh as pleasant as his own at the sight of his twinkling light above and in the confusion of their departure Gaston too slipped forth ↑~~out~~ ↑away↓↓ he would stay neither to test impressions nor taste the [1 cm] ↑dainty↓ supper ↑▲in effect↓ he had renewed old acquaintance. Yes! the house, the style, was the man. [**End 26 r Hou**]

Chap: ix.[1]

A poison–daisy.

The earth with her bars was about me.
or ~~Sweet, sweet, sweet, poison, for the age's tooth!~~

[0.5 cm] That laugh in the moon-lit street was partly at sight of a well-known object,—*assez reco↑▲i↓gnoissable pour estre doré, et de velours jaune garny d'argent,*—the carriage of ~~the~~ Queen ↑▲Margaret↓ of Navarre, who had stepped forth lightly at the street-corner and, gliding along the shadowed side of the way, ~~was~~ presently ~~ascending~~ ↑▲ascended↓ Jasmin's stairs, by appointment, to solicit in person the favours of that reluctant youth. "At the Court of France 'tis the women ↑▲solicit the men":—s<S>o, savage old Jeanne d'Albret↓ ~~at the Fench court: so ▲ the mother of Henry the Fourth~~ had warned ↑▲her son, Margaret's husband,↓ ~~him~~ when he first came ~~thither~~ ↑▲to Paris, ~~whence↓~~ from which he [**End 1 r**] ↑2↓ was now far enough away in his rude little mountainous dominion. ↑▲"Queen Margot," [1 cm illeg cancln] ↑▲Marguerite↓—pearl, or daisy,<—>so=called,̶as if for the very purpose of suggesting satiric fancy, but with a↑?↓ ↑▲a↓ face, at all events,▲↓ ~~Marguerite↓2↑ "Queen Margot"↓↑ ▲with a↑?↓ face at least ↑all events↓~~ as irreproachably white as the moon-light, unlike the ~~ladies~~ ↑▲women↓ of her ~~day~~ ↑▲time,↓ is used to go unmasked on the very boldest errands. She, certainly, is by no means ↑=↓ an empty sheath! Call her ↑rather↓ rather, amid the many classic revivals of the ↑▲hour, ↑~~that day↓↓ time, in thoughts~~ ↑▲memories↓ of "the magnificent, ancient, empresses, of time past, as Suetonius and others describe them," delightfully ↑by↓ to her loyal ~~chevalier~~ ↑▲biographer↓ Brantome:—Call her a new ↑a↓ and perhaps lovelier Faustine.<,> ↑▲at home and popular among men of the sword.↓ Like

---

1. This chapter consists of 29 leaves—28 recto only, 1 both sides; consecutive pagination in upper right corner begins with folio 2. Pencil headings in an unknown hand the in upper right corner of fol. 1 are: *? G de L* and, beneath and further right, (9). Paper: fols. [1]–5, (9" x 7") COLLARD; fols. 6–7 (9" x 7 7/16") cobalt; fols. 8, 10–17 (9" x 7 1/8") TOWGOOD'S; fols. 9, 18–29 (9" x 7 7/16") cobalt.

Chap: iX.

A poison-daisy.

The earth with her bars was about me.

~~or Sweet, sweet, sweetly poison, for the age's tooth!~~

That laugh in the moon-lit street was partly at

sight of a well-known object, — assez recognoissable pour

estre doré, et de velours jaune garny d'argent, — the

Margaret

carriage of ~~the~~ Queen of Navarre, who had stepped forth

lightly at the street-corner and, gliding along the shadowed

                                        ascended

side of the way, ~~who~~ presently ~~ascending~~ Jasmin's stairs, by

appointment, to solicit in person the favours of that

reluctant youth. "At the Court of France 'tis the women

solicit the men." — So, savage old Jeanne d'Albret

~~not the French court is the mother of Henry the Fourth~~ had

her son, Margaret's husband,   to Paris, ~~where~~

warned ~~him~~ when he first came ~~thither~~ from which he

Fig. 6

Faustine, she had ↑▲had ~~her~~↓ "a share in the moving of armies;↑"↓ might have been called like her, in dubious sense, ~~the~~↑?↓ ↑"↓m<M>*other* of the a<A>rmy."—[**End 2 r**]

↑3↓ ¶. By no means an empty sheath! She had been just in time to catch sight of the retreating Gaston, whose features are not quite new to her. At supper, amid witty ~~succession~~ amendments on ↑of↓ the lie to be ready for use next day against any compromising rumours of her presence here at so late an hour, she asks his name; and awaits him, all[2] herself, not long after, as, under Jasmin's guidance, he mounts ~~the~~ ↑▲a private↓ staircase of the Louvre, to learn in intimate exposure as much as he ↑▲will↓ ~~cares~~ of the most beautiful, ~~and~~ ↑▲as also↓ the most accessible, of the ↑▲great↓ ladies of ↑▲that day.↓ ~~her time.~~

[1 cm] The martial aptitudes in this embodiment of loveliness and love—↑▲of the ↑~~of the~~↓↓ seed of ~~Venus~~ ↑▲Venus ↑Mars↓↓ and ~~of Mars~~ ↑▲of Mars ↑~~Venus~~↓↓—Brantome ↑▲has attested↓ ~~attests~~ [**End 3 r**] ↑4↓ with boundless admiration: "her share in the moving of armies": how prosperously at the age of twenty-two her cunning had seconded her courage in a certain warlike mission to Flanders: how even in the long later years of banishment or imprisonment at Usson grim fortress of Louis the Eleventh amid the volcanic mountains of Auvergne her imperative genius had never deserted the

---

2. From *all* to *Had* (247:8–248:18), folio 5 verso represents an earlier textual variant (possibly part of an entire chapter draft), cancelled and replaced with an expanded version:

↑3↓ all herself ~~next~~ ↑not long after↓ day as under Jasmin's guidance he mounts the staircase of the Louvre to learn in intimate exposure as much as he cares of perhaps the most beautiful certainly the most accessible of the ↑great↓ ladies of °°that ~~time~~ ↑°°her day.↓

[1 cm] The ↑~~military~~↓ martial ↑▲spirit↓ aptitudes ↓in↑↓ ~~of~~ this embodiment ↑~~incorporation~~↓ of loveliness and love ↑▲of the ↑{~~daughter~~↓↓ seed of {~~Venus~~↓2↑ ↑{Mars}↓ and {of↑?↓ Mars {↑↑ ↑{Venus}↓:—Brantome her loyal biographer {~~has~~ attest{ed↑{s}↓ ~~that~~ with boundless admiration: "her share in the moving of armies": how [4 cm]: how [4 cm]. That ↑courtly↓ writer who had been neither more nor less than a mirror of the men and women of his day ↑generation ↑age↓↓, their attraction power and grace, had withdrawn himself from their actual presence about the time of Gaston's ~~coming~~ ↑settling in↓ to Paris. Had [**End 5 v**]

Pencil here is in Pater's hand. The whole of the page is canceled in Pater's usual fashion (two bent vertical parallel strokes) with one horizontal stroke also through the seventh primary line.

adulterous[3] impossible Queen of Navarre not to be Queen of France.—What would you have? Even in incomparable pearls as experts know there is always deduction to be made: *il y a toujours à redire.* Well! on those ramparts of cold black lightning-struck lava she had very soon been in command. "In a little time," says Brantome, "the keeper of the ~~prisoner found him~~ [End 4 r] ↑5↓ ~~en devint prisonnier en peu de temps, says Brantome Pauvre homme! que pensoit-il faire? Vouloir tenir prison captive en sa prison celle qui de ses yeux et de son beau visage peut assujettir en ses liens et chaines tout le reste du monde comme ung forcat!~~ ↑"the ↑▲very↓ keeper of the~~ prison found himself her prisoner."[22] What had he thought of doing,"[22] Poor Wretch!<?> Did he think to hold captive in his cells, the woman whose eyes, whose comely countenance were locks and chains with which she could set fast all the rest of the world like a slave at the oar"?

[¶] That courtly writer, ~~who ▲ had been~~ ↑▲whose observant mind was↓ neither more nor less than a mirror ~~of~~ ↑▲held up to↓ the men and women of his ~~day~~ ↑▲generation,↓ their attractive power and grace, had withdrawn himself from their actual presence about the time of Gaston's coming to Paris. Had good or evil chance brought ~~Gaston~~ ↑▲him↓ just then into ↑▲Brantome's↓ ~~his~~ company or even into the company of his written books ↑(name them- as-[1 cm])↓ Pierre de Bourdeilles ↑▲or↓ ~~and~~ de Brantome [End 5 r] ↑6↓ incapable as he seems by nature and training of any kind whatever of "second" thoughts must inevitably ↑certainly↓ have reinforced the ↑those↓ earlier theoretic or abstract influences upon him of Bruno and ↑cf.16.↓ Montaigne. For it is precisely according to their intention, their abstract prejudgment ↑conception↓ of things that the chronicler ↑author of↓ records ↑represents↓ the living world of persons and their deeds around him *paints* it we may truly say so lively so gaudy ~~are~~ ↑▲are↓ the hues of his vocabulary his palette. The mere habit and carriage of Brantome himself upon that ↑the↓ stage of Parisian life would have concurred ↑alike↓ with the "new gospel" of the philosophic monk and ↑as↓ with the Gascon ↑▲worldling's↓ ~~worl~~ summarised experience of the world in a challenge to make ↑free↓ trial a free

---

3. HOU slip: Pater copies Lalanne's footnote of an affair in Brantôme's portrait of Marguerite (8:82 n.1):

> *Marg.* in Usson, / —composes a chanson, pour / l'un de ses amants, / fils d'un chaudronnier / d'Auvergne. / [¶] ↑Its object↓—he might be heir to a kingdom, or / son of a—her desire was / the same—the / element of, indefinable, but irresistible / desire—like thirst.

Pater's handwriting spirals around the right, top, and left margins.

realisation of the doctrine of "indifference" a ↑of↓ moral indifference. The business of war [**End 6 r**] ↑7↓ Brantome had learned under that "great captain, Monsieur François de Guise", 'hough in his day King Charles the Ninth that sincere lover of letters who had ↑had↓ a true literary gift of his own had valued in him not so much the soldier as the unflagging story-teller. "Gentleman in ordinary of the King's Chamber," "born a mere gentleman," as he ~~says~~ ↑observes↓ of another "he had the heart of an emperor in his bowels." "To every place where illustrious rivals contested the prize of glory" he had made his way. Mars and Love he says "make war alike: the one and the other has his sword, his clarion, his camp." He frequents both, yielding himself always easily genially and with no misgiving to the world on its march careless what the issues may be so only ↑for his part↓ he feels it to be in motion. Unembarrassed by abstract questions, a lover of [**End 7 r**] ↑8↓ every sort of hazard, he passes ~~easily~~ ↑▲lightly↓ over what may ↑might↓ ~~shock~~ shock others in the ↑▲undeniable↓ mere brilliancy of men's doings the brilliancy of their sins of their generosity. *Ces beaux faicts!*—those gallant deeds, he has seen, or read of in history:—there is nothing in all that, ↑~~il n'y a rien en tout cela,~~↓ he would ~~say~~ protest "but what I could achieve as gallantly, at a push!" ↑~~que je n'executerois-je aussi bravement que eux à la nécessité~~↓ Chagrinned in some way ~~at the court of~~ ↑▲by↓ Charles's successor he shut up or parted with °his court braveries and in the retirement of °~~his~~ ↑▲a↓ country-house turned finally at about the age of thirty-five from the actual world to feed in memory on its carefully hived sweetness with a pen in ↑°his↓ hand he could ↑use↓ use as ~~dexterously~~ ↑gaudily↓ ↑brilliantly↓↓ ↓adroitly↑ ↑▲adroitly, as gaudily,↓ as the [**End 8 r**] ↑9↓ sword. He is visibly anxious for "name and fame" in transmitting to his executors the manuscript work of his remaining years. When he is gone they will print his ~~wo~~ books fruit as he boasts of his own shining natural abilities *faits et composés de son esprit et de son invention.* "The said books will be found in velvet covers of various shades respectively together with a large volume of "Ladies" covered that in green velvet all curiously [2.5 cm] ↑gardés↓ and fairly corrected. Fine things are to be found there: grave histories, in effect, stories, high speech, witty sayings, such as no one will ↑▲omit↓ ~~omit~~ to read, methinks, that has once peeped within." Those books, the [3 cm] ↑(titles)↓, the [3 cm], the [3 cm], were not published till [2.5 cm], [2.5 cm] years after Gaston's end [**End 9 r**] ↑10↓ ~~Gaston's death~~ ↑decease↓ and it was ↑had been↓ just as he came thither that the writer, ↑▲~~Brantome,~~↓ °~~himself~~ had ↑▲quitted↓ ~~deserted~~ Paris. Failing Brantôme however, and his ↑▲gallery↓ ~~collection~~ of ↑▲eloquent↓ ~~speak~~• ~~ing~~ portraits, there still was ↑▲the original,↓ the living thing ↑~~original~~↓

°itself, ↑▲precisely↓ as he had left it:—but left it, ↑▲however,↓ (observe!) under a genial ↑▲genial sun-shine↓ sun-°light, sunset as it proved, which truly was now turned to colours very different from those of any kind of normal day, or night.

[¶] Such ↑Those↓ wild fervours of love and battle, of ˙crime ↑sin↓, such as, to ↑for ↑with↓↓ Brantome and his like, are ↑▲count↓ as but ordinary ↑the ordinary level ↓degree↑ of↓ blood-heat, have their reactions. As upon Charles himself on the morrow of the great ˙crime, a sort of [End 10 r] ↑11↓ [2.5 cm] ↑atome↓ of nervous prostration had settled visibly on Paris, with ↑▲certain sullen↓ effects of °sullen ↑infected ↑morbid↓↓ colour if not immediately agreeable at least profoundly interesting for ↑to↓ the ↑▲duly↓ duly[?] ↑attu↓ trained aesthetic sense. Art ↑▲art achieved, and ↑achieved art↓↓ reaching just now the ↑its↓ last refinements, the finest intelligence of its own motives and capacity must needs minister to the fashionable tastes ↑mood↑s↓↓ of the day in ↑with↓ somewhat low-pitched ↑low-pitched ↑terne↓↓ "symphonies" in black and grey not easy to achieve with↑?↓ "harmonies"↑?↓ in iron and steel, or at best ↑▲the gayest↓ in steel and silver ↑▲↓[?] rusted↑y↓ steel tarnished silver↓. Iron ↑▲armlets, necklaces, necklets, iron chains, how daintily ↑finely↓ decorative we may understand, ↑conceive,↓ became the fashion among ↑with↓, well! among Les belles ferroniéres [*sic*], in an age ↑▲year ↑the years↓↓ which saw or felt all [End 11 r] ↑12↓[4] around the first beginnings of "The League" and cherished ↑preferred↓ ↑▲ever↓ in the precious metals the °sullen ↑cloudy↓ lustres of ↑▲the baser↓ baser.ones. ↑▲*[5] The night-mare work of Bernard ↑de ↑de↓ Palissy ↑▲is↓ in fact ↑truth↓ fairly representative of ↑▲the the that ↑that his↓↓ its age. Like that masquerade figure of his shading half-blindedly its one ↑▲own↓ little candle, one picked ↑groped↓ one's way mentally morally about all-accomplished Paris as ↑▲if↓ in the rambling purlieus↑? ↑purlieus↓↓ of ↑▲some↑?↓↓ a great↑?↓ ↑▲vast↓ theatre ↑▲among ↑amid↓↓ the traps, ↑▲the↓ and ↑▲the↓ lofts and ↑the↓ stairways ↑▲ladders ↑side↓↓ and peep-holes upon the artificially ↑▲illumined↓ lighted stage ↑stage-play in which↓ where the actors not seldom reached the height

---

4. A fragment of a slip with a perforated edge and violet border, originally glued to the sheet, remains in the upper left of the head margin.

5. Asterisked BNC slip correlates with careted asterisk in text:

   ↑*↓ [0.25 illeg cancln] i<I>t was as if they gloried ↑▲felt some sensible↓ affinity / in ↑for↓ colours of the earth earthy, / of the sodden earth in ↑▲under↓ rain & / or in decay—& took ↑▲wh.↓ made / silver look like iron.

Overleaf, inverted, recorded in Emendations & Variants 316.36:19–34.

of real lust real madness and in real ↑▲fury↓ ~~anger~~ drew swords on one another. Partly moulding, in part ~~a mere follower of~~ ↑▲the ↑a↓ merely obsequious to↓ [**End 12 r**] ↑13↓ the preferences of ~~the~~ ↑▲its↓ day the taste of the reign of Henry the Third was but the ↑▲appropriate↓ ~~natural~~ last ~~term~~ ↑▲word↓ of an art from the first largely derivative, ~~the~~ ↑▲that↓ so carefully "forced" Renaissance art ↑▲dear to↓ ~~of~~ the French court, which borrowing from Italy, its patience, its subtlety and refinement, ~~they~~ had not cared or not been able to derive ↑▲also↓ its gay ↑buoyant↓ red natural ↑▲life-blood↓ ~~life's blood~~. In Raffaelle in Titian even in the ↑▲dreamy↓ ~~mystic~~ Umbrians the thoughtful Lombards how full the pulsation how stalwart the growth. ↑~~which~~ ~~the~~↓ The artists of ↑▲the new↓ *Italy in France* had contrived to infect ↑~~but~~ ~~infected~~↓ it with the visible [3 cm] ↑malaise↓ which went properly with their own moral perhaps physical "caducity":—~~the~~ exotic [**End 13 r**] ↑14↓ ↑▲contemporary↓ writers ~~of~~ [2 cm illeg cancln] ↑~~the day~~↓ had introduced the ↑that↓ word. ~~Even~~ t<T>he old intransigeant native art itself in Jean Cousin for ~~its~~ ↑▲instance↓ had lost its "Gallic" gaiety. Well! °even↑?↓ the ↑▲most powerful↓ ~~best~~ art ↑▲the hand of↓ Veronese °~~even~~ ↑▲°himself↓ must needs after all ↑▲be↓ content<ed> °~~itself not~~ not with broad day but, ↑▲at best with a sort of↓ ~~with an~~ algebraic system of symbols thereof<.> ↑in ↑and↓↓ ~~a kind of~~°~~compromise~~ (with night). ~~To~~ ↑▲And ↑So So,↓↓ Gaston ~~looking~~ ↑▲as he looked↓ back upon these years seemed to have been dealing in them ~~perhaps~~ not with facts at all ↑▲perhaps↓ but only with "effects" of art ~~but certainly~~ ↑at ~~any rate~~↓ at the clearest ↑best↓ ~~with~~ ↑under↓ that sort of merely pictorial daylight in which the artist ↑▲can but ↑~~and do ↑can↑ but↓↓ ~~others~~ make ~~terms~~ ↑terms ↑~~a compromise~~↓↓ with darkness.

[1.5 cm] For there was ~~that~~ ↑▲much ↑~~something~~↓↓ in ~~the~~ ↑▲his own↓ mental condition ~~of~~ [**End 14 r**] ↑15↓ ~~Gaston~~ at this ↑that↓ time, ↑▲in↑ his ↑▲own↓ changed sense of life which ~~made him~~°~~sympathetic to~~ ↑▲made him sympathetic with ↑~~was in alliance~~↓↓ those ↑~~that ↑the↑ ↑this↑ peculiarity in↓ peculiarities of the surrounding atmosphere. The ~~morne~~ ↑more↓ ~~terne~~ ↑▲sombre ↑~~sombre triste~~↓↓ air of Paris↑?↓ ↑▲as if of that↑?↓ ashen hue which is proper to penitence ↑~~as if of the ashen hue proper to penitence a penitent penitents~~↓↓ ~~on the morrow of its~~ ↑the↓ ~~great crime was congruous~~ ↑concurred with↓ befitted certain ↑some↓ remorseful ↑▲shadings↓ ~~currents~~ of ↑in↓ his own thought ↑~~thoughts~~↓ a certain sense of broken ↑br↓ ideal there a ↑the↓ haunting desire to *repair*, ~~a wounded~~ ↑▲an offended ~~froissé~~↓ moral delicacy which ↑if↓ however exaggerated was inalienably a part of himself, as the search for the child ceasing he settled down↑?↓ into ~~the~~ ↑▲a↓ mere spectator ~~driven~~ ↑▲thrust, ↑forced↓↓ it might ↑~~would~~↓ seem, from action

upon contemplation in ~~this~~ ↑a~~that~~↓ a world where while action seemed so
dubious so °compromising [**End 15 r**] ↑16↓ to ~~a~~ ↑▲the↓ scrupulous
conscience there was still so much to see, to understand, perforce to admire.
As he °~~took~~ ↑▲assumed ↑~~chose~~↓↓ his place to watch ~~perhaps~~ to ° take his
share, ↑▲perhaps,↓ to take at least an intellectual part as sympathetic as might
be in the dramatic action ~~around~~ ↑▲before↓ him, ~~those~~ ↑▲the ↑~~the~~
utterance↓↓ voices of ↑▲Giordano↓ Bruno ↑{cf.6.}↓ and ↑▲of Monsr de↓
Montaigne were ↑was↓ indeed ~~was~~ almost physically ↑▲in his ears↓ ~~audible
to ↑for↓ him~~ both alike recommending though from ~~quite~~ opposite points in
the speculative circle their ~~theory~~ ↑▲doctrine ↑~~that philosophy~~↓↓ of
"indifference": ↑▲yes! of moral indifference. It↓ ~~which~~ presented itself ↑▲in
fact as ↑~~seemed to present~~↓↓ ~~as nothing~~ ↑▲neither more nor↓ less than the
↑an↓ ~~exactly~~ ↑nicely↓ weighted ↑▲theoretic↓ equivalent to the ↑▲actual↓
situation.

[¶] Readers will ~~remember~~ ↑▲call to mind↓ that place in the Odyssey where
[**End 16 r**] ↑17↓ Ulysses approaches the palace of Circe ↑▲as in that
memorable tapestry ~~of~~ ↑tapestried scene↓ on the wall of Monsr de Montaigne's
study, its pleasant-seeming▲↓ ~~its pleasant-seeming~~ solitude in the midst of the
magic island the ~~delightful~~ ↑▲clear voice↓ singing which makes one forget
everything beside, ↑▲as she suddenly ↑▲appears at↓ ~~flings wide~~ ↑▲is seen
from↓ the ↑▲doorway↓ ~~doors~~ and ↑▲calls↓ to *him*:↓

ἡ δ' αἶψ' ἐξελθοῦσα θύρας ὤιξε φαεινὰς
καὶ κάλει·

~~Such~~ ↑▲Just such↓ singing welcomed Gaston now seemed to draw him
magnetically up the spiral Gothic stair-case of the old palace of the Louvre to
the modish and modern half Italian apartments of Queen Margaret. From the
various levels ↑▲of the ascent ↑as he ascended↓↓ "the city of pleasure"
(consciously ~~it~~ Paris was already that) ~~was~~ ↑▲became↓ more and more
↑▲completely↓ ~~entirely~~ visible in what was artistically ↑▲perhaps the most
fortunate↓ ~~the happiest~~ moment of its history. The red-tiled, fantastically
crested [**End 17 r**] ↑18↓ houses wound along deep and narrow lanes close
about the vast monastic precincts the vast "hotels" and palaces all alike
climbing for light as high as they could in the thickly over-built space
between *La Cité* old Roman Lutetia with its gothic towers of *Notre-Dame* on
the island in the divided Seine and the bowery ↑bosky↓ circle of clerical or
seigneurial gardens beyond the fiercely marked line of rampart bristling with
iron. The sun-light seemed to rest by preference on the broad white cheerful

masses of the half-classic Renaissance masonry which ↑▲had↓ h̶a̶d̶ pushed their way amid the sombre medieval brickwork threatening to supersede the Middle a<A>ge and ↑with↓ its sad memories altogether ↑but ↑though↓↓ with still uncompleted towers abrupt galleries and stair-ways [**End 18 r**] ↑19↓ into the air.

[¶] Immediately below filling the atmosphere with the acrid perfume of coarse wild flowers the old disused t̶i̶t̶e̶ ↑tile↓ beds ↑field↓ stretched away to the delicately pillared central *pavillon* of the Tuileries. Nothing was finished. You heard the crisp sounds of the chisel even now ↑then↓ at work. The fresh daintily carved cornices, ran into the hanging masses of unwrought masonry, as daringly as the weeds might have done ↑do↓ into masses of hanging ruin. This ↑The↓ very staircase up which Gaston and his companion seemed drawn now by the ↑a↓ shrill dominant singing above them was itself but a remnant of the m<M>iddle Age emphatic upon the voluptuously smoothed surface of the Medicean facade com- [**End 19 r**] ↑20↓ pleted by the eminent Pierre↑?↓ ↑de↓ l'Escot on two sides only of the old feudal court-yard. The Louvre of the Valois, where the "Matins of Paris" had begun, to the inmost recesses of which their bloody service had penetrated the few favoured Huguenot courtiers rushing for shelter to Margaret's chamber under her coverlet ↑of Margaret↓ "because they were used" said popular satire:—the visitor to Paris may fancy ↑conceive↓ the place ↑as↓ intermediate between the forbidding circular donjons of Louis the Eleventh and the later official splendours of Richelieu and the Napoleons the foundations of those ancient feudal towers still remaining traced ↑out now↓, instructively, ↑in white↓ on the m̶e̶n̶ nineteenth century ↑asphalt↓ pavement.

[¶] A̶ t̶h̶e̶ ↑▲At the↓ sound of male footsteps the royal lady was astir and [**End 20 r**] ↑21↓ flinging wide the doors upon them suddenly like Homer's sorceress thrilled her curious visitors who trod their way softly into what seemed ↑might seem↓ the dimness the discreet order the perfume of some religious rite just ↑▲concluding↓ c̶o̶n̶c̶l̶u̶ as the virginal treble music died away. It was ↑nothing less than↓ an oratory this so ↑very↓ entirely characteristic apartment of Queen Margaret with its relics and rich reliquaries its recesses for devotion, ↑▲was↓ partly also a student's chamber as seriously arranged for its purpose as any monastic *scriptorium*: the tapestries (profanely storied, it must be said) excluding daylight might seem appropriate as a security also against the intrusion upon this charmed circle ↑area↓ of any quite simple thoughts from the world without. In fact its cunning occupant had well considered [**End 21 r**] ↑22↓ her business understood the best way of presenting her personal gifts, and might, for ↑with↓ other than clerkly reasons ↑motives↓ be shy even at this remote height of undraped windows. Clerkly this supreme ↑sovereign↓ beauty of her day certainly was; writing, writing constantly with a sort of really classic instinct for the genius of her native tongue and this ↑that↓ clerkliness did but add the more to the impression of cunning and wizardry about her again like that of Homer's Circe—δεινὴ θεός. On those classic pages which have survived her taking all the world into her confidence about all her people and herself doubtless with much adroit suppression of truth amid their seeming candour yet ↑though by way of what some may think↓ a quite "ruinous" apology some may think all so far as language is concerned is ~~clear~~ [?] [**End 22 r**] ↑23↓ clear straight-forward and—prosaic!

[0.5 cm] Friendly Brantome had seen many strangers come to France, to the French court expressly to gaze on that unique beauty of which the fame was gone through all Europe. He finds it pleasant to remember her (how many years afterwards!) at Blois on one particular day ↑occasion↓, with "her ~~palm~~"palm" how at a certain procession he and others had no profit of their devotions—our Palm-sunday devotions—*car nous y vasquames* [sic] *peu pour contemplir* [sic] *ceste princesse et nous y ravir plus qu'au service divin.* "Bacchus" he observes in another place ~~alw~~ always ready for quaint prattle about the old pagan gods,—Bacchus gives men fine blood Ceres fair flesh: but (here is the point) could have [**End 23 r**] ↑24↓ given neither one nor the other so long as men and women lived not on bread and wine but on chesnuts or acorns. Certainly Queen Margaret's beauty qui est telle que le beau parler de maistre Jehan Chartier, le suttilité de Maistre Jehan de Meun, et la main de Foucquet ne sauroyoient dire, escrire ne paindre, being nevertheless a carnal product of the carnal things of Ceres and Bacchus—carnal, as the massive white throat testifies—came of fine living, of fine feeding, so to call it ↑to speak candidly↓ of very dainty meal and wine through many generations of those who had lived "softly" as a matter of course "in kings' houses." The paleness Ronsard and his friends had cherished in their girlish mistresses had been a pale- [**End 24 r**] ↑25↓ ness not less used than **that of white wild-flowers to open air French sun-light: **that of Margaret on the other hand with her Italian derivation a quality which ↑at least↓ out of Italy at least will never seem altogether a thing of nature. With all the blue-veined well-compact lustre of flawless ↑perfectly compact↓ physical health it was the pallor nevertheless of a thing kept studiously like white lilac or roses in winter from the common air or you might fancy in the dark, and there was almost oriental blue richness blackness in the king-fisher wings or waves of hair which over-shadowed it ↑ce beau visage blanc↓ so abundantly yet with lines so jealously observed along the proud firm smooth flesh ce beau visage blanc making you think with ↑by↓ its trans- [**End 25 r**] ↑26↓ parent shadows of cool places around—yes! around dangerously deep water-pools amid a great heat. Like such water the black eyes surprised you by their clear dark blue when in ~~ful~~ full sunlight for a moment as the trees opened above.

[1.5 cm] That this beauty admirable ↑excellent↓ as Gaston found it had the character ↑air↓ of an instrument of ↑for↓ men's perdition about it was ↑had been↓ the observation ↑remark↓ of an unfriendly perhaps disappointed male visitor. But it was a devoted friend of Margaret's own sex who dying and desiring to die piously must needs thrust her from the bedside: Retirez-vous Madame, je vous prie, car il me faut prier et songer à mon Dieu, et vous ne me faites que ramentevoir le monde quand je [**End 26 r**] ↑27↓ vous regarde.

[¶] Of many minor arts at their perfection in that ↑artistic↓ age perhaps perhaps [*sic*] the most characteristic is the enamel of Limoges [1 cm] ↑with↓ its exquisitely ↑delicately↓ pencilled miniatures delicately veined brightly jewelled ↑and↓ detached in sharp outline on the lustrous or dark-blue surface like a solitary reflection in a mirror. Why had the dainty powers of ♦hand involved in it come to just this or stopped just here one asks before the ↑now↓ priceless achievements of this seemingly ↑irrecoverably↓ lost art—hard or as it is at its best ~~surely~~ harsh surely in spite of the manifold refinements of handling which delight ↑the↓ connoisseur↑s↓ in such matters ↑things↓— connoisseurs such as Margaret herself the panels [**End 27 r**] ↑28↓ of whose apartment where the only quite fresh or natural colours were to be found ↑only↓ in some out-of-the-way material—green ivory, green garnets, white peacocks' feathers—had been filled with sumptuous plaques from the hand of Leonard the Limousin himself. And (the thought occurred to Gaston) she had herself perhaps a superficial resemblance to this stuff as he sat and watched her and Jasmin at play with chessmen wrought in ↑of↓ it—a miracle of artistic dexterity in their way. She might have been the cunning *Bella Donna* whose physiognomy [1 cm illeg. cancln] haunts so much of the art-work of that age the visible form and ↑or↓ presentment of an unseen force moulding ↑and↓ remoulding after its own pattern all one saw around one in that choice [**End 28 r**] ↑29↓ little world of Paris where she ↑had↓ played so large a part—δεινὴ θεός!—the genius of cruel or unkindly as opposed to kindly love. [**End 29 r**]

Chapter X.

An Eros.

"The earth with her bars was about me".

The physiology of love, from the days of Plato to our

own — the days of Stendhal and Michelet — has had its students

analysing more or less ingeniously, the phenomena of its diseased

or healthy action, not always with entire theoretic disinterestedness,

yet driving, amid the complexities the thousand-fold casuis-

tries of what is after all the most practical of subjects, at

the very practical distinction of a blessing or a curse in it —

Eros or Anteros. The essence of such distinction however has

perhaps been touched most truly by William Blake in his

fantastically wise little poem of _The Cloud and the Pebble_

Fig. 7

Chapter X.[1]

Anteros.

"The earth with her bars was about me."

[1 cm] The physiology of love, from the days of Plato to our own—the days of Stendhal and Michelet—has had its students analysing, more or less ingeniously, the phenomena of its diseased or healthy action, not always with entire theoretic disinterestedness, yet driving, amid the complexities the thousand-fold casuistries of what is after all the most practical of subjects, at the very practical distinction of a blessing or a curse in it—Eros or Anteros. The essence of such distinction however has perhaps been touched most truly by William Blake in his fantastically wise little poem of *The Clod and the Pebble* [**End 1 r**] ↑2↓ when ↑where↓ he contrasts the Love which must needs please another with that which can only please itself the loves↑L↓ which respectively must serve or be served be possessed or in possession the Love that would fain do costly sacrifice with the ↑that↓ Love which ↑that↓ would so willingly extort it. Unselfish love ↑as↓ we know has its flights its extraordinary [3 cm] ↑passages↓ and even more the selfish ↑even more↓ its caprices of self-pleasing of demand on the voluntary yet so ruinous servility of others: their bodily and ↑or↓ mental decrease—their suicide Let [*sic*] us say!—as just one grain of incense, consumed, wholly consumed, on the red coal. Such impious claim to sovereignty centres of course in the consciousness of some inalienable incommunicable personal distinction most properly of that physical beauty which flushes [**End 2 r**] ↑3↓ the veins and therewith his imagination his reason his force of will with physical appetite scarcely anything man covets being in ultimate analysis desirable by him except through links of association however remote of identification however

---

1. This chapter consists of 41 leaves, all recto only; consecutive pagination in upper right corner begins with folio 2. Pencil headings in an unknown hand in the upper right corner of fol. 1 are: *? G de L* and, beneath, *(10)*. Paper: fols. [1]–7, 8–16 (8 7/8" x 7 7/16"), cobalt edged; fol. 7 (9" x 7 1/8") TOWGOOD'S; fols. 17–25 (9" x 7") COLLARD; fols. 36–41 (9" x 7 7/16"), cobalt edged.

supposititious with the desire of the bodily eye. [9 cm] ² ↑*Fastus inest pulchris, sequiturque superbia formam.*↓ How many enigmas on the stage of human life are really covered by the recondite relationships of what we may call erotic humility to erotic pride.

[0.5 cm] In the age of the Valois among people of an extraordinary force of will ready to assert to the utmost the whole of what they felt and were an age of courtiers and ceremonial of continual self-presentation therefore which with senses re- [**End 3 r**] ↑4↓ fined by a lovely though decadent art felt the full significance of personality in its sensible manifestations,—in such an age, we might perhaps trace the steps by which the desire of physical of carnal beauty becomes a sort of religion a profane and cruel religion as cruel religions there are or have been. Was such sentiment wasteful despotic and strangely exclusive where it is present at all a natural and normal condition of certain types of human mind at all times or the wholly artificial creation of a somewhat visionary art and poetry invading a phase of actual life from which ordinary motives had deceased ↑departed↓: or had it come, already in full development, from Italy (as infection comes, wrapped up with costly furni- [**End 4 r**] ↑5↓ ture and the like) to set a fashion, and remodel everything else after its own new pattern? Had it escaped from the grave of antiquity, reopened there with all that antiquity had known the over-powering literature the sins the exotic sin which imperial Rome in its days of decadence had learned from those old-world subjects who were become in turn the masters of its thought, sins like those of Tyre and Sidon which neither the blood of primitive martyrs nor the consecrations of the Middle Age had yet purged ↑detached↓ from its very stones? So the student of moral ideas of historic fact may ask shocked or merely curious. There at all events it was: Amor, L'Amour, in every form of selfish pity and terror of sorrow and joy "enthroned in the land of [**End 5 r**] ↑6↓ oblivion" of forgetfulness of all beside itself the carnal consuming and essentially wolfish love though so humanely learned in the remotest delicacies of human form the shading of the eyelid the ~~curv~~ ↑ᴧcurvature↓ of the lip colours lines as immaculate seemingly as those of opening flowers the love or lust that will not be contented with anything less than the consumption the destruction of its object as if it had been a literal π eating and drinking of it which meant only to pluck all that to take another like a flower from ~~the~~ ↑its↓ stalk or a grape from the wall suck

---

2. Here a fractional line indicates that the following interlined quotation is to be set off from the text.

out the juice and fling away the rent skin chiefly by way of gaining pleasant assurance to itself of its own sovereignty. [**End 6 r**]

↑7 6↓ [1 cm] Its sovereignty enthroned for the moment in the person, ↑▲the reprobate beauty,↓ of Margaret the ↑that↓ golden daisy of France golden ↑▲or yellow↓ or at least not white ↑but then ↑though (↑?↓ even↓↓ liturgically yellow or gold though ↑however↓ dusky does duty for white:) moy, as she writes, qui suis fille de roy et soeur de roys, herself indeed queen queen Margot of little Navarre but who thought it not worth while to secure ↑▲by average decency ↑of life↓↓ the throne of France: preferred ↑▲rather↓ to be queen ↑▲empress deity if it might be↓ of men's hearts and found ↑▲in plenty↓ her willing devoted thirsty subjects. Yes! there were ↑▲the virginal↓ the really white flowers ↑of both sexes↑?↓↓ whose floral perfection ↑like some↓ triumph of the gardener's art ↑▲of the old Adam ~~who had brought~~ ↑▲bringing↓ his curious skill so far↓ might be thought to justify ~~the~~ ↑▲the heated shade, the morbid sad ↑triste ↑terne↓↓ "secondary" colours, ~~in~~ all that was ↑~~all that was artificial in~~↓ artificial or medicated ~~light and~~ ↑▲in the↓ air of the world around them, upon which, ↑▲like veritably spiritual things in their transformed earthiness,↓ they stole opened spread themselves so gracefully ↑▲easily↓ superbly for an hour, yet with ↑so delightful↓ a delightful sense of ↓mystery, as if drawing ↓they drew↑ their nurture from nethermost darkness.↑ [**End 7 r**] ↑8↓ They swarmed here these ↑those↓ luscious heavy-petalled blossoms these momentarily beautiful faces lips eyes with your ↑own↓ eyes on which one ↑you↓ might forget or desire to forget all beside ↑and↓ over which for the like of Margaret some cruel assertion of empire might have the sweetness of an embrace. From forgotten old houses in remote corners of France like choice furniture or untouched portraits they were ↑had↓ come on demand. And in ↑and with the lapse of↓ a month or a year in this singular atmosphere the exotic personality the hand the eye the lip the inflammable fancy within of which these were eloquent had had ↑even↓ surpassed the utmost imaginings of the exotic fine art which had discovered to others and ↑as↓ to themselves their high aesthetic value. You seemed to await ↑expect↓ to know ↑have known↓ something of them [**End 8 r**] ↑9↓ before they came after a few minutes intercourse to have known them always. They filled a place made ready for them by the books the pictures the very fashions of the day nay more than filled it they superseded all this ~~delightfully~~ ↑daringly.↓ Was there ◆here ↑And was ↑And might this be↓↓ perhaps the fulfilment of Gaston's early boyish dreams of [2 cm] ↑(repeat)↓ ◆awaiting him ◆here ↑~~here~~↓—somewhere among these faces pathetic appealing in spite of their pride passing so constantly about him by day ↑and↓ at night steadily fixed ↑steadily↓ upon the dark wall of the brain? ↑(? weeping &c.)↓

[¶] Unkindly or cruel love the worship of the body the religion of physical beauty with its congenital and appropriate fanaticism, ↑a↓ servitude based on the most potent form of that relationship of the weak to the strong noted by Aristotle as the elementary [**End 9 r**] ↑10↓ ground of slavery in human nature itself—most potent as being ↑because↓ in effect the relation ↑servitude↓ of the insane to the sane—the "impassioned love of passion" love for love's sake as a doctrine and a discipline a science and a fine art all in one its evocative power over what finely educated senses must straightway declare •de •lightful desirable in the sphere of imageries colour music words refining the very lips that uttered them the anatomy of the thing of his own free experience the strange delight of such servitude for the master and stranger still for the servant in it was for a time for months that grew to years almost exclusively to occupy the mind of Gaston at home in this singular place ↑like↓ Circe's enchanted island or like the maze on the ↑that↓ old cathedral floor at [**End 10 r**] ↑11↓ Chartres such mazes as savage fingers not ↑no↓ less than the finest ↑ones↓ have been led to trace likest of all to that labyrinth of land and water of streams and pathways in the background of [3 cm], revolving perpetually into themselves. An air of casuistry about it stimulating pleasantly the reflective action of the brain as its romance coaxed the fancy that ↑t~~hat~~ odd savour of a↓ remote and curious scholarship in ↑of↓ love in which Queen Margaret seemed a graduate a doctor had from the a fascination for the studious youth himself before all things a scholar a fastidious scholar whose ↑His own↓ conscious clerkly distinction was in truth to the taste of the day to Margaret as the final expression of the taste of the ↑that ↑her↓↓ day the hour the moment the present moment for which alone professedly those who [**End 11 r**] ↑12↓ were of it thought and wrought. For both of them as both alike absorbed students fellow-students there was certainly a wonderful charm when as with the poet of the *Vita Nuova* with Petrarch with sinful Abelard of old here in Paris such grave ~~thoughts~~ ↑▲thoughts↓ as seem naturally alien from carnal love enter its service put on its livery become its accomplices. The trim discreet almost priestly scholar correcting annotating the great lady's manuscripts nominally a very proper secretary was conscious of while he suggested to her the question (of a kind seductive to ↑for↓ the thoughtful) in what precise ↑exact↓ proportions a cool grave self-possessed intelligence might coexist with the physical throb of youth could conspire with ↑▲it↓ as he ↑Gaston↓ came and went on his learned business, entertaining and himself entertained, [**End 12 r**] ↑13↓ in what for ↑by↓ his good fortune was a kind of mutual indifference. For, as with physical delicacies, if you wished to sip, as you might wine, to enjoy ⁺in veritable connoisseurship the singularly attempered character of the so gifted Margaret a calm though kindly indifference was in fact the proper condition for doing so—an indifference which would have formed in truth one of the three constituent chapters in that book of ↑on↓ the physiology of love ↑which↓ she might have penned with triumphant suitability to the humour of her generation.

[0.5 cm] The unkindness of the ↑its↓ two other chapters—of that cruel eagerness to consume the reluctant lover and ↑then↓ of that cruel weariness of the ↑a↓ lover found too facile which allowed nay [**End 13 r**] ↑14↓ encouraged him to consume to destroy himself in ↑by↓ sacrifice delightful surely in its degree to him also—these chapters in Margaret's supposed physiology↑P↓ of love↑L↓ Gaston read ↑we may ↑might↓ say↓ carefully to the end as one might really read a book occupied that is to say often feverishly ↑▲enough↓ in brain-work with philosophic or sophistic ↑casuistic↓ questions concerning for instance the entanglement of beauty with evil to what extent one might succeed in disentangling them or failing that how far one may warm and water the dubious double root watch for the ↑its↓ flower or retain the ~~hoper~~ ↑hope↓ or the memory or the mere tokens of it in one's keeping.↑?↓ Amid a hundred palpable though quickly evanescent sympathies attachments affections operative as if through a mere touch in the dark a form seen but for [**End 14 r**] ↑15↓ a few moments ↑or↓ a name only with the fancied ↑voice and↓ eyes and hands ↑voice↓ that might pertain to it he found himself at times almost as suppliant as ~~as~~ ↑the↓ people about him to what claimed for service on bended knee and ↑with↓ consciously self-forgetful heart. Enthralled constantly by the spectacle before him more and more exclusively detached by it from the claim↑s↓ of anything beside yet chilled to the heart by a wretched sense of brevity, of decay and hasting in it he lived ever in dread of some great and over-powering ↑over-whelming ↑[1 cm illeg canceln] ↓↓ temptation. Was it he in fact who suffered ↑the↓ exclusion ↑the↓ detachment thus paying a penalty? Was there something some one he had disloyally neglected who had now put him aside deserted him in just distress or anger and pain fluttering [**End 15 r**] ↑16↓ away from him as from a soiled place and now he must bear the consequences? In omnibus his peccaverunt adhuc: said the Psalmist: et ↑Et↓ defecerunt in vanitate dies eorum: Therefore their days did He consume in vanity, and their years in festinatione,—in distresful hasting no-whither. Was ↑And was↓ it really thus ↑▲after all?↓ ~~with him~~ Was it so with him? ↑himself?↓

[1 cm] If ~~Queen~~ Queen Margaret's chamber was ~~a some~~ like a some place of strange worship ~~away from us as from what whither one could not discover if Margarets room~~[?] ~~and if again whither one could not discover if whither that held good in any way or other to an~~ [End 16 r] ↑17 ↓<6>5↓ ~~If Margaret's chamber was like a place of strange worship,~~ herself at once ↑its↓ idol and priestess, its chief relic was as ghastly as church relics ↑▲usually↓ are, ~~lying there~~ ↑▲exposed↓ ~~among the best prized objects of her personal property,~~ a dead man's face, ↑▲with the stamp of ↑stamped with ~~its~~ his violent end,↓ mummied and brown, lying ↑set↓ there ↑exposed↓ among the best prized objects of her ↑the lady's↓ personal ↑property↓ mounted in a kind of shrine or pyx of jewellers' ↑good goldsmiths'↓ work, ↑and↓ set with gems ↑picked↓ from her ↑milady's↓ own ornaments. ↑jewel-case.↓ Just that species of ↑Precisely ↓such↑ fantastic↓ love, love as a servitude, ↑an idolatry,↓ a "voluntary humily [*sic*], had been ↑come↓ ↑naturally↓ to the humour ↑appetite ↑liking↓↓ of one Jacques La Mole, gay-flowering sprig from an old stock rooted deep in the province of [2 cm], as he ↑▲first↓ sauntered hopefully into Paris on a path which crossed at [End 17 r] ↑18 ~~17 16~~↓ last at the fatal point ↑of conjunction↓, on the fatal day and hour, the determined ↑so incisive inexorable↓ path of Margaret then also at her freshest and henceforth his soul's one queen ↑the ~~sole~~ monarch of his soul↓, whereupon ↑and thereupon↓ the whole ↑entire↓ sheaf of his gifts and gaieties had kindled into fire, a pyramid of sweet aromatic fire ↑▲flame moving to its end↓ before her. ↑as she went onward.↓ Plotting recklessly with the ↑madman's↓ hare-brained wit he had in that world of ~~accomplished~~ ↑very cunning↓ plots, ↑▲in fact↓ almost as openly ↑frankly↓ as he unsheathed always for her sake his first youthful sword, ↑for her↓ he played for her a wild game for [1.5 cm] years, in which ↑▲not ~~even he could~~↓ even he, ~~could hardly fancy~~ ↑▲not even ↑▲love's fanatic<s>↑s↓↓ could maintain↓ he had won the prize he played for. ↑at stake.↓ In due ↑Shortly in↓ course of time ↑years↓ you see him pass into ↑▲a sordid↓ prison, ↑into↓ dim torture-chambers in the keeping of those who will rack the [End 18 r] ↑19 ~~18 17~~↓ young limbs this way and that to squeeze out if they may ↑can↓ truth about the doings of more stealthy enemies than he of the powers that are and when he emerges again to suffer in public, ↑and↓ as if voluntarily ↑▲by way of a slight offering↓ to fling his life to her, sitting there to watch she has no effective or natural sympathy ~~with~~ ↑for↓ the young man, with form already ruined his shattered arm making shift to fling cap in air gaily ↑gallantly↓, does watch however, ↑puts out no hand to save

him, but yet ↓only↑↓ and makes a point of carrying the severed head³ ↑▴thus offered and duly accepted by her↓ away with her, to be set amid ↑to set ↑sets it among↓↓ her choicest gifts ↑received↓ tribute winnings. Ci-gît &c. [4.5 cm] and [2 cm] have mercy ~~of~~ on his soul ↑or↓ on what remains ↑be-f ↑may ↑still be left↓ remain ~~be-f↓↓~~ unconsumed of it. [**End 19 r**]

↑20 ~~19~~ ~~18~~↓ [0.5 cm] There ↑then↓ now ever in the presence of Margaret, actually upon an altar with unbleached ↑funeral↓ wax lights amid the curtained space of her little oratory, ↑like↓ the smirched moth⁴ beside ↑upon↓ the candle was the ugly brown face, made ↑thus ↑so↓↓ ugly for her sake.⁵ The dainty ↑graceful↓ Jasmin sees it there as usual recoils instinctively ↑▴hates the ↑very↓ place where it is kept seems to detect the scent↓ ~~wishes to be gone~~ of it here there underneath pleasanter ones ↑perfumes↓ wishes to be gone ↑as usual↓ having in truth no great care for Margaret one of her reluctant [2 cm] ↑subjects ↑lovers or claimees↓↓, as he will find to his cost ↑for which he will pay the cost↓ almost as [2 cm] ↑ruefully↓, ~~in~~ in which

---

3. HOU slip:
   —↑▴she is↓ not to be contented with / a lock of the abundant↑?↓ / hair cut ~~by the~~ ↑▴[0.5 illeg cancln] ↓dextrously↑↓ away / from the neck by the (T.O. / executioner— / [¶]—the last of so many careful / toilets and hair- / dressings for her / sake,

The "(T.O." notation ("Turn Over") is in the right margin.

Overleaf, four primary half-lines, right half of sheet with vertical strikeout, and the continuation, interlined and inverted in relation to the canceled lines:

   but carries away &c.

The canceled text is an earlier draft of precisely this incident (105:2–5):

   , in a dim torture / ...ry limb & squeeze out / more subtle ↑stealt[h]y↓ enemies of / ...d when he emerges again

4. Both sides of a BNC slip pertain:
   La Mole— brevity—[   ] & / he fluttered right into it—into / its [   ]— & there was his / brown face, the ↓▾central↑ relic of M's / — · —the moth, the candle, / it was [illeg.] to watch.

Overleaf, inverted:
   —the moth & the / candle—of course / the candle is / unsympathetic

5. BNC slip:
   It was a ↑the↓ / —the primitive, the↑?↓ precise / sensible ↑visible↓ counterpart analogue / to the *thoughts* about death, wh. / had haunted him ↑all↓ thro' these / later years in Paris— the the[?]—/ ↑,the — of↓ —Margaret

Overleaf, inverted, Dip. 13 n.4.

matter he will pay ↑be cast in↓ the cost almost as heavily as that former too
ready ↑prompt↓ lover, former ↑whilom↓ ~~ovner~~ owner of ~~eyes and~~ ↑▲these
↑the↓ embalmed↓ lips and eyes so winning and eloquent once [**End 20 r**] ↑21
~~20 19~~↓ so repulsive now.

[¶] Yet Jasmin too so light of step picking his way through the ↑an unclean↓
world ↑as if ◆on ↑along↓ a silken list↓ with a daintiness which makes almost
every one he meets instinctively ↑concede ↓give↑ ↑yield↓ him the nicer
↓best↑ side↓ he too has done does his share ↑part↓ in crushing live ↑living↓
sentient things ◆on ↑there in↓ his brief passage, though he has no care
↑liking↓ for ghastly relics in the ↑his↓ pleasant ↑house places↓ chambers of
his house ↑memory↓ or his memory. ↑house.↓—

[0.5] About this time for the diversion of Paris the ↑a↓ [3 cm] ↑choice↓
company of Italian players brought there ↑thither↓ by King Henry presented
there in↑?↓ masquerade↑?↓ by way of ↑a↓ "mystery" or "morality" their own
version of a legend we ↑people since↓ have come to know well ~~since~~ the
legend of Tannhäus↑s↓er. The [**End 21 r**] ↑22 ~~20<1>~~↓ ↑romantic↓ knight as
we remember on his dreamy medieval way ↑journey stumbles↓ amid the
↑eery old↓ cliffs and ~~rocks~~ woods of Germany stumbles into the hiding-place
of Venus herself not dead but still alive though when ↑if↓ she peeps ↑peeped↓
forth she sees ↑would see↓ a Gothic church steeple. Well! once for all
Tannhausser [*sic*] **g** is hers gives her his heart himself a gift ↑thing↓ not to be
recovered ↑recoverable had back again↓ makes ↑his ↑an↓↓ effort↑s↓ to break
the spell finds his way ↑goes↓ to Rome seeking absolution from the Pope
returns ↑again however↓ to the cave and his heart there all the time as if to
hell as we feel ↑and to hell so to speak↓ forever though a pretty afterthought
hints at final restoration. ↑B↓[6]

[¶] Those Italian players took the story ↑their subject↓ a little from ↑on↓ one
[**End 22 r**] ↑23 ~~21<2>~~↓ side so to speak ↑put the ↑?↓ Venustas the quality of
Venus not on a goddess but on a god and↓ made the adoring fanatical lover
a woman, ~~old~~ ↑the↓ old Eve mother of us all as through many forms she takes
↑her way↓ through the world, ↑ever↓ one and the same from age to age, with
desire towards [2.5 cm] ruling over her, betrayed again and again into the ▲
realm of some irrepressible male deity ↑idol↓, ↑supposed↓ in this particular
case to be [3.5 cm], seeking ↑she seeks↓ now and then if it may be the
ministry of some wholesomer ↑kind of↓ religion, but always returning

---

6. Beta symbol

↑again↓ at last underground to her ~~idol and~~ ↑madness and idolatry↓ usually, as was truly said, to nurse ~~the~~ her deity in sickness. ↑Well!↓ The ↑Franco-↓Italian version followed ↑her↓ then ↑the ↑self-immolating↓ longing feminine soul↓ from age to age always the same (↑the↓ constant repetition ↑of its sad fortunes↓ was the force [**End 23 r**] ↑24 2<3>2↓ of the thing) with such fantastic knowledge as stage-players in that loosely pedantic age could come by of the ways the looks ↑the raiment↓ of men and women in old Assyria transformed quickly ↑mistily↓ on the stage to ancient Egypt, Judaea Corinth Rome to humanity as these ↑like this very↓ theatrical performers ↑company did↓ presenting a single piece in all the towns and provinces in turn onward to modern ↑medieval↓ Nuremberg and modern Venice and coming down to the last generation ↑discreetly↓ stopped at today ↑their own↓ not from lack of contemporary instance as the reader knows ↑is aware↓ but ↑as↓ leaving the theme confidently to the fancy the experience of a ↑fashionable↓ Parisian audience late in the sixteenth century. [**End 24 r**]

↑25 ~~24~~ ~~23~~↓ [1 cm] Only, be it remembered, such feminine ↑female↓ souls are not necessarily lodged in women's bosoms. In ↑an ↑a certain↓ episode of↓ Jasmin's fantastic experience the ↑▲idolatrous or↓ servile disposi•tion ↑attitude↓ ~~had sheathed itself~~ ↑~~been~~ ↑was↓ ~~unveiled~~ unveiled itself↓ in the person of a lad who ~~realising~~ ↑had realised↓ towards him ↑as it were↓ the s very genius of slavery as a natural affec•tion of ↑the↓ human mind. See them together ↑just able to walk ↑move↓ away from one another ↑in play↓ for a few minutes↓ at the door of the farm-house, ~~foster-brothers~~ in the old French country, foster-brothers Jasmin fleurdelisè and Raoul as delicately made as he though less softly clad the wild flower ↑if↓ it be really ~~clad~~ wild is not ↑essentially↓ less delicate ↑essentially↓ than the growth ↑garden flower↓ of the garden ↑gardens↓ if it be really wild. Raoul ↑▲↑~~come~~ ~~down through generations of cottagers on the~~ ↑come through generations of cottagers↓ ↑▲on the↓ wholesome woodside↓ ~~in this country where the latter~~ ↑~~come hither in this small~~ ↓where nice wild-flowers↑↓ naturally abound, ↑▲seems↓ ~~is~~ [**End 25 r**] ↑2<6>5 ~~24~~↓ ↑▲indeed↓ cut so to speak on the same pattern and of the same stuff as his play-fellow from the manor-house, yet ~~one will be a↑?↓~~master ~~indeed~~ ↑▲somehow, by some natural sway part tendency in the inward↓ unseen ↑elementary↓ settlement of things one will be ↑the a↓ master indeed↑?↓ ↑and↓ the other ↑a↓ "servant of servants" to his brother. What strange disturbance is, ↑this within him, like the [1.5 cm] ↑battling↓ of a wounded bird in his bosom,↓ when Jasmin leaves him ↑the place↓ for the first time, this surprising ↑overwhelming↓ discovery ↑in a moment↓ that the other who is ↑seems↓ already afar on his ↑far off along the↓ road homewards, is necessary to his being, the sickness with which he turns round ↑back↓ to his own place in the world ↑an hour since ↓ago↑↓ so delightful ↑sufficient but just now↓ an hour since ↑ago↓ this ↑the↓ determination ↑his one solace ↓comfort↑ is ~~in~~ ↑suddenly formed, yet ↑but↓ unalterable determination—↓ to find his own solace↓ to nurse at any price the hope of seeing ↑to see↓ him ↑J.↓ again. ↑with unchanged regard ↑ways towards↓ himself.↓ He is told that the other will forget him that it must [**End 26 r**] ↑27 ~~2~~<6>5↓ and ought to be so in his unimaginable home in ↑far up there at↓ the great ↑fine↓ castle lined with silk and gold, [1 cm illeg canceln] yet ↑he↓ ruminates ↑wonders ↑ponders↓↓ what he ↑the ↑that other↓↓ may be doing there now ↑and now↓ there or there. Yes! doubtless↓2↑ forgetful↓1↑ of him ↑himself↓. A few hours ↑days↓ ago he could ↑would↓ not have thought ↑understood ↑believed↓↓ that thus it would ↑could↓ be with him this dislocation of himself of a part of himself, ~~seeking now~~ ↑its↓ like a thing cut in two yet alive still as Plato fancied, seeking seeking blindly to be one again with its fellow its self.

[¶] The castle↑C↓ however after all is not so far off is ↑distantly↓ visible in the distance up there on the rising ground though ↑while ↑where↓↓ he is down in the cottage, and he does see his lord [**End 27 r**] ↑28 ~~27 26~~↓ again from time to time ↑and actually↓ with a sort of kindness on both sides, the luxury of pride on this ↑one↓ side working reciprocally ↑and↓ with perfect ↑reciprocity and↓ ease about ↑around↓ the luxury of ~~pri~~ humility on the ↑that↓ other, nature itself having ~~foremed~~ ↑formed↓ some to rule and some to serve. For so decided ~~are~~ ↑is↓ the opposition of the mutual instincts which determine this ↑such↓ relationship found to be that we might ↑may↓ surely suppose ~~them~~ it a ↑them the↓ result of some original primitive purely ↑animal and↓ physical ↑or animal↓ divergency in the cerebral ↑molecule or↓ germ. parted asunder ↑~~necessarily~~↓ set over against each other more and more with ↑at in↓ each generation the ↑fatally↓ fixed and fatally opposites in a necessary "strife" ↑contention↓ and subsequent [1 cm] ↑?↓ collusion↓ of soul like two distinct yet, [2 cm] ↑as ↑the↓ older doctrinaires supposed fancied↓ natural species ↑now↓. Yes! the [**End 28 r**] ↑29 ~~28 27~~↓ [3 cm] ↑seigneurial↓ species of soul and the servile species, a mass of instincts susceptibilities consequent issues built up ↑gathered ↑massed↓↓ gradually ↑from of old↓ through generations of forefathers whose habitation ↑abode↓ had been in meagre cottages, ↑in their lords' stables, in↓ dark-cells, torture chambers surviving in ↑with↓ all fitness in the modest person of the ↑this↓ young serf↓2↑ or servitor↓1↑ in ~~15~~ fifteen-hundred-and [3 cm], side by side with the perfectly blown flower of the old primitive or eternal germ of mastery of the natural superior in Jasmin. The servitor ↑His servant↓ loves him admires loves the more would willingly ↑fain↓ serve him in some ↑very↓ costly manner, as he returns finer daintier each time from school, from court, from incredible foreign lands ↑places↓, a ↑perfect↓ mystery of superiority, like [**End 29 r**] ↑30 ~~29 28~~↓ some young pontiff in his silk and lace and [1.5 cm] goudron to ↑in↓ the view of that ↑loyal↓ simple ↑confident↓ creature, feeling that odd ↑strange↓ ache within when the other ↑of course↓ departs again ↑of course↓, not less through habit but more than at ↑the↓ first anticipating now ↑every ↑each↓ time↓ the tale of emptied days as it will be told over again as freshly as ever from point to point ~~from~~ for him ↑thus↓ deserted thus by his comrade, his master. He thinks of all the pleasures the glories ↑that the other ↑he↓↓ goes to his own ↑indeed↓ and right for him and ↑but↓ is not envious. And now ↑as he comes again now↓ as he comes again ↑coming again↓ he makes his ↑the↓ servitor though he ~~is~~ [?] cannot handle a ↑the↓ pen a sort of poet[7] at last ↑as he↓ consciously associating ↑associates↓ that gallant presence with the ↑▲flashes, the↓ changeful beauty and pride, of ↑all↓ other outward things, the [**End 30 r**] ↑31 ~~30 29~~↓ lily and the rose on Our Lady's altar the moving ocean of fresh green leaves the immaculate snow. Drilled by his own loyal painstaking into a fit attendant enough, like some choice kind of dog, he is permitted at last to his unspeakable delight to follow his ↑~~young~~↓ lord to Paris throws himself without question into the young man's ways ↑life↓ there its ↑his↓ friendships hatreds intrigues and ↑r [?]↓ at length as fate leads ↑at length↓ his heart big ↑aflame ↑wild↓↓ with the ~~heart~~ ↑mere↓ hope to please such a master to the uttermost ↑and in costliest fashion↓ follows out ↑up↓ some fancied ♦passing quarrel of his tracks out ↑hunts down↓ with ↑a↓ suddenly developed cunning and does ↑takes↓ his lord's justice ↑vengeance↓ on the body ↑person↓ of a young [2.5 cm] ↑seigneur↓ of higher rank than Jasmin's own. Lightly ↑In↓ [**End 31 r**] ↑32 ~~31 30~~↓ in the inattention with the indifference of spirit which follow ↑follows↓ a great ~~deep~~ ↑deed↓ he ↑lightly↓ permits himself to be taken red-handed with from ↑guilty of↓ a crime, the murder of a [2 cm] by a servant, for which he must ↑will↓ be "broken on the wheel" ↑certainly↓ to the ♦passing regret of Jasmin though he shudders ↑shocked↓ at ↑such↓ a crime like his ↑as that↓. They crowd in ↑the indifferent world↓ where he is to "suffer" on the hot fine morning the ↑an↓

---

7. HOU slip:

~~=how he connected~~[?] ~~himself / with sudden~~ [1.5 cm illeg cancln] ~~itself~~= / ~~becomes a poet~~ / becomes in his dumb, ↑half=↓ choked / way, a poet dumb, but in all / but action—a poet—

Overleaf, not applicable

indifferent world going to market ↑or↓ returning ↑on their way home↓ from
marriages ↑a wedding↓ on their way to funerals taking their cakes to the
baker or their cattle to the butcher↑y↓ regretful only not to be able to stay and
see it out people ↑wholly↓ unused to enquire about ↑question↓ the justness
of "public "acts of "justice"[8]: a pavement of heads children who thought he
must indeed ↑"be↓ wicked [**End 32 r**] ↑33 3̶<̶2̶>̶1̶↓ to have suffered so" or that
he didn't ↑couldn't↓ feel the blows or hid their faces and wept religious
persons who would have ↑prolonged his lifetime↓ kept him alive between
those blows or d̶ added to their number, to secure a truly penitent passage for
him from the ↑this↓ world this world of racking eyes about him ~~under the
heat~~ in the Place de Greve. ~~under the~~ ↑*under]~~ ↑amid↓↓ ↑▲Amid this↓ heat
of a ↑the↓ gaudy thirsty June morning.<,> ~~There~~ ↑▲how↓ enviable the ↑those
more↓ aristocratic sight-seers who sit at ↑nicely ↑carefully↓↓ shaded
windows, or ↑and those who↓ have found standing place ~~under the~~ ↑in that↓
long shadow across the square of the tower ↑belfry↓ of the ↑old↓ Hotel de
Ville, where ~~th~~ ↑all has been made↓ ready for the sufferer. He, for one ↑at
least ↑at all events↓↓ emerging from his ↑the↓ shadowy prison gate seemed
even now ↑thus↓ to find ↑a momentary relief pleasantness↓ the warmth
↑heat↓ the sun-light the wide=air ↑air;↓ [**End 33 r**] ↑34 3̶3̶ 3̶2̶↓ ↑and↓ shivers
perhaps ↑partly↓ with cold↑?↓ as they strip away his scanty clothing. Under
the constraint of these ↑the↓ few↓2↑ last↓1↑ days he is become humbler than
a little child ↑is pressed↑?↓ onward↓ may be handled turned this way and that
as passively as a ↑dead↓ child already dead. A priest ~~comes~~ ↑of course↓ stands
↑as↓ near him ↑as may be↓ but he doesn't listen looks only for the master in
his [2 cm] might mistake another for him. When they bind him ↑at last↓ to
the great ↑fixed↓ upright wheel, like Saint Andrew on his cross, ↑not
blindfold↓ facing the multitude having the ↑only his↓ loose white shirt upon
him at the bosom (that ↑it↓ will be nothing in the way of the iron bar) the
women ↑perhaps↓ for the first time in his brief life, ↑in a luxury of grief↓ feel
that he belongs or ↑ought↓ to belong to them, ↑to their proper world↓ Amor
Lacrimosus, bound ↑there↓ to the wheel, like a rose on the trellis. [**End 34 r**]
↑35 3̶4̶ 3̶3̶↓ The executioners forgot the [2.5 cm] ↑rag↓ for binding
↑blindfolding↓ the lad's eyes; a handkerchief a score of handkerchiefs are
passed through ↑pressed ◆handed over the heads of↓ the crowd. People
speculate with [2 cm] breath on the effect of the first blow of the iron bar ↑in
◆hands of iron↓ across the legs are hushed as if ~~to~~ ↑for↓ distant music or ~~some
utmost~~ ↑an eloquent↓ voice as they wait ↑await ↑listen↓↓ for ↑the sound of↓

8. Pater is trying a phrase of three different lengths.

the second the third ↑next and the next this way and that with pause between↓ over the extended arms, the stomach for the last stroke upon the open bosom which does not always kill immediately the body with every ~~bone~~ ↑bone limb↓ broken hanging there ↑▲to die after all in the course of nature↓ till the ~~surgeons come~~ public [1.5 cm] come who will reduce it to ashes. As people pass away around it they hardly know whether it breathes still a few only get near enough to ascertain the truth of a ↑the↓ ↓relieving↑ rumour passing ↑which passes↓ through the ↓crowd that the sufferer ↑boyish criminal↓ is dead. ~~Yet etc.~~↑ [**End 35 r**]

↑36↓ [1 cm] Yet Jasmin shuddered at could not bear the neighbourhood of the relic Margaret had snatched triumphantly from a scene like ↑such as↓ that the kind of scene which gave the key-note for the entire↑?↓ scenery ↑key-note as it was for the entire scenery↓ of the whole world here about him to [1 cm] and his thoughts at this time a great ~~pla~~ Place de Greve. Again and again revolutionists tried to purge it ↑of↓ that Parisian one ↑of its↓ but with ↑by↓ fresh crimes of their own.

[1 cm] "Intention," the mental act by which you peer into and exhaust the infinitude of qualities lying within the compass of a single ↑▲object or↓ phenomenon is ever necessarily (so ↑as↓ logicians tell you) "↑?↓ in inverse proportion to "extension" to any larger or more liberal survey of the area which the name of such object or phenomenon ↑generally↓ denotes. [**End 36 r**] ↑37↓ The ~~The~~ interests, the one interest, revolving perpetually round and round again into itself which occupied the thoughts of Gaston at this time had a marked exclusiveness. Observe, touch, taste of all things, indifferently!—So his philosophic guides had steadily recommended—guides he might ⁕seem indeed to have encountered ↑quite↓ casually on the ↑his↓ way, whose judgments ↑⁕theories↓ nevertheless presented to him as he then actually was seemed to come ↑to him↓ with nothing less than axiomatic force.

[¶] Yet it was to this their advocacy of a ↑the↓ ~~la~~ larger ↑larger↓ and ↑more↓ liberal acceptance of life had in fact committed him—to this exclusive preoccupation with what was certainly but a limited department of the great garden and ↑As↓ as he looked back afterwards it was [**End 37 r**] ↑38↓ noticeable that just here for him life had contracted to its ~~uttermost.~~ ↑▲narrowest.↓ As he contemplated ever more and more intently a single exotic sentiment ↑with↓ its interpretation in art in literature in life, other interests manifold once his dropped ↑fell↓ away around it leaving it there alone thrusting it ~~four~~ forward upon him as if in an otherwise empty world,

⁺but yes! with the bell of doom hanging there under the sunless sky in In vanitate in festinatione deficiunt dies—anni.

[1 cm] Presenting itself at first as ↑only ↑⁺but↓↓ the proper antidote to the too narrow and scrupulous conscience of a religious childhood a restrained youth the theory of "indifference" had ⁺but subjected him to a sort of conscience more exclusive still to this impas- [**End 38 r**] ↑39↓ sioned love of passion—call it what you will. Amans amavi [3 cm] so in ever-revolving circle through every tense of the verb to love did ↑does↓ Augustine describe ↑describes↓ the like of it in himself. Here certainly for a while had been ↑was↓ for him ↑w↓ the single the ↑and↓ all-exclusive touch-stone of reality of value in things. Not the conscious art only the literature the music of the age but the very furniture about one was full of it and of nothing else—the ↑▲wine↓ w̶i̶n̶e̶ one drank the cup that held it the platter you ↑one↓ took it from and above all those graceful fashions ↑with↓ perhaps the loveliest ↑masculine↓ dress the world has seen how faithfully how daintily it ↑followed↓ displayed yet made a mystery of the form ↑person the natural form↓ within relieved the finely bred much cared ↑▲for↓ hand and head. And then the shoes. ↑The very shoes↓ Common people's [**End 39 r**] ↑40↓ seemed to belong to what soiled ↑▲them↓ these designed rather to mark with scornful emphasis dainty opposition to the earth they trod on.

[¶] And Gaston glancing across the ↑his↓ mirror (how that age elaborated ↑doated on↓ its mirrors!) ↑Gaston↓ saw himself also closely enough conformed to the aesthetic demand of the day that he too had taken the impress and colour of the ↑his↓ age the hue ↑(↓like the insect on the tree↑)↓ of what mentally he fed on. With the jealousy the exclusiveness of the herbalist for instance who must complete his series at any cost or of the grammarian or any other specialist it was as if he gathering under lock and key in the hot-house of an over-excited fancy a collection of very rare flowers from ↑of↓ human life. Nay! [**End 40 r**] ↑41↓ this tiny red drop ↑at the bottom of the cup↓ so to figure it into which the whole world seemed expressed at the bottom of the cup who should say it was not worth all beside? Its ↑And its↓ hue infected not merely all objects of sense but the sense itself. ⁺With the ↑The↓ eye, the fancy, the ⁺very fibre and fabric of his brain ↑being↓ saturated ⁺with ↑by↓ it, "the earth with her bars↑"↓ was ↑"↓about" him in his very sleep and at this time, after fifteen years' using, the ↑that↓ little prayer↑P↓ for peace↑P↓, ↑p[?]↓ as useless ↑at last,↓ or insincere or perhaps profane ↑for a while↓ departed for a while from his lips. [**End 41 r**]

Chapter XI. [1]

[1 cm] Was Margaret after all indeed the mirror of the age ↑her time↓, or that other, her brother, on the throne? In an age so spontaneous and sincere, in its devotion to antiquity carrying ↑wearing↓ its well-dusted antique lore like some fresh flower of to-day, the features of "The Tyrant" as [3 cm] ↑Suetonius↓ or ↑and↓ [4 cm] ↑Lampridius↓ had conceived him must of course ↑have↓ come in evidence to be welcomed or otherwise along with other types. Would it have been with a shudder or with a sense of encouragement at the discovery of a spirit ↑so↓ akin to his own with a blush or only a satiric laugh perhaps the whirligig of things coming round again to the same point so funnily that in the ↑Latin↓ pages of [7.5 cm] ↑Lampridius Dion Herodianus↓ or in a ↑new↓ French version of the old Greek of [1.5 cm], King Henry [**End 1 r**] ↑2↓ might recognise his likeness under a portrait in which sinful ↑vicious↓ inclinations and a kind of reprobate beauty are blent in proportions of which we can scarcely ↑hardly↓ get at the secret? Many resemblances to himself in the shameful young Roman emperor who had polluted afresh by taking it the impiously divine name of Elagabalus he could not fail to notice. Fondling of a woman he afterwards banishes to a remote Syrian town but who as the sister of an empress had tasted something of the fla splendours of an ↑the↓ imperial court like the French queen-mother like Catherine ↑now↓ all cunning ↑now↓ or all audacity always without scruple for the child she has early dedicated to the service of an impure religion in the magnificent temple of the [1.5 cm] ↑Sun-god↓ at [3 cm], at fifteen he issues from [**End 2 r**] ↑3↓ that ↑the↓ mystic shelter of his boyhood himself like a fascinating idol in her hands. He delights the eyes of the debauched soldiery as they see him gracefully performing the functions of his office delights their very souls when victims ↑thus↓ of a clever *coup d'etat* they accept him as at

---

1. This untitled chapter consists of 44 leaves, all recto only; pin-holes in upper left corner. On two lines in the upper right of fol. 1 in faint pencil in an unknown hand are: *G de L*; underneath is a circled *11*. Paper: fols. [1]–6, 31 (9" x 7 7/16") cobalt edged; fols. 30, 32, 34 (9" x 7 3/16") cobalt-vermilion edged; fols. 7–29, 33, 35–44 (9" x 7") COLLARD.

Chapter XI.

her tone
Was Margaret after all indeed the mirror of the age, or
that other, her brother, on the throne? In an age so spontaneous
in airing
and sincere, in its devotion to antiquity carrying its well-dusted
antique lore like some fresh flower of to-day, the features of "The
Suetonius and Lampridius
Tyrant" as   or   had conceived him must of
have
course come in evidence to be welcomed or otherwise along with other
types. Would it have been with a shudder or with a sense of encourage-
so
ment at the discovery of a spirit akin to his own with a blush or only
a satiric laugh perhaps the whirligig of things coming round again
Latin   Lampridius Dion
to the same point so funnily that in the pages of
Herodianus   new
          or in a French version of the old Greek of   King Henry

Fig. 8

least the illegitimate son of their late indulgent murdered emperor as their emperor to be with passing flashes of the courage of the military gifts they can really understand.

[0.5 cm] He is still notwithstanding true to his ↑priestly↓ education himself a priest at heart ↑a↓ priest of the hot mad Assyrian sun-god whose worship is a prostitution whose name Elagabalus ↑▲ adding to it the whole gaudy load of official names and titles,↓ he has taken for his own by whose favour surely he is now on his ~~way~~ imperial progress till with the assent the acclamation of a senate ↑and↓ a populace doating in [**End 3 r**] ↑4↓ their turn on the lax florid sentimental features still [2 cm] ↑extant↓ on his coins, on the strange voluptuous Syrian nature, his ↑the↓ wild dances and barbaric ~~hy~~ hymns, his supposed [2.5 cm] ↑possession↓ of magic gifts his ↑the↓ largess doubtless of carefully hoarded wealth he stands on the Palatine hill, a ↑his ↑the↓ ↓ jewelled mitre glittering on his head, to lay there the foundations of a ↑the↓ temple for ↑of↓ his own tutelary deity, for whom he is jealous ↑and↓ who is to ↑shall↓ cast the native gods of Rome into obscurity. But, like the young French monarch returning from ~~Cracow~~ ↑Warsaw↓ to Paris, he had loitered, fatally for himself, on that so delightful journey. The roses had seemed to come down on him from above and from the earth at the touch of his feet of his chariot-wheels All he comes in contact with blossoms or is transformed [**End 4 r**] ↑5↓ into gold. Only, somewhere among them like Henry of France he has left behind ↑him↓ his understanding ↑and↓ appears ~~some times~~ ↑at times↓ a madman. His people soon tire of a frantic superstition such as this he appears really attached to of the lad's cruelties his ↑of a↓ sensual cruelty apparently for its own sake, of the grave folly which establishes a senate of women under the presidency of his mother an earlier Catherine de Medici to decide ↑for the decision of↓ questions of attire and etiquette his marriage to a Vestal virgin his polygamy his coarse favouritism the dreamy profanity with which he solemnises the nuptials of his impure god to Pallas of Troy, to Urania, to ↑▲all↓ the goddesses of Italy the secret human sacrifices the open murders. He could hardly have sinned so much in the time, objects the [**End 5 r**] ↑6↓ shrewder student of what historic writers liked so well doubtless to tell of him. For, alas! for the degeneracy of a later age, of a Northern latitude, in this matter of life as a fine art (one of the minor merely decorative ↑▲or amusing↓ arts) Elagabus [*sic*] had managed to pack his whole ↑entire↓ story into the incredibly brief term of three years and died at eighteen along with the ↑still↓ doating mother cut to pieces suddenly by the swords of his former admirers the victim of art of his poetry his own poetic soul ↑▲ you might almost say↓ of his religion! ~~you may~~ ↑might↓ ~~say~~

[¶] King Henry's masquerade his gloomy theatrical reproduction of the part of the insane young Roman emperor had a run after all of not less than [3 cm] years. He dies by the hand of ↑▲ an assassin, a fanatic ↑al↓↓ ↓monk at the age of [2 cm], in Gaston's [1.5 cm] th² year, with taste surfeited,↑ **[End 6 r]** ↑7↓ ↑one ‸might fancy, of such toys as he really cared for. Meantime ↑▲the storm↓ gathering↓ around, ~~adding~~ ↑▲joining↓ cloud to cloud does but enhance ↑▲at least↓ for ~~a~~ ↑the↓ sensitive spectator<s> ↑s↓ the theatrical effect of ↑▲~~of~~ the thing,↓ ~~a little flashily~~ ↑▲~~a tiny~~ ↑▲a tiny,↓ flowery,↓ ↑▲madly ↑~~madly~~↓↓ lighted island, ~~its~~ ↑▲whence the ↑~~of which the~~↓↓ music and satiric laughter ~~is~~ ↑are↓ heard across the black waves which must presently engulf it ↑~~like a gay flower tossed upon them~~↓. Gay as those revellers seem, ↑▲at heart ↑~~in their hearts~~↓↓ they have ↑▲at heart↓ the melancholy proper to ↑▲the insane.↓ ~~madmen.~~ Pluck one of them by the sleeve, and you'll hear also the ↑▲weeping↓ ~~tears~~ of the madman ↑▲for a moment↓ aware of his madness and what must °come of it. But ↑▲as ↑since↓↓ we are, ↑▲all, ~~of us~~ or the more sensitive of us,↓ educated ~~formed transformed~~ °~~come~~ ↑▲are brought↓ to be what we are ↑▲in ↑▲a↓ large measure↓ ~~largely~~ by what we *see*, perforce or by chance or choice, sympathetically or otherwise, ~~and~~ ↑and↓ to °follow for a few pages that ~~singular~~ singularly blent ~~scene~~ ↓actors↑ ~~will further~~ ↑▲scenery, may further↓ the interpretation **[End 7 r]** ↑8↓ of Gaston's character as he stands there for a while to watch ↑▲the actors;↓ so closely that for a time he seemed actually to be of their company ~~full of some~~ ↑▲fascinated by the↓ sense of ↑▲~~curious~~ a certain ↑~~of a strange~~↓↓ beauty there he could not wholly ↑~~hardly~~↓ have explained even to himself, of the ↑▲saving ↑~~saving effect~~ ↑gaiety↓↓↓ ~~redeeming~~ ‸~~grace it~~ ↑▲animation and gaiety, it↓ might be, with which a worthless thing was done, the ↑▲pathetic↓ grace ~~the~~ ↑~~unconscious~~↓ ~~pathos~~ with which the doomed↑2↓ the infatuated↑1↓ pass to their destruction ↑▲?as he was ‸always↓ on the alert also ‸always for the redeeming ↑▲traits↓ in vitiated human nature. The estimate of an age, ↑▲of↓ its characteristics, ~~by~~ ↑▲as seen in ↑~~through~~↓↓ its effects ↑s↓ upon a sensitive mind:—↑▲that,↓ after all, ~~that~~ is the utmost we can come by ↑even↓ in converse with even the strictest ↑▲of historians.↓ ~~historian.~~

[1 cm] *Votre etat baie de tous cotés, comme une vieille masure.* **[End 8 r]** ↑9↓ *Ou sont vos noblesses? Ou sont vos soldats? Votre trone est à qui veut le prendre.*

---

2. Superscript canceled; to be a word rather than in numerals.

Vous touchez la ruine.[3]—It was the warning of ↑(Louis of Nassau)↓ a shrewd
↑▲man of affairs ↑politician↓↓ not unfriendly to the throne of the Valois in
the year next after the ↑that ~~of~~↓ fatal year ↑one↓ of Saint Bartholomew. Ten
years had ↑▲since↓ passed by and now the faithful chronicler of his time
Pierre de l'Estoile ↑▲noting ~~its~~↓ ~~recording~~ events from day to ~~day~~ ↑day↓
seemingly with no prejudices records that ↑precisely how ↑~~notes how~~↓↓ Le
Roi ↑▲is comme &c.↓ faisait tous les jours festins nouveaux, comme si son
Estat eut été le plus paisible du monde. ~~He did it however~~ ↑~~He did thus~~
~~however~~ ↑~~But he was doing~~↓↓ a<A>s if blinded ↑however↓ by heaven or by
himself, ↑▲he was doing ↑did↓ thus↓ with an all but empty purse, on the
verge of public bankruptcy. ↑▲"On n'entendait parler que des choses
effroyables." *, ++↓[4] The historian **[End 9r]** ↑10↓ ~~notes~~ ↑▲observes ~~just now~~↓
about this time that la huitième guerre civile avait commencé,—the eighth:
but ~~as we~~ ↑▲and, in fact, we↓ know that for a whole generation war civil war
had been like ↑▲a part of the ↑~~almost~~↓↓ ~~an~~ established condition of things
↑~~life~~↓, its shocking incidents mixed up with the perennial picturesque of
nature, ↑▲and↓ the pretty artifices ↑s↓ of that ~~dainty~~ ↑?↓ gracefully self-
indulgent age. Smoldering like a fire, creeping like a serpent among the corn,
raising its metal coil here or there in declared battle, war, or ↑▲the spirit of
it,↓ ~~its spirit~~ its immediate causes ↑▲~~the spirit of it~~ ↓↑?↓ ~~was~~↓ were everywhere,
in men's families, in men's very selves, ~~was~~↑?↓ in Gaston for instance, ↑▲a
war↓ between that ↑a↓ ~~profound~~ ↑▲profoundly ~~rot~~ rooted↓ sensuousness
↑▲within ↑~~in him~~↓↓ which ~~kept~~ ↑▲held↓ him there to ↑▲gazing↓ ~~watch~~
sympathetically ↑▲year after year ~~on~~ on what↓ ~~a scene from~~ ↑the sins↓ **[End
10 r]** ↑11↓ ~~which~~ the religious mysticism which ~~was~~ ↑▲~~made~~ ↑formed↓↓ the

---

3. HOU slip with verticle strikeout:

> *~~Louis of Nassau to Ch. IX.~~ /* 1573. ↑to the throne[?] of [illeg]↓ "Vous touchez la ruine;
> / votre etat baie de tous cotés, / lezardé comme une vieille / masure. . . Ou sont vos /
> noblesses? Ou sont vos / soldats? Ce trone est à / qui veut le prendre."— / That was in
> —. And now &c.

Overleaf, Dip. 11 n.4, second transcription.

4. Two HOU slips. The first only tentatively correlates with asterisk:

> ↑*↓ La science de D. n'est plus en / la terre — exclaims the central / chronicler of these y[rs].

The second correlates more definitely with symbol:

> ++ It was as if they felt knew— / these people, Cath. her flying cortege &c.— / their hour,
> the end of their world / all but upon them and were now / bent desperately now, on
> gathering / up, what they really cared for most— / they & their like, the fragments that /
> remained, under the threatening ferment[?], / to the curious eye, revealing char[r].

Overleaf, Dip. 11 n.3.

other half of his nature, bid him fly from ~~to take ref~~ ↑▲turn ↑~~far away for~~ for immediate↓↓ refuge in the wounds of [4 cm]. The reader sees him it is to be hoped pleased ↓⁊★↑ ↑▲or at least interested↓ yet ~~sorrowing~~ ↑▲~~sorrowful~~ regretful, sorrowfully↓ ~~sorrowing~~ puzzled for himself and others, curious, indulgent, ↑▲~~and~~ ↑not ↑▲however↓ very self-indulgent and↓↓ certainly not with a ↑▲made-up↓ ~~mind~~[?] mind. And on the larger scene of battle too ↑also various↓ ~~long-sm~~ ↑▲long-smoldering↓ oppositions had formed at last very definitely into two ↑~~deadly~~↓ °~~parties~~ ↑▲~~hostile~~ camps↓ hostile ↑▲even↓ to ~~the~~ death. The ↑▲eighth civil⁊↓ war, ↑the war↓ of the three Henries des trois Henri had commenced says the historian. ~~Only~~ ↑▲But in truth↓ among the many parties ↑▲into which↓ ~~of~~ France was split ~~the party~~ ↑Henry the↓ Third and what friends he had scarcely counted for ↑▲one at all.↓ ~~one~~ ↑▲*↓[5] It was ~~over the crushed person~~ ↑▲beside ↑▲any question of↓ the insignificant claims↓ of Henri de Valois ↑▲and ↑▲all ~~all~~ ~~almost~~ but over his↓ ~~that~~ [End 11 r] ↑12↓ ↑▲crushed person, that↓ Henri de ↑▲Guise↓ ~~Navarre~~ and Henri de Navarre ↑▲were to↓ ~~would~~ fight ~~it~~ ↑★~~their battle~~ their battle↓ out their battle.

[¶] —"The Cause" under ↑led by↓ Henri de Navarre "The League" by ↑under↓ Henri de Guise ~~those leaders in truth identifying themselves with their respective factions~~ ↑▲loosely representative, respectively, of the↑?↓ Huguenots of the↑?↓ Catholics:—It would be↓ impossible for the King to identify himself with ↑take the leadership of↓ either though ↑perhaps↓ half ironically called upon ↑invited↓[6] to do so by one and the other. The Huguenots are less than a tenth part of the popula•tion ↑French people↓ but rich↑2↓ and shrewd↑1↓ ↑far↓ beyond that propor•tion ↑the Reformation↓ *armed* ↑P↓protestantism Their catholic neighbours are really afraid of these people ↑men↓ who ↑will↓ pray ↑▲openly↓ after their own manner ↑fashion↓ in defiance of law but ↑who↓ pray standing upright in their ~~armoury~~[?] ↑armour↓. The crime or accident [End 12 r] ↑13↓ ↑▲of the Eve ~~o~~ ↑~~the Eve~~↓↓

---

5. BERG slip correlates with asterisk:

> ~~The~~ * The League being set now / so decisively against "The Cause" / you might think that legitimate / royalty as a third party might / ally itself to either to each in turn / according to ~~Catherine's old~~ with the / futile subtlety of old Catherine's / hopeless policy. No! Those The / ~~T.O.~~ / other two will squeeze / number thee out "of the way" between / them

The canceled "T.O." (Turn Over) is at bottom, left. Overleaf, not applicable (canceled draft of "Lacedaemon," *Plato and Platonism*). Perhaps because overleaf was filled, the last three lines instead circle around the right, top and left margins.

6. Holograph has a transposition symbol enclosing "↑perhaps↓ half ironically" and "called upon ↑invited↓"

of Saint Bartholomew has left their general condition ↑▲unchanged↓ adding
only a profound sense of wrong. As Catherine knew ce sont des chats ↑▲the
Queen mother "They were cats," as the Queen ↑▲-mother, Catherine,↓
knew—"those Huguenots!—▲↓ que vos Huguenots qui se trouvent toujours
sur leurs pieds. From ↑All over↓ side ↑end↓ to side ↑end↓ of France they are
gathering ↑drawing↓ more ↑and more↓ compactly together hope to conquer
France for the Reformation failing that are ready to dismember it ↑her↓ f by
the conquest of a part.

¶. You may read in [3 cm] ↑a certain old Suabian chronicler whose grimy
↑blacksmith's↓ hands handled ↑a pen forcibly↓↓ how [8 cm] ↑how a famous
Italian smith↓ made ↑constructed↓ a singular iron flower ↑of iron↓ It was like
the ↑▲stealthy↓ formation of the League over against the ↑▲those↓ Huguenots
une armée l'hommes sortant de la terre ↑of terrible armed men↓. They
love↑d↓ those ↑genial↓ old Swiss and South German *workmen ↑masters↓ to
curl↓1↑ ↑↑smooth↓2↑↓ and curl↓3↑↓ their rude↓2↑ ↑harsh↓1↑↓ metal into
[**End 13 r**] ↑14↓ trellis ↑*work↓ of honeysuckle spiked↑y↓ lilies bossy roses:↓
and °°the like and ↑▲now↓ here was an ↑a cunning↓ Italian more than
emulating their worthy art and↑?↓ ↑▲being↓ determined for once to do** the
like while keeping ↑retaining↓ ↑under the ↑undulous?↓ leaves↓ all iron's
native poignancy ↑defiance ↑keenness↓↓ and [3.5 cm] ↑defiance↓. How he
contrived polished veiled his machinery you were tempted to feel ↑▲try
↑with↓ the finger↓ amid the ↑▲graceful ↑convolutions↓↓ foliage touched the
hidden spring perchance ↑▲and found↓ felt your wrist ↑▲held ↑imprisoned↓↓
in a moment in a circle of bristling points while the central stamen slid from
its sheath upon ↑through the↓ your hand, like a great poignard ↑from its
sheath,↓ or the fang of a steely serpent. [¶] Starting ↑Flashing suddenly↓ like
that upon the Huguenots upon King Henry the League "the ↑The↓ Holy
Union for [6 cm]",[7] had been ↑as cunningly contrived↓ shaped adapted to its
end, ↑▲(the aggrandisement ↓of the house of Lorr↑ ↑the supremacy↓↓ the
supremacy ↓▾in fact, the final accession to the throne of France,↑ of the house
of [**End 14 r**] ↑15↓ Lorraine ↑somewhat ↑somewhat↓ hypocritically↓ of
catholicism ↑▲only↓ ↑and↓ so far ↑only↓ as was compatible with that:) ↑▲had
been cunningly shaped to its end↓ in ↑secresy↓ secret<sy> for years, and was

---

7. BERG slip:

La Sainte Union—for / ↑▲giving↓ effect to, a certain &c.

Overleaf with verticle strikeout:

—vrais Hug^ts, qui savonent / mieux le metier de / se diffendre que d' / assaillir.

at last after a shock of incredible conflicting rumour ↑▲now •actually↓ in ~~actual~~ evidence first of all in Picardy, ↑patient humble and ↑of↓ devout ~~catholicism and↓~~ ↑▲its ↑▲broad↓ ~~green~~ ↓slow↑ waves ↑▲of corn & grass↓ and statey [*sic*] grey churches↓ in large sympathy with the sky Picardy, where ↑▲~~where~~ catholicism still seems a thing of ↓the soil↑↓ ~~where~~ the earth ↑▲itself↓ so to speak ↑▲still↓ ~~in~~ ↑▲is ever ↑still↓↓ naturally green with it. It ↑?↓ was not ~~certainly~~ for the Pope ↑▲certainly↓: he ~~discredits~~ ↑▲disavows↓ it with many another false or ambiguous volunteer ↑▲in his service;~~?~~ [?]↓ nor for the king, ~~ironically~~ ↑▲though satirically↓ challenged to assume its ↑the↓ headship ↑▲—of the Sainte Union↓ if a true ~~catholic~~ ↑▲son of the church↓ he be; nor for ~~France~~ the clergy ~~nor~~ whose fanaticism it ~~cajoles~~ ↑▲is ready to betrays;↓ nor for Christ, nor, as it pretends, for the poor whom h\<H\>e loved ↑ "the impoverished French people"; "the poor of France!"—▲↓ nor for France ↑▲which↓ it is ↑as↓ ready ~~like~~ ↑▲to sell to Spain ↓as↑↓ the Huguenot to dismember nor even for any section of it, nor in the proper sense **[End 15 r]** ↑16↓ for any political interest at all, but ↑▲simply↓ bent on taking advantage of all men's religious or other ~~devotion~~ ↑enthusiasm↓ by the way, ~~an~~ ↑▲the↓ unscrupulous [1.5 illeg canceln] ↑▲conspiracy↓ of a family, a family with a nest of murderous ↑▲enmities within↓ ~~jealousies in~~ its own bosom, ↑▲something of↓ the unnatural ↑▲tragic↓ horror of ~~a~~ ↑▲an ↑some↓ old↓ Greek play ↑~~tragedy.~~↓. With that unerring relentlessness for once which fiction supposes in ↑▲the↓ ~~a~~ "secret society" ↑▲, as such;↓ it spreads from Picardy to Normandy to Champagne[8] from North to South into the streets of Paris closes gradually ↑▲and ↑~~but~~↓ therefore↓ all the more firmly locks itself together round the court the throne the person of the king from whose light head it would pluck the crown has its Judith, or [1.5 cm], or [1 cm], in the person of the [3 cm] ↑Duchesse [1.5 cm] ?(omit)↓[9] actually ↓ostentatiously↑ resident in Paris who ↑. She↓ **[End 16 r]** ↑17↓ carries at her girdle, ↑▲strange ↑odd

---

8. HOU slip, first four lines canceled with a single vertical strikeout, the fifth line with a horizontal strikeout:

> 1576. The League—of / the Nivernais, Languedoc, / Champagne, Normandy, / etc. etc. / ~~at first ratified by the K.~~ /— ↑for "a certain wide-spread desire that / there sh^d be but <u>one</u> rel^n in / the ~~country;~~ land."

9. Pin-holes in two HOU slips match pin-holes between primary lines 10 and 11 in holograph:

> #1 La duchesse de Montpensier, / soeur de Duc de Guise, / la furie de la Ligue—
>
> #2 The duchesse de Montpensier / is the soeur furieuse of H. / de Guise.—the "Judith / of the party," the Ligue—

heirloom,↓↓ the scissors which made a ↑▲tonsured ↑~~gave the~~↓↓ monk ~~a monk~~ ↑▲of the of the *fainéant*,↓ and shall do the same ↑like↓ for Henry the Third.

[1.5 cm] The court ↑▲as↓ we saw ↑▲with↓ its sweet-lipped leader ↑~~head~~↓ its ↑▲Queen↓ Margot was gracefully pedantic classical ready to sell anything ↑▲to sell↓ itself for a ↑~~really~~↓ ~~old~~ song really old and its enemies catch a trick ↑▲so taking↓ for the moment ~~so taking~~ in learned but not ↑▲necessarily↓ ~~always~~ far-fetched parallels ↑▲minatory↓ significant ~~minatory~~ ↑menacing↓ between ↑▲the↓ present and ↑▲the↓ past in ↑▲ancient ↑at ancient↓↓ Rome, or ↑▲say! ~~even~~ ↓in↑↓ ancient Tyre ~~even~~, ↑even ↑say!↓ or in [2 cm]. ↑▲They ~~had~~↓ had their theories ↑▲also, in an age ↑also↓ ambitious of metaphysic views↓ ~~abstract yet poetic yet~~ ↑in either case also ↑either way↓↓ ~~practical in~~ ↑▲abstract theories yet practical in↓ this that they give to ↑▲vague or↓ passing enmities↑y↓ or discontent↑s↓ that ↑▲intellectual coherence, that↓ unity of idea, by which they ↑▲may↓ appeal to the imagination. ~~The~~ ↑▲A certain old↓ theory for instance du gouvernement des gens ↑sires↓ du fleur [**End 17 r**] ↑18↓ de Lys ↑▲that [1.5 cm] ~~favoured by~~ ↑recommends↓↓ ~~is in favour with~~ ↑▲recommends itself to↓ the house of Lorraine. ↑▲Legitimately, ↑~~It is necessary~~↓↓ France must of necessity ↑necessarily↓ be governed by a member of the royal family but not necessarily by its hereditary ↑▲~~hereditary head~~ head↓: and ~~it reinforces~~ that ↑▲convenient↓ ~~flattering~~ theory ↑▲is reinforced↓ by an appeal still more disquieting to recondite historic fact. Older ↑~~Older~~↓ than the house↑H↓ of Capet, ↑▲the House of Lorraine,↓ ~~it is they it is~~ Henri de Guise and his natural ↑▲issue↓ ~~heirs who~~ are the legitimate heirs ↑▲not merely ↑▲of↓ the personal rights↓ of Charlemagne but of the apostolic ↑▲benediction↓ ~~patronage~~ upon him the patronage of the Roman see to which, Observe! ↑~~See!~~↓↓ we are faithful. ~~The moment~~ ↑▲And ↑a<A>nd now↓ the opportunity ↑occasion↓↓ is come ~~to restore~~ ↑▲at last for a restoration of↓ the crown to its legitimate ~~inheritors.~~ ↑owners. ↑heirs↓↓ Nay! they represent, in a past older ↑dimmer↓ ~~even~~ than Charlemagne ↑~~even~~↓ even: [8 cm] ↑Pharamond Clodion le Chevelu↓ Retourne, Chilpéric! Clovis, reveille-toi! says the Anonymous Sonnet, chalked <on> ~~on~~ the walls, the house-doors, of Paris, on the doors of the Louvre. [**End 18 r**]

↑19↓ [0.5 cm] Le tuer ou le tondre, to ↑▲h~~um~~<s>b<l>ay↓ the usurping °tyrant ↑~~le faineant prebendier~~[?] ↑who ↑▲fails even of↓ ~~has not of even~~ the conventional ~~claim~~ ↓title to reign↑↓↓, ↑▲or make him a monk, a capucin,↓ with those shears of ↑▲the new Judith,↓ —— Montpensier lui faire suivre sa vocation ~~et en faire un capucin~~: there are genuine precedents for either course in our old French history. Pope Sixtus the Fifth who does not think much of what the Leaguers and their like ~~claim~~ ↑▲boast boast ↑pretend↓ ↓ to be doing for *him* asked at length ↑last↓ s'il serait bon d'attenter à la vie du Roi answers of course ↑▲honestly↓ with a ↑de↓ decided negative. Old ↑▲Jewish↓ °~~Testament~~ history, ↑however↓ old Roman history, ↑▲however,↓ seemed to ↑dare to↓ give a different answer to Huguenot and to certain new-fangled "republicans" ↑at ↓of↑ that early date↓ as to the ↑▲↑▲the right↓ righteous↓ ~~proper~~ treatment of Tyrants and the ↑Henry's↓ end ↑▲of Henry the Third↓ might ↓▼already↑ be ✢ foreseen.

[1.5 cm] ~~And~~ ↑▲For↓ to the classic ↑▲fantasy↑ies↓ ↓ ~~fancies~~ of a court paganised under [**End 19 r**] ↑20↓ the ~~masque~~ ↑▲°~~pretense~~ mask ↑a ~~semblance~~↓ of catholic zeal, to the antique poetic ~~of~~ ↑or↓ pedantic ↑antique↓ °pretensions of the ↑▲rival↓ Guises, the Huguenots ↑▲reading their b<B>ible in French, oppose↓ in their turn, like our ↑▲own↓ English puritans, ardent defenders of the Evangele of the New Testament ~~as~~ ↑▲though↓ they profess ↑▲to be,↓ ~~a~~ certain ↑kind of↓ grim reminiscences↑s↓ of the Old, and were ↑but seemed↓ terribly in earnest about ~~its~~ ↑▲them.↓ Tyrannicide, ~~surely is duty~~ ↑▲assassination that is to say assassination, is *duty*, surely,↓ nay! heroic piety in certain cases about which ↑protestant↓ "armed protestants<ism>" may ~~devel~~ [?] develope a ↑their↓ protestant casuistry. Men's thoughts were then hard at work all around on the nature ↑the↓ and basis of royal and all other authority, ↑▲on the very basis of society itself. ↑son d ait↓ ↓ ~~To those~~ ↑▲Those↓ fervid Hebrew ↑▲fantasies ↑reminiscences↓ ↓ ~~memories~~ of the past meet half-way a wholly different range of ↑range formed↓ opinion<s>↑s↓ ↑▲thoughts ↑theory full-fledged↓ which anticipate the future. ↑▲*↓[10] ↑▲of "~~social contract,~~"↓ f<F>ull-fledged ↑▲republican theories↓ ~~revolutionary~~ ↓of "social contract," Elective Monarchy, la "sacro-sainte autorité de ↓l'assemblée nationale,"—↑↑[**End 20 r**] ↑21↓ ~~theory↑ies↓ presenting~~) ↑▲present ↑which presents↓ ↓ themselves ↑itself↓ in folios or pamphlets or audacious ↑fervid↓ talk and ~~give~~ ↑▲lend↓ a sufficiently ↑▲decisively threatening ↑menacing↓ ↓ ~~minatory~~ import ↑significance↓ to the assembling of the States-general with immense popular enthusiasm at Blois, whither °already his people's prisoner

---

10. Two BNC slips, one asterisked, correlate with a careted asterisk on folio 20.

#1 * Those forcible, metallic / words, [   ], are / heard in a new connexion. / Les rois &c.
Overleaf inverted, material not applicable (canceled draft of "Lacedaemon," *Plato and Platonism*).

#2 —Les rois tiennent leur couronne / du peuple, & peuvent le "forfaire" / pour félonie envers le peuple, / comme un vassal "forfait" / son fief envers son seigneur. / ~~those terrible words in such a / new connexion".~~

go King Henry ~~proceeds~~ ↑goes↓ to preside ~~as if~~ °~~already~~↑?↓ playing the
desperate hand of Louis the Sixteenth ▲— to preside ↑~~goes to~~↓ over the
debates which may end in "improving away" himself. ↑~~Even~~↓ The ↑very↓
League itself "for mutual protection sans nulle acception de personnes" had
already mastered ↑~~learned to use~~↓ some↑?↓ of the revolutionary slang of
'ninety-three.

[¶] And our brother of Alençon Anjou and the rest, ~~M~~ [?]↑?↓ *Monsieur* our
sullen younger brother? ↑!↓ — ~~how~~ ↑▲how↓ far may we count on [**End 21 r**]
↑22↓ the loyalty the family sentiment of ↑▲one of↓ our own blood our own
naughty blood who should we fail of ↑▲legitimate↓ offspring is the natural
↑heir↓ heir to our throne but ↑our natural heir and ↓yet↓↑ who sees us too
still young ↑only a little older than himself ↑but a few years ~~more than his
own~~↓↓ and wedded to maiden health fresh from the fields [2 cm] ↑of↓. So
↑acutely↓ well in fact does he understand the advantages the temptations of
his position that he is terribly afraid lest we be beforehand with *his* life ↑♦very
existence↓ and adding ↑to add↓ to our perplexities is for ever escaping from
an affectionate home as from a prison to ~~his own town of Angers~~ ↑our avowed
enemies in↓ England or the Netherlands or ~~in~~ ↑within↓ the bounds of France
or at our ♦very doors. Our mother truly does not fail in the blind ↑rabid↓ love
of a cat for her offspring of herself but is failing in whatever dubious political
craft ↑▲may once have▲↓ been [**End 22 r**] ↑23↓ ~~she had~~ ↑~~once possessed~~↓
hers, her old tricks which no longer deceive, ↑▲is anxious↓ still however to
manage for us to occupy us with delightful aesthetic fatuities that the ↑▲all↓
serious business ↑things↓ of life may be left to her and ↑~~in lapsing into futile
superstition~~↓ has blundered badly more than once of late ↑~~is no more of
importance~~↓. Our version ↑▲then↓ of Elagabalus in the North ↑~~then~~↓ is ~~then~~
not an unmixed success. Of the personal gifts appropriate to that part we are
undoubtedly possessed but circumstance ↑▲the↓ accidents we cannot compel
~~goes~~ ↑▲go↓ for ↑▲more↓ than half in the production of ↑▲such↓ magnetic
effects ↑▲as↓ that wonderful progress from Syria to Rome ↑▲or↓ the
brillianc<y>~~ies~~↑y↓[?]↓ of our own youth. We are Christians after all of a sort
not pagans, ↑▲very craven ones indeed↓ hampered at every move ↑▲at ↓~~all
events~~↑ least↓ by the susceptibilities ~~at least~~ of others and in a Northern
latitude every thing moves slowly. ↑while [**End 23 r**] ↑24↓ rapidity↓ ~~Rapidity~~
of ↑in the↓ action in passion[?] was ↑▲as ↓may↑ be perceived↓ ~~an~~ ↑▲an↓
essential ~~to~~ ↑in↓ the success of the °piece which the ↑▲that blood-stained↓
flowery ~~bloody~~ young Roman↑?↓ emperor ↑~~had~~↓ played ↑▲out↓ to the ↑its↓

end in three years.[11] The mistake of prolonging a~thing~ ↑▲such a ◇ piece↓
beyond the ↑▲natural↓ life of its floral decorations is nothing less than
ruinous. ↑▲Des lors says the historian d̶e̶s̶ le roi était comme seul.↓ To whom
shall we turn?

[¶] Well! With o̶u̶r̶ Louise at o̶u̶r̶ ↑▲one's↓ side ↑princesse si belle & bien
formée↓ still of course to the hope of offspring of our own. A cry, ↑▲a w̶a̶l̶
↓wail,↑ poignant as↓ like that of ↑biblical↓ Leah, a̶n̶d̶ ↑or↓ Rachel, goes up
from every church in France, ↑w̶i̶t̶h̶↓ that Le Roi ↑a̶n̶d̶↓ pourroit ↑▲tost avoir
belle et abondante lignée,↓ and gives a kind of shrill startling sharply
expressed outward accent to Gaston's silent ↑o̶w̶n̶↓ preoccupation with the
fate of his own ↑t̶h̶e̶↓ lost child to↑?↓ his increasing desire, as the years
increase, that he might be ↑feel↓ less alone, a̶s̶ ↑▲while↓ those **[End 24 r]**
↑25↓ haunting ↑t̶h̶a̶t̶ ̶h̶a̶u̶n̶t̶i̶n̶g̶ ↑dreamy↓ c̶h̶o̶r̶u̶s̶ ̶o̶f̶ ̶c̶h̶i̶l̶d̶r̶e̶n̶'s̶↓ voices of the
children grown ↑now↓ to youth now come to him ↑◇somewhat↓ too
reproachfully ↑to ↓be borne↑ bear↓ out of ◇some dim background of the
world immediately about him with its ↑▲manifold ↑m̶a̶n̶y̶↓↓ outrages o̶f̶ on h̶i̶s̶
human kindness. King and Q̶u̶e̶e̶n̶ ↑Consort↓ proceed once more to the
sanctuary of his youth to↑?↓ the church of Chartres to the feet of Our Lady
under↑U↓ the earth↑E↓ ↑as↓ to the hem of her veritable garment there, take
away ↑▲with them ↑i̶n̶ ̶e̶x̶c̶h̶a̶n̶g̶e̶ ̶f̶o̶r̶ ↑▲her↓ i̶m̶a̶g̶e̶ ̶a̶l̶l̶ ̶i̶n̶ ̶s̶i̶l̶v̶e̶r̶ ̶g̶i̶l̶t̶↓↓ the copy
of it to be worn by themselves in n̶e̶w̶[?] faith.

[¶] But in vain! Ostentatiously, in late Lent after a too prolonged carnival
↑▲l̶<L>eurs m̶<M>ajestés↓ t̶h̶e̶ ̶k̶i̶n̶g̶ visit in turn every church in Paris to hear
m̶<M>ass↑M̶↓ i̶n̶ ̶t̶h̶a̶t̶ ↑▲with a special↓ "intention" that male offspring m̶i̶g̶h̶t̶
↑may↓ be given them ↑▲as they so greatly desire—the male line which may
succeed↓ "p̶o̶u̶r̶ ̶l̶a̶ ̶d̶o̶n̶n̶e̶r̶ ̶l̶a̶ ̶m̶a̶s̶l̶e̶ ̶l̶i̶g̶n̶é̶e̶ ̶q̶u̶e̶ **[End 25 r]** ↑26↓ t̶a̶n̶t̶ ̶i̶l̶s̶
d̶e̶s̶i̶r̶o̶i̶e̶n̶t̶—l̶a̶ ̶m̶a̶s̶l̶e̶ ̶l̶i̶g̶n̶é̶e̶ ̶q̶u̶i̶ ̶p̶e̶u̶s̶t̶ ̶s̶u̶c̶c̶é̶d̶e̶r̶ ̶à̶ ̶l̶a̶ ̶c̶o̶u̶r̶o̶n̶n̶e̶ ̶d̶e̶ ̶F̶r̶a̶n̶c̶e̶.̶↑ to
the crown of France.↓ H̶e̶ ↑▲Henry↓ dedicates a new ↑▲or fresh↓ piece of The
True Cross replacing an older relic stolen ↑▲lately ↑o̶f̶ ̶l̶a̶t̶e̶↓↓ from La ↑The
T̶h̶e̶↓ Sainte Chapelle ↑the chapel of o̶<O>ur "Palace," ↑d̶u̶ ̶P̶a̶l̶a̶i̶s̶↓↓ fallen
doubtless into miserable Italian keeping to the great consternation of Parisians
always ↑e̶v̶e̶r̶↓ devout at least ↑▲up↓ to that level. Hypocrite! thinks his
people as they see him pass ↑▲in[12] somewhat a̶b̶j̶e̶c̶t̶l̶y̶↓ abject devotion, along

---

11. As here in *years*, Pater sometimes overwrites his final cursive s with a roman text
type *s*; is this mere doodling? an aesthetic improvement? or a fair copy habit so a
careless compositor will not overlook it?

12. This has a very light strikeout, perhaps not quite intended?

the foul streets ~~m~~ ↑muttering ↑▲prayers↓ as best he can↓ amid a ↑▲is
pressing↓ crowd of sordid "penitents". ~~But~~ ↑▲~~Only~~ ↑Still,↓↓ there ↑▲really↓
are complexities of human temper ↑▲at times↓ a little beyond the *people*.
True! Meantime ↑▲observes the chronicler, not withstanding all its miseries,
they manage to be gay in Paris to laugh↓2↑ and dance↓1↑ ↑~~laughing low,~~
↑~~laughed low, gracefully, timidly or amorously,~~↓ ~~not always timidly,~~
~~amorously~~↓ ~~of course~~ he says; amorously of course↓ ~~non obstant toutes ces~~
~~miseris, on ne laisse de s'égayer à Paris d'y rire & danser,~~ to put the last
refinements ~~into that~~ ↑▲upon the↓ low octave of colour, ↑▲prevalent ↑then
prevailing↓↓ couleurs de sacristie[13] ↑▲almost↓ **[End 26 r]** ↑27↓ art's latest
triumph surely in bringing by ~~fine~~ ↑▲a subtle↓ economy ~~effects so rich &~~ out
of so little, ↑▲effects so rich.*[14] —Brown satin grey silk enriched with black
velvet set up with rich dark fancy stones & ~~fine~~ [?] ~~place~~ ↑▲heavy unbleached
lace!↓ What a flutter of expectation ↑▲~~among~~ ↑along↓ the ↑double↓ rows of
courtiers↓ when ↑▲—↓ enters the presence chamber in ~~his~~ ↑▲this ↑that↓↓
new toilet, contrasting ↑~~of~~ ↑~~contrast~~↓↓, the white aristocratic paté of his face,
while the silent unheeding ↑▲~~"the tyrant"~~↓ monarch ↑▲"the tyrant"↓[15]
heedlessly cons—a Latin grammar! ~~the [2.5 cm] of his boyhood,~~ ↑&
~~apprendu à decliner~~ qui sembloit, says [2 cm], presager la declinaison de son

---

13. HOU slip, three primary lines on right-hand side of canceled page correlate with
primary line 12, folio 26, and lines 1–3, folio 27:

> . . .f colour ↑coleurs [*sic*] de sacristié↓ / ...y so ↑rich↓ a beauty out of so little. / ...riched
> with black velvet set up

Overleaf, Dip. 13 n.23, second slip.

14. Asterisked BNC slip correlates with asterisk in text; first line only in pencil
(except for asterisk, dash, and overwritten capital in ink):

> ↑*↓—a<A> banquet in one colour, / or a ~~torch~~ combat by torch-light / between ↑of↓ 14
> blancs contre / 14 jaunes, in the courtyard / of the Louvre. ↑or↓ If ~~only the~~ ↑those↓ /
> comedians we have ordered / from Venise w^d ↑▲but↓ come to teach / us ~~the full~~ / ~~meaning~~
> ~~of life~~ what little remains / to be learned of the / full meaning of life!

Another BNC slip (unruled paper) may have served as a two-word reminder for the
material interpolated here at this asterisk: couleurs foncés

15. HOU slip (in the "Hobbes," bMS Eng 1150 [18]), appears to compare Henri with
Herod, represented in Wilde's *Salomé*, published in Paris in 1893, as a frightened
tyrant without male progeny. Pater would have been aware of it in rehearsal, June
1892:

> Henri de Valois—
>
> Vilain Herodes—

Pater placed a 0.25 cm vertical stroke under each character in Henri's name, as if
attempting to find a numerical and, perhaps, symbolic connection between the kings.

Etat. ↑▲ is actually learning anew to decline, keeps all the world waiting for
that. Had ↑And had↓ not ↑another↓ that ↑▲other↓ delightful young decadent
emperor, [2 cm] ↑▲Byzantine↓ kept his ↑▲the↓ grey-beard↑ed↓ ministers
waiting while he fed his↑?↓ favourite↑?the↓ pigeons, studied their ↑▲dietetic
whims, their ↓markings, their dainty tumbles over the jasper floor,↑ dainty
[1.5 cm] over the jasper floor, ↑▲knowing↓ the dietetic wings ↑whims↓ of his
feathered guests [End 27 r] ↑28↓ their [2 cm] ↑pirouettes↓ over [2 cm], their
marking↑s↓; an achievement of nature, a↑?↓ spectacle for infinite power,
infinite leisure, worth surely all protocols movement of armies and the like;
all the world beside. For foil contrast pour rehausser the effect of all this
↑that↓ across these ↑those↓ dim col couleurs de sacristie as if revealed by
↑▲sudden↓ lantern ↑▲under some sudden↓ flash amid ↑into↓ the shadows the
uniforms↑s↓ ↑▲crude, truculent, ↑the↓ barbaric of the ↑harsh barbaric
truculent crude↓ ↓ of our Swiss guards who serve us, a regiment of mercenary
↑foreign↓ guards already in attendance again as ↑▲like↓ a presage of 'ninety-
three against revolutionary outrage on our ↑the↓ sacred person. Nay! our
aesthetic doings shall have a purpose beyond ↑▲a ↑merely↓ any merely↓
momentary satisfaction. Pentecost that day we have always piously observed
as ↑▲so conspicuously our day ↑the fast over, so conspicuous↓ ↓ of good-
fortunes↑s↓ shall be [End 28 r] ↑29↓ further honoured by a new order of
knighthood, a band of ↑▲young men tall and↓ "proper" ↑▲dear to our hearts,
and↓ young men devoted to us, who may defend us—ces épees
dorées—should ↑▲in the↓ undisguised ♦hand-to-♦hand battle in one's very
chamber, ↑▲to which ↑▲we↓ seems to be ↑▲coming↓ ↓coming↑ at hand↓
among these rambling stairs and narrow passages of our hotel, ↑▲or prison,
de Saint Pol.[16] The copes insignia &↑ like a bastille apparel of the ↑Order,
&c.↓ Copes its copes, [1.5 cm] ↑▲with &c.↓ you might ↑see↓ them still
↑▲see↓ not long since in the m↑M↓usée des Souverains de France, [1 cm]
↑along↓ with the of S. Louis & [2 cm] and [2.5 cm].

¶. Fear wild sudden fear the principal ↑chief↓ performer stricken b [?] by
↑with↓ it:—that ↑is↓ of course ↑a distinctly quite ↑a proper ↑highly↓ ↓↓ is an
appropriate effect in such a ↑tragi-comedy↓ ↑↑a↓ tragi-comic↓ scene of tragi-

---

16. HOU slip:

   —retreats, more & more, to a / capital within Paris—Pol. / a Bastille—with [   ], & the /
   tombs of [   ]—or leaves P. / altogether, [illeg] himself at [   ], at / —[   ].

Overleaf, canceled with a single vertical strikeout:

   —le despotisme du "Grand Turc" / etait le gouvernement [illeg] / aux yeux de Calvin[?]:
   & de la / plupart des souverains / d'occident.

comedy, the ↑▲sort of↓ effect to which orchestra and ↑~~expectant~~↓ spectators ~~are~~ gradually attune themselves. As if ~~the~~ [End 29 r] ↑30↓ angry heaven itself in the form of a beggar forced its way in to threaten, through the serried guards amid all↑?↓ the morbid luxury↑ies↓ of the ↑this↓ bankrupt court comes the bold remonstrance of a single just man here or there representing the wretched condition of "the poor" that is to say of the people of France.[17] Pour dix qui vivent grassement ici il y en a dix mille qui ont disette. In still less considerate form the ~~same~~ ↑same↓ reproach penetrates to the royal cabinet as anonymous printed matter pasquinades in French or Latin, ↑that irrepressible↓ la liberté Francoise de parler now chatting through a press whose agency is already everywhere. ↑o<O>utside the↓ The *learned and curious were already collecting the↑?↓ handbills tracts sheets for posting all over Paris very popular in intention though often [End 30 r] ↑31↓ quaintly *learned in ↑the↓ form nay ↑or↓ even in the very language in which they were written:—*Le Reveille-nation* [*sic*] journal of the Huguenots who could cut as sharply with the pen ↑▲as with the sword↓ says L'Estoile ~~as with the sword silly~~ ↑▲who has soiled many of his pages with ~~the silly~~ ↑such↓ lying or truthful satire of the day—silly↓ acrostics which repack the letters of the royal name La Vie de la Royne-Mere qu'on appelle ~~vulgg~~ vulgairement La Vie de Sainte Catherine She herself read and laughed at could have ↑done it better↓ ~~a~~ something to it. Rithmes parlant des roines Frédégondes↑s↓ Brunehilde Jezebel.—Des bruits de Paris c'est à-dire menteries yet they pass from hand to hand ↑▲things erewhile people would not have dared to whisper, printed now↓. And about this time, exhumée pour ainsi dire du tombeau de son auteur Le Discours de la Servitude volontaire that terrible declaration de La Boetie against royalty is published for the first time.—A circle of hissing ↓tongues all about round the court and its gaieties with set steel fangs of set ↓steel below.↑↑ [End 31 r]

↑32↓ [1 cm] The reader perhaps remembers ↑perhaps↓ the ~~case~~ sad plight ↑case↓ of the traveller who must needs ~~sleep die or~~ sleep for a few hours an hour as he traverses a desolate forest The place abounds in ~~ancts~~ ↑ants↓ terrible red ants. He ↑But he↓ gathers ↑therefore↓ ~~carefully~~ the brush wood

---

17. BERG slip with vertical strikeout; two sets of double pinholes:

Lettre touchante sur la captivité / des enfants de France—↑▲i.e.↓ of Francis 1st— / Cabinet historique de M. Louis / Paris: Sept 1856. to find it there, ↓even↑ / *Humanity's* ↑▲very[?]↓ soft[?]—how touching↓ under royal trappings— / how *touching* to find it, there ↑so,↓ — —/ instances.

Overleaf, Dip. 11 n.20.

carefully together in a great circle on the open ↑a clear↓ space and lights a
great fire all round him to keep them ↑the insects↓ away. He ↑Then he↓ lies
down to sleep in the midst but wakes with the hissing of a circle of venomous
serpents all round his blazing ring only waiting ~~as~~[?] for ↑till↓ the fire to burn
↑burns↓ itself out.

[0.5 cm] Strange! It is this conscious or unconscious imitator of faineant ~~old
Roman or bzantine~~ [sic] ~~emperor people who becomes for the first time in
France out of mem~~= [End 32 r]

↑33~~2~~↓ [0.5 cm] Strange! It is this conscious↓2↑ or unconscious↓+↓
↑▲imitator↓ ~~imitation~~ of fainéant old Roman or Byzantine emperor-deities
who becomes "majesty"↑? pl:↓ for the first time ↑▲in France↓ ~~to be adored~~
↑shrouds himself↓ half in personal vanity half in fear ↑▲shrouds himself to be
adored↓ changes the old easy ~~familiarity~~ ↑accessibility↓ of a↑?↓ French
monarchs into a ↑▲curious↓ system of etiquette ~~into~~ ↑through↓ which it is
difficult for ordinary ~~men~~ ↑▲people↓ to penetrate. ~~They put~~ t<T>he people of
Paris the poor ↑have↓ their suspicions ↑▲and↓ ↑and↓ with more or less
shrewdness↓ ~~put their own~~ put their own ↑▲disloyal ↑~~harsh unfriendly~~↓↓
construction on the studied mystery of their master's ↑▲life↓ ~~days~~ disseminate
↑▲their↓ rumours. He makes a shadow where he goes artfully. ~~Curious~~ ↑Great
is ↑~~New~~↓↓ gossip; ~~unfounded in~~ ↑&↓ ↑the↓ mystery↑ious↓, even if it be not
the ~~mysterious~~ mystery of↓ ~~in~~ hidden crime ~~may do much to sap a weak
throne.~~ ↑,gives ↑secures↓ its full further advantage to gossip.▲↓ Meantime the
rival Henry Henri de Guise ↑already ↑now↓↓ veritable Roi [End 33 r] ↑34↓
de Paris,[18] comes hither on his selfish business leader of that solemn league
and covenant yet with florid abundant face and hair and like the sun ↑and↓
as ~~he~~ if he made the flowers they threw about him to grow there playing his
part with a delightful ease and a kind of jovial natural royalty over common
people. Parisians ↑▲always↓ sympathetic ↑straightway↓ ever at home
↑straightway↓ with a cheerful countenance like ↑▲him none the less↓ for that
manly or brutal ↑▲scar across↓ the check. That it repeats ↑oddly↓ the accident
of his father's youth ↑who had been↓ Le Balafrè before him ↑▲doubles the
prestige of the thing↓ It is like a sign impressed—by heaven ↑—↓ or hell.
They credit him as people ↑▲will do sometimes credit creatures only a very

---

18. BNC slip; Pater's allusion to Henri de Guise as "veritable Roi de Paris" anticipates
a moment the novel does not reach—the king's words at Guise's assassination (1588):
~~a note on k. of P. je suis~~ / roi de ~~F,~~ he says ~~with relief,~~ / J'ai ~~tué le roi de P.~~ / (Je suis Roi de
F. cries H.III. / ~~over the corpse of H. de G.~~ / j'ai over his corpse ~~now~~ / j'ai tué le Roi de P.)

little stronger than themselves↓ with almost diabolical personal force.—Is it powder of gold, or of steel, that he takes in his meat?—Bon Prince! Meantime the flowers rain ↑are rained↓ gently upon him. He is almost ↑well nigh↓ stifled with the close pressure of affection. The simple rubbed their chapelets ↑▲contre lui↓ pour les sanctifier.

↓[1 cm] I have dwelt thus at length on what was visible in Paris jus [*sic*] then, on the ↑▲mere historic scene there,↓↑ [**End 34 r**] ↑35 33↓ ↑▲forgetful it might it is seem of the company of Gaston ↑~~have apparently deserted my friend Gaston~~ ↑~~deserting it might seem our↓↓↓ ~~there because~~ ? but only because I ↓▾do↑ suppose him thoughtfully looking on ↑▲with us, all along ↓the while,↑↓ ~~as ▲ one even~~ ↑▲as essentially a creature of the eye, even ↑~~creatures of the eye as we are↓↓~~ more likely than others to be shaped by the things he sees. With ↑▲a look↓2↑,↓ a manner↓1↑, ↑▲a manner of speaking also ↑~~an utterance↓↓~~ which infallibly win royal kindness he penetrates that ↑awful↓ singular reserve, ↑does but feel↓ ~~only feels~~ at rest, ↑▲a certain ↑~~a certain [1 cm] and repose↓↓~~ repose ↑of temper↓, amid the dainty ↑▲selections and↓ adjustments ~~that~~ ↑▲which↓ prevail ↑▲amid these↓ ~~there, the~~ last pale lustres of the court of the Valois, ~~the~~ awed ↑▲sometimes ↑awed↓↓ by its deeper ↑~~deep ?↓~~ shadows, ↑▲its ↓the↑ darkness↓↓ wistful curious, ↑yet ↑but↓↓ himself certainly uncontaminate as if invisibly shielded ~~but~~ ↑▲and ↑~~above all↓↓~~ always with ~~a~~ ↑~~an immense↓~~ great pity, ↑~~an immense↓~~ a great indulgence. ~~J'ay une merveilleuse lacheté vers~~ ↑M. had said↓ ~~la misericorde et mansuetude. There are half-domestic animals which~~ J'ay une merveilleuse lachetè ↑▲says↓ ~~M. de M. had said,~~ ↑▲says his tutor, M. de Montaigne (might have said for him)↓ vers la misericorde et mansuetude. [**End 35 r**]

↑36 34↓ [0.5 cm] There are ↑▲certain↓ half domestic animals which come ↑creep ↑draw↓↓ very near to men's ↓lives their firesides only to be the objects of their hatred; the last of↑ the Valois ~~with their~~ made ↑▲set Gaston↓ ~~made G~~ think ↑thinking↓ of them. ↑▲The tyrant—[0.5 cm],↓Le tyran aux abois it was like ↑such↓ an animal ↑one of these animals↓ and one ↑he↓ pitied it as one does ↑must↓ pity the very rat wh. sheds tears ↑▲at last, they ~~they~~ say who know it best.↓ And then according to his habit he looked back and saw ↑▲in thought, his contemporary↓ ~~and saw~~ the hopeful ↑~~eloquent &~~ ↑"spirituel"↓ brave↓ child ↑lad↓, ↑▲eloquent and brave, "spirituel",↓ in this man, ~~man~~ whose name was to be ↑was to be↓ infamous: ~~That~~ ↑and that↓ he could do so without effort was ~~surely~~ a proof ↑▲surely↓ of ~~moral discernment~~ ↑surviving moral capacity↓ as if ↑▲some discerning↓ ~~an~~ artist from ↑this↓, the ~~harsh~~ ↑▲malignant↓ caricatures ↑▲which↓ remain as the veritable likeness of ↑~~as the~~

~~likeness veritable~~ ↑in truth▲↓ ↓↓ ~~wh. have rem^d of~~ so vain ↓personable↑ a monarch ~~actually~~ ↑▲were to ↑~~were to by original~~ ↑e^d↓ ↓↓ put together for himself ↑▲such a↓ ~~that~~ portrait ↑▲of Henry the 3rd, as ~~it~~ happens ↑▲to↓ have been preserved↓ ~~wh. really remains of him~~ ↑<H>↓, in a certain old ↑▲picture↓ gallery, ~~in~~ not far from Venice: ~~winning~~ ↑▲winsome ↑~~delightful~~↓↓ lad ↑▲there!↓ ↑puer ingenui vultus ingenuique pudoris.↓ You had but to look ↑▲closely, kindly, ↑▲even now,↓ and↓ ~~at it &~~ there were redeeming touches ~~in~~ ↑▲amid↓ the ruin to which ~~it~~ ↑▲he↓ was ↓▼actually↑ come ↑~~wh. had overtaken it~~▼↓. [End 36 r]

↑37 ~~35~~↓ [0.5 cm] To a ↑the↓ disciple of Montaigne ↑(? only below)↓, his doctrine of the "ondoyancy" of life ↑man ↑the world↓↓, it would ↑ ⁕came↓ ⁕come ↑▲naturally↓ of course ~~naturally~~ to note the unexpected taking place in us after all reassuringly to the discredit of many an obvious forecast about human ↑men's↓ souls those surprises ↑which↓ in man as in nature Montaigne had taught him to prize ↑in man as in nature↓ the mixture of motives, the afterthoughts, ↑the returning↓ returns upon one's self, ↑the↓ repentances, saving inconsistencies [2 cm] ↑returns ↑returning↓↓ upon one's self, [9 cm] ↑of the conscience of right↓ dews of paradise [4.5 cm] ↑call them in fact ↑say [1 cm] after all↓↓ penetrating even to hell, which leave seemingly damned souls at the worst ↑but↓ dubious ones ↑after all.↓. The devil, the [4 cm], says [3 cm] is [2.5 cm], and as such ↑monstrous character↓ an ennuyant ~~and~~ ↑because an a really↓ inexpressive character [End 37 r] ↑38 ~~36~~↓ and for one's own sake ↑merely↓ as a ↑mere↓ spectator seeking ↑claiming ↑who claims↓↓ at least to be interested one is ↑we are↓ anxious to find those ↑▲saving↓ inconsistencies in evil which reassure one ↑us as↓ with the ↑a↓ hopeful sense that there are ↑indication of latent↓ redeeming ↑regenerating↓ forces ↑↑still↓ at work ↑very deep perhaps it may be↓ somewhere ↓here or there below the surface↑↓ which to regenerate after all in ways beyond our limited calculations ↑power of calculation.↓. It brought him ↑therefore ↑then↓↓ a flattering sense of his philosophic capacity that he could note without prejudice the kindly [2.5 cm] ↑self-denying assiduities↓ of royalty about a childish death-bed at ↑~~about~~↓ this time. It was pitiful enough indeed to think of what became ↑of some↓ other children, ↑stricken↓ made ↑left ↑forced↓↓ to suffer in early life ↑their earliest days↓, a large ↑so large↓ part of the penalty of the political crimes ↑offences↓ or mere unsuccess of their fathers, ↑the degraded pauper↓ the young children of [2 cm] Montgomery↓?2↑, of ↑or↓ Coligni↓?1↑. ↑Little↓ Madame [End 38 r] ↑3<9>7↓ Elizabeth, the little daughter of [2.5 cm], she at least for one felt the [2.5 cm] of ↑what sweetness there was↓ in Henry's kindness. The courtly array about her bed of suffering

↑all the order &c.↓ had for once its justification in pleasing distracting a sick child. [58 cm]¹⁹ The white queen her mother of the tiny creature ↑princess↓ soon after departed finally alone to her ↑old German↓ home in Germany. It ↑That↓ was like another child's funeral amid natural regrets ↑with universal regret↓ ~~in such~~ ↑amid↓ ↑for for↓↓ a ↑~~whole~~↓ train of ↑such↓ white deaths ²⁰so to call them of women and children amid red ones. Ah! how people wept in that Paris which [**End 39 r**] ↑40 ~~38 28~~↓ meant to have sold itself for the minor graces of life. And here was this ↑the↓ other queen ↑praying↓ full of ↑various ↑contending↓↓ terror↑s, that the king her husband may ↓repudiate her and ↓the like↑↑↓. Ah! Pity of Heaven, of [2 cm], of [3 cm] Chartres, m<M>e donnez mâslè lignée!

[1 cm] There was one artist ↑in France↓ to whom though he knew how to be a courtier a sort of primitive greatness ↑had↓ still remained something of the ↑~~the~~ proper and↓ the natural dignity of art and life [3 cm] ↑had still remained↓ amid in the midst of a this ↑that↓ ♦world of self-complaisant ↑cent ↑satisfied↓↓ decadence in both. Let him give us on parting ↑before ↑ere we part↓↓ from it a glimpse of **g** [9.5 cm] ↑those the ever-surviving ↓persisting persistent↑ moral forces in things↓, such as he afforded on occasion ↑from time to time↓ with the ↑an↓ effect of ↑an↓ ironic contrast to the age of Henry the 3rd and↑?↓ without which no picture of that age would ↑could ↑can↓↓

---

19. Three and a half primary lines are vacant here, a left-margin dot reserving the three empty rows. Two HOU slips pertain, the second with a quotation from L'Estoile (1:239) on both sides:

> #1 The little princess— / —with perhaps mistaken scruples / they tried to make her / understand she was / dying, but didn't succeed. / ~~tho~~ tho' she admitted in / truth her inability to say her / long prayer—said her short on[e]— & then.

Overleaf, material from *Plato and Platonism* not applicable.

> #2 Wed. Ap. 2. 1578. / —mourust en l'hotel d'Anjou, à P.— / m^me Marie-Isabel de France, ~~fill~~ / fille unique & legitime du feu roy Ch. 9, / agée de 5 à 6 ans, qui fut pleurée / & regrettée à cause de son gentil esprit / & la bonté & douceur—on the 9th— / son corps, de l'hotel auquel elle estoit / decedée, fut porté en l'eglise de P. [**End r**] avec magnificence & appareil / fort hon[n]orable: et le lendemain / fut fait solennel service en la- / dite église—puis, le lendemain / son corps, mis dans un coche, / fust mené à S Denis, & la [sic] enterré, *sans autre solennité.*

Tipsy accents in this scribble have been realigned silently; italics in the final phrase are Pater's.

20. BERG slip:

—a series of white funerals— / ↑one↓ they seemed to be always passing / along—

Overleaf, Dip. 11 n.17.

be complete. Jean Cousin a kind ↑sort↓ of Mi- **[End 40 r]** ↑41 39↓ chelangelo
in France has like him an imagination ↑like his↓ occupied not by the low-
pulsed middle-•life ↓period↑ ↑so to call it↓ of his own day, but with [1.5 cm]
↑the ↑its↓↓ energetic origins and issues [4 cm] ↑of of human life ↑destiny↓↓,
the Creation of Adam & Eve [5.5 cm] ↑Eva Pandora↓ the Last Judgment: the
naked realities ↑so to speak↓ of human life ↑destiny↓ displayed to ↑in↓ a
•world which had come to find dress the most important thing in life and
draped sculpture more significant than the nude. Here ↑indeed ↑in fact
↓truth↑ ↑under a certain Italian influence↓↓↓ all the little things of •life
↑existence↓ had ↑were↓ become wonderfully ↑marvellously↓ b̶u̶t̶ refined but
with a refinement ↑however↓ which had been ↑was in truth↓ but the
garment's hem, the outermost [2.5 cm] ↑aura↓ of the great art of Italy itself
& it was to ↑this↓ that ↑the soul of↓ Cousin ↑had↓ reverted or rather
↑perhaps↓ to the old Gothic **[End 41]** ↑42 4̶0̶ 2̶9̶↓ vigour of ↑his↓ native
France itself. For he had in fact a preference, predilection not explained by
the mere conditions of demand and supply i̶n̶ ↑at↓ that moment, for work in
that conspicuously medieval and French medium ↑art ↑manufacture↓↓ of
stained ↑painting on↓ glass, though he refined ↑immeasurably↓ at every point
in that ↑the↓ process beyond ↑upon↓ any ↑all↓ earlier achievements in it.
While he knows more than all the old secrets of its [2 cm] and ruby and gold
he can also draw with the truth and largeness of a master and ↑though↓ still
with an eye to the particular destination of his work ↑design ↑drawing↓↓. He
can also think incisively ↑profoundly↓ and has again like Michelangelo, l̶i̶k̶e̶
t̶h̶e̶ ↑▴and in sympathy with the finer[?] spirit of that↓ age generally his
dreams of old Roman greatness ↑like that from the realisation of which his
hand has just now rested.↓. Today then King and court with **[End 42 r]** ↑43
4̶1̶↓ whom ↑though they are so little fitted to understand him ↑unfitted as
though they are for more than a superficial understanding of him ↓his aims↑↓
the aged artist master has ↑nevertheless has↓ his credit, proceed to ↑in gay
summer weather fitted for the excursion↓ to the old chapel of the castle in the
forest of Vincennes to gaze on his ↑t̶o̶ the↓ latest ↑skill↓ achievement ↑of his
art.↓ there in the colours they love. The new window gleams out under [7.5
cm] ↑amid the shadows of the old gothic chapel↓ a marvel of many coloured
gold [1 cm] ↑clear as crystal, as ↑like↓ in the Apocalyptic ↑vision itself
↑breaking into the darkness of the old↓↓↓ and they listen readily while the
old man ↑aged painter ↑deferentially, with ironic deference is it?↓↓ explains
the subject, ↑"I can always leave off talking when I hear a master play!"↓
about concerning which̶,̶ ̶w̶h̶a̶t̶ ̶t̶h̶e̶ ̶s̶p̶l̶e̶n̶d̶i̶d̶ ̶c̶r̶o̶w̶n̶e̶d̶ ̶f̶i̶g̶u̶r̶e̶ ̶i̶s̶ ̶d̶o̶i̶n̶g̶ ↑though
↑▴like veritable connoisseurs↓ they profess an almost exclusive care for form

and↓ handling in art, they are straightway curious.—What the glorious crowned figure ↑splendid figure with crown & sceptre↓ is doing: ⸺A ↑Augustus̶ The Sibyl &c.↓ A fine subject in fact, perhaps the greatest an artist ↑art↓ can deal with, though certainly still [1 cm] ↑not yet worn-out↓ by artists: the Sibyl, summing up all [6 cm]: Augustus [6 cm]: the Mother and the Child, all the pathos of [3.5 cm] ↑human flesh↓ which **[End 43 r]** ↑44 4̶2̶↓ the eternal Son has now wrapt about himself. Aye! a gospel subject the speaker asserts to t̶h̶e̶i̶r̶ ↑the↓ ignorant questions with which, with rapturous comments on the [2 cm], they begin presently to divert ↑discountenance ↑distract Cousin's↓↓ the further speech of the old man who seems indeed ↑*↓[21] [12 cm] For their master is ↑being↓ visibly put out [3 cm] Augustus, was supposed to have merited [5.5 cm] ↑is one horn of the royal dilemma↓ and the light [2.5 cm] glares actually on the other, the opposite, form of it with the effect of an ↑unkindly↓ ironic contrast like a slap ↑blow↓ in the face, with ↑as from↓ the lightning-flash the thunder-clap which suddenly darkens the place on the June evening at which modern royalty, t̶h̶o̶u̶g̶h̶ in a ↑wicked↓ rage, ↑pulls out a rattling rosary and↓ begins to patter to itself, with the air ↑mien↓ of a veritable coward: a model of such as the artist perhaps took note for professional use. **[End 44 r]**

---

21. This asterisk does not appear to match any available slips.

||

Chapter XII.
A Wedding.

(for motto, an epitaph)

To crown the lad's good fortune a husband of the Queen's
                    but
lineage has been found for Jasmin's pretty penniless sister
and glad for once to find himself _in loco parentis_ he was
astir almost with the first light of the flighty march mor-
                            away
ning to prepare himself for the duty of giving the bride away.
With thoughts almost insanely preoccupied by the marriage
          making   as
relation and taking pleasure for the serious business of life
                         always
Henry and those who led or were led by him ~~also~~ made
the most of weddings and contrived to spend a long time upon
                  this   now
them. The significance of the day actually come at last,

Fig. 9

Chapter XII. ¹

A Wedding.

(for motto, an epitaph)

[1 cm] To crown the lad's good fortune a husband of the Queen's lineage has been found for Jasmin's pretty ↑but↓ penniless sister and glad for once to find himself *in loco parentis* he was astir almost with the first light of the flighty March morning to prepare himself for the duty of giving ↑away↓ the bride away. With thoughts almost insanely preoccupied by the marriage relation and taking ↑♦making↓ pleasure for ↑as↓ the serious business of life Henry and those who led or were led by him ~~almo~~ ↑always↓ ♦made the most of weddings and contrived to spend a long time upon them. The significance of the ↑this↓ day ↑now↓ actually come at last, [**End 1 r**] ↑2↓² bringing this ↑that↓ final sacred distinction to him and his, flushes Jasmin's face suddenly as he wakes from the ↑his↓ perfectly dreamless sleep of youth, collects his thoughts ↑in a moment↓, springs from the bed and looks forth anxious ~~of~~ ↑▲first↓ of all about ↑concerning↓ the weather. While he slept the world visible from his window had arrayed itself in virgin white. The grey spires of *Saint Germain*

---

1. This is the most fragmentary of the holograph chapters, consisting of nine leaves, three with writing on recto only and six on both sides (only one overleaf pertains to *Gaston*). No pencil markings, no brand watermarks, no pin holes. BNC paper: fols. [1]–5 (8 7/8" x 7 3/16") cobalt edged; fol. 7 (8 15/16" x 7 3/16") has traces of blue. HOU paper: fol. 6 (8 7/8" x 7 1/4") shows a trace of vermilion edge; fols. 7–8 (8 3/4" x 7") have traces of cobalt edges. The BNC folios are all at the same "latest" stage of revision; the HOU folios derive from two earlier stages of revision (which I shall term "initial" and "intermediate") and are paginated 6[r]/3[v] (both drafts "intermediate"), 7r and 8r (both "initial"). Overleaf, fol. 1, not applicable (a canceled, unpublished translation from Plato's *Republic*, Book 5).

2. Overleaf, not applicable (canceled, unpublished translation from Plato's *Republic*, Book 5).

des Pres had lodged the crisp snow-flakes on their way along the³ North-east wind blowing steadily since nightfall and stood there more monastically ↑chaste ↑cold stern↓ ↓ than ever panelled and picked out afresh on that side he could have fancied with snow-white Italian marble.

[¶] The silver, and white linen, the purple and white flowers, of [**End 2 r**] ↑3↓ the wedding table, are scarcely less virginal, set there ready for the royal and other guests in the long low chamber of the *Palais des Thermes* the *Hotel* which the Abbot of Cluny had inserted so daintily into ↑amid↓ the ~~old~~ smoke-black hollows of the haunted old Roman bath of the Emperor Julian. ~~The reader who may~~ ↑Should the reader ↑~~If the~~↓ ↓ visit the place he is recommended to acquaint himself with its fantastic change of fortunes. ↑The Abbot left↓ [18 cm] who, by royal favour, will keep house there for awhile rent-free. Bride and bridegroom, the aged cardinal [2.5 cm] who officiates [6 cm] waited long ↑for Jasmin,↓ in the [2.5 cm] gothic chapel ↑for Jasmin↓ ~~one by one~~ made shift at last to perform the due ceremonies ˙without him ↑in his absence↓ with an uncomfortable [**End 3 r**] ↑4↓ sense of incompleteness in the rite though royalty as such paternal over all persons ↑its subjects↓ good-naturedly takes upon itself the duty of giving ↑away↓ the bride away a genuine country lass ↑and here↓ like a caged bird here too much fluttered↑?↓ to be ↑quite↓ aware what is done ↑doing↓ with her. ~~But as~~ ↑As↓ they pass from the restraint of the sacred place a babble of wonderment ensues. But for his duty towards the bride pale now as the snowdrops half-fainting at the breakfast table with fatigue and fear the king himself would have gone to seek him in his lodgings. Refusing meantime ↑meanwhile↓ to take his place he sends instead two pages two wedding posies of silken flowers detached from his very person. Let loose from "the presence" into the reviving air they trip

---

3. An "intermediate" draft HOU 3 v, including text from BNC 2 r and 3 r, is transcribed here. This HOU draft is cancelled with two parallel vertical lines:

↑3↓ the North-east ~~window~~ ↑wind↓ blowing steadily since night-fall and stood ↑rose↓ there more monastically chaste ↑stern ↑cold↓ ↓ than ever panelled and pi˙cked out afresh on that side ↑aspect↓ you might fancy ↑he could have fancied↓ with white ↑snowy ↑snow-white ↑fle˙ckless↓ ↓ ↓ Italian marble.

[0.5 cm] The silver and white linen, the purple & white flowers of the wedding table, are scarcely less virginal set there ready for the long ↑the↓ royal and other guests in the long ↑low↓ chamber of the palais des thermes, the hotel which the abbot of Cluny had inserted so daintily into the old black ↑smoke black↓ hollows of Julian's baths ↑—hollows of the ↑haunted↓ old Roman bath B[Beta symbol] of emp↑J.↓. The reader who visits the place today is recommended to peep into ↑acquaint himself with↓ with odd [2.5 cm] ↑changes↓ of its fortunes. [3.5 cm] ↑The abbot left↓ [**End 3 v HOU**]

↑fly↓ over the crisp snow the buckram of their [**End 4 r**] ↑5↓ court dress yielding this way and that to natural boyish movement ↑within it↓ with a gracefully comic air of ruffled feathers, making those who watch them from the window laugh even now as they fly ↑run↓ more speedily than would have been credited though↑?↓ on tip-toe and glancing suspiciously at their satin shoes.

[0.5 cm] Jasmin as we know had not forgotten his duty was not likely to forget of that kind had been full of it over-night and up betimes could hardly occupy the interval by the most leisurely of toilets pausing now and then to examine the pictures from his old nursery on the wall himself at six years old as [1.5 cm] Handling the his ↑hand↓ mirror very carefully not to break it ominously at such a moment he compares the infant face with his own [**End 5 r**] ↑6↓[4] and just then a red dash ↑across it↓ of foggy sun-light across it makes him think with a little laugh of that evening ↑twilight↓ not so long ago when he "had met himself."

[¶] The ↑Even the↓ toilet even of an exquisite ↑a Parisian↓ at the court ↑even in the reign↓ of Henry the Third does not last for ever. ↑▲The beautiful male dress of the day is complete ↑▲the head stiff in the collar starched heavily with rice.↓↓ There was no more to do. ↑be done.↓ Just ↑and just↓ then the lad becomes ↑feels↓ aware ↑of↓ an empty stomach. His ↑and his↓ valet serves ↑and summons his valet to ~~him~~ serve ↑who serves↓ him with↓ him with a little ↑▲delicate↓ bread and wine ↑▲himself↓ tasting the latter first pour faire l'essai as is done always in these murderous treacherous days with persons of importance. And at last ↑At last then↓ he descends the stair ↑stairs himself↓ looks forth from the door ↑along into the street↓ for the chair which is to[5]

---

4. Here begins HOU 6 r, uncancelled and textually continuous with BNC 5 r and 7 r; this page from an "intermediate" draft may have been incorporated unrevised into the "latest" BNC draft because it followed BNC 5 r without overlapping and because the BNC revision had very nearly come to the end of its rough copy. Overleaf, the canceled HOU 3 v.

5. In part, the "early" draft HOU 7 r corresponds, at an earlier stage of revision, to the penultimate and final primary lines of the "intermediate" draft HOU 6 r and to all of the BNC "latest" draft 7 r that ends after seven primary lines. This material is cancelled from the top by a single vertical line terminated by a horizontal stroke through primary line 9. The lowest three uncancelled primary lines of HOU 7 r continue the chapter with new material in an "early" state and are given in the diplomatic transcription of the chapter. The upper nine cancelled lines are transcribed here as a variant for HOU 6 r and BNC 7 r:

carry him to the wedding not due however for half an hour yet ↑to come↓ as he notes by the much-prized watch at his [**End 6 r HOU**] ↑7↓ [6]which stopped half-crushed in his hand a few minutes later marking at least for others the term ↑critical point↓ of his little destiny. The snow ~~driven~~ ↑on the ground↓ is still freezing Impatient at the delay he will try his foot upon the dry clean ↑untouched↓ crisp particles in the delicious↑?↓ frosty virgin air. Like an opal a mass of opals his white satin holds its own is not shamed ↑even face to face with the virgin snow↓ flashes rather against the level morning sunlight against ↑upon↓ the hard white road-way. [**End 7 r**]

[1 cm] With a kind of ↑ultimate↓ indifference on both sides how pleasant ↑how [1 cm] of time↓ could Margaret Queen Margot be with ↑to↓ those into whose ~~in~~ intimacy ↑with whom ↑whom the fortune of the hour brought↓ ↓ contact the fortune of the day ↑hour↓ brought her. ↑▲* ++↓ But, ↑Only,↓ if [**End 7 r HOU**] ↑8↓[7] if ↑her heart moved at eye or hand↓ that curse ↑malediction↓ of her love, entered into the [2 cm], it was equally fatal to slave or rebel, to La Mole as he lifted [2 cm], to Jasmin now, in his 19th year, ↑▲⊙↓ (as he sets forth, in profound peace with himself and all things, self-centered, ↑free from any embarrassing lien on any person besides↓ ~~or~~ devoted if to any one to ↑the king↓ his king, who has used him so kindly.) [**End 8 r HOU**].

↑7↓ to carry him to the [2 cm] not due ↑however↓ for half an hour yet to come, as he notes by the ↑priceless↓ watch at his [1.5 cm]; which stopped [3 cm] a few minutes after marking ↑for others at least,↓ the precise point of his ↑little↓ destiny. The snow, driven up [2 cm] and [2.5 cm] is still freezing ↑hard dry↓ [1.5 cm]; impatient; he will try his foot upon it in the ↑through this↓ delicious ↑frosty↓ virgin air. ↑—delightful to try one's foot upon the dry clean untouched crisp particles.↓ Like an opal a mass ↑crust↓ of opals in his white satin; ↑holds its own↓ is not shamed flashes rather on against ↑even face to face with↓ the hard white ↑foot,↓ road-way.

6. Overleaf, not applicable (canceled draft on the Parthenon sculptures).

7. An uncancelled "early" HOU draft 8 r continues the narrative in fragmentary form.

Book iii. [1]

Ch: 13. — Mi–carême. [2]

"He shall drink &c.."

[¶] The foreground of life ↑things↓, its sins, its beauty and sorrows, the
°effective ↑▲spectacular↓ contrasts of the actors↓2↑, the incidents↓1↑ from
which one could not take one's eyes ~~from~~:—the reader it is hoped ~~sees~~
↑▲↑▲can↓ still see↓ Gaston ~~still in~~ ↑▲also through↓ the admiration and
↑▲distress↓ ~~pity~~, the perplexity also, aroused ↑exited[3]↓ in him as he gazes ~~on
the external scene before him in truth~~ ↑thereon, so absorbed ↑▲preoccupied↓
in truth ↑~~which the external scene arouses in him in truth~~ so ~~preoccupied~~↓↓
with its immediate °effects—that he finds but scant ↑scanty↓ opportunity
↑occasion↓ for ↑consideration of ↑pondering ↑noting↓↓↓ what ↑▲at some
other↓ ~~may be~~ time might ~~be~~ ↑▲have ↑▲been↓ discernible ↑▲by him↓
~~recognisable↓~~ in the ↑a↓ more or less remote background ↑▲where ↑with
the↓↓ ~~in which~~ ↑▲it must be said↓ the religion of his youth ↑~~now little more~~↓
is now little more than a vanishing point. ~~Recollecting~~ [3 cm] ↑~~from time to
time~~↓ ↓Its ↓old↑ formalities recurring↑ to his mind, now and again, [**End 1
r**] ↑2↓ he admitted to himself, with mixed feelings, that in all probability he
~~had~~ ↑▲must have↓ long since ↑~~have~~↓ ceased to be ~~in~~ ↑▲in what he had been
taught to ↑▲identify as↓ ~~call↓~~ "a state of grace", ~~and the~~ ↑while that↓ little
prayer↑P↓ for peace↑P↓ ↑▲from the Roman Vespers↓ had ↑was↓ ~~faded~~
↑departed ↑deserted↓↓ from his lips.

---

1. This is the only reference to a division of *Gaston* into books (and does not appear
in Clara's copy); this heading, in the upper left corner, is separated from the chapter
number and title by a diagonal line. In the upper right of fol. 1 on two lines in faint
pencil in an unknown hand are: *G de L*; underneath *(4)*.

2. The chapter consists of 21 leaves on recto only; pin-holes in upper left corner.
Paper is 9" x 7" COLLARD throughout.

3. Pater often, but not invariably, created a cursive *x* by the *sc* maneuver which
required the pen to be lifted from the paper only once; in consequence, the *c* is lost
here by haplography.

Ch: 13. — Mi-carême.

"He shall drink it."

~~things~~

The foreground of life, its suns, its beauty and sorrows,

spectacular

the ~~effective~~ contrasts of the actors, the incidents from which

one could not take one's eyes ~~from~~ :— the reader it is hoped
com
still see   ~~also~~ through   distress
Gaston ~~still in~~ the admiration and ~~fuss~~, the per-
                excited
plexity also, aroused in him as he gazes
                         therein, so absorbed
preoccupied
in truth
Scene before him   in truth   with its immediate effects
                                noticing
                ~~seems~~ occasion pondering at some other
that he finds but scant opportunity for what   such
                     consideration of
have   her
discernible
time might in the more or less remote background, which
                                                      where
it must be said
the religion of his youth is now little more than a vanishing

point. Recollecting   to his mind, now and again,
Its sometimes recurring
Ad

Fig. 10

[¶] T͟h͟e͟ ↑The ↑Those↓↓ misgivings ⬦which o͟f͟-͟c͟o͟u͟r͟s͟e͟ in a nature like ↑such as↓ his survive o͟f͟-͟c͟o͟u͟r͟ ↑of course↓ positive ↑s[?]↓ belief were apt ↑▲also↓ to accumulate ↑▲upon him↓ in the darkness following ↑▲naturally upon ↑whereon↓ ⬦which↓ mere physical daylight in its turn would dissipate ↑p͟u͟t͟ t͟h͟e͟m͟-͟t͟o͟-͟f͟l͟i͟g͟h͟t͟↓ them⁴ altogether for a while, ↑t͟i͟m͟e͟,͟↓ and ↑it was on a m͟o͟r͟n͟i͟n͟g͟-͟i͟n͟-͟s͟p͟r͟i͟n͟g͟↓ one spring morning⁵ ↑that↓ Gaston l͟e͟f͟t͟ ↑having left↓ his bed earlier than was ↑▲now↓ his ↑habit↓ w͟o͟n͟t͟-͟n͟o͟w͟-͟a͟n͟d͟ ↑h͟e͟↓ ↑Gaston ↑he↓↓ paced ↑and came pacing↓ the streets of Paris, to air a haunted fancy so to speak, ↑▲himself ↑▲after i͟n͟ a few moments' exercise ↓walking↑↓ all↓ alive to its ↑the↓ early freshness and m͟i͟g͟h͟t͟ ↑very↓ glad might one say *grateful* ⁇ as he p͟a͟s͟s͟e͟s͟ ↑crosses↓ from side to side to walk continu- [**End 2 r**] ↑3↓ ously in the sun, Yes! *grateful*, to be thus alive.

[¶] [1 cm] There were no signs however of early ↑or late↓ rising in the spot to which at length his ↑after a while this↓ cheerful circuit ↑below ↑along the↓↓ brought him though in one sense the most populous↑?—↓ in Paris, the ↑ancient ↑old↓↓ Cemetery of the Innocents with its [5 cm] ↑▲*milliers* ↑*sur milliers*↓ *de cadavres*↓, over which the yellow light was creeping ↑winning its way↓ kindly, its ↑the↓ lowliest graves ↑then↓ casting long shadows.—They haunted him ↑▲every where↓ still those Innocents, the ↑▲young↓ children slain or lost: who in irony surely had lent their name to this ↑▲most aged↓ place, with its shocking ↑defiant unashamed↓⁷ presentment, of mortality by day, i͟t͟s͟-͟e͟q͟u͟a͟l͟l͟y͟-͟d͟e͟f͟i͟a͟n͟t͟-͟d͟e͟f͟i͟a͟n͟t͟-͟a͟n͟d͟-͟u͟n͟a͟s͟h͟a͟m͟e͟d͟ ↑of the ⬦sins ↑misdeeds↓ of the living by night the thieves, [2 cm] courtesans↓, who haunted this place of ill

---

4. Two BNC slips when joined create three primary lines with two vertical strikeouts correlating, in Pater's redrafting, with primary lines 8–12, folio 2, and line 1, folio 3:

   them, & one spring morning G. left his bed earlier than was his habit ↑wont↓ now and paced the streets of P., enjoying ↑alive to the of i͟t͟s͟-͟e͟a͟r͟l͟y͟-͟f͟r͟e͟s͟h͟n͟e͟s͟s͟↓-͟a͟n͟d͟-͟g͟l͟a͟d͟,͟-͟s͟h͟a͟l͟l͟-͟↑͟m͟i͟g͟h͟t͟↓͟ o͟n͟e͟-͟s͟a͟y͟-͟g͟r͟a͟t͟e͟f͟u͟l͟?͟-͟t͟o͟-͟b͟e͟-͟a͟l͟i͟v͟e͟. It

Left slip overleaf, inverted, Dip. 13 n.8, #1; right slip overleaf, inverted, Dip. 10 n.5.

5. BNC slip in pencil:

   The — ↑scene at 7ᵃᵐ↓ — the —the — / were links of a chain, / afterwards well-knit together / by, fasten— land-marks / in the life of his— who / was now

6. Underlining canceled and then restored

7. BNC slip, left bottom of sheet, three primary lines with vertical strikeout—a very preliminary drafting correlating with primary lines 7–10, folio 3:

   [illeg] fancy still, [   ] / might ↑wᵈ↓ have told him, that / tality, its ↑defiant↓ unashamed [   ],

Overleaf inverted, Dip. 13 n.11.

fame, ~~as if~~ [5 cm illeg canceln] ~~or~~ sheltered by its horrors, or relishing the
more ↑better↓ [**End 3 r**] ↑4↓ the dregs of sin amid the coarser ↑coarse or
crude↓ associations of death, the grave-↑▲diggers' careless doings ↑ways↓,↓
the corrupt↓2↑colours, the odour↑s↓↓1↑.[8] La belle[9] Huissiére, at all events
↑least↓, had found a ↑her↓ a permanent lodging at last, Gaston read her
~~epitaphy~~ ↑epitaph↓ on the unclean ↑neglected ↑weathered↓↓ stone.— [21
cm] Let the reader think of what he may have seen of ancient historic
churchyards ↑grave-↓ of [2 cm] Prague, [5 cm] ↑the Elyiam[?][10]↓ Arles, S.
Pancras, if he likes, as ~~he~~ ↑Gaston↓ walks there amid [2 cm], with the hot
↑increasing↓ sunshine [3 cm] ↑increasing heat of the↓ upon the ↑his↓
pathway, upon himself, but thrust it ↑▲all that↓ back ↑▲deep↓ into the
grotesque gloom of the middle age. Ah! they needed long changing there
↑▲those ↑▲old↓ soiled bodies↓ in the dark through those ↑these↓ endless
unnoted mornings, ↑and↓ the [2 cm] [**End 4 r**] ↑5↓ ones long in making;
though the earth for its ↑her↓ part seemed anxious to give them up ↑its
ragged dead ↓already↑↓ or ↓▾to be↑ at best ↑least to be ↓but↑↓ a careless
keeper of ~~them.~~ ↑the bones↓ having made its own ↑proper ↑natural↓↓ use of
the body's juices. As if mistaking the jubilant sunshine of this first summer
day for the resurrection morning, ~~one~~ ↑the↓ occupant of an ↑a nameless↓ old
↑stone coffin had tumbled forth. ~~upon the~~ Hanging [++] [2 cm] in↓ ↑▲an
↑▲immense↓ aubepine of immemorial↓ ~~Above it, hanging~~ age flowered above
it; ♦had↑?↓ flowered, as if with a second youth of late years, miraculously it
♦had seemed to the crowds who had come to visit it, ↑being arrosée, rajeunié,
fortifiée,↓ drinking fresh light with ↑strength to blossom anew ↓from↑↓ the
blood of the ↑heretic it had come by↓, after the ↑▲carnage↓ of S. B. ↑▲The

---

8. Two BNC slips pertain:

　　#1: ↑odours↓—Yes! in certain ~~lurking~~ / airs—↑wh.↓ that ↑had↓ lurked too / long ~~in~~ ↑on↓
　　↓▾about↑ certain places here.

Overleaf, inverted, left half of transcription, Dip. 13 n.4.

　　#2:—sur cette terre pestiféré du / grande cimitiére [sic] des Innocents, / la nuit erraient des
　　filles, / logeaient près [sic] des charniers, / & faisaient l'amour sur / les tombes. / ~~like la
　　belle [　　] when epitaph~~ / read.

Overleaf not applicable (canceled draft of "The Genius of Plato," *Plato and Platonism*).

9. Under the *b* there are several pencil dots and faint lines.

10. "Alyscamps" is lightly written in pencil in Clara's transcription in an unidentified
hand.

patient ↑industrious↓ L'Estoile has chronicled↑?↓ the fact, ↑and surmise: *↓[11] As if for a parable it sent up clear ↑immaculate ↑sparkling↓↓ water ↑too↓ too from its very midst ↑the ↑very↓ midst of its ↓the↑↑this↓ defilements↓. And was it ↑also↓ by way of parable that J. G. in his turn had carved ↑constructed ↑designed↓↓ this graceful fountain to utilise it ↑for the thirsty, or ↑or to quench↓ the [1.5 cm] ↑benitiers↓, little [1.5 cm] ↑holy water fonts↓ at the graves?↓—↑with↓ just those particular imageries ↓youth & vigour↑ the nymphs you may still **[End 5 r]** ↑6↓ see amid their native reeds and water-lilies at. In the low-rippling ↑lines of↓ of the low white marble reliefs they seem to be flowing ↑in motion↓ with the water amid wh. they are yet so firmly, ↑carnally↓ voluptuously, embodied. Perhaps he ↑J. G.↓ only meant to lift ↑cheer↓ the ↑▲gloom of the↓ place with his those ↑these↓ graceful [2.5 cm] ↑creatures ↑things↓↓ though he had but emphasised it by ↑passing↓ contrast. [31 cm] ↑(what Adam of Brescia, says)↓[12]

¶. Reading the epitaphs ↑as he goes carelessly ↑steps casually↓↓, even then for the most part formal or trivial ↑but↓ with here and there a veritable cry of distress ↑of the dead for the dead↓, he too comes presently as if by accident to "the brook in the way": ↑(quote It^n words)↓ finds it, feels those drops of water welcome in this Inf^{no}, or Purg^r say of Paris in the sounds, the lights, wh. enfold **[End 6 r]** ↑7↓ him take possession of him as he enters a ʼcertain↓ church ↑door↓ at the roadside one of those ↑rich↓ late ↑later↓ Gothic ↑flowery↓ churches in which ↑which then enriched↓ Paris was then rich, ↑and↓ in which ↑the last↓ dainty arts, fittest it might seem for [2.5 cm], spent themselves on divine service. The well-informed visitor to Paris will have visited ↑remember ↓perhaps↑↓ S. [2 cm], S^t [2 cm], S̸ Medard, and [6 cm] ↑take a hint from them↓ their dainty morsls [*sic*] of stained glass ↑the jubé↓ of the genius of that ↑the↓ refined place, [3.5 cm] ↑in which Gaston↓, for a moment becomes once more the creature of the influences of his consecrated boyhood. ~~(Traits of St Agnes; ending with the glass [4 cm])~~ ~~It was like religion tempering~~ ↑subduing↓ ~~itself~~ with [7.5 cm] ↑~~indulgence~~, ↑the↓ ~~infinite patience of superiority↓~~, and a kind of heavenly courtesy, to a petulant↓ 2↑ or

---

11. Asterisked BNC slip correlates with asterisk in text:

   * ~~all a<A>bout the graves~~ / Left to itself, the church- / yard earth abounded with / veritable country- ↑field-↓ flowers, of / the more acrid coarser ♦kinds, / with a ♦ sort of savage abundance / of pollen, flung around about / them.

   Inverted overleaf, transcription in Dip. 13 n.7.

12. Pater marks his 31 cm space with three reference dots on the left-hand side of each blank line.

~~wayward~~↓↑↑~~soul.~~ ↑⊖Its builder very happy, or very acute, for while it
adapted as if in[13] under ~~subduing~~ ↑▲mere↓ awkward necessity to the lines of
the adjoining streets its irregularities were full of expression. ↑▲*. ~~no soul, of~~
~~man, or thing, or place,↑ nothing is ever~~[?] ~~like another, it seemed to say.~~ be
as formal as you will.} ~~Had the~~ ↓▾An acute↑ artist ↓▾might have↑ conceived
~~a~~ [End 7 r] ↑8↓ ↑just such a↓ curious system of proportions ↑as he was here
committed to↓ for their own sake, or welcomed the site wh. determined them
for him ↑~~inf~~ enforced them on him↓.[14] To ↑A ↑The↓↓ the more careful gaze
there was ↑seemed to find ↑seemed to be↓↓ some special fineness ↑of
[indeterminate cms]↓, self-recollection; in the lines of ↑jubé↓ and ↑arch,↓ as
if the wayward free fancies of the artist ↑builder↓ workman had been
effectually called upon to recollect themselves here,—where they were ↑he
was↓ & what they were doing. And it ↑this↓ had this effect it gave what ↑for
the mere formal style of ↓the place↑↓ would otherwise have been but a ↑one↓
sanctuary among many others like ↑not unlike↓ it, a cachet of its own, ↑as
regards ↑and towards↓↓ for the soul of Gaston, ↑here↓ today the *peculiarity*
which won him. ↑⚹↓ Crowded for foot-hold, on the odd & angular
↑irregular↓ space among the roads ↑streets↓ around, it went, as if spirally
↑one-sidedly↓, as best it might, but with ↑markedly↓ united [End 8 r] ↑9↓
determination high ↑all the higher↓ into the air above them. The light fell
pleasantly ↑softly placidly↓ on the remote high stone spaces[15]: and the glass,
it was ↑windows they were↓ like the ↑natural↓ soft colouring ↑brightness↓
of a fine day. It was like religion, ↑▲like the cath: ch:, subduing↓ tempering
itself with indulgence, the infinite patience of an infinite superiority to a
petulant ↑the wayward↓ or wayward ↑petulant↓ soul.

↑¶.↑?↓↓ The people of Paris says one ↑Mérimée↓ were at that date ↑a cette
epoque day↓ horriblement fanatique: its ↑the↓ pulpits ↑of P.↓ rang just then
with fanatical leaguist sermons: but the [4 cm] ↑movement, however,↓ wh.
makes fanatics of the coarse, lighting on finer souls produces there the ↑its↓
finish of rel[n]: ↑its fairer flowers↓ and the ↑that↓ age had its ↑revival↓ or

---

13. Word circled

14. Here is faint pencil 2 cm line, nearly vertical, probably by Clara to mark a pause
in her transcribing; it became the *de facto* end of her transcription. Minor
abridgements or emendations of wording in her transcription have not been
footnoted; major augmentations adopted as emendations of the Edition Text are
recorded in Emendations & Variants.

15. BNC slip (unruled paper) may pertain:

    —how the spaces of the ch. / seemed stained with / X[n] doct.—with the / blood of [   ]—

ritualism also, as we should call it: ↑▲its curés ↑who were miracles of personal devotion,↓; its churches where worship was ~~of~~ more select, [2.5 cm] ↓careful than elsewhere,↑ careful↓ its revival of [1.5 cm]; with a more [2 cm] ↑correct↓ consideration than had prevailed till now ↑of late↓ for ↑of↓ sacred **[End 9 r]** ↑10↓ seasons, points of ritual, above all with a great development of such church music as lifted[16] the age of [1.5 cm]. Our ↑The↓ ritualistic Gaston, then is reminded,[17] by [3.5 cm] ↑the rose-purple↓, the "flowers of pensive ↑▲hope", a certain ↑reserved↓ gaiety breaking thro' the Lenten severity↓ that it is the season of mi-carême ↑? name of the Sunday.↓ with its [2 cm] ↑thoughts↓ of manna ↑in the wilderness &c. (repeti[]n) ↑of the miraculous feeding of the fainting multitudes Repeti[]n↓↓ and yields himself as he would ↑could↓ do ↑did↓ more readily than most men to its suggestions. ↑▲*[18] ↑Respiremus—let us take breath a little, recover our strength, pleads the collect.↓ As the ↑The↓ door closes on the world behind him ↑but↓ it is like coming ↑it↓ into the open air ↑▲like leaving a mad-house,↓: not he alone had thought of the people who gave it its colour, its ~~its~~ character ↑▲e.g.↓ as a sort of aveuglis [*sic*], or madmn[*sic*], ↑▲desperate,↓ of himself ↑as↓ infected ↑▲it might be ↑perhaps ↑~~perh~~↓↓↓ with their disease ↑misfortune.↓. Well! the ritual of today was full not of miraculous feeding only, but of the cure of the sick, ↑and↓ the insane ↑of demons cast out. ↑the casting out of demons.↓↓. The epistle, still on that **[End 10 r]** ↑11↓ peculiar line of thought, explained, how A^m had 2 sons—unum de ancillâ, et unum de libero, and how he that was born after the flesh persecuted &c.. And as he thus lingered, seated himself, at least to gaze as an outsider might for a few minutes ↑half an hour↓ on what the accident of his ↑morning's↓ walk had thus presented so ↑as if↓ generously for his refreshment, ↑his↓ thought finds ↑go ↑▲goes↓ back↓ its their ↑find takes its↓ way back stade upon stade, the [1.5 cm], the [1.5 cm], the [1.5 cm], to descend ↑and rest↓ at last in ↑upon↓ the midst ↑the midst↓

---

16. Appears to be a conversion of *uplifted* into *lifted*

17. BNC slip; two primary half-lines, bottom left of sheet, with vertical strikeout, correlates loosely to primary lines 2–4, folio 10:

.Thn, (ritualism) a more[?] / , the [ ], remind G. that

Overleaf, Dip. 13 n.20.

18. BNC slip presumably correlates with the careted asterisk in the text:

—this lover of pensive places, / of the sanctuary especially / where humanity lays aside its / vulgarity at least for a / while—at at least looks / its best for a while—& if one / addresses you it is proper to / say reply hush!—lingers reaches / irresistibly to look, to listen.

Overleaf, Dip. 13 n.19.

of his consecrated boyhood, when thoughts like ↑such as↓ these had been so familiar ↑come so familiarly ↓readily↑ ↑naturally↓↓ to him. Decorated or soiled, as he is with, well! the vanities, that can hardly belong here ↑to a place ↓beautiful and venerable place↑ like this↓, he seems to see that[19] other world with the place ↑▲he has but deserted for a time still↓ kept for him there; ~~the place he has~~ **[End 11 r]** ↑12↓ as one selected ↑determined ↑pre-destined↓↓ from eternity ↑in spite of all↓ to sit thereon ↑there ↑~~with~~ ↑among↓ with the elect↓↓ in spite of all. ↑*↓ The gospel in ↑for↓ the proper Mass ↑Mass proper for the day↓ tells[20] of the lad and the ~~homely~~ provision he had made ↑▲or induced others to make↓ for his carnal refreshment: lifted now to so wondrous use, ↑a service↓ so wonderful ↑unparalleled↓. A ↑▲carefully↓ sensuous boy surely with his loaves and fishes, yet with a hunger for divine ↑eternal↓ things which had brought him so far. What had become of him? and of this incident ↑strange↓ privilege ↑accorded him↓ of his early youth ↑life↓. Had it remained as the hour of the redemption of his body and soul, or only as an almost incredible incident of a dreamy youth ↑boyhood↓ upon wh. as he looked upon which, and [4 cm] ↑the sentiment it recalled↓ he could but say ↑exclaim↓ my wickednesses are gone over my head!

[¶] The proper Mass of ↑But the Mass proper to↓ the day over ↑completed↓ a less ↑sweetly ↑graciously↓↓ [2 cm] office begins. **[End 12 r]** ↑13↓ In a little while ↑the church ↑place↓ transforms itself ↓under the hands of↑↓ diligent sacristans↑?↓ transform the place ↑church↓ into a house of official ↑heartless ↑strident ↑emphatic↓ earthly↓↓ mourning, crudely black and white, and from the depths of the great ↑brass brazen↓ *serpents* groan the first notes of the funeral psalm, the funeral service of a not undecorated ↑undistinguished↓ soldier ↑military ↓officer↑↓, as the great white satin scutcheons, spread amply over ↑on↓ the funeral ↑velvet↓ pall indicate. A ↑little↓ band of men ↑↑the↓

---

19. BNC slip; three primary half-lines, bottom left corner of sheet, with vertical strikeout, correlating with primary lines 11–12, folio 11, and primary lines 1–6, folio 12:

> that other / him, to have an empty place / time: My place among ↑▲selected from everlasting ↑as one determined to↓↓ keep / life. ↑The Gospel told of the loaves↓ A sensuous boy surely, yet with a ↓what became of him—had the lov

Overleaf, Dip. 13 n.18.

20. BNC slip; correlates with primary lines 1–2, folio 12:

> *Oculi omnium—Aperis: is for / =the gradual, followed by / the gospel [   ]. ↓wh.↑ It tells ↓▼appropriately↑ of

Overleaf, Dip. 13 n.17.

soldiers of his regiment↓ are on duty ↑in ↑their↓ uniforms↓ form a ↑the↓
guard of honour around [1 cm] ↑the ↑heavy↓ coffin↓ and at its head ↑foot↓
↑also↓ braced stiffly ↑also↓ in new ↑fresh↓ boyish uniform ↑stands ↓the son
of the deceased↑↓ a lad of seventeen ↑sixteen years↓ perhaps of modest yet
manful features ↑bearing↓ and having such as those haunting creatures
↑nestlings↓ to Gaston's fancy were now almost ↑well-nigh↓ grown to be
almost as we know to his bodily ear.[21] Yes! to his bodily ear today ↑verily it
might seem; with palpable accent↓.—Why, by what ill-timed ↑disfavour↓, had
he [**End 13 r**] ↑14↓ wandered ↑roved↓ hither ↑this morning↓ to be touched
↑moved↓ shocked uselessly by another's grief ↑distress↓; for as[22] they lift the
coffin ↑at last awkwardly↓, the Mass for the Dead being now over with a
↑harsh ↑cruel ↑hollow↓ grating over the↓↓ across stones, the ↑that↓ lad (the
↑that↓ young Frenchman!) ↑who had stood ↓kept↑ his place ↑footing↓ there
so manfully throughout↓ loses suddenly ↑lost all on a sudden↓ his forced
composure ↑doubled himself↓ and his face in ↑on↓ his sleeve literally lifted
up his voice and wept ↑aloud↓.[23]

[¶] After all the cry ↑The cry↓ of another's grief ↑after all↓ after ↑of↓ a very
youthful grief which ere the day was ↑to be↓ over w^d perhaps ↑might in all
likelihood↓ ~~to~~ be succeeded ↑replaced superseded↓ by other thoughts
comfortable enough did but make ↑leave↓ Gaston all the readier to follow his
way ↑route↓ further ↑from home↓ as he had undertaken ↑designed↓ to do in
fulfilment of a certain old promise to visit a friend, far beyond these ↑the↓

---

21. BNC slip; three primary half-lines, right half of sheet with vertical strikeout,
correlating to primary lines 9–11, folio 13:

   desc. [   ], such as / . . . own to be, for G's haunting / to his bodily ear. Yes! to his
Overleaf, Dip. 13 n.23.

22. BNC slip (on light blue paper textured with darker blue threads, unruled);
written with the same finer pen-point as the chapter manuscript at this place;
correlating with primary lines 2–3, folio 14:

   —as the [   ] lifts [   ], they / ground[?] arms with a harsh / rattle on the church pavement

23. BNC slip; correlates with primary lines 6–7, folio 14:

   N.B. Link the funeral scene / to the ch^yard. Such grief, / wild grief, still alive. / Say this à
   propos of the / epitaphs—then repeat / it (in one sentence) later.

Overleaf, Dip. 13 n.21.

Also a HOU slip, only tentatively applicable:

   12. *Begins*, with the weeping / of young man (desc. him) / *Ends*, with the weeping of / the
   child turned to / delightful laughter.

Overleaf, Dip. 11 n.13.

gloomy [3 cm] ↑boundaries ↑borders↓↓ of Paris, to Fon- [**End 14 r**]
tainebleau, then a frequent residence ↑favourite place of retirement↓ of the
court. He meant to leave ↑Paris↓ altogether soon its close streets, its colours
of corruption ↑decay↓, its sin, its nightmares, ↑into the "peaceful sanctuary
of his youth"↓ and even this temporary escape from it was irresistibly cheerful
↑reassuring↓ as the wheels passed lightly over the way ↑route ↑roads↓↓
southwestwaards [*sic*] ↑?↓. The very suburbs ↑Even the suburban streets↓ as
he drove away at that fresh early hour seemed ↑already↓ to anticipate the
♦country ↑be full of ↑pleasant↓ country thoughts↓ a scent of watering is
↑was↓ in the air: ↑▲more & more ↓as↑↓ the prospect widens, the peace, the
gaiety of the ♦country reigns sole in his ♦thoughts. The very work-people, the
wayfarers ↑toiling travellers on foot↓, the very beggars, in a series of [1.5 cm]
vignettes, seemed graceful ↑blond↓, well-clad, light footed. The [3.5 cm]
↑acacias↓ at the road-side ↑along the road↓ held ↑lifted↓ their bouquets of
tender ♦green ↑verdure↓ as high as they could [**End 15 r**] ↑16↓ into the ↑mid-
↑late↓↓ April sun, below them the etroits sentiers, between the vines, pass
into ↑wᵈ take one ↓deeper↑↓ into the♦ country♦ side ↑—vines, the winding
village stˢ of [0.5] of [0.5] an almost ↑all but↓ ↓hived[?] in them↑↓. The
finger of the early ↑fresh↓ morning breeze was ↑restless↓ everywhere in this
eblouissant ↑over ↓through↑ the dazzling↓ symphony in white and green.
Still recording painting [1.5 cm] ↑noting within↓ the notes in it more
↑directly↓ congruous with his own leading sentiments he notes a young man
resting that the boy who ↑he↓ accompanies may rest under the ↑in ↑the↓ rare
shade↓: they seem as gaie and babillard as the young birds, yet as he thoughts
↑thinks↓ resemble himself. As he comes towards the end of his journey he
notes the thing ↑blond &↓ again ↑for a moment ↓as he passes↑↓ in the
garden now of a riant miniature Itⁿ villa beyond the gilt ↑trellis↓ ironworld
↑work↓, ↑with its↓ [1.5 cm] ↑: there they stand ↓blond, matutinal,↑↓ among
[2 cm] making an ↑blond↓ idyll of the carefully tended ↑kept↓ garden beds
& grass [**End 16 r**] ↑17↓ the paths ↑pathways↓ of fine sand. ↑And↓ Over the
↑this↓ friendly↓2↑ ↑gentil↓1↑↓ campagne at last the forest at last with its grey
rocks, its immemorial oaks & beeches of Pharamond & [1.5 cm] Sᵗ Louis,
spread moutonnés over gentle hill & vale under universal shadowless
sunlight, till the golden green ↑stood↓ triumphant upon the large noonday
blue.

[¶] Towards afternoon ↑evening↓ would he ↑care to↓ visit asks his hospitable
friend a rare place of which he has ↑holds↓ the key: le cabinet [3.5 cm] ↑des
peintures du roi↓ royal—of laughing ↑riant↓ F. I. The works of [1.5 cm], and
[2.5 cm], and [1.5 cm], above all of the great Milanese master L. de V. hang

just as he had left them, ↑at ↑by↓ the orders of↓ in the days of F. the 1ˢᵗ. It was a favourable moment ↑time ↑hour↓↓ for seeing [**End 17 r**] ↑18↓ them, this slanting afternoon light.

[0.5 cm] The expansion of the animal spirits in Gaston, as he passed today, through the light and air of the ↑his↓ route to Fontainebleau ↑this white place↓ was like a ↑the↓ physical parallel to the mental relief, ↑to↓ a certain larger ↑and↓ richer genial sense of things, of which this creature of the eye now became aware in himself as he yielded ↑yielding↓ straightway to the influence of what he saw on the walls around him. He surrendered ↑surrendered his taste,↓ to the ↑happy ↑genial↓↓ spell of Itⁿ art the power of L. and [1.5 cm], ↑& their↓ its peculiar reading of life. The Renaissance of Italy transferred to France, in a hundred minute ↑minor↓ [2.5 cm] forming [1.5 cm] ↑coloring life↓, had, in fact, as all that ↑is↓ really grows ↑growing↓ will do conformed ↑itself↓ to the soil [1.5 cm], ↑allying↓ had↑?↓ [**End 18 r**] ↑19↓ itself to, ↑and↓ was become the servant ↑minister↓ of what reigned already in men's hearts or fancy ↑ies↓ there, the cruel ↑barren, unkindly↓, the [1.5 cm] ↑unkindly↓ love, which centered, ↑▲in M's [2 cm],↓ in the [2 cm] broken on the wheel ↑not gone↓ in the Palace de Grêve. How potent had been the spell [4 cm] ↑over Gaston's↓. Passing now ↑Looking today↓ from the derivative to the source, ↑or↓ to the rock whence it was hewn G. ↑he↓ found amid a development of form and colour and poetic suggestion ↑so much↓ richer far than this Northern one, the ↑a↓ larger heart also, the genius not of a cruel ↑an unkindly ↑as we call barren earth unkindly↓↓, but of a kindly love, the ↑a↓ manifestation of of nature and man ↑as if↓ under the genial light of [2 cm] ↑God's↓ immediate presence. The reader will ↑may↓ estimate for himself the influence ↑importance ↑significance↓↓ of such a ↑this↓ discovery in ↑for↓ one in ↑for ↑to↓↓ whom art, and the [1.5 cm] ↑sensible ↑distinctions, preferences↓↓ of art, had ↑were ↑was↓↓ become a [**End 19 r**] ↑20↓ kind of ↑the substitute for↓ conscience, dislocated or dissipated by a ↑the↓ negative phʸ ↑of↓. its ↑what a↓ force it had for ↑in↓ the future [2 cm], colouring ↑▲so to speak↓ of his experience ↑soul ↑spirit↓↓: it gave for a coherency to the increasing ↑growing↓ suggestions of his ↑G's↓ own mind and experience ↑purpose↓. His visit to this place actually set him on a long series of explorations among the art-treasures of Paris itself, what there might be like it there to see to hold converse with thro' the eye,—a large ↑cheering↓ resource during the rest ↑remainder↓ of the time he stayed ↑remained↓ there—and was like the later stage of a long education. Kindness, the kindness of [1.5 cm] to [1.5 cm], stimulated by ↑forgetting itself in↓ the sight ↑admiration ↑love↓↓ of physical ↑visible↓ beauty, [5 cm] ↑the eyes, the lips↓

kindling into creation ↑kindled to the reproduction↓, of its like, renewing the world, handing on, as a pledge ↑ground↓ of love and kindness [**End 20 r**] ↑21↓ for ever, ↑▲the beauty wh. had kindled it↓ the likeness ↑of↓,↑or↓ an improvement upon itself, kindling a like love in turn, linking ↑genially ↑kindly ↑filially↓2↑ paternally↓1↑,↓↓↓ age to age, the young to the old, marriage, maternity, childhood and youth, ↑—the kindness by wh. [1 cm] cherishes the failing heart in —,↓ consecrated by ↑indefeasible↓ union with the [2.5 cm], who looks favourably also on the virginity the restraint wh. guards ↑in fact secures↓ the purity, the ardency ↑therefore↓ of the creative flame: that ↑this↓ was what Gaston found in those untouched revelations of the mind of [l.5] & [2.5]; the ↑those↓ mature Italian masters and it [1 cm] ↑? promoting↓ still further his [1.5 cm] ↑that increasing↓ preoccupation with the perennial ↑the greater unchangeable↓ interests of life with wh. he enters ↑entered↓ upon this ↑the ↓coming↑↓ new and later phase of his own later ↑maturer↓ manhood. ↑Here↓ Art according to its proper ↑ministry ↑purpose ↑function↓↓↓ was ↑had been↓ here at once the ↑an↓ interpretation and ↑an↓ idealisation of life. [**End 21 r**]

❦ TEXTUAL EMENDATIONS
& VARIANTS

With the exceptions noted below, this section records emendations of, and the principal variants to, the copy texts; namely, to the **BERG** holograph, Chapters 1–5, 7; to Shadwell's **1896** edition, Chapter 6; and to the **BNC/HOU** (Brasenose/Houghton) holographs, Chapters 8–13. The Edition Text for *Gaston* is compared with the 1888 *Macmillan's Magazine* (for Chapters 1–5), with the *Fortnightly Review* (for Chapter 7), with Shadwell's 1896 edition (for Chapters 1–5 and 7), and with Clara Pater's transcription (**CP**) of her brother's first 7 pages, Chapter 13. The 1910 Library Edition is of negligible interest; essentially a reprinting of Shadwell's edition, it merely corrects one or two misprints and imposes slightly modified house rules for hyphenation of compound words and the placement of punctuation relative to closing quotation marks.

The lemma is enclosed in a *scroll bracket* to indicate a copy text *emendation* and in a *square bracket* to mark a *variant*.

EMENDATIONS (CHAPTERS 1–13)

Emendations in the copy text of wording, orthography, and paragraphing are recorded, although regularization of chapter headings is not recorded. Emendations of punctuation within sentences cannot be recorded since both the **BERG** and **BNC/HOU** copy texts are incompletely punctuated. Also, I silently capitalize the frequently-appearing "Huguenot" or "Protestant" because Pater's practice is inconsistent. (But Pater's nineteenth-century lower-casing of "catholic" is retained, as it was in MM and **1896**—Chapter 6 excepted: there **1896** uses capitals. Because the holograph is lost, I allow that textual anomaly to remain.) Emendations of such details as the italicization of foreign words are recorded for Chapters 1–7 but, because Pater had not finalized this or similar details in the unpublished manuscripts, cannot be recorded for Chapters 8–13; however, the Diplomatic Transcriptions serve as the emendations/variants record for that material. Additionally, I silently emend the Chapter 6 copy text to follow the conventions of **1910** in the placement of punctuation relative to quotation marks. (I assume Shadwell removed this chapter from the **BERG** and lost it at the printer's—all other **1896** chapters may have been set directly from his emendations of magazine pages; puzzlingly, Shadwell suggests he found

Chapter 6 among the less-polished **BNC/HOU** drafts, differentiating it from the "largely revised" Chapter 7.)

Elsewhere, Pater's less-finished manuscripts are sporadically marked with *'s and ++'s, indicating points at which additional material was intended to be inserted. Eighteen detached slips accompany the *Gaston* manuscript and several others are at Harvard's Houghton Library and the New York Public Library, Berg Collection. Some are irrelevant to *Gaston* and some are merely background notes for the novel, but others clearly were intended to be inserted in the narrative's next drafting. In a few instances the asterisks match; in other cases the relevance of the material to the text is clear. Manuscript slips pertaining to Chapters 1–7 are included here as variants (transcribed diplomatically); slips pertaining to Chapters 8–13 are reproduced as variants in the notes to the Diplomatic Transcriptions and, if relevant, are used to emend the Edition Text. Such emendations are noted here, though minor augmentations such as expansions of Pater's abbreviations are not noted. Finally, my conjectured readings for lacunae are marked as emendations within brackets directly in the Edition Text; and their analytic rationales are given in the Explanatory Annotations rather than here among the more mechanical or functional particulars.

Although I permit Pater a few more hypenations than his *Macmillan's Magazine* (**MM**) editor would have condoned, variations in usage, such as sporadic obsolete spellings, create difficulties: "chestnut" in Chapter 4, but "chesnuts" in Chapter 9. Pater probably was merely following **MM**'s modern house rules in Chapter 4; left to his own devices, he gravitated towards the quaint. But editors are expected to crack the Grim Whip of Consistency, so an 1890s-style "modernity" will temper his predilection for the old-fashioned.

VARIANTS (CHAPTERS 1–7)

All the extensive or interpretively relevant verbal variations in the printed editions, together with the principal uncareted interlineations in the Berg manuscript copy text, are recorded; but minor variations of wording or differences in punctuation, orthography (including hyphenation, capitalization, italics), typography and paragraphing are omitted. Documentation of Pater's continuous retouching of the published versions of *Marius the Epicurean* was first made by Edmund Chandler (*Pater on Style*, 1958), who asserted that bulk of Pater's variants were difficult to interpret. But because Chapters 8–13 are posthumously published, the Diplomatic Transcriptions will present a full record of alternative wordings.

CHAPTER 1

Copy text: **BERG holograph**

1:16   south-west} South-west **BERG, MM**   south-west **1896**

1:17–20   Latour, . . . lightsome home] Latour, ~~nesting there century after century, it recorded~~ ↑*very↓ ~~significantly~~ ↑it bore significant record of↓ ~~the effectiveness of~~ ↑the effectiveness of↓ their brotherly union, ↑*from age to age↓ ↑century after century, as indeed promotion~~ as they rested there.~~century after century.*↓ ~~less by way of invasion of the rights of others than by the improvement of all gentler sentiments within.~~ From the sumptuous monuments of their last resting-place, backward ~~to every~~ ↑*the every= day↓ object<s> ~~which had encircled them in~~ ↑*this↓ that ↑*to the very stones of this↓ more lightsome home **BERG**   Latour, nesting there century after century, it recorded significantly the effectiveness of their brotherly union, less by way of invasion of the rights of others than by the improvement of all gentler sentiments within. From the sumptuous monuments of their last resting-place, backwards to every object which had encircled them in that warmer and more lightsome home **MM, 1896**

2:13–14   suggested the building here of] now suggested to the younger, himself already wistfully recalling, as from the past, the kindly motion and noise of the place like a sort of audible sunlight, the building of **MM, 1896**

2:14   Château} Chateau **BERG**   Château **MM, 1896**

2:35–36}   Between paragraphs, Pater's holograph intentionally leaves a blank space of one line; this has been edited out because nowhere else in the holographs is such typographical spacing indicated. Shadwell moved this spacing to 6:15–16 (see below).

3:3–4   In the church of Saint Hubert,] Here, in the church of Saint Hubert, church of their parish, and of their immemorial patronage, though ↑it lay at a considerable distance from their abode, **MM, 1896**

3:33   harvest] harvest under this cloudless sky **MM**

4:12   associations] associations, as well secular as religious, **MM**

4:14   of a divine sanction} of ~~some~~ ↑some ↑a↓↓ <a> [1.5 cm] ↑divine↓ sanction **BERG** of a divine sanction **MM, 1896**

4:27   kind . . . inherited, he] kind, that with many characteristics of obvious inheritance he **MM** kind; that, together with many characteristics obviously inherited, he **1896**

4:37   that might} which might **BERG**; Pater interlined *that* over both this and the preceding *which*; that is a habitual compositional pattern indicating that in one instance he will use a *which* and in the other a *that*, but that he has not yet decided which will be which, only that both will not be *that* nor will both be *which*. I therefore follow the MM reading that gives the second *which* as *that*.

5:3–4   "clericature," he made a great demand on] clericature, his proposal made a demand on all **MM, 1896**

5:7–8 and one half . . . time] and of which, at that time, one half of the benefices were **MM; 1896 agrees but deletes commas.**

5:8–10 In effect . . . their old] But actually the event came to be a dedication on their part not unlike those old biblical ones—an offering in old **MM; 1896 agrees but adds commas.**

5:23 astray, *ovis quæ periit*] astray, *sicut ovis quæ periit* **MM, 1896**

5:33 youth,] youth, and of something else perhaps besides that, **MM**

6:1–3 manfully. . . . . between] manfully, though he kneels meekly enough and remains, with his head bowed forward, at the knees of the seated bishop who recites the appointed prayers, amid **MM** manfully; though he kneels meekly enough, and remains, with his head bowed forward, at the knees of the seated bishop who recites the appointed prayers, between **1896**

6:6 ever!] ever! who had thus hastened to lay down the hair of his head for the divine love. **MM, 1896**

6:15–16 **Between the paragraphs, the text of 1896 leaves extra space.**

6:16 their road homewards,] their cheerful, unenclosed road, **MM** their cheerful, un-enclosed road, **1896**

6:28 Château d'Amour} *Château d'Amour* **BERG; the other three instances in the holograph do not italicize the name; therefore, I give the Roman here, as in MM, 1896.**

6:30 of fancy, of sentiment] of refined or fantastic sentiment **MM, 1896**

6:34 ¶ It] ¶ With minds full of their recent business it **MM, 1896**

7:6 travellers} travillers **BERG; Pater's misspelling**

7:13 from} to **BERG, MM** from **1896**

7:16–17 the power . . . imagination] the imaginative power of fortuitous circumstance **MM**

8:5 down a lute . . . notes,] down from the wall and struck out the notes of a lute, **MM, 1896**

8:10 Wars} War **BERG** Wars **MM, 1896; writers (Pater among them) note that there were eight wars, and the collective designation is always in the plural.**

8:13 vengeance for the treacherous murder of his father.} vengeance on †for↓ the treacherous murder of his father. **BERG** vengeance on a treacherous murder. **MM** vengeance on the treacherous murder of his father. **1896**

8:15   the religious war} that ↑the↓ Religious War **BERG** the Religious War **MM** the religious war **1896; since the reference is to warfare generally, I adopt the 1896 lower-case form.**

8:17   culture; it filled} culture it ↑It↓ filled **BERG; Pater was still debating one or two sentences.** culture, and filled **MM, 1896 agrees but uses semicolon**

8:18   heady fanaticism] heady ↑religious↓ fanaticism **BERG**   heady religious fanaticism **MM, 1896**

8:30   convictions. Yet religion, the assumed ground] convictions. The wisest perhaps, like Michel de L'Hôpital, withdrew themselves from a conflict in which not a single actor has the air of quite pure intentions; while religion, itself the supposed ground **MM; 1896 agrees, but deletes a comma and changes** *supposed* **to** *assumed.*

8:31–32   the leaders . . . forward] the parties, the leaders, at once violent and cunning, who are more pretentious **MM; 1896 agrees, but changes** *more* **to** *most*

8:38   year 1562} year 1862 **BERG** year 1562 **MM, 1896.**

9:8   its professed motives.] its assumed motives. **MM** the assumed motives of that strife. **1896**

11:34–35   natures and amid happier circumstances,] natures, through the concurrence of happier circumstance, **MM, 1896**

13:6   WALTER PATER. **MM**

13:7   (*To be continued.*) **MM**

CHAPTER 2

Copy text: **BERG holograph**

14:11   Our Lady's Church] "I had almost said even as they." **MM** OUR LADY'S CHURCH. "I had almost said even as they." **1896**

14:19   shift—*sacra camisia*—which] shift which **MM, 1896**

14:29   and could never precisely detach his earlier vision] and his earlier vision was a thing he could never precisely recover, or disentangle from **MM, 1896**

15:13   along, in] along, cross-bearer and acolyte, in **MM, 1896**

15:37–38   churches. There] churches. ↑As at the present day, there↓ There **BERG** churches: there **MM, 1896**

16:12   Deux-manoirs} Deux-Manoirs **BERG; the second element in the compound elsewhere is lower case.**

16:16   feet} **word omitted in BERG, clearly an error of mechanical copying.** feet MM, **1896**

16:31–32   Physical twilight we most of us love, in its season.] We love, most of us, physical twilight. **MM, 1896**

17:20   uncalculated} un-calculated **BERG**   uncalculated **1896**; MM **shows** *un-calculated* **as an end-of-line hyphenation, possibly mechanically copied by Pater.**

17:21–22   thoughts. Alien at a thousand points from his pre-conceptions of life, it presented itself, in] thoughts, proposing itself importunately, in **MM**; **1896 agrees, but adds a comma.**

17:24–25   a thing to be judged] a thing, alien at a thousand points from his preconceptions of life, to be judged **MM, 1896**

17:28   manners. And how] manners, as to which a grave national assembly, more than three centuries before the States-General of 1789, had judged French youth of quality somewhat behind-hand, recommending king and nobles to take better care for the future of their education, "to the end that, enlightened and *moralized*, they might know their duties, and be less likely to abuse their privileges." ¶ And how **MM**; **1896 agrees with MM, but with three emendations:** behindhand, *moralised*, privileges".

17:37   aesthetic sense in} aesthetic [2 cm] ↑sense↓ in **BERG**   aesthetic sense in **MM, 1896**

18:17   Exmes} **a lacuna in BERG in place of a name;** Exmes MM, **1896**

19:20   Sémur's} Semur's **BERG**   Sémur's MM, **1896**

19:39–20:1   associated his companions, added] associated his companions ↑so full of artificial enjoyment↓, added **BERG**   associated them, so full of artificial enjoyment for the well-to-do, added **MM**   associated his companions, so full of artificial enjoyment for the well-to-do, added **1896**

20:11   conclusively with this so tangible world, its suppositions] conclusively with its suppositions **MM**

20:39–21:7   With a real sense . . . absurd."] The nephew of his predecessor in the the see, with a real sense of the divine world, but as something immeasurably distant, he had been brought by a maladroit worldly good fortune a little too close to its immediate and visible embodiments. Afar, you might trace the divine agency on its way. But to touch, to handle it, with these fleshly hands—well! with Monseigneur it was not to believe because the thing was "incredible or absurd." **MM**   The nephew of his predecessor in the see, with a real sense of the divine world but as something immeasurably distant, Monseigneur Guillard had been brought by maladroit worldly good-fortune a little too close to its immediate and visible embodiments. From afar, you might trace the divine agency on its way. But to touch, to handle it, with these fleshly hands:—well! for Monseigneur, that was by no means to believe because the thing was "incredible, or absurd". **1896**

21:15–16   own? He asked himself at all events, from time to time, could] own? Only, could **MM, 1896**

21:16   a real sun] a real sun ⌈(a Latin phrase⌋ **BERG**

21:36–37   peach-blossom and wine] peach-blossom and vine **MM; however, the MM chapter title reads** *WINE.*

23:32–33   beauty in these things, like an effect of magic as being won from] beauty, like magicians' work, like an effect of magic as being extorted from **MM** beauty in these things, like magicians' work, like an effect of magic as being extorted from **1896**

24:7   others proceed] others to proceed **BERG** others proceed **MM, 1896**

24:9   *coulevrines*] *coulev-* rines **BERG, end-of-line hyphenation** *coulevrines* **MM, 1896**

24:16–17   A tear] A tear ⌈few tears⌋ **BERG**

24:36   WALTER PATER. **MM**

24:37   (*To be continued.*) **MM**

CHAPTER 3

Copy text: **BERG holograph**

25:30   more clearly] more [1.5 cm] ⌈clearly⌋ **BERG** more easily **MM, 1896**

26:24   the flush and refledging] the flush⌈?⌋ and⌈?⌋ refledging ⌈the flush⌋ **BERG**

26:30   Skylark] Skylard **BERG** Skylark **MM, 1896**

26:31   golden-green] golden green **BERG** golden-green **MM, 1896**

27:1   mouthpiece] mouth-piece **BERG; MM hyphenates the word at the end of a line and Pater assumed it to be compound (a less frequent usage)** mouthpiece **1896.**

27:7   pretension] pretention **BERG** pretension **MM, 1896**

27:14   indeed, put on . . . a docile] indeed, on its mettle about "scholarship," though actually of listless humour among books that certainly stirred the past, makes a docile **MM; and 1896 agrees, except for comma placement:** "scholarship",

28:19   could count the] could the **BERG** could count the **MM, 1896**

28:36   with him as] with as **BERG** with him as **MM, 1896**

29:38   days} day **BERG** days **MM, 1896**

30:12   the relex action} the ↑reflex↓ action **BERG** the reflex action **MM, 1896**

30:25   leisure} pleasure **BERG** leisure **MM, 1896**

30:31   other, and were} other were **BERG** other, and were **MM, 1896**

30:33   captainless} captain-less **BERG** captainless **MM, 1896**

31:8   mistletoe} misletoe **BERG, MM (an obsolete spelling for 1890s)** mistletoe
          1896

31:21   oak tree} oak-tree **BERG** oak tree **MM, 1896**

33:4   pedantic *Jeux*] pedantic ↑society of the↓ "*Jeux* **BERG**

33:7   melted down church] melted down ↑the precious metal of↓ church **BERG**

34:29   eagerly-sought} eagerly sought **BERG** eagerly-sought **MM, 1896**

35:25   were} well **BERG** were **MM, 1896**

35:34   in due sufficiency.} in ~~sufficien~~ ↑due↓ sufficiency. **BERG** in due sufficiency.
          MM, 1896

36:19–34   **BNC SLIP with vertical strikeout may pertain to this passage (horizontally cancelled lines probably pertain to another study):**

> Pleiad: it's the *outlines* of the beautiful— / the love of beauty realised as a sort of
> rel^n— / with this minute *care & scruple*— / This he finds, as an actually existent
> enterprise there, going on / in the world—its *conscience & self-consciousness*. /[¶]
> ~~? trans^{ms} of Plato. / His surprise in finding a plan of the / church life, already~~
> ~~familiar, among / them.~~

Overleaf, inverted, Dip.Transcrip. 9.250:n.5.

37:13   WALTER PATER. **MM**

37:14   (*To be continued.*) **MM**

CHAPTER 4

Copy text: **BERG holograph**

39:2   terrors, if it} terrors, it **BERG** terrors, if it **MM, 1896**

39:17   night-hawk} night-hush ↑night-jar↓ **BERG (a night-jar is a hawk)** night-hush
          MM night-hawk **1896**

39:18   honeysuckle} honey-suckle **BERG** honeysuckle **MM, 1896**

39:30   strange] strange ⌐dreamy⌐ **BERG**

40:18   Black Angers, white Saumur] Black Angus, candescent Saumur **MM**   Black
Angers, white Saumur **1896, 1910**

40:34   earth itself? As] earth itself? It was a landscape, certainly, which did not merely
accept the sun, but flashed it back gratefully from those white gracious carven houses
that were like a natural part of it. As **MM; 1896 identical except for:** the white,
gracious, carven houses,

40:39   palatial abodes challenged] palatial abodes, never out of sight, high on the river
banks, challenged **MM; 1896 agrees throughout except for:** bank

41:28–29   stalks of the ixias, like] stalks, like **MM**

41:39   touches. A forbidden] touches—an inky accent upon the painted surface—a
forbidden **MM**   touches; a forbidden **1896**

41:39   inmates} **accidentally omitted in BERG** inmates **MM, 1896**

42:37–38   curiosity. ¶ In those] curiosity. ¶ [extra space between paragraphs] Three
different forms of composition have, under different conditions, prevailed—three
distinct literary methods—in the presentation of philosophic thought: earliest, the
metrical form, when philosophy was still a thing of intuition, sanguine, imaginative,
often obscure, and became a *poem* "concerning nature" after the manner of Pythagoras
"his golden verses"; precisely the opposite way to that, when native intuition had
shrunk into dogmatic system, the dry bones of which rattle in one's ear with Aristotle
or Aquinas as a formal *treatise*; the true philosophic temper, the proper human
complexion in this subject, lying between these opposites as the third essential form
of its literature, the *essay*—that characteristic model of our own time, so rich and
various in special apprehensions of truth, but of so vague and dubious sense of their
ensemble and issues. Characteristic modern form of philosophic literature, the essay
came into use at what was really the invention of the relative or "modern spirit", in
the Renaissance of the sixteenth century. The reader sees already that these three
methods are no mere literary accidents dependent on the choice of particular writers,
but necessities of literary form strictly determined by matter as corresponding to three
essentially different ways in which the human mind relates itself to truth. If oracular
verse, stimulant, but enigmatic, is the proper vehicle of enthusiastic intuition; if the
treatise with its ambitious array of premise and conclusion is the natural output of
scholastic all-sufficiency; so the form of the essay as we have it in Montaigne, the
representative essayist, inventor of the name as in essence of the thing—of the essay
in its seemingly modest aim, its really large and venturous possibilities—is indicative
of his peculiar function with regard to that age, as in truth the commencement of our
own. It supplies precisely the literary form necessary to a mind for which truth itself
is but a possibility, realisable not as general and open conclusion but rather as elusive
effect of a particular experience—to a mind which, noting faithfully those random

lights which meet it by the way, must needs content itself with suspense of judgment at the end of the intellectual journey, to the very last asking *Que sçais-je?* **MM**; **rewritten, this passage was incorporated in** *Plato*, **pp. 174–76.**

44:9   converse of which} ↑▲converse of↓ from **BERG** converse from which **MM, 1896**

44:10–11   for Plato, for Socrates . . . the essential] for Plato, the essential **MM**

44:17–18 connexion to be supposed by the reader, the Essays] connexion to be supposed by the reader, ↑constituting their characteristic difficulty,↓ the the Essays **BERG** connexion to be supposed, constituting their characteristic difficulty, the essays **MM** connexion to be supposed by the reader, constituting their characteristic difficulty, the Essays **1896**

45:16–17   life. ¶ In] life. It was a flattery to have been sent hither. ¶ In **MM**

45:30–31 wisdom that was coming to be his own, from] wisdom ↑ripe and placid↓ that was coming to be his own, from **BERG** wisdom that was coming to be his own, ripe and placid, from **MM; 1896 agrees except for:** —from

46:4   told deeply} told [4 cm] ↑deeply↓ **BERG** told emphatically **MM, 1896**

46:14–16 :such were . . . traits of character,] :~~was what this quietly enthusiastic~~ ~~enthusiastic reader would formulate the sum of his studies of books and things~~ ↑▲such were the ↑so↓ terms ~~in which this quietly Gaston,~~ [1.5 cm] ~~was ready to~~ [1 cm] ~~sum up~~ ↑in which Gaston, reflecting on his long unsuspicious sojourn here <t>here,↓ detached for himself, from the habits, the random traits of cha-▲↓ racter, **BERG** —such was the sense of this open book, of all books and things: that was what this quietly enthusiastic reader was ready to assert as the sum of his studies: disturbingly, as Gaston found, reflecting on his long unsuspicious sojourn there, and detaching from the habits, the random traits of character, **MM; 1896 agrees except for:** things. That was what

46:38   WALTER PATER. **MM**

46:39   (*To be continued.*) **MM**

CHAPTER 5

Copy text: **BERG holograph**

47:14   nature!—so deep} nature so deep **BERG** nature! So deep **MM** nature!—so deep **1896**

47:24   radical diversity] diversity **MM**

47:21–24 A Houghton slip, canceled with a single vertical strikeout, incorporates five lines from the right side of an earlier draft:

> measure of evidence of truth / . . . tom what was that but of / moral and m
> mental view / opinion what but diversity of / various in kind and degree

47:22 custom!—what} custom what BERG; punctuation is reconstructed consistent with emendation 47:14 custom! What MM custom!—What 1896

48:4–5 at home, on its native soil, it is] at home it was MM

48:37 men} "men BERG, opening mark not matched with a closing one men MM, 1896

49:15 oversee} over-see BERG oversee MM, 1896; Cotton's word unhyphenated also.

49:38–39 was consistent . . . . Even] was congruous with his sympathetic belief in the native gifts of youth. Even MM; 1896 agrees with BERG, except it renders *capabilities* as *capability*

50:3–4 nature:—the shrewd wisdom of an un-lettered] nature—the mere self-will of men, the shrewd wisdom of an unlettered MM; 1896 agrees except for: nature:—

51:2–3 On this . . . surpassed;] ↑▲On this single point, antiquity itself had been surpassed;▲↓ ~~That had remained with him as his one fixed st~~ BERG. Apparently Pater's eye jumped back to 51:1. Although the MM sentence commences *It had remained*, perhaps Pater recopied *That had remained* either because he already had entered this correction on the printed page (as he had done with the MM "Child in the House," now at Worcester College), or was *not* revising from the printed page but was using copy returned from the printer (subsequently revised or with *That had* as its original phrase altered in proof), or else may have been utilizing a draft from which the printer's fair copy derived. Cf. 59:6–9.

52:23 Romans. Perhaps could] Romans, somewhat conventionally; and Montaigne was fond of assuring people suddenly that could MM; 1896 agrees except *suddenly* is in commas.

53:1 years} months BERG; emended to agree with MM, 1896; Montaigne was married in 1565; this chapter, set in 1571, already ascribes to him four of the six children ultimately born from the union.

53:34 composition"? He would] composition"? (Was good faith, just there, calling bad faith to work in its vineyard?) He would MM

53:39–54:3 BNC slip, from the right half of a canceled page with three primary lines and interlineations:

↑but not what I seek↓ my expectation & the journey of my / me fashion")—doubt, finally ↑at last↓, / ↑t—as the best of pillows to sleep on.↓ in fact G. did sleep well, ~~then~~

54:25   what was "properly} what "properly **BERG** what was "properly **MM, 1896**

54:34–35   —"I have . . . . tomorrow."] **Italicized in MM but not in Montaigne or Cotton's translation.**

55:10–11   it might be} **This phrase is repeated in holograph, Pater's eye jumping backwards to recopy the same words.**

57:19–20   sensation in these unpremeditated thoughts which seemed] sensation here, which to Gaston seemed **MM** sensation in these unpremeditated thoughts, which to Gaston seemed **1896**

58:5   hardly escape so} hardly ↑a soul↓ so **BERG** hardly escape so **MM, 1896**

58:8–9   old-fashioned construction] old-fashioned and so hopeful construction **MM**

58:21–27   age, attracted him. . . . For}] age, attracted him . . . objects ↑and experiences↓ of the this indubitable. . . . For **BERG** age, seemed to him, in his present humour, less a receptivity towards problematic heavenly lights that might find their way to one from infinite skies, than towards the pleasant quite finite objects and experiences of the indubitable world of sense so close around him. It presented itself to him as that general license, over against the world's challenge to try it, which his own warm and curious appetite demanded of the theorist just then. For **MM** age, attracted him, in his present humour, not so much in connexion with those problematic heavenly lights that might find their way to one from infinite skies, as with the pleasant, quite finite, objects and experiences of the indubitable world of sense, so close around him. Over against the world's challenge to make trial of it, here was that general licence, which his own warm and curious appetite just then demanded of the moral theorist. For **1896**

58:33   century, to Pascal, Montaigne was] century he was **MM**

59:6–9   Was this all . . . preparation?} **Absent in BERG and MM but found in 1896. The sentence may have been deleted by Pater or the MM editor when the serialization was discontinued; if Pater later recopied the magazine text, he may have neglected to reinsert it.**

59:13   WALTER PATER **MM**

CHAPTER 6

Copy text: **1896** Shadwell edition

60:21   *Iliad*} Iliad **1896**

61:10   *Noces Vermeilles*} Noces Vermeilles **1896**

64:17   a while} awhile **1896** a while **1910**

66:21   Châtillon} Chatillon **1896**

CHAPTER 7

Copy text: **Berg holograph**

68:8–11   Chapter VII *The Lower Pantheism*] GIORDANO BRUNO. PARIS: 1586. **FR**

68:14–17   "*Jetzo*, . . .—HEINE.} **The epigraph does not appear in BERG; instead, Pater marks the missing lines in his manuscript with four precisely spaced reference dots on the left-hand side, where each missing line should begin; in FR the epigraph is unitalicized and in quotation marks; in 1896 it is also unitalicized but is not in quotation marks. (If the epigraph was added at FR proof stage and if Pater was transcribing either his fair copy returned from the printer or a copy earlier in the stemma, this might explain the holograph lacuna; the other explanation is that Pater was searching for another epigraph—but, then, why one with the identical number of lines?)**

68:19–70:2   Those who were curious . . . inspiration.] **Not in FR but in BERG, 1896**

69:8   *m'amie*} **Emended from L'Estoile's** *ma mie* **(as also in BERG, 1896), a not infrequent erroneous orthography used after** *ma*. **Since** *mie* **means** *crumb, very little bit*, **it is remotely possible this could be a nursery term of endearment; however, Baird (2:636) translates the word as** *friend*.

69:25   Pentecostal} ↑P↓pentecostal **BERG** Pentecostal **1896**

70:3–14   On the Feast of the Pentecost . . . a scene."] **The initial 41 words of the FR essay, up to the first semicolon in the second sentence of the essay, are integrated with this Berg paragraph.**

70:8   sky—like] sky above the old grey walls; like **1896**

70:15–71:5   Charles's last words . . . an hour.] **Not in FR but in BERG, 1896**

70:24   Whitsun-Monday} Whitsun-monday **BERG** Whit-Monday **1896**; **properly capitalized, the BERG form is an acceptable variant of Shadwell's emendation.**

71:6–7   on a Whitsunday afternoon . . . to one, who,] **Here the BERG version links up at the first semicolon in FR's second sentence: and it was on a Whit-Sunday afternoon that curious Parisians had the opportunity of listening to one who, FR** on a Whitsunday afternoon, amid the gaudy red hues of the season, that Gaston listened to one, who, **1896**

71:10–12 operations, and . . . . The] operation. The **FR**

71:13 Order} order **BERG** Order **FR, 1896**

71:18–21 still. What . . . fact. Men] still. Men **FR**

71:26 University itself into the background. For] university into a perhaps not unmerited background; for **FR**

72:10 Order} order **BERG** Order **FR, 1896**

72:35–36 Empedocles . . . that] Empedocles, Pythagoras, who had enjoyed the original divine sense of things, above all, Parmenides, that **FR** Empedocles, for instance, and Pythagoras, who had been nearer the original sense of things; Parmenides, above all, that **1896**

73:2 *l'antica filosofia Italiana*} unitalicized in **BERG**; italicized in **FR, 1896**

73:15 consciousness} con- **BERG** consciousness **FR, 1896; Pater forgot to complete the word on his next line when copying.**

73:18–19 His assisting Spirit, who, in truth, is the Creator of things in and by His} his assisting Spirit, who, in truth, is the creator of things in and by his **BERG** his assisting Spirit, who, in truth, creates all things in and by his **FR** His assisting Spirit, who, in truth, is the Creator of things, in and by His **1896**

74:7–8 also, together . . . Gaston for one, to be] also to be **FR; 1896 follows BERG but deletes:** for one

75:4 physical or sensuous ardours] physical ardours **FR**

75:14 *Furori,*} *Furori,*" **BERG** *Furori,* **FR, 1896**

75:17 earlier, physically erotic, impulses] earlier physical impulses **FR**

75:20–21 no original lack of the sensuous or poetic fire.] no ~~lack~~ ↑▲original deficiency ↑lack↓↓ of ~~the natural stuff~~ ↑in ↑the↓ sensuous or poetic↓ fire. **BERG** no lack of the natural stuff out of which such mystic transferences must be made. **FR, 1896**

75:33 sense} [3 cm] ↑sense↓ **BERG** sense **FR, 1896**

76:7 of old gothic carvers} of [2.5 cm] ↑old gothic↓ carvers **BERG** of gothic carvers **FR** of old gothic carvers **1896**

77:25–26 occupy. [¶] That] occupy, an echo of the creative word of God himself, "*Qui innumero numero innumerorum nomina dicit.*" [¶] That **FR**

79:7–8 a very new religion indeed, yet a *religion.*] a new religion. **FR** a religion; very new indeed, yet a *religion.* **1896**

79:11–12 **A HOU slip, canceled with a single vertical line, generally pertains:**

B. his enthusiasm for ancient / lit. —his penchant for versi- / fication ==his admiration / for Parmenides== / He passes from ch. doct. to / Joachim &c. —finds it larger— / then, in old Gks, catches the / same rumour, larger, older / still—came & asserted / it in that strange / Paris.

80:2–3 presented himself . . . to-day] presented himself in the comely Dominican habit. The eyes which in their last sad protest against stupidity would mistake, or miss altogether, the image of the Crucified, were to-day **FR** presented himself to his audience in the comely Dominican habit. The reproachful eyes were to-day **1896**

80:8 an occasional peevish cloud} an ⌈occasional⌉ peevish cloud **BERG** a peevish cloud **FR, 1896**

80:17–18 and was hardly . . . contemned.] and, with all his contempt for the "asinine" vulgar, was not fastidious. **FR**

80:27 that age of the Renaissance.] the age, according to the fashion of that ornamental paganism which the Renaissance indulged. **FR**

80:37 of a} of of a **BERG** of **FR, 1896**

81:1 Gaston] Parisians **FR**

81:11 "Installation of the Ass,"] "constellation of the Ass," **FR** "installation of the ass", **1896**

81:21–38 The *Shadows* . . . "opposites"?] **Paragraph not is FR, but is an addendum for the novel; 1896 agrees with Berg with minor finicky divergences.**

82:2 difference between Rome} difference Rome **BERG** difference between Rome **FR, 1896**

82:15 sometimes] ever **FR**

83:1–4 distinction, the . . . art?] distinction, to the "opposed points," the "fenced opposites" of which many, certainly, then present, in that Paris of the last of the Valois, could never by any possibility become "indifferent," between the precious and the base, aesthetically—between what was right and wrong, as matter of art? **FR; 1896 agrees with BERG with one change: to Gaston for instance,**

83:5 WALTER PATER. **FR**

CHAPTER 8

Copy texts: **BNC and HOU holographs**

86:18   house} ↑▲house↓ **BNC pencil augmentation**

87:17   faded} fade **BNC**

87:39   Colombe} Colomb **BNC**

88:25   But again} But Again **BNC.**

88:30   *Melancholia}* *Melancolia* **BNC (an obsolete spelling); Pater used** *Melancholia* **in** *Studies in the History of the Renaissance* **(p. 116).**

89:20   *godronné}* *goudronné* **BNC;** *goudron* **is pine-tar, but it is less likely Pater meant tarred (i.e., smeared or coated) with a ground of attached pearls than a** *godronné* **surface ornamented with a loop or swag design.**

CHAPTER 9

Copy text: **BNC holograph**

95:8–10   It was as if . . . like iron.} **Asterisked BNC slip correlates with an asterisk above a caret here in the text.**

98:13   chestnuts} chesnuts **BNC; obsolete spelling emended to agree with BERG 4.42:21.**

CHAPTER 10

Copy text: **BNC holograph**

107:35   godron} goudron **BNC; see also 8.89:20.**

CHAPTER 11

Copy text: **BNC holograph**

113:33–37   It was as if . . . character.} **Marked BNC slip correlates with its notation in the text.**

114:18–21   The League . . . between them.} **Asterisked BNC slip correlates with an asterisk in the text.**

116:2–3   de Montpensier . . . de Guise,} **Double pin-holes in HOU slip match pin-holes in text.**

116:30　La duchesse de Montpensier} —— Montpensier **BNC**

117:12–14　*Les rois* . . . connexion.} Two BNC slips, the asterisk of one correlates with a careted asterisk in the text.

118:34　in} ~~in~~ BNC; a tentative strikeout.

119:2–6　A banquet . . . life!} Asterisked BNC slip correlates with an asterisk in the text.

119:29　Saint Paul} Saint Pol BNC; apparently Pater's phonetic spelling.

120:9　*Le Réveille-matin*} *Le Reveille-nation* BNC; either a slip of the pen or Pater misread his handwritten notes.

120:14　added} a BNC; an instance of major suspension.

121:14　just} jus **BNC**

122:22　Gabriel Montgomery} [2cm] Montgomery **BNC**

122:26–29　The little princess . . . *douceur.*} Two BNC slips, the second a quotation from L'Estoile (1:239), correlate with left-margin dots reserving three and a half primary lines.

CHAPTER 12

Copy texts: **BNC and HOU holographs**

127:9　twenty-ninth year} 19th year BNC; but Jasmin would have been nineteen about the time of the St. Bartholomew's Massacre, a decade before this incident in the story.

CHAPTER 13

Copy text: **BNC holograph**

128:14　"He shall . . . brook in the way."} "He shall drink &c.." BNC "He shall drink of the brook in the way." **CP**

128:20　excited} exited BNC; an instance of minor contraction.

129:6　the thieves, the courtesans} the thieves, [2 cm] courtesans BNC

129:9–11　—*sur cette terre* . . . *sur les tombes.*} Augmentation from BNC slip.

129:14–19　*Ce fut* . . . *âme.*} **CP**

129:22 Alyscamps [at]} **CP**

129:32 luxuriantly . . . walls,} **CP**

129:33–34 filling its hollows with nests of fiery crimson} **CP**

130:10–12 Left to itself . . . about them.} **Asterisked BNC slip correlates with asterisk in the text.** Left to itself the churchyard earth abounded with veritable field-flowers of the more acrid coarser kinds, with a sort of savage abundance of pattern all about the graves. **CP; Clara misinterprets Pater's index marking under** *sort* **as cross-bars on the l's of** *pollen* **beneath, so she infers the word was** *pattern*; **given that a "pattern" can hardly be "flung" (assuming that she deciphered Pater's verb, which looks vaguely like an electric discharge between two wires), she was was obliged to reconstruct the sentence using words on the slip that had been canceled.**

130:16 imageries of youth and vigour, the} imageries ↓youth & vigour↑ the **BNC** particular [ ] imageries, the **CP**

130:21–22 contrast—what Adam of Brescia says:} contrast. ↑(what Adam of Brescia, says)↓ **BNC** contrast. **CP One could argue Pater did not intend to identify the speaker, only to cite his words.**

130:30–35 way": . . . —finds} way": ↑(quote It^n words)↓ finds **BNC** way": finds **CP, with notation + *Dante* in her left head margin.**

131:5 builder was very} builder very **BNC** builder was very **CP**

131:7 its very enforced irregularities} its irregularities **BNC** its very enforced irregularities **CP**

131:7–9 No soul . . . place, nothing is ever like another, it seemed to say, be as formal as you will.} ~~no soul, of man, or thing, or place, nothing is ever like another, it seemed to say.~~ be as formal as you will. **BNC** No soul of man, or thing, or place, it seemed to say, is really like another mechanically. **CP**

131:28–29 revivial of ritualism} revival or ritualism **BNC**

131:38–132:2 —this lover . . . to listen.} **BNC slip corrrelates with an asterisk in the text; a canceled asterisk, folio 8, seems to have been an earlier possible place for this insertion.**

133:20 southeastwards} southwestwaards [sic] **BNC; this is the direction of Chartres and La Beauce, but not the direction of Fontainebleau.**

❧ APPENDIX

Pater's Paper

Pater wrote in tannin ink on similar but not identically-sized "quarto" sheets of laid writing-paper (which, when held to the light, shows vertical wire-marks and horizontal chain-lines imitating the mold in old handmade paper). Each of Pater's sheets has twenty three very faint horizontal blue-grey rulings ("lined" paper) with head and tail margins. By writing on alternate lines Pater obtains his twelve primary lines per page. Either the right or left vertical edge of each leaf is uneven, the result of being torn from a copy-book of folded and stitched leaves; the holes left by the original sewings are observable on a number of the rough edges. Pater probably appreciated the resulting approximation in his torn-out sheets to the "deckle edge" characteristic of handmade paper (his paper was made on a machine with a "dandy roll" that produced the laid watermarkings). Some of his portfolios had trimmed edges tinted cobalt blue or marbled cobalt and vermilion (color intensity varies from sheet to sheet).

One is tempted to ask at what stage of the novel did Pater use which kind of sheet? Certain of the torn edges conspicuously match (e.g., Chapter 10, fol.22 r and 10, 26 r), a fact that would be relevant to unraveling compositional sequence only if one were sure that Pater consumed his sheets methodically for each draft and then substituted revised pages with equal uniformity. One might then deduce an order of composition according to some variation on a pattern of conjugates produced by the signatures: 4th and 5th, 3rd and 6th, 2nd and 7th, 1st and 8th, or whatever. Though one supposes Pater tore the sheet out before writing on it, one cannot say whether he followed a pattern or not—similarities in some torn margins indicate that sometimes he removed several sheets at once. Despite these uncertainties, minute kernels of fact may yet be gleaned. For example, in Chapter 11, 39 r (originally paginated as 37) and 40 v (originally paginated overleaf also as 38 and 28) are conjugate leaves. From this one may deduce that 28 was likely only a slip of the pen for 38 (otherwise, why wasn't 39 r also originally paginated not only as 37 but also as 27?). Again in this chapter, folios 27 r, 28 r and 29 r are all torn similarly (hence probably with the same hand movement); the latter two are conjugates of folios 33 r and 35 r. But 27 r seems to have no mate, perhaps because the text on what would have been its conjugate sheet is a later draft. Indeed, 30 r, 31 r, 32 r and 34 r are on different paper. Might one thus infer that for this chapter, text on these differing sheets is an interpolated revision?

The measurements of the sheets described below are not unique to *Gaston*; indeed, a few of these sheets were salvaged from other writing projects, the original text canceled and the verso used for the novel. The vertical dimension of Pater's sheets is generally nine inches—none are longer, a very few are as short as 8 3/4". Horizontal dimensions and other characteristics differ somewhat more markedly. The widest sheet is 7 7/16". (Since all sheets are torn along one vertical edge, material variation makes horizontal measurements imprecise; indeed, even the machine trimming may not have met tolerances of 1/16".) In the 7 7/16" width, the cut edges—top, fore, and foot—are tinted cobalt blue, now very much faded. (A sub-category of this type has a vertical measurement of 8 7/8".) An intermediate width sheet is 7 3/16"; its three cut edges are marbled cobalt blue and vermilion (thus each sheet shows these colors at randomly alternating intervals). Tinting is strongest on the top edge, less obvious on the vertical edge, and only a trace of blue with the very scantiest trace of red on the bottom.

Two narrower types measure 7 1/8" and 7" horizontally, neither with tinting but displaying watermark brandnames in block letters. The brandname of the former, on two lines, is TOWGOOD'S FINE; this sheet is entirely confined to Chapter 9, except for a single sheet in Chapter 10, fol. 7. The brandname of the latter is J COLLARD LONDON FINE, on three lines (aligned at 90° to the ruling). The usually so constrained Pater recklessly ignored this watermarked indication of recto/verso in selecting a side to on which to write. In addition to the "cobalt" edged (standard or short), the "cobalt-vermilion" edged, the "Collard," and the "Towgood" (all these characteristic of the BNC manuscripts), the Berg sheets represent some slightly different combinations of sizes, from 8 7/8" to 9" vertical x 7" to 7 3/8" horizontal, some edges cobalt tinted and some untinted. Finally, the Houghton *Gaston* displays two very short sheets, 8 3/4" vertical x 7" horizontal, cobalt edged, both salvaged from the drafts of other works.

Pater's slips generally derive from sheets conforming to the above specifications; thus a slip 2 1/4" x 3 1/2" would have been created by tearing the familiar 9" x 7" sheet once vertically and quartering each strip horizontally. Indeed, one BNC slip also has the final four characters in "COLLARD," a "DON" (partial "D") from "LONDON," and the final "E" in "FINE"; another such slip from the Berg has "OWGO" and "FIN," clearly a partial "TOWGOOD'S FINE." Only one BNC slip on atypically light-blue notepaper is very much smaller than the others.

Clara's laid paper is quite unlike her brother's. In her copy of Chapter 13, fols. 1–3, 5–6 have 21 ruled lines and measure 8 1/16" vertical x 6 1/2" horizontal; left edges very slightly rough; cut edges are untinted; no brand watermarks. Folio 4 is laid, faintly blue in hue throughout, unruled, measures 8" vertical x 6 3/8" horizontal and has Britannia as a brand watermark, a female figure grasping a staff/spear in an oval frame under a crown.

No text has been lost through simple wear, but the holograph does show deterioration. Corners and the protruding edges of the largest sheets exhibit abrasions or worse; first and last pages of chapters are sometimes badly rubbed. The paper (either its fibers or, more probably, its resin for hard-sizing) is photosensitive and at one time must have lain in some disarray exposed to direct sunlight; in consequence, the holograph now exhibits a number of darkened margins (how this could have occurred in an English climate is a total mystery but since the paper in more than one library shows it, it must have originated before the manuscript was separated). Many of the BNC and Berg leaves have pin holes in upper left corners, indicating old fastenings (double pin holes on a few slips indicate they were pinned to a particular page); rust spots from paper clips occasionally are seen on sheets and slips. From its pristine cobalt-and-vermilion panache covered with Pater's elegantly black, often robust characters, it is now divided between continents in dispirited piles of grayish drab.

Notes

Notes

Notes

Notes

Notes

Notes

Notes